A Christmas Carol
and Other Christmas Books

KT-467-793

CHARLES DICKENS

A Christmas Carol

and Other Christmas Books

Edited with an Introduction and Notes by

ROBERT DOUGLAS-FAIRHURST

OXFORD
UNIVERSITY PRESS

BISHOPSTOWN
LIBRARY

OXFORD

UNIVERSITY PRESS

Great Clarendon Street, Oxford OX2 6DP

Oxford University Press is a department of the University of Oxford.
It furthers the University's objective of excellence in research, scholarship,
and education by publishing worldwide in

Oxford New York

Auckland Cape Town Dar es Salaam Hong Kong Karachi
Kuala Lumpur Madrid Melbourne Mexico City Nairobi
New Delhi Shanghai Taipei Toronto

With offices in

Argentina Austria Brazil Chile Czech Republic France Greece
Guatemala Hungary Italy Japan Poland Portugal Singapore
South Korea Switzerland Thailand Turkey Ukraine Vietnam

Oxford is a registered trade mark of Oxford University Press
in the UK and in certain other countries

Published in the United States
by Oxford University Press Inc., New York

Editorial material © Robert Douglas-Fairhurst 2006

The moral rights of the author have been asserted
Database right Oxford University Press (maker)

First published 2006

All rights reserved. No part of this publication may be reproduced,
stored in a retrieval system, or transmitted, in any form or by any means,
without the prior permission in writing of Oxford University Press,
or as expressly permitted by law, or under terms agreed with the appropriate
reprographics rights organization. Enquiries concerning reproduction
outside the scope of the above should be sent to the Rights Department,
Oxford University Press, at the address above

You must not circulate this book in any other binding or cover
and you must impose the same condition on any acquirer

British Library Cataloguing in Publication Data

Data available

Library of Congress Cataloging in Publication Data
Dickens, Charles, 1812–1870.
A Christmas carol and other Christmas books / Charles Dickens ;
edited with an introduction and notes by Robert Douglas-Fairhurst.
    v. cm. — (Oxford world's classics)
Includes bibliographical references.
    Contents: A Christmas carol — The chimes — The cricket on the hearth —
The battle of life — The haunted man.
    1. Christmas stories, English. I. Douglas-Fairhurst, Robert.
II. Title. III. Series: Oxford world's classics (Oxford University Press)
    PR4557.A2D68 2006
    823'.8—dc22   2006008854

Typeset by RefineCatch Limited, Bungay, Suffolk
Printed in Great Britain by
Clays Ltd., St Ives plc

ISBN 0–19–920474–8   978–0–19–920474–8

1

BISHOPSTOWN
LIBRARY

CONTENTS

CORK CITY LIBRARY	
06079775	
HJ	22/03/2007
	£12.99

INTRODUCTION

ON 2 January 1840, Dickens wrote to his printers, Bradbury and Evans, to thank them for their annual Christmas gift of a turkey. He chose his words with care:

My Dear Sirs,

I determined not to thank you for the Turkey until it was quite gone, in order that you might have a becoming idea of its astonishing capabilities.

The last remnant of that blessed bird made its appearance at breakfast yesterday—I repeat it, yesterday—the other portions having furnished forth seven grills, one boil, and a cold lunch or two . . .[1]

It is a generous letter, fully in keeping with the generosity of the people he is addressing. Still, like many people who write to express their thanks for unexpected or unwanted Christmas gifts, it seems that Dickens could not resist poking gentle fun at the purchasers' taste, not least by hinting that sending him a turkey the size of a small child was perhaps being generous to a fault. Is there a note of reproach in 'My Dear Sirs'? There is certainly more than one sense in which a turkey that hangs around for a week might be thought of as 'that blessed bird', as is clear from Dickens's decision to pump up 'turkey' into 'Turkey', the double insistence on its final reappearance 'yesterday—I repeat it, yesterday', and the drawn-out sentence that describes the many attempts made by the Dickens household to finish it off ('seven grills, one boil, and a cold lunch or two'), like a chorus of 'The Twelve Days of Christmas' in which partridges in pear trees and swans a-swimming have been usurped by this one 'blessed bird'. Even the reference to the turkey's 'astonishing capabilities' seems suspended between wonder and worry, as if a turkey that produced so many leftovers came close to being a real-life version of those enchanted objects and creatures—pots overflowing with porridge, or geese laying limitless supplies of golden eggs—that throng the pages of fairy-tales.

Four years later, Dickens had written something that possessed still more 'astonishing capabilities'. *A Christmas Carol in Prose: Being*

[1] *The Letters of Charles Dickens*, Pilgrim Edition, ed. Madeline House *et al.*, 12 vols. (Oxford: Clarendon Press, 1965–2002), i. 1.

a Ghost Story of Christmas was first published just before Christmas in 1843, and since then it has never been out of print. Originally written as a tract for the times, this cautionary tale about the ongoing tussle between greed and goodness has been thought of as timely whenever it has been read. Enjoyed by its first readers as a modern expression of the spirit of Christmas—as modern as Christmas cards, which were sent for the first time in the same year as the *Carol*'s publication—it has since become popular for quite different reasons: the sense of tradition it is thought to embody, a reminder of the simple pleasures that seem to have been lost sight of in the seasonal scrum of shoppers, an annual invitation to the pleasures of nostalgia.[2] Reproduced so often, and in so many different forms, it has become as much a part of Christmas as mince pies or turkey, with the key difference that, as Martin Heidegger argued was true of all classic works, it has never been 'used up'.[3] There have been dozens of films, starring everyone from Laurence Olivier and Ralph Richardson to Mr Magoo and Mickey Mouse, operas and ballets, an all-black musical (*Comin' Uptown*, which opened on Broadway in 1979), Benjamin Britten's 1947 *Men of Goodwill: Variations on 'A Christmas Carol'*, even a BBC mime version in 1973 starring Marcel Marceau.[4] So regular are the annual returns of the *Carol* to our stages and screens, in fact, that it has become something like a secular ritual, an alternative Christmas story to its more obviously religious rival, in which the three wise men are replaced by three instructive spirits, and the pilgrimage to a child in a manger is replaced by a visit to the house of Tiny Tim. Even people who have never read the *Carol* know the story of Scrooge, the miserable old skinflint who repents after being visited by the Ghost of Christmas Past, the Ghost of Christmas Present, and the Ghost of Christmas Yet to Come. So widely and deeply has this story entered the popular

[2] A renewal of interest in Christmas during the first half of the nineteenth century is suggested by the number of books and essays published on the topic, including Robert Seymour, *The Book of Christmas* (1835) (Seymour had been Dickens's first illustrator for *The Pickwick Papers*), Thomas Kibble Hervey, *The Book of Christmas* (1836), William Sandys, *Christmastide: Its History, Festivities, and Carols* (1852), and a satirical essay that may have been a direct influence on Dickens's depiction of Scrooge, Douglas Jerrold's 'How Mr. Chokepear keeps a merry Christmas', *Punch* (December 1841).

[3] Martin Heidegger, *Poetry, Language, Thought*, trans. Albert Hofstadter (New York: Harper and Row, 1971).

[4] See Fred Guilda, *A Christmas Carol and its Adaptations* (London: McFarland & Co., 2000).

imagination that phrases such as 'Bah! Humbug!' have floated free of their original context and acquired the force of common proverbs, while Scrooge himself has entered the language as a piece of cultural shorthand 'used allusively to designate a miserly, tight-fisted person or killjoy' (*OED*, 'Scrooge').

This can make it hard to read, even for the first time, without the uncanny feeling that it is both familiar and strange, ancient and modern. Like any story that has developed the power of a myth, as Virginia Woolf once observed,[5] we tend to know the *Carol* even before we know how to read, and our knowledge comes from many different sources, with the result that any attempt to assess what Dickens actually wrote can be an experience as hazy and disorientating as Scrooge's first impressions of the Ghost of Christmas Past: 'what was light one instant, at another time was dark, so the figure itself fluctuated in its distinctness' (p. 28). And yet, to read his original story closely is to realize that, even though at first it may seem to lack the zip and glitz of later adaptations—there are no Cockney dance routines in the snow, no bustling crowd scenes full of cheeky urchins, no Muppets belting out big musical numbers— Dickens's plot cannot properly be separated from the strange and haunting power of his narrative style. In both the local details and overall shape of his writing, Dickens sets out to show his readers that what happens in the *Carol* is intimately bound up with how it is described as happening.

To take just one example, the story of Scrooge's mean-spirited solitude being replaced by open-hearted sociability is echoed in a style marked by narrative generosity. Repeatedly, the narrator lingers over examples of human activities that show companionability spreading from one person to another—Bob Cratchit joining some strangers for a slide on the ice, or Scrooge's nephew playing games with his friends and relatives—in a way that is as involuntary and catching as a cough. Even the natural world, far from being indifferent to these activities, seems to be working on a similar principle of benevolent overflow, with fog that busies itself 'pouring in at every chink and keyhole', or 'great, round, pot-bellied baskets of chestnuts' that tumble out on to the street 'in their apoplectic opulence'— a cheering alternative to the water-plug, as solitary and frozen as

[5] 'David Copperfield' (1925), repr. in Stephen Wall (ed.), *Charles Dickens: A Critical Anthology* (Harmondsworth: Penguin, 1970), 273.

Scrooge, with its 'overflowings sullenly congealed, and turned to misanthropic ice' (p. 15). Whether moving or static, animate or inanimate, everyone and everything appears to be spilling over, breaking out, extending beyond itself. Dickens's narrator, too, repeatedly sets out to convince us that the world we share is, or should be, one of liberality, plenitude, intimate connectedness. Whether he is describing Scrooge's character ('a squeezing, wrenching, grasping, scraping, clutching, covetous, old sinner!'), or the weather ('cold, bleak, biting'), or the objects that make up Marley's chain ('cash-boxes, keys, padlocks, ledgers, deeds, and heavy purses wrought in steel'), rarely is one detail given when three or four or more will do, as Dickens crams every sentence with alternatives and supplements, like a set of thesaurus entries spread out across the page (pp. 10, 19). Indeed, there are times when the *Carol* reads more like an extended shopping-list than a book, as when Dickens describes the throne of the Ghost of Christmas Present, made up of 'turkeys, geese, game, poultry, brawn, great joints of meat, sucking-pigs, long wreaths of sausages, mince-pies, plum-puddings, barrels of oysters, red-hot chestnuts, cherry-cheeked apples, juicy oranges, luscious pears, immense twelfth-cakes, and seething bowls of punch' (p. 43). That's quite a mouthful, even for a reader, and one of the problems Dickens confronted when inserting such lists into the *Carol*, with all the wide-eyed enthusiasm of a small child leaving a note for Santa, is that they might not be properly absorbed into the story as a whole; however lip-smacking each item might be individually, put together like this they run the risk of producing a nasty case of narrative indigestion. Faced with the prize turkey Scrooge sends to the Cratchits, a suspicious reader might then wonder whether Dickens was winking at his readers about the nature of the story he had produced for them. 'He could never have stood upon his legs, that bird', we are told by the narrator, voicing Scrooge's gleeful thoughts, 'He would have snapped 'em short off in a minute, like sticks of sealing-wax' (p. 79). An oddly self-conscious thing to say at this stage of a story, perhaps, when the writer is close to wrapping up his manuscript and sending it off to the printers, especially given how spindly Dickens's plot is when compared to the top-heavy nature of his style, chiselled with italics and spattered with exclamation-marks ('It *was* a Turkey!'). But it takes a confident writer to joke about what he is up to, and a swaggeringly confident one to tease his readers with the thought that he might not be up to it. And sure enough, the delighted lists that stretch across the *Carol*'s pages serve as a valuable reminder that, even when Dickens's prose risks sounding strained or anxious, he is fully in control.

Writing in an accretive style was nothing new for Dickens; from the start of his career, he had been alternately celebrated and condemned as a writer unusually fond of what George Orwell described as 'the *unnecessary detail*'.[6] However, never before had he set out so deliberately to bring together his style and his narrative subject. As the *Carol* develops, even details that at first appear superfluous, narrative grace notes, are revealed to be part of a pattern, 'a genial shadowing forth', designed to alert the eyes and ears of Dickens's readers to the dangers of assuming that anything or anyone is as 'self-contained' as Scrooge supposes himself to be (pp. 47, 10). The light that spills out of the shop windows, for example, which 'made pale faces ruddy as they passed', sets the tone for light to become a central image of the different ways in which human beings, too, might reach out beyond the boundaries of the self: the 'positive light' that issues from Fezziwig's calves when he dances, which is echoed in his power 'to make our service light or burdensome'; the light-house, which offers a model of cheerful solidarity in the face of chilly adversity; the 'light hearts' of Scrooge's creditors when they think he is dead; the precious burden of Tiny Tim, willingly taken on by his father, for whom 'he was very light to carry'; finally, Scrooge signalling his redemption by whooping that he is 'as light as a feather' (p. 78). Gently but insistently, Dickens educates his readers into the need to make connections in a world that might otherwise shiver into isolated fragments. It is the same idea and the same technique he would later develop in novels such as *Bleak House*, where his listing of objects and urgent cross-referencing of ideas would again reflect his pleasure in the sprawling multitudinousness of the world and his anxious desire to keep that sprawl in check. At this stage in his career, however, writing the first narrative that he had planned as 'a little *whole*', Dickens seems more confident in his ability to keep his imagination from overspilling the boundaries of his plot, and less worried about his ability to find a style to match the dense weave of

---

[6] 'The outstanding, unmistakable mark of Dickens's writing is the *unnecessary detail* . . . His imagination overwhelms everything, like a kind of weed', George Orwell, 'Charles Dickens', *Inside the Whale* (1940), repr. ibid., 308.

affection and obligation that should bind together the rich with the poor, the living with the dead. And the writer with his readers? Who better to remind us that other people are 'fellow-passengers to the grave, and not another race of creatures bound on other journeys' (p. 12), as Scrooge's nephew puts it, than a writer whose story has asked generations of readers to make the same journey, as each pair of eyes travels across the page to meet that clinching final sentence, at once conclusive and all-embracing, 'God bless Us, Every One'?

The hope that nobody is beyond the reach of this blessing is one that Dickens animates from the start. As Graham Holderness has observed, even when Scrooge is at his most crabbed and cussed, grimly fantasizing about Christmas revellers being buried with stakes of holly through their hearts, he is rendered largely harmless by the narrative in which he finds himself: 'The medium in which he exists—the prose of the tale—is so alive and crackling with the energy and vitality of imagination and humour that it gives us assurance that the menace of Scrooge can be dealt with.'[7] In this generous atmosphere, even his encounter with his former business partner starts to sound less like a spine-tingling haunting than an old music-hall act, 'Scrooge and Marley', going through a creaky routine:

'You don't believe in me,' observed the Ghost.

'I don't,' said Scrooge.

'What evidence would you have of my reality beyond that of your senses?'

'I don't know,' said Scrooge.

'Why do you doubt your senses?'

'Because,' said Scrooge, 'a little thing affects them. A slight disorder of the stomach makes them cheats. You may be an undigested bit of beef, a blot of mustard, a crumb of cheese, a fragment of an underdone potato. There's more of gravy than the grave about you, whatever you are.' (p. 21)

Not a very good joke, perhaps, but clear evidence of the *Carol*'s theatrical qualities, in which characters repeatedly seem to speak to each other with an ear cocked for the response of a larger audience, and the first hint that Scrooge is capable of being converted, with that playful shift from 'gravy' to 'grave' showing how easily one thing can be transformed into something quite different. (Dickens is already practising what he will go on to preach: Scrooge's joke owes

---

[7] 'Imagination in *A Christmas Carol*', *Études Anglaises*, 32 (1979), 28–45 (39).

something to Falstaff's confession that his face reveals the effects not of gravity but of 'gravy, gravy, gravy'.[8]) 'Scrooge was not much in the habit of cracking jokes', the narrator goes on to explain, 'nor did he feel, in his heart, by any means waggish then. The truth is, that he tried to be smart, as a means of distracting his own attention, and keeping down his terror' (p. 21). One might make much the same claim about Dickens, who, like many of his contemporaries, routinely mocked the belief in ghosts as a lingering trace of the uncivilized past, but also found it impossible to shake more primitive feelings of dread out of his mind or voice. Dickens was not unusual in being unsure about how seriously to take such apparitions: the *Carol's* ghosts first materialized in the same decade as spiritualism, which divided audiences across Britain and America into those who eagerly attended séances to hear the voices of the dead, and those who questioned the spirits with much the same scepticism that Scrooge reveals in his interrogation of Marley. However, Dickens had especially good reasons for being troubled by the idea that the dead might refuse to stay dead. In April 1842, just over a year before he described Marley's ghost dragging his heavy chain across the floor, he had visited the shackled prisoners in the Western Penitentiary in Pittsburgh, Pennsylvania, and wrote to John Forster of being haunted by 'a horrible thought': '*What if ghosts be one of the terrors of these jails?* . . . The utter solitude by day and night; the hours of darkness; the silence of death; the mind for ever brooding on melancholy themes, and having no relief . . . The more I think of it, the more certain I feel that not a few of these men . . . are nightly visited by spectres.'[9] Perhaps it is not surprising that Dickens was troubled by the idea that prisoners were haunted by the ghosts of the past. After all, having to face hours of solitary and silent brooding was also his chosen fate as a writer, and there are good reasons for thinking that some of the 'melancholy themes' that weave in and out of his fiction—the blighting wrongs done to children; the need for imaginative escape; the hope that the controlled world of fiction might redeem the more disorderly world of fact—were the unsettled ghosts of his own past. But like all good comedians, Dickens was adept at laughing at the ideas he found most troubling, and in the *Carol* he caught a tone perfectly suspended between humour and

---

[8] *King Henry IV, Part II*, I. ii. 161.   [9] *Letters*, iii. 181.

horror, a comedy of terrors, that would allow him to contemplate the awfulness of dying unloved and alone while simultaneously distracting his attention with gags and bits of slapstick.

For the rest of his career, these tones would shift and swerve unpredictably against one another, like a narrative double-act of wise-cracking comedian and solemn sidekick, but at this stage they are carefully balanced. Only when Scrooge's character is no longer at odds with the generous tone of the story in which he finds himself will his conversion be complete, as he celebrates his return to the land of the living by launching himself into 'a splendid laugh, a most illustrious laugh. The father of a long, long line of brilliant laughs!'—a description that not only delightedly enacts the idea of echoing laughter in its self-generating repetitions, but also confirms that in the future Scrooge will be equally capable of laughing and making others laugh (p. 78). It is the final proof of an idea that Dickens has been investigating throughout the *Carol*. What does Scrooge learn about himself? Precisely what Dickens's readers are expected to learn about themselves, which is that even activities with the potential to isolate people from one another, including the act of reading, can be transformed into models of reciprocity and trust. Even if 'nothing ever happened on this globe, for good, at which some people did not have their fill of laughter at the outset' (p. 83), the possibility that laughter can divide people from one another does not cancel out the possibility that it can also bring them together, like the singing of a Christmas carol. Only by realizing that our actions are 'for good' in the twin sense of being both morally improving and permanent can we prevent ourselves from becoming like those pitiful ghosts that Scrooge sees whirling through the night air, like new Victorian arrivals in Dante's *Inferno*: 'The misery with them all was, clearly, that they sought to interfere, for good, in human matters, and had lost the power for ever' (p. 26).

We know that Dickens's ear was caught by one carol in particular, because in the opening pages a small boy, 'gnawed and mumbled by the hungry cold as bones are gnawed by dogs', stoops down at Scrooge's keyhole 'to regale him with a Christmas carol', and the one he chooses to try his luck is 'God Rest You Merry, Gentlemen' (p. 15). It is one of the shortest and strangest examples in Dickens's work of the adult novelist encountering his unhappy childhood self. It is also a curious example of Dickens's memory being overpowered by his imagination. Even before he published his story, this was a Christmas carol that was in the air: in 1833, William Sandys noted that 'In the metropolis a solitary itinerant may be occasionally heard in the streets, croaking out "God rest you merry, gentlemen," or some other old carol.'[10] One might then expect the ears of Dickens's readers to have been snagged by his misquotation, because what the small boy sings through Scrooge's keyhole is not 'God rest you merry, gentlemen' but 'God bless you merry gentleman! | May nothing you dismay!' Not a bad change if you're looking for some loose change, and if it is a mistake then it is a forgivable one, given that subsequent verses of the carol offer us a 'blessed babe', a 'blessed morn', and a 'blessed Angel', even if they do not go so far as a 'blessed bird'. But the slight shift in direction also quietly hints at the narrative trajectory of the *Carol* as a whole, in which Scrooge's new-found joy will spill over into cries of 'a merry Christmas' to strangers in the street, and the narrator's final words will expand the ideal family of the Cratchits to include his readers past, present, and yet to come: 'God bless Us, Every One!' (p. 83). At the same time, it offers the first clue that this is 'A Ghost Story of Christmas' in which nobody is expected to be seriously scared by Scrooge's spectral visitors, and certainly not in the way that Dickens imagined the nightmares of those Pennsylvanian prisoners. Like the flapping sheets and mechanical wails of a ghost-train, Scrooge's spirits haunt him in a sequence that is carefully plotted; the thrills are organized into an orderly sequence; the risks are stage-managed. Although the phrase 'God rest you' gains an edge of menace with the appearance of Marley's endlessly wandering ghost, in a scene that ripples uneasily with echoes of *Hamlet*, a pun such as 'gravy'/'grave' shows Dickens reassuring his readers that they need not be in any serious alarm that this story will veer away from a comic resolution: 'God rest you merry, gentlemen, | Let nothing you dismay.'

'The dire neglect of soul and body'

There was certainly plenty to cause Dickens dismay as he started to plan the *Carol* in 1843. He had recently visited a ragged school, established in a dilapidated house in the swarming slums of Saffron

---

[10] William Sandys, *Christmas Carols, Ancient and Modern* (London: Richard Bentley, 1833), p. cxxv; 'God Rest You Merry, Gentlemen' is reproduced on pp. 102–4.

Hill (the precise location, he later claimed, of Fagin's den in *Oliver Twist*), and had been appalled by what he found: 'a sickening atmosphere, in the midst of taint and dirt and pestilence: with all the deadly sins let loose, howling and shrieking at the doors.' 'I have very seldom seen', Dickens told the philanthropist Angela Burdett-Coutts, 'in all the strange and dreadful things I have seen in London and elsewhere, anything so shocking as the dire neglect of soul and body exhibited in these children.' Many of them earned a living through thieving or prostitution; others crept away at night to shelter 'under the dry arches of bridges and viaducts; under porticoes; sheds and carts; to outhouses; in sawpits; on staircases'; all were steeped in misery and squalor.[11] But who or what could rescue these pitiful creatures from the 'profound ignorance and perfect barbarism' into which they had been born? And how could Dickens's middle-class readers be brought to realize that Ignorance and Want—the 'meagre, ragged, scowling, wolfish' children who appear to Scrooge from beneath the robe of the Ghost of Christmas Present—were as much their responsibility as their own more pampered offspring? These were among the questions that Dickens returned to in a speech three weeks later at the Manchester Athenaeum, in which he again underlined the need for education to drive away ignorance, 'the most prolific parent of misery and crime', and ended with an appeal for workers and employers to come together in recognition of their 'mutual duty and responsibility'.[12] And so the public themes of *A Christmas Carol* started to fit together in Dickens's mind: education; charity; home.

There were also more private impulses at work. Sales of *Martin Chuzzlewit*, the novel in which he had set out to explore 'the number and variety of humour and vices that have their roots in selfishness', had started to flag. Dickens's decision to send his 'hero', Martin Chuzzlewit, off to America half-way through the serialization had done little to increase his popularity, and Dickens's publishers had started murmuring about a contractual clause that permitted them to subtract money from his income if the novel's sales did not meet the expectations set up by his handsome advance. A career that had been flourishing a year or two previously was threatening to unravel

[11] *Letters*, iii. 562–4.
[12] See John Butt, 'Dickens's Christmas Books', in *Pope, Dickens and Others* (Edinburgh: Edinburgh University Press, 1969), 136.

before his eyes. Nor was his private life in much better shape. His wife Catherine was expecting another child, and although it would be unfair to think that she was solely responsible for this state of affairs, the prospect of another mouth to feed cast Dickens into a state of mind that alternated between gloom and fury, saddled with 'a Donkey' of a wife and a father who insisted on cadging money off anyone who wanted to keep on good terms with his famous son. At one point, Dickens confessed, he dreamed of a baby being skewered on a toasting-fork: hardly the dream of a man looking forward to an extra mouth to feed. (Not that it embarrassed Dickens into keeping it to himself: this was also the dream in which 'a private gentleman and a particular friend' is announced to be 'as dead Sir . . . as a door-nail', so providing him with one of the opening sentences of his new book: 'Old Marley was as dead as a door-nail.') Even by his own standards he was restless and dissatisfied, involved in so many parallel careers—novelist, journalist, public speaker, social campaigner, and more—that his life seemed to be turning into a perpetual fidget. At the same time, his body had started to give out the first warning signals that it was not as keen as his mind to be involved in so much at once, with the appearance of intermittent facial spasms which he put down to 'rheumatism', but which seem just as likely to have been an angry nervous tic. And all the while there were the voices in his head: the characters who, he said, clustered around his desk as he wrote, clamouring for his attention, like ghosts who could only be laid to rest once they had been set down on the page. 'I seem to hear the people talking again', he told a French journalist at the time. By this he seems to have meant primarily that his head was still echoing with the voices of the people he had met on his recent trip to America, but it is hard to be sure, not least because Dickens himself did not always seem to know whether his characters were believable because they had been copied from life, or because the world was becoming as grotesque and fantastical as one of his stories. What does seem clear is that, given his recent sales figures, he would have been forgiven for wondering whether he had misheard what they had to say for themselves.

One word that looms up out of the first paragraph of the *Carol* is the capitalized ' 'Change': 'Scrooge's name was good upon 'Change for anything he chose to put his hand to.' Here ' 'Change' is short-hand for the Exchange, the centre of London's financial market in which Scrooge makes his money, but if Scrooge is 'good' for anything he puts his hand to, then what of other professions that involve putting one's name to bits of paper? What are writers good for? What is their business in life? Not easy questions to answer, especially by a writer who seemed unsure where his career was heading. And so he went back. Back to the cheerful tone of his biggest commercial success, *The Pickwick Papers*, from which he borrowed the interpolated tale of the gravedigger Gabriel Grub, 'an ill-conditioned, cross-grained, surly fellow—a morose and lonely man, who consorted with nobody but himself', converted by some mischievous goblins who show him visions of the past and future. Back to the thundering voice of Carlyle, with Scrooge's thin-lipped response to the men collecting charitable donations ('Are there no prisons? . . . And the Union workhouses? . . . The Treadmill and the Poor Law are in full vigour, then?') replaying and replying to Carlyle's sarcastic question in *Chartism* (1840): 'Are there not treadmills, gibbets; even hospitals, poor-rates, New-Poor Laws?' (pp. 13–14). Back to the world of the pantomime, Dickens's first and most lasting theatrical love, in which a Benevolent Spirit would magically transform the characters or their setting, creating a fairy-tale world in which, as Dickens recalled in 'A Christmas Tree' (1850), 'Everything is capable, with the greatest ease, of being changed into Anything, and "Nothing is, but thinking makes it so." ' Finally, back to the money-grubbing world of *Martin Chuzzlewit*, which Dickens was completing at the same time he was working on the *Carol*, and which had made him realize that there were more subtle ways of sending people abroad than merely packing them off to America. As Marley explains, 'It is required of every man . . . that the spirit within him should walk abroad among his fellow-men, and travel far and wide'—a form of self-projection one might expect writers to be especially skilled at, as the narrator of the *Carol* claims to be 'standing in the spirit at your elbow', but also one that Dickens wanted to show was at the heart of all the other ways in which one person might affect another 'for good' (pp. 22, 28). As he set to work on the *Carol*, Forster records with what 'a strange mastery it seized him',[13] laughing and crying aloud as he wrote, sending himself abroad with each movement of his hand across the page. And then,

[13] John Forster, *The Life of Charles Dickens* (1872–4), ed. with notes by A. J. Hoppé, 2 vols. (London: Dent, 1966), i. 283.

once he had finished his work for the day, he would be off, pacing the city streets through the night, sometimes covering ten or fifteen miles at a time. Perhaps he was attempting to wind himself ever tighter in the coils of the city. Perhaps he was attempting to pick up enough speed to escape its gravitational pull. All that can be said for certain is that motion and emotion were curiously tangled together in Dickens's mind,[14] and that if at the start of the *Carol* Scrooge is something of a self-parody of Dickens's fears about himself—the solitariness, the unhappy childhood, the desire for money—by the end Dickens had successfully brought him into line with a far more optimistic view of himself, as he bursts out into the street ready to send himself abroad imaginatively as well as physically, as light-hearted as he is light-footed.

The *Carol* took Dickens a little over six weeks to complete, and he wrote the final pages at the beginning of December, following it with 'The End' and three emphatic double underlinings. Then, he said, he 'broke out like a Madman': a whirl of parties, conjuring performances and dancing, as if he secretly worried that there would be something unhealthily Scrooge-like about staying in one place for too long during the festive season.[15] The book itself needed to be ready in time for the Christmas market, and Dickens kept his customary sharp eye on every aspect of its production. Priced at a relatively modest five shillings, it was handsomely (and seasonally) bound in red cloth, with gilt-edged pages, four hand-coloured etchings provided by John Leech, and four additional black and white wood engravings. Dickens had chosen to publish the book at his own expense, hoping that he would make more money by receiving a percentage of the profits than he would by accepting a one-off payment, and his anxiety is clear in the strained mood of self-congratulation that starts to appear in his letters: the *Carol* was a modern fairy-tale that would drive out 'the dragon of ignorance from its hearth'; it was a 'Sledge hammer' that would 'come down with twenty times the force—twenty thousand times the force'.[16] Financially, Dickens's nervousness was well

---

[14] George Augustus Sala, one of Dickens's protégés as a young journalist on *Household Words*, reported that 'It was one of Mr. Dickens's maxims that a given amount of mental exertion should be counteracted by a commensurate amount of bodily fatigue'; *Dickens: Interviews and Recollections*, ed. Philip Collins, 2 vols. (London: Macmillan, 1981), ii. 199.

[15] *Letters*, iv. 3.

[16] *Letters*, iii. 461.

founded: although the *Carol* had sold some 6,000 copies by Christmas Eve, and kept on selling well into the New Year, the high cost of production meant that he received less than a quarter of the profits he had been expecting. In every other way, though, the publication was an unprecedented success.

The critics were almost uniformly kind. One or two murmured that Dickens's genial tone was maybe a little overbearing, his hospitality a little suffocating—a view later echoed by G. K. Chesterton, who noted that Dickens 'tended sometimes to pile up the cushions until none of the characters could move'—but otherwise the reviews were full of praise for his skill in producing a conversion story that was also squarely aimed at changing the hearts and minds of its readers.[17] Francis Jeffrey applauded the *Carol*'s 'genuine *goodness*'; the usually sharp-tongued Theodore Martin argued that it was 'finely felt, and calculated to work much social good'; Thackeray described it with envy-tinged admiration as 'a national benefit, and to every man and woman who reads it a personal kindness'; even Margaret Oliphant, who came up with the faintest praise of all, later characterizing Dickens's book as 'the apotheosis of turkey and plum pudding', admitted that 'it moved us all in those days as if it had been a new gospel'.[18] Many of the ways in which the *Carol* moved its readers have since passed into critical folklore. Jane Welsh Carlyle reported that 'visions of Scrooge' had so worked on her husband's 'nervous organisation' that 'he has been seized with a perfect *convulsion* of hospitality, and had actually insisted on *improvising two* dinner parties'. A Mr Fairbanks, who attended a Christmas Eve reading of the *Carol* in Boston in 1867, was so moved that thereafter he closed his factory on Christmas Day and sent every worker a turkey. 'Dickens' *Christmas Carol* helps the poultry business amazingly,' as one wag noted in *Wilkes's Spirit of the Times* (21 December 1867). 'Everybody who reads it and who has money immediately rushes off and buys a turkey for the poor.'[19] Wherever one looks in the period,

---

[17] G. K. Chesterton, *Charles Dickens* (London: Methuen, 1906, repr. 1943), 128.

[18] *Dickens: The Critical Heritage*, ed. Philip Collins (London: Routledge, 1971), 147–50.

[19] See Paul Davis, *The Lives and Times of Ebenezer Scrooge* (New Haven: Yale University Press, 1990). Carlyle later had a change of heart, complaining that Dickens 'thought men ought to be buttered up, and the world made soft and accommodating for them, and all sorts of fellows have turkey for their Christmas dinner', *Dickens: Interviews and Recollections*, i. 63–4.

in fact, there are examples of the *Carol* being read as a good book that also did much good. Nor were its practical effects only of the charitable kind. By the end of February 1844, there were eight rival theatrical productions of the *Carol* running simultaneously in London, while replies from other writers started to appear in print, including W. M. Swepstone's *Christmas Shadows* (1850), Horatio Alger's *Job Warner's Christmas* (1863), and Louisa May Alcott's *A Christmas Dream, and How It Came True* (1882), like a set of variations on the theme of redemption: some of them describing Scrooge's new life as a reformed man, and others less charitably showing where, in the writer's humble opinion, Dickens's story needed to be put right.

Dickens himself seemed equally unable to leave his story alone, periodically returning to it during the rest of his career to tweak the phrasing or fiddle with the punctuation. But perhaps this is not surprising when one considers the central place that Christmas occupied in his career. From his early short essay 'A Christmas Dinner' in *Sketches by Boz* (1836) to his incomplete final novel *The Mystery of Edwin Drood* (1870), in which an uncle appears to have murdered his nephew on Christmas Day, Christmas is sunk into his imagination like a watermark. Year after year his mind would strike off in different directions; year after year he would return to the same imaginative centre, as Christmas exerted its gravitational pull. 'We all come home, or ought to come home, for a short holiday,' he writes in 'A Christmas Tree', and the scattered evidence of his stories suggests that Christmas provided him with something similar in his writing: a short holiday from the relentless grind of producing monthly instalments of the latest novel; a return to his imaginative roots; a home-key. 'Christmas was always a time which in our home was looked forward to with eagerness and delight', his daughter Mamie recalled, while his son Henry agreed that Christmas in the Dickens household 'was a great time, a really jovial time, and my father was always at his best, a splendid host, bright and jolly as a boy and throwing his heart and soul into everything that was going on'. However rosy these recollections, others observed that Dickens's enjoyment of Christmas seemed more determined, even ruthless, than one might expect from someone with a genuinely boyish sense of fun: whether he was learning a new conjuring trick, or mastering the steps to a dance, his son Charles noted, there was always the same 'alarming thoroughness with which he always threw himself into everything he had occasion to take up'.[20] If Christmas was a time for returning to the world of childhood, it was also a time for asserting control over it, measuring how far he had travelled from a period that he tended to look back on with the same self-pity that stirs Scrooge when he encounters his younger self: 'a lonely boy was reading near a feeble fire; and Scrooge ... wept to see his poor forgotten self as he used to be' (p. 31).

The four Christmas Books that were written to capitalize on the success of the *Carol*, in particular, allowed Dickens to reflect on what had changed in the previous year and what had remained constant. All of them attempted to follow the pattern set down by their popular predecessor, by weaving urgent social questions—the plight of agricultural labourers; the self-satisfied exhortations of political economists; the young women driven to suicide by poverty and hypocrisy—into a story of conversion. In *The Chimes: A Goblin Story of Some Bells that Rang an Old Year Out and a New Year In* (1844), the spirits of the chimes forcibly remind good-hearted messenger Trotty Veck of the danger in believing that the poor are 'born bad', by showing him his power to affect the future of those he loves. *The Cricket on the Hearth: A Fairy Tale of Home* (1845) emerged from Dickens's plan to launch a periodical called 'The Cricket', intended to put the homely ideals of the *Carol* into wider circulation, and its story of a marriage put under strain by suspicions of infidelity combined a melodramatic plot with the 'vein of glowing, heart, generous, mirthful, beaming reference in everything to Home and Fireside' that he had earlier identified with his '*Carol* philosophy'.[21] *The Battle of Life: A Love Story* (1846) reworked many of the same ingredients into a still less believable plot, as Marion Jeddler sacrifices her lover to her sister, and her good example converts her cynical father into a model of beaming gratitude. Finally, after a pause of two years during which Dickens was working on *Dombey and Son* (despite being 'very loath to lose the money. And still more so to leave any gap at Christmas firesides which I ought to fill'), there appeared *The Haunted Man and the Ghost's Bargain: A Fancy for Christmas Time*

---

[20] *My Father As I Recall Him* (Westminster: Roxburgh Press, 1896), 26; *My Father As I Knew Him* (London: William Heinemann, 1934), 44; *Dickens: Interviews and Recollections*, i. 133.
[21] Forster, *Life*, i. 301.

(1848), which concerns an embittered scholar, Redlaw, who is offered forgetfulness by his ghostly double, and is brought to recognize that without his memories of suffering he is unable to sympathize with anyone else—a story with 'a good Christmas tendency', Dickens claimed.

The later Christmas Books were popular with the public, who bought them in their thousands, and to begin with, at least, Dickens was confident in their power to be as effective as the *Carol*, crowing in one letter that *The Chimes* 'has a grip upon the very throat of the public'. The critics were less convinced. *The Times* described *The Cricket on the Hearth* as 'a twaddling manifestation of silliness almost from the first page to the last', and *The Battle of Life*, even when compared to 'the deluge of trash' that Dickens had inspired other writers to produce for the growing Christmas market, as '*the worst . . . the very worst*'. If the *Carol* had been seen as simple-hearted, its sequels were largely dismissed by reviewers as simple-minded, despite the undiminished applause of the public: a divergence of views, according to one weary notice of *The Battle of Life*, that only went to confirm the time-honoured truth that 'book-buyers and reviewers do not always entertain similar opinions'.[22] Even Dickens was not convinced that a seasonal offering like *The Battle of Life* was quite as generous as it made out, confessing to Forster 'I really do not know what this story is worth.' The verdict of posterity has been 'not much', but the later Christmas Books are still worth reading carefully for the light—and the shadows—they cast on Dickens's more famous works. Sometimes this is a matter of fleeting echoes, so that to eyes grown used to Dickens's development as a novelist, these stories offer good examples of his peculiar imaginative combination of fecundity and thrift, as ideas that are worked out later in far more confident and convincing detail are here presented as narrative doodles, thin in themselves but pregnant with possibility. (*The Battle of Life*, for example, was a title that Dickens liked so much he even considered reusing it for his later novel on the theme of heroic self-sacrifice, before settling on *A Tale of Two Cities* as a less confusing choice.) Sometimes it is a matter of a shared obsession with a single idea, such as the security and intimacy of home, and the repeated problems Dickens faced in trying to describe happy homes in the

---

[22] *Dickens: The Critical Heritage*, 154–76.

here and now, given his tendency to think of home as an ideal that has either been lost or has yet to come into being. (Consider the cry of Scrooge's sister, 'I have come to bring you home, dear brother . . . To bring you home, home, home' (p. 33), which, as is so often the case with Dickens's prose when it slips into the rhythms of verse, seems oddly suspended between mourning and magical incantation.) But the key reason for reading the Christmas Books, for all their melodramatic contortions and sentimental spasms, is that they represent Dickens's most concentrated and sustained investigation into the benefits and dangers of fiction: how it works, what we use it for, and why the world of books, while offering a model of the real world, can never take its place.

'No one was more intensely fond than Dickens of old nursery tales,' Forster wrote in his description of the *Carol*'s composition, 'and he had a secret delight in feeling that he was here only giving them a higher form.'[23] There was certainly a strong association in Dickens's mind between fairy-tales and Christmas, both of which he connected with the idea of conversion. Stories of religious conversion had occupied a popular market niche for a number of years, but Dickens was unusual in assuming that being converted to a new way of life was intimately bound up with the transformative powers of the imagination—powers which were the special privilege of children, and which were especially stimulated by such books as those Scrooge sees his younger self reading: the *Arabian Nights*, old romances, *Robinson Crusoe*. The links between religious conversion and imaginative transformation, tract and fairy-tale, make themselves felt in the *Carol* from the first page to the last, beginning with a playful variation on the traditional 'Once upon a time' ('Marley was dead, to begin with') and ending with Tiny Tim's 'God bless Us, Every One!'—a prayer that holds under its breath the question of how far the traditional 'they lived happily ever after' might stretch. However, as Dickens continues to test the idea in his later Christmas Books, the pleasures of reading come under greater scrutiny; the power of the imagination comes into doubt.

David Copperfield, in a strongly autobiographical passage, records how as a child David finds himself in a 'blessed little room' containing a small collection of books, from whose pages 'Roderick Random,

[23] Forster, *Life*, i. 371.

Peregrine Pickle, Humphrey Clinker, Tom Jones, The Vicar of Wakefield, Don Quixote, Gil Blas, and Robinson Crusoe, came out, a glorious host, to keep me company. They kept alive my fancy, and my hope of something beyond that place and time.'[24] Again, one notices a biblical strain weaving in and out of Dickens's writing— 'blessed . . . glorious host'—but a few years earlier, in *The Cricket on the Hearth*, he had warned that those who live exclusively in a world of fancy risk being deluded rather than blessed. Caleb Plummer constructs stories for his blind daughter Bertha with all the care of a novelist: to her ears, at least, his shabby clothes are magnificent; his employer is a paragon of benevolence; their house is a palace. Over time, their conversations have taken on the form of a sentimental routine, in which Bertha asks her father leading questions to which he replies with a heavy heart but a cheerful voice, conjuring up a fantasy for her to live in that is only on nodding terms with the real world. As Scott Moncrieff has noted, Dickens takes some care to distinguish his own imaginative skill from that of his hero: 'Caleb's poor inventive powers have produced a limited repertoire of descriptions, which he and his daughter repeat to each other, almost like a pathetic vaudeville team.'[25] But this does not entirely remove the disturbing parallel between their imaginative collusion and Dickens's relationship with his reader; nor does it prevent questioning shadows from being cast back across Dickens's attempts in the earlier Christmas Books to reconcile the twin demands of realism and romance, describing the world both as it is and as one might wish it to be. There is not much to separate Caleb's attempt to brighten up their miserable life and Dickens's buoyant descriptions of the Cratchits' scanty Christmas dinner. 'But that's the worst of my calling,' Caleb confesses, 'I'm always deluding myself and swindling myself' (p. 192). Not unlike the novelist. One of the key words of the Christmas Books is 'fancy', which for Dickens designated the mind's power to make the real world more like the possible worlds of fiction. But how far should the writer go in disguising the truth so as to make it more palatable? At what point does the exercise of fancy become merely fanciful?

Dickens rarely asks such questions directly, but they continue to bubble uneasily under the surface of stories that otherwise seem

---

[24] *David Copperfield* (1849–50), ch. 4.
[25] 'The Cricket in the Study', *Dickens Studies Annual*, 22 (1993), 137–53 (150).

wholly self-assured, even a little smug. Some of this unease seems to have been provoked by Dickens's inability to predict or control how his fiction would be understood once it had been released into the literary market-place. It certainly does not suggest any great confidence in the interpretative powers of his readers that Trotty Veck's only response to his newspaper in *The Chimes* is that it is 'full of obserwations', or that the model reader in *The Battle of Life* is a woman whose entire library is kept engraved on a thimble and a nutmeg-grater, or that her husband attempts to follow her mouthed warning about Michael Warden 'with looks of deep amazement and perplexity . . . answered her signals with other signals expressive of the deepest distress and confusion—followed the motions of her lips—guessed half aloud "milk and water," "monthly warning," "mice and walnuts"—and couldn't approach her meaning' (p. 306). More awkward still seems to have been Dickens's growing sense that, for himself as much as for his readers, these stories were too orderly, too neat to be true to the complexity of the problems he was addressing: the responses of readers; the responsibilities of writers; the dangers of misinterpretation. Indeed, the more often he returned to Christmas in these books, the more self-conscious he seems to have become about what lay behind his work as a novelist, and whether a set of short stories would help his development or turn out to be no more than a form of narrative stuttering. The problem with writing a story inspired by those he read as a boy was that he might not be refreshing his creative powers so much as driving them back. It was a dilemma that can be heard at every level of the Christmas Books: the reduction of complex moral arguments to neat formulas, such as Clemency Newcome's 'For-get and For-give' and 'Do as you—would—be—done by'; the wary repetitions of 'little', a word that is returned to like someone touching a bruise; the miniaturization of social debates down to a single family group, producing the spectacle of a writer who was to be characterized by Ruskin as 'the leader of the steam-whistle party *par excellence*',[26] in recognition of his forward-thinking views, spending the opening six pages of *The Cricket on the Hearth* describing a singing competition between the merry little cricket and a kettle 'Hum, hum, hum—m—m' ing on the hob. Clearly there were large questions that needed to be tackled,

[26] Letter to Charles Eliot Norton (19 June 1870), repr. in *Dickens: The Critical Heritage*, 443–4.

and Dickens needed a larger form in which to take them on. It may not be a coincidence, then, that the final Christmas Book was published at the end of 1848, only a few weeks before he started to work on the novel that would give these concerns—the power of the past to shape identity, the effects of reading fiction, the limits of the imagination—their most ambitious literary shape: *David Copperfield*.

Sending himself abroad

By 1849 Dickens no longer had the time or energy to publish a separate story each Christmas, although many of the ideas he had first explored in the Christmas Books continued to send out shockwaves into the later novels. The boy named as 'Ignorance' in the *Carol*, for example, on whose brow is written Doom 'unless the writing be erased', would be rewritten as *Bleak House*'s Jo, who 'don't know nothink'. The sympathetic portrait in *The Cricket on the Hearth* of an older man wooing and marrying a much younger woman is one that Dickens would return to with the brooding force of an obsession in the years to come: Dr Strong in *David Copperfield*, Arthur Clennam in *Little Dorrit*, Joe Gargery in *Great Expectations*. Most self-consciously, the idea of being chained to one's past, which had extended its own links from Marley's ghost in the *Carol*, to the hope of Redlaw in *The Haunted Man* that he might destroy the 'golden links' of his 'intertwisted chain of feelings and associations', would later re-emerge in *Great Expectations*, as Abel Magwitch stumbles out of the mist on Christmas Day to be freed from his shackles by Pip, an action that is later revealed to have been 'the first link' of 'the long chain' that binds their lives together. But although Dickens was increasingly preoccupied with editing the journals *Household Words* (1850–9) and *All the Year Round* (1859–70), which had taken over many of the social functions he associated with his '*Carol* philosophy', he continued to write stories that were intended for Christmas, even if, like many of the later Christmas Books, they were not centrally about Christmas. His best contributions, though, such as 'What Christmas Is, As We Grow Older' (see Appendix 1), were both at once. The essay was first published in 1851 as Dickens's leading article for the annual Christmas number of *Household Words*, with the aim that it should 'strike the chord of the season'. As this was the first in a series of stories especially commissioned for the

Christmas issue, it strikes something more like the first note in a broken chord, but the aim is clear enough: like the Christmas songs described the previous year in Tennyson's *In Memoriam* ('Our voices took a higher range; | Once more we sang: "They do not die | Nor lose their mortal sympathy, | Nor change to us, although they change" '),[27] these stories were supposed to appeal to feelings of community by showing how well different voices could blend together. That was the theory, anyway. In practice, despite his attempts to cosy up to his readers with titles such as 'A Round of Stories by the Christmas Fire' (1852), Dickens gradually became disillusioned with this model of publication. His stated reasons for doing so were predictable enough: there was a 'want of cohesion or originality' in his fellow contributors, so that in the cold light of print what had originally been idealized as a neat 'round' of stories ended up as something far lumpier and more lop-sided. However, Dickens may also have had another reason to be dissatisfied. In 1853, he had given a public reading of the *Carol*, and here at last he had discovered a solution to the problem of how best to reach his audience: he would do it in person. How better to assure himself that he had created a mutually responsive relationship of storyteller and listener than by inviting his readers to cluster around him, like an extended family or 'a group of friends, listening to a tale told by a winter fire'?[28] In all, between 1853 and 1870, he gave no fewer than 127 performances of the *Carol*, by far his most popular full-length reading, in an abbreviated version (see Appendix 2) that allowed him to bring together a diverse readership into a single body of listeners, and then fire them with an affection for Dickens and for each other, creating a perfect Christmas on demand. (One might note in passing how often the words 'hearth' and 'heart' appear in close proximity in the Christmas Books, as if trying to blend into a single ideal of domestic warmth.) Of course, such readings did not answer all the questions Dickens had raised in 1843; some questions, like some ghosts, are easier to raise than to appease. But here, standing by his reading-desk, Dickens was finally doing what Scrooge vows to do, by living in the past, present, and future all at once. He was young Scrooge, the small boy 'intent upon his reading'; he was old Scrooge,

[27] *In Memoriam*, XXX.
[28] See Philip Collins's introduction to *Charles Dickens: The Public Readings* (Oxford: Clarendon Press, 1975).

changing before the audience's eyes in the charmed circle of the performance; he was Scrooge after the end of the story, offering himself to the public in the hope of doing them some good. It was a performance fully in keeping with his understanding of the spirit of Christmas: summoning the ghosts of the past; healing the wounds opened up by time; transforming the world to fit the shape of his imagination.

Is that too optimistic as a description? One should be wary of romanticizing the gruelling nature of the public readings: these were the performances, after all, that left Dickens frail and exhausted, and quite possibly hastened his early death, a driven man who could go no further. One should be equally wary of romanticizing the effect of the Christmas Books themselves: more than one commentator has pointed out that Dickens, described by Walter Bagehot as 'a sentimental radical',[29] was far better at affecting the mood of the nation than he was at creating any serious pressure for social change. (Lenin walked out of a production of *The Cricket on the Hearth* at the Moscow Arts Theatre in 1922 because, according to his wife, 'Dickens's middle-class sentimentality began to get on his nerves'.)[30] Give or take a turkey or two, Dickens's skill at playing on his audience's heartstrings did not necessarily lead to much loosening of their purse-strings. But if one had to find an image of what he was trying to achieve in the Christmas Books, one could do worse than pause over this picture of the novelist conjuring up stories at his reading-desk. 'The Inimitable', his face illuminated by the flaring gas-jets, gripping the public by the throat. Standing at their elbow. Sending himself abroad.

[29] Repr. in Wall (ed.), *Charles Dickens*, 136.

[30] Nadezhda Krupskaya, *Memories of Lenin* (London: Lawrence and Wishart, 1942), 299; the incident is discussed by Michael Patrick Hearn in *The Annotated Christmas Carol* (New York: W. W. Norton, 2004), p. ciii.

NOTE ON THE TEXT

THE Christmas Books were first published individually as illustrated volumes each December from 1843 to 1848, with the exception of 1847, when Dickens was too preoccupied with amateur theatricals and the final instalments of *Dombey and Son* to satisfy public demand for what had rapidly become a popular annual tradition. *A Christmas Carol* appeared in 1843, *The Chimes* in 1844, *The Cricket on the Hearth* in 1845, *The Battle of Life* in 1846, and *The Haunted Man* in 1848. In these volumes Dickens experimented with a form of 'rhetorical' punctuation that was based more on speech-rhythms than on grammatical sense, although he did not apply it consistently, and abandoned it in later editions, possibly because the success of his public reading versions of the Christmas Books encouraged him to separate public performance from the experience of silent reading. The Christmas Books appeared together for the first time in the 1852 Cheap Edition, originally in seventeen weekly numbers, then in four monthly parts, and finally as a single volume, for which Dickens added a revised Preface. For the 1868 Charles Dickens Edition, Dickens made some minor corrections and revisions, and supplied new descriptive running headlines. This is the edition which represents his final published intentions for the Christmas Books, and it forms the basis of the text printed here. Printer's errors have been silently corrected, although no attempt has been made to update standard nineteenth-century forms of spelling and punctuation that appear consistently in the original texts; the running headlines have not been reproduced.

The manuscripts of *A Christmas Carol*, *The Cricket on the Hearth*, and *The Battle of Life* are in the Pierpont Morgan Library, New York; a facsimile edition of *A Christmas Carol* was published by the Folio Press in 1970, and another by the Pierpont Morgan Library in 1993. The manuscript of *The Chimes* is in the Forster Collection of the Victoria and Albert Museum, London, along with Dickens's corrected proof-copy. The manuscript of *The Haunted Man*, formerly in the Pforzheimer Library, New York, is now in private hands. Dickens's public reading versions of four of the

Christmas Books—*A Christmas Carol, The Chimes, The Cricket on the Hearth*, and (left in an unfinished state) *The Haunted Man*—are reproduced in *Charles Dickens: The Public Readings*, edited by Philip Collins (Oxford: Clarendon Press, 1975). 'What Christmas Is, As We Grow Older' (Appendix 1) was first published as the leading article in the Christmas number of *Household Words* for 1851. The pages from Dickens's reading version of *A Christmas Carol* (Appendix 2) are reproduced from his prompt-book copy held by the New York Public Library; a facsimile edition was published in 1971 edited by Philip Collins.

Note on the illustrations

Dickens was forced to make several changes to the appearance of *A Christmas Carol* during the publication of the first edition. His original plan had been to use green endpapers, but the printing process ended up producing a drab olive colour that failed to suggest a suitably festive mood, so for the second issue they were quickly altered to yellow; this colour then clashed with the title page, which had to be changed to red and blue. The title page and four of the illustrations by John Leech (reproduced below on pp. 4, 20, 45, and 76) were expensively but crudely hand coloured, which was intended to make the edition look luxurious while keeping the price down to an affordable five shillings. Dickens professed himself to be satisfied with the results, but he did not repeat the experiment in the later Christmas Books, which included black and white illustrations (of variable size and quality) by a range of Victorian artists, including Daniel Maclise, Clarkson Stanfield, Richard Doyle, and John Tenniel. This Oxford World's Classics edition reproduces all of John Leech's original illustrations to *A Christmas Carol*, and a selection of the illustrations to *The Chimes, The Cricket on the Hearth, The Battle of Life*, and *The Haunted Man*, as follows: John Leech, pp. 139, 160, 187, 241, 346, 389; Daniel Maclise, pp. 84, 162, 244, 287, 320; John Tenniel, p. 322.

SELECT BIBLIOGRAPHY

Biographies and reference works

Peter Ackroyd, *Dickens* (London: Sinclair Stevenson, 1990).

Philip Collins (ed.), *Dickens: The Critical Heritage* (London: Routledge, 1971).

—— *Dickens: Interviews and Recollections*, 2 vols. (London: Macmillan, 1981).

John Forster, *The Life of Charles Dickens*, 3 vols. (1872–4), ed. with notes by A. J. Hoppé (London: Dent, 1966).

Ruth F. Glancy (ed.), *Dickens's Christmas Books, Christmas Stories, and Other Short Fiction. An Annotated Bibliography* (New York: Garland Publishing, 1985).

Michael Patrick Hearn (ed.), *The Annotated Christmas Carol* (New York and London: W. W. Norton, 1976).

Andrew Sanders, *Authors in Context: Charles Dickens* (Oxford: Oxford University Press, 2003).

Paul Schlicke (ed.), *The Oxford Reader's Companion to Dickens* (Oxford: Oxford University Press, 1999).

Related writings by Dickens

Charles Dickens: The Public Readings, ed. Philip Collins (Oxford: Clarendon Press, 1975).

A Christmas Carol: The Public Reading Version. A Facsimile of the Author's Prompt-copy, ed. Philip Collins (New York: New York Public Library, 1971).

A Christmas Carol and Other Christmas Writings, ed. Michael Slater (London: Penguin, 2003). Includes the essays 'Christmas Festivities', 'A Christmas Tree', and 'What Christmas Is, As We Grow Older', and Christmas episodes from *The Pickwick Papers* ('The Story of the Goblins Who Stole a Sexton') and *Master Humphrey's Clock*.

The Pilgrim Edition of the Letters of Charles Dickens, 12 vols. (Oxford: Clarendon Press, 1965–2002). The letters most relevant to the composition of the Christmas Books are concentrated in volumes iii–v.

The Speeches of Charles Dickens, ed. K. J. Fielding (Oxford: Clarendon Press, 1960).

Critical studies of the Christmas Books

John Butt, 'Dickens's Christmas Books', in *Pope, Dickens and Others* (Edinburgh: Edinburgh University Press, 1969).

G. K. Chesterton, 'Dickens and Christmas', in *Charles Dickens* (London: Methuen, 1906).

Jane R. Cohen, 'The Illustrators of the Christmas Books', in *Charles Dickens and His Original Illustrators* (Columbus, Oh.: Ohio State University Press, 1980).

George H. Ford, 'Dickens and the Voices of Time', *Nineteenth-Century Fiction*, 24 (1970), 428–48.

Humphry House, *The Dickens World* (Oxford: Oxford University Press, 1941).

S. A. Muresianu, *The History of the Victorian Christmas Book* (New York: Garland Publishing, 1987).

Robert L. Patten, ' "A Surprising Transformation": Dickens and the Hearth', in U. C. Knoepflmacher and G. B. Tennyson (eds.), *Nature and the Victorian Imagination* (Berkeley: University of California Press, 1977), 153–70.

Harry Stone, 'The Christmas Books: Giving Nursery Tales a Higher Form', in *Dickens and the Invisible World: Fairy Tales, Fantasy and Novel-Making* (Bloomington, Ind.: Indiana University Press, 1979).

Deborah Thomas, *Dickens and the Short Story* (Philadelphia: University of Pennsylvania Press, 1982).

Kathleen Tillotson, 'The Middle Years from the *Carol* to *Copperfield*', *Dickens Memorial Lectures 1970*, a special supplement to *The Dickensian*, 65 (1970), 7–19.

Edmund Wilson, 'Dickens: the Two Scrooges', in *The Wound and the Bow* (London: W. H. Allen & Co., 1941).

A Christmas Carol

Philip Collins, 'Carol Philosophy, Cheerful Views', *Études Anglaises*, 23 (1970), 158–67.

Paul Davis, *The Lives and Times of Ebenezer Scrooge* (New Haven: Yale University Press, 1990).

The Dickensian, 89: 3 (Winter 1993). Special issue commemorating the 150th anniversary of *A Christmas Carol*'s first publication; essays include J. Hillis Miller, 'The Genres of *A Christmas Carol*', 193–206, and Michael Slater, 'The Triumph of Humour: The *Carol* Revisited', 184–92.

Ruth Glancy, 'Dickens and Christmas: His Framed-Tale Themes', *Nineteenth-Century Fiction*, 35 (1980), 53–72.

Fred Guida, *A Christmas Carol and its Adaptations: A Critical Examination of Dickens's Story and its Productions on Screen and Television* (Jefferson, NC: McFarland & Co. Inc., 2000).

Graham Holderness, 'Imagination in *A Christmas Carol*', *Études Anglaises*, 32 (1979), 28–45.

Robert L. Patten, 'Dickens Time and Again', *Dickens Studies Annual*, 2 (1972), 163–96.

John Sutherland, 'How Do the Cratchits Cook Scrooge's Turkey?', in *Who Betrays Elizabeth Bennett? Further Puzzles in Classical Fiction* (Oxford: Oxford University Press, 1999), 49–54.

The Chimes

Marilyn J. Kurata, 'Fantasy and Realism: A Defence of *The Chimes*', *Dickens Studies Annual*, 13 (1984), 19–34.

Michael Shelden, 'Dickens, "The Chimes", and the Anti-Corn Law League', *Victorian Studies*, 25 (1982), 329–53.

Michael Slater, 'Dickens (and Forster) at work on *The Chimes*', *Dickens Studies*, 2 (1966), 106–40.

—— 'Dickens's Tract for the Times', in *Dickens 1970* (London: Chapman and Hall, 1970).

—— 'Carlyle and Jerrold into Dickens: A Study of *The Chimes*', *Nineteenth-Century Fiction*, 24 (1970), 506–26.

Sheila Smith, 'John Overs to Charles Dickens: A Working-Man's Letter and Its Implications', *Victorian Studies*, 18 (1974), 195–217.

The Cricket on the Hearth

Sylvia Manning, 'Dickens, January, and May', *The Dickensian*, 71 (1975), 67–74.

Scott Moncrieff, '*The Cricket* in the Study', *Dickens Studies Annual*, 22 (1993), 137–53.

The Battle of Life

Katherine Carolan, '*The Battle of Life*, a Love Story', *The Dickensian*, 69 (1973), 105–10.

Ruth Glancy, 'The Shaping of *The Battle of Life*: Dickens's Manuscript Revisions', *Dickens Studies Annual*, 17 (1988), 67–89.

The Haunted Man

Ruth Glancy, 'Dickens at Work on *The Haunted Man*', *Dickens Studies Annual*, 15 (1986), 65–85.

Malcolm Morley, 'Pepper and *The Haunted Man*', *The Dickensian*, 48 (1952), 185–90.

Harry Stone, 'Dickens's Artistry in *The Haunted Man*', *South Atlantic Quarterly*, 61 (1962), 492–505.

—— 'The Love Pattern in Dickens's Novels', in Robert B. Partlow Jr.

(ed.), *Dickens the Craftsman: Strategies of Presentation* (Carbondale, Ill.: Southern Illinois University Press, 1970).

Further reading in Oxford World's Classics

Charles Dickens, *Barnaby Rudge*, ed. Clive Hurst, with introduction by Jon Mee and Iain McCalman.

—— *Bleak House*, ed. Stephen Gill.

—— *David Copperfield*, ed. Nina Burgis, with introduction by Andrew Sanders.

—— *Dombey and Son*, ed. Alan Horsman, with introduction by Dennis Walder.

—— *Great Expectations*, ed. Margaret Cardwell, with introduction by Kate Flint.

—— *Hard Times*, ed. Paul Schlicke.

—— *Little Dorrit*, ed. Harvey Peter Sucksmith.

—— *Martin Chuzzlewit*, ed. Margaret Cardwell.

—— *The Mystery of Edwin Drood*, ed. Margaret Cardwell.

—— *Nicholas Nickleby*, ed. Paul Schlicke.

—— *The Old Curiosity Shop*, ed. Elizabeth M. Brennan.

—— *Oliver Twist*, ed. Stephen Gill.

—— *Our Mutual Friend*, ed. Michael Cotsell.

—— *The Pickwick Papers*, ed. James Kinsley.

—— *A Tale of Two Cities*, ed. Andrew Sanders.

E. T. A. Hoffmann, *The Golden Pot and Other Tales*, trans. Ritchie Robertson.

Andrew Sanders, *Charles Dickens* (Authors in Context).

A CHRONOLOGY OF CHARLES DICKENS

Dickens's major fictions are indicated by bold type.

Life	*Historical and Cultural Background*
1809 (13 June) John Dickens, a clerk in the Navy Pay Office, marries Elizabeth Barrow.	
1810 (28 Oct.) Frances Dickens ('Fanny') born.	
1811	Prince of Wales becomes Prince Regent. W. M. Thackeray born. Jane Austen, *Sense and Sensibility*
1812 (7 Feb.) Charles Dickens born at Mile End Terrace, Landport, Portsea (now 393 Old Commercial Road, Portsmouth).	Luddite riots. War between Britain and the United States. Napoleon's retreat from Moscow. Robert Browning and Edward Lear born. Lord Byron, *Childe Harold's Pilgrimage*, i and ii (completed 1818)
1813	Robert Southey becomes Poet Laureate. Napoleon defeated at Leipzig. Austen, *Pride and Prejudice*; Byron, *The Bride of Abydos*, *The Giaour*; P. B. Shelley, *Queen Mab*
1814 Birth (Mar.) and death (Sept.) of Alfred Allen Dickens.	Napoleon exiled to Elba. Austen, *Mansfield Park*; Sir Walter Scott, *Waverley*; William Wordsworth, *The Excursion*
1815 (1 Jan.) Dickens family moves to London.	Escape of Napoleon; Battle of Waterloo. Anthony Trollope born. Thomas Robert Malthus, *An Inquiry into Rent*; Scott, *Guy Mannering*
1816 (Apr.) Letitia Dickens born.	Charlotte Brontë born. Austen, *Emma*; S. T. Coleridge, *Christabel and Other Poems*; Thomas Love Peacock, *Headlong Hall*; Scott, *The Antiquary*, *Old Mortality*
1817 (Apr.) Dickens family settles in Chatham.	Jane Austen dies. Byron, *Manfred*; Coleridge, *Biographia Literaria*; John Keats, *Poems*; Robert Owen, *Report to the Committee on the Poor Law*; Scott, *Rob Roy*

Life	Historical and Cultural Background
1818	Emily Brontë born. Austen, *Northanger Abbey*, *Persuasion* (posth.); Keats, *Endymion*; Peacock, *Nightmare Abbey*; Scott, *The Heart of Midlothian*; Mary Shelley, *Frankenstein*
1819 (Sept.) Harriet Dickens born.	Princess Victoria born. Peterloo 'Massacre' (11 deaths). A. H. Clough, Mary Anne Evans (George Eliot), Charles Kingsley, John Ruskin born. Byron, *Don Juan*, i–ii (continued till 1824); Scott, *The Bride of Lammermoor*; Wordsworth, *Peter Bell*, *The Waggoner*
1820 Frederick Dickens ('Fred') born.	Death of George III; accession of Prince Regent as George IV. Trial of Queen Caroline. Anne Brontë born. John Clare, *Poems, Descriptive of Rural Life*; Keats, *Lamia, Isabella, The Eve of St Agnes and Other Poems*; Malthus, *Principles of Political Economy*; Charles Robert Maturin, *Melmoth the Wanderer*; P. B. Shelley, *The Cenci, Prometheus Unbound*; Scott, *Ivanhoe*
1821 CD goes to school run by William Giles.	Greek War of Independence starts. Napoleon dies. Keats dies. Clare, *The Village Minstrel and Other Poems*; Thomas De Quincey, *Confessions of an English Opium Eater*; Pierce Egan, *Life in London*; Thomas Moore, *Irish Melodies*; Scott, *Kenilworth*; P. B. Shelley, *Adonais*; Southey, *A Vision of Judgement*
1822 (Mar.) Alfred Lamert Dickens born; Harriet Dickens dies. CD stays in Chatham when family moves to Camden Town, London; rejoins them later, but his education is discontinued.	Shelley dies. Matthew Arnold born. Byron, *The Vision of Judgement*
1823 (Dec.) Family moves to 4 Gower Street North, where Mrs Dickens fails in her attempt to run a school.	Building of present British Museum begins. Coventry Patmore born. Charles Lamb, *Essays of Elia*; Scott, *Quentin Durward*

Life	*Historical and Cultural Background*
1824 (late Jan. or early Feb.) CD sent to work at Jonathan Warren's blacking warehouse, Hungerford Stairs; (20 Feb.) John Dickens arrested and imprisoned for debt in the Marshalsea till 28 May; CD in lodgings; family moves to Somers Town.	National Gallery founded in London. Repeal of acts forbidding formation of trades unions. Byron dies. Wilkie Collins born. James Hogg, *The Private Memoirs and Confessions of a Justified Sinner*; Walter Savage Landor, *Imaginary Conversations* (completed 1829); Scott, *Redgauntlet*
1825 (9 Mar.) John Dickens retires from Navy Pay Office with a pension; (Mar./Apr.) CD leaves Warren's and recommences his schooling at Wellington House Academy.	Stockton–Darlington railway opens. Hazlitt, *Table-Talk*, *The Spirit of the Age*; Alessandro Manzoni, *I promessi sposi*
1826 John Dickens works as Parliamentary correspondent for *The British Press*.	University College London and Royal Zoological Society founded. J. Fenimore Cooper, *The Last of the Mohicans*; Benjamin Disraeli, *Vivian Grey* (completed 1827); Mary Shelley, *The Last Man*
1827 (Mar.) Family evicted for non-payment of rates; CD becomes a solicitor's clerk; (Nov.) Augustus Dickens born.	Battle of Navarino. William Blake dies. Clare, *The Shepherd's Calendar*; De Quincey, 'On Murder Considered as One of the Fine Arts'
1828 John Dickens works as reporter for *The Morning Herald*.	Duke of Wellington PM. George Meredith, D. G. Rossetti, Leo Tolstoy born. Pierce Egan, *Finish to the Adventures of Tom, Jerry and Logic*
1829 CD works at Doctors' Commons as a shorthand reporter.	Catholic Emancipation Act; Robert Peel establishes Metropolitan Police.
1830 (8 Feb.) Admitted as reader to British Museum; (May) falls in love with Maria Beadnell.	George IV dies; William IV succeeds. Opening of Manchester–Liverpool Railway. July revolution in France; accession of Louis-Philippe as emperor. Greece independent. Hazlitt dies. Christina Rossetti born. William Cobbett, *Rural Rides*; Sir Charles Lyell, *Principles of Geology* (completed 1832); Alfred Tennyson, *Poems, Chiefly Lyrical*

Life	*Historical and Cultural Background*
1831 Composes poem 'The Bill of Fare'; starts work as reporter for *The Mirror of Parliament*.	Reform Bill. Major cholera epidemic. Michael Faraday's electro-magnetic current. Peacock, *Crotchet Castle*; Edgar Allan Poe, *Poems*; Stendhal, *Le Rouge et le noir*
1832 Becomes Parliamentary reporter on the *True Sun*.	Lord Grey PM. First Reform Act. Jeremy Bentham, Crabbe, Goethe, and Scott die. Charles Lutwidge Dodgson (Lewis Carroll) born. Goethe, *Faust*, ii; Mary Russell Mitford, *Our Village*; Tennyson, *Poems*; Frances Trollope, *Domestic Manners of the Americans*
1833 Concludes relationship with Maria Beadnell; first story, 'A Dinner at Poplar Walk' (later called 'Mr Minns and his Cousin') published in *Monthly Magazine*.	First steamship crosses the Atlantic. Abolition of slavery in all British colonies (from Aug. 1834). Factory Act forbids employment of children under 9. First government grant for schools. Oxford Movement starts. Robert Browning, *Pauline*; John Henry Newman, 'Lead, Kindly Light' and (with others) the first *Tracts for the Times*
1834 (Jan.–Feb.) Six more stories appear in *Monthly Magazine*; (Aug.) meets Catherine Hogarth; becomes reporter on *The Morning Chronicle*, which publishes (Sept.–Dec.) first five 'Street Sketches'; (Dec.) moves to Furnival's Inn, Holborn.	Robert Owen's Grand National Trades Union. 'Tolpuddle Martyrs' transported to Australia. Lord Melbourne PM; then Peel. Workhouses set up under Poor Law Amendment Act. Coleridge, Lamb, and Malthus die. William Morris born. Balzac, *Eugénie Grandet*; Thomas Carlyle, *Sartor Resartus*; Harriet Martineau, *Illustrations of Political Economy*
1835 (?May) Engaged to Catherine Hogarth ('Kate'); publishes stories, sketches, and scenes in *Monthly Magazine*, *Evening Chronicle*, and *Bell's Life in London*.	Lord Melbourne PM. Municipal Corporations Act reforms local government. Cobbett and James Hogg die. Browning, *Paracelsus*; Alexis de Tocqueville, *La Démocratie en Amérique*

Life	*Historical and Cultural Background*
1836 (Feb.) Takes larger chambers in Furnival's Inn; (8 Feb.) *Sketches by Boz, First Series* published; (31 Mar.) first monthly number of *Pickwick Papers* issued; (2 Apr.) marries Catherine Hogarth; (June) publishes *Sunday Under Three Heads*; leaves the *Morning Chronicle* (Nov.); (17 Dec.) *Sketches by Boz, Second Series*; (?Dec.) meets John Forster.	Beginning of Chartism. First London train (to Greenwich). Forms of telegraph used in England and America. Augustus Pugin's *Contrasts* advocates Gothic style of architecture. Browning, 'Porphyria's Lover'; Nicolai Gogol, *The Government Inspector*; Frederick Marryat, *Mr Midshipman Easy*
1837 (1 Jan.) First monthly number of *Bentley's Miscellany*, edited by CD, published; (6 Jan.) birth of first child, Charles ('Charley'); (31 Jan.) serialization of *Oliver Twist* begins in *Bentley's*; (3 Mar.) *Is She His Wife?* produced at the St James's; (Apr.) family moves to 48 Doughty Street; (7 May) sudden death of his sister-in-law, Mary Hogarth, at 17; CD suspends publication of *Pickwick Papers* and *Oliver Twist* for a month; (Aug.–Sept.) first family holiday in Broadstairs; (17 Nov.) *Pickwick Papers* published in one volume.	William IV dies; Queen Victoria succeeds. Carlyle, *The French Revolution*; Isaac Pitman, *Stenographic Short-Hand*; J. G. Lockhart, *Memoirs of the Life of Sir Walter Scott*
1838 (Jan.–Feb.) Visits Yorkshire schools with Hablot Browne ('Phiz'); (6 Mar.) second child, Mary ('Mamie'), born; (31 Mar.) monthly serialization of *Nicholas Nickleby* begins; (9 Nov.) *Oliver Twist* published in three volumes.	Isambard Kingdom Brunel's *Great Western* inaugurates regular steamship service between England and USA. London–Birmingham railway completed. Irish Poor Law. Anti-Corn Law League founded by Richard Cobden. People's Charter advocates universal suffrage. Carlyle, *Sartor Resartus*; John Ruskin, *The Poetry of Architecture*; R. S. Surtees, *Jorrocks's Jaunts and Jollities*; Wordsworth, *Sonnets*

Life	Historical and Cultural Background
1839 (31 Jan.) Resigns editorship of *Bentley's*; (23 Oct.) *Nicholas Nickleby* published in one volume; (29 Oct.) third child, Kate ('Katey'), born; (Dec.) family moves to 1 Devonshire Terrace, Regent's Park.	Opium War between Britain and China. Chartist riots. Louis Daguerre and W. H. Fox Talbot independently develop photography. Carlyle, *Chartism*; Darwin, *Journal of Researches into the Geology and Natural History of . . . Countries Visited by HMS Beagle*; Harriet Martineau, *Deerbrook*
1840 (4 Apr.) First weekly issue of *Master Humphrey's Clock* (also published monthly) in which *The Old Curiosity Shop* is serialized from 25 Apr.; (1 June) moves family to Broadstairs; (11 Oct.) returns to London; (15 Oct.) *Master Humphrey's Clock*, Vol. I published.	Queen Victoria marries Prince Albert. Maoris yield sovereignty of New Zealand to Queen Victoria by Treaty of Waitangi. Rowland Hill introduces penny postage. Fanny Burney dies.
1841 (8 Feb.) Fourth child, Walter, born; *The Old Curiosity Shop* concluded and *Barnaby Rudge* commenced in *Master Humphrey's Clock* (6 and 13 Feb.); operated on for fistula (without anaesthetic). *Master Humphrey's Clock*, Vols. II and III published (Apr. and Dec.); one-volume editions of *The Old Curiosity Shop* and *Barnaby Rudge* published (15 Dec.).	Peel PM. Hong Kong and New Zealand proclaimed British. *Punch* founded. W. H. Ainsworth, *Old St Paul's*; Browning, *Pippa Passes*; Carlyle, *On Heroes, Hero-Worship, and the Heroic in History*; R. W. Emerson, *Essays*. Dion Boucicault's *London Assurance* acted
1842 (Jan.–June) CD and Catherine visit North America; (Aug.–Sept.) with family in Broadstairs; (Oct.–Nov.) visits Cornwall with Forster and others; (19 Oct.) *American Notes* published; (31 Dec.) first monthly number of *Martin Chuzzlewit* published.	End of wars with China and Afghanistan. Mines Act: no underground work by women or by children under 10. Chadwick report on sanitary condition of the working classes. Chartist riots. Copyright Act. Stendhal dies. Browning, *Dramatic Lyrics*; Gogol, *Dead Souls*; Thomas Babington Macaulay, *Lays of Ancient Rome*; Tennyson, *Poems*

Life	*Historical and Cultural Background*
1843 (19 Dec.) *A Christmas Carol* published.	British annexation of Sind and Natal. I. K. Brunel's *Great Britain*, the first ocean screw-steamer, launched. Southey dies; Wordsworth becomes Poet Laureate. Carlyle, *Past and Present*; Thomas Hood, 'Song of the Shirt'; Macaulay, *Essays*; J. S. Mill, *System of Logic*; Ruskin, *Modern Painters*, i (completed 1860)
1844 (15 Jan.) Fifth child, Francis, born; (16 July) takes family to Genoa; one-volume edition of *Martin Chuzzlewit* published; (30 Nov.–8 Dec.) returns to London to read *The Chimes* (published 16 Dec.) to his friends.	Factory Act restricts working hours of women and children. 'Rochdale Pioneers' found first co-operative society. Ragged School Union. William Barnes, *Poems of Rural Life in the Dorset Dialect*; E. B. Barrett, *Poems*; Disraeli, *Coningsby*; Dumas, *Les Trois Mousquetaires*; A. W. Kinglake, *Eōthen*
1845 Travels in Italy with Catherine before returning to London from Genoa; (20 Sept.) directs and acts in first performance of the Amateur Players, Ben Jonson's *Every Man In His Humour*; (28 Oct.) sixth child, Alfred, born; (20 Dec.) *The Cricket on the Hearth* published.	Disappearance of Sir John Franklin's expedition to find a North-West Passage from the Atlantic to the Pacific. War with Sikhs. 1845–9: potato famine in Ireland: 1 million die; 8 million emigrate. Thomas Hood and Sydney Smith die. Browning, *Dramatic Romances and Lyrics*; Disraeli, *Sybil*; Engels, *Condition of the Working Class in England*; Poe, *The Raven and other Poems*, *Tales of Mystery and Imagination*
1846 (21 Jan.–9 Feb.) Edits *The Daily News*; (May) *Pictures from Italy* published; (31 May) leaves with family for Switzerland via the Rhine; (11 June) settles in Lausanne; (30 Sept.) monthly serialization of *Dombey and Son* commences; (16 Nov.) family moves to Paris; (Dec.) *The Battle of Life* published.	Corn Laws repealed; Peel resigns; Lord John Russell PM. Ether first used as a general anaesthetic. Robert Browning and Elizabeth Barrett marry secretly and leave for Italy. Balzac, *La Cousine Bette*; *Poems by Currer, Ellis and Acton Bell* (i.e. Charlotte, Emily, and Anne Brontë); Edward Lear, *Book of Nonsense*

Life | *Historical and Cultural Background*

1847 (28 Feb.) Returns from Paris; (18 Apr.) seventh child, Sydney, is born; (June–Sept.) with family at Broadstairs; (27–8 July) performs in Manchester and Liverpool with the Amateurs; (Nov.) Urania Cottage, Miss Coutts's 'Home for Homeless Women', in whose administration CD is involved, opened in Shepherd's Bush.

Factory Act limits working day for women and young persons to 10 hours. James Simpson discovers anaesthetic properties of chloroform. Louis Napoleon escapes to England from prison.
A. Brontë, *Agnes Grey*; C. Brontë, *Jane Eyre*; E. Brontë, *Wuthering Heights*; Tennyson, *The Princess*. J. M. Morton's *Box and Cox* acted

1848 (12 Apr.) One-volume edition of *Dombey and Son* published; (May–July) the Amateurs perform in London, Manchester, Liverpool, Birmingham, Edinburgh, and Glasgow; (2 Sept.) sister Fanny dies; (19 Dec.) *The Haunted Man* published.

Outbreak of cholera in London. Public Health Act. End of Chartist Movement. Pre-Raphaelite Brotherhood founded. 'The Year of Revolutions' in Europe. Louis Napoleon becomes President of France. Emily Brontë, Branwell Brontë die.
A. Brontë, *The Tenant of Wildfell Hall*; Elizabeth Gaskell, *Mary Barton*; Marx and Engels, *Communist Manifesto*; J. S. Mill, *Principles of Political Economy*; Thackeray, *Vanity Fair*

1849 (16 Jan.) Eighth child, Henry ('Harry'), born; (30 Apr.) monthly serialization of *David Copperfield* begins; (July–Oct.) with family at Bonchurch, Isle of Wight.

Revolt against the British in Montreal. Punjab annexed. Rome proclaimed a republic; later taken by the French. Suppression of Communist riots in Paris. Californian gold rush. Anne Brontë, E. A. Poe die.
C. Brontë, *Shirley*; Sir John Herschel, *Outlines of Astronomy*; Macaulay, *History of England*, i–ii (unfinished at his death, in 1859); Ruskin, *The Seven Lamps of Architecture*

1850 (30 Mar.) First issue of *Household Words*, a weekly journal edited and contributed to by CD; (16 Aug.) ninth child, Dora, born; (Aug.–Oct.) at Broadstairs; (15 Nov.) one-volume edition of *David Copperfield* published.

Restoration of Roman Catholic hierarchy in England. Factory Act: 60-hour week for women and young persons. Public Libraries Act. Dover–Calais telegraph cable laid. Balzac and Wordsworth die. Tennyson becomes Poet Laureate.
E. B. Browning, 'Sonnets from the Portuguese', in *Poems*; Nathaniel Hawthorne, *The Scarlet Letter*; Tennyson, *In Memoriam A.H.H.*; Thackeray, *The History of Pendennis*; Wordsworth, *The Prelude* (posth.)

	Life	*Historical and Cultural Background*
1851	(25 Jan.) *A Child's History of England* starts serialization in *Household Words*; (31 Mar.) John Dickens dies; (14 Apr.) Dora dies suddenly, aged 8 months; (May) directs and acts in Bulwer-Lytton's *Not So Bad As We Seem* before the Queen, in aid of the Guild of Literature and Art; (May–Oct.) last family holiday at Broadstairs; (Nov.) moves to Tavistock House.	Great Exhibition in the Crystal Palace, Hyde Park. Fall of French Second Republic. Gold found in Australia. George Borrow, *Lavengro*; Henry Mayhew, *London Labour and the London Poor*; Herman Melville, *Moby Dick*; George Meredith, *Poems*; Ruskin, *The King of the Golden River*, *The Stones of Venice*, i (completed 1853)
1852	(28 Feb.) Monthly serialization of ***Bleak House*** begins; (14 Apr.) birth of tenth child, Edward ('Plorn'); (Feb.–Sept.) provincial performances of *Not So Bad As We Seem*; (July–Oct.) family stays in Dover.	Lord Derby becomes PM; then Lord Aberdeen. Louis Napoleon proclaimed Emperor Napoleon III. 1852–6: David Livingstone crosses Africa. Tom Moore and the Duke of Wellington die. M. P. Roget, *Roget's Thesaurus of English Words and Phrases*; Harriet Beecher Stowe, *Uncle Tom's Cabin*; Thackeray, *Henry Esmond*
1853	(June–Oct.) Family stays in Boulogne; (12 Sept.) one-volume edition of ***Bleak House*** published; (Oct.–Dec.) in Switzerland and Italy with Wilkie Collins and Augustus Egg; (10 Dec.) *A Child's History of England* concluded in *Household Words*; (27–30 Dec.) gives public readings of *A Christmas Carol* and *The Cricket on the Hearth* in Birmingham.	Arnold, *Poems*; C. Brontë, *Villette*; Gaskell, *Ruth*, *Cranford*; Surtees, *Mr Sponge's Sporting Career*
1854	(28–30 Jan.) Visits Preston; (1 Apr.–12 Aug.) weekly serialization of ***Hard Times*** in *Household Words*; (June–Oct.) family stays in Boulogne; (7 Aug.) ***Hard Times*** published in one volume; (Dec.) reads *A Christmas Carol* in Reading, Sherborne, and Bradford.	Reform of the Civil Service. France and Britain join Turkey against Russia in the Crimean War; battles of Alma, Balaclava, Inkerman and siege of Sebastopol; Florence Nightingale goes to Scutari. Patmore, *The Angel in the House*, i (completed 1862); Tennyson, 'The Charge of the Light Brigade'; H. D. Thoreau, *Walden*

Life	*Historical and Cultural Background*
1855 (Feb.) Meets Maria Winter (née Beadnell) again; (27 Mar.) reads *A Christmas Carol* in Ashford, Kent; (June) directs and acts in Collins's *The Lighthouse* at Tavistock House; family stays in Folkestone, where CD reads *A Christmas Carol* on 5 Oct.; (15 Oct.) settles family in Paris; (1 Dec.) monthly serialization of *Little Dorrit* begins; (Dec.) reads *A Christmas Carol* at Peterborough and Sheffield.	Lord Palmerston PM. Newspaper tax abolished. *Daily Telegraph*, first London penny newspaper, founded. Fall of Sebastopol. 1855–6: G. J. Mendel discovers laws of heredity. Charlotte Brontë and Mary Russell Mitford die. R. Browning, *Men and Women*; Gaskell, *North and South*; Longfellow, *Hiawatha*; Tennyson, *Maud and other Poems*; Thackeray, *The Newcomes*, *The Rose and the Ring*; A. Trollope, *The Warden*; Walt Whitman, *Leaves of Grass*
1856 (Mar.) Buys Gad's Hill Place, Kent; (29 Apr.) family returns from Paris; (June–Sept.) family stays in Boulogne.	End of Crimean War. Britain annexes Oudh; Sir Henry Bessemer patents his steel-making process. Synthetic colours invented. Henry Irving's first stage appearance. National Gallery founded in London. Mrs Craik (Dinah Maria Mulock), *John Halifax, Gentleman*; Flaubert, *Madame Bovary*
1857 (Jan.) Directs and acts in Collins's *The Frozen Deep* at Tavistock House; (13 Feb.) moves to Gad's Hill Place; (30 May) *Little Dorrit* published in one volume; Walter leaves for service with the East India Company; (June–July) visited by Hans Andersen; gives three public readings of *A Christmas Carol*; (July–Aug.) performances of *The Frozen Deep* in London and, with Ellen Ternan, her sister, and mother in the cast, in Manchester.	Divorce courts established in England. Arnold becomes Professor of Poetry at Oxford. Museum—later, the Victoria and Albert Museum—opened in South Kensington. Beginning of Indian mutiny; siege and relief of Lucknow. Baudelaire, *Les Fleurs du mal*; C. Brontë, *The Professor* (posth.); E. B. Browning, *Aurora Leigh*; Gaskell, *The Life of Charlotte Brontë*; Hughes, *Tom Brown's Schooldays*; Livingstone, *Missionary Travels and Researches in South Africa*; A. Trollope, *Barchester Towers*

Life	*Historical and Cultural Background*
1858 (19 Jan.; 26 Mar; 15 Apr.) Reads *A Christmas Carol* for charity; (29 Apr.–22 July) series of 17 public readings; (May) separation from Catherine; (7 and 12 June) publishes 'personal' statement about it in *The Times* and *Household Words*; (Aug.) *Reprinted Pieces* published; (Aug.–Nov.) first provincial reading tour, extending to Ireland and Scotland (85 readings); (24 Dec.) first series of London Christmas readings begins.	Derby PM. Indian Mutiny suppressed; powers of East India Company transferred to the Crown. Queen Victoria proclaimed Empress of India. Launch of I. K. Brunel's *Great Eastern*. Darwin and A. R. Wallace give joint paper on evolution. R. M. Ballantyne, *The Coral Island*; Clough, *Amours de Voyage*; Eliot, *Scenes of Clerical Life*; A. Trollope, *Doctor Thorne*
1859 (30 Apr.) Begins to edit *All the Year Round* in which *A Tale of Two Cities* appears weekly till 26 November; (28 May) final number of *Household Words*; (Oct.) gives 14 readings on second provincial tour; (21 Nov.) *A Tale of Two Cities* published in one volume; (24 Dec.) begins series of three London Christmas readings.	Palmerston PM. Franco-Austrian War: Austrians defeated at Solferino. War of Italian Liberation. The abolitionist John Brown hanged for treason at Charlestown, Virginia. Thomas de Quincey, Leigh Hunt, and Lord Macaulay die. Darwin, *On the Origin of Species by Means of Natural Selection*; Eliot, *Adam Bede*; Edward FitzGerald, *Rubáiyát of Omar Khayyám*; J. S. Mill, *On Liberty*; Samuel Smiles, *Self-Help*; Tennyson, *Idylls of the King*
1860 (17 July) Katey marries Charles Collins; (27 July) CD's brother Alfred dies, at 38; (21 Aug.) sells Tavistock House; (Oct.) settles permanently at Gad's Hill; (1 Dec.) weekly serialization of *Great Expectations* begins in *All the Year Round*, continuing till 3 Aug. 1861.	Abraham Lincoln elected US president; Carolina secedes from the Union. Collins, *The Woman in White*; Eliot, *The Mill on the Floss*; Faraday, *Various Forces of Matter*. Boucicault's *The Colleen Bawn* acted
1861 (Mar.–Apr.) Series of 6 London readings; (6 July) *Great Expectations* published in three volumes; (Oct.–Jan. 1862) gives 46 readings on third provincial tour; (19 Nov.) Charley marries Elizabeth ('Bessie') Evans: CD refuses to be present.	Abolition of Paper Tax. Prince Albert dies. Victor Emmanuel becomes King of Italy. Serfdom abolished in Russia. Outbreak of American Civil War. E. B. Browning and A. H. Clough die. Mrs Isabella Mary Beeton, *Book of Household Management*; Eliot, *Silas Marner*; J. S. Mill, *Utilitarianism*; F. T. Palgrave, *The Golden Treasury*; Reade, *The Cloister and the Hearth*; A. Trollope, *Framley Parsonage*; Mrs Henry Wood, *East Lynne*

	Life	*Historical and Cultural Background*
1862	(Feb.–May) Exchanges Gad's Hill Place for a house in London but also uses rooms at the office of *All the Year Round*; (Mar.–June) London readings; (June–Oct.) makes several visits to France; (Oct.) settles Mamie and her aunt, Georgina Hogarth, in Paris; (Dec.) returns to Gad's Hill for Christmas.	Famine among Lancashire cotton workers. Bismarck becomes Chancellor of Prussia. Thoreau dies. Mary Elizabeth Braddon, *Lady Audley's Secret*; Hugo, *Les Misérables*; Meredith, *Modern Love*; Christina Rossetti, *Goblin Market and Other Poems*; Herbert Spencer, *First Principles*; Turgenev, *Fathers and Sons*
1863	(Jan.) Gives 3 readings for charity at British Embassy in Paris; (Feb. and Aug.) makes further visits to France; (Mar.–May) London readings; (13 Sept.) Elizabeth Dickens dies; (31 Dec.) Walter dies in Calcutta, India, aged 22.	Beginning of work on London underground railway. Lincoln's Gettysburg Address; emancipation of US slaves. Thackeray and Frances Trollope die. Eliot, *Romola*; Margaret Oliphant, *Salem Chapel*
1864	(1 May) Monthly serialization of *Our Mutual Friend* begins; (27 June–6 July) probably in France; (Nov.) in France.	Karl Marx organizes first Socialist International in London. Louis Pasteur publishes his theory of germs as the cause of disease. International Red Cross founded. John Clare, W. S. Landor, R. S. Surtees, and Hawthorne die. Sheridan Le Fanu, *Uncle Silas*; Newman, *Apologia pro Vita Sua*; Tennyson, *Enoch Arden and Other Poems*; Trollope, *The Small House at Allington, Can You Forgive Her?*
1865	(Feb.–June) Three trips to France; (Feb.–Apr.) first attack of lameness from swollen left foot; (29 May) sees Alfred off to Australia; (9 June) returning from France with Ellen Ternan and her mother, is in fatal railway accident at Staplehurst, Kent; (Sept.) visit to France; (20 Oct.) *Our Mutual Friend* published in two volumes.	Russell PM. William Booth founds Christian Mission in Whitechapel, known from 1878 as the Salvation Army. Completion of transatlantic cable. End of American Civil War. Abraham Lincoln assassinated. Elizabeth Gaskell dies. Arnold, *Essays in Criticism, First Series*; Lewis Carroll, *Alice's Adventures in Wonderland*

Life	*Historical and Cultural Background*
1866 (Apr.–June) Readings in London and the provinces; (June) CD's brother Augustus Dickens dies in Chicago, aged 38.	Derby PM. Second Reform Bill. Fenians active in Ireland: Habeas Corpus suspended. Elizabeth Garrett opens dispensary for women. Dr T. J. Barnardo opens home for destitute children in London's East End. Peacock and John Keble die.
	Fyodor Dostoevsky, *Crime and Punishment*; Eliot, *Felix Holt, the Radical*; Gaskell, *Wives and Daughters* (posth., unfinished); Swinburne, *Poems and Ballads*, First Series
1867 (Jan.–May) Readings in England and Ireland; (Nov.) begins American reading tour in Boston; (Dec.) *No Thoroughfare*, written jointly with Collins, published in *All the Year Round*.	Fenian outrages in England. Second Reform Act. Factory Act. Joseph Lister practises antiseptic surgery. Building of Royal Albert Hall commenced.
	Arnold, 'Dover Beach', 'Thyrsis', in *New Poems*; Walter Bagehot, *The English Constitution*; Henrik Ibsen, *Peer Gynt*; Karl Marx, *Das Kapital*, i; Trollope, *The Last Chronicle of Barset*; Emile Zola, *Thérèse Raquin*
1868 (22 Apr.) Sails home from New York, having cancelled planned readings in the USA and Canada; (26 Sept.) Plorn sails to Australia to join Alfred; (Oct.) Harry enters Trinity College, Cambridge; CD begins Farewell Reading Tour; CD's brother Fred dies, aged 48.	Disraeli PM; Gladstone PM. Trades' Union Congress founded. Basutoland annexed.
	Louisa May Alcott, *Little Women*; Collins, *The Moonstone*; Queen Victoria, *Leaves from a Journal of Our Life in the Highlands*
1869 (5 Jan.) Introduces 'Sikes and Nancy' into his repertoire; (22 Apr.) serious illness forces CD to break off reading tour after 74 readings.	Girton College for Women founded. Suez Canal opened.
	Arnold, *Culture and Anarchy*; R. D. Blackmore, *Lorna Doone*; R. Browning, *The Ring and the Book*; J. S. Mill, *On the Subjection of Women*; Leo Tolstoy, *War and Peace*; Trollope, *Phineas Finn*, *He Knew He Was Right*; Paul Verlaine, *Fêtes galantes*
1870 (Jan.– Mar.) Farewell readings in London; (9 Mar.) received by Queen Victoria; (1 Apr.) first of six completed numbers of *The Mystery of Edwin Drood* issued; (9 June) dies, aged 58, following a cerebral haemorrhage, at Gad's Hill; (14 June) buried in Westminster Abbey.	Gladstone's Irish Land Act. Married Women's Property Act gives wives the right to their own earnings. Elementary Education Act for England and Wales. Outbreak of Franco-Prussian War: Napoleon III defeated and exiled; siege of Paris (till 1871).
	E. C. Brewer, *Dictionary of Phrase and Fable*; D. G. Rossetti, *Poems*

CHRISTMAS BOOKS

PREFACE

THE narrow space within which it was necessary to confine these Christmas Stories when they were originally published, rendered their construction a matter of some difficulty, and almost necessitated what is peculiar in their machinery. I could not attempt great elaboration of detail, in the working out of character within such limits. My chief purpose was, in a whimsical kind of masque which the good humour of the season justified, to awaken some loving and forbearing thoughts, never out of season in a Christian land.

Mr. Fezziwig's Ball

A CHRISTMAS CAROL.

IN PROSE.

BEING

A Ghost Story of Christmas.

BY

CHARLES DICKENS.

WITH ILLUSTRATIONS BY JOHN LEECH.

LONDON

CHAPMAN & HALL, 186, STRAND.

PREFACE

I HAVE endeavoured in this Ghostly little book to raise the Ghost of an Idea which shall not put my readers out of humour with themselves, with each other, with the season, or with me. May it haunt their houses pleasantly, and no one wish to lay it.

Their faithful Friend and Servant,

C. D.

December, 1843.

CONTENTS

STAVE I

MARLEY was dead, to begin with. There is no doubt whatever about that. The register of his burial was signed by the clergyman, the clerk, the undertaker, and the chief mourner. Scrooge signed it. And Scrooge's name was good upon 'Change,* for anything he chose to put his hand to.

Old Marley was as dead as a door-nail.

Mind! I don't mean to say that I know, of my own knowledge, what there is particularly dead about a door-nail. I might have been inclined, myself, to regard a coffin-nail as the deadest piece of ironmongery in the trade. But the wisdom of our ancestors* is in the simile; and my unhallowed hands shall not disturb it, or the Country's done for. You will therefore permit me to repeat, emphatically, that Marley was as dead as a door-nail.

Scrooge knew he was dead? Of course he did. How could it be otherwise? Scrooge and he were partners for I don't know how many years. Scrooge was his sole executor, his sole administrator, his sole assign, his sole residuary legatee,* his sole friend, and sole mourner. And even Scrooge was not so dreadfully cut up by the sad event, but that he was an excellent man of business on the very day of the funeral, and solemnised it with an undoubted bargain.

The mention of Marley's funeral brings me back to the point I started from. There is no doubt that Marley was dead. This must be distinctly understood, or nothing wonderful can come of the story I am going to relate. If we were not perfectly convinced that Hamlet's Father died before the play began, there would be nothing more remarkable in his taking a stroll at night,* in an easterly wind, upon his own ramparts, than there would be in any other middle-aged gentleman rashly turning out after dark in a breezy spot—say Saint Paul's Churchyard for instance—literally to astonish his son's weak mind.

Scrooge never painted out Old Marley's name. There it stood, years afterwards, above the warehouse door: Scrooge and Marley. The firm was known as Scrooge and Marley. Sometimes people new to the business called Scrooge Scrooge, and sometimes Marley, but he answered to both names. It was all the same to him.

Oh! But he was a tight-fisted hand at the grindstone, Scrooge! a squeezing, wrenching, grasping, scraping, clutching, covetous, old sinner! Hard and sharp as flint, from which no steel had ever struck out generous fire; secret, and self-contained, and solitary as an oyster. The cold within him froze his old features, nipped his pointed nose, shrivelled his cheek, stiffened his gait; made his eyes red, his thin lips blue; and spoke out shrewdly in his grating voice. A frosty rime was on his head, and on his eyebrows, and his wiry chin. He carried his own low temperature always about with him; he iced his office in the dog-days;* and didn't thaw it one degree at Christmas.

External heat and cold had little influence on Scrooge. No warmth could warm, no wintry weather chill him. No wind that blew was bitterer than he, no falling snow was more intent upon its purpose, no pelting rain less open to entreaty. Foul weather didn't know where to have him.* The heaviest rain, and snow, and hail, and sleet, could boast of the advantage over him in only one respect. They often 'came down'* handsomely, and Scrooge never did.

Nobody ever stopped him in the street to say, with gladsome looks, 'My dear Scrooge, how are you? When will you come to see me?' No beggars implored him to bestow a trifle, no children asked him what it was o'clock, no man or woman ever once in all his life inquired the way to such and such a place, of Scrooge. Even the blind men's dogs appeared to know him; and when they saw him coming on, would tug their owners into doorways and up courts; and then would wag their tails as though they said, 'No eye at all is better than an evil eye, dark master!'

But what did Scrooge care! It was the very thing he liked. To edge his way along the crowded paths of life, warning all human sympathy to keep its distance, was what the knowing ones call 'nuts'* to Scrooge.

Once upon a time—of all the good days in the year, on Christmas Eve—old Scrooge sat busy in his counting-house. It was cold, bleak, biting weather: foggy withal: and he could hear the people in the court outside, go wheezing up and down, beating their hands upon their breasts, and stamping their feet upon the pavement stones to warm them. The city clocks had only just gone three, but it was quite dark already—it had not been light all day—and candles were flaring in the windows of the neighbouring offices, like ruddy smears upon the palpable brown air. The fog came pouring in at every chink and keyhole, and was so dense without, that although the court was of the narrowest, the houses opposite were mere phantoms. To see the dingy cloud come drooping down, obscuring everything, one might have thought that Nature lived hard by, and was brewing on a large scale.

The door of Scrooge's counting-house was open that he might keep his eye upon his clerk, who in a dismal little cell beyond, a sort of tank, was copying letters. Scrooge had a very small fire, but the clerk's fire was so very much smaller that it looked like one coal. But he couldn't replenish it, for Scrooge kept the coal-box in his own room; and so surely as the clerk came in with the shovel, the master predicted that it would be necessary for them to part. Wherefore the clerk put on his white comforter, and tried to warm himself at the candle; in which effort, not being a man of a strong imagination, he failed.

'A merry Christmas, uncle! God save you!' cried a cheerful voice. It was the voice of Scrooge's nephew, who came upon him so quickly that this was the first intimation he had of his approach.

'Bah!' said Scrooge, 'Humbug!'*

He had so heated himself with rapid walking in the fog and frost, this nephew of Scrooge's, that he was all in a glow; his face was ruddy and handsome; his eyes sparkled, and his breath smoked again.

'Christmas a humbug, uncle!' said Scrooge's nephew. 'You don't mean that, I am sure?'

'I do,' said Scrooge. 'Merry Christmas! What right have you to be merry? What reason have you to be merry? You're poor enough.'

'Come, then,' returned the nephew gaily. 'What right have you to be dismal? What reason have you to be morose? You're rich enough.'

Scrooge having no better answer ready on the spur of the moment, said 'Bah!' again; and followed it up with 'Humbug.'

'Don't be cross, uncle!' said the nephew.

'What else can I be,' returned the uncle, 'when I live in such a world of fools as this? Merry Christmas! Out upon merry Christmas! What's Christmas time to you but a time for paying bills without money; a time for finding yourself a year older, but not an hour richer; a time for balancing your books and having every item in 'em through a round dozen of months presented dead against you? If I could work my will,' said Scrooge indignantly, 'every idiot who goes about with "Merry Christmas" on his lips, should be boiled with his own pudding, and buried with a stake of holly through his heart. He should!'

'Uncle!' pleaded the nephew.

'Nephew!' returned the uncle, sternly, 'keep Christmas in your own way, and let me keep it in mine.'

'Keep it!' repeated Scrooge's nephew. 'But you don't keep it.'

'Let me leave it alone, then,' said Scrooge. 'Much good may it do you! Much good it has ever done you!'

'There are many things from which I might have derived good, by which I have not profited, I dare say,' returned the nephew. 'Christmas among the rest. But I am sure I have always thought of Christmas time, when it has come round—apart from the veneration due to its sacred name and origin, if anything belonging to it can be apart from that—as a good time; a kind, forgiving, charitable, pleasant time; the only time I know of, in the long calendar of the year, when men and women seem by one consent to open their shut-up hearts freely, and to think of people below them as if they really were fellow-passengers to the grave, and not another race of creatures bound on other journeys. And therefore, uncle, though it has never put a scrap of gold or silver in my pocket, I believe that it *has* done me good, and *will* do me good; and I say, God bless it!'

The clerk in the tank involuntarily applauded. Becoming immediately sensible of the impropriety, he poked the fire, and extinguished the last frail spark for ever.

'Let me hear another sound from *you*,' said Scrooge, 'and you'll keep your Christmas by losing your situation! You're quite a powerful speaker, sir,' he added, turning to his nephew. 'I wonder you don't go into Parliament.'

'Don't be angry, uncle. Come! Dine with us tomorrow.'

Scrooge said that he would see him—yes, indeed he did. He went the whole length of the expression, and said that he would see him in that extremity first.

'But why?' cried Scrooge's nephew. 'Why?'

'Why did you get married?' said Scrooge.

'Because I fell in love.'

'Because you fell in love!' growled Scrooge, as if that were the only one thing in the world more ridiculous than a merry Christmas. 'Good afternoon!'

'Nay, uncle, but you never came to see me before that happened. Why give it as a reason for not coming now?'

'Good afternoon,' said Scrooge.

'I want nothing from you; I ask nothing of you; why cannot we be friends?'

'Good afternoon,' said Scrooge.

'I am sorry, with all my heart, to find you so resolute. We have never had any quarrel, to which I have been a party. But I have made the trial in homage to Christmas, and I'll keep my Christmas humour to the last. So A Merry Christmas, uncle!'

'Good afternoon!' said Scrooge.

'And A Happy New Year!'

'Good afternoon!' said Scrooge.

His nephew left the room without an angry word, notwithstanding. He stopped at the outer door to bestow the greetings of the season on the clerk, who, cold as he was, was warmer than Scrooge; for he returned them cordially.

'There's another fellow,' muttered Scrooge; who overheard him: 'my clerk, with fifteen shillings a-week, and a wife and family, talking about a merry Christmas. I'll retire to Bedlam.'*

This lunatic, in letting Scrooge's nephew out, had let two other people in. They were portly gentlemen, pleasant to behold, and now stood, with their hats off, in Scrooge's office. They had books and papers in their hands, and bowed to him.

'Scrooge and Marley's, I believe,' said one of the gentlemen, referring to his list. 'Have I the pleasure of addressing Mr. Scrooge, or Mr. Marley?'

'Mr. Marley has been dead these seven years,' Scrooge replied. 'He died seven years ago, this very night.'

'We have no doubt his liberality is well represented by his surviving partner,' said the gentleman, presenting his credentials.

It certainly was; for they had been two kindred spirits. At the ominous word 'liberality,' Scrooge frowned, and shook his head, and handed the credentials back.

'At this festive season of the year, Mr. Scrooge,' said the gentleman, taking up a pen, 'it is more than usually desirable that we should make some slight provision for the Poor and destitute, who suffer greatly at the present time. Many thousands are in want of common necessaries; hundreds of thousands are in want of common comforts, sir.'

'Are there no prisons?' asked Scrooge.

'Plenty of prisons,' said the gentleman, laying down the pen again.

'And the Union workhouses?'* demanded Scrooge. 'Are they still in operation?'

'They are. Still,' returned the gentleman, 'I wish I could say they were not.'

'The Treadmill and the Poor Law are in full vigour, then?' said Scrooge.

'Both very busy, sir.'

'Oh! I was afraid, from what you said at first, that something had occurred to stop them in their useful course,' said Scrooge. 'I'm very glad to hear it.'

'Under the impression that they scarcely furnish Christian cheer of mind or body to the multitude,' returned the gentleman, 'a few of us are endeavouring to raise a fund to buy the Poor some meat and drink, and means of warmth. We choose this time, because it is a time, of all others, when Want is keenly felt, and Abundance rejoices. What shall I put you down for?'

'Nothing!' Scrooge replied.

'You wish to be anonymous?'

'I wish to be left alone,' said Scrooge. 'Since you ask me what I wish, gentlemen, that is my answer. I don't make merry myself at Christmas and I can't afford to make idle people merry. I help to support the establishments I have mentioned—they cost enough; and those who are badly off must go there.'

'Many can't go there; and many would rather die.'

'If they would rather die,' said Scrooge, 'they had better do it, and decrease the surplus population.* Besides—excuse me—I don't know that.'

'But you might know it,' observed the gentleman.

'It's not my business,' Scrooge returned. 'It's enough for a man to understand his own business, and not to interfere with other people's. Mine occupies me constantly. Good afternoon, gentlemen!'

Seeing clearly that it would be useless to pursue their point, the gentlemen withdrew. Scrooge resumed his labours with an improved opinion of himself, and in a more facetious temper than was usual with him.

Meanwhile the fog and darkness thickened so, that people ran about with flaring links,* proffering their services to go before horses in carriages, and conduct them on their way. The ancient tower of a church, whose gruff old bell was always peeping slily down at

Scrooge out of a gothic window in the wall, became invisible, and struck the hours and quarters in the clouds, with tremulous vibrations afterwards as if its teeth were chattering in its frozen head up there. The cold became intense. In the main street, at the corner of the court, some labourers were repairing the gas-pipes, and had lighted a great fire in a brazier, round which a party of ragged men and boys were gathered: warming their hands and winking their eyes before the blaze in rapture. The water-plug being left in solitude, its overflowings sullenly congealed, and turned to misanthropic ice. The brightness of the shops where holly sprigs and berries crackled in the lamp heat of the windows, made pale faces ruddy as they passed. Poulterers' and grocers' trades became a splendid joke: a glorious pageant, with which it was next to impossible to believe that such dull principles as bargain and sale had anything to do. The Lord Mayor, in the stronghold of the mighty Mansion House, gave orders to his fifty cooks and butlers to keep Christmas as a Lord Mayor's household should; and even the little tailor, whom he had fined five shillings on the previous Monday for being drunk and bloodthirsty in the streets, stirred up tomorrow's pudding in his garret, while his lean wife and the baby sallied out to buy the beef.

Foggier yet, and colder! Piercing, searching, biting cold. If the good Saint Dunstan had but nipped the Evil Spirit's nose with a touch of such weather as that, instead of using his familiar weapons, then indeed he would have roared to lusty purpose.* The owner of one scant young nose, gnawed and mumbled by the hungry cold as bones are gnawed by dogs, stooped down at Scrooge's keyhole to regale him with a Christmas carol: but at the first sound of

> 'God bless you merry gentleman!
> May nothing you dismay!'*

Scrooge seized the ruler with such energy of action, that the singer fled in terror, leaving the keyhole to the fog and even more congenial frost.

At length the hour of shutting up the counting-house arrived. With an ill-will Scrooge dismounted from his stool, and tacitly admitted the fact to the expectant clerk in the Tank, who instantly snuffed his candle out, and put on his hat.

'You'll want all day to-morrow, I suppose?' said Scrooge.

'If quite convenient, sir.'

'It's not convenient,' said Scrooge, 'and it's not fair. If I was to stop half-a-crown for it, you'd think yourself ill-used, I'll be bound?'

The clerk smiled faintly.

'And yet,' said Scrooge, 'you don't think *me* ill-used, when I pay a day's wages for no work.'

The clerk observed that it was only once a year.

'A poor excuse for picking a man's pocket every twenty-fifth of December!' said Scrooge, buttoning his great-coat to the chin. 'But I suppose you must have the whole day. Be here all the earlier next morning.'*

The clerk promised that he would; and Scrooge walked out with a growl. The office was closed in a twinkling, and the clerk, with the long ends of his white comforter dangling below his waist (for he boasted no great-coat), went down a slide on Cornhill,* at the end of a lane of boys, twenty times, in honour of its being Christmas Eve, and then ran home to Camden Town as hard as he could pelt, to play at blindman's-buff.*

Scrooge took his melancholy dinner in his usual melancholy tavern; and having read all the newspapers, and beguiled the rest of the evening with his banker's-book, went home to bed. He lived in chambers which had once belonged to his deceased partner. They were a gloomy suite of rooms, in a lowering pile of building up a yard, where it had so little business to be, that one could scarcely help fancying it must have run there when it was a young house, playing at hide-and-seek with other houses, and forgotten the way out again. It was old enough now, and dreary enough, for nobody lived in it but Scrooge, the other rooms being all let out as offices. The yard was so dark that even Scrooge, who knew its every stone, was fain to grope with his hands. The fog and frost so hung about the black old gateway of the house, that it seemed as if the Genius of the Weather sat in mournful meditation on the threshold.

Now, it is a fact, that there was nothing at all particular about the knocker on the door, except that it was very large. It is also a fact, that Scrooge had seen it, night and morning, during his whole residence in that place; also that Scrooge had as little of what is called fancy about him as any man in the city of London, even including—which is a bold word—the corporation, aldermen, and livery.* Let it also be borne in mind that Scrooge had not bestowed one thought on Marley, since his last mention of his seven-years' dead partner that afternoon. And then let any man explain to me, if he can, how it happened that Scrooge, having his key in the lock of the door, saw in the knocker, without its undergoing any intermediate process of change—not a knocker, but Marley's face.*

Marley's face. It was not in impenetrable shadow as the other objects in the yard were, but had a dismal light about it, like a bad lobster in a dark cellar. It was not angry or ferocious, but looked at Scrooge as Marley used to look: with ghostly spectacles turned up on its ghostly forehead. The hair was curiously stirred, as if by breath or hot-air; and, though the eyes were wide open, they were perfectly motionless. That, and its livid colour, made it horrible; but its horror seemed to be in spite of the face and beyond its control, rather than a part of its own expression.

As Scrooge looked fixedly at this phenomenon, it was a knocker again.

To say that he was not startled, or that his blood was not conscious of a terrible sensation to which it had been a stranger from infancy, would be untrue. But he put his hand upon the key he had relinquished, turned it sturdily, walked in, and lighted his candle.

He *did* pause, with a moment's irresolution, before he shut the door; and he *did* look cautiously behind it first, as if he half-expected to be terrified with the sight of Marley's pigtail sticking out into the hall. But there was nothing on the back of the door, except the screws and nuts that held the knocker on, so he said 'Pooh, pooh!' and closed it with a bang.

The sound resounded through the house like thunder. Every room above, and every cask in the wine-merchant's cellars below, appeared to have a separate peal of echoes of its own. Scrooge was not a man to be frightened by echoes. He fastened the door, and walked across the hall, and up the stairs; slowly too: trimming his candle as he went.

You may talk vaguely about driving a coach-and-six up a good old flight of stairs, or through a bad young Act of Parliament;* but I mean to say you might have got a hearse up that staircase, and taken it broadwise, with the splinter-bar* towards the wall and the door towards the balustrades: and done it easy. There was plenty of width for that, and room to spare; which is perhaps the reason why Scrooge thought he saw a locomotive hearse going on before him in the gloom. Half-a-dozen gas-lamps out of the street wouldn't have lighted the entry too well, so you may suppose that it was pretty dark with Scrooge's dip.*

Up Scrooge went, not caring a button for that. Darkness is cheap, and Scrooge liked it. But before he shut his heavy door, he walked through his rooms to see that all was right. He had just enough recollection of the face to desire to do that.

Sitting-room, bed-room, lumber-room. All as they should be. Nobody under the table, nobody under the sofa; a small fire in the grate; spoon and basin ready; and the little saucepan of gruel (Scrooge had a cold in his head) upon the hob. Nobody under the bed; nobody in the closet; nobody in his dressing-gown, which was hanging up in a suspicious attitude against the wall. Lumber-room as usual. Old fire-guard, old shoes, two fish-baskets, washing-stand on three legs, and a poker.

Quite satisfied, he closed his door, and locked himself in; double-locked himself in, which was not his custom. Thus secured against surprise, he took off his cravat; put on his dressing-gown and slippers, and his nightcap; and sat down before the fire to take his gruel.

It was a very low fire indeed; nothing on such a bitter night. He was obliged to sit close to it, and brood over it, before he could extract the least sensation of warmth from such a handful of fuel. The fire-place was an old one, built by some Dutch merchant long ago, and paved all round with quaint Dutch tiles, designed to illustrate the Scriptures. There were Cains and Abels, Pharaohs' daughters, Queens of Sheba, Angelic messengers descending through the air on clouds like feather-beds, Abrahams, Belshazzars, Apostles putting off to sea in butter-boats, hundreds of figures to attract his thoughts; and yet that face of Marley, seven years dead, came like the ancient Prophet's rod,* and swallowed up the whole. If each smooth tile had been a blank at first, with power to shape some picture on its surface from the disjointed fragments of his thoughts, there would have been a copy of old Marley's head on every one.

'Humbug!' said Scrooge; and walked across the room.

After several turns, he sat down again. As he threw his head back in the chair, his glance happened to rest upon a bell, a disused bell, that hung in the room, and communicated for some purpose now forgotten with a chamber in the highest story of the building. It was with great astonishment, and with a strange, inexplicable dread, that as he looked, he saw this bell begin to swing. It swung so softly in the outset that it scarcely made a sound; but soon it rang out loudly, and so did every bell in the house.

This might have lasted half a minute, or a minute, but it seemed an hour. The bells ceased as they had begun, together. They were succeeded by a clanking noise, deep down below; as if some person were dragging a heavy chain over the casks in the wine merchant's cellar. Scrooge then remembered to have heard that ghosts in haunted houses were described as dragging chains.

The cellar-door flew open with a booming sound, and then he heard the noise much louder, on the floors below; then coming up the stairs; then coming straight towards his door.

'It's humbug still!' said Scrooge. 'I won't believe it.'

His colour changed though, when, without a pause, it came on through the heavy door, and passed into the room before his eyes. Upon its coming in, the dying flame leaped up, as though it cried, 'I know him; Marley's Ghost!' and fell again.

The same face: the very same. Marley in his pigtail, usual waistcoat, tights and boots; the tassels on the latter bristling, like his pigtail, and his coat-skirts, and the hair upon his head. The chain he drew was clasped about his middle. It was long, and wound about him like a tail; and it was made (for Scrooge observed it closely) of cash-boxes, keys, padlocks, ledgers, deeds, and heavy purses wrought in steel. His body was transparent; so that Scrooge, observing him, and looking through his waistcoat, could see the two buttons on his coat behind.

Scrooge had often heard it said that Marley had no bowels,* but he had never believed it until now.

No, nor did he believe it even now. Though he looked the phantom through and through, and saw it standing before him; though he felt the chilling influence of its death-cold eyes; and marked the very texture of the folded kerchief bound about its head and chin, which wrapper he had not observed before; he was still incredulous, and fought against his senses.

'How now!' said Scrooge, caustic and cold as ever. 'What do you want with me?'

'Much!'—Marley's voice, no doubt about it.

'Who are you?'

'Ask me who I *was*.'

Marley's Ghost

'Who *were* you then?' said Scrooge, raising his voice. 'You're particular, for a shade.' He was going to say '*to* a shade,'* but substituted this, as more appropriate.

'In life I was your partner, Jacob Marley.'

'Can you—can you sit down?' asked Scrooge, looking doubtfully at him.

'I can.'

'Do it, then.'

Scrooge asked the question, because he didn't know whether a ghost so transparent might find himself in a condition to take a chair; and felt that in the event of its being impossible, it might involve the necessity of an embarrassing explanation. But the ghost sat down on the opposite side of the fireplace, as if he were quite used to it.

'You don't believe in me,' observed the Ghost.

'I don't,' said Scrooge.

'What evidence would you have of my reality beyond that of your senses?'

'I don't know,' said Scrooge.

'Why do you doubt your senses?'

'Because,' said Scrooge, 'a little thing affects them. A slight disorder of the stomach makes them cheats. You may be an undigested bit of beef, a blot of mustard, a crumb of cheese, a fragment of an underdone potato. There's more of gravy than of grave about you, whatever you are!'

Scrooge was not much in the habit of cracking jokes, nor did he feel, in his heart, by any means waggish then. The truth is, that he tried to be smart, as a means of distracting his own attention, and keeping down his terror; for the spectre's voice disturbed the very marrow in his bones.

To sit, staring at those fixed glazed eyes, in silence for a moment, would play, Scrooge felt, the very deuce with him. There was something very awful, too, in the spectre's being provided with an infernal atmosphere of its own. Scrooge could not feel it himself, but this was clearly the case; for though the Ghost sat perfectly motionless, its hair, and skirts, and tassels, were still agitated as by the hot vapour from an oven.

'You see this toothpick?' said Scrooge, returning quickly to the charge, for the reason just assigned; and wishing, though it were only for a second, to divert the vision's stony gaze from himself.

'I do,' replied the Ghost.

'You are not looking at it,' said Scrooge.

'But I see it,' said the Ghost, 'notwithstanding.'

'Well!' returned Scrooge, 'I have but to swallow this, and be for the rest of my days persecuted by a legion of goblins, all of my own creation. Humbug, I tell you! humbug!'

At this the spirit raised a frightful cry, and shook its chain with such a dismal and appalling noise, that Scrooge held on tight to his chair, to save himself from falling in a swoon. But how much greater was his horror, when the phantom taking off the bandage round its head,* as if it were too warm to wear in-doors, its lower jaw dropped down upon its breast!

Scrooge fell upon his knees, and clasped his hands before his face.

'Mercy!' he said. 'Dreadful apparition, why do you trouble me?'

'Man of the worldly mind!' replied the Ghost, 'do you believe in me or not?'

'I do,' said Scrooge. 'I must. But why do spirits walk the earth, and why do they come to me?'

'It is required of every man,' the Ghost returned, 'that the spirit within him should walk abroad among his fellow-men, and travel far and wide; and if that spirit goes not forth in life, it is condemned to do so after death. It is doomed to wander through the world—oh, woe is me!—and witness what it cannot share, but might have shared on earth, and turned to happiness!'

Again the spectre raised a cry, and shook its chain and wrung its shadowy hands.

'You are fettered,' said Scrooge, trembling. 'Tell me why?'

'I wear the chain I forged in life,' replied the Ghost. 'I made it link by link, and yard by yard; I girded it on of my own free will, and of my own free will I wore it. Is its pattern strange to *you*?'

Scrooge trembled more and more.

'Or would you know,' pursued the Ghost, 'the weight and length of the strong coil you bear yourself? It was full as heavy and as long as this, seven Christmas Eves ago. You have laboured on it, since. It is a ponderous chain!'

Scrooge glanced about him on the floor, in the expectation of finding himself surrounded by some fifty or sixty fathoms of iron cable: but he could see nothing.

'Jacob,' he said, imploringly. 'Old Jacob Marley, tell me more. Speak comfort to me, Jacob!'

'I have none to give,' the Ghost replied. 'It comes from other regions, Ebenezer Scrooge, and is conveyed by other ministers, to other kinds of men. Nor can I tell you what I would. A very little more, is all permitted to me. I cannot rest, I cannot stay, I cannot linger anywhere. My spirit never walked beyond our counting-house—mark me!—in life my spirit never roved beyond the narrow limits of our money-changing hole; and weary journeys lie before me!'

It was a habit with Scrooge, whenever he became thoughtful, to put his hands in his breeches pockets. Pondering on what the Ghost had said, he did so now, but without lifting up his eyes, or getting off his knees.

'You must have been very slow about it, Jacob,' Scrooge observed, in a business-like manner, though with humility and deference.

'Slow!' the Ghost repeated.

'Seven years dead,' mused Scrooge. 'And travelling all the time!'

'The whole time,' said the Ghost. 'No rest, no peace. Incessant torture of remorse.'

'You travel fast?' said Scrooge.

'On the wings of the wind,' replied the Ghost.

'You might have got over a great quantity of ground in seven years,' said Scrooge.

The Ghost, on hearing this, set up another cry, and clanked its chain so hideously in the dead silence of the night, that the Ward* would have been justified in indicting it for a nuisance.

'Oh! captive, bound, and double-ironed,' cried the phantom, 'not to know, that ages of incessant labour, by immortal creatures, for this earth must pass into eternity before the good of which it is susceptible is all developed. Not to know that any Christian spirit working kindly in its little sphere, whatever it may be, will find its mortal life too short for its vast means of usefulness. Not to know that no space of regret can make amends for one life's opportunity misused! Yet such was I! Oh! such was I!'

'But you were always a good man of business, Jacob,' faltered Scrooge, who now began to apply this to himself.

'Business!' cried the Ghost, wringing its hands again. 'Mankind was my business. The common welfare was my business; charity, mercy, forbearance, and benevolence, were, all, my business. The dealings of my trade were but a drop of water in the comprehensive ocean of my business!'

It held up its chain at arm's length, as if that were the cause of all its unavailing grief, and flung it heavily upon the ground again.

'At this time of the rolling year,' the spectre said, 'I suffer most. Why did I walk through crowds of fellow-beings with my eyes turned down, and never raise them to that blessed Star which led the Wise Men to a poor abode! Were there no poor homes to which its light would have conducted *me*!'

Scrooge was very much dismayed to hear the spectre going on at this rate, and began to quake exceedingly.

'Hear me!' cried the Ghost. 'My time is nearly gone.'

'I will,' said Scrooge. 'But don't be hard upon me! Don't be flowery, Jacob! Pray!'

'How it is that I appear before you in a shape that you can see, I may not tell. I have sat invisible beside you many and many a day.'

It was not an agreeable idea. Scrooge shivered, and wiped the perspiration from his brow.

'That is no light part of my penance,' pursued the Ghost. 'I am here to-night to warn you, that you have yet a chance and hope of escaping my fate. A chance and hope of my procuring, Ebenezer.'

'You were always a good friend to me,' said Scrooge. 'Thank'ee!'

'You will be haunted,' resumed the Ghost, 'by Three Spirits.'

Scrooge's countenance fell almost as low as the Ghost's had done.

'Is that the chance and hope you mentioned, Jacob?' he demanded, in a faltering voice.

'It is.'

'I—I think I'd rather not,' said Scrooge.

'Without their visits,' said the Ghost, 'you cannot hope to shun the path I tread. Expect the first to-morrow, when the bell tolls One.'*

'Couldn't I take 'em all at once, and have it over, Jacob?' hinted Scrooge.

'Expect the second on the next night at the same hour. The third upon the next night when the last stroke of Twelve has ceased to vibrate. Look to see me no more; and look that, for your own sake, you remember what has passed between us!'

When it had said these words, the spectre took its wrapper from the table, and bound it round its head, as before. Scrooge knew this, by the smart sound its teeth made, when the jaws were brought together by the bandage. He ventured to raise his eyes again, and found his supernatural visitor confronting him in an erect attitude, with its chain wound over and about its arm.

The apparition walked backward from him; and at every step it took, the window raised itself a little, so that when the spectre reached it, it was wide open.

It beckoned Scrooge to approach, which he did. When they were within two paces of each other, Marley's Ghost held up its hand, warning him to come no nearer. Scrooge stopped.

Not so much in obedience, as in surprise and fear: for on the raising of the hand, he became sensible of confused noises in the air; incoherent sounds of lamentation and regret; wailings inexpressibly sorrowful and self-accusatory. The spectre, after listening for a

moment, joined in the mournful dirge; and floated out upon the bleak, dark night.

Scrooge followed to the window: desperate in his curiosity. He looked out.

The air was filled with phantoms, wandering hither and thither in restless haste, and moaning as they went. Every one of them wore chains like Marley's Ghost; some few (they might be guilty governments) were linked together; none were free. Many had been personally known to Scrooge in their lives. He had been quite familiar with one old ghost, in a white waistcoat, with a monstrous iron safe attached to its ankle, who cried piteously at being unable to assist a wretched woman with an infant, whom it saw below, upon a door-step. The misery with them all was, clearly, that they sought to interfere, for good, in human matters, and had lost the power for ever.

Whether these creatures faded into mist, or mist enshrouded them, he could not tell. But they and their spirit voices faded together; and the night became as it had been when he walked home.

Scrooge closed the window, and examined the door by which the Ghost had entered. It was double-locked, as he had locked it with his own hands, and the bolts were undisturbed. He tried to say 'Humbug!' but stopped at the first syllable. And being, from the emotion he had undergone, or the fatigues of the day, or his glimpse of the Invisible World,* or the dull conversation of the Ghost, or the lateness of the hour, much in need of repose; went straight to bed, without undressing, and fell asleep upon the instant.

STAVE II

THE FIRST OF THE THREE SPIRITS

WHEN Scrooge awoke, it was so dark, that looking out of bed, he could scarcely distinguish the transparent window from the opaque walls of his chamber. He was endeavouring to pierce the darkness with his ferret eyes, when the chimes of a neighbouring church struck the four quarters. So he listened for the hour.

To his great astonishment the heavy bell went on from six to seven, and from seven to eight, and regularly up to twelve; then stopped. Twelve! It was past two when he went to bed. The clock was wrong. An icicle must have got into the works. Twelve!

He touched the spring of his repeater,* to correct this most preposterous clock. Its rapid little pulse beat twelve; and stopped.

'Why, it isn't possible,' said Scrooge, 'that I can have slept through a whole day and far into another night. It isn't possible that anything has happened to the sun, and this is twelve at noon!'

The idea being an alarming one, he scrambled out of bed, and groped his way to the window. He was obliged to rub the frost off with the sleeve of his dressing-gown before he could see anything; and could see very little then. All he could make out was, that it was still very foggy and extremely cold, and that there was no noise of people running to and fro, and making a great stir, as there unquestionably would have been if night had beaten off bright day, and taken possession of the world. This was a great relief, because 'three days after sight of this First of Exchange pay to Mr. Ebenezer Scrooge or his order,' and so forth, would have become a mere United States' security* if there were no days to count by.

Scrooge went to bed again, and thought, and thought, and thought it over and over and over, and could make nothing of it. The more he thought, the more perplexed he was; and the more he endeavoured not to think, the more he thought.

Marley's Ghost bothered him exceedingly. Every time he resolved within himself, after mature inquiry, that it was all a dream, his mind flew back again, like a strong spring released, to its first position, and presented the same problem to be worked all through, 'Was it a dream or not?'

Scrooge lay in this state until the chime had gone three quarters more, when he remembered, on a sudden, that the Ghost had warned him of a visitation when the bell tolled one. He resolved to lie awake until the hour was passed; and, considering that he could no more go to sleep than go to Heaven, this was perhaps the wisest resolution in his power.

The quarter was so long, that he was more than once convinced he must have sunk into a doze unconsciously, and missed the clock. At length it broke upon his listening ear.

'Ding, dong!'

'A quarter past,' said Scrooge, counting.

'Ding, dong!'

'Half-past!' said Scrooge.

'Ding, dong!'

'A quarter to it,' said Scrooge.

'Ding, dong!'

'The hour itself,' said Scrooge, triumphantly, 'and nothing else!'

He spoke before the hour bell sounded, which it now did with a deep, dull, hollow, melancholy ONE. Light flashed up in the room upon the instant, and the curtains of his bed were drawn.

The curtains of his bed were drawn aside, I tell you, by a hand. Not the curtains at his feet, nor the curtains at his back, but those to which his face was addressed. The curtains of his bed were drawn aside; and Scrooge, starting up into a half-recumbent attitude, found himself face to face with the unearthly visitor who drew them: as close to it as I am now to you, and I am standing in the spirit at your elbow.

It was a strange figure—like a child: yet not so like a child as like an old man, viewed through some supernatural medium, which gave him the appearance of having receded from the view, and being diminished to a child's proportions. Its hair, which hung about its neck and down its back, was white as if with age; and yet the face had not a wrinkle in it, and the tenderest bloom was on the skin. The arms were very long and muscular; the hands the same, as if its hold were of uncommon strength. Its legs and feet, most delicately formed, were, like those upper members, bare. It wore a tunic of the purest white; and round its waist was bound a lustrous belt, the sheen of which was beautiful. It held a branch of fresh green holly in its hand; and, in singular contradiction of that wintry emblem, had its dress trimmed with summer flowers. But the strangest thing about it was, that from the crown of its head there sprung a bright clear jet of light, by which all this was visible; and which was doubt-less the occasion of its using, in its duller moments, a great extinguisher for a cap, which it now held under its arm.

Even this, though, when Scrooge looked at it with increasing steadiness, was *not* its strangest quality. For as its belt sparkled and glittered now in one part and now in another, and what was light one instant, at another time was dark, so the figure itself fluctuated in its distinctness: being now a thing with one arm, now with one leg, now with twenty legs, now a pair of legs without a head, now a head without a body: of which dissolving parts, no outline would be visible in the dense gloom wherein they melted away.* And in the very wonder of this, it would be itself again; distinct and clear as ever.

'Are you the Spirit, sir, whose coming was foretold to me?' asked Scrooge.

'I am!'

The voice was soft and gentle. Singularly low,* as if instead of being so close beside him, it were at a distance.

'Who, and what are you?' Scrooge demanded.

'I am the Ghost of Christmas Past.'

'Long Past?' inquired Scrooge: observant of its dwarfish stature.

'No. Your past.'

Perhaps Scrooge could not have told anybody why, if anybody could have asked him; but he had a special desire to see the Spirit in his cap; and begged him to be covered.

'What!' exclaimed the Ghost, 'would you so soon put out, with worldly hands, the light I give? Is it not enough that you are one of those whose passions made this cap, and force me through whole trains of years to wear it low upon my brow!'

Scrooge reverently disclaimed all intention to offend or any knowledge of having wilfully 'bonneted'* the Spirit at any period of his life. He then made bold to inquire what business brought him there.

'Your welfare!' said the Ghost.

Scrooge expressed himself much obliged, but could not help thinking that a night of unbroken rest would have been more conducive to that end. The Spirit must have heard him thinking, for it said immediately:

'Your reclamation, then. Take heed!'

It put out its strong hand as it spoke, and clasped him gently by the arm.

'Rise! and walk with me!'

It would have been in vain for Scrooge to plead that the weather and the hour were not adapted to pedestrian purposes; that bed was warm, and the thermometer a long way below freezing; that he was clad but lightly in his slippers, dressing-gown, and nightcap; and that he had a cold upon him at that time. The grasp, though gentle as a woman's hand, was not to be resisted. He rose: but finding that the Spirit made towards the window, clasped his robe in supplication.

'I am a mortal,' Scrooge remonstrated, 'and liable to fall.'

'Bear but a touch of my hand *there*,' said the Spirit, laying it upon his heart, 'and you shall be upheld in more than this!'

As the words were spoken, they passed through the wall, and stood upon an open country road, with fields on either hand. The city had entirely vanished. Not a vestige of it was to be seen. The darkness and the mist had vanished with it, for it was a clear, cold, winter day, with snow upon the ground.

'Good Heaven!' said Scrooge, clasping his hands together, as he looked about him. 'I was bred in this place. I was a boy here!'

The Spirit gazed upon him mildly. Its gentle touch, though it had been light and instantaneous, appeared still present to the old man's sense of feeling. He was conscious of a thousand odours floating in the air, each one connected with a thousand thoughts, and hopes, and joys, and cares long, long, forgotten!

'Your lip is trembling,' said the Ghost. 'And what is that upon your cheek?'

Scrooge muttered, with an unusual catching in his voice, that it was a pimple; and begged the Ghost to lead him where he would.

'You recollect the way?' inquired the Spirit.

'Remember it!' cried Scrooge with fervour; 'I could walk it blindfold.'

'Strange to have forgotten it for so many years!' observed the Ghost. 'Let us go on.'

They walked along the road, Scrooge recognising every gate, and post, and tree; until a little market-town appeared in the distance, with its bridge, its church, and winding river. Some shaggy ponies now were seen trotting towards them with boys upon their backs, who called to other boys in country gigs and carts, driven by farmers. All these boys were in great spirits, and shouted to each other, until the broad fields were so full of merry music, that the crisp air laughed to hear it!

'These are but shadows of the things that have been,' said the Ghost. 'They have no consciousness of us.'

The jocund travellers came on; and as they came, Scrooge knew and named them every one. Why was he rejoiced beyond all bounds to see them! Why did his cold eye glisten, and his heart leap up* as they went past! Why was he filled with gladness when he heard them give each other Merry Christmas, as they parted at cross-roads and bye-ways, for their several homes! What was merry Christmas to Scrooge? Out upon merry Christmas! What good had it ever done to him?

'The school is not quite deserted,' said the Ghost. 'A solitary child, neglected by his friends, is left there still.'

Scrooge said he knew it. And he sobbed.

They left the high-road, by a well-remembered lane, and soon approached a mansion of dull red brick, with a little weathercock-surmounted cupola on the roof, and a bell hanging in it. It was a large house, but one of broken fortunes; for the spacious offices were little used, their walls were damp and mossy, their windows broken, and their gates decayed. Fowls clucked and strutted in the stables; and the coach-houses and sheds were over-run with grass. Nor was it more retentive of its ancient state, within; for entering the dreary hall, and glancing through the open doors of many rooms, they found them poorly furnished, cold, and vast. There was an earthy savour in the air, a chilly bareness in the place, which associated itself somehow with too much getting up by candle-light, and not too much to eat.

They went, the Ghost and Scrooge, across the hall, to a door at the back of the house. It opened before them, and disclosed a long, bare, melancholy room, made barer still by lines of plain deal forms* and desks. At one of these a lonely boy was reading near a feeble fire; and Scrooge sat down upon a form, and wept to see his poor forgotten self as he used to be.

Not a latent echo in the house, not a squeak and scuffle from the mice behind the panelling, not a drip from the half-thawed water-spout in the dull yard behind, not a sigh among the leafless boughs of one despondent poplar, not the idle swinging of an empty store-house door, no, not a clicking in the fire, but fell upon the heart of Scrooge with a softening influence, and gave a freer passage to his tears.*

The Spirit touched him on the arm, and pointed to his younger self, intent upon his reading. Suddenly a man, in foreign garments: wonderfully real and distinct to look at: stood outside the window, with an axe stuck in his belt, and leading by the bridle an ass laden with wood.

'Why, it's Ali Baba!* Scrooge exclaimed in ecstasy. 'It's dear old honest Ali Baba! Yes, yes, I know! One Christmas time, when yonder solitary child was left here all alone, he *did* come, for the first time, just like that. Poor boy! And Valentine,' said Scrooge, 'and his wild brother, Orson;* there they go! And what's his name, who was put down in his drawers, asleep, at the Gate of Damascus; don't you see him! And the Sultan's Groom turned upside down by the Genii; there he is upon his head! Serve him right. I'm glad of it. What business had *he* to be married to the Princess!'*

To hear Scrooge expending all the earnestness of his nature on such subjects, in a most extraordinary voice between laughing and crying; and to see his heightened and excited face; would have been a surprise to his business friends in the city, indeed.

'There's the Parrot!' cried Scrooge. 'Green body and yellow tail, with a thing like a lettuce growing out of the top of his head; there he is! Poor Robin Crusoe, he called him, when he came home again after sailing round the island. 'Poor Robin Crusoe, where have you been, Robin Crusoe?' The man thought he was dreaming, but he wasn't. It was the Parrot, you know. There goes Friday, running for his life to the little creek!* Halloa! Hoop! Halloo!'

Then, with a rapidity of transition very foreign to his usual character, he said, in pity for his former self, 'Poor boy!' and cried again.

'I wish,' Scrooge muttered, putting his hand in his pocket, and looking about him, after drying his eyes with his cuff: 'but it's too late now.'

'What is the matter?' asked the Spirit.

'Nothing,' said Scrooge. 'Nothing. There was a boy singing a Christmas Carol at my door last night. I should like to have given him something: that's all.'

The Ghost smiled thoughtfully, and waved its hand: saying as it did so, 'Let us see another Christmas!'

Scrooge's former self grew larger at the words, and the room became a little darker and more dirty. The panels shrunk, the windows cracked; fragments of plaster fell out of the ceiling, and the naked laths were shown instead; but how all this was brought about, Scrooge knew no more than you do. He only knew that it was quite correct; that everything had happened so; that there he was, alone again, when all the other boys had gone home for the jolly holidays.

He was not reading now, but walking up and down despairingly. Scrooge looked at the Ghost, and with a mournful shaking of his head, glanced anxiously towards the door.

It opened; and a little girl, much younger than the boy, came darting in, and putting her arms about his neck, and often kissing him, addressed him as her 'Dear, dear brother.'

'I have come to bring you home, dear brother!' said the child, clapping her tiny hands, and bending down to laugh. 'To bring you home, home, home!'

'Home, little Fan?' returned the boy.

'Yes!' said the child, brimful of glee. 'Home, for good and all. Home, for ever and ever. Father is so much kinder than he used to be, that home's like Heaven! He spoke so gently to me one dear night when I was going to bed, that I was not afraid to ask him once more if you might come home; and he said Yes, you should; and sent me in a coach to bring you. And you're to be a man!' said the child, opening her eyes, 'and are never to come back here; but first, we're to be together all the Christmas long, and have the merriest time in all the world.'

'You are quite a woman, little Fan!' exclaimed the boy.

She clapped her hands and laughed, and tried to touch his head; but being too little, laughed again, and stood on tiptoe to embrace him. Then she began to drag him, in her childish eagerness, towards the door; and he, nothing loth to go, accompanied her.

A terrible voice in the hall cried, 'Bring down Master Scrooge's box, there!' and in the hall appeared the school-master himself, who glared on Master Scrooge with a ferocious condescension, and threw him into a dreadful state of mind by shaking hands with him. He then conveyed him and his sister into the veriest old well of a shivering best-parlour that ever was seen, where the maps upon the wall, and the celestial and terrestrial globes in the windows, were waxy with cold. Here he produced a decanter of curiously light wine, and a block of curiously heavy cake, and administered instalments of those dainties to the young people: at the same time, sending out a meagre servant to offer a glass of 'something' to the postboy, who answered that he thanked the gentleman, but if it was the same tap as he had tasted before, he had rather not. Master Scrooge's trunk being by this time tied on to the top of the chaise, the children bade the school-master good-bye right willingly; and getting into it, drove gaily down the garden-sweep: the quick wheels dashing the hoar-frost and snow from off the dark leaves of the evergreens like spray.

'Always a delicate creature, whom a breath might have withered,' said the Ghost. 'But she had a large heart!'

'So she had,' cried Scrooge. 'You're right. I will not gainsay it, Spirit. God forbid!'

'She died a woman,' said the Ghost, 'and had, as I think, children.'

'One child,' Scrooge returned.

'True,' said the Ghost. 'Your nephew!'

Scrooge seemed uneasy in his mind; and answered briefly, 'Yes.'

Although they had but that moment left the school behind them, they were now in the busy thoroughfares of a city, where shadowy passengers passed and re-passed; where shadowy carts and coaches battled for the way, and all the strife and tumult of a real city were. It was made plain enough, by the dressing of the shops, that here too it was Christmas time again; but it was evening, and the streets were lighted up.

The Ghost stopped at a certain warehouse door, and asked Scrooge if he knew it.

'Know it!' said Scrooge. 'Was I apprenticed here!'

They went in. At sight of an old gentleman in a Welsh wig,* sitting behind such a high desk, that if he had been two inches taller he must have knocked his head against the ceiling, Scrooge cried in great excitement:

'Why, it's old Fezziwig! Bless his heart; it's Fezziwig alive again!'

Old Fezziwig laid down his pen, and looked up at the clock, which pointed to the hour of seven. He rubbed his hands; adjusted his capacious waistcoat; laughed all over himself, from his shoes to his organ of benevolence,* and called out in a comfortable, oily, rich, fat, jovial voice:

'Yo ho, there! Ebenezer! Dick!'

Scrooge's former self, now grown a young man, came briskly in, accompanied by his fellow-'prentice.

'Dick Wilkins, to be sure!' said Scrooge to the Ghost. 'Bless me, yes. There he is. He was very much attached to me, was Dick. Poor Dick! Dear, dear!'

'Yo ho, my boys!' said Fezziwig. 'No more work to-night. Christmas Eve, Dick. Christmas, Ebenezer! Let's have the shutters up,' cried old Fezziwig, with a sharp clap of his hands, 'before a man can say Jack Robinson!'

You wouldn't believe how those two fellows went at it! They charged into the street with the shutters—one, two, three—had 'em up in their places—four, five, six—barred 'em and pinned 'em—seven, eight, nine—and came back before you could have got to twelve, panting like race-horses.

'Hilli-ho!' cried old Fezziwig, skipping down from the high desk, with wonderful agility. 'Clear away, my lads, and let's have lots of room here! Hilli-ho, Dick! Chirrup, Ebenezer!'

Clear away! There was nothing they wouldn't have cleared away, or couldn't have cleared away, with old Fezziwig looking on. It was done in a minute. Every movable was packed off, as if it were dismissed from public life for evermore; the floor was swept and watered, the lamps were trimmed, fuel was heaped upon the fire; and the warehouse was as snug, and warm, and dry, and bright a ball-room, as you would desire to see upon a winter's night.

In came a fiddler with a music-book, and went up to the lofty desk, and made an orchestra of it, and tuned like fifty stomach-aches. In came Mrs. Fezziwig, one vast substantial smile. In came the three Miss Fezziwigs, beaming and lovable. In came the six young followers whose hearts they broke. In came all the young men and women employed in the business. In came the housemaid, with her cousin, the baker. In came the cook, with her brother's particular friend, the milkman. In came the boy from over the way, who was suspected of not having board enough from his master; trying to hide himself behind the girl from next door but one, who was proved to have had her ears pulled by her mistress. In they all came, one after another; some shyly, some boldly, some gracefully, some awkwardly, some pushing, some pulling; in they all came, anyhow and everyhow. Away they all went, twenty couple at once; hands half round and back again the other way; down the middle and up again; round and round in various stages of affectionate grouping: old top couple always turning up in the wrong place; new top couple starting off again, as soon as they got there; all top couples at last, and not a bottom one to help them! When this result was brought about, old Fezziwig, clapping his hands to stop the dance, cried out, 'Well done!' and the fiddler plunged his hot face into a pot of porter,* especially provided for that purpose. But scorning rest, upon his reappearance, he instantly began again, though there were no dancers yet, as if the other fiddler had been carried home, exhausted, on a shutter, and he were a bran-new man resolved to beat him out of sight, or perish.

There were more dances, and there were forfeits, and more dances, and there was cake, and there was negus,* and there was a great piece of Cold Roast, and there was a great piece of Cold Boiled, and there were mince-pies, and plenty of beer. But the great effect of the evening came after the Roast and Boiled, when the fiddler (an artful dog, mind! The sort of man who knew his business better than you or I could have told it him!) struck up 'Sir Roger de Coverley.'* Then old Fezziwig stood out to dance with Mrs. Fezziwig. Top couple, too; with a good stiff piece of work cut out for them; three or four and twenty pair of partners; people who were not to be trifled with; people who *would* dance, and had no notion of walking.

But if they had been twice as many—ah, four times—old Fezziwig would have been a match for them, and so would Mrs. Fezziwig. As to *her*, she was worthy to be his partner in every sense of the term. If that's not high praise, tell me higher, and I'll use it. A positive light appeared to issue from Fezziwig's calves. They shone in every part of the dance like moons. You couldn't have predicted, at any given time, what would have become of them next. And when old Fezziwig and Mrs. Fezziwig had gone all through the dance; advance and retire, both hands to your partner, bow and curtsey, corkscrew, thread-the-needle, and back again to your place; Fezziwig 'cut'*—cut so deftly, that he appeared to wink with his legs, and came upon his feet again without a stagger.

When the clock struck eleven, this domestic ball broke up. Mr. and Mrs. Fezziwig took their stations, one on either side of the door, and shaking hands with every person individually as he or she went out, wished him or her a Merry Christmas. When everybody had retired but the two 'prentices, they did the same to them; and thus the cheerful voices died away, and the lads were left to their beds; which were under a counter in the back-shop.

During the whole of this time, Scrooge had acted like a man out of his wits. His heart and soul were in the scene, and with his former self. He corroborated everything, remembered everything, enjoyed everything, and underwent the strangest agitation. It was not until now, when the bright faces of his former self and Dick were turned from them, that he remembered the Ghost, and became conscious that it was looking full upon him, while the light upon its head burnt very clear.

'A small matter,' said the Ghost, 'to make these silly folks so full of gratitude.'

'Small!' echoed Scrooge.

The Spirit signed to him to listen to the two apprentices, who were pouring out their hearts in praise of Fezziwig: and when he had done so, said,

'Why! Is it not? He has spent but a few pounds of your mortal money: three or four perhaps. Is that so much that he deserves this praise?'

'It isn't that,' said Scrooge, heated by the remark, and speaking unconsciously like his former, not his latter, self. 'It isn't that, Spirit. He has the power to render us happy or unhappy; to make our service light or burdensome; a pleasure or a toil. Say that his power lies in words and looks; in things so slight and insignificant that it is impossible to add and count 'em up: what then? The happiness he gives, is quite as great as if it cost a fortune.'

He felt the Spirit's glance, and stopped.

'What is the matter?' asked the Ghost.

'Nothing particular,' said Scrooge.

'Something, I think?' the Ghost insisted.

'No,' said Scrooge, 'No. I should like to be able to say a word or two to my clerk just now. That's all.'

His former self turned down the lamps as he gave utterance to the wish; and Scrooge and the Ghost again stood side by side in the open air.

'My time grows short,' observed the Spirit. 'Quick!'

This was not addressed to Scrooge, or to any one whom he could see, but it produced an immediate effect. For again Scrooge saw himself. He was older now; a man in the prime of life. His face had not the harsh and rigid lines of later years; but it had begun to wear the signs of care and avarice. There was an eager, greedy, restless motion in the eye, which showed the passion that had taken root, and where the shadow of the growing tree would fall.

He was not alone, but sat by the side of a fair young girl in a mourning-dress: in whose eyes there were tears, which sparkled in the light that shone out of the Ghost of Christmas Past.

'It matters little,' she said, softly. 'To you, very little. Another idol has displaced me; and if it can cheer and comfort you in time to come, as I would have tried to do, I have no just cause to grieve.'

'What Idol has displaced you?' he rejoined.

'A golden one.'*

'This is the even-handed dealing of the world!' he said. 'There is nothing on which it is so hard as poverty; and there is nothing it professes to condemn with such severity as the pursuit of wealth!'

'You fear the world too much,' she answered, gently. 'All your other hopes have merged into the hope of being beyond the chance of its sordid reproach. I have seen your nobler aspirations fall off one by one, until the master-passion, Gain, engrosses you. Have I not?'

'What then?' he retorted. 'Even if I have grown so much wiser, what then? I am not changed towards you.'

She shook her head.

'Am I?'

'Our contract is an old one. It was made when we were both poor and content to be so, until, in good season, we could improve our worldly fortune by our patient industry. You *are* changed. When it was made, you were another man.'

'I was a boy,' he said impatiently.

'Your own feeling tells you that you were not what you are,' she returned. 'I am. That which promised happiness when we were one in heart, is fraught with misery now that we are two. How often and how keenly I have thought of this, I will not say. It is enough that I *have* thought of it, and can release you.'

'Have I ever sought release?'

'In words. No. Never.'

'In what, then?'

'In a changed nature; in an altered spirit; in another atmosphere of life; another Hope as its great end. In everything that made my love of any worth or value in your sight. If this had never been between us,' said the girl, looking mildly, but with steadiness, upon him; 'tell me, would you seek me out and try to win me now? Ah, no!'

He seemed to yield to the justice of this supposition, in spite of himself. But he said with a struggle, 'You think not.'

'I would gladly think otherwise if I could,' she answered, 'Heaven knows! When *I* have learned a Truth like this, I know how strong and irresistible it must be. But if you were free to-day, to-morrow, yesterday, can even I believe that you would choose a dowerless girl—you who, in your very confidence with her, weigh everything by Gain: or, choosing her, if for a moment you were false enough to your one guiding principle to do so, do I not know that your repentance and regret would surely follow? I do; and I release you. With a full heart, for the love of him you once were.'

He was about to speak; but with her head turned from him, she resumed.

'You may—the memory of what is past half makes me hope you will—have pain in this. A very, very brief time, and you will dismiss the recollection of it, gladly, as an unprofitable dream, from which it happened well that you awoke. May you be happy in the life you have chosen!'

She left him, and they parted.

'Spirit!' said Scrooge, 'show me no more! Conduct me home. Why do you delight to torture me?'

'One shadow more!' exclaimed the Ghost.

'No more!' cried Scrooge. 'No more. I don't wish to see it. Show me no more!'

But the relentless Ghost pinioned him in both his arms, and forced him to observe what happened next.

They were in another scene and place; a room, not very large or handsome, but full of comfort. Near to the winter fire sat a beautiful young girl, so like that last that Scrooge believed it was the same, until he saw *her*, now a comely matron, sitting opposite her daughter. The noise in this room was perfectly tumultuous, for there were more children there, than Scrooge in his agitated state of mind could count; and, unlike the celebrated herd in the poem,* they were not forty children conducting themselves like one, but every child was conducting itself like forty. The consequences were uproarious beyond belief; but no one seemed to care; on the contrary, the mother and daughter laughed heartily, and enjoyed it very much; and the latter, soon beginning to mingle in the sports, got pillaged by the young brigands most ruthlessly. What would I not have given to be one of them! Though I never could have been so rude, no, no! I wouldn't for the wealth of all the world have crushed that braided hair, and torn it down; and for the precious little shoe, I wouldn't have plucked it off, God bless my soul! to save my life. As to measuring her waist in sport, as they did, bold young brood, I couldn't have done it; I should have expected my arm to have grown round it for a punishment, and never come straight again. And yet I should have dearly liked, I own, to have touched her lips; to have questioned her, that she might have opened them; to have looked upon the lashes of her downcast eyes, and never raised a blush; to have let loose waves of hair, an inch of which would be a keepsake beyond price: in

short, I should have liked, I do confess, to have had the lightest
licence of a child, and yet to have been man enough to know its value.

But now a knocking at the door was heard, and such a rush
immediately ensued that she with laughing face and plundered dress
was borne towards it the centre of a flushed and boisterous group,
just in time to greet the father, who came home attended by a man
laden with Christmas toys and presents. Then the shouting and
the struggling, and the onslaught that was made on the defenceless
porter! The scaling him with chairs for ladders to dive into his
pockets, despoil him of brown-paper parcels, hold on tight by
his cravat, hug him round his neck, pommel his back, and kick his
legs in irrepressible affection! The shouts of wonder and delight
with which the development of every package was received! The
terrible announcement that the baby had been taken in the act of
putting a doll's frying-pan into his mouth, and was more than suspected of having swallowed a fictitious turkey, glued on a wooden
platter! The immense relief of finding this a false alarm! The joy, and
gratitude, and ecstasy! They are all indescribable alike. It is enough
that by degrees the children and their emotions got out of the parlour and by one stair at a time, up to the top of the house; where they
went to bed, and so subsided.

And now Scrooge looked on more attentively than ever, when the
master of the house, having his daughter leaning fondly on him, sat
down with her and her mother at his own fireside; and when he
thought that such another creature, quite as graceful and as full of
promise, might have called him father, and been a spring-time in the
haggard winter of his life, his sight grew very dim indeed.

'Belle,' said the husband, turning to his wife with a smile, 'I saw an
old friend of yours this afternoon.'

'Who was it?'

'Guess!'

'How can I? Tut, don't I know,' she added in the same breath,
laughing as he laughed. 'Mr. Scrooge.'

'Mr. Scrooge it was. I passed his office window; and as it was not
shut up, and he had a candle inside, I could scarcely help seeing him.
His partner lies upon the point of death, I hear; and there he sat
alone. Quite alone in the world, I do believe.'

'Spirit!' said Scrooge in a broken voice, 'remove me from this
place.'

'I told you these were shadows of the things that have been,' said the Ghost. 'That they are what they are, do not blame me!'

'Remove me!' Scrooge exclaimed, 'I cannot bear it!'

He turned upon the Ghost, and seeing that it looked upon him with a face, in which in some strange way there were fragments of all the faces it had shown him, wrestled with it. 'Leave me! Take me back. Haunt me no longer!'

In the struggle, if that can be called a struggle in which the Ghost with no visible resistance on its own part was undisturbed by any effort of its adversary, Scrooge observed that its light was burning high and bright; and dimly connecting that with its influence over him, he seized the extinguisher-cap, and by a sudden action pressed it down upon its head.

The Spirit dropped beneath it, so that the extinguisher covered its whole form; but though Scrooge pressed it down with all his force, he could not hide the light, which streamed from under it, in an unbroken flood upon the ground.

He was conscious of being exhausted, and overcome by an

irresistible drowsiness; and, further, of being in his own bed-room. He gave the cap a parting squeeze, in which his hand relaxed; and had barely time to reel to bed, before he sank into a heavy sleep.

STAVE III

THE SECOND OF THE THREE SPIRITS

Awaking in the middle of a prodigiously tough snore, and sitting up in bed to get his thoughts together, Scrooge had no occasion to be told that the bell was again upon the stroke of One. He felt that he was restored to consciousness in the right nick of time, for the especial purpose of holding a conference with the second messenger despatched to him through Jacob Marley's intervention. But, finding that he turned uncomfortably cold when he began to wonder which of his curtains this new spectre would draw back, he put them every one aside with his own hands, and lying down again, established a sharp look-out all round the bed. For, he wished to challenge the Spirit on the moment of its appearance, and did not wish to be taken by surprise, and made nervous.

Gentlemen of the free-and-easy sort,* who plume themselves on being acquainted with a move or two, and being usually equal to the time-of-day,* express the wide range of their capacity for adventure by observing that they are good for anything from pitch-and-toss* to manslaughter; between which opposite extremes, no doubt, there lies a tolerably wide and comprehensive range of subjects. Without venturing for Scrooge quite as hardily as this, I don't mind calling on you to believe that he was ready for a good broad field of strange appearances, and that nothing between a baby and rhinoceros would have astonished him very much.

Now, being prepared for almost anything, he was not by any means prepared for nothing; and, consequently, when the Bell struck One, and no shape appeared, he was taken with a violent fit of trembling. Five minutes, ten minutes, a quarter of an hour went by, yet nothing came. All this time, he lay upon his bed, the very core and centre of a blaze of ruddy light, which streamed upon it when the clock proclaimed the hour; and which, being only light, was more alarming than a dozen ghosts, as he was powerless to make out what it meant, or would be at; and was sometimes apprehensive that he might be at that very moment an interesting case of spontaneous combustion,* without having the consolation of knowing it. At last, however, he began to think—as you or I would have thought at first; for it is always the person not in the predicament who knows what ought to have been done in it, and would unquestionably have done it too—at last, I say, he began to think that the source and secret of this ghostly light might be in the adjoining room, from whence, on further tracing it, it seemed to shine. This idea taking full possession of his mind, he got up softly and shuffled in his slippers to the door.

The moment Scrooge's hand was on the lock, a strange voice called him by his name, and bade him enter. He obeyed.

It was his own room. There was no doubt about that. But it had undergone a surprising transformation. The walls and ceiling were so hung with living green, that it looked a perfect grove; from every part of which, bright gleaming berries glistened. The crisp leaves of holly, mistletoe, and ivy reflected back the light, as if so many little mirrors had been scattered there; and such a mighty blaze went roaring up the chimney, as that dull petrification of a hearth had never known in Scrooge's time, or Marley's, or for many and many a winter season gone. Heaped up on the floor, to form a kind of throne, were turkeys, geese, game, poultry, brawn, great joints of meat, sucking-pigs, long wreaths of sausages, mince-pies, plum-puddings, barrels of oysters, red-hot chestnuts, cherry-cheeked apples, juicy oranges, luscious pears, immense twelfth-cakes,* and seething bowls of punch, that made the chamber dim with their delicious steam. In easy state upon this couch, there sat a jolly Giant, glorious to see; who bore a glowing torch, in shape not unlike Plenty's horn, and held it up, high up, to shed its light on Scrooge, as he came peeping round the door.

'Come in!' exclaimed the Ghost. 'Come in! and know me better, man!'

Scrooge entered timidly, and hung his head before this Spirit. He was not the dogged Scrooge he had been; and though the Spirit's eyes were clear and kind, he did not like to meet them.

'I am the Ghost of Christmas Present,' said the Spirit. 'Look upon me!'

Scrooge reverently did so. It was clothed in one simple green robe, or mantle, bordered with white fur. This garment hung so loosely on the figure, that its capacious breast was bare, as if disdaining to be warded or concealed by any artifice. Its feet, observable beneath the ample folds of the garment, were also bare; and on its head it wore no other covering than a holly wreath, set here and there with shining icicles. Its dark brown curls were long and free; free as its genial face, its sparkling eye, its open hand, its cheery voice, its unconstrained demeanour, and its joyful air. Girded round its middle was an antique scabbard; but no sword was in it, and the ancient sheath was eaten up with rust.

'You have never seen the like of me before!' exclaimed the Spirit.

'Never,' Scrooge made answer to it.

'Have never walked forth with the younger members of my family; meaning (for I am very young) my elder brothers born in these later years?' pursued the Phantom.

'I don't think I have,' said Scrooge. 'I am afraid I have not. Have you had many brothers, Spirit?'

'More than eighteen hundred,' said the Ghost.

'A tremendous family to provide for!' muttered Scrooge.

The Ghost of Christmas Present rose.

'Spirit,' said Scrooge submissively, 'conduct me where you will. I went forth last night on compulsion, and I learnt a lesson which is working now. To-night, if you have aught to teach me, let me profit by it.'

'Touch my robe!'

Scrooge did as he was told, and held it fast.

Holly, mistletoe, red berries, ivy, turkeys, geese, game, poultry, brawn, meat, pigs, sausages, oysters, pies, puddings, fruit, and punch, all vanished instantly. So did the room, the fire, the ruddy glow, the hour of night, and they stood in the city streets on Christmas morning, where (for the weather was severe) the people made a rough, but brisk and not unpleasant kind of music, in scraping the snow from the pavement in front of their dwellings, and from the tops of their houses, whence it was mad delight to the boys to see it come plumping down into the road below, and splitting into artificial little snow-storms.

The house fronts looked black enough, and the windows blacker, contrasting with the smooth white sheet of snow upon the roofs, and with the dirtier snow upon the ground; which last deposit had been ploughed up in deep furrows by the heavy wheels of carts and

Scrooge's third Visitor

waggons; furrows that crossed and re-crossed each other hundreds of times where the great streets branched off; and made intricate channels, hard to trace in the thick yellow mud and icy water. The sky was gloomy, and the shortest streets were choked up with a dingy mist, half thawed, half frozen, whose heavier particles descended in a shower of sooty atoms, as if all the chimneys in Great Britain had, by one consent, caught fire, and were blazing away to their dear hearts' content. There was nothing very cheerful in the climate or the town, and yet was there an air of cheerfulness abroad that the clearest summer air and brightest summer sun might have endeavoured to diffuse in vain.

For, the people who were shovelling away on the house-tops were jovial and full of glee; calling out to one another from the parapets, and now and then exchanging a facetious snowball—better-natured missile far than many a wordy jest—laughing heartily if it went right and not less heartily if it went wrong. The poulterers' shops were still half open, and the fruiterers' were radiant in their glory. There were great, round, pot-bellied baskets of chestnuts, shaped like the waistcoats of jolly old gentlemen, lolling at the doors, and tumbling out into the street in their apoplectic opulence. There were ruddy, brown-faced, broad-girthed Spanish Onions, shining in the fatness of their growth like Spanish Friars, and winking from their shelves in wanton slyness at the girls as they went by, and glanced demurely at the hung-up mistletoe. There were pears and apples, clustered high in blooming pyramids; there were bunches of grapes, made in the shopkeepers' benevolence to dangle from conspicuous hooks, that people's mouths might water gratis as they passed; there were piles of filberts, mossy and brown, recalling, in their fragrance, ancient walks among the woods, and pleasant shufflings ankle deep through withered leaves; there were Norfolk Biffins,* squab and swar-thy, setting off the yellow of the oranges and lemons, and, in the great compactness of their juicy persons, urgently entreating and beseeching to be carried home in paper bags and eaten after dinner. The very gold and silver fish,* set forth among these choice fruits in a bowl, though members of a dull and stagnant-blooded race, appeared to know that there was something going on; and, to a fish, went gasping round and round their little world in slow and passionless excitement.

The Grocers'! oh the Grocers'! nearly closed, with perhaps two shutters down, or one; but through those gaps such glimpses! It was not alone that the scales descending on the counter made a merry sound, or that the twine and roller parted company so briskly, or that the canisters were rattled up and down like juggling tricks, or even that the blended scents of tea and coffee were so grateful to the nose, or even that the raisins were so plentiful and rare, the almonds so extremely white, the sticks of cinnamon so long and straight, the other spices so delicious, the candied fruits so caked and spotted with molten sugar as to make the coldest lookers-on feel faint and subsequently bilious. Nor was it that the figs were moist and pulpy, or that the French plums blushed in modest tartness from their highly-decorated boxes, or that everything was good to eat and in its Christmas dress; but the customers were all so hurried and so eager in the hopeful promise of the day, that they tumbled up against each other at the door, crashing their wicker baskets wildly, and left their purchases upon the counter, and came running back to fetch them, and committed hundreds of the like mistakes, in the best humour possible; while the Grocer and his people were so frank and fresh that the polished hearts with which they fastened their aprons behind might have been their own, worn outside for general inspection, and for Christmas daws to peck at* if they chose.

But soon the steeples called good people all, to church and chapel, and away they came, flocking through the streets in their best clothes, and with their gayest faces. And at the same time there emerged from scores of bye-streets, lanes, and nameless turnings, innumerable people, carrying their dinners to the bakers' shops.* The sight of these poor revellers appeared to interest the Spirit very much, for he stood with Scrooge beside him in a baker's doorway, and taking off the covers as their bearers passed, sprinkled incense on their dinners from his torch. And it was a very uncommon kind of torch, for once or twice when there were angry words between some dinner-carriers who had jostled each other, he shed a few drops of water on them from it, and their good humour was restored directly. For they said, it was a shame to quarrel upon Christmas Day. And so it was! God love it, so it was!

In time the bells ceased, and the bakers were shut up; and yet there was a genial shadowing forth of all these dinners and the progress of their cooking, in the thawed blotch of wet above each baker's oven; where the pavement smoked as if its stones were cooking too.

'Is there a peculiar flavour in what you sprinkle from your torch?' asked Scrooge.

'There is. My own.'

'Would it apply to any kind of dinner on this day?' asked Scrooge.

'To any kindly given. To a poor one most.'

'Why to a poor one most?' asked Scrooge.

'Because it needs it most.'

'Spirit,' said Scrooge, after a moment's thought, 'I wonder you, of all the beings in the many worlds about us, should desire to cramp these people's opportunities of innocent enjoyment.'

'I!' cried the Spirit.

'You would deprive them of their means of dining every seventh day, often the only day on which they can be said to dine at all,' said Scrooge. 'Wouldn't you?'

'I!' cried the Spirit.

'You seek to close these places on the Seventh Day?'* said Scrooge. 'And it comes to the same thing.'

'*I* seek!' exclaimed the Spirit.

'Forgive me if I am wrong. It has been done in your name, or at least in that of your family,' said Scrooge.

'There are some upon this earth of yours,' returned the Spirit, 'who lay claim to know us, and who do their deeds of passion, pride, ill-will, hatred, envy, bigotry, and selfishness in our name, who are as strange to us and all our kith and kin, as if they had never lived. Remember that, and charge their doings on themselves, not us.'

Scrooge promised that he would; and they went on, invisible, as they had been before, into the suburbs of the town. It was a remarkable quality of the Ghost (which Scrooge had observed at the baker's), that notwithstanding his gigantic size, he could accommodate himself to any place with ease; and that he stood beneath a low roof quite as gracefully and like a supernatural creature, as it was possible he could have done in any lofty hall.

And perhaps it was the pleasure the good Spirit had in showing off this power of his, or else it was his own kind, generous, hearty nature, and his sympathy with all poor men, that led him straight to Scrooge's clerk's; for there he went, and took Scrooge with him, holding to his robe; and on the threshold of the door the Spirit smiled, and stopped to bless Bob Cratchit's dwelling with the sprinkling of his torch. Think of that! Bob had but fifteen 'Bob'* a-week himself;

he pocketed on Saturdays but fifteen copies of his Christian name; and yet the Ghost of Christmas Present blessed his four-roomed house!

Then up rose Mrs. Cratchit, Cratchit's wife, dressed out but poorly in a twice-turned gown,* but brave in ribbons, which are cheap and make a goodly show for sixpence; and she laid the cloth, assisted by Belinda Cratchit, second of her daughters, also brave in ribbons; while Master Peter Cratchit plunged a fork into the saucepan of potatoes, and getting the corners of his monstrous shirt collar (Bob's private property, conferred upon his son and heir in honour of the day) into his mouth, rejoiced to find himself so gallantly attired, and yearned to show his linen in the fashionable Parks. And now two smaller Cratchits, boy and girl, came tearing in, screaming that outside the baker's they had smelt the goose, and known it for their own; and basking in luxurious thoughts of sage and onion, these young Cratchits danced about the table, and exalted Master Peter Cratchit to the skies, while he (not proud, although his collars nearly choked him) blew the fire, until the slow potatoes bubbling up, knocked loudly at the saucepan-lid to be let out and peeled.

'What has ever got your precious father then?' said Mrs. Cratchit. 'And your brother, Tiny Tim! And Martha warn't as late last Christmas Day by half-an-hour?'

'Here's Martha, mother!' said a girl, appearing as she spoke.

'Here's Martha, mother!' cried the two young Cratchits. 'Hurrah! There's *such* a goose, Martha!'

'Why, bless your heart alive, my dear, how late you are!' said Mrs. Cratchit, kissing her a dozen times, and taking off her shawl and bonnet for her with officious zeal.

'We'd a deal of work to finish up last night,' replied the girl, 'and had to clear away this morning, mother!'

'Well! Never mind so long as you are come,' said Mrs. Cratchit. 'Sit ye down before the fire, my dear, and have a warm, Lord bless ye!'

'No, no! There's father coming,' cried the two young Cratchits, who were everywhere at once. 'Hide, Martha, hide!'

So Martha hid herself, and in came little Bob, the father, with at least three feet of comforter exclusive of the fringe, hanging down before him; and his threadbare clothes darned up and brushed, to look seasonable; and Tiny Tim upon his shoulder. Alas for Tiny Tim, he bore a little crutch, and had his limbs supported by an iron frame!

'Why, where's our Martha?' cried Bob Cratchit, looking round.

'Not coming,' said Mrs. Cratchit.

'Not coming!' said Bob, with a sudden declension in his high spirits; for he had been Tim's blood horse* all the way from church, and had come home rampant. 'Not coming upon Christmas Day!'

Martha didn't like to see him disappointed, if it were only in joke; so she came out prematurely from behind the closet door, and ran into his arms, while the two young Cratchits hustled Tiny Tim, and bore him off into the wash-house, that he might hear the pudding singing in the copper.*

'And how did little Tim behave?' asked Mrs. Cratchit, when she had rallied Bob on his credulity, and Bob had hugged his daughter to his heart's content.

'As good as gold,' said Bob, 'and better. Somehow he gets thoughtful, sitting by himself so much, and thinks the strangest things you ever heard. He told me, coming home, that he hoped the people saw him in the church, because he was a cripple, and it might be pleasant to them to remember upon Christmas Day, who made lame beggars walk, and blind men see.'*

Bob's voice was tremulous when he told them this, and trembled more when he said that Tiny Tim was growing strong and hearty.

His active little crutch was heard upon the floor, and back came Tiny Tim before another word was spoken, escorted by his brother and sister to his stool before the fire; and while Bob, turning up his cuffs—as if, poor fellow, they were capable of being made more shabby—compounded some hot mixture in a jug with gin and lemons, and stirred it round and round and put it on the hob to simmer; Master Peter, and the two ubiquitous young Cratchits went to fetch the goose, with which they soon returned in high procession.

Such a bustle ensued that you might have thought a goose the rarest of all birds; a feathered phenomenon, to which a black swan was a matter of course—and in truth it was something very like it in that house. Mrs. Cratchit made the gravy (ready beforehand in a little saucepan) hissing hot; Master Peter mashed the potatoes with incredible vigour; Miss Belinda sweetened up the apple-sauce; Martha dusted the hot plates; Bob took Tiny Tim beside him in a tiny corner at the table; the two young Cratchits set chairs for every-body, not forgetting themselves, and mounting guard upon their posts, crammed spoons into their mouths, lest they should shriek for goose before their turn came to be helped. At last the dishes were set on, and grace was said. It was succeeded by a breathless pause, as Mrs. Cratchit, looking slowly all along the carving-knife, prepared to plunge it in the breast; but when she did, and when the long expected gush of stuffing issued forth, one murmur of delight arose all round the board, and even Tiny Tim, excited by the two young Cratchits, beat on the table with the handle of his knife, and feebly cried Hurrah!

There never was such a goose. Bob said he didn't believe there ever was such a goose cooked. Its tenderness and flavour, size and cheapness, were the themes of universal admiration. Eked out by apple-sauce and mashed potatoes, it was a sufficient dinner for the whole family; indeed, as Mrs. Cratchit said with great delight (surveying one small atom of a bone upon the dish), they hadn't ate it all at last! Yet every one had had enough, and the youngest Cratchits in particular, were steeped in sage and onion to the eyebrows! But now, the plates being changed by Miss Belinda, Mrs. Cratchit left the room alone—too nervous to bear witnesses—to take the pudding up and bring it in.

Suppose it should not be done enough! Suppose it should break in turning out! Suppose somebody should have got over the wall of the back-yard, and stolen it, while they were merry with the goose—a supposition at which the two young Cratchits became livid! All sorts of horrors were supposed.

Hallo! A great deal of steam! The pudding was out of the copper. A smell like a washing-day! That was the cloth. A smell like an eating-house and a pastrycook's next door to each other, with a laundress's next door to that! That was the pudding! In half a minute Mrs. Cratchit entered—flushed, but smiling proudly—with the pudding, like a speckled cannon-ball, so hard and firm, blazing in half of half-a-quartern* of ignited brandy, and bedight with Christmas holly stuck into the top.

Oh, a wonderful pudding! Bob Cratchit said, and calmly too, that he regarded it as the greatest success achieved by Mrs. Cratchit since their marriage. Mrs. Cratchit said that now the weight was off her mind, she would confess she had had her doubts about the quantity of flour. Everybody had something to say about it, but nobody said or thought it was at all a small pudding for a large family. It would have been flat heresy to do so. Any Cratchit would have blushed to hint at such a thing.

At last the dinner was all done, the cloth was cleared, the hearth swept, and the fire made up. The compound in the jug being tasted, and considered perfect, apples and oranges were put upon the table, and a shovel-full of chestnuts on the fire. Then all the Cratchit family drew round the hearth, in what Bob Cratchit called a circle, meaning half a one; and at Bob Cratchit's elbow stood the family display of glass. Two tumblers, and a custard-cup without a handle.

These held the hot stuff from the jug, however, as well as golden goblets would have done; and Bob served it out with beaming looks, while the chestnuts on the fire sputtered and cracked noisily. Then Bob proposed:

'A Merry Christmas to us all, my dears. God bless us!' Which all the family re-echoed.

'God bless us every one!' said Tiny Tim, the last of all.

He sat very close to his father's side upon his little stool. Bob held his withered little hand in his, as if he loved the child, and wished to keep him by his side, and dreaded that he might be taken from him.

'Spirit,' said Scrooge, with an interest he had never felt before, 'tell me if Tiny Tim will live.'

'I see a vacant seat,' replied the Ghost, 'in the poor chimney-corner, and a crutch without an owner, carefully preserved. If these shadows remain unaltered by the Future, the child will die.'

'No, no,' said Scrooge. 'Oh, no, kind Spirit! say he will be spared.'

'If these shadows remain unaltered by the Future, none other of my race,' returned the Ghost, 'will find him here. What then? If he be like to die, he had better do it, and decrease the surplus population.'

Scrooge hung his head to hear his own words quoted by the Spirit, and was overcome with penitence and grief.

'Man,' said the Ghost, 'if man you be in heart, not adamant, forbear that wicked cant until you have discovered What the surplus is, and Where it is. Will you decide what men shall live, what men shall die? It may be, that in the sight of Heaven, you are more worthless and less fit to live than millions like this poor man's child. Oh God! to hear the Insect on the leaf pronouncing on the too much life among his hungry brothers in the dust!'

Scrooge bent before the Ghost's rebuke, and trembling cast his eyes upon the ground. But he raised them speedily, on hearing his own name.

'Mr. Scrooge!' said Bob; 'I'll give you Mr. Scrooge, the Founder of the Feast!'

'The Founder of the Feast indeed!' cried Mrs. Cratchit, reddening. 'I wish I had him here. I'd give him a piece of my mind to feast upon, and I hope he'd have a good appetite for it.'

'My dear,' said Bob, 'the children! Christmas Day.'

'It should be Christmas Day, I am sure,' said she, 'on which one drinks the health of such an odious, stingy, hard, unfeeling man as Mr. Scrooge. You know he is, Robert! Nobody knows it better than you do, poor fellow!'

'My dear,' was Bob's mild answer, 'Christmas Day.'

'I'll drink his health for your sake and the Day's,' said Mrs. Cratchit, 'not for his. Long life to him! A merry Christmas and a happy new year! He'll be very merry and very happy, I have no doubt!'

The children drank the toast after her. It was the first of their proceedings which had no heartiness. Tiny Tim drank it last of all, but he didn't care twopence for it. Scrooge was the Ogre of the family. The mention of his name cast a dark shadow on the party, which was not dispelled for full five minutes.

After it had passed away, they were ten times merrier than before, from the mere relief of Scrooge the Baleful being done with. Bob Cratchit told them how he had a situation in his eye for Master Peter which would bring in, if obtained, full five-and-sixpence weekly. The two young Cratchits laughed tremendously at the idea of Peter's being a man of business; and Peter himself looked thoughtfully at the fire from between his collars, as if he were deliberating what particular investments he should favour when he came into the receipt of that bewildering income. Martha, who was a poor apprentice at a milliner's, then told them what kind of work she had to do, and how many hours she worked at a stretch, and how she meant to lie abed to-morrow morning for a good long rest;* to-morrow being a holiday she passed at home. Also how she had seen a countess and a lord some days before, and how the lord 'was much about as tall as Peter'; at which Peter pulled up his collars so high that you couldn't have seen his head if you had been there. All this time the chestnuts and the jug went round and round; and by-and-bye they had a song, about a lost child travelling in the snow, from Tiny Tim, who had a plaintive little voice, and sang it very well indeed.

There was nothing of high mark in this. They were not a handsome family; they were not well dressed; their shoes were far from being water-proof; their clothes were scanty; and Peter might have known, and very likely did, the inside of a pawnbroker's. But they were happy, grateful, pleased with one another, and contented with the time; and when they faded, and looked happier yet in the bright sprinklings of the Spirit's torch at parting, Scrooge had his eye upon them, and especially on Tiny Tim, until the last.

By this time it was getting dark, and snowing pretty heavily; and as Scrooge and the Spirit went along the streets, the brightness of the roaring fires in kitchens, parlours, and all sorts of rooms, was wonderful. Here, the flickering of the blaze showed preparations for a cosy dinner, with hot plates baking through and through before the fire, and deep red curtains, ready to be drawn to shut out cold and darkness. There all the children of the house were running out into the snow to meet their married sisters, brothers, cousins, uncles, aunts, and be the first to greet them. Here, again, were shadows on the window-blind of guests assembling; and there a group of handsome girls, all hooded and fur-booted, and all chattering at once, tripped lightly off to some near neighbour's house; where, woe upon the single man who saw them enter—artful witches, well they knew it—in a glow!

But, if you had judged from the numbers of people on their way to friendly gatherings, you might have thought that no one was at home to give them welcome when they got there, instead of every house expecting company, and piling up its fires half-chimney high. Blessings on it, how the Ghost exulted! How it bared its breadth of breast, and opened its capacious palm, and floated on, outpouring, with a generous hand, its bright and harmless mirth on everything within its reach! The very lamplighter, who ran on before, dotting the dusky street with specks of light, and who was dressed to spend the evening somewhere, laughed out loudly as the Spirit passed, though little kenned the lamplighter that he had any company but Christmas!

And now, without a word of warning from the Ghost, they stood upon a bleak and desert moor, where monstrous masses of rude stone were cast about, as though it were the burial-place of giants,* and water spread itself wheresoever it listed, or would have done so, but for the frost that held it prisoner; and nothing grew but moss and furze, and coarse rank grass. Down in the west the setting sun had left a streak of fiery red, which glared upon the desolation for an instant, like a sullen eye, and frowning lower, lower, lower yet, was lost in the thick gloom of darkest night.

'What place is this?' asked Scrooge.

'A place where Miners live, who labour in the bowels of the earth,' returned the Spirit. 'But they know me. See!'

A light shone from the window of a hut, and swiftly they advanced towards it. Passing through the wall of mud and stone, they found a cheerful company assembled round a glowing fire. An old, old man and woman, with their children and their children's children, and another generation beyond that, all decked out gaily in their holiday attire. The old man, in a voice that seldom rose above the howling of the wind upon the barren waste, was singing them a Christmas song—it had been a very old song when he was a boy—and from time to time they all joined in the chorus. So surely as they raised their voices, the old man got quite blithe and loud; and so surely as they stopped, his vigour sank again.

The Spirit did not tarry here, but bade Scrooge hold his robe, and passing on above the moor, sped—whither? Not to sea? To sea. To Scrooge's horror, looking back, he saw the last of the land, a frightful range of rocks, behind them; and his ears were deafened by the thundering of water, as it rolled and roared, and raged among the dreadful caverns it had worn, and fiercely tried to undermine the earth.

Built upon a dismal reef of sunken rocks, some league or so from shore, on which the waters chafed and dashed, the wild year through, there stood a solitary lighthouse. Great heaps of sea-weed clung to its base, and storm-birds—born of the wind one might suppose, as sea-weed of the water—rose and fell about it, like the waves they skimmed.

But even here, two men who watched the light had made a fire, that through the loophole in the thick stone wall shed out a ray of brightness on the awful sea. Joining their horny hands over the rough table at which they sat, they wished each other Merry Christmas in their can of grog,* and one of them: the elder, too, with his face all damaged and scarred with hard weather, as the figure-head of an old ship might be: struck up a sturdy song that was like a Gale in itself.

Again the Ghost sped on, above the black and heaving sea—on, on—until, being far away, as he told Scrooge, from any shore, they lighted on a ship. They stood beside the helmsman at the wheel, the look-out in the bow, the officers who had the watch; dark, ghostly figures in their several stations; but every man among them hummed a Christmas tune, or had a Christmas thought, or spoke below his breath to his companion of some by-gone Christmas Day, with homeward hopes belonging to it. And every man on board, waking or sleeping, good or bad, had had a kinder word for another on that day than on any day in the year; and had shared to some extent in its festivities; and had remembered those he cared for at a distance, and had known that they delighted to remember him.

It was a great surprise to Scrooge, while listening to the moaning of the wind, and thinking what a solemn thing it was to move on through the lonely darkness over an unknown abyss, whose depths were secrets as profound as Death: it was a great surprise to Scrooge, while thus engaged, to hear a hearty laugh. It was a much greater surprise to Scrooge to recognise it as his own nephew's, and to find himself in a bright, dry, gleaming room, with the Spirit standing smiling by his side, and looking at that same nephew with approving affability!

'Ha, ha!' laughed Scrooge's nephew. 'Ha, ha, ha!'

If you should happen, by any unlikely chance, to know a man more blest in a laugh than Scrooge's nephew, all I can say is, I should like to know him too. Introduce him to me, and I'll cultivate his acquaintance.

It is a fair, even-handed, noble adjustment of things, that while there is infection in disease and sorrow, there is nothing in the world so irresistibly contagious as laughter and good-humour. When Scrooge's nephew laughed in this way: holding his sides, rolling his head, and twisting his face into the most extravagant contortions: Scrooge's niece, by marriage, laughed as heartily as he. And their assembled friends being not a bit behindhand, roared out lustily.

'Ha, ha! Ha, ha, ha, ha!'

'He said that Christmas was a humbug, as I live!' cried Scrooge's nephew. 'He believed it too!'

'More shame for him, Fred!' said Scrooge's niece, indignantly. Bless those women; they never do anything by halves. They are always in earnest.

She was very pretty: exceedingly pretty. With a dimpled, surprised-looking, capital face; a ripe little mouth, that seemed made to be kissed—as no doubt it was; all kinds of good little dots about her chin, that melted into one another when she laughed; and the sunniest pair of eyes you ever saw in any little creature's head. Altogether she was what you would have called provoking, you know; but satisfactory, too. Oh, perfectly satisfactory.

'He's a comical old fellow,' said Scrooge's nephew, 'that's the truth; and not so pleasant as he might be. However, his offences carry their own punishment, and I have nothing to say against him.'

'I'm sure he is very rich, Fred,' hinted Scrooge's niece. 'At least you always tell *me* so.'

'What of that, my dear!' said Scrooge's nephew. 'His wealth is of no use to him. He don't do any good with it. He don't make himself comfortable with it. He hasn't the satisfaction of thinking—ha, ha, ha!—that he is ever going to benefit US with it.'

'I have no patience with him,' observed Scrooge's niece. Scrooge's niece's sisters, and all the other ladies, expressed the same opinion.

'Oh, I have!' said Scrooge's nephew. 'I am sorry for him; I couldn't be angry with him if I tried. Who suffers by his ill whims! Himself, always. Here, he takes it into his head to dislike us, and he won't come and dine with us. What's the consequence? He don't lose much of a dinner.'

'Indeed, I think he loses a very good dinner,' interrupted Scrooge's niece. Everybody else said the same, and they must be allowed to have been competent judges, because they had just had dinner; and, with the dessert upon the table, were clustered round the fire, by lamplight.

'Well! I'm very glad to hear it,' said Scrooge's nephew, 'because I haven't great faith in these young housekeepers. What do *you* say, Topper?'

Topper had clearly got his eye upon one of Scrooge's niece's sisters, for he answered that a bachelor was a wretched outcast, who had no right to express an opinion on the subject. Whereat Scrooge's niece's sister—the plump one with the lace tucker:* not the one with the roses—blushed.

'Do go on, Fred,' said Scrooge's niece, clapping her hands. 'He never finishes what he begins to say! He is such a ridiculous fellow!'

Scrooge's nephew revelled in another laugh, and as it was impossible to keep the infection off; though the plump sister tried hard to do it with aromatic vinegar; his example was unanimously followed.

'I was only going to say,' said Scrooge's nephew, 'that the consequences of his taking a dislike to us, and not making merry with us, is, as I think, that he loses some pleasant moments, which could do him no harm. I am sure he loses pleasanter companions than he can find in his own thoughts, either in his mouldy old office, or his dusty chambers. I mean to give him the same chance every year, whether he likes it or not, for I pity him. He may rail at Christmas till he dies, but he can't help thinking better of it—I defy him—if he finds me going there, in good temper, year after year, and saying, Uncle Scrooge, how are you? If it only puts him in the vein to leave his poor clerk fifty pounds, *that's* something; and I think I shook him yesterday.'

It was their turn to laugh now at the notion of his shaking Scrooge. But being thoroughly good-natured, and not much caring what they laughed at, so that they laughed at any rate, he encouraged them in their merriment, and passed the bottle joyously.

After tea, they had some music. For they were a musical family, and knew what they were about, when they sung a Glee or Catch,* I can assure you: especially Topper, who could growl away in the bass like a good one, and never swell the large veins in his forehead, or get red in the face over it. Scrooge's niece played well upon the harp; and played among other tunes a simple little air (a mere nothing: you might learn to whistle it in two minutes), which had been familiar to the child who fetched Scrooge from the boarding-school, as he had been reminded by the Ghost of Christmas Past. When this strain of music sounded, all the things that Ghost had shown him, came upon his mind; he softened more and more; and thought that if he could have listened to it often, years ago, he might have cultivated the kindnesses of life for his own happiness with his own hands, without resorting to the sexton's spade that buried Jacob Marley.

But they didn't devote the whole evening to music. After a while they played at forfeits; for it is good to be children sometimes, and never better than at Christmas, when its mighty Founder was a child himself. Stop! There was first a game at blind-man's buff. Of course there was. And I no more believe Topper was really blind than I believe he had eyes in his boots. My opinion is, that it was a done thing between him and Scrooge's nephew; and that the Ghost of Christmas Present knew it. The way he went after that plump sister in the lace tucker, was an outrage on the credulity of human nature.

Knocking down the fire-irons, tumbling over the chairs, bumping against the piano, smothering himself among the curtains, wherever she went, there went he! He always knew where the plump sister was. He wouldn't catch anybody else. If you had fallen up against him (as some of them did), on purpose, he would have made a feint of endeavouring to seize you, which would have been an affront to your understanding, and would instantly have sidled off in the direction of the plump sister. She often cried out that it wasn't fair; and it really was not. But when at last, he caught her; when, in spite of all her silken rustlings, and her rapid flutterings past him, he got her into a corner whence there was no escape; then his conduct was the most execrable. For his pretending not to know her; his pretending that it was necessary to touch her head-dress, and further to assure himself of her identity by pressing a certain ring upon her finger, and a certain chain about her neck; was vile, monstrous! No doubt she told him her opinion of it, when, another blind-man being in office, they were so very confidential together, behind the curtains.

Scrooge's niece was not one of the blind-man's buff party, but was made comfortable with a large chair and a footstool, in a snug corner, where the Ghost and Scrooge were close behind her. But she joined in the forfeits, and loved her love to admiration with all the letters of the alphabet.* Likewise at the game of How, When, and Where,* she was very great, and to the secret joy of Scrooge's nephew, beat her sisters hollow: though they were sharp girls too, as Topper could have told you. There might have been twenty people there, young and old, but they all played, and so did Scrooge; for wholly forgetting in the interest he had in what was going on, that his voice made no sound in their ears, he sometimes came out with his guess quite loud, and very often guessed quite right, too; for the sharpest needle, best Whitechapel,* warranted not to cut in the eye, was not sharper than Scrooge; blunt as he took it in his head to be.

The Ghost was greatly pleased to find him in this mood, and looked upon him with such favour, that he begged like a boy to be allowed to stay until the guests departed. But this the Spirit said could not be done.

'Here is a new game,' said Scrooge. 'One half hour, Spirit, only one!'

It was a Game called Yes and No, where Scrooge's nephew had to think of something, and the rest must find out what; he only answering to their questions yes or no, as the case was. The brisk fire of questioning to which he was exposed, elicited from him that he was thinking of an animal, a live animal, rather a disagreeable animal, a savage animal, an animal that growled and grunted sometimes, and talked sometimes, and lived in London, and walked about the streets, and wasn't made a show of, and wasn't led by anybody, and didn't live in a menagerie, and was never killed in a market, and was not a horse, or an ass, or a cow, or a bull, or a tiger, or a dog, or a pig, or a cat, or a bear. At every fresh question that was put to him, this nephew burst into a fresh roar of laughter; and was so inexpressibly tickled, that he was obliged to get up off the sofa and stamp. At last the plump sister, falling into a similar state, cried out:

'I have found it out! I know what it is, Fred! I know what it is!'

'What is it?' cried Fred.

'It's your Uncle Scro-o-o-o-oge!'

Which it certainly was. Admiration was the universal sentiment, though some objected that the reply to 'Is it a bear?' ought to have been 'Yes'; inasmuch as an answer in the negative was sufficient to have diverted their thoughts from Mr. Scrooge, supposing they had ever had any tendency that way.

'He has given us plenty of merriment, I am sure,' said Fred, 'and it would be ungrateful not to drink his health. Here is a glass of mulled wine ready to our hand at the moment; and I say, "Uncle Scrooge!"'

'Well! Uncle Scrooge!' they cried.

'A Merry Christmas and a Happy New Year to the old man, whatever he is!' said Scrooge's nephew. 'He wouldn't take it from me, but may he have it, nevertheless. Uncle Scrooge!'

Uncle Scrooge had imperceptibly become so gay and light of heart, that he would have pledged the unconscious company in return, and thanked them in an inaudible speech, if the Ghost had given him time. But the whole scene passed off in the breath of the last word spoken by his nephew; and he and the Spirit were again upon their travels.

Much they saw, and far they went, and many homes they visited, but always with a happy end. The Spirit stood beside sick beds, and they were cheerful; on foreign lands, and they were close at home; by struggling men, and they were patient in their greater hope; by poverty, and it was rich. In almshouse, hospital, and jail, in misery's every refuge, where vain man in his little brief authority* had not made fast the door, and barred the Spirit out, he left his blessing, and taught Scrooge his precepts.

It was a long night, if it were only a night; but Scrooge had his doubts of this, because the Christmas Holidays appeared to be condensed into the space of time they passed together. It was strange, too, that while Scrooge remained unaltered in his outward form, the Ghost grew older, clearly older. Scrooge had observed this change, but never spoke of it, until they left a children's Twelfth Night party, when, looking at the Spirit as they stood together in an open place, he noticed that its hair was grey.

'Are spirits' lives so short?' asked Scrooge.

'My life upon this globe is very brief,' replied the Ghost. 'It ends to-night.'

'To-night!' cried Scrooge.

'To-night at midnight. Hark! The time is drawing near.'

The chimes were ringing the three quarters past eleven at that moment.

'Forgive me if I am not justified in what I ask,' said Scrooge, looking intently at the Spirit's robe, 'but I see something strange, and not belonging to yourself, protruding from your skirts. Is it a foot or a claw?'

'It might be a claw, for the flesh there is upon it,' was the Spirit's sorrowful reply. 'Look here.'

From the foldings of its robe, it brought two children; wretched, abject, frightful, hideous, miserable. They knelt down at its feet, and clung upon the outside of its garment.

'Oh, Man! look here. Look, look, down here!' exclaimed the Ghost.

They were a boy and girl. Yellow, meagre, ragged, scowling, wolf-ish; but prostrate, too, in their humility. Where graceful youth should have filled their features out, and touched them with its freshest tints, a stale and shrivelled hand, like that of age, had pinched, and twisted them, and pulled them into shreds. Where angels might have sat enthroned, devils lurked, and glared out menacing. No change, no degradation, no perversion of humanity, in any grade, through all the mysteries of wonderful creation, has monsters half so horrible and dread.

Scrooge started back, appalled. Having them shown to him in this

way, he tried to say they were fine children, but the words choked themselves, rather than be parties to a lie of such enormous magnitude.

'Spirit! are they yours!' Scrooge could say no more.

'They are Man's,' said the Spirit, looking down upon them. 'And they cling to me, appealing from their fathers. This boy is Ignorance. This girl is Want. Beware them both, and all of their degree, but most of all beware this boy, for on his brow I see that written which is Doom, unless the writing be erased. Deny it!' cried the Spirit, stretching out its hand towards the city. 'Slander those who tell it ye! Admit it for your factious purposes, and make it worse. And abide the end!'

'Have they no refuge or resource?' cried Scrooge.

'Are there no prisons?' said the Spirit, turning on him for the last time with his own words. 'Are there no workhouses?'

The bell struck twelve.

Scrooge looked about him for the Ghost, and saw it not. As the last stroke ceased to vibrate, he remembered the prediction of old Jacob Marley, and lifting up his eyes, beheld a solemn Phantom, draped and hooded, coming, like a mist along the ground, towards him.

STAVE IV

THE LAST OF THE SPIRITS

THE Phantom slowly, gravely, silently approached. When it came near him, Scrooge bent down upon his knee; for in the very air through which this Spirit moved it seemed to scatter gloom and mystery.

It was shrouded in a deep black garment, which concealed its head, its face, its form, and left nothing of it visible save one out-stretched hand. But for this it would have been difficult to detach its figure from the night, and separate it from the darkness by which it was surrounded.

He felt that it was tall and stately when it came beside him, and that its mysterious presence filled him with a solemn dread. He knew no more, for the Spirit neither spoke nor moved.

'I am in the presence of the Ghost of Christmas Yet To Come?' said Scrooge.

The Spirit answered not, but pointed onward with its hand.

'You are about to show me shadows of the things that have not happened, but will happen in the time before us,' Scrooge pursued. 'Is that so, Spirit?'

The upper portion of the garment was contracted for an instant in its folds, as if the Spirit had inclined its head. That was the only answer he received.

Although well used to ghostly company by this time, Scrooge feared the silent shape so much that his legs trembled beneath him, and he found that he could hardly stand when he prepared to follow it. The Spirit paused a moment, as observing his condition, and giving him time to recover.

But Scrooge was all the worse for this. It thrilled him with a vague uncertain horror, to know that behind the dusky shroud, there were ghostly eyes intently fixed upon him, while he, though he stretched his own to the utmost, could see nothing but a spectral hand and one great heap of black.

'Ghost of the Future!' he exclaimed, 'I fear you more than any spectre I have seen. But as I know your purpose is to do me good, and as I hope to live to be another man from what I was, I am prepared to bear you company, and do it with a thankful heart. Will you not speak to me?'

It gave him no reply. The hand was pointed straight before them.

'Lead on!' said Scrooge. 'Lead on! The night is waning fast, and it is precious time to me, I know. Lead on, Spirit!'

The Phantom moved away as it had come towards him. Scrooge followed in the shadow of its dress, which bore him up, he thought, and carried him along.

They scarcely seemed to enter the city; for the city rather seemed to spring up about them, and encompass them of its own act. But there they were, in the heart of it; on 'Change, amongst the merchants; who hurried up and down, and chinked the money in their pockets, and conversed in groups, and looked at their watches, and trifled thoughtfully with their great gold seals; and so forth, as Scrooge had seen them often.

The Spirit stopped beside one little knot of business men. Observing that the hand was pointed to them, Scrooge advanced to listen to their talk.

'No,' said a great fat man with a monstrous chin, 'I don't know much about it, either way. I only know he's dead.'

'When did he die?' inquired another.

'Last night, I believe.'

'Why, what was the matter with him?' asked a third, taking a vast quantity of snuff out of a very large snuff-box. 'I thought he'd never die.'

'God knows,' said the first, with a yawn.

'What has he done with his money?' asked a red-faced gentleman with a pendulous excrescence on the end of his nose, that shook like the gills of a turkey-cock.

'I haven't heard,' said the man with the large chin, yawning again. 'Left it to his company, perhaps. He hasn't left it to *me*. That's all I know.'

This pleasantry was received with a general laugh.

'It's likely to be a very cheap funeral,' said the same speaker; 'for upon my life I don't know of anybody to go to it. Suppose we make up a party and volunteer?'

'I don't mind going if a lunch is provided,' observed the gentleman with the excrescence on his nose. 'But I must be fed, if I make one.'

Another laugh.

'Well, I am the most disinterested among you, after all,' said the first speaker, 'for I never wear black gloves,* and I never eat lunch. But I'll offer to go, if anybody else will. When I come to think of it, I'm not at all sure that I wasn't his most particular friend; for we used to stop and speak whenever we met. Bye, bye!'

Speakers and listeners strolled away, and mixed with other groups. Scrooge knew the men, and looked towards the Spirit for an explanation.

The Phantom glided on into a street. Its finger pointed to two persons meeting. Scrooge listened again, thinking that the explanation might lie here.

He knew these men, also, perfectly. They were men of business: very wealthy, and of great importance. He had made a point always of standing well in their esteem: in a business point of view, that is; strictly in a business point of view.

'How are you?' said one.

'How are you?' returned the other.

'Well!' said the first. 'Old Scratch* has got his own at last, hey?'

'So I am told,' returned the second. 'Cold, isn't it?'

'Seasonable for Christmas time. You're not a skater, I suppose?'

'No. No. Something else to think of. Good morning!'

Not another word. That was their meeting, their conversation, and their parting.

Scrooge was at first inclined to be surprised that the Spirit should attach importance to conversations apparently so trivial; but feeling assured that they must have some hidden purpose, he set himself to consider what it was likely to be. They could scarcely be supposed to have any bearing on the death of Jacob, his old partner, for that was Past, and this Ghost's province was the Future. Nor could he think of any one immediately connected with himself, to whom he could apply them. But nothing doubting that to whomsoever they applied they had some latent moral for his own improvement, he resolved to treasure up every word he heard, and everything he saw; and especially to observe the shadow of himself when it appeared. For he had an expectation that the conduct of his future self would give him the clue he missed, and would render the solution of these riddles easy.

He looked about in that very place for his own image; but another man stood in his accustomed corner, and though the clock pointed to his usual time of day for being there, he saw no likeness of himself among the multitudes that poured in through the Porch. It gave him little surprise, however; for he had been revolving in his mind a change of life, and thought and hoped he saw his new-born resolutions carried out in this.

Quiet and dark, beside him stood the Phantom, with its outstretched hand. When he roused himself from his thoughtful quest, he fancied from the turn of the hand, and its situation in reference to himself, that the Unseen Eyes were looking at him keenly. It made him shudder, and feel very cold.

They left the busy scene, and went into an obscure part of the town, where Scrooge had never penetrated before, although he recognised its situation, and its bad repute. The ways were foul and narrow; the shops and houses wretched; the people half-naked, drunken, slipshod, ugly. Alleys and archways, like so many cesspools, disgorged their offences of smell, and dirt, and life, upon the straggling streets; and the whole quarter reeked with crime, with filth, and misery.

Far in this den of infamous resort, there was a low-browed, beetling* shop, below a pent-house roof, where iron, old rags, bottles, bones, and greasy offal, were bought. Upon the floor within, were piled up heaps of rusty keys, nails, chains, hinges, files, scales, weights, and refuse iron of all kinds. Secrets that few would like to scrutinise were bred and hidden in mountains of unseemly rags, masses of corrupted fat, and sepulchres of bones. Sitting in among the wares he dealt in, by a charcoal stove, made of old bricks, was a grey-haired rascal, nearly seventy years of age; who had screened himself from the cold air without, by a frousy curtaining of miscellaneous tatters, hung upon a line; and smoked his pipe in all the luxury of calm retirement.

Scrooge and the Phantom came into the presence of this man, just as a woman with a heavy bundle slunk into the shop. But she had scarcely entered, when another woman, similarly laden, came in too; and she was closely followed by a man in faded black, who was no less startled by the sight of them, than they had been upon the recognition of each other. After a short period of blank astonishment, in which the old man with the pipe had joined them, they all three burst into a laugh.

'Let the charwoman alone to be the first!' cried she who had entered first. 'Let the laundress alone to be the second; and let the undertaker's man alone to be the third. Look here, old Joe, here's a chance! If we haven't all three met here without meaning it!'

'You couldn't have met in a better place,' said old Joe, removing his pipe from his mouth. 'Come into the parlour. You were made free of it long ago, you know; and the other two an't strangers. Stop till I shut the door of the shop. Ah! How it skreeks! There an't such a rusty bit of metal in the place as its own hinges, I believe; and I'm sure there's no such old bones here, as mine. Ha, ha! We're all suitable to our calling, we're well matched. Come into the parlour. Come into the parlour.'

The parlour was the space behind the screen of rags. The old man raked the fire together with an old stair-rod, and having trimmed his smoky lamp (for it was night), with the stem of his pipe, put it in his mouth again.

While he did this, the woman who had already spoken threw her bundle on the floor, and sat down in a flaunting manner on a stool; crossing her elbows on her knees, and looking with a bold defiance at the other two.

'What odds then! What odds, Mrs. Dilber?' said the woman. 'Every person has a right to take care of themselves. *He* always did.'

'That's true, indeed!' said the laundress. 'No man more so.'

'Why then, don't stand staring as if you was afraid, woman; who's the wiser? We're not going to pick holes in each other's coats,* I suppose?'

'No, indeed!' said Mrs. Dilber and the man together. 'We should hope not.'

'Very well, then!' cried the woman. 'That's enough. Who's the worse for the loss of a few things like these? Not a dead man, I suppose.'

'No, indeed,' said Mrs. Dilber, laughing.

'If he wanted to keep 'em after he was dead, a wicked old screw',* pursued the woman, 'why wasn't he natural in his lifetime? If he had been, he'd have had somebody to look after him when he was struck with Death, instead of lying gasping out his last there, alone by himself.'

'It's the truest word that ever was spoke,' said Mrs. Dilber. 'It's a judgment on him.'

'I wish it was a little heavier judgment,' replied the woman; 'and it should have been, you may depend upon it, if I could have laid my hands on anything else. Open that bundle, old Joe, and let me know the value of it. Speak out plain. I'm not afraid to be the first, nor afraid for them to see it. We knew pretty well that we were helping ourselves, before we met here, I believe. It's no sin. Open the bundle, Joe.'

But the gallantry of her friends would not allow of this; and the man in faded black, mounting the breach first, produced *his* plunder. It was not extensive. A seal or two, a pencil-case, a pair of sleeve-buttons, and a brooch of no great value, were all. They were severally examined and appraised by old Joe, who chalked the sums he was disposed to give for each, upon the wall, and added them up into a total when he found there was nothing more to come.

'That's your account,' said Joe, 'and I wouldn't give another sixpence, if I was to be boiled for not doing it. Who's next?'

Mrs. Dilber was next. Sheets and towels, a little wearing apparel, two old-fashioned silver teaspoons, a pair of sugar-tongs, and a few boots. Her account was stated on the wall in the same manner.

'I always give too much to ladies. It's a weakness of mine, and that's the way I ruin myself,' said old Joe. 'That's your account. If you asked me for another penny, and made it an open question, I'd repent of being so liberal and knock off half-a-crown.'

'And now undo *my* bundle, Joe,' said the first woman.

Joe went down on his knees for the greater convenience of opening it, and having unfastened a great many knots, dragged out a large and heavy roll of some dark stuff.

'What do you call this?' said Joe. 'Bed-curtains!'

'Ah!' returned the woman, laughing and leaning forward on her crossed arms. 'Bed-curtains!'

'You don't mean to say you took 'em down, rings and all, with him lying there?' said Joe.

'Yes I do,' replied the woman. 'Why not?'

'You were born to make your fortune,' said Joe, 'and you'll certainly do it.'

'I certainly shan't hold my hand, when I can get anything in it by reaching it out, for the sake of such a man as He was, I promise you, Joe,' returned the woman coolly. 'Don't drop that oil upon the blankets, now.'

'His blankets?' asked Joe.

'Whose else's do you think?' replied the woman. 'He isn't likely to take cold without 'em, I dare say.'

'I hope he didn't die of anything catching? Eh?' said old Joe, stopping in his work, and looking up.

'Don't you be afraid of that,' returned the woman. 'I an't so fond of his company that I'd loiter about him for such things, if he did. Ah! you may look through that shirt till your eyes ache; but you won't find a hole in it, nor a threadbare place. It's the best he had, and a fine one too. They'd have wasted it, if it hadn't been for me.'

'What do you call wasting of it?' asked old Joe.

'Putting it on him to be buried in, to be sure,' replied the woman with a laugh. 'Somebody was fool enough to do it, but I took it off again. If calico an't good enough for such a purpose, it isn't good enough for anything. It's quite as becoming to the body. He can't look uglier than he did in that one.'

Scrooge listened to this dialogue in horror. As they sat grouped about their spoil, in the scanty light afforded by the old man's lamp, he viewed them with a detestation and disgust, which could hardly have been greater, though they had been obscene demons, marketing the corpse itself.

'Ha, ha!' laughed the same woman, when old Joe, producing a flannel bag with money in it, told out their several gains upon the ground. 'This is the end of it, you see! He frightened every one away from him when he was alive, to profit us when he was dead! Ha, ha, ha!'

'Spirit!' said Scrooge, shuddering from head to foot. 'I see, I see. The case of this unhappy man might be my own. My life tends that way, now. Merciful Heaven, what is this!'

He recoiled in terror, for the scene had changed, and now he almost touched a bed: a bare, uncurtained bed: on which, beneath a

ragged sheet, there lay a something covered up, which, though it
was dumb, announced itself in awful language.

The room was very dark, too dark to be observed with any accur-
acy, though Scrooge glanced round it in obedience to a secret
impulse, anxious to know what kind of room it was. A pale light,
rising in the outer air, fell straight upon the bed; and on it, plundered
and bereft, unwatched, unwept, uncared for, was the body of this man.

Scrooge glanced towards the Phantom. Its steady hand was
pointed to the head. The cover was so carelessly adjusted that the
slightest raising of it, the motion of a finger upon Scrooge's part,
would have disclosed the face. He thought of it, felt how easy it
would be to do, and longed to do it; but had no more power to
withdraw the veil* than to dismiss the spectre at his side.

Oh cold, cold, rigid, dreadful Death, set up thine altar here, and
dress it with such terrors as thou hast at thy command: for this is
thy dominion!* But of the loved, revered, and honoured head, thou
canst not turn one hair to thy dread purposes, or make one feature
odious. It is not that the hand is heavy and will fall down when
released; it is not that the heart and pulse are still; but that the
hand WAS open, generous, and true; the heart brave, warm, and
tender; and the pulse a man's. Strike, Shadow, strike! And see his
good deeds springing from the wound, to sow the world with life
immortal!

No voice pronounced these words in Scrooge's ears, and yet he
heard them when he looked upon the bed. He thought, if this man
could be raised up now, what would be his foremost thoughts?
Avarice, hard-dealing, griping cares? They have brought him to a
rich end, truly!

He lay, in the dark empty house, with not a man, a woman, or a
child, to say that he was kind to me in this or that, and for the
memory of one kind word I will be kind to him. A cat was tearing at
the door, and there was a sound of gnawing rats beneath the hearthstone. What *they* wanted in the room of death, and why they were so
restless and disturbed, Scrooge did not dare to think.

'Spirit!' he said, 'this is a fearful place. In leaving it, I shall not
leave its lesson, trust me. Let us go!'

Still the Ghost pointed with an unmoved finger to the head.

'I understand you,' Scrooge returned, 'and I would do it, if I
could. But I have not the power, Spirit. I have not the power.'

Again it seemed to look upon him.

'If there is any person in the town, who feels emotion caused by this man's death,' said Scrooge quite agonised, 'show that person to me, Spirit, I beseech you!'

The Phantom spread its dark robe before him for a moment, like a wing; and withdrawing it, revealed a room by daylight, where a mother and her children were.

She was expecting some one, and with anxious eagerness; for she walked up and down the room; started at every sound; looked out from the window; glanced at the clock; tried, but in vain, to work with her needle; and could hardly bear the voices of the children in their play.

At length the long-expected knock was heard. She hurried to the door, and met her husband; a man whose face was careworn and depressed, though he was young. There was a remarkable expression in it now; a kind of serious delight of which he felt ashamed, and which he struggled to repress.

He sat down to the dinner that had been hoarding for him by the fire; and when she asked him faintly what news (which was not until after a long silence), he appeared embarrassed how to answer.

'Is it good?' she said, 'or bad?'—to help him.

'Bad,' he answered.

'We are quite ruined?'

'No. There is hope yet, Caroline.'

'If *he* relents,' she said, amazed, 'there is! Nothing is past hope, if such a miracle has happened.'

'He is past relenting,' said her husband. 'He is dead.'

She was a mild and patient creature if her face spoke truth; but she was thankful in her soul to hear it, and she said so, with clasped hands. She prayed forgiveness the next moment, and was sorry; but the first was the emotion of her heart.

'What the half-drunken woman whom I told you of last night, said to me, when I tried to see him and obtain a week's delay; and what I thought was a mere excuse to avoid me; turns out to have been quite true. He was not only very ill, but dying, then.'

'To whom will our debt be transferred?'

'I don't know. But before that time we shall be ready with the money; and even though we were not, it would be a bad fortune indeed to find so merciless a creditor in his successor. We may sleep to-night with light hearts, Caroline!'

Yes. Soften it as they would, their hearts were lighter. The children's faces, hushed and clustered round to hear what they so little understood, were brighter; and it was a happier house for this man's death! The only emotion that the Ghost could show him, caused by the event, was one of pleasure.

'Let me see some tenderness connected with a death,' said Scrooge; 'or that dark chamber, Spirit, which we left just now, will be for ever present to me.'

The Ghost conducted him through several streets familiar to his feet; and as they went along, Scrooge looked here and there to find himself, but nowhere was he to be seen. They entered Poor Bob Cratchit's house; the dwelling he had visited before; and found the mother and the children seated round the fire.

Quiet. Very quiet. The noisy little Cratchits were as still as statues in one corner, and sat looking up at Peter, who had a book before him. The mother and her daughters were engaged in sewing. But surely they were very quiet!

' "And He took a child, and set him in the midst of them." '*

Where had Scrooge heard those words? He had not dreamed them. The boy must have read them out, as he and the Spirit crossed the threshold. Why did he not go on?

The mother laid her work upon the table, and put her hand up to her face.

'The colour hurts my eyes,' she said.

The colour? Ah, poor Tiny Tim!

'They're better now again,' said Cratchit's wife. 'It makes them weak by candlelight; and I wouldn't show weak eyes to your father when he comes home, for the world. It must be near his time.'

'Past it rather,' Peter answered, shutting up his book. 'But I think he has walked a little slower than he used, these few last evenings, mother.'

They were very quiet again. At last she said, and in a steady, cheerful voice, that only faltered once:

'I have known him walk with—I have known him walk with Tiny Tim upon his shoulder, very fast indeed.'

'And so have I,' cried Peter. 'Often.'

'And so have I,' exclaimed another. So had all.

'But he was very light to carry,' she resumed, intent upon her work, 'and his father loved him so, that it was no trouble: no trouble. And there is your father at the door!'

She hurried out to meet him; and little Bob in his comforter—he had need of it, poor fellow—came in. His tea was ready for him on the hob, and they all tried who should help him to it most. Then the two young Cratchits got upon his knees and laid, each child a little cheek, against his face, as if they said, 'Don't mind it, father. Don't be grieved!'

Bob was very cheerful with them, and spoke pleasantly to all the family. He looked at the work upon the table, and praised the industry and speed of Mrs. Cratchit and the girls. They would be done long before Sunday, he said.

'Sunday! You went to-day, then, Robert?' said his wife.

'Yes, my dear,' returned Bob. 'I wish you could have gone. It would have done you good to see how green a place it is. But you'll see it often. I promised him that I would walk there on a Sunday. My little, little child!' cried Bob. 'My little child!'

He broke down all at once. He couldn't help it. If he could have helped it, he and his child would have been farther apart perhaps than they were.

He left the room, and went up-stairs into the room above, which was lighted cheerfully, and hung with Christmas. There was a chair set close beside the child, and there were signs of some one having been there, lately. Poor Bob sat down in it, and when he had thought a little and composed himself, he kissed the little face. He was reconciled to what had happened, and went down again quite happy.

They drew about the fire, and talked; the girls and mother working still. Bob told them of the extraordinary kindness of Mr. Scrooge's nephew, whom he had scarcely seen but once, and who, meeting him in the street that day, and seeing that he looked a little—'just a little down you know,' said Bob, inquired what had happened to distress him. 'On which,' said Bob, 'for he is the pleasantest-spoken gentleman you ever heard, I told him. "I am heartily sorry for it, Mr. Cratchit," he said, "and heartily sorry for your good wife." By the bye, how he ever knew *that*, I don't know.'

'Knew what, my dear?'

'Why, that you were a good wife,' replied Bob.

'Everybody knows that!' said Peter.

'Very well observed, my boy!' cried Bob. 'I hope they do. "Heartily sorry," he said, "for your good wife. If I can be of service to you in any way," he said, giving me his card, "that's where I live. Pray come to me." Now, it wasn't', cried Bob, 'for the sake of anything he might be able to do for us, so much as for his kind way, that this was quite delightful. It really seemed as if he had known our Tiny Tim, and felt with us.'

'I'm sure he's a good soul!' said Mrs. Cratchit.

'You would be surer of it, my dear,' returned Bob, 'if you saw and spoke to him. I shouldn't be at all surprised—mark what I say!—if he got Peter a better situation.'

'Only hear that, Peter,' said Mrs. Cratchit.

'And then,' cried one of the girls, 'Peter will be keeping company with some one, and setting up for himself.'

'Get along with you!' retorted Peter, grinning.

'It's just as likely as not,' said Bob, 'one of these days; though there's plenty of time for that, my dear. But however and whenever we part from one another, I am sure we shall none of us forget poor Tiny Tim—shall we—or this first parting that there was among us?'

'Never, father!' cried they all.

'And I know,' said Bob, 'I know, my dears, that when we recollect how patient and how mild he was; although he was a little, little child; we shall not quarrel easily among ourselves, and forget poor Tiny Tim in doing it.'

'No, never, father!' they all cried again.

'I am very happy,' said little Bob, 'I am very happy!'

Mrs. Cratchit kissed him, his daughters kissed him, the two young Cratchits kissed him, and Peter and himself shook hands. Spirit of Tiny Tim, thy childish essence was from God!

'Spectre,' said Scrooge, 'something informs me that our parting moment is at hand. I know it, but I know not how. Tell me what man that was whom we saw lying dead?'

The Ghost of Christmas Yet To Come conveyed him, as before—though at a different time, he thought: indeed, there seemed no order in these latter visions, save that they were in the Future—into the resorts of business men, but showed him not himself. Indeed, the Spirit did not stay for anything, but went straight on, as to the end just now desired, until besought by Scrooge to tarry for a moment.

'This court,' said Scrooge, 'through which we hurry now, is where my place of occupation is, and has been for a length of time. I see the house. Let me behold what I shall be, in days to come!'

The Spirit stopped; the hand was pointed elsewhere.

'The house is yonder,' Scrooge exclaimed. 'Why do you point away?'

The inexorable finger underwent no change.

Scrooge hastened to the window of his office, and looked in. It was an office still, but not his. The furniture was not the same, and the figure in the chair was not himself. The Phantom pointed as before.

He joined it once again, and wondering why and whither he had gone, accompanied it until they reached an iron gate. He paused to look round before entering.

A churchyard. Here, then, the wretched man whose name he had now to learn, lay underneath the ground. It was a worthy place. Walled in by houses; overrun by grass and weeds, the growth of vegetation's death, not life; choked up with too much burying;* fat with repleted appetite. A worthy place!

The Spirit stood among the graves, and pointed down to One. He advanced towards it trembling. The Phantom was exactly as it had been, but he dreaded that he saw new meaning in its solemn shape.

'Before I draw nearer to that stone to which you point,' said Scrooge, 'answer me one question. Are these the shadows of the things that Will be, or are they shadows of things that May be, only!'

Still the Ghost pointed downward to the grave by which it stood.

'Men's courses will foreshadow certain ends, to which, if per-severed in, they must lead,' said Scrooge. 'But if the courses be departed from, the ends will change. Say it is thus with what you show me!'

The Spirit was immovable as ever.

Scrooge crept towards it, trembling as he went; and following the finger, read upon the stone of the neglected grave his own name, EBENEZER SCROOGE.

'Am *I* that man who lay upon the bed?' he cried, upon his knees.

The finger pointed from the grave to him, and back again.

'No, Spirit! Oh, no, no!'

The finger still was there.

'Spirit!' he cried, tight clutching at its robe, 'hear me! I am not the man I was. I will not be the man I must have been but for this intercourse. Why show me this, if I am past all hope!'

The Last of the Spirits

For the first time the hand appeared to shake.

'Good Spirit,' he pursued, as down upon the ground he fell before it: 'Your nature intercedes for me, and pities me. Assure me that I yet may change these shadows you have shown me, by an altered life!'

The kind hand trembled.

'I will honour Christmas in my heart, and try to keep it all the year. I will live in the Past, the Present, and the Future. The Spirits of all Three shall strive within me. I will not shut out the lessons that they teach. Oh, tell me I may sponge away the writing on this stone!'

In his agony, he caught the spectral hand. It sought to free itself, but he was strong in his entreaty, and detained it. The Spirit, stronger yet, repulsed him.

Holding up his hands in a last prayer to have his fate reversed, he saw an alteration in the Phantom's hood and dress. It shrunk, collapsed, and dwindled down into a bedpost.

STAVE V

THE END OF IT

YES! and the bedpost was his own. The bed was his own, the room was his own. Best and happiest of all, the Time before him was his own, to make amends in!

'I will live in the Past, the Present, and the Future!' Scrooge repeated, as he scrambled out of bed. 'The Spirits of all Three shall strive within me. Oh Jacob Marley! Heaven, and the Christmas Time be praised for this! I say it on my knees, old Jacob, on my knees!'

He was so fluttered and so glowing with his good intentions, that his broken voice would scarcely answer to his call. He had been sobbing violently in his conflict with the Spirit, and his face was wet with tears.

'They are not torn down,' cried Scrooge, folding one of his bed-curtains in his arms, 'they are not torn down, rings and all. They are here—I am here—the shadows of the things that would have been, may be dispelled. They will be. I know they will!'

His hands were busy with his garments all this time; turning them inside out, putting them on upside down, tearing them, mislaying them, making them parties to every kind of extravagance.

'I don't know what to do!' cried Scrooge, laughing and crying in the same breath; and making a perfect Laocoön* of himself with his stockings. 'I am as light as a feather, I am as happy as an angel, I am as merry as a schoolboy. I am as giddy as a drunken man. A merry Christmas to everybody! A happy New Year to all the world! Hallo here! Whoop! Hallo!'

He had frisked into the sitting-room, and was now standing there: perfectly winded.

'There's the saucepan that the gruel was in!' cried Scrooge, starting off again, and going round the fire-place. 'There's the door, by which the Ghost of Jacob Marley entered! There's the corner where the Ghost of Christmas Present, sat! There's the window where I saw the wandering Spirits! It's all right, it's all true, it all happened. Ha, ha, ha!'

Really, for a man who had been out of practice for so many years, it was a splendid laugh, a most illustrious laugh. The father of a long, long line of brilliant laughs!

'I don't know what day of the month it is!' said Scrooge. 'I don't know how long I've been among the Spirits. I don't know anything. I'm quite a baby. Never mind. I don't care. I'd rather be a baby. Hallo! Whoop! Hallo here!'

He was checked in his transports by the churches ringing out the lustiest peals he had ever heard. Clash, clang, hammer; ding, dong, bell. Bell, dong, ding; hammer, clang, clash! Oh, glorious, glorious!

Running to the window, he opened it, and put out his head. No fog, no mist; clear, bright, jovial, stirring, cold; cold, piping for the blood to dance to; Golden sunlight; Heavenly sky; sweet fresh air; merry bells. Oh, glorious! Glorious!

'What's to-day?' cried Scrooge, calling downward to a boy in Sunday clothes, who perhaps had loitered in to look about him.

'Eh?' returned the boy, with all his might of wonder.

'What's to-day, my fine fellow?' said Scrooge.

'To-day!' replied the boy. 'Why, CHRISTMAS DAY.'

'It's Christmas Day!' said Scrooge to himself. 'I haven't missed it. The Spirits have done it all in one night. They can do anything they like. Of course they can. Of course they can. Hallo, my fine fellow!'

'Hallo!' returned the boy.

'Do you know the Poulterer's, in the next street but one, at the corner?' Scrooge inquired.

'I should hope I did,' replied the lad.

'An intelligent boy!' said Scrooge. 'A remarkable boy! Do you know whether they've sold the prize Turkey that was hanging up there?—Not the little prize Turkey: the big one?'

'What, the one as big as me?' returned the boy.

'What a delightful boy!' said Scrooge. 'It's a pleasure to talk to him. Yes, my buck!'

'It's hanging there now,' replied the boy.

'Is it?' said Scrooge. 'Go and buy it.'

'Walk-ER!'* exclaimed the boy.

'No, no,' said Scrooge, 'I am in earnest. Go and buy it, and tell 'em to bring it here, that I may give them the direction where to take it. Come back with the man, and I'll give you a shilling. Come back with him in less than five minutes and I'll give you half-a-crown!'

The boy was off like a shot. He must have had a steady hand at a trigger who could have got a shot off half so fast.

'I'll send it to Bob Cratchit's!' whispered Scrooge, rubbing his hands, and splitting with a laugh. 'He sha'n't know who sends it. It's twice the size of Tiny Tim. Joe Miller* never made such a joke as sending it to Bob's will be!'

The hand in which he wrote the address was not a steady one, but write it he did, somehow, and went down-stairs to open the street door, ready for the coming of the poulterer's man. As he stood there, waiting his arrival, the knocker caught his eye.

'I shall love it, as long as I live!' cried Scrooge, patting it with his hand. 'I scarcely ever looked at it before. What an honest expression it has in its face! It's a wonderful knocker!—Here's the Turkey. Hallo! Whoop! How are you! Merry Christmas!'

It *was* a Turkey! He never could have stood upon his legs, that bird. He would have snapped 'em short off in a minute, like sticks of sealing-wax.

'Why, it's impossible to carry that to Camden Town,' said Scrooge. 'You must have a cab.'

The chuckle with which he said this, and the chuckle with which he paid for the Turkey, and the chuckle with which he paid for the cab, and the chuckle with which he recompensed the boy, were only to be exceeded by the chuckle with which he sat down breathless in his chair again, and chuckled till he cried.

Shaving was not an easy task, for his hand continued to shake very much; and shaving requires attention, even when you don't dance while you are at it. But if he had cut the end of his nose off, he would have put a piece of sticking-plaister over it, and been quite satisfied.

He dressed himself 'all in his best,' and at last got out into the streets. The people were by this time pouring forth, as he had seen them with the Ghost of Christmas Present; and walking with his hands behind him, Scrooge regarded every one with a delighted smile. He looked so irresistibly pleasant, in a word, that three or four good-humoured fellows said, 'Good morning, sir! A merry Christmas to you!' And Scrooge said often afterwards, that of all the blithe sounds he had ever heard, those were the blithest in his ears.

He had not gone far, when coming on towards him he beheld the portly gentleman, who had walked into his counting-house the day before, and said, 'Scrooge and Marley's, I believe?' It sent a pang across his heart to think how this old gentleman would look upon him when they met; but he knew what path lay straight before him, and he took it.

'My dear sir,' said Scrooge, quickening his pace, and taking the old gentleman by both his hands. 'How do you do? I hope you succeeded yesterday. It was very kind of you. A merry Christmas to you, sir!'

'Mr. Scrooge?'

'Yes,' said Scrooge. 'That is my name, and I fear it may not be pleasant to you. Allow me to ask your pardon. And will you have the goodness'—here Scrooge whispered in his ear.

'Lord bless me!' cried the gentleman, as if his breath were taken away. 'My dear Mr. Scrooge, are you serious?'

'If you please,' said Scrooge. 'Not a farthing less. A great many back-payments are included in it, I assure you. Will you do me that favour?'

'My dear sir,' said the other, shaking hands with him. 'I don't know what to say to such munifi——'

'Don't say anything, please,' retorted Scrooge. 'Come and see me. Will you come and see me?'

'I will!' cried the old gentleman. And it was clear he meant to do it.

'Thank'ee,' said Scrooge. 'I am much obliged to you. I thank you fifty times. Bless you!'

He went to church, and walked about the streets, and watched the people hurrying to and fro, and patted children on the head, and questioned beggars, and looked down into the kitchens of houses, and up to the windows, and found that everything could yield him pleasure. He had never dreamed that any walk—that anything—could give him so much happiness. In the afternoon he turned his steps towards his nephew's house.

He passed the door a dozen times, before he had the courage to go up and knock. But he made a dash, and did it:

'Is your master at home, my dear?' said Scrooge to the girl. Nice girl! Very.

'Yes, sir.'

'Where is he, my love?' said Scrooge.

'He's in the dining-room, sir, along with mistress. I'll show you up-stairs, if you please.'

'Thank'ee. He knows me,' said Scrooge, with his hand already on the dining-room lock. 'I'll go in here, my dear.'

He turned it gently, and sidled his face in, round the door. They were looking at the table (which was spread out in great array); for these young housekeepers are always nervous on such points, and like to see that everything is right.

'Fred!' said Scrooge.

Dear heart alive, how his niece by marriage started! Scrooge had forgotten, for the moment, about her sitting in the corner with the footstool, or he wouldn't have done it, on any account.

'Why bless my soul!' cried Fred, 'who's that?'

'It's I. Your uncle Scrooge. I have come to dinner. Will you let me in, Fred?'

Let him in! It is a mercy he didn't shake his arm off. He was at home in five minutes. Nothing could be heartier. His niece looked just the same. So did Topper when *he* came. So did the plump sister, when *she* came. So did every one when *they* came. Wonderful party, wonderful games, wonderful unanimity, wonderful happiness!

But he was early at the office next morning. Oh, he was early there. If he could only be there first, and catch Bob Cratchit coming late! That was the thing he had set his heart upon.

And he did it; yes, he did! The clock struck nine. No Bob. A quarter past. No Bob. He was full eighteen minutes and a half behind his time. Scrooge sat with his door wide open, that he might see him come into the Tank.

His hat was off, before he opened the door; his comforter too. He was on his stool in a jiffy; driving away with his pen, as if he were trying to overtake nine o'clock.

'Hallo!' growled Scrooge, in his accustomed voice, as near as he could feign it. 'What do you mean by coming here at this time of day?'

'I am very sorry, sir,' said Bob. 'I *am* behind my time.'

'You are?' repeated Scrooge. 'Yes. I think you are. Step this way, sir, if you please.'

'It's only once a year, sir,' pleaded Bob, appearing from the Tank. 'It shall not be repeated. I was making rather merry yesterday, sir.'

'Now, I'll tell you what, my friend,' said Scrooge, 'I am not going to stand this sort of thing any longer. And therefore,' he continued,

leaping from his stool, and giving Bob such a dig in the waistcoat that he staggered back into the Tank again: 'and therefore I am about to raise your salary!'

Bob trembled, and got a little nearer to the ruler. He had a momentary idea of knocking Scrooge down with it, holding him, and calling to the people in the court for help and a strait-waistcoat.

'A merry Christmas, Bob!' said Scrooge, with an earnestness that could not be mistaken, as he clapped him on the back. 'A merrier Christmas, Bob, my good fellow, than I have given you for many a year! I'll raise your salary, and endeavour to assist your struggling family, and we will discuss your affairs this very afternoon, over a Christmas bowl of smoking bishop,* Bob! Make up the fires, and buy another coal-scuttle before you dot another i, Bob Cratchit!'

Scrooge was better than his word. He did it all, and infinitely more; and to Tiny Tim, who did NOT die, he was a second father. He became as good a friend, as good a master, and as good a man, as the good old city knew, or any other good old city, town, or borough, in the good old world. Some people laughed to see the alteration in him, but he let them laugh, and little heeded them; for he was wise enough to know that nothing ever happened on this globe, for good, at which some people did not have their fill of laughter in the outset; and knowing that such as these would be blind anyway, he thought it quite as well that they should wrinkle up their eyes in grins, as have the malady in less attractive forms. His own heart laughed; and that was quite enough for him.

He had no further intercourse with Spirits, but lived upon the Total Abstinence Principle,* ever afterwards; and it was always said of him, that he knew how to keep Christmas well, if any man alive possessed the knowledge. May that be truly said of us, and all of us! And so, as Tiny Tim observed, God bless Us, Every One!

The Spirits of the Bells

THE CHIMES

A Goblin Story

OF

SOME BELLS THAT RANG AN OLD YEAR OUT

AND A NEW YEAR IN

FIRST QUARTER

THERE are not many people—and as it is desirable that a story-teller and a story-reader should establish a mutual understanding as soon as possible, I beg it to be noticed that I confine this observation neither to young people nor to little people, but extend it to all conditions of people: little and big, young and old: yet growing up, or already growing down again—there are not, I say, many people who would care to sleep in a church. I don't mean at sermon-time in warm weather (when the thing has actually been done, once or twice), but in the night, and alone. A great multitude of persons will be violently astonished, I know, by this position, in the broad bold Day. But it applies to Night. It must be argued by night, and I will undertake to maintain it successfully on any gusty winter's night appointed for the purpose, with any one opponent chosen from the rest, who will meet me singly in an old churchyard, before an old church-door; and will previously empower me to lock him in, if needful to his satisfaction, until morning.

For the night-wind has a dismal trick of wandering round and round a building of that sort, and moaning as it goes; and of trying, with its unseen hand, the windows and the doors; and seeking out some crevices by which to enter. And when it has got in; as one not finding what it seeks, whatever that may be, it wails and howls to issue forth again: and not content with stalking through the aisles, and gliding round and round the pillars, and tempting the deep organ, soars up to the roof, and strives to rend the rafters: then flings itself despairingly upon the stones below, and passes, muttering, into the vaults. Anon, it comes up stealthily, and creeps along the walls, seeming to read, in whispers, the Inscriptions sacred to the Dead. At some of these, it breaks out shrilly, as with laughter; and at others, moans and cries as if it were lamenting. It has a ghostly sound too, lingering within the altar; where it seems to chaunt, in its wild way, of Wrong and Murder done, and false Gods worshipped, in defiance of the Tables of the Law, which look so fair and smooth, but are so flawed and broken. Ugh! Heaven preserve us, sitting snugly round the fire! It has an awful voice, that wind at Midnight, singing in a church!

But, high up in the steeple! There the foul blast roars and whis-tles! High up in the steeple, where it is free to come and go through many an airy arch and loophole, and to twist and twine itself about the giddy stair, and twirl the groaning weathercock, and make the very tower shake and shiver! High up in the steeple, where the belfry is, and iron rails are ragged with rust, and sheets of lead and copper, shrivelled by the changing weather, crackle and heave beneath the unaccustomed tread; and birds stuff shabby nests into corners of old oaken joists and beams; and dust grows old and grey; and speckled spiders, indolent and fat with long security, swing idly to and fro in the vibration of the bells, and never loose their hold upon their thread-spun castles in the air, or climb up sailor-like in quick alarm, or drop upon the ground and ply a score of nimble legs to save one life! High up in the steeple of an old church, far above the light and murmur of the town and far below the flying clouds that shadow it, is the wild and dreary place at night: and high up in the steeple of an old church,* dwelt the Chimes I tell of.

They were old Chimes, trust me. Centuries ago, these bells had been baptized by bishops: so many centuries ago, that the register of their baptism was lost long, long before the memory of man, and no one knew their names. They had had their Godfathers and Godmothers, these Bells (for my own part, by the way, I would rather incur the responsibility of being Godfather to a Bell than a Boy), and had their silver mugs no doubt, besides. But Time had mowed down their sponsors, and Henry the Eighth had melted down their mugs;* and they now hung, nameless and mugless, in the church-tower.

Not speechless, though. Far from it. They had clear, loud, lusty, sounding voices, had these Bells; and far and wide they might be heard upon the wind. Much too sturdy Chimes were they, to be dependent on the pleasure of the wind, moreover; for, fighting gal-lantly against it when it took an adverse whim, they would pour their cheerful notes into a listening ear right royally; and bent on being heard on stormy nights, by some poor mother watching a sick child, or some lone wife whose husband was at sea, they had been some-times known to beat a blustering Nor' Wester; aye, 'all to fits,' as Toby Veck said;—for though they chose to call him Trotty Veck, his name was Toby, and nobody could make it anything else either (except Tobias) without a special act of parliament; he having been as lawfully christened in his day as the Bells had been in theirs, though with not quite so much of solemnity or public rejoicing.

For my part, I confess myself of Toby Veck's belief, for I am sure he had opportunities enough of forming a correct one. And whatever Toby Veck said, I say. And I take my stand by Toby Veck, although he *did* stand all day long (and weary work it was) just outside the church-door. In fact he was a ticket-porter,* Toby Veck, and waited there for jobs.

And a breezy, goose-skinned, blue-nosed, red-eyed, stony-toed, tooth-chattering place it was, to wait in, in the winter-time, as Toby Veck well knew. The wind came tearing round the corner—especially the east wind—as if it had sallied forth, express, from the confines of the earth, to have a blow at Toby. And oftentimes it seemed to come upon him sooner than it had expected, for bouncing round the corner, and passing Toby, it would suddenly wheel round again, as if it cried 'Why, here he is!' Incontinently his little white apron would be caught up over his head like a naughty boy's garments, and his feeble little cane would be seen to wrestle and struggle unavailingly in his hand, and his legs would undergo tremendous agitation, and Toby himself all aslant, and facing now in this direction, now in that, would be so banged and buffeted, and touzled, and worried, and hustled, and lifted off his feet, as to render it a state of things but one degree removed from a positive miracle, that he wasn't carried up bodily into the air as a colony of frogs or snails or other very portable creatures sometimes are, and rained down again, to the great astonishment of the natives, on some strange corner of the world where ticket-porters are unknown.

But, windy weather, in spite of its using him so roughly, was, after all, a sort of holiday for Toby. That's the fact. He didn't seem to wait so long for a sixpence in the wind, as at other times; the having to fight with that boisterous element took off his attention, and quite freshened him up, when he was getting hungry and low-spirited. A hard frost too, or a fall of snow, was an Event; and it seemed to do him good, somehow or other—it would have been hard to say in what respect though, Toby! So wind and frost and snow, and perhaps a good stiff storm of hail, were Toby Veck's red-letter days.

Wet weather was the worst; the cold, damp, clammy wet, that wrapped him up like a moist great-coat—the only kind of great-coat Toby owned, or could have added to his comfort by dispensing with.

Wet days, when the rain came slowly, thickly, obstinately down; when the street's throat, like his own, was choked with mist; when smoking umbrellas passed and re-passed, spinning round and round like so many teetotums,* as they knocked against each other on the crowded footway, throwing off a little whirlpool of uncomfortable sprinklings; when gutters brawled and waterspouts were full and noisy; when the wet from the projecting stones and ledges of the church fell drip, drip, drip, on Toby, making the wisp of straw on which he stood mere mud in no time; those were the days that tried him. Then indeed, you might see Toby looking anxiously out from his shelter in an angle of the church wall—such a meagre shelter that in summer time it never cast a shadow thicker than a good-sized walking-stick upon the sunny pavement—with a disconsolate and lengthened face. But coming out, a minute afterwards, to warm himself by exercise, and trotting up and down some dozen times, he would brighten even then, and go back more brightly to his niche.

They called him Trotty from his pace, which meant speed if it didn't make it. He could have Walked faster perhaps; most likely; but rob him of his trot, and Toby would have taken to his bed and died. It bespattered him with mud in dirty weather; it cost him a world of trouble; he could have walked with infinitely greater ease; but that was one reason for his clinging to it so tenaciously. A weak, small, spare old man, he was a very Hercules, this Toby, in his good intentions. He loved to earn his money. He delighted to believe—Toby was very poor, and couldn't well afford to part with a delight—that he was worth his salt. With a shilling or an eighteenpenny message or small parcel in hand, his courage always high, rose higher. As he trotted on, he would call out to fast Postmen ahead of him, to get out of the way; devoutly believing that in the natural course of things he must inevitably overtake and run them down; and he had perfect faith—not often tested—in his being able to carry anything that man could lift.

Thus, even when he came out of his nook to warm himself on a wet day, Toby trotted. Making, with his leaky shoes, a crooked line of slushy footprints in the mire; and blowing on his chilly hands and rubbing them against each other, poorly defended from the searching cold by threadbare mufflers of grey worsted, with a private apartment only for the thumb, and a common room or tap* for the rest of the fingers; Toby, with his knees bent and his cane beneath his arm, still trotted. Falling out into the road to look up at the belfry when the Chimes resounded, Toby trotted still.

He made this last excursion several times a day, for they were company to him; and when he heard their voices, he had an interest in glancing at their lodging-place, and thinking how they were moved, and what hammers beat upon them. Perhaps he was the more curious about these Bells, because there were points of resemblance between themselves and him. They hung there, in all weathers, with the wind and rain driving in upon them; facing only the outsides of all those houses; never getting any nearer to the blazing fires that gleamed and shone upon the windows, or came puffing out of the chimney tops; and incapable of participation in any of the good things that were constantly being handed, through the street doors and the area railings, to prodigious cooks. Faces came and went at many windows: sometimes pretty faces, youthful faces, pleasant faces: sometimes the reverse: but Toby knew no more (though he often speculated on these trifles, standing idle in the streets) whence they came, or where they went, or whether, when the lips moved, one kind word was said of him in all the year, than did the Chimes themselves.

Toby was not a casuist—that he knew of, at least—and I don't mean to say that when he began to take to the Bells, and to knit up his first rough acquaintance with them into something of a closer and more delicate woof, he passed through these considerations one by one, or held any formal review or great field-day in his thoughts. But what I mean to say, and do say is, that as the functions of Toby's body, his digestive organs for example, did of their own cunning, and by a great many operations of which he was altogether ignorant, and the knowledge of which would have astonished him very much, arrive at a certain end; so his mental faculties, without his privity or concurrence, set all these wheels and springs in motion, with a thousand others, when they worked to bring about his liking for the Bells.

And though I had said his love, I would not have recalled the word, though it would scarcely have expressed his complicated feeling. For, being but a simple man, he invested them with a strange and solemn character. They were so mysterious, often heard and never seen; so high up, so far off, so full of such a deep strong melody, that he regarded them with a species of awe; and sometimes when he looked up at the dark arched windows in the tower, he half expected to be beckoned to by something which was not a Bell, and yet was what he had heard so often sounding in the Chimes. For all this, Toby scouted with indignation a certain flying rumour that the Chimes were haunted, as implying the possibility of their being connected with any Evil thing. In short, they were very often in his ears, and very often in his thoughts, but always in his good opinion; and he very often got such a crick in his neck by staring with his mouth wide open, at the steeple where they hung, that he was fain to take an extra trot or two, afterwards, to cure it.

The very thing he was in the act of doing one cold day, when the last drowsy sound of Twelve o'clock, just struck, was humming like a melodious monster of a Bee, and not by any means a busy bee, all through the steeple!

'Dinner-time, eh!' said Toby, trotting up and down before the church. 'Ah!'

Toby's nose was very red, and his eyelids were very red, and he winked very much, and his shoulders were very near his ears, and his legs were very stiff, and altogether he was evidently a long way upon the frosty side of cool.

'Dinner-time, eh!' repeated Toby, using his right-hand muffler like an infantine boxing-glove, and punishing his chest for being cold. 'Ah-h-h-h!'

He took a silent trot, after that, for a minute or two.

'There's nothing,' said Toby, breaking forth afresh—but here he stopped short in his trot, and with a face of great interest and some alarm, felt his nose carefully all the way up. It was but a little way (not being much of a nose) and he had soon finished.

'I thought it was gone,' said Toby, trotting off again. 'It's all right, however. I am sure I couldn't blame it if it was to go. It has a precious hard service of it in the bitter weather, and precious little to look forward to; for I don't take snuff myself. It's a good deal tried, poor creetur, at the best of times; for when it *does* get hold of a pleasant whiff or so (which an't too often), it's generally from somebody else's dinner, a-coming home from the baker's.'

The reflection reminded him of that other reflection, which he had left unfinished.

'There's nothing,' said Toby, 'more regular in its coming round than dinner-time, and nothing less regular in its coming round than dinner. That's the great difference between 'em. It's took me a long time to find it out. I wonder whether it would be worth any gentleman's while, now, to buy that obserwation for the Papers; or the Parliament!'

Toby was only joking, for he gravely shook his head in self-depreciation.

'Why! Lord!' said Toby. 'The Papers is full of obserwations as it is; and so's the Parliament. Here's last week's paper, now'; taking a very dirty one from his pocket, and holding it from him at arm's length; 'full of obserwations! Full of obserwations! I like to know the news as well as any man,' said Toby, slowly; folding it a little smaller, and putting it in his pocket again: 'but it almost goes against the grain with me to read a paper now. It frightens me almost. I don't know what we poor people are coming to. Lord send we may be coming to something better in the New Year nigh upon us!'

'Why, father, father!' said a pleasant voice, hard by.

But Toby, not hearing it, continued to trot backwards and forwards: musing as he went, and talking to himself.

'It seems as if we can't go right, or do right, or be righted,' said Toby. 'I hadn't much schooling, myself, when I was young; and I can't make out whether we have any business on the face of the earth, or not. Sometimes I think we must have—a little; and sometimes I think we must be intruding. I get so puzzled sometimes that I am not even able to make up my mind whether there is any good at all in us, or whether we are born bad. We seem to be dreadful things; we seem to give a deal of trouble; we are always being complained of and guarded against. One way or other, we fill the papers. Talk of a New Year!' said Toby, mournfully. 'I can bear up as well as another man at most times; better than a good many, for I am as strong as a lion, and all men an't; but supposing it should really be that we have no right to a New Year—supposing we really *are* intruding——'

'Why, father, father!' said the pleasant voice again.

Toby heard it this time; started; stopped; and shortening his sight, which had been directed a long way off as seeking the enlightenment in the very heart of the approaching year, found himself face to face with his own child, and looking close into her eyes.

Bright eyes they were. Eyes that would bear a world of looking in, before their depth was fathomed. Dark eyes, that reflected back the eyes which searched them; not flashingly, or at the owner's will, but with a clear, calm, honest, patient radiance, claiming kindred with that light which Heaven called into being. Eyes that were beautiful and true, and beaming with Hope. With Hope so young and fresh; with Hope so buoyant, vigorous, and bright, despite the twenty years of work and poverty on which they had looked; that they became a voice to Trotty Veck, and said: 'I think we have some business here—a little!'

Trotty kissed the lips belonging to the eyes, and squeezed the blooming face between his hands.

'Why, Pet,' said Trotty. 'What's to do? I didn't expect you to-day, Meg.'

'Neither did I expect to come, father,' cried the girl, nodding her head and smiling as she spoke. 'But here I am! And not alone; not alone!'

'Why you don't mean to say,' observed Trotty, looking curiously at a covered basket which she carried in her hand, 'that you——'

'Smell it, father dear,' said Meg. 'Only smell it!'

Trotty was going to lift up the cover at once, in a great hurry, when she gaily interposed her hand.

'No, no, no,' said Meg, with the glee of a child. 'Lengthen it out a little. Let me just lift up the corner; just the lit-tle ti-ny cor-ner, you know,' said Meg, suiting the action to the word with the utmost gentleness, and speaking very softly, as if she were afraid of being overheard by something inside the basket; 'there. Now. What's that?'

Toby took the shortest possible sniff at the edge of the basket, and cried out in a rapture:

'Why, it's hot!'

'It's burning hot!' cried Meg. 'Ha, ha, ha! It's scalding hot!'

'Ha, ha, ha!' roared Toby, with a sort of kick. 'It's scalding hot!'

'But what is it, father?' said Meg. 'Come. You haven't guessed what it is. And you must guess what it is. I can't think of taking it out, till you guess what it is. Don't be in such a hurry! Wait a minute! A little bit more of the cover. Now guess!'

Meg was in a perfect fright lest he should guess right too soon; shrinking away, as she held the basket towards him; curling up her pretty shoulders; stopping her ear with her hand, as if by so doing she could keep the right word out of Toby's lips; and laughing softly the whole time.

Meanwhile Toby, putting a hand on each knee, bent down his nose to the basket, and took a long inspiration at the lid; the grin upon his withered face expanding in the process, as if he were inhaling laughing gas.*

'Ah! It's very nice,' said Toby. 'It an't—I suppose it an't Polonies?'*

'No, no, no!' cried Meg, delighted. 'Nothing like Polonies!'

'No,' said Toby, after another sniff. 'It's—it's mellower than Polonies. It's very nice. It improves every moment. It's too decided for Trotters. An't it?'

Meg was in an ecstasy. He could not have gone wider of the mark than Trotters—except Polonies.

'Liver?' said Toby, communing with himself. 'No. There's a mildness about it that don't answer to liver. Pettitoes?* No. It an't faint enough for pettitoes. It wants the stringiness of Cocks' heads. And I know it an't sausages. I'll tell you what it is. It's chitterlings!'*

'No, it an't!' cried Meg, in a burst of delight. 'No, it an't!'

'Why, what am I a-thinking of!' said Toby, suddenly recovering a position as near the perpendicular as it was possible for him to assume. 'I shall forget my own name next. It's tripe!'

Tripe it was; and Meg, in high joy, protested he should say, in half a minute more, it was the best tripe ever stewed.

'And so,' said Meg, busying herself exultingly with the basket, 'I'll lay the cloth at once, father; for I have brought the tripe in a basin, and tied the basin up in a pocket-handkerchief; and if I like to be proud for once, and spread that for a cloth, and call it a cloth, there's no law to prevent me; is there, father?'

'Not that I know of, my dear,' said Toby. 'But they're always a-bringing up some new law or other.'

'And according to what I was reading you in the paper the other day, father; what the Judge said, you know; we poor people are supposed to know them all. Ha, ha! What a mistake! My goodness me, how clever they think us!'

'Yes, my dear,' said Trotty; 'and they'd be very fond of any one of us that *did* know 'em all. He'd grow fat upon the work he'd get, that man, and be popular with the gentlefolks in his neighbourhood. Very much so!'

'He'd eat his dinner with an appetite, whoever he was, if it smelt like this,' said Meg, cheerfully. 'Make haste, for there's a hot potato beside, and half a pint of fresh-drawn beer in a bottle. Where will you dine, father? On the Post, or on the Steps? Dear, dear, how grand we are. Two places to choose from!'

'The steps to-day, my Pet,' said Trotty. 'Steps in dry weather. Post in wet. There's a greater conveniency in the steps at all times, because of the sitting down; but they're rheumatic in the damp.'

'Then here,' said Meg, clapping her hands, after a moment's bustle; 'here it is, all ready! And beautiful it looks! Come, father. Come!'

Since his discovery of the contents of the basket, Trotty had been standing looking at her—and had been speaking too—in an abstracted manner, which showed that though she was the object of his thoughts and eyes, to the exclusion even of tripe, he neither saw nor thought about her as she was at that moment, but had before him some imaginary rough sketch or drama of her future life. Roused, now, by her cheerful summons, he shook off a melancholy shake of the head which was just coming upon him, and trotted to her side. As he was stooping to sit down, the Chimes rang.

'Amen!' said Trotty, pulling off his hat and looking up towards them.

'Amen to the Bells, father?' cried Meg.

'They broke in like a grace, my dear,' said Trotty, taking his seat. 'They'd say a good one, I am sure, if they could. Many's the kind thing they say to me.'

'The Bells do, father?' laughed Meg, as she set the basin, and a knife and fork, before him. 'Well!'

'Seem to, my Pet,' said Trotty, falling to with great vigour. 'And where's the difference? If I hear 'em, what does it matter whether they speak it or not? Why bless you, my dear,' said Toby, pointing at the tower with his fork, and becoming more animated under the influence of dinner, 'how often have I heard them bells say, "Toby Veck, Toby Veck, keep a good heart, Toby! Toby Veck, Toby Veck, keep a good heart, Toby!" A million times? More!'

'Well, I never!' cried Meg.

She had, though—over and over again. For it was Toby's constant topic.

'When things is very bad,' said Trotty; 'very bad indeed, I mean; almost at the worst; then it's "Toby Veck, Toby Veck, job coming soon, Toby! Toby Veck, Toby Veck, job coming soon, Toby!" That way.'

'And it comes—at last, father,' said Meg, with a touch of sadness in her pleasant voice.

'Always,' answered the unconscious Toby. 'Never fails.'

While this discourse was holding, Trotty made no pause in his attack upon the savoury meat before him, but cut and ate, and cut and drank, and cut and chewed, and dodged about, from tripe to hot potato, and from hot potato back again to tripe, with an unctuous and unflagging relish. But happening now to look all round the street—in case anybody should be beckoning from any door or window for a porter—his eyes, in coming back again, encountered Meg: sitting opposite to him, with her arms folded: and only busy in watching his progress with a smile of happiness.

'Why, Lord forgive me!' said Trotty, dropping his knife and fork. 'My dove! Meg! why didn't you tell me what a beast I was?'

'Father?'

'Sitting here,' said Trotty, in penitent explanation, 'cramming, and stuffing, and gorging myself; and you before me there, never so much as breaking your precious fast, nor wanting to, when——'

'But I have broken it, father,' interposed his daughter, laughing, 'all to bits. I have had my dinner.'

'Nonsense,' said Trotty. 'Two dinners in one day! It an't possible! You might as well tell me that two New Year's Days will come together, or that I have had a gold head all my life, and never changed it.'

'I have had my dinner, father, for all that,' said Meg, coming nearer to him. 'And if you'll go on with yours, I'll tell you how and where; and how your dinner came to be brought; and—and something else besides.'

Toby still appeared incredulous; but she looked into his face with her clear eyes, and laying her hand upon his shoulder, motioned him to go on while the meat was hot. So Trotty took up his knife and fork again, and went to work. But much more slowly than before, and shaking his head, as if he were not at all pleased with himself.

'I had my dinner, father,' said Meg, after a little hesitation, 'with—with Richard. His dinner-time was early; and as he brought his dinner with him when he came to see me, we—we had it together, father.'

Trotty took a little beer, and smacked his lips. Then he said, 'Oh!'—because she waited.

'And Richard says, father——' Meg resumed. Then stopped.

'What does Richard say, Meg?' asked Toby.

'Richard says, father——' Another stoppage.

'Richard's a long time saying it,' said Toby.

'He says then, father,' Meg continued, lifting up her eyes at last, and speaking in a tremble, but quite plainly; 'another year is nearly gone, and where is the use of waiting on from year to year, when it is so unlikely we shall ever be better off than we are now? He says we are poor now, father, and we shall be poor then, but we are young now, and years will make us old before we know it. He says that if we wait: people in our condition: until we see our way quite clearly, the way will be a narrow one indeed—the common way—the Grave, father.'

A bolder man than Trotty Veck must needs have drawn upon his boldness largely, to deny it. Trotty held his peace.

'And how hard, father, to grow old, and die, and think we might have cheered and helped each other! How hard in all our lives to love each other; and to grieve, apart, to see each other working, changing, growing old and grey. Even if I got the better of it, and forgot him (which I never could), oh father dear, how hard to have a heart so full as mine is now, and live to have it slowly drained out every drop, without the recollection of one happy moment of a woman's life, to stay behind and comfort me, and make me better!'

Trotty sat quite still. Meg dried her eyes, and said more gaily: that is to say, with here a laugh, and there a sob, and here a laugh and sob together:

'So Richard says, father; as his work was yesterday made certain for some time to come, and as I love him, and have loved him full three years—ah! longer than that, if he knew it!—will I marry him on New Year's Day; the best and happiest day, he says, in the whole year, and one that is almost sure to bring good fortune with it. It's a short notice, father—isn't it?—but I haven't my fortune to be settled, or my wedding dresses to be made, like the great ladies, father, have I? And he said so much, and said it in his way; so strong and earnest, and all the time so kind and gentle; that I said I'd come and talk to you, father. And as they paid the money for that work of mine this morning (unexpectedly, I am sure!) and as you have fared very poorly for a whole week, and as I couldn't help wishing there should be something to make this day a sort of holiday to you as well as a dear and happy day to me, father, I made a little treat and brought it to surprise you.'

'And see how he leaves it cooling on the step!' said another voice.

It was the voice of this same Richard, who had come upon them unobserved, and stood before the father and daughter; looking down upon them with a face as glowing as the iron on which his stout sledge-hammer daily rung. A handsome, well-made, powerful young-ster he was; with eyes that sparkled like the red-hot droppings from a furnace fire; black hair that curled about his swarthy temples rarely; and a smile—a smile that bore out Meg's eulogium on his style of conversation.

'See how he leaves it cooling on the step!' said Richard. 'Meg don't know what he likes. Not she!'

Trotty, all action and enthusiasm, immediately reached up his hand to Richard, and was going to address him in a great hurry, when the house-door opened without any warning, and a footman very nearly put his foot into the tripe.

'Out of the vays here, will you! You must always go and be a-settin on our steps, must you! You can't go and give a turn to none of the neighbours never, can't you! *Will* you clear the road, or won't you?'

Strictly speaking, the last question was irrelevant, as they had already done it.

'What's the matter, what's the matter!' said the gentleman for whom the door was opened; coming out of the house at that kind of light-heavy pace—that peculiar compromise between a walk and a jog-trot—with which a gentleman upon the smooth down-hill of life, wearing creaking boots, a watch-chain, and clean linen, *may* come out of his house: not only without any abatement of his dignity, but with an expression of having important and wealthy engagements elsewhere. 'What's the matter! What's the matter!'

'You're always a-being begged, and prayed, upon your bended knees you are,' said the footman with great emphasis to Trotty Veck, 'to let our door-steps be. Why don't you let 'em be? CAN'T you let 'em be?'

'There! That'll do, that'll do!' said the gentleman. 'Halloa there! Porter!' beckoning with his head to Trotty Veck. 'Come here. What's that? Your dinner?'

'Yes, sir,' said Trotty, leaving it behind him in a corner.

'Don't leave it there,' exclaimed the gentleman. 'Bring it here, bring it here. So! This is your dinner, is it?'

'Yes, sir,' repeated Trotty, looking with a fixed eye and a watery mouth, at the piece of tripe he had reserved for a last delicious tit-bit; which the gentleman was now turning over and over on the end of the fork.

Two other gentlemen had come out with him. One was a low-spirited gentleman of middle age, of a meagre habit, and a disconsolate face; who kept his hands continually in the pockets of his scanty pepper-and-salt* trousers, very large and dog's-eared from that custom; and was not particularly well brushed or washed. The other, a full-sized, sleek, well-conditioned gentleman, in a blue coat with bright buttons, and a white cravat. This gentleman had a very red face, as if an undue proportion of the blood in his body were squeezed up into his head; which perhaps accounted for his having also the appearance of being rather cold about the heart.

He who had Toby's meat upon the fork, called to the first one by the name of Filer; and they both drew near together. Mr. Filer being exceedingly short-sighted, was obliged to go so close to the remnant of Toby's dinner before he could make out what it was, that Toby's heart leaped up into his mouth. But Mr. Filer didn't eat it.

'This is a description of animal food, Alderman,' said Filer, making little punches in it, with a pencil-case, 'commonly known to the labouring population of this country, by the name of tripe.'

The Alderman laughed, and winked; for he was a merry fellow, Alderman Cute.* Oh, and a sly fellow too! A knowing fellow. Up to everything. Not to be imposed upon. Deep in the people's hearts! He knew them, Cute did. I believe you!

'But who eats tripe?' said Mr. Filer, looking round. 'Tripe is without an exception the least economical, and the most wasteful article of consumption that the markets of this country can by possibility produce. The loss upon a pound of tripe has been found to be, in the boiling, seven-eighths of a fifth more than the loss upon a pound of any other animal substance whatever. Tripe is more expensive, properly understood, than the hothouse pine-apple. Taking into account the number of animals slaughtered yearly within the bills of mortality* alone; and forming a low estimate of the quantity of tripe which the carcases of those animals, reasonably well butchered, would yield; I find that the waste on that amount of tripe, if boiled, would victual a garrison of five hundred men for five months of thirty-one days each, and a February over. The Waste, the Waste!'

Trotty stood aghast, and his legs shook under him. He seemed to have starved a garrison of five hundred men with his own hand.

'Who eats tripe?' said Mr. Filer, warmly. 'Who eats tripe?'

Trotty made a miserable bow.

'You do, do you?' said Mr. Filer. 'Then I'll tell you something. You snatch your tripe, my friend, out of the mouths of widows and orphans.'

'I hope not, sir,' said Trotty, faintly. 'I'd sooner die of want!'

'Divide the amount of tripe before-mentioned, Alderman,' said Mr. Filer, 'by the estimated number of existing widows and orphans, and the result will be one pennyweight of tripe to each. Not a grain is left for that man. Consequently, he's a robber.'*

Trotty was so shocked, that it gave him no concern to see the Alderman finish the tripe himself. It was a relief to get rid of it, anyhow.

'And what do you say?' asked the Alderman, jocosely, of the red-faced gentleman in the blue coat. 'You have heard friend Filer. What do *you* say?'

'What's it possible to say?' returned the gentleman. 'What *is* to be said? Who can take any interest in a fellow like this,' meaning Trotty; 'in such degenerate times as these? Look at him. What an object! The good old times, the grand old times, the great old times! *Those* were the times for a bold peasantry, and all that sort of thing. Those were the times for every sort of thing, in fact. There's nothing now-a-days. Ah!' sighed the red-faced gentleman. 'The good old times, the good old times!'*

The gentleman didn't specify what particular times he alluded to; nor did he say whether he objected to the present times, from a disinterested consciousness that they had done nothing very remark-able in producing himself.

'The good old times, the good old times,' repeated the gentleman. 'What times they were! They were the only times. It's of no use talking about any other times, or discussing what the people are in *these* times. You don't call these, times, do you? I don't. Look into Strutt's Costumes,* and see what a Porter used to be, in any of the good old English reigns.'

'He hadn't, in his very best circumstances, a shirt to his back, or a stocking to his foot; and there was scarcely a vegetable in all England for him to put into his mouth,' said Mr. Filer. 'I can prove it, by tables.'

But still the red-faced gentleman extolled the good old times, the grand old times, the great old times. No matter what anybody else said, he still went turning round and round in one set form of words concerning them; as a poor squirrel turns and turns in its revolving cage; touching the mechanism, and trick of which, it has probably quite as distinct perceptions, as ever this red-faced gentleman had of his deceased Millennium.

It is possible that poor Trotty's faith in these very vague Old Times was not entirely destroyed, for he felt vague enough, at that moment. One thing, however, was plain to him, in the midst of his distress; to wit, that however these gentlemen might differ in details, his misgivings of that morning, and of many other mornings, were well founded. 'No, no. We can't go right or do right,' thought Trotty in despair. 'There is no good in us. We are born bad!'

But Trotty had a father's heart within him; which had somehow got into his breast in spite of this decree; and he could not bear that Meg, in the blush of her brief joy, should have her fortune read by these wise gentlemen. 'God help her,' thought poor Trotty. 'She will know it soon enough.'

He anxiously signed, therefore, to the young smith, to take her away. But he was so busy, talking to her softly at a little distance, that he only became conscious of this desire, simultaneously with Alderman Cute. Now, the Alderman had not yet had his say, but *he* was a philosopher, too—practical, though! Oh, very practical— and, as he had no idea of losing any portion of his audience, he cried, 'Stop!'

'Now, you know,' said the Alderman, addressing his two friends, with a self-complacent smile upon his face which was habitual to him, 'I am a plain man, and a practical man; and I go to work in a plain practical way. That's my way. There is not the least mystery or difficulty in dealing with this sort of people if you only understand 'em, and can talk to 'em in their own manner. Now, you Porter! Don't you ever tell me, or anybody else, my friend, that you haven't always enough to eat, and of the best; because I know better. I have tasted your tripe, you know, and you can't "chaff"* me. You understand what "chaff" means, eh? That's the right word, isn't it? Ha, ha, ha! Lord bless you,' said the Alderman, turning to his friends again, 'it's the easiest thing on earth to deal with this sort of people, if you understand 'em.'

Famous man for the common people, Alderman Cute! Never out of temper with them! Easy, affable, joking, knowing gentleman!

'You see, my friend,' pursued the Alderman, 'there's a great deal of nonsense talked about Want—"hard up," you know; that's the phrase, isn't it? ha! ha! ha!—and I intend to Put it Down. There's a certain amount of cant in vogue about Starvation, and I mean to Put it Down. That's all! Lord bless you,' said the Alderman, turning to his friends again, 'you may Put Down anything among this sort of people, if you only know the way to set about it.'

Trotty took Meg's hand and drew it through his arm. He didn't seem to know what he was doing though.

'Your daughter, eh?' said the Alderman, chucking her familiarly under the chin.

Always affable with the working classes, Alderman Cute! Knew what pleased them! Not a bit of pride!

'Where's her mother?' asked that worthy gentleman.

'Dead,' said Toby. 'Her mother got up linen; and was called to Heaven when She was born.'

'Not to get up linen *there*, I suppose,' remarked the Alderman pleasantly.

Toby might or might not have been able to separate his wife in Heaven from her old pursuits. But query: If Mrs. Alderman Cute had gone to Heaven, would Mr. Alderman Cute have pictured her as holding any state or station there?

'And you're making love to her, are you?' said Cute to the young smith.

'Yes,' returned Richard quickly, for he was nettled by the question. 'And we are going to be married on New Year's Day.'

'What do you mean!' cried Filer sharply. 'Married!'

'Why, yes, we're thinking of it, Master,' said Richard. 'We're rather in a hurry, you see, in case it should be Put Down first.'

'Ah!' cried Filer, with a groan. 'Put *that* down, indeed, Alderman, and you'll do something. Married! Married!! The ignorance of the first principles of political economy on the part of these people; their improvidence; their wickedness; is, by Heavens! enough to—Now look at that couple, will you!'

Well? They were worth looking at. And marriage seemed as reasonable and fair a deed as they need have in contemplation.

'A man may live to be as old as Methuselah,'* said Mr. Filer, 'and may labour all his life for the benefit of such people as those; and may heap up facts on figures, facts on figures, facts on figures, mountains high and dry; and he can no more hope to persuade 'em that they have no right or business to be married, than he can hope to persuade 'em that they have no earthly right or business to be born. And *that* we know they haven't. We reduced it to a mathematical certainty long ago!'*

Alderman Cute was mightily diverted, and laid his right forefinger on the side of his nose, as much as to say to both his friends, 'Observe me, will you! Keep your eye on the practical man!'—and called Meg to him.

'Come here, my girl!' said Alderman Cute.

The young blood of her lover had been mounting, wrathfully, within the last few minutes; and he was indisposed to let her come. But, setting a constraint upon himself, he came forward with a stride as Meg approached, and stood beside her. Trotty kept her hand within his arm still, but looked from face to face as wildly as a sleeper in a dream.

'Now, I'm going to give you a word or two of good advice, my girl,' said the Alderman, in his nice easy way. 'It's my place to give advice, you know, because I'm a Justice. You know I'm a Justice, don't you?'

Meg timidly said, 'Yes.' But everybody knew Alderman Cute was a Justice! O dear, so active a Justice always! Who such a mote of brightness in the public eye, as Cute!

'You are going to be married, you say,' pursued the Alderman. 'Very unbecoming and indelicate in one of your sex! But never mind that. After you are married, you'll quarrel with your husband and come to be a distressed wife. You may think not; but you will, because I tell you so. Now, I give you fair warning, that I have made up my mind to Put distressed wives Down. So, don't be brought before me. You'll have children—boys. Those boys will grow up bad, of course, and run wild in the streets, without shoes and stockings. Mind, my young friend! I'll convict 'em summarily, every one, for I am determined to Put boys without shoes and stockings, Down. Perhaps your husband will die young (most likely) and leave you with a baby. Then you'll be turned out of doors, and wander up and down the streets. Now, don't wander near me, my dear, for I am resolved to Put all wandering mothers Down. All young mothers, of all sorts and kinds, it's my determination to Put Down. Don't think to plead illness as an excuse with me; or babies as an excuse with me; for all sick persons and young children (I hope you know the church-service,* but I'm afraid not) I am determined to Put Down. And if you attempt, desperately, and ungratefully, and impiously, and fraudulently attempt, to drown yourself, or hang yourself, I'll have no pity for you, for I have made up my mind to Put all suicide Down!* If there is one thing,' said the Alderman, with his self-satisfied smile, 'on which I can be said to have made up my mind more than on another, it is to Put suicide Down. So don't try it on. That's the phrase, isn't it? Ha, ha! now we understand each other.'

Toby knew not whether to be agonised or glad, to see that Meg had turned a deadly white, and dropped her lover's hand.

'And as for you, you dull dog,' said the Alderman, turning with even increased cheerfulness and urbanity to the young smith, 'what are you thinking of being married for? What do you want to be married for, you silly fellow? If I was a fine, young, strapping chap like you, I should be ashamed of being milksop enough to pin myself to a woman's apron-strings! Why, she'll be an old woman before you're a middle-aged man! And a pretty figure you'll cut then, with a draggle-tailed wife and a crowd of squalling children crying after you wherever you go!'

O, he knew how to banter the common people, Alderman Cute!

'There! Go along with you,' said the Alderman, 'and repent. Don't make such a fool of yourself as to get married on New Year's Day. You'll think very differently of it, long before next New Year's Day: a trim young fellow like you, with all the girls looking after you. There! Go along with you!'

They went along. Not arm in arm, or hand in hand, or interchanging bright glances; but, she in tears; he, gloomy and down-looking. Were these the hearts that had so lately made old Toby's leap up from its faintness? No, no, The Alderman (a blessing on his head!) had Put *them* Down.

'As you happen to be here,' said the Alderman to Toby, 'you shall carry a letter for me. Can you be quick? You're an old man.'

Toby, who had been looking after Meg, quite stupidly, made shift to murmur out that he was very quick, and very strong.

'How old are you?' inquired the Alderman.

'I'm over sixty, sir,' said Toby.

'O! This man's a great deal past the average age, you know,' cried Mr. Filer, breaking in as if his patience would bear some trying, but this really was carrying matters a little too far.

'I feel I'm intruding, sir,' said Toby. 'I—I misdoubted it this morning. Oh dear me!'

The Alderman cut him short by giving him the letter from his pocket. Toby would have got a shilling too; but Mr. Filer clearly showing that in that case he would rob a certain given number of persons of ninepence-halfpenny a-piece, he only got sixpence; and thought himself very well off to get that.

Then the Alderman gave an arm to each of his friends, and walked off in high feather; but, he immediately came hurrying back alone, as if he had forgotten something.

'Porter!' said the Alderman.

'Sir!' said Toby.

'Take care of that daughter of yours. She's much too handsome.'

'Even her good looks are stolen from somebody or other, I suppose,' thought Toby, looking at the sixpence in his hand, and thinking of the tripe. 'She's been and robbed five hundred ladies of a bloom a-piece, I shouldn't wonder. It's very dreadful!'

'She's much too handsome, my man,' repeated the Alderman. 'The chances are, that she'll come to no good, I clearly see. Observe what I say. Take care of her!' With which, he hurried off again.

'Wrong every way. Wrong every way!' said Trotty, clasping his hands. 'Born bad. No business here!'

The Chimes came clashing in upon him as he said the words. Full, loud, and sounding—but with no encouragement. No, not a drop.

'The tune's changed,' cried the old man, as he listened. 'There's not a word of all that fancy in it. Why should there be? I have no business with the New Year nor with the old one neither. Let me die!'

Still the Bells, pealing forth their changes, made the very air spin. Put 'em down, Put 'em down! Good old Times, Good old Times! Facts and Figures, Facts and Figures! Put 'em down, Put 'em down! If they said anything they said this, until the brain of Toby reeled.

He pressed his bewildered head between his hands, as if to keep it from splitting asunder. A well-timed action, as it happened; for finding the letter in one of them, and being by that means reminded of his charge, he fell, mechanically, into his usual trot, and trotted off.

THE SECOND QUARTER

THE letter Toby had received from Alderman Cute, was addressed to a great man in the great district of the town. The greatest district of the town. It must have been the greatest district of the town, because it was commonly called 'the world' by its inhabitants.

The letter positively seemed heavier in Toby's hand, than another letter. Not because the Alderman had sealed it with a very large coat of arms and no end of wax, but because of the weighty name on the superscription, and the ponderous amount of gold and silver with which it was associated.

'How different from us!' thought Toby, in all simplicity and earnestness, as he looked at the direction. 'Divide the lively turtles in the bills of mortality, by the number of gentlefolks able to buy 'em; and whose share does he take but his own! As to snatching tripe from anybody's mouth—he'd scorn it!'

With the involuntary homage due to such an exalted character, Toby interposed a corner of his apron between the letter and his fingers.

'His children,' said Trotty, and a mist rose before his eyes; 'his daughters—Gentlemen may win their hearts and marry them; they may be happy wives and mothers; they may be handsome like my darling M—e—'

He couldn't finish the name. The final letter swelled in his throat, to the size of the whole alphabet.

'Never mind,' thought Trotty. 'I know what I mean. That's more than enough for me.' And with this consolatory rumination, trotted on.

It was a hard frost, that day. The air was bracing, crisp, and clear. The wintry sun, though powerless for warmth, looked brightly down upon the ice it was too weak to melt, and set a radiant glory there. At other times, Trotty might have learned a poor man's lesson from the wintry sun; but he was past that, now.

The Year was Old, that day. The patient Year had lived through the reproaches and misuses of its slanderers, and faithfully performed its work. Spring, summer, autumn, winter. It had laboured through the destined round, and now laid down its weary head to die. Shut

out from hope, high impulse, active happiness, itself, but active messenger of many joys to others, it made appeal in its decline to have its
toiling days and patient hours remembered, and to die in peace.
Trotty might have read a poor man's allegory in the fading year; but
he was past that, now.

And only he? Or has the like appeal been ever made, by seventy
years at once upon an English labourer's head, and made in vain!

The streets were full of motion, and the shops were decked out
gaily. The New Year, like an Infant Heir to the whole world, was
waited for, with welcomes, presents, and rejoicings. There were
books and toys for the New Year, glittering trinkets for the New Year,
dresses for the New Year, schemes of fortune for the New Year; new
inventions to beguile it. Its life was parcelled out in almanacks and
pocket-books; the coming of its moons, and stars, and tides, was
known beforehand to the moment; all the workings of its seasons
in their days and nights, were calculated with as much precision as
Mr. Filer could work sums in men and women.

The New Year, the New Year. Everywhere the New Year! The Old
Year was already looked upon as dead; and its effects were selling
cheap, like some drowned mariner's aboardship. Its patterns were
Last Year's, and going at a sacrifice, before its breath was gone. Its
treasures were mere dirt, beside the riches of its unborn successor!

Trotty had no portion, to his thinking, in the New Year or the Old.

'Put 'em down, Put 'em down! Facts and Figures, Facts and
Figures! Good old Times, Good old Times! Put 'em down, Put
'em down!'—his trot went to that measure, and would fit itself to
nothing else.

But, even that one, melancholy as it was, brought him, in due
time, to the end of his journey. To the mansion of Sir Joseph Bowley,
Member of Parliament.

The door was opened by a Porter. Such a Porter! Not of Toby's
order. Quite another thing. His place was the ticket* though; not
Toby's.

This Porter underwent some hard panting before he could speak;
having breathed himself by coming incautiously out of his chair,
without first taking time to think about it and compose his mind.
When he had found his voice—which it took him a long time to do,
for it was a long way off, and hidden under a load of meat—he said in
a fat whisper,

'Who's it from?'

Toby told him.

'You're to take it in, yourself,' said the Porter, pointing to a room at the end of a long passage, opening from the hall. 'Everything goes straight in, on this day of the year. You're not a bit too soon; for the carriage is at the door now, and they have only come to town for a couple of hours, a' purpose.'

Toby wiped his feet (which were quite dry already) with great care, and took the way pointed out to him; observing as he went that it was an awfully grand house, but hushed and covered up, as if the family were in the country. Knocking at the room-door, he was told to enter from within; and doing so found himself in a spacious library, where, at a table strewn with files and papers, were a stately lady in a bonnet; and a not very stately gentleman in black who wrote from her dictation; while another, and an older, and a much statelier gentleman, whose hat and cane were on the table, walked up and down, with one hand in his breast, and looked complacently from time to time at his own picture—a full length; a very full length—hanging over the fireplace.

'What is this!' said the last-named gentleman. 'Mr. Fish, will you have the goodness to attend?'

Mr. Fish begged pardon, and taking the letter from Toby, handed it, with great respect.

'From Alderman Cute, Sir Joseph.'

'Is this all? Have you nothing else, Porter?' inquired Sir Joseph.

Toby replied in the negative.

'You have no bill or demand upon me—my name is Bowley, Sir Joseph Bowley—of any kind from anybody, have you?' said Sir Joseph. 'If you have, present it. There is a cheque-book by the side of Mr. Fish. I allow nothing to be carried into the New Year. Every description of account is settled in this house at the close of the old one. So that if death was to—to——'

'To cut,' suggested Mr. Fish.

'To sever, sir,' returned Sir Joseph, with great asperity, 'the cord of existence—my affairs would be found, I hope, in a state of preparation.'

'My dear Sir Joseph!' said the lady, who was greatly younger than the gentleman. 'How shocking!'

'My lady Bowley,' returned Sir Joseph, floundering now and then, as in the great depth of his observations, 'at this season of the year we should think of—of—ourselves. We should look into our—our accounts. We should feel that every return of so eventful a period in human transactions, involves a matter of deep moment between a man and his—and his banker.'

Sir Joseph delivered these words as if he felt the full morality of what he was saying; and desired that even Trotty should have an opportunity of being improved by such discourse. Possibly he had this end before him in still forbearing to break the seal of the letter, and in telling Trotty to wait where he was, a minute.

'You were desiring Mr. Fish to say, my lady—' observed Sir Joseph.

'Mr. Fish has said that, I believe,' returned his lady, glancing at the letter. 'But, upon my word, Sir Joseph, I don't think I can let it go after all. It is so very dear.'

'What is dear?' inquired Sir Joseph.

'That Charity, my love. They only allow two votes for a subscription of five pounds. Really monstrous!'

'My lady Bowley,' returned Sir Joseph, 'you surprise me. Is the luxury of feeling in proportion to the number of votes; or is it, to a rightly constituted mind, in proportion to the number of applicants, and the wholesome state of mind to which their canvassing reduces them? Is there no excitement of the purest kind in having two votes to dispose of among fifty people?'

'Not to me, I acknowledge,' replied the lady. 'It bores one. Besides, one can't oblige one's acquaintance. But you are the Poor Man's Friend,* you know, Sir Joseph. You think otherwise.'

'I *am* the Poor Man's Friend,' observed Sir Joseph, glancing at the poor man present. 'As such I may be taunted. As such I have been taunted. But I ask no other title.'

'Bless him for a noble gentleman!' thought Trotty.

'I don't agree with Cute here, for instance,' said Sir Joseph, holding out the letter. 'I don't agree with the Filer party. I don't agree with any party. My friend the Poor Man has no business with anything of that sort, and nothing of that sort has any business with him. My friend the Poor Man, in my district, is my business. No man or body of men has any right to interfere between my friend and me. That is the ground I take. I assume a—a paternal character towards my friend. I say, "My good fellow, I will treat you paternally." '

Toby listened with great gravity, and began to feel more comfortable.

'Your only business, my good fellow,' pursued Sir Joseph, looking abstractedly at Toby; 'your only business in life is with me. You needn't trouble yourself to think about anything. I will think for you; I know what is good for you; I am your perpetual parent. Such is the dispensation of an all-wise Providence! Now, the design of your creation is—not that you should swill, and guzzle, and associate your enjoyments, brutally, with food'; Toby thought remorsefully of the tripe; 'but that you should feel the Dignity of Labour. Go forth erect into the cheerful morning air, and—and stop there. Live hard and temperately, be respectful, exercise your self-denial, bring up your family on next to nothing, pay your rent as regularly as the clock strikes, be punctual in your dealings (I set you a good example; you will find Mr. Fish, my confidential secretary, with a cash-box before him at all times); and you may trust to me to be your Friend and Father.'

'Nice children, indeed, Sir Joseph!' said the lady, with a shudder. 'Rheumatisms, and fevers, and crooked legs, and asthmas, and all kinds of horrors!'

'My lady,' returned Sir Joseph, with solemnity, 'not the less am I the Poor Man's Friend and Father. Not the less shall he receive encouragement at my hands. Every quarter-day he will be put in communication with Mr. Fish. Every New Year's Day, myself and friends will drink his health. Once every year, myself and friends will address him with the deepest feeling. Once in his life, he may even perhaps receive—in public, in the presence of the gentry—a Trifle from a Friend. And when, upheld no more by these stimulants, and the Dignity of Labour, he sinks into his comfortable grave, then, my lady'—here Sir Joseph blew his nose—'I will be a Friend and a Father—on the same terms—to his children.'

Toby was greatly moved.

'O! You have a thankful family, Sir Joseph!' cried his wife.

'My lady,' said Sir Joseph, quite majestically, 'Ingratitude is known to be the sin of that class. I expect no other return.'

'Ah! Born bad!' thought Toby. 'Nothing melts us.'

'What man can do, *I* do,' pursued Sir Joseph. 'I do my duty as the Poor Man's Friend and Father; and I endeavour to educate his mind, by inculcating on all occasions the one great moral lesson which that class requires. That is, entire Dependence on myself. They have no business whatever with—with themselves. If wicked and designing persons tell them otherwise, and they become impatient and discontented, and are guilty of insubordinate conduct and black-hearted ingratitude—which is undoubtedly the case—I am their Friend and Father still. It is so Ordained. It is in the nature of things.'

With that great sentiment, he opened the Alderman's letter, and read it.

'Very polite and attentive, I am sure!' exclaimed Sir Joseph. 'My lady, the Alderman is so obliging as to remind me that he has had "the distinguished honour"—he is very good—of meeting me at the house of our mutual friend Deedles, the banker; and he does me the favour to inquire whether it will be agreeable to me to have Will Fern put down.'*

'*Most* agreeable!' replied my Lady Bowley. 'The worst man among them! He has been committing a robbery, I hope?'

'Why no,' said Sir Joseph, referring to the letter. 'Not quite. Very near. Not quite. He came up to London, it seems, to look for employment (trying to better himself—that's his story), and being found at night asleep in a shed, was taken into custody, and carried next morning before the Alderman. The Alderman observes (very properly) that he is determined to put this sort of thing down; and that if it will be agreeable to me to have Will Fern put down, he will be happy to begin with him.'

'Let him be made an example of, by all means,' returned the lady. 'Last winter, when I introduced pinking and eyelet-holing* among the men and boys in the village, as a nice evening employment, and had the lines,

> O let us love our occupations,
> Bless the squire and his relations,
> Live upon our daily rations,
> And always know our proper stations,

set to music on the new system,* for them to sing the while; this very Fern—I see him now—touched that hat of his, and said, "I humbly ask your pardon, my lady, but *an't* I something different from a great girl?" I expected it, of course; who can expect anything but insolence and ingratitude from that class of people! That is not to the purpose, however. Sir Joseph! Make an example of him!'

'Hem!' coughed Sir Joseph. 'Mr. Fish, if you'll have the goodness to attend——'

Mr. Fish immediately seized his pen, and wrote from Sir Joseph's dictation.

'Private. My dear Sir. I am very much indebted to you for your courtesy in the matter of the man William Fern, of whom, I regret to add, I can say nothing favourable. I have uniformly considered myself in the light of his Friend and Father, but have been repaid (a common case I grieve to say) with ingratitude, and constant opposition to my plans. He is a turbulent and rebellious spirit. His character will not bear investigation. Nothing will persuade him to be happy when he might. Under these circumstances, it appears to me, I own, that when he comes before you again (as you informed me he promised to do to-morrow, pending your inquiries, and I think he may be so far relied upon), his committal for some short term as a Vagabond,* would be a service to society, and would be a salutary example in a country where—for the sake of those who are, through good and evil report, the Friends and Fathers of the Poor, as well as with a view to that, generally speaking, misguided class themselves—examples are greatly needed. And I am,' and so forth.

'It appears,' remarked Sir Joseph when he had signed this letter, and Mr. Fish was sealing it, 'as if this were Ordained: really. At the close of the year, I wind up my account and strike my balance, even with William Fern!'

Trotty, who had long ago relapsed, and was very low-spirited, stepped forward with a rueful face to take the letter.

'With my compliments and thanks,' said Sir Joseph. 'Stop!'

'Stop!' echoed Mr. Fish.

'You have heard, perhaps,' said Sir Joseph, oracularly, 'certain remarks into which I have been led respecting the solemn period of time at which we have arrived, and the duty imposed upon us of settling our affairs, and being prepared. You have observed that I don't shelter myself behind my superior standing in society, but that Mr. Fish—that gentleman—has a cheque-book at his elbow, and is in fact here, to enable me to turn over a perfectly new leaf, and enter on the epoch before us with a clean account. Now, my friend, can you lay your hand upon your heart, and say, that you also have made preparations for a New Year?'

'I am afraid, sir,' stammered Trotty, looking meekly at him, 'that I am a—a—little behind-hand with the world.'

'Behind-hand with the world!' repeated Sir Joseph Bowley, in a tone of terrible distinctness.

'I am afraid, sir,' faltered Trotty, 'that there's a matter of ten or twelve shillings owing to Mrs. Chickenstalker.'

'To Mrs. Chickenstalker!' repeated Sir Joseph, in the same tone as before.

'A shop, sir,' exclaimed Toby, 'in the general line. Also a—a little money on account of rent. A very little, sir. It oughtn't to be owing, I know, but we have been hard put to it, indeed!'

Sir Joseph looked at his lady, and at Mr. Fish, and at Trotty, one after another, twice all round. He then made a despondent gesture with both hands at once, as if he gave the thing up altogether.

'How a man, even among this improvident and impracticable race; an old man; a man grown grey; can look a New Year in the face, with his affairs in this condition; how he can lie down on his bed at night, and get up again in the morning, and——There!' he said, turning his back on Trotty. 'Take the letter. Take the letter!'

'I heartily wish it was otherwise, sir,' said Trotty, anxious to excuse himself. 'We have been tried very hard.'

Sir Joseph still repeating 'Take the letter, take the letter!' and Mr. Fish not only saying the same thing, but giving additional force to the request by motioning the bearer to the door, he had nothing for it but to make his bow and leave the house. And in the street, poor Trotty pulled his worn old hat down on his head, to hide the grief he felt at getting no hold on the New Year, anywhere.

He didn't even lift his hat to look up at the Bell tower when he came to the old church on his return. He halted there a moment, from habit: and knew that it was growing dark, and that the steeple rose above him, indistinct and faint, in the murky air. He knew, too, that the Chimes would ring immediately; and that they sounded to his fancy, at such a time, like voices in the clouds. But he only made the more haste to deliver the Alderman's letter, and get out of the way before they began; for he dreaded to hear them tagging 'Friends and Fathers, Friends and Fathers,' to the burden they had rung out last.

Toby discharged himself of his commission, therefore, with all possible speed, and set off trotting homeward. But what with his pace, which was at best an awkward one in the street; and what with his hat, which didn't improve it; he trotted against somebody in less than no time, and was sent staggering out into the road.

'I beg your pardon, I'm sure!' said Trotty, pulling up his hat in great confusion, and between the hat and the torn lining, fixing his head into a kind of bee-hive. 'I hope I haven't hurt you.'

As to hurting anybody, Toby was not such an absolute Samson, but that he was much more likely to be hurt himself: and indeed, he had flown out into the road, like a shuttlecock. He had such an opinion of his own strength, however, that he was in real concern for the other party: and said again,

'I hope I haven't hurt you?'

The man against whom he had run; a sun-browned, sinewy, country-looking man, with grizzled hair, and a rough chin; stared at him for a moment, as if he suspected him to be in jest. But, satisfied of his good faith, he answered:

'No, friend. You have not hurt me.'

'Nor the child, I hope?' said Trotty.

'Nor the child,' returned the man. 'I thank you kindly.'

As he said so, he glanced at a little girl he carried in his arms, asleep: and shading her face with the long end of the poor handkerchief he wore about his throat, went slowly on.

The tone in which he said 'I thank you kindly,' penetrated Trotty's heart. He was so jaded and foot-sore, and so soiled with travel, and looked about him so forlorn and strange, that it was a comfort to him to be able to thank any one: no matter for how little. Toby stood gazing after him as he plodded wearily away, with the child's arm clinging round his neck.

At the figure in the worn shoes—now the very shade and ghost of shoes—rough leather leggings, common frock, and broad slouched hat, Trotty stood gazing, blind to the whole street. And at the child's arm, clinging round its neck.

Before he merged into the darkness the traveller stopped; and looking round, and seeing Trotty standing there yet, seemed undecided whether to return or go on. After doing first the one and then the other, he came back, and Trotty went half-way to meet him.

'You can tell me, perhaps,' said the man with a faint smile, 'and if you can I am sure you will, and I'd rather ask you than another—where Alderman Cute lives.'

'Close at hand,' replied Toby. 'I'll show you his house with pleasure.'

'I was to have gone to him elsewhere to-morrow.' said the man, accompanying Toby, 'but I'm uneasy under suspicion, and want to clear myself, and to be free to go and seek my bread—I don't know where. So, maybe he'll forgive my going to his house to-night.'

'It's impossible,' cried Toby with a start, 'that your name's Fern!'

'Eh!' cried the other, turning on him in astonishment.

'Fern! Will Fern!' said Trotty.

'That's my name,' replied the other.

'Why then,' cried Trotty, seizing him by the arm, and looking cautiously round, 'for Heaven's sake don't go to him! Don't go to him! He'll put you down as sure as ever you were born. Here! come up this alley, and I'll tell you what I mean. Don't go to *him*.'

His new acquaintance looked as if he thought him mad; but he bore him company nevertheless. When they were shrouded from observation, Trotty told him what he knew, and what character he had received, and all about it.

The subject of his history listened to it with a calmness that surprised him. He did not contradict or interrupt it, once. He nodded his head now and then—more in corroboration of an old and worn-out story, it appeared, than in refutation of it; and once or twice threw back his hat, and passed his freckled hand over a brow, where every furrow he had ploughed seemed to have set its image in little. But he did no more.

'It's true enough in the main,' he said, 'master, I could sift grain from husk here and there, but let it be as 'tis. What odds? I have gone against his plans; to my misfortun'. I can't help it; I should do the like to-morrow. As to character, them gentlefolks will search and search, and pry and pry, and have it as free from spot or speck in us, afore they'll help us to a dry good word!—Well! I hope they don't lose good opinion as easy as we do, or their lives is strict indeed, and hardly worth the keeping. For myself, master, I never took with that hand'—holding it before him—'what wasn't my own; and never held it back from work, however hard, or poorly paid. Whoever can deny it, let him chop it off! But when work won't maintain me like a human creetur; when my living is so bad, that I am Hungry, out of doors and in; when I see a whole working life begin that way, go on that way, and end that way, without a chance or change; then I say to the gentlefolks "Keep away from me! Let my cottage be. My doors is dark enough without your darkening of 'em more. Don't look for me to come up into the Park to help the show when there's a Birthday, or a fine Speechmaking, or what not. Act your Plays and Games without me, and be welcome to 'em, and enjoy 'em. We've nowt to do with one another. I'm best let alone!" '

Seeing that the child in his arms had opened her eyes, and was looking about her in wonder, he checked himself to say a word or two of foolish prattle in her ear, and stand her on the ground beside him. Then slowly winding one of her long tresses round and round his rough forefinger like a ring, while she hung about his dusty leg, he said to Trotty:

'I'm not a cross-grained man by natur', I believe; and easy satisfied, I'm sure. I bear no ill-will against none of 'em. I only want to live like one of the Almighty's creeturs. I can't—I don't—and so there's a pit dug between me, and them that can and do. There's others like me. You might tell 'em off by hundreds and by thousands, sooner than by ones.'

Trotty knew he spoke the Truth in this, and shook his head to signify as much.

'I've got a bad name this way,' said Fern; 'and I'm not likely, I'm afeared, to get a better. 'Tan't lawful to be out of sorts, and I AM out of sorts, though God knows I'd sooner bear a cheerful spirit if I could. Well! I don't know as this Alderman could hurt *me* much by sending me to jail; but without a friend to speak a word for me, he might do it; and you see—!' pointing downward with his finger, at the child.

'She has a beautiful face,' said Trotty.

'Why, yes!' replied the other in a low voice, as he gently turned it up with both his hands towards his own, and looked upon it steadfastly. 'I've thought so, many times. I've thought so, when my hearth was very cold, and cupboard very bare. I thought so t'other night, when we were taken like two thieves. But they—they shouldn't try the little face too often, should they, Lilian? That's hardly fair upon a man!'

He sunk his voice so low, and gazed upon her with an air so stern and strange, that Toby, to divert the current of his thoughts, inquired if his wife were living.

'I never had one,' he returned, shaking his head. 'She's my

brother's child: a orphan. Nine year old, though you'd hardly think it; but she's tired and worn out now. They'd have taken care of her, the Union*—eight-and-twenty mile away from where we live— between four walls (as they took care of my old father when he couldn't work no more, though he didn't trouble 'em long); but I took her instead, and she's lived with me ever since. Her mother had a friend once, in London here. We are trying to find her, and to find work too; but it's a large place. Never mind. More room for us to walk about in, Lilly!'

Meeting the child's eyes with a smile which melted Toby more than tears, he shook him by the hand.

'I don't so much as know your name,' he said, 'but I've opened my heart free to you, for I'm thankful to you; with good reason. I'll take your advice, and keep clear of this—'

'Justice,' suggested Toby.

'Ah!' he said. 'If that's the name they give him. This Justice. And to-morrow will try whether there's better fortun' to be met with, somewheres near London. Good night. A Happy New Year!'

'Stay!' cried Trotty, catching at his hand, as he relaxed his grip. 'Stay! The New Year never can be happy to me, if we part like this. The New Year never can be happy to me, if I see the child and you, go wandering away, you don't know where, without a shelter for your heads. Come home with me! I'm a poor man, living in a poor place; but I can give you lodging for one night and never miss it. Come home with me! Here! I'll take her!' cried Trotty, lifting up the child. 'A pretty one! I'd carry twenty times her weight, and never know I'd got it. Tell me if I go too quick for you. I'm very fast. I always was!' Trotty said this, taking about six of his trotting paces to one stride of his fatigued companion; and with his thin legs quivering again, beneath the load he bore.

'Why, she's as light,' said Trotty, trotting in his speech as well as in his gait; for he couldn't bear to be thanked, and dreaded a moment's pause; 'as light as a feather. Lighter than a Peacock's feather—a great deal lighter. Here we are and here we go! Round this first turning to the right, Uncle Will, and past the pump, and sharp off up the passage to the left, right opposite the public-house. Here we are and here we go! Cross over, Uncle Will, and mind the kidney pieman at the corner! Here we are and here we go! Down the Mews here, Uncle Will, and stop at the black door, with "T. Veck, Ticket Porter," wrote upon a board; and here we are and here we go, and here we are indeed, my precious Meg, surprising you!'

With which words Trotty, in a breathless state, set the child down before his daughter in the middle of the floor. The little visitor looked once at Meg; and doubting nothing in that face, but trusting everything she saw there; ran into her arms.

'Here we are and here we go!' cried Trotty, running round the room, and choking audibly. 'Here, Uncle Will, here's a fire you know! Why don't you come to the fire! Oh here we are and here we go. Meg, my precious darling, where's the kettle! Here it is and here it goes, and it'll bile in no time!'

Trotty really had picked up the kettle somewhere or other in the course of his wild career, and now put it on the fire: while Meg, seating the child in a warm corner, knelt down on the ground before her, and pulled off her shoes, and dried her wet feet on a cloth. Ay, and she laughed at Trotty too—so pleasantly, so cheerfully, that Trotty could have blessed her where she kneeled; for he had seen that, when they entered, she was sitting by the fire in tears.

'Why, father!' said Meg. 'You're crazy to-night, I think. I don't know what the Bells would say to that. Poor little feet. How cold they are!'

'Oh, they're warmer now!' exclaimed the child. 'They're quite warm now!'

'No, no, no,' said Meg. 'We haven't rubbed 'em half enough. We're so busy. So busy! And when they're done, we'll brush out the damp hair; and when that's done, we'll bring some colour to the poor pale face with fresh water; and when that's done, we'll be so gay, and brisk, and happy—!'

The child, in a burst of sobbing, clasped her round the neck; caressed her fair cheek with its hand; and said, 'Oh Meg! oh dear Meg!'

Toby's blessing could have done no more. Who could do more!

'Why, father!' cried Meg, after a pause.

'Here I am and here I go, my dear!' said Trotty.

'Good gracious me!' cried Meg. 'He's crazy! He's put the dear child's bonnet on the kettle, and hung the lid behind the door!'

'I didn't go for to do it, my love,' said Trotty, hastily repairing this mistake. 'Meg, my dear!'

Meg looked towards him and saw that he had elaborately stationed himself behind the chair of their male visitor, where with many mysterious gestures he was holding up the sixpence he had earned.

'I see, my dear,' said Trotty, 'as I was coming in, half an ounce of tea lying somewhere on the stairs; and I'm pretty sure there was a bit of bacon too. As I don't remember where it was exactly, I'll go myself and try to find 'em.'

With this inscrutable artifice, Toby withdrew to purchase the viands he had spoken of, for ready money, at Mrs. Chickenstalker's; and presently came back, pretending he had not been able to find them, at first, in the dark.

'But here they are at last,' said Trotty, setting out the tea-things, 'all correct! I was pretty sure it was tea, and a rasher. So it is. Meg, my pet, if you'll just make the tea, while your unworthy father toasts the bacon, we shall be ready, immediate. It's a curious circumstance,' said Trotty, proceeding in his cookery, with the assistance of the toasting-fork, 'curious, but well known to my friends, that I never care, myself, for rashers, nor for tea. I like to see other people enjoy 'em,' said Trotty, speaking very loud, to impress the fact upon his guest, 'but to me, as food, they're disagreeable.'

Yet Trotty sniffed the savour of the hissing bacon—ah!—as if he liked it; and when he poured the boiling water in the tea-pot, looked lovingly down into the depths of that snug cauldron, and suffered the fragrant steam to curl about his nose, and wreathe his head and face in a thick cloud. However, for all this, he neither ate nor drank, except at the very beginning, a mere morsel for form's sake, which he appeared to eat with infinite relish, but declared was perfectly uninteresting to him.

No. Trotty's occupation was, to see Will Fern and Lilian eat and drink; and so was Meg's. And never did spectators at a city dinner or court banquet find such high delight in seeing others feast: although it were a monarch or a pope: as those two did, in looking on that night. Meg smiled at Trotty, Trotty laughed at Meg. Meg shook her head, and made belief to clap her hands, applauding Trotty; Trotty conveyed, in dumbshow, unintelligible narratives of how and when and where he had found their visitors, to Meg; and they were happy. Very happy.

'Although,' thought Trotty, sorrowfully, as he watched Meg's face; 'that match is broken off, I see!'

'Now, I'll tell you what,' said Trotty after tea. 'The little one, she sleeps with Meg, I know.'

'With good Meg!' cried the child, caressing her. 'With Meg.'

'That's right,' said Trotty. 'And I shouldn't wonder if she kiss Meg's father, won't she? *I*'m Meg's father.'

Mightly delighted Trotty was, when the child went timidly towards him, and having kissed him, fell back upon Meg again.

'She's as sensible as Solomon,'* said Trotty. 'Here we come and here we—no, we don't—I don't mean that—I—what was I saying, Meg, my precious?'

Meg looked towards their guest, who leaned upon her chair, and with his face turned from her, fondled the child's head, half hidden in her lap.

'To be sure,' said Toby. 'To be sure! I don't know what I'm rambling on about, to-night. My wits are wool-gathering,* I think. Will Fern, you come along with me. You're tired to death, and broken down for want of rest. You come along with me.'

The man still played with the child's curls, still leaned upon Meg's chair, still turned away his face. He didn't speak, but in his rough coarse fingers, clenching and expanding in the fair hair of the child, there was an eloquence that said enough.

'Yes, yes,' said Trotty, answering unconsciously what he saw expressed in his daughter's face. 'Take her with you, Meg. Get her to bed. There! Now, Will, I'll show you where you lie. It's not much of a place: only a loft; but, having a loft, I always say, is one of the great conveniences of living in a mews; and till this coach-house and stable gets a better let, we live here cheap. There's plenty of sweet hay up there, belonging to a neighbour; and it's as clean as hands, and Meg, can make it. Cheer up! Don't give way. A new heart for a New Year, always!'

The hand released from the child's hair, had fallen, trembling, into Trotty's hand. So Trotty, talking without intermission, led him out as tenderly and easily as if he had been a child himself.

Returning before Meg, he listened for an instant at the door of her little chamber; an adjoining room. The child was murmuring a simple Prayer before lying down to sleep; and when she had remembered Meg's name, 'Dearly, Dearly'—so her words ran—Trotty heard her stop and ask for his.

It was some short time before the foolish little old fellow could compose himself to mend the fire, and draw his chair to the warm hearth. But when he had done so, and had trimmed the light, he took his newspaper from his pocket, and began to read. Carelessly at first, and skimming up and down the columns; but with an earnest and a sad attention, very soon.

For this same dreaded paper re-directed Trotty's thoughts into the channel they had taken all that day, and which the day's events had so marked out and shaped. His interest in the two wanderers had set him on another course of thinking, and a happier one, for the time; but being alone again, and reading of the crimes and violences of the people, he relapsed into his former train.

In this mood, he came to an account (and it was not the first he had ever read) of a woman who had laid her desperate hands not only on her own life but on that of her young child.* A crime so terrible, and so revolting to his soul, dilated with the love of Meg, that he let the journal drop, and fell back in his chair, appalled!

'Unnatural and cruel!' Toby cried. 'Unnatural and cruel! None but people who were bad at heart, born bad, who had no business on the earth, could do such deeds. It's too true, all I've heard to-day; too just, too full of proof. We're Bad!'

The Chimes took up the words so suddenly—burst out so loud, and clear, and sonorous—that the Bells seemed to strike him in his chair.

And what was that, they said?

'Toby Veck, Toby Veck, waiting for you Toby! Toby Veck, Toby Veck, waiting for you Toby! Come and see us, come and see us, Drag him to us, drag him to us, Haunt and hunt him, haunt and hunt him, Break his slumbers, break his slumbers! Toby Veck, Toby Veck, door open wide Toby, Toby Veck, Toby Veck, door open wide Toby—' then fiercely back to their impetuous strain again, and ringing in the very bricks and plaster on the walls.

Toby listened. Fancy, fancy! His remorse for having run away from them that afternoon! No, no. Nothing of the kind. Again, again, and yet a dozen times again. 'Haunt and hunt him, haunt and hunt him, Drag him to us, drag him to us!' Deafening the whole town!

'Meg,' said Trotty softly: tapping at her door. 'Do you hear anything?'

'I hear the Bells, father. Surely they're very loud to-night.'

'Is she asleep?' said Toby, making an excuse for peeping in.

'So peacefully and happily! I can't leave her yet though, father. Look how she holds my hand!'

'Meg,' whispered Trotty. 'Listen to the Bells!'

She listened, with her face towards him all the time. But it underwent no change. She didn't understand them.

Trotty withdrew, resumed his seat by the fire, and once more listened by himself. He remained here a little time.

It was impossible to bear it; their energy was dreadful.

'If the tower-door is really open,' said Toby, hastily laying aside his apron, but never thinking of his hat, 'what's to hinder me from going up into the steeple and satisfying myself? If it's shut, I don't want any other satisfaction. That's enough.'

He was pretty certain as he slipped out quietly into the street that he should find it shut and locked, for he knew the door well, and had so rarely seen it open, that he couldn't reckon above three times in all. It was a low arched portal, outside the church, in a dark nook behind a column; and had such great iron hinges, and such a monstrous lock, that there was more hinge and lock than door.

But what was his astonishment when, coming bare-headed to the church; and putting his hand into this dark nook, with a certain misgiving that it might be unexpectedly seized, and a shivering propensity to draw it back again; he found that the door, which opened outwards, actually stood ajar!

He thought, on the first surprise, of going back; or of getting a light, or a companion, but his courage aided him immediately, and he determined to ascend alone.

'What have I to fear?' said Trotty. 'It's a church! Besides, the ringers may be there, and have forgotten to shut the door.'

So he went in, feeling his way as he went, like a blind man; for it was very dark. And very quiet, for the Chimes were silent.

The dust from the street had blown into the recess; and lying there, heaped up, made it so soft and velvet-like to the foot, that there was something startling, even in that. The narrow stair was so close to the door, too, that he stumbled at the very first; and shutting the door upon himself, by striking it with his foot, and causing it to rebound back heavily, he couldn't open it again.

This was another reason, however, for going on. Trotty groped his way, and went on. Up, up, up, and round, and round; and up, up, up; higher, higher, higher up!

It was a disagreeable staircase for that groping work; so low and narrow, that his groping hand was always touching something; and it often felt so like a man or ghostly figure standing up erect and making room for him to pass without discovery, that he would rub the smooth wall upward searching for its face, and downward searching for its feet, while a chill tingling crept all over him. Twice or thrice, a door or niche broke the monotonous surface; and then it seemed a gap as wide as the whole church; and he felt on the brink of an abyss, and going to tumble headlong down, until he found the wall again.

Still up, up, up; and round and round; and up, up, up; higher, higher, higher up!

At length, the dull and stifling atmosphere began to freshen: presently to feel quite windy: presently it blew so strong, that he could hardly keep his legs. But he got to an arched window in the tower, breast high, and holding tight, looked down upon the house-tops, on the smoking chimneys, on the blurr and blotch of lights (towards the place where Meg was wondering where he was and calling to him perhaps), all kneaded up together in a leaven of mist and darkness.

This was the belfry, where the ringers came. He had caught hold of one of the frayed ropes which hung down through apertures in the oaken roof. At first he started, thinking it was hair; then trembled at the very thought of waking the deep Bell. The Bells themselves were higher. Higher, Trotty, in his fascination, or in working out the spell upon him, groped his way. By ladders now, and toilsomely, for it was steep, and not too certain holding for the feet.

Up, up, up; and climb and clamber; up, up, up; higher, higher, higher up!

Until, ascending through the floor, and pausing with his head just raised above its beams, he came among the Bells. It was barely possible to make out their great shapes in the gloom; but there they were. Shadowy, and dark, and dumb.

A heavy sense of dread and loneliness fell instantly upon him, as he climbed into this airy nest of stone and metal. His head went round and round. He listened, and then raised a wild 'Holloa!'

Holloa! was mournfully protracted by the echoes.

Giddy, confused, and out of breath, and frightened, Toby looked about him vacantly, and sunk down in a swoon.

THIRD QUARTER

BLACK are the brooding clouds and troubled the deep waters, when the Sea of Thought, first heaving from a calm, gives up its Dead. Monsters uncouth and wild, arise in premature, imperfect resurrection; the several parts and shapes of different things are joined and mixed by chance; and when, and how, and by what wonderful degrees, each separates from each, and every sense and object of the mind resumes its usual form and lives again, no man—though every man is every day the casket of this type of the Great Mystery—can tell.*

So, when and how the darkness of the night-black steeple changed to shining light; when and how the solitary tower was peopled with a myriad figures; when and how the whispered 'Haunt and hunt him,' breathing monotonously through his sleep or swoon, became a voice exclaiming in the waking ears of Trotty, 'Break his slumbers'; when and how he ceased to have a sluggish and confused idea that such things were, companioning a host of others that were not; there are no dates or means to tell. But, awake and standing on his feet upon the boards where he had lately lain, he saw this Goblin Sight.

He saw the tower, whither his charmed footsteps had brought him, swarming with dwarf phantoms, spirits, elfin creatures of the Bells. He saw them leaping, flying, dropping, pouring from the Bells without a pause. He saw them, round him on the ground; above him, in the air; clambering from him, by the ropes below; looking down upon him, from the massive iron-girded beams; peeping in upon him, through the chinks and loopholes in the walls; spreading away and away from him in enlarging circles, as the water ripples give way to a huge stone that suddenly comes plashing in among them. He saw them, of all aspects and all shapes. He saw them ugly, handsome, crippled, exquisitely formed. He saw them young, he saw them old, he saw them kind, he saw them cruel, he saw them merry, he saw them grim; he saw them dance, and heard them sing; he saw them tear their hair, and heard them howl. He saw the air thick with them. He saw them come and go, incessantly. He saw them riding downward, soaring upward, sailing off afar, perching near at hand, all restless and all violently active. Stone, and brick, and slate, and tile, became transparent to him as to them. He saw them *in* the houses, busy at the sleepers' beds. He saw them soothing people in their dreams; he saw them beating them with knotted whips; he saw them yelling in their ears; he saw them playing softest music on their pillows; he saw them cheering some with the songs of birds and the perfume of flowers; he saw them flashing awful faces on the troubled rest of others, from enchanted mirrors which they carried in their hands.

He saw these creatures, not only among sleeping men but waking also, active in pursuits irreconcilable with one another, and possessing or assuming natures the most opposite. He saw one buckling on innumerable wings to increase his speed; another loading himself with chains and weights, to retard his. He saw some putting the hands of clocks forward, some putting the hands of clocks backward, some endeavouring to stop the clock entirely. He saw them representing, here a marriage ceremony, there a funeral; in this chamber an election, in that a ball; he saw, everywhere, restless and untiring motion.

Bewildered by the host of shifting and extraordinary figures, as well as by the uproar of the Bells, which all this while were ringing, Trotty clung to a wooden pillar for support, and turned his white face here and there, in mute and stunned astonishment.

As he gazed, the Chimes stopped. Instantaneous change! The whole swarm fainted! their forms collapsed, their speed deserted them; they sought to fly, but in the act of falling died and melted into air. No fresh supply succeeded them. One straggler leaped down pretty briskly from the surface of the Great Bell, and alighted on his feet, but he was dead and gone before he could turn round. Some few of the late company who had gambolled in the tower, remained there, spinning over and over a little longer; but these became at every turn more faint, and few, and feeble, and soon went the way of the rest. The last of all was one small hunchback, who had got into an echoing corner, where he twirled and twirled, and floated by himself a long time; showing such perseverance, that at last he dwindled to a leg and even to a foot, before he finally retired; but he vanished in the end, and then the tower was silent.

Then and not before, did Trotty see in every Bell a bearded figure of the bulk and stature of the Bell—incomprehensibly, a figure and the Bell itself. Gigantic, grave, and darkly watchful of him, as he stood rooted to the ground.

Mysterious and awful figures! Resting on nothing; poised in the night air of the tower, with their draped and hooded heads merged in the dim roof; motionless and shadowy. Shadowy and dark, although he saw them by some light belonging to themselves—none else was there—each with its muffled hand upon its goblin mouth.

He could not plunge down wildly through the opening in the floor; for all power of motion had deserted him. Otherwise he would have done so—aye, would have thrown himself, head foremost, from the steeple-top, rather than have seen them watching him with eyes that would have waked and watched although the pupils had been taken out.

Again, again, the dread and terror of the lonely place, and of the wild and fearful night that reigned there, touched him like a spectral hand. His distance from all help; the long, dark, winding, ghost-beleaguered way that lay between him and the earth on which men lived; his being high, high, high, up there, where it had made him dizzy to see the birds fly in the day; cut off from all good people, who at such an hour were safe at home and sleeping in their beds; all this struck coldly through him, not as a reflection but a bodily sensation. Meantime his eyes and thoughts and fears, were fixed upon the watchful figures; which, rendered unlike any figures of this world by the deep gloom and shade enwrapping and enfolding them, as well as by their looks and forms and supernatural hovering above the floor, were nevertheless as plainly to be seen as were the stalwart oaken frames, cross-pieces, bars and beams, set up there to support the Bells. These hemmed them, in a very forest of hewn timber; from the entanglements, intricacies, and depths of which, as from among the boughs of a dead wood blighted for their phantom use, they kept their darksome and unwinking watch.

A blast of air—how cold and shrill!—came moaning through the tower. As it died away, the great Bell, or the Goblin of the Great Bell, spoke.

'What visitor is this!' it said. The voice was low and deep, and Trotty fancied that it sounded in the other figures as well.

'I thought my name was called by the Chimes!' said Trotty, raising his hands in an attitude of supplication. 'I hardly know why I am here, or how I came. I have listened to the Chimes these many years. They have cheered me often.'

'And you have thanked them?' said the Bell.

'A thousand times!' said Trotty.

'How?'

'I am a poor man,' faltered Trotty, 'and could only thank them in words.'

'And always so?' inquired the Goblin of the Bell. 'Have you never done us wrong in words?'

'No!' cried Trotty eagerly.

'Never done us foul, and false, and wicked wrong, in words?' pursued the Goblin of the Bell.

Trotty was about to answer, 'Never!' But he stopped, and was confused.

'The voice of Time', said the Phantom, 'cries to man, Advance! Time is for his advancement and improvement; for his greater worth, his greater happiness, his better life; his progress onward to that goal within its knowledge and its view, and set there, in the period when Time and He began. Ages of darkness, wickedness, and violence, have come and gone—millions uncountable, have suffered, lived, and died—to point the way before him. Who seeks to turn him back, or stay him on his course, arrests a mighty engine which will strike the meddler dead; and be the fiercer and the wilder, ever, for its momentary check!'

'I never did so to my knowledge, sir,' said Trotty. 'It was quite by accident if I did. I wouldn't go to do it, I'm sure.'

'Who puts into the mouth of Time, or of its servants,' said the Goblin of the Bell, 'a cry of lamentation for days which have had their trial and their failure, and have left deep traces of it which the blind may see—a cry that only serves the present time, by showing men how much it needs their help when any ears can listen to regrets for such a past—who does this, does a wrong. And you have done that wrong, to us, the Chimes.'

Trotty's first excess of fear was gone. But he had felt tenderly and gratefully towards the Bells, as you have seen; and when he heard himself arraigned as one who had offended them so weightily, his heart was touched with penitence and grief.

'If you knew,' said Trotty, clasping his hands earnestly—'or perhaps you do know—if you know how often you have kept me company; how often you have cheered me up when I've been low; how you were quite the plaything of my little daughter Meg (almost the only one she ever had) when first her mother died, and she and me were left alone; you won't bear malice for a hasty word!'

'Who hears in us, the Chimes, one note bespeaking disregard, or stern regard, of any hope, or joy, or pain, or sorrow, of the many-sorrowed throng; who hears us make response to any creed that gauges human passions and affections, as it gauges the amount of miserable food on which humanity may pine and wither; does us wrong. That wrong you have done us!' said the Bell.

'I have!' said Trotty. 'Oh forgive me!'

'Who hears us echo the dull vermin of the earth: the Putters Down of crushed and broken natures, formed to be raised up higher than such maggots of the time can crawl or can conceive,' pursued the Goblin of the Bell; 'who does so, does us wrong. And you have done us wrong!'

'Not meaning it,' said Trotty. 'In my ignorance. Not meaning it!'

'Lastly, and most of all,' pursued the Bell. 'Who turns his back upon the fallen and disfigured of his kind; abandons them as vile; and does not trace and track with pitying eyes the unfenced precipice by which they fell from good—grasping in their fall some tufts and shreds of that lost soil, and clinging to them still when bruised and dying in the gulf below; does wrong to Heaven and man, to time and to eternity. And you have done that wrong!'

'Spare me,' cried Trotty, falling on his knees; 'for Mercy's sake!'

'Listen!' said the Shadow.

'Listen!' cried the other Shadows.

'Listen!' said a clear and childlike voice, which Trotty thought he recognised as having heard before.

The organ sounded faintly in the church below. Swelling by degrees, the melody ascended to the roof, and filled the choir and nave. Expanding more and more, it rose up, up; up, up; higher, higher, higher up; awakening agitated hearts within the burly piles of oak, the hollow bells, the iron-bound doors, the stairs of solid stone; until the tower walls were insufficient to contain it, and it soared into the sky.

No wonder that an old man's breast could not contain a sound so vast and mighty. It broke from that weak prison in a rush of tears; and Trotty put his hands before his face.

'Listen!' said the Shadow.

'Listen!' said the other Shadows.

'Listen!' said the child's voice.

A solemn strain of blended voices, rose into the tower.

It was a very low and mournful strain—a Dirge—and as he listened, Trotty heard his child among the singers.

'She is dead!' exclaimed the old man. 'Meg is dead! Her Spirit calls to me. I hear it!'

'The Spirit of your child bewails the dead, and mingles with the dead—dead hopes, dead fancies, dead imaginings of youth,' returned the Bell, 'but she is living. Learn from her life, a living truth. Learn from the creature dearest to your heart, how bad the bad are born. See every bud and leaf plucked one by one from off the fairest stem, and know how bare and wretched it may be. Follow her! To desperation!'

Each of the shadowy figures stretched its right arm forth, and pointed downward.

'The Spirit of the Chimes is your companion,' said the figure. 'Go! It stands behind you!'

Trotty turned, and saw—the child! The child Will Fern had carried in the street; the child whom Meg had watched, but now, asleep!

'I carried her myself, to-night,' said Trotty. 'In these arms!'

'Show him what he calls himself,' said the dark figures, one and all.

The tower opened at his feet. He looked down, and beheld his own form, lying at the bottom, on the outside: crushed and motionless.

'No more a living man!' cried Trotty. 'Dead!'

'Dead!' said the figures all together.

'Gracious Heaven! And the New Year—'

'Past,' said the figures.

'What!' he cried, shuddering. 'I missed my way, and coming on the outside of this tower in the dark, fell down—a year ago?'

'Nine years ago!' replied the figures.

As they gave the answer, they recalled their outstretched hands; and where their figures had been, there the Bells were.

And they rung; their time being come again. And once again, vast multitudes of phantoms sprung into existence; once again, were incoherently engaged, as they had been before; once again, faded on the stopping of the Chimes; and dwindled into nothing.

'What are these?' he asked his guide. 'If I am not mad, what are these?'

'Spirits of the Bells. Their sound upon the air,' returned the child. 'They take such shapes and occupations as the hopes and thoughts of mortals, and the recollections they have stored up, give them.'

'And you,' said Trotty wildly. 'What are you?'

'Hush, hush!' returned the child. 'Look here!'

In a poor, mean room; working at the same kind of embroidery which he had often, often seen before her; Meg, his own dear daughter, was presented to his view. He made no effort to imprint his kisses on her face; he did not strive to clasp her to his loving heart; he knew that such endearments were, for him, no more. But he held his trembling breath, and brushed away the blinding tears, that he might look upon her; that he might only see her.

Ah! Changed. Changed. The light of the clear eye, how dimmed. The bloom, how faded from the cheek. Beautiful she was, as she had ever been, but Hope, Hope, Hope, oh where was the fresh Hope that had spoken to him like a voice!

She looked up from her work, at a companion. Following her eyes, the old man started back.

In the woman grown, he recognised her at a glance. In the long silken hair, he saw the self-same curls; around the lips, the child's expression lingering still. See! In the eyes, now turned inquiringly on Meg, there shone the very look that scanned those features when he brought her home!

Then what was this, beside him!

Looking with awe into its face, he saw a something reigning there: a lofty something, undefined and indistinct, which made it hardly more than a remembrance of that child—as yonder figure might be—yet it was the same: the same: and wore the dress.

Hark. They were speaking!

'Meg,' said Lilian, hesitating. 'How often you raise your head from your work to look at me!'

'Are my looks so altered, that they frighten you?' asked Meg.

'Nay, dear! But you smile at that, yourself! Why not smile, when you look at me, Meg?'

'I do so. Do I not?' she answered: smiling on her.

'Now you do,' said Lilian, 'but not usually. When you think I'm busy, and don't see you, you look so anxious and so doubtful, that I hardly like to raise my eyes. There is little cause for smiling in this hard and toilsome life, but you were once so cheerful.'

'Am I not now!' cried Meg, speaking in a tone of strange alarm, and rising to embrace her. 'Do *I* make our weary life more weary to you, Lilian!'

'You have been the only thing that made it life,' said Lilian, fervently kissing her; 'sometimes the only thing that made me care to live so, Meg. Such work, such work! So many hours, so many days, so many long, long nights of hopeless, cheerless, never-ending work—not to heap up riches, not to live grandly or gaily, not to live upon enough, however coarse; but to earn bare bread; to scrape together just enough to toil upon, and want upon, and keep alive in us the consciousness of our hard fate! Oh Meg, Meg!' she raised her voice and twined her arms about her as she spoke, like one in pain. 'How can the cruel world go round, and bear to look upon such lives!'

'Lilly!' said Meg, soothing her, and putting back her hair from her wet face. 'Why, Lilly! You! So pretty and so young!'

'Oh Meg!' she interrupted, holding her at arm's-length, and looking in her face imploringly. 'The worst of all, the worst of all! Strike me old, Meg! Wither me, and shrivel me, and free me from the dreadful thoughts that tempt me in my youth!'

Trotty turned to look upon his guide. But the Spirit of the child had taken flight. Was gone.

Neither did he himself remain in the same place; for Sir Joseph Bowley, Friend and Father of the Poor, held a great festivity at Bowley Hall, in honour of the natal day of Lady Bowley. And as Lady Bowley had been born on New Year's Day (which the local newspapers considered an especial pointing of the finger of Providence to number One, as Lady Bowley's destined figure in Creation), it was on a New Year's Day that this festivity took place.

Bowley Hall was full of visitors. The red-faced gentleman was there, Mr. Filer was there, the great Alderman Cute was there— Alderman Cute had a sympathetic feeling with great people, and had considerably improved his acquaintance with Sir Joseph Bowley on the strength of his attentive letter: indeed had become quite a friend of the family since then—and many guests were there. Trotty's ghost was there, wandering about, poor phantom, drearily; and looking for its guide.

There was to be a great dinner in the Great Hall. At which Sir Joseph Bowley, in his celebrated character of Friend and Father of the Poor, was to make his great speech. Certain plum-puddings were to be eaten by his Friends and Children in another Hall first; and, at a given signal, Friends and Children flocking in among their Friends and Fathers, were to form a family assemblage, with not one manly eye therein unmoistened by emotion.

But there was more than this to happen. Even more than this. Sir Joseph Bowley, Baronet and Member of Parliament, was to play a match at skittles—real skittles—with his tenants!*

'Which quite reminds me,' said Alderman Cute, 'of the days of old King Hal, stout King Hal, bluff King Hal.* Ah. Fine character!'

'Very,' said Mr. Filer, dryly. 'For marrying women and murdering 'em. Considerably more than the average number of wives, by the bye.'

'You'll marry the beautiful ladies, and not murder 'em, eh?' said Alderman Cute to the heir of Bowley, aged twelve. 'Sweet boy! We shall have this little gentleman in Parliament now,' said the Alderman, holding him by the shoulders, and looking as reflective as he could, 'before we know where we are. We shall hear of his successes at the poll; his speeches in the House; his overtures from Governments; his brilliant achievements of all kinds; ah! we shall make our little orations about him in the Common Council, I'll be bound; before we have time to look about us!'

'Oh, the difference of shoes and stockings!' Trotty thought. But his heart yearned towards the child, for the love of those same shoeless and stockingless boys, predestined (by the Alderman) to turn out bad, who might have been the children of poor Meg.

'Richard,' moaned Trotty, roaming among the company, to and fro; 'where is he? I can't find Richard! Where is Richard?'

Not likely to be there, if still alive! But Trotty's grief and solitude confused him; and he still went wandering among the gallant company, looking for his guide, and saying, 'Where is Richard? Show me Richard!'

He was wandering thus, when he encountered Mr. Fish, the confidential Secretary: in great agitation.

'Bless my heart and soul!' cried Mr. Fish. 'Where's Alderman Cute? Has anybody seen the Alderman?'

Seen the Alderman? Oh dear! Who could ever help seeing the Alderman? He was so considerate, so affable, he bore so much in mind the natural desires of folks to see him, that if he had a fault, it was the being constantly On View. And wherever the great people were, there, to be sure, attracted by the kindred sympathy between great souls, was Cute.

Several voices cried that he was in the circle round Sir Joseph. Mr. Fish made way there; found him; and took him secretly into a window near at hand. Trotty joined them. Not of his own accord. He felt that his steps were led in that direction.

'My dear Alderman Cute,' said Mr. Fish. 'A little more this way. The most dreadful circumstance has occurred. I have this moment received the intelligence. I think it will be best not to acquaint Sir Joseph with it till the day is over. You understand Sir Joseph, and will give me your opinion. The most frightful and deplorable event!'

'Fish!' returned the Alderman. 'Fish! My good fellow, what is the matter? Nothing revolutionary, I hope! No—no attempted interference with the magistrates?'

'Deedles, the banker,' gasped the Secretary. 'Deedles Brothers— who was to have been here to-day—high in office in the Goldsmiths' Company—'

'Not stopped!' exclaimed the Alderman. 'It can't be!'

'Shot himself.'

'Good God!'

'Put a double-barrelled pistol to his mouth, in his own counting house,' said Mr. Fish, 'and blew his brains out. No motive. Princely circumstances!'

'Circumstances!' exclaimed the Alderman. 'A man of noble fortune. One of the most respectable of men. Suicide, Mr. Fish! By his own hand!'

'This very morning,' returned Mr. Fish.

'Oh the brain, the brain!' exclaimed the pious Alderman, lifting up his hands. 'Oh the nerves, the nerves; the mysteries of this machine called Man! Oh the little that unhinges it: poor creatures that we are! Perhaps a dinner, Mr. Fish. Perhaps the conduct of his son, who, I have heard, ran very wild, and was in the habit of drawing bills upon him without the least authority! A most respectable man. One of the most respectable men I ever knew! A lamentable instance, Mr. Fish. A public calamity! I shall make a point of wearing the deepest mourning. A most respectable man! But there is One above. We must submit, Mr. Fish. We must submit!'

What, Alderman! No word of Putting Down? Remember, Justice,

your high moral boast and pride. Come, Alderman! Balance those scales. Throw me into this, the empty one, no dinner, and Nature's founts in some poor woman, dried by starving misery and rendered obdurate to claims for which her offspring *has* authority in holy mother Eve. Weigh me the two, you Daniel,* going to judgment, when your day shall come! Weigh them, in the eyes of suffering thousands, audience (not unmindful) of the grim farce you play. Or supposing that you strayed from your five wits—it's not so far to go, but that it might be—and laid hands upon that throat of yours, warning your fellows (if you have a fellow) how they croak their comfortable wickedness to raving heads and stricken hearts. What then?

The words rose up in Trotty's breast, as if they had been spoken by some other voice within him. Alderman Cute pledged himself to Mr. Fish that he would assist him in breaking the melancholy catastrophe to Sir Joseph when the day was over. Then, before they parted, wringing Mr. Fish's hand in bitterness of soul, he said, 'The most respectable of men!' And added that he hardly knew (not even he), why such afflictions were allowed on earth.

'It's almost enough to make one think, if one didn't know better,' said Alderman Cute, 'that at times some motion of a capsizing nature was going on in things, which affected the general economy of the social fabric. Deedles Brothers!'

The skittle-playing came off with immense success. Sir Joseph knocked the pins about quite skilfully; Master Bowley took an innings at a shorter distance also; and everybody said that now, when a Baronet and the Son of a Baronet played at skittles, the country was coming round again, as fast as it could come.

At its proper time, the Banquet was served up. Trotty involuntarily repaired to the Hall with the rest, for he felt himself conducted thither by some stronger impulse than his own free will. The sight was gay in the extreme; the ladies were very handsome; the visitors delighted, cheerful, and good-tempered. When the lower doors were opened, and the people flocked in, in their rustic dresses, the beauty of the spectacle was at its height; but Trotty only murmured more and more, 'Where is Richard? He should help and comfort her! I can't see Richard!'

There had been some speeches made; and Lady Bowley's health had been proposed; and Sir Joseph Bowley had returned thanks, and had made his great speech, showing by various pieces of evidence that he was the born Friend and Father, and so forth; and had given as a Toast, his Friends and Children, and the Dignity of Labour; when a slight disturbance at the bottom of the Hall attracted Toby's notice. After some confusion, noise, and opposition, one man broke through the rest, and stood forward by himself.

Not Richard. No. But one whom he had thought of, and had looked for, many times. In a scantier supply of light, he might have doubted the identity of that worn man, so old, and grey, and bent; but with a blaze of lamps upon his gnarled and knotted head, he knew Will Fern as soon as he stepped forth.

'What is this!' exclaimed Sir Joseph, rising. 'Who gave this man admittance? This is a criminal from prison! Mr. Fish, sir, *will* you have the goodness—'

'A minute!' said Will Fern. 'A minute! My Lady, you was born on this day along with a New Year. Get me a minute's leave to speak.'

She made some intercession for him. Sir Joseph took his seat again, with native dignity.

The ragged visitor—for he was miserably dressed—looked round upon the company, and made his homage to them with a humble bow.

'Gentlefolks!' he said. 'You've drunk the Labourer.* Look at me!'

'Just come from jail,' said Mr. Fish.

'Just come from jail,' said Will. 'And neither for the first time, nor the second, nor the third, nor yet the fourth.'

Mr. Filer was heard to remark testily, that four times was over the average; and he ought to be ashamed of himself.

'Gentlefolks!' repeated Will Fern. 'Look at me! You see I'm at the worst. Beyond all hurt or harm; beyond your help; for the time when your kind words or kind actions could have done ME good,'—he struck his hand upon his breast, and shook his head, 'is gone, with the scent of last year's beans or clover on the air. Let me say a word for these,' pointing to the labouring people in the Hall; 'and when you're met together, hear the real Truth spoke out for once.'

'There's not a man here,' said the host, 'who would have him for a spokesman.'

'Like enough, Sir Joseph. I believe it. Not the less true, perhaps, is what I say. Perhaps that's a proof on it. Gentlefolks, I've lived many a year in this place. You may see the cottage from the sunk fence over yonder. I've seen the ladies draw it in their books, a hundred times. It looks well in a picter, I've heerd say; but there an't weather in picters, and may be 'tis fitter for that, than for a place to live in. Well! I lived there. How hard—how bitter hard, I lived there, I won't say. Any day in the year, and every day, you can judge for your own selves.'

He spoke as he had spoken on the night when Trotty found him in the street. His voice was deeper and more husky, and had a trembling in it now and then; but he never raised it passionately, and seldom lifted it above the firm stern level of the homely facts he stated.

' 'Tis harder than you think for, gentlefolks, to grow up decent, commonly decent, in such a place. That I growed up a man and not a brute, says something for me—as I was then. As I am now, there's nothing can be said for me or done for me. I'm past it.'

'I am glad this man has entered,' observed Sir Joseph, looking round serenely. 'Don't disturb him. It appears to be Ordained. He is an example: a living example. I hope and trust, and confidently expect, that it will not be lost upon my Friends here.'

'I dragged on,' said Fern, after a moment's silence, 'somehow. Neither me nor any other man knows how; but so heavy, that I couldn't put a cheerful face upon it, or make believe that I was anything but what I was. Now, gentlemen—you gentlemen that sits at Sessions—when you see a man with discontent writ on his face, you says to one another, "He's suspicious. I has my doubts," says you, "about Will Fern. Watch that fellow!" I don't say, gentlemen, it ain't quite nat'ral, but I say 'tis so; and from that hour, whatever Will Fern does, or lets alone—all one—it goes against him.'

Alderman Cute stuck his thumbs in his waistcoat-pockets, and leaning back in his chair, and smiling, winked at a neighbouring chandelier. As much as to say, 'Of course! I told you so. The common cry! Lord bless you, we are up to all this sort of thing—myself and human nature.'

'Now, gentlemen,' said Will Fern, holding out his hands, and flushing for an instant in his haggard face, 'see how your laws are made to trap and hunt us when we're brought to this. I tries to live elsewhere. And I'm a vagabond. To jail with him! I comes back here. I goes a-nutting in your woods, and breaks—who don't?—a limber branch or two. To jail with him! One of your keepers sees me in the broad day, near my own patch of garden, with a gun. To jail with him! I has a nat'ral angry word with that man, when I'm free again.

To jail with him! I cuts a stick. To jail with him! I eats a rotten apple or a turnip. To jail with him! It's twenty mile away; and coming back I begs a trifle on the road. To jail with him! At last, the constable, the keeper—anybody—finds me anywhere, a-doing anything. To jail with him, for he's a vagrant, and a jail-bird known; and jail's the only home he's got.'

The Alderman nodded sagaciously, as who should say, 'A very good home too.'

'Do I say this to serve MY cause!' cried Fern. 'Who can give me back my liberty, who can give me back my good name, who can give me back my innocent niece? Not all the Lords and Ladies in wide England. But, gentlemen, gentlemen, dealing with other men like me, begin at the right end. Give us, in mercy, better homes when we're a-lying in our cradles; give us better food when we're a-working for our lives; give us kinder laws to bring us back when we're a-going wrong; and don't set. Jail, Jail, Jail, afore us, everywhere we turn. There an't a condescension you can show the Labourer then, that he won't take, as ready and as grateful as a man can be; for he has a patient, peaceful, willing heart. But you must put his rightful spirit in him first; for whether he's a wreck and ruin such as me, or is like one of them that stand here now, his spirit is divided from you at this time. Bring it back, gentlefolks, bring it back! Bring it back, afore the day comes when even his Bible changes in his altered mind, and the words seem to him to read, as they have sometimes read in my own eyes—in Jail: "Whither thou goest, I can Not go; where thou lodgest, I do Not lodge; thy people are Not my people; Nor thy God my God!" '*

A sudden stir and agitation took place in the Hall. Trotty thought at first, that several had risen to eject the man; and hence this change in its appearance. But another moment showed him that the room and all the company had vanished from his sight, and that his daughter was again before him, seated at her work. But in a poorer, meaner garret than before; and with no Lilian by her side.

The frame at which she had worked, was put away upon a shelf and covered up. The chair in which she had sat, was turned against the wall. A history was written in these little things, and in Meg's grief-worn face. Oh! who could fail to read it!

Meg strained her eyes upon her work until it was too dark to see the threads; and when the night closed in, she lighted her feeble

candle and worked on. Still her old father was invisible about her; looking down upon her; loving her—how dearly loving her!—and talking to her in a tender voice about the old times, and the Bells. Though he knew, poor Trotty, though he knew she could not hear him.

A great part of the evening had worn away, when a knock came at her door. She opened it. A man was on the threshold. A slouching, moody, drunken sloven, wasted by intemperance and vice, and with his matted hair and unshorn beard in wild disorder; but with some traces on him, too, of having been a man of good proportion and good features in his youth.

He stopped until he had her leave to enter; and she, retiring a pace or two from the open door, silently and sorrowfully looked upon him. Trotty had his wish. He saw Richard.

'May I come in, Margaret?'

'Yes! Come in. Come in!'

It was well that Trotty knew him before he spoke; for with any doubt remaining on his mind, the harsh discordant voice would have persuaded him that it was not Richard but some other man.

There were but two chairs in the room. She gave him hers, and stood at some short distance from him, waiting to hear what he had to say.

He sat, however, staring vacantly at the floor; with a lustreless and stupid smile. A spectacle of such deep degradation, of such abject hopelessness, of such a miserable downfall, that she put her hands before her face and turned away, lest he should see how much it moved her.

Roused by the rustling of her dress, or some such trifling sound, he lifted his head, and began to speak as if there had been no pause since he entered.

'Still at work, Margaret? You work late.'

'I generally do.'

'And early?'

'And early.'

'So she said. She said you never tired; or never owned that you tired. Not all the time you lived together. Not even when you fainted, between work and fasting. But I told you that, the last time I came.'

'You did,' she answered. 'And I implored you to tell me nothing more; and you made me a solemn promise, Richard, that you never would.'

'A solemn promise,' he repeated, with a drivelling laugh and vacant stare. 'A solemn promise. To be sure. A solemn promise!' Awakening, as it were, after a time; in the same manner as before; he said with sudden animation:

'How can I help it, Margaret? What am I to do? She has been to me again!'

'Again!' cried Meg, clasping her hands. 'O, does she think of me so often! Has she been again!'

'Twenty times again,' said Richard. 'Margaret, she haunts me. She comes behind me in the street, and thrusts it in my hand. I hear her foot upon the ashes when I'm at my work (ha, ha! that an't often), and before I can turn my head, her voice is in my ear, saying, "Richard, don't look round. For Heaven's love, give her this!" She brings it where I live; she sends it in letters; she taps at the window and lays it on the sill. What *can* I do? Look at it!'

He held out in his hand a little purse, and chinked the money it enclosed.

'Hide it,' said Meg. 'Hide it! When she comes again, tell her, Richard, that I love her in my soul. That I never lie down to sleep, but I bless her, and pray for her. That, in my solitary work, I never cease to have her in my thoughts. That she is with me, night and day. That if I died to-morrow, I would remember her with my last breath. But, that I cannot look upon it!'

He slowly recalled his hand, and crushing the purse together, said with a kind of drowsy thoughtfulness:

'I told her so. I told her so, as plain as words could speak. I've taken this gift back and left it at her door, a dozen times since then. But when she came at last, and stood before me, face to face, what could I do?'

'You saw her!' exclaimed Meg. 'You saw her! O, Lilian, my sweet girl! O, Lilian, Lilian!'

'I saw her,' he went on to say, not answering, but engaged in the same slow pursuit of his own thoughts. 'There she stood: trembling! "How does she look, Richard? Does she ever speak of me? Is she thinner? My old place at the table: what's in my old place? And the frame she taught me our old work on—has she burnt it, Richard?" There she was. I heard her say it.'

Meg checked her sobs, and with the tears streaming from her eyes, bent over him to listen. Not to lose a breath.

With his arms resting on his knees; and stooping forward in his chair, as if what he said were written on the ground in some half legible character, which it was his occupation to decipher and connect; he went on.

' "Richard, I have fallen very low; and you may guess how much I have suffered in having this sent back, when I can bear to bring it in my hand to you. But you loved her once, even in my memory, dearly. Others stepped in between you; fears, and jealousies, and doubts, and vanities, estranged you from her; but you did love her, even in my memory!" I suppose I did,' he said, interrupting himself for a moment. 'I did! That's neither here nor there. "O Richard, if you ever did; if you have any memory for what is gone and lost, take it to her once more. Once more! Tell her how I laid my head upon your shoulder, where her own head might have lain, and was so humble to you, Richard. Tell her that you looked into my face, and saw the beauty which she used to praise, all gone: all gone: and in its place, a poor, wan, hollow cheek, that she would weep to see. Tell her everything, and take it back, and she will not refuse again. She will not have the heart!" '

So he sat musing, and repeating the last words, until he woke again, and rose.

'You won't take it, Margaret?'

She shook her head, and motioned an entreaty to him to leave her.

'Good night, Margaret.'

'Good night!'

He turned to look upon her; struck by her sorrow, and perhaps by the pity for himself which trembled in her voice. It was a quick and rapid action; and for the moment some flash of his old bearing kindled in his form. In the next he went as he had come. Nor did this glimmer of a quenched fire seem to light him to a quicker sense of his debasement.

In any mood, in any grief, in any torture of the mind or body, Meg's work must be done. She sat down to her task, and plied it. Night, midnight. Still she worked.

She had a meagre fire, the night being very cold; and rose at intervals to mend it. The Chimes rang half-past twelve while she was thus engaged; and when they ceased she heard a gentle knocking at the door. Before she could so much as wonder who was there, at that unusual hour, it opened.

O Youth and Beauty, happy as ye should be, look at this. O Youth and Beauty, blest and blessing all within your reach, and working out the ends of your Beneficent Creator, look at this!

She saw the entering figure; screamed its name; cried 'Lilian!'

It was swift, and fell upon its knees before her: clinging to her dress.

'Up, dear! Up! Lilian! My own dearest!'

'Never more, Meg; never more! Here! Here! Close to you, holding to you, feeling your dear breath upon my face!'

'Sweet Lilian! Darling Lilian! Child of my heart—no mother's love can be more tender—lay your head upon my breast!'

'Never more, Meg. Never more! When I first looked into your face, you knelt before me. On my knees before you, let me die. Let it be here!'

'You have come back. My Treasure! We will live together, work together, hope together, die together!'

'Ah! Kiss my lips, Meg; fold your arms about me; press me to your bosom; look kindly on me; but don't raise me. Let it be here. Let me see the last of your dear face upon my knees!'

O Youth and Beauty, happy as ye should be, look at this! O Youth and Beauty, working out the ends of your Beneficent Creator, look at this!

'Forgive me, Meg! So dear, so dear! Forgive me! I know you do, I see you do, but say so, Meg!'

She said so, with her lips on Lilian's cheek. And with her arms twined round—she knew it now—a broken heart.

'His blessing on you, dearest love. Kiss me once more! He suffered her to sit beside His feet, and dry them with her hair.* O Meg, what Mercy and Compassion!'

As she died, the Spirit of the child returning, innocent and radiant, touched the old man with its hand, and beckoned him away.

FOURTH QUARTER

SOME new remembrance of the ghostly figures in the Bells; some faint impression of the ringing of the Chimes; some giddy consciousness of having seen the swarm of phantoms reproduced and reproduced until the recollection of them lost itself in the confusion of their numbers; some hurried knowledge, how conveyed to him he knew not, that more years had passed; and Trotty, with the Spirit of the child attending him, stood looking on at mortal company.

Fat company, rosy-cheeked company, comfortable company. They were but two, but they were red enough for ten. They sat before a bright fire, with a small low table between them; and unless the fragrance of hot tea and muffins lingered longer in that room than in most others, the table had seen service very lately. But all the cups and saucers being clean, and in their proper places in the corner-cupboard; and the brass toasting-fork hanging in its usual nook and spreading its four idle fingers out as if it wanted to be measured for a glove; there remained no other visible tokens of the meal just finished, than such as purred and washed their whiskers in the person of the basking cat, and glistened in the gracious, not to say the greasy, faces of her patrons.

This cosy couple (married, evidently) had made a fair division of the fire between them, and sat looking at the glowing sparks that dropped into the grate; now nodding off into a doze; now waking up again when some hot fragment, larger than the rest, came rattling down, as if the fire were coming with it.

It was in no danger of sudden extinction, however; for it gleamed not only in the little room, and on the panes of window-glass in the door, and on the curtain half drawn across them, but in the little shop beyond. A little shop, quite crammed and choked with the abundance of its stock; a perfectly voracious little shop, with a maw as accommodating and full as any shark's. Cheese, butter, firewood, soap, pickles, matches, bacon, table-beer, peg-tops, sweetmeats, boys' kites, bird-seed, cold ham, birch brooms, hearth-stones, salt, vinegar, blacking, red-herrings, stationery, lard, mushroom-ketchup, staylaces, loaves of bread, shuttle-cocks, eggs, and slate pencil; everything was fish that came to the net of this greedy little shop, and all articles were in its net. How many other kinds of petty merchandise were there, it would be difficult to say; but balls of packthread, ropes of onions, pounds of candles, cabbage-nets, and brushes, hung in bunches from the ceiling, like extraordinary fruit; while various odd canisters emitting aromatic smells, established the veracity of the inscription over the outer door, which informed the public that the keeper of this little shop was a licensed dealer in tea, coffee, tobacco, pepper, and snuff.

Glancing at such of these articles as were visible in the shining of the blaze, and the less cheerful radiance of two smoky lamps which burnt but dimly in the shop itself, as though its plethora sat heavy on their lungs; and glancing, then, at one of the two faces by the parlour-fire; Trotty had small difficulty in recognising in the stout old lady, Mrs. Chickenstalker: always inclined to corpulency, even in the days when he had known her as established in the general line, and having a small balance against him in her books.

The features of her companion were less easy to him. The great broad chin, with creases in it large enough to hide a finger in; the astonished eyes, that seemed to expostulate with themselves for sinking deeper and deeper into the yielding fat of the soft face; the nose afflicted with that disordered action of its functions which is generally termed The Snuffles; the short thick throat and labouring chest, with other beauties of the like description; though calculated to impress the memory, Trotty could at first allot to nobody he had ever known: and yet he had some recollection of them too. At length, in Mrs. Chickenstalker's partner in the general line, and in the crooked and eccentric line of life, he recognised the former porter of Sir Joseph Bowley; an apoplectic innocent, who had connected himself in Trotty's mind with Mrs. Chickenstalker years ago, by giving him admission to the mansion where he had confessed his obligations to that lady, and drawn on his unlucky head such grave reproach.

Trotty had little interest in a change like this, after the changes he had seen; but association is very strong sometimes; and he looked involuntarily behind the parlour-door, where the accounts of credit customers were usually kept in chalk. There was no record of his name. Some names were there, but they were strange to him, and infinitely fewer than of old; from which he argued that the porter was an advocate of ready money transactions, and on coming into the business had looked pretty sharp after the Chickenstalker defaulters.

So desolate was Trotty, and so mournful for the youth and promise of his blighted child, that it was a sorrow to him, even to have no place in Mrs. Chickenstalker's ledger.

'What sort of a night is it, Anne?' inquired the former porter of Sir Joseph Bowley, stretching out his legs before the fire, and rubbing as much of them as his short arms could reach; with an air that added, 'Here I am if it's bad, and I don't want to go out if it's good.'

'Blowing and sleeting hard,' returned his wife; 'and threatening snow. Dark. And very cold.'

'I'm glad to think we had muffins,' said the former porter, in the tone of one who had set his conscience at rest. 'It's a sort of night that's meant for muffins. Likewise crumpets. Also Sally Lunns.'*

The former porter mentioned each successive kind of eatable, as if he were musingly summing up his good actions. After which he rubbed his fat legs as before, and jerking them at the knees to get the fire upon the yet unroasted parts, laughed as if somebody had tickled him.

'You're in spirits, Tugby, my dear,' observed his wife.

The firm was Tugby, late Chickenstalker.

'No,' said Tugby. 'No. Not particular. I'm a little elewated. The muffins came so pat!'

With that he chuckled until he was black in the face; and had so much ado to become any other colour, that his fat legs took the strangest excursions into the air. Nor were they reduced to anything like decorum until Mrs. Tugby had thumped him violently on the back, and shaken him as if he were a great bottle.

'Good gracious, goodness, lord-a-mercy bless and save the man!' cried Mrs. Tugby, in great terror. 'What's he doing?'

Mr. Tugby wiped his eyes, and faintly repeated that he found himself a little elewated.

'Then don't be so again, that's a dear good soul,' said Mrs. Tugby, 'if you don't want to frighten me to death, with your struggling and fighting!'

Mr. Tugby said he wouldn't; but his whole existence was a fight, in which, if any judgment might be founded on the constantly-increasing shortness of his breath, and the deepening purple of his face, he was always getting the worst of it.

'So it's blowing, and sleeting, and threatening snow; and it's dark, and very cold, is it, my dear?' said Mr. Tugby, looking at the fire, and reverting to the cream and marrow* of his temporary elevation.

'Hard weather indeed,' returned his wife, shaking her head.

'Aye, aye! Years', said Mr. Tugby, 'are like Christians in that respect. Some of 'em die hard; some of 'em die easy. This one hasn't many days to run, and is making a fight for it. I like him all the better. There's a customer, my love!'

Attentive to the rattling door, Mrs. Tugby had already risen.

'Now then!' said that lady, passing out into the little shop. 'What's wanted? Oh! I beg your pardon, sir, I'm sure. I didn't think it was you.'

She made this apology to a gentleman in black, who, with his wristbands tucked up, and his hat cocked loungingly on one side, and his hands in his pockets, sat down astride on the table-beer barrel, and nodded in return.

'This is a bad business up-stairs, Mrs. Tugby,' said the gentleman. 'The man can't live.'

'Not the back-attic can't!' cried Tugby, coming out into the shop to join the conference.

'The back-attic, Mr. Tugby,' said the gentleman, 'is coming down-stairs fast, and will be below the basement very soon.'

Looking by turns at Tugby and his wife, he sounded the barrel with his knuckles for the depth of beer, and having found it, played a tune upon the empty part.

'The back-attic, Mr. Tugby,' said the gentleman: Tugby having stood in silent consternation for some time: 'is Going.'

'Then,' said Tugby, turning to his wife, 'he must Go, you know, before he's Gone.'

'I don't think you can move him,' said the gentleman, shaking his head. 'I wouldn't take the responsibility of saying it could be done, myself. You had better leave him where he is. He can't live long.'

'It's the only subject', said Tugby, bringing the butter-scale down upon the counter with a crash, by weighing his fist on it, 'that we've ever had a word upon; she and me; and look what it comes to! He's going to die here, after all. Going to die upon the premises. Going to die in our house!'

'And where should he have died, Tugby?' cried his wife.

'In the workhouse,' he returned. 'What are workhouses made for?'

'Not for that,' said Mrs. Tugby, with great energy. 'Not for that! Neither did I marry you for that. Don't think it, Tugby. I won't have it. I won't allow it. I'd be separated first, and never see your face again. When my widow's name stood over that door, as it did for many years: this house being known as Mrs. Chickenstalker's far and wide, and never known but to its honest credit and its good report: when my widow's name stood over that door, Tugby, I knew him as a handsome, steady, manly, independent youth; I knew her as the sweetest-looking, sweetest-tempered girl, eyes ever saw; I knew her father (poor old creetur, he fell down from the steeple walking in his sleep, and killed himself), for the simplest, hardest-working, childest-hearted man, that ever drew the breath of life; and when I turn them out of house and home, may angels turn me out of Heaven. As they would! And serve me right!'

Her old face, which had been a plump and dimpled one before the changes which had come to pass, seemed to shine out of her as she said these words; and when she dried her eyes, and shook her head and her handkerchief at Tugby, with an expression of firmness which it was quite clear was not to be easily resisted, Trotty said, 'Bless her! Bless her!'

Then he listened, with a panting heart, for what should follow. Knowing nothing yet, but that they spoke of Meg.

If Tugby had been a little elevated in the parlour, he more than balanced that account by being not a little depressed in the shop, where he now stood staring at his wife, without attempting a reply; secretly conveying, however—either in a fit of abstraction or as a precautionary measure—all the money from the till into his own pockets, as he looked at her.

The gentleman upon the table-beer cask, who appeared to be some authorised medical attendant upon the poor, was far too well accustomed, evidently, to little differences of opinion between man and wife, to interpose any remark in this instance. He sat softly whistling, and turning little drops of beer out of the tap upon the ground, until there was a perfect calm: when he raised his head, and said to Mrs. Tugby, late Chickenstalker:

'There's something interesting about the woman, even now. How did she come to marry him?'

'Why that', said Mrs. Tugby, taking a seat near him, 'is not the least cruel part of her story, sir. You see they kept company, she and Richard, many years ago. When they were a young and beautiful couple, everything was settled, and they were to have been married on a New Year's Day. But, somehow, Richard got it into his head, through what the gentlemen told him, that he might do better, and that he'd soon repent it, and that she wasn't good enough for him, and that a young man of spirit had no business to be married. And the gentlemen frightened her, and made her melancholy, and timid of his deserting her, and of her children coming to the gallows, and of its being wicked to be man and wife, and a good deal more of it.

And in short, they lingered and lingered, and their trust in one another was broken, and so at last was the match. But the fault was his. She would have married him, sir, joyfully. I've seen her heart swell, many times afterwards, when he passed her in a proud and careless way; and never did a woman grieve more truly for a man, than she for Richard when he first went wrong.'

'Oh! he went wrong, did he?' said the gentleman, pulling out the vent-peg of the table-beer, and trying to peep down into the barrel through the hole.

'Well, sir, I don't know that he rightly understood himself, you see. I think his mind was troubled by their having broke with one another; and that but for being ashamed before the gentlemen, and perhaps for being uncertain too, how she might take it, he'd have gone through any suffering or trial to have had Meg's promise and Meg's hand again. That's my belief. He never said so; more's the pity! He took to drinking, idling, bad companions: all the fine resources that were to be so much better for him than the Home he might have had. He lost his looks, his character, his health, his strength, his friends, his work: everything!'

'He didn't lose everything, Mrs. Tugby,' returned the gentleman, 'because he gained a wife; and I want to know how he gained her.'

'I'm coming to it, sir, in a moment. This went on for years and years; he sinking lower and lower; she enduring, poor thing, miseries enough to wear her life away. At last, he was so cast down, and cast out, that no one would employ or notice him; and doors were shut upon him, go where he would. Applying from place to place, and door to door; and coming for the hundredth time to one gentleman who had often and often tried him (he was a good workman to the very end); that gentleman, who knew his history, said, "I believe you are incorrigible; there is only one person in the world who has a chance of reclaiming you; ask me to trust you no more, until she tries to do it." Something like that, in his anger and vexation.'

'Ah!' said the gentleman. 'Well?'

'Well, sir, he went to her, and kneeled to her; said it was so; said it ever had been so; and made a prayer to her to save him.'

'And she?—Don't distress yourself, Mrs. Tugby.'

'She came to me that night to ask me about living here. "What he was once to me." she said, "is buried in a grave, side by side with what I was to him. But I have thought of this; and I will make the

trial. In the hope of saving him; for the love of the light-hearted girl
(you remember her) who was to have been married on a New Year's
Day; and for the love of her Richard.' And she said he had come to
her from Lilian, and Lilian had trusted to him, and she never could
forget that. So they were married; and when they came home here,
and I saw them, I hoped that such prophecies as parted them when
they were young, may not often fulfil themselves as they did in this
case, or I wouldn't be the makers of them for a Mine of Gold.'

The gentleman got off the cask, and stretched himself, observing:

'I suppose he used her ill, as soon as they were married?'

'I don't think he ever did that,' said Mrs. Tugby, shaking her head,
and wiping her eyes. 'He went on better for a short time; but, his
habits were too old and strong to be got rid of; he soon fell back a
little; and was falling fast back, when his illness came so strong upon
him. I think he has always felt for her. I am sure he has. I have seen
him, in his crying fits and tremblings, try to kiss her hand; and I have
heard him call her "Meg," and say it was her nineteenth birthday.
There he has been lying, now, these weeks and months. Between him
and her baby, she has not been able to do her old work; and by not
being able to be regular, she has lost it, even if she could have done it.
How they have lived, I hardly know!'

'*I* know,' muttered Mr. Tugby; looking at the till, and round the
shop, and at his wife; and rolling his head with immense intelligence.
'Like Fighting Cocks!'*

He was interrupted by a cry—a sound of lamentation—from the
upper story of the house. The gentleman moved hurriedly to the door.

'My friend,' he said, looking back, 'you needn't discuss whether
he shall be removed or not. He has spared you that trouble, I believe.'

Saying so, he ran up-stairs, followed by Mrs. Tugby; while
Mr. Tugby panted and grumbled after them at leisure: being rendered more than commonly short-winded by the weight of the till, in
which there had been an inconvenient quantity of copper. Trotty,
with the child beside him, floated up the staircase like mere air.

'Follow her! Follow her! Follow her!' He heard the ghostly voices
in the Bells repeat their words as he ascended. 'Learn it from the
creature dearest to your heart!'

It was over. It was over. And this was she, her father's pride and
joy! This haggard, wretched woman, weeping by the bed, if it
deserved that name, and pressing to her breast, and hanging down

her head upon, an infant. Who can tell how spare, how sickly, and how poor an infant! Who can tell how dear!

'Thank God!' cried Trotty, holding up his folded hands. 'O, God be thanked! She loves her child!'

The gentleman, not otherwise hard-hearted or indifferent to such scenes, than that he saw them every day, and knew that they were figures of no moment in the Filer sums—mere scratches in the working of these calculations—laid his hand upon the heart that beat no more, and listened for the breath, and said, 'His pain is over. It's better as it is!' Mrs. Tugby tried to comfort her with kindness. Mr. Tugby tried philosophy.

'Come, come!' he said, with his hands in his pockets, 'you mustn't give way, you know. That won't do. You must fight up. What would have become of me if *I* had given way when I was porter, and we had as many as six runaway carriage-doubles* at our door in one night! But I fell back upon my strength of mind, and didn't open it!'

Again Trotty heard the voices, saying, 'Follow her!' He turned towards his guide, and saw it rising from him, passing through the air. 'Follow her!' it said. And vanished.

He hovered round her; sat down at her feet; looked up into her face for one trace of her old self; listened for one note of her old pleasant voice. He flitted round the child: so wan, so prematurely old, so dreadful in its gravity, so plaintive in its feeble, mournful, miserable wail. He almost worshipped it. He clung to it as her only safeguard; as the last unbroken link that bound her to endurance. He set his father's hope and trust on the frail baby; watched her every look upon it as she held it in her arms; and cried a thousand times, 'She loves it! God be thanked, she loves it!'

He saw the woman tend her in the night; return to her when her grudging husband was asleep, and all was still; encourage her, shed tears with her, set nourishment before her. He saw the day come, and the night again; the day, the night; the time go by; the house of death relieved of death; the room left to herself and to the child; he heard it moan and cry; he saw it harass her, and tire her out, and when she slumbered in exhaustion, drag her back to consciousness, and hold her with its little hands upon the rack; but she was constant to it, gentle with it, patient with it. Patient! Was its loving mother in her inmost heart and soul, and had its Being knitted up with hers as when she carried it unborn.

All this time, she was in want: languishing away, in dire and pining want. With the baby in her arms, she wandered here and there, in quest of occupation; and with its thin face lying in her lap, and looking up in hers, did any work for any wretched sum; a day and night of labour for as many farthings as there were figures on the dial. If she had quarrelled with it; if she had neglected it; if she had looked upon it with a moment's hate; if, in the frenzy of an instant, she had struck it! No. His comfort was, She loved it always.

She told no one of her extremity, and wandered abroad in the day lest she should be questioned by her only friend: for any help she received from her hands, occasioned fresh disputes between the good woman and her husband; and it was new bitterness to be the daily cause of strife and discord, where she owed so much.

She loved it still. She loved it more and more. But a change fell on the aspect of her love. One night.

She was singing faintly to it in its sleep, and walking to and fro to hush it, when her door was softly opened, and a man looked in.

'For the last time,' he said.

'William Fern!'

'For the last time.'

He listened like a man pursued: and spoke in whispers.

'Margaret, my race is nearly run. I couldn't finish it, without a parting word with you. Without one grateful word.'

'What have you done?' she asked: regarding him with terror.

He looked at her, but gave no answer.

After a short silence, he made a gesture with his hand, as if he set her question by; as if he brushed it aside; and said:

'It's long ago, Margaret, now: but that night is as fresh in my memory as ever 'twas. We little thought, then,' he added, looking round, 'that we should ever meet like this. Your child, Margaret? Let me have it in my arms. Let me hold your child.'

He put his hat upon the floor, and took it. And he trembled as he took it, from head to foot.

'Is it a girl?'

'Yes.'

He put his hand before its little face.

'See how weak I'm grown, Margaret, when I want the courage to look at it! Let her be, a moment. I won't hurt her. It's long ago, but—What's her name?'

'Margaret,' she answered, quickly.

'I'm glad of that,' he said. 'I'm glad of that!'

He seemed to breathe more freely; and after pausing for an instant, took away his hand, and looked upon the infant's face. But covered it again, immediately.

'Margaret!' he said; and gave her back the child. 'It's Lilian's.'

'Lilian's!'

'I held the same face in my arms when Lilian's mother died and left her.'

'When Lilian's mother died and left her!' she repeated, wildly.

'How shrill you speak! Why do you fix your eyes upon me so? Margaret!'

She sunk down in a chair, and pressed the infant to her breast, and wept over it. Sometimes, she released it from her embrace, to look anxiously in its face: then strained it to her bosom again. At those times, when she gazed upon it, then it was that something fierce and terrible began to mingle with her love. Then it was that her old father quailed.

'Follow her!' was sounded through the house. 'Learn it, from the creature dearest to your heart!'

'Margaret,' said Fern, bending over her, and kissing her upon the brow: 'I thank you for the last time. Good night. Good bye! Put your hand in mine, and tell me you'll forget me from this hour, and try to think the end of me was here.'

'What have you done?' she asked again.

'There'll be a Fire to-night,'* he said, removing from her. 'There'll be Fires this winter-time, to light the dark nights, East, West, North, and South. When you see the distant sky red, they'll be blazing. When you see the distant sky red, think of me no more; or, if you do, remember what a Hell was lighted up inside of me, and think you see its flames reflected in the clouds. Good night. Good bye!'

She called to him; but he was gone. She sat down stupefied, until her infant roused her to a sense of hunger, cold, and darkness. She paced the room with it the live-long night, hushing it and soothing it. She said at intervals, 'Like Lilian, when her mother died and left her!' Why was her step so quick, her eye so wild, her love so fierce and terrible, whenever she repeated those words?

'But it is Love,' said Trotty. 'It is Love. She'll never cease to love it. My poor Meg.'

She dressed the child next morning with unusual care—ah, vain expenditure of care upon such squalid robes!—and once more tried to find some means of life. It was the last day of the Old Year. She tried till night and never broke her fast. She tried in vain.

She mingled with an abject crowd, who tarried in the snow, until it pleased some officer appointed to dispense the public charity (the lawful charity; not that once preached upon a Mount),* to call them in, and question them, and say to this one, 'Go to such a place,' to that one, 'Come next week'; to make a football of another wretch, and pass him here and there, from hand to hand, from house to house, until he wearied and lay down to die;* or started up and robbed, and so became a higher sort of criminal, whose claims allowed of no delay. Here, too, she failed.

She loved her child, and wished to have it lying on her breast. And that was quite enough.

It was night: a bleak, dark, cutting night: when, pressing the child close to her for warmth, she arrived outside the house she called her home. She was so faint and giddy, that she saw no one standing in the doorway until she was close upon it, and about to enter. Then she recognised the master of the house, who had so disposed himself— with his person it was not difficult—as to fill up the whole entry.

'O!' he said softly. 'You have come back?'

She looked at the child, and shook her head.

'Don't you think you have lived here long enough without paying any rent? Don't you think that, without any money, you've been a pretty constant customer at this shop, now?' said Mr. Tugby.

She repeated the same mute appeal.

'Suppose you try and deal somewhere else,' he said. 'And suppose you provide yourself with another lodging. Come! Don't you think you could manage it?'

She said in a low voice, that it was very late. To-morrow.

'Now I see what you want,' said Tugby; 'and what you mean. You know there are two parties in this house about you, and you delight in setting 'em by the ears. I don't want any quarrels; I'm speaking softly to avoid a quarrel; but if you don't go away, I'll speak out loud, and you shall cause words high enough to please you. But you shan't come in. That I am determined.'

She put her hair back with her hand, and looked in a sudden manner at the sky, and the dark lowering distance.

'This is the last night of an Old Year, and I won't carry ill-blood and quarrellings and disturbances into a New One, to please you nor anybody else,' said Tugby, who was quite a retail Friend and Father. 'I wonder you an't ashamed of yourself, to carry such practices into a New Year. If you haven't any business in the world, but to be always giving way, and always making disturbances between man and wife, you'd be better out of it. Go along with you.'

'Follow her! To desperation!'

Again the old man heard the voices. Looking up, he saw the figures hovering in the air, and pointing where she went, down the dark street.

'She loves it!' he exclaimed, in agonised entreaty for her. 'Chimes! she loves it still!'

'Follow her!' The shadows swept upon the track she had taken, like a cloud.

He joined in the pursuit; he kept close to her; he looked into her face. He saw the same fierce and terrible expression mingling with her love, and kindling in her eyes. He heard her say, 'Like Lilian! To be changed like Lilian!' and her speed redoubled.

O, for something to awaken her! For any sight, or sound, or scent, to call up tender recollections in a brain on fire! For any gentle image of the Past to rise before her!

'I was her father! I was her father!' cried the old man, stretching out his hands to the dark shadows flying on above. 'Have mercy on her, and on me! Where does she go? Turn her back! I was her father!'

But they only pointed to her, as she hurried on; and said, 'To desperation! Learn it from the creature dearest to your heart!'

A hundred voices echoed it. The air was made of breath expended in those words. He seemed to take them in, at every gasp he drew. They were everywhere, and not to be escaped. And still she hurried on; the same light in her eyes, the same words in her mouth, 'Like Lilian! To be changed like Lilian!'

All at once she stopped.

'Now turn her back!' exclaimed the old man, tearing his white hair. 'My child! Meg! Turn her back! Great Father, turn her back!'

In her own scanty shawl, she wrapped the baby warm. With her fevered hands she smoothed its limbs, composed its face, arranged its mean attire. In her wasted arms she folded it, as though she never would resign it more. And with her dry lips, kissed it in a final pang, and last long agony of Love.

Putting its tiny hand up to her neck, and holding it there, within her dress, next to her distracted heart, she set its sleeping face against her: closely, steadily, against her: and sped onward to the River.

To the rolling River, swift and dim, where Winter Night sat brooding like the last dark thoughts of many who had sought a refuge there before her. Where scattered lights upon the banks gleamed sullen, red, and dull, as torches that were burning there, to show the way to Death. Where no abode of living people cast its shadow on the deep, impenetrable, melancholy shade.

To the River! To that portal of Eternity, her desperate footsteps tended with the swiftness of its rapid waters running to the sea. He tried to touch her as she passed him, going down to its dark level: but the wild distempered form, the fierce and terrible love, the desperation that had left all human check or hold behind, swept by him like the wind.

He followed her. She paused a moment on the brink, before the dreadful plunge. He fell down on his knees, and in a shriek addressed the figures in the Bells now hovering above them.

'I have learnt it!' cried the old man. 'From the creature dearest to my heart! O, save her, save her!'

He could wind his fingers in her dress; could hold it! As the words escaped his lips, he felt his sense of touch return, and knew that he detained her.

The figures looked down steadfastly upon him.

'I have learnt it!' cried the old man. 'O, have mercy on me in this hour, if, in my love for her, so young and good, I slandered Nature in the breasts of mothers rendered desperate! Pity my presumption, wickedness, and ignorance, and save her.'

He felt his hold relaxing. They were silent still.

'Have mercy on her!' he exclaimed, 'as one in whom this dreadful crime has sprung from Love perverted; from the strongest, deepest Love we fallen creatures know! Think what her misery must have been, when such seed bears such fruit! Heaven meant her to be good. There is no loving mother on the earth who might not come to this, if such a life had gone before. O, have mercy on my child, who, even at this pass, means mercy to her own, and dies herself, and perils her immortal soul, to save it!'

She was in his arms. He held her now. His strength was like a giant's.

'I see the Spirit of the Chimes among you!' cried the old man, singling out the child, and speaking in some inspiration, which their looks conveyed to him. 'I know that our inheritance is held in store for us by Time. I know there is a sea of Time to rise one day, before which all who wrong us or oppress us will be swept away like leaves. I see it, on the flow! I know that we must trust and hope, and neither doubt ourselves, nor doubt the good in one another. I have learnt it from the creature dearest to my heart. I clasp her in my arms again. O Spirits, merciful and good, I take your lesson to my breast along with her! O Spirits, merciful and good, I am grateful!'

He might have said more; but the Bells, the old familiar Bells, his own dear, constant, steady friends, the Chimes, began to ring the joy-peals for a New Year: so lustily, so merrily, so happily, so gaily, that he leapt upon his feet, and broke the spell that bound him.

'And whatever you do, father,' said Meg, 'don't eat tripe again, without asking some doctor whether it's likely to agree with you; for how you *have* been going on, Good gracious!'

She was working with her needle, at the little table by the fire; dressing her simple gown with ribbons for her wedding. So quietly happy, so blooming and youthful, so full of beautiful promise, that he uttered a great cry as if it were an Angel in his house; then flew to clasp her in his arms.

But he caught his feet in the newspaper, which had fallen on the hearth; and somebody came rushing in between them.

'No!' cried the voice of this same somebody; a generous and jolly voice it was! 'Not even you. Not even you. The first kiss of Meg in the New Year is mine. Mine! I have been waiting outside the house, this hour, to hear the Bells and claim it. Meg, my precious prize, a happy year! A life of happy years, my darling wife!'

And Richard smothered her with kisses.

You never in all your life saw anything like Trotty after this. I don't care where you have lived or what you have seen; you never in all your life saw anything at all approaching him! He sat down in his chair and beat his knees and cried; he sat down in his chair and beat his knees and laughed; he sat down in his chair and beat his knees and laughed and cried together; he got out of his chair and hugged Meg; he got out of his chair and hugged Richard; he got out of his chair and hugged them both at once; he kept running up to Meg, and squeezing her fresh face between his hands and kissing it, going from her backwards not to lose sight of it, and running up again like a figure in a magic lantern; and whatever he did, he was constantly sitting himself down in his chair, and never stopping in it for one single moment; being—that's the truth—beside himself with joy.

'And to-morrow's your wedding-day, my pet!' cried Trotty. 'Your real, happy wedding-day!'

'To-day!' cried Richard, shaking hands with him. 'To-day. The Chimes are ringing in the New Year. Hear them!'

They WERE ringing! Bless their sturdy hearts, they WERE ringing! Great Bells as they were; melodious, deep-mouthed, noble Bells; cast in no common metal; made by no common founder; when had they ever chimed like that, before!

'But to-day, my pet,' said Trotty. 'You and Richard had some words to-day.'

'Because he's such a bad fellow, father,' said Meg. 'An't you, Richard? Such a headstrong, violent man! He'd have made no more of speaking his mind to that great Alderman, and putting *him* down I don't know where, than he would of——'

'—Kissing Meg,' suggested Richard. Doing it too!

'No. Not a bit more,' said Meg. 'But I wouldn't let him, father. Where would have been the use!'

'Richard, my boy!' cried Trotty. 'You was turned up Trumps originally; and Trumps you must be, till you die! But you were crying by the fire to-night, my pet, when I came home! Why did you cry by the fire?'

'I was thinking of the years we've passed together, father. Only that. And thinking that you might miss me, and be lonely.'

Trotty was backing off to that extraordinary chair again, when the child, who had been awakened by the noise, came running in half-dressed.

'Why, here she is!' cried Trotty, catching her up. 'Here's little Lilian! Ha ha ha! Here we are and here we go! O here we are and here we go again! And here we are and here we go! and Uncle Will too!' Stopping in his trot to greet him heartily. 'O, Uncle Will, the vision that I've had to-night, through lodging you! O, Uncle Will, the obligations that you've laid me under, by your coming, my good friend!'

Before Will Fern could make the least reply, a band of music burst into the room, attended by a lot of neighbours, screaming 'A Happy New Year, Meg!' 'A Happy Wedding!' 'Many of 'em!' and other fragmentary good wishes of that sort. The Drum (who was a private friend of Trotty's) then stepped forward, and said:

'Trotty Veck, my boy! It's got about, that your daughter is going to be married to-morrow. There an't a soul that knows you that don't wish you well, or that knows her and don't wish her well. Or that knows you both, and don't wish you both all the happiness the New Year can bring. And here we are, to play it in and dance it in, accordingly.'

Which was received with a general shout. The Drum was rather drunk, by-the-bye; but never mind.

'What a happiness it is, I'm sure,' said Trotty, 'to be so esteemed! How kind and neighbourly you are! It's all along of my dear daughter. She deserves it!'

They were ready for a dance in half a second (Meg and Richard at the top); and the Drum was on the very brink of leathering away with all his power; when a combination of prodigious sounds was heard outside, and a good-humoured comely woman of some fifty years of age, or thereabouts, came running in, attended by a man bearing a stone pitcher of terrific size, and closely followed by the marrow-bones and cleavers,* and the bells; not *the* Bells, but a portable collection on a frame.

Trotty said, 'It's Mrs. Chickenstalker!' And sat down and beat his knees again.

'Married, and not tell me, Meg!' cried the good woman. 'Never! I couldn't rest on the last night of the Old Year without coming to wish you joy. I couldn't have done it, Meg. Not if I had been bed-ridden. So here I am; and as it's New Year's Eve, and the Eve of your wedding too, my dear, I had a little flip* made, and brought it with me.'

Mrs. Chickenstalker's notion of a little flip, did honour to her character. The pitcher steamed and smoked and reeked like a volcano; and the man who had carried it, was faint.

'Mrs. Tugby!' said Trotty, who had been going round and round her, in an ecstasy.—'I *should* say, Chickenstalker—Bless your heart and soul! A happy New Year, and many of 'em! Mrs. Tugby,' said Trotty when he had saluted her;—'I *should* say, Chickenstalker— This is William Fern and Lilian.'

The worthy dame, to his surprise, turned very pale and very red.

'Not Lilian Fern whose mother died in Dorsetshire!'* said she.

Her uncle answered 'Yes,' and meeting hastily, they exchanged some hurried words together; of which the upshot was, that Mrs. Chickenstalker shook him by both hands; saluted Trotty on his cheek again of her own free will; and took the child to her capacious breast.

'Will Fern!' said Trotty, pulling on his right-hand muffler. 'Not the friend you was hoping to find?'

'Ay!' returned Will, putting a hand on each of Trotty's shoulders. 'And like to prove a'most as good a friend, if that can be, as one I found.'

'O!' said Trotty. 'Please to play up there. Will you have the goodness!'

To the music of the band, the bells, the marrow-bones and cleavers, all at once; and while the Chimes were yet in lusty operation out of doors; Trotty, making Meg and Richard second couple, led off Mrs. Chickenstalker down the dance, and danced it in a step unknown before or since; founded on his own peculiar trot.

Had Trotty dreamed? Or are his joys and sorrows, and the actors in them, but a dream; himself a dream; the teller of this tale a dreamer, waking but now? If it be so, O listener, dear to him in all his visions, try to bear in mind the stern realities from which these shadows come; and in your sphere—none is too wide, and none too limited for such an end—endeavour to correct, improve, and soften them. So may the New Year be a happy one to you, happy to many more whose happiness depends on you! So may each year be happier than the last, and not the meanest of our brethren or sisterhood debarred their rightful share, in what our Great Creator formed them to enjoy.

THE
CRICKET ON THE HEARTH
A Fairy Tale of Home

TO

LORD JEFFREY*

THIS LITTLE STORY IS INSCRIBED

WITH

THE AFFECTION AND ATTACHMENT

OF HIS FRIEND

THE AUTHOR

December, 1845.

CHIRP THE FIRST

THE kettle began it! Don't tell me what Mrs. Peerybingle said. I know better. Mrs. Peerybingle may leave it on record to the end of time that she couldn't say which of them began it; but, I say the kettle did. I ought to know, I hope! The kettle began it, full five minutes by the little waxy-faced Dutch clock in the corner, before the Cricket uttered a chirp.

As if the clock hadn't finished striking, and the convulsive little Haymaker* at the top of it, jerking away right and left with a scythe in front of a Moorish Palace, hadn't mowed down half an acre of imaginary grass before the Cricket joined in at all!

Why, I am not naturally positive. Every one knows that. I wouldn't set my own opinion against the opinion of Mrs. Peerybingle, unless I were quite sure, on any account whatever. Nothing should induce me. But, this is a question of fact. And the fact is, that the kettle began it, at least five minutes before the Cricket gave any sign of being in existence. Contradict me, and I'll say ten.

Let me narrate exactly how it happened. I should have proceeded to do so in my very first word, but for this plain consideration—if I am to tell a story I must begin at the beginning; and how is it possible to begin at the beginning, without beginning at the kettle?

It appeared as if there were a sort of match, or trial of skill, you must understand, between the kettle and the Cricket. And this is what led to it, and how it came about.

Mrs. Peerybingle, going out into the raw twilight, and clicking over the wet stones in a pair of pattens* that worked innumerable rough impressions of the first proposition in Euclid* all about the yard—Mrs. Peerybingle filled the kettle at the water-butt. Presently returning, less the pattens (and a good deal less, for they were tall and Mrs. Peerybingle was but short), she set the kettle on the fire. In doing which she lost her temper, or mislaid it for an instant; for, the water being uncomfortably cold, and in that slippy, slushy, sleety sort of state wherein it seems to penetrate through every kind of substance, patten rings included—had laid hold of Mrs. Peerybingle's toes, and even splashed her legs. And when we rather plume ourselves (with reason too) upon our legs, and keep ourselves particularly neat in point of stockings, we find this, for the moment, hard to bear.

Besides, the kettle was aggravating and obstinate. It wouldn't allow itself to be adjusted on the top bar; it wouldn't hear of accommodating itself kindly to the knobs of coal; it *would* lean forward with a drunken air, and dribble, a very Idiot of a kettle, on the hearth. It was quarrelsome, and hissed and spluttered morosely at the fire. To sum up all, the lid, resisting Mrs. Peerybingle's fingers, first of all turned topsy-turvy, and then, with an ingenious pertinacity deserving of a better cause, dived sideways in—down to the very bottom of the kettle. And the hull of the Royal George* has never made half the monstrous resistance to coming out of the water, which the lid of that kettle employed against Mrs. Peerybingle, before she got it up again.

It looked sullen and pig-headed enough, even then; carrying its handle with an air of defiance, and cocking its spout pertly and mockingly at Mrs. Peerybingle, as if it said, 'I won't boil. Nothing shall induce me!'

But Mrs. Peerybingle, with restored good humour, dusted her chubby little hands against each other, and sat down before the kettle, laughing. Meantime, the jolly blaze uprose and fell, flashing and gleaming on the little Haymaker at the top of the Dutch clock, until one might have thought he stood stock still before the Moorish Palace, and nothing was in motion but the flame.

He was on the move, however; and had his spasms, two to the second, all right and regular. But, his sufferings when the clock was going to strike, were frightful to behold; and when a Cuckoo looked out of a trapdoor in the Palace, and gave note six times, it shook him, each time, like a spectral voice—or like a something wiry, plucking at his legs.

It was not until a violent commotion and a whirring noise among the weights and ropes below him had quite subsided, that this terrified Haymaker became himself again. Nor was he startled without reason; for these rattling, bony skeletons of clocks are very disconcerting in their operation, and I wonder very much how any set of men, but most of all how Dutchmen, can have had a liking to invent them. There is a popular belief that Dutchmen love broad cases and much clothing for their own lower selves; and they might know better than to leave their clocks so very lank and unprotected, surely.

Now it was, you observe, that the kettle began to spend the evening. Now it was, that the kettle, growing mellow and musical, began to have irrepressible gurglings in its throat, and to indulge in short vocal snorts, which it checked in the bud, as if it hadn't quite made up its mind yet, to be good company. Now it was that after two or three such vain attempts to stifle its convivial sentiments, it threw off all moroseness, all reserve, and burst into a stream of song so cosy and hilarious, as never maudlin nightingale yet formed the least idea of.

So plain too! Bless you, you might have understood it like a book—better than some books you and I could name, perhaps. With its warm breath gushing forth in a light cloud which merrily and gracefully ascended a few feet, then hung about the chimney-corner as its own domestic Heaven, it trolled its song with that strong energy of cheerfulness, that its iron body hummed and stirred upon the fire; and the lid itself, the recently rebellious lid—such is the influence of a bright example —performed a sort of jig, and clattered like a deaf and dumb young cymbal that had never known the use of its twin brother.

That this song of the kettle's was a song of invitation and welcome to somebody out of doors: to somebody at that moment coming on, towards the snug small home and the crisp fire: there is no doubt whatever. Mrs. Peerybingle knew it, perfectly, as she sat musing before the hearth. It's a dark night, sang the kettle, and the rotten leaves are lying by the way; and, above, all is mist and darkness, and, below, all is mire and clay; and there's only one relief in all the sad and murky air; and I don't know that it is one, for it's nothing but a glare; of deep and angry crimson, where the sun and wind together; set a brand upon the clouds for being guilty of such weather; and the widest open country is a long dull streak of black; and there's hoar-frost on the finger-post, and thaw upon the track; and the ice it isn't water, and the water isn't free; and you couldn't say that anything is what it ought to be; but he's coming, coming, coming!——

And here, if you like, the Cricket DID chime in! with a Chirrup, Chirrup, Chirrup of such magnitude, by way of chorus; with a voice so astoundingly disproportionate to its size, as compared with the kettle; (size! you couldn't see it!) that if it had then and there burst itself like an over-charged gun, if it had fallen a victim on the spot, and chirruped its little body into fifty pieces, it would have seemed a natural and inevitable consequence, for which it had expressly laboured.

The kettle had had the last of its solo performance. It persevered with undiminished ardour; but the Cricket took first fiddle and kept it. Good Heaven, how it chirped! Its shrill, sharp, piercing voice resounded through the house, and seemed to twinkle in the outer darkness like a star. There was an indescribable little trill and tremble in it, at its loudest, which suggested its being carried off its legs, and made to leap again, by its own intense enthusiasm. Yet they went very well together, the Cricket and the kettle. The burden of the song was still the same; and louder, louder, louder still, they sang it in their emulation.

The fair little listener—for fair she was, and young: though something of what is called the dumpling shape; but I don't myself object to that—lighted a candle, glanced at the Haymaker on the top of the clock, who was getting in a pretty average crop of minutes; and looked out of the window, where she saw nothing, owing to the darkness, but her own face imaged in the glass. And my opinion is (and so would yours have been) that she might have looked a long way, and seen nothing half so agreeable. When she came back, and sat down in her former seat, the Cricket and the kettle were still keeping it up, with a perfect fury of competition. The kettle's weak side clearly being, that he didn't know when he was beat.

There was all the excitement of a race about it. Chirp, chirp, chirp! Cricket a mile ahead. Hum, hum, hum—m—m! Kettle making play in the distance, like a great top. Chirp, chirp, chirp! Cricket round the corner. Hum, hum, hum—m—m! Kettle sticking to him in his own way; no idea of giving in. Chirp, chirp, chirp! Cricket fresher than ever. Hum, hum, hum—m—m! Kettle slow and steady. Chirp, chirp, chirp! Cricket going in to finish him. Hum, hum, hum—m—m! Kettle not to be finished. Until at last they got so jumbled together, in the hurry-skurry, helter-skelter, of the match, that whether the kettle chirped and the Cricket hummed, or the Cricket chirped and the kettle hummed, or they both chirped and both hummed, it would have taken a clearer head than yours or mine to have decided with anything like certainty. But of this, there is no doubt: that the kettle and the Cricket, at one and the same moment, and by some power of amalgamation best known to themselves, sent, each, his fireside song of comfort streaming into a ray of the candle that shone out through the window, and a long way down the lane. And this light, bursting on a certain person who, on the instant, approached towards it through the gloom, expressed the whole thing to him, literally in a twinkling, and cried, 'Welcome home, old fellow! Welcome home, my boy!'

This end attained, the kettle, being dead beat, boiled over, and was taken off the fire. Mrs. Peerybingle then went running to the door, where, what with the wheels of a cart, the tramp of a horse, the voice of a man, the tearing in and out of an excited dog, and the surprising and mysterious appearance of a baby, there was soon the very What's-his-name to pay.

Where the baby came from, or how Mrs. Peerybingle got hold of it in that flash of time, *I* don't know. But a live baby there was in Mrs. Peerybingle's arms; and a pretty tolerable amount of pride she seemed to have in it, when she was drawn gently to the fire, by a sturdy figure of a man, much taller and much older than herself, who had to stoop a long way down, to kiss her. But she was worth the trouble. Six foot six, with the lumbago, might have done it.

'Oh goodness, John!' said Mrs. P. 'What a state you are in with the weather!'

He was something the worse for it, undeniably. The thick mist hung in clots upon his eyelashes like candied thaw; and between the fog and fire together, there were rainbows in his very whiskers.

'Why, you see, Dot,' John made answer, slowly, as he unrolled a shawl from about his throat; and warmed his hands; 'it—it an't exactly summer weather. So, no wonder.'

'I wish you wouldn't call me Dot, John. I don't like it,' said Mrs. Peerybingle: pouting in a way that clearly showed she *did* like it, very much.

'Why what else are you?' returned John, looking down upon her with a smile, and giving her waist as light a squeeze as his huge hand and arm could give. 'A dot and'—here he glanced at the baby—'a dot and carry*—I won't say it, for fear I should spoil it; but I was very near a joke. I don't know as ever I was nearer.'

He was often near to something or other very clever, by his own account: this lumbering, slow, honest John; this John so heavy, but so light of spirit; so rough upon the surface, but so gentle at the core; so dull without, so quick within; so stolid, but so good! Oh Mother Nature, give thy children the true poetry of heart that hid itself in this poor Carrier's breast—he was but a Carrier by the way—and we can bear to have them talking prose, and leading lives of prose; and bear to bless thee for their company!

It was pleasant to see Dot, with her little figure, and her baby in her arms: a very doll of a baby: glancing with a coquettish thoughtfulness at the fire, and inclining her delicate little head just enough on one side to let it rest in an odd, half-natural, half-affected, wholly nestling and agreeable manner, on the great rugged figure of the Carrier. It was pleasant to see him, with his tender awkwardness, endeavouring to adapt his rude support to her slight need, and make his burly middle-age a leaning-staff not inappropriate to her blooming youth. It was pleasant to observe how Tilly Slowboy, waiting in the background for the baby, took special cognizance (though in her earliest teens) of this grouping; and stood with her mouth and eyes wide open, and her head thrust forward, taking it in as if it were air. Nor was it less agreeable to observe how John the Carrier, reference being made by Dot to the aforesaid baby, checked his hand when on the point of touching the infant, as if he thought he might crack it; and bending down, surveyed it from a safe distance, with a kind of puzzled pride, such as an amiable mastiff might be supposed to show, if he found himself, one day, the father of a young canary.

'An't he beautiful, John? Don't he look precious in his sleep?'

'Very precious,' said John. 'Very much so. He generally *is* asleep, an't he?'

'Lor, John! Good gracious no!'

'Oh,' said John, pondering. 'I thought his eyes was generally shut. Halloa!'

'Goodness, John, how you startle one!'

'It an't right for him to turn 'em up in that way!' said the astonished Carrier, 'is it? See how he's winking with both of 'em at once! And look at his mouth! Why he's gasping like a gold and silver fish!'

'You don't deserve to be a father, you don't,' said Dot, with all the dignity of an experienced matron. 'But how should you know what little complaints children are troubled with, John! You wouldn't so much as know their names, you stupid fellow.' And when she had turned the baby over on her left arm, and had slapped its back as a restorative, she pinched her husband's ear, laughing.

'No,' said John, pulling off his outer coat. 'It's very true, Dot. I don't know much about it. I only know that I've been fighting pretty

stiffly with the wind to-night. It's been blowing north-east, straight
into the cart, the whole way home.'

'Poor old man, so it has!' cried Mrs. Peerybingle, instantly becoming very active. 'Here! Take the precious darling, Tilly, while I make
myself of some use. Bless it, I could smother it with kissing it, I
could! Hie then, good dog! Hie, Boxer, boy! Only let me make the tea
first, John; and then I'll help you with the parcels, like a busy bee.
'How doth the little'*—and all the rest of it, you know, John. Did you
ever learn "how doth the little," when you went to school, John?'

'Not to quite know it,' John returned. 'I was very near it once. But
I should only have spoilt it, I dare say.'

'Ha, ha,' laughed Dot. She had the blithest little laugh you ever
heard. 'What a dear old darling of a dunce you are, John, to be sure!'

Not at all disputing this position, John went out to see that the boy
with the lantern, which had been dancing to and fro before the door
and window, like a Will of the Wisp, took due care of the horse; who
was fatter than you would quite believe, if I gave you his measure, and
and so old that his birthday was lost in the mists of antiquity. Boxer,
feeling that his attentions were due to the family in general, and
must be impartially distributed, dashed in and out with bewildering
inconstancy; now, describing a circle of short barks round the horse,
where he was being rubbed down at the stable-door; now, feigning to
make savage rushes at his mistress, and facetiously bringing himself
to sudden stops; now, eliciting a shriek from Tilly Slowboy, in the
low nursing-chair near the fire, by the unexpected application of his
moist nose to her countenance; now, exhibiting an obtrusive interest
in the baby; now, going round and round upon the hearth, and lying
down as if he had established himself for the night; now, getting up
again, and taking that nothing of a fag-end of a tail of his, out into
the weather, as if he had just remembered an appointment, and was
off, at a round trot, to keep it.

'There! There's the teapot, ready on the hob!' said Dot; as briskly
busy as a child at play at keeping house. 'And there's the old knuckle
of ham; and there's the butter; and there's the crusty loaf, and all!
Here's the clothes-basket for the small parcels, John, if you've got
any there—where are you, John? Don't let the dear child fall under
the grate, Tilly, whatever you do!'

It may be noted of Miss Slowboy, in spite of her rejecting the
caution with some vivacity, that she had a rare and surprising

talent for getting this baby into difficulties: and had several times imperilled its short life, in a quiet way peculiarly her own. She was of a spare and straight shape, this young lady, insomuch that her garments appeared to be in constant danger of sliding off those sharp pegs, her shoulders, on which they were loosely hung. Her costume was remarkable for the partial development, on all possible occasions, of some flannel vestment of a singular structure; also for affording glimpses, in the region of the back, of a corset, or pair of stays, in colour a dead-green. Being always in a state of gaping admiration at everything, and absorbed, besides, in the perpetual contemplation of her mistress's perfections and the baby's, Miss Slowboy, in her little errors of judgment, may be said to have done equal honour to her head and to her heart; and though these did less honour to the baby's head, which they were the occasional means of bringing into contact with deal doors, dressers, stair-rails, bed-posts, and other foreign substances, still they were the honest results of Tilly Slowboy's constant astonishment at finding herself so kindly treated, and installed in such a comfortable home. For, the maternal and paternal Slowboy were alike unknown to Fame, and Tilly had been bred by public charity, a foundling; which word, though only differing from fondling by one vowel's length, is very different in meaning, and expresses quite another thing.

To have seen little Mrs. Peerybingle come back with her husband, tugging at the clothes-basket, and making the most strenuous exertions to do nothing at all (for he carried it), would have amused you almost as much as it amused him. It may have entertained the Cricket too, for anything I know; but, certainly, it now began to chirp again, vehemently.

'Heyday!' said John, in his slow way. 'It's merrier than ever, to-night, I think.'

'And it's sure to bring us good fortune, John! It always has done so. To have a Cricket on the Hearth, is the luckiest thing in all the world!'*

John looked at her as if he had very nearly got the thought into his head, that she was his Cricket in chief, and he quite agreed with her. But, it was probably one of his narrow escapes, for he said nothing.

'The first time I heard its cheerful little note, John, was on that night when you brought me home—when you brought me to my new home here; its little mistress. Nearly a year ago. You recollect, John?'

O yes. John remembered. I should think so!

'Its chirp was such a welcome to me! It seemed so full of promise and encouragement. It seemed to say, you would be kind and gentle with me, and would not expect (I had a fear of that, John, then) to find an old head on the shoulders of your foolish little wife.'

John thoughtfully patted one of the shoulders, and then the head, as though he would have said No, no; he had had no such expectation; he had been quite content to take them as they were. And really he had reason. They were very comely.

'It spoke the truth, John, when it seemed to say so; for you have ever been, I am sure, the best, the most considerate, the most affectionate of husbands to me. This has been a happy home, John; and I love the Cricket for its sake!'

'Why so do I then,' said the Carrier. 'So do I, Dot.'

'I love it for the many times I have heard it, and the many thoughts its harmless music has given me. Sometimes, in the twilight, when I have felt a little solitary and down-hearted, John—before baby was here to keep me company and make the house gay—when I have thought how lonely you would be if I should die; how lonely I should be if I could know that you had lost me, dear; its Chirp, Chirp, Chirp upon the hearth, has seemed to tell me of another little voice, so sweet, so very dear to me, before whose coming sound my trouble vanished like a dream. And when I used to fear—I did fear once, John, I was very young you know—that ours might prove to be an ill-assorted marriage, I being such a child, and you more like my guardian than my husband; and that you might not, however hard you tried, be able to learn to love me, as you hoped and prayed you might; its Chirp, Chirp, Chirp has cheered me up again, and filled me with new trust and confidence. I was thinking of these things to-night, dear, when I sat expecting you; and I love the Cricket for their sake!'

'And so do I,' repeated John. 'But, Dot? *I* hope and pray that I might learn to love you? How you talk! I had learnt that, long before I brought you here, to be the Cricket's little mistress, Dot!'

She laid her hand, an instant, on his arm, and looked up at him with an agitated face, as if she would have told him something. Next moment she was down upon her knees before the basket, speaking in a sprightly voice, and busy with the parcels.

'There are not many of them to-night, John, but I saw some

goods behind the cart, just now; and though they give more trouble, perhaps, still they pay as well; so we have no reason to grumble, have we? Besides, you have been delivering, I dare say, as you came along?'

'Oh yes,' John said. 'A good many.'

'Why what's this round box? Heart alive, John, it's a wedding-cake!'

'Leave a woman alone to find out that,' said John, admiringly. 'Now a man would never have thought of it. Whereas, it's my belief that if you was to pack a wedding-cake up in a tea-chest, or a turn-up bedstead, or a pickled salmon keg, or any unlikely thing, a woman would be sure to find it out directly. Yes; I called for it at the pastry-cook's.'

'And it weighs I don't know what—whole hundred-weights!' cried Dot, making a great demonstration of trying to lift it. 'Whose is it, John? Where is it going?'

'Read the writing on the other side,' said John.

'Why, John! My Goodness, John!'

'Ah! who'd have thought it!' John returned.

'You never mean to say,' pursued Dot, sitting on the floor and shaking her head at him, 'that it's Gruff and Tackleton the toymaker!'

John nodded.

Mrs. Peerybingle nodded also, fifty times at least. Not in assent— in dumb and pitying amazement; screwing up her lips the while with all their little force (they were never made for screwing up; I am clear of that), and looking the good Carrier through and through, in her abstraction. Miss Slowboy, in the mean time, who had a mechanical power of reproducing scraps of current conversation for the delectation of the baby, with all the sense struck out of them, and all the nouns changed into the plural number, inquired aloud of that young creature, Was it Gruffs and Tackletons the toymakers then, and Would it call at Pastry-cooks for wedding-cakes, and Did its mothers know the boxes when its fathers brought them homes; and so on.

'And that is really to come about!' said Dot. 'Why, she and I were girls at school together, John.'

He might have been thinking of her, or nearly thinking of her, perhaps, as she was in that same school time. He looked upon her with a thoughtful pleasure, but he made no answer.

'And he's as old! As unlike her!—Why, how many years older than you, is Gruff and Tackleton, John?'

'How many more cups of tea shall I drink to-night at one sitting, than Gruff and Tackleton ever took in four, I wonder!' replied John, good-humouredly, as he drew a chair to the round table, and began at the cold ham. 'As to eating, I eat but little; but that little I enjoy, Dot.'

Even this, his usual sentiment at meal times, one of his innocent delusions (for his appetite was always obstinate, and flatly contradicted him), awoke no smile in the face of his little wife, who stood among the parcels, pushing the cake-box slowly from her with her foot, and never once looked, though her eyes were cast down too, upon the dainty shoe she generally was so mindful of. Absorbed in thought, she stood there, heedless alike of the tea and John (although he called to her, and rapped the table with his knife to startle her), until he rose and touched her on the arm; when she looked at him for a moment, and hurried to her place behind the teaboard, laughing at her negligence. But not as she had laughed before. The manner and the music were quite changed.

The Cricket, too, had stopped. Somehow the room was not so cheerful as it had been. Nothing like it.

'So, these are all the parcels, are they, John?' she said, breaking a long silence, which the honest Carrier had devoted to the practical illustration of one part of his favourite sentiment—certainly enjoying what he ate, if it couldn't be admitted that he ate but little. 'So these are all the parcels; are they, John?'

'That's all,' said John. 'Why—no—I—' laying down his knife and fork, and taking a long breath. 'I declare—I've clean forgotten the old gentleman!'

'The old gentleman?'

'In the cart,' said John. 'He was asleep, among the straw, the last time I saw him. I've very nearly remembered him, twice, since I came in; but he went out of my head again. Halloa! Yahip there! Rouse up! That's my hearty!'

John said these latter words outside the door, whither he had hurried with the candle in his hand.

Miss Slowboy, conscious of some mysterious reference to The Old Gentleman,* and connecting in her mystified imagination certain associations of a religious nature with the phrase, was so disturbed, that hastily rising from the low chair by the fire to seek protection near the skirts of her mistress, and coming into contact as she crossed the doorway with an ancient Stranger, she instinctively made a charge or butt at him with the only offensive instrument within her reach. This instrument happening to be the baby, great commotion and alarm ensued, which the sagacity of Boxer rather tended to increase; for, that good dog, more thoughtful than its master, had, it seemed, been watching the old gentleman in his sleep, lest he should walk off with a few young poplar trees that were tied up behind the cart; and he still attended on him very closely, worrying his gaiters in fact, and making dead sets at the buttons.

'You're such an undeniable good sleeper, sir,' said John, when tranquillity was restored; in the meantime the old gentleman had stood, bareheaded and motionless, in the centre of the room; 'that I have half a mind to ask you where the other six* are—only that would be a joke, and I know I should spoil it. Very near though,' murmured the Carrier, with a chuckle; 'very near!'

The Stranger, who had long white hair, good features, singularly bold and well defined for an old man, and dark, bright, penetrating eyes, looked round with a smile, and saluted the Carrier's wife by gravely inclining his head.

His garb was very quaint and odd—a long, long way behind the time. Its hue was brown, all over. In his hand he held a great brown club or walking-stick; and striking this upon the floor, it fell asunder, and became a chair. On which he sat down, quite composedly.

'There!' said the Carrier, turning to his wife. 'That's the way I found him, sitting by the roadside! Upright as a milestone. And almost as deaf.'

'Sitting in the open air, John!'

'In the open air,' replied the Carrier, 'just at dusk. "Carriage Paid," he said; and gave me eighteenpence. Then he got in. And there he is.'

'He's going, John, I think!'

Not at all. He was only going to speak.

'If you please, I was to be left till called for,' said the Stranger, mildly. 'Don't mind me.'

With that, he took a pair of spectacles from one of his large pockets, and a book from another, and leisurely began to read. Making no more of Boxer than if he had been a house lamb!*

The Carrier and his wife exchanged a look of perplexity. The Stranger raised his head; and glancing from the latter to the former, said,

'Your daughter, my good friend?'

'Wife,' returned John.

'Niece?' said the Stranger.

'Wife,' roared John.

'Indeed?' observed the Stranger. 'Surely? Very young!'

He quietly turned over, and resumed his reading. But, before he could have read two lines, he again interrupted himself to say:

'Baby, yours?'

'John gave him a gigantic nod; equivalent to an answer in the affirmative, delivered through a speaking trumpet.

'Girl?'

'Bo-o-oy!' roared John.

'Also very young, eh?'

Mrs. Peerybingle instantly struck in. 'Two months and three da-ays! Vaccinated just six weeks ago-o! Took very fine-ly! Considered, by the doctor, a remarkably beautiful chi-ild! Equal to the general run of children at five months o-old! Takes notice, in a way quite won-der-ful! May seem impossible to you, but feels his legs al-ready!'

Here the breathless little mother, who had been shrieking these short sentences into the old man's ear, until her pretty face was crimsoned, held up the Baby before him as a stubborn and triumph-ant fact; while Tilly Slowboy, with a melodious cry of 'Ketcher, Ketcher'—which sounded like some unknown words, adapted to a popular Sneeze—performed some cow-like gambols round that all unconscious Innocent.

'Hark! He's called for, sure enough,' said John. 'There's somebody at the door. Open it, Tilly.'

Before she could reach it, however, it was opened from without; being a primitive sort of door, with a latch, that any one could lift if he chose—and a good many people did choose, for all kinds of neighbours liked to have a cheerful word or two with the Carrier, though he was no great talker himself. Being opened, it gave admission to a little, meagre, thoughtful, dingy-faced man, who seemed to have made himself a greatcoat from the sack-cloth covering of some old box; for, when he turned to shut the door, and keep the weather

out, he disclosed upon the back of that garment, the inscription G &
T in large black capitals. Also the word GLASS in bold characters.

'Good evening John!' said the little man. 'Good evening Mum.
Good evening Tilly. Good evening Unbeknown! How's Baby Mum?
Boxer's pretty well I hope?'

'All thriving, Caleb,' replied Dot. 'I am sure you need only look at
the dear child, for one, to know that.'

'And I'm sure I need only look at you for another,' said Caleb.

He didn't look at her though; he had a wandering and thoughtful
eye which seemed to be always projecting itself into some other time
and place, no matter what he said; a description which will equally
apply to his voice.

'Or at John for another,' said Caleb. 'Or at Tilly, as far as that goes.
Or certainly at Boxer.'

'Busy just now, Caleb?' asked the Carrier.

'Why, pretty well, John,' he returned, with the distraught air of a
man who was casting about for the Philosopher's stone,* at least.
'Pretty much so. There's rather a run on Noah's Arks at present. I
could have wished to improve upon the Family, but I don't see how
it's to be done at the price. It would be a satisfaction to one's mind,
to make it clearer which was Shems and Hams, and which was
Wives. Flies an't on that scale neither, as compared with elephants
you know! Ah! well! Have you got anything in the parcel line for
me, John?'

The Carrier put his hand into a pocket of the coat he had taken
off; and brought out, carefully preserved in moss and paper, a tiny
flower-pot.

'There it is!' he said, adjusting it with great care. 'Not so much as
a leaf damaged. Full of buds!'

Caleb's dull eye brightened, as he took it, and thanked him.

'Dear, Caleb,' said the Carrier. 'Very dear at this season.'

'Never mind that. It would be cheap to me, whatever it cost,'
returned the little man. 'Anything else, John?'

'A small box,' replied the Carrier. 'Here you are!'

' "For Caleb Plummer," ' said the little man, spelling out the
direction. ' "With Cash." With Cash, John? I don't think it's for me.'

'With Care,' returned the Carrier, looking over his shoulder.
'Where do you make out cash?'

'Oh! To be sure!' said Caleb. 'It's all right. With care! Yes, yes;

that's mine. It might have been with cash, indeed, if my dear Boy in the Golden South Americas had lived, John. You loved him like a son; didn't you? You needn't say you did. *I* know, of course. "Caleb Plummer. With care." Yes, yes, it's all right. It's a box of dolls' eyes for my daughter's work. I wish it was her own sight in a box, John.'

'I wish it was, or could be!' cried the Carrier.

'Thank'ee,' said the little man. 'You speak very hearty. To think that she should never see the Dolls—and them a-staring at her, so bold, all day long! That's where it cuts. What's the damage,* John?'

'I'll damage you,' said John, 'if you inquire. Dot! Very near?'

'Well! it's like you to say so,' observed the little man. 'It's your kind way. Let me see. I think that's all.'

'I think not,' said the Carrier. 'Try again.'

'Something for our Governor, eh?' said Caleb, after pondering a little while. 'To be sure. That's what I came for; but my head's so running on them Arks and things! He hasn't been here, has he?'

'Not he,' returned the Carrier. 'He's too busy, courting.'

'He's coming round though,' said Caleb; 'for he told me to keep on the near side of the road going home, and it was ten to one he'd take me up. I had better go, by the bye.—You couldn't have the goodness to let me pinch Boxer's tail, Mum, for half a moment, could you?'

'Why, Caleb! what a question!'

'Oh never mind, Mum,' said the little man. 'He mightn't like it perhaps. There's a small order just come in, for barking dogs; and I should wish to go as close to Natur' as I could, for sixpence. That's all. Never mind, Mum.'

It happened opportunely, that Boxer, without receiving the proposed stimulus, began to bark with great zeal. But, as this implied the approach of some new visitor, Caleb, postponing his study from the life to a more convenient season, shouldered the round box, and took a hurried leave. He might have spared himself the trouble, for he met the visitor upon the threshold.

'Oh! You are here, are you? Wait a bit. I'll take you home. John Peerybingle, my service to you. More of my service to your pretty wife. Handsomer every day! Better too, if possible! And younger,' mused the speaker, in a low voice; 'that's the Devil of it!'

'I should be astonished at your paying compliments, Mr.

Tackleton,' said Dot, not with the best grace in the world; 'but for your condition.'

'You know all about it then?'

'I have got myself to believe it, somehow,' said Dot.

'After a hard struggle, I suppose?'

'Very.'

Tackleton the Toy-merchant, pretty generally known as Gruff and Tackleton—for that was the firm, though Gruff had been bought out long ago; only leaving his name, and as some said his nature, according to its Dictionary meaning, in the business—Tackleton the Toy-merchant was a man whose vocation had been quite misunderstood by his Parents and Guardians. If they had made him a Money Lender, or a sharp Attorney, or a Sheriff's Officer, or a Broker, he might have sown his discontented oats in his youth, and, after having had the full run of himself in ill-natured transactions, might have turned out amiable, at last, for the sake of a little freshness and novelty. But, cramped and chafing in the peaceable pursuit of toy-making, he was a domestic Ogre, who had been living on children all his life, and was their implacable enemy. He despised all toys; wouldn't have bought one for the world; delighted, in his malice, to insinuate grim expressions into the faces of brown-paper farmers who drove pigs to market, bellmen who advertised lost lawyers' consciences, movable old ladies who darned stockings or carved pies; and other like samples of his stock in trade. In appalling masks; hideous, hairy, red-eyed Jacks in Boxes; Vampire Kites; demoniacal Tumblers who wouldn't lie down, and were perpetually flying forward, to stare infants out of countenance; his soul perfectly revelled. They were his only relief and safety-valve. He was great in such inventions. Anything suggestive of a Pony-nightmare* was delicious to him. He had even lost money (and he took to that toy very kindly) by getting up Goblin slides for magic-lanterns, whereon the Powers of Darkness were depicted as a sort of supernatural shell-fish, with human faces. In intensifying the portraiture of Giants, he had sunk quite a little capital; and, though no painter himself, he could indicate, for the instruction of his artists, with a piece of chalk, a certain furtive leer for the countenances of those monsters, which was safe to destroy the peace of mind of any young gentleman between the ages of six and eleven, for the whole Christmas or Midsummer Vacation.

What he was in toys, he was (as most men are) in other things. You may easily suppose, therefore, that within the great green cape, which reached down to the calves of his legs, there was buttoned up to the chin an uncommonly pleasant fellow; and that he was about as choice a spirit, and as agreeable a companion, as ever stood in a pair of bull-headed-looking boots with mahogany-coloured tops.

Still, Tackleton, the toy-merchant, was going to be married. In spite of all this, he was going to be married. And to a young wife too, a beautiful young wife.

He didn't look much like a bridegroom, as he stood in the Carrier's kitchen, with a twist in his dry face, and a screw in his body, and his hat jerked over the bridge of his nose, and his hands tucked down into the bottoms of his pockets, and his whole sarcastic ill-conditioned self peering out of one little corner of one little eye, like the concentrated essence of any number of ravens. But, a Bridegroom he designed to be.

'In three days' time. Next Thursday. The last day of the first month in the year. That's my wedding-day,' said Tackleton.

Did I mention that he had always one eye wide open, and one eye nearly shut; and that the one eye nearly shut, was always the expressive eye? I don't think I did.

'That's my wedding-day!' said Tackleton, rattling his money.

'Why, it's our wedding-day too,' exclaimed the Carrier.

'Ha, ha!' laughed Tackleton. 'Odd! You're just such another couple. Just!'

The indignation of Dot at this presumptuous assertion is not to be described. What next? His imagination would compass the possibility of just such another Baby, perhaps. The man was mad.

'I say! A word with you,' murmured Tackleton, nudging the Carrier with his elbow, and taking him a little apart. 'You'll come to the wedding? We're in the same boat, you know.'

'How in the same boat?' inquired the Carrier.

'A little disparity, you know,' said Tackleton, with another nudge. 'Come and spend an evening with us, beforehand.'

'Why?' demanded John, astonished at this pressing hospitality.

'Why?' returned the other. 'That's a new way of receiving an invitation. Why, for pleasure—sociability, you know, and all that!'

'I thought you were never sociable,' said John, in his plain way.

'Tchah! It's of no use to be anything but free with you, I see,' said Tackleton. 'Why, then, the truth is you have a—what tea-drinking people call a sort of a comfortable appearance together, you and your wife. We know better, you know, but—'

'No, we don't know better,' interposed John. 'What are you talking about?'

'Well! We *don't* know better, then,' said Tackleton. 'We'll agree that we don't. As you like; what does it matter? I was going to say, as you have that sort of appearance, your company will produce a favourable effect on Mrs. Tackleton that will be. And, though I don't think your good lady's very friendly to me, in this matter, still she can't help herself from falling into my views, for there's a compactness and cosiness of appearance about her that always tells, even in an indifferent case. You'll say you'll come?'

'We have arranged to keep our Wedding-Day (as far as that goes) at home,' said John. 'We have made the promise to ourselves these six months. We think, you see, that home—'

'Bah! what's home?' cried Tackleton. 'Four walls and a ceiling! (why don't you kill that Cricket? *I* would! I always do. I hate their noise.) There are four walls and a ceiling at my house. Come to me!'

'You kill your Crickets, eh?' said John.

'Scrunch 'em, sir,' returned the other, setting his heel heavily on the floor. 'You'll say you'll come? It's as much your interest as mine, you know, that the women should persuade each other that they're quiet and contented, and couldn't be better off. I know their way. Whatever one woman says, another woman is determined to clinch, always. There's that spirit of emulation among 'em, sir, that if your wife says to my wife, "I'm the happiest woman in the world, and mine's the best husband in the world, and I dote on him," my wife will say the same to yours, or more, and half believe it.'

'Do you mean to say she don't, then?' asked the Carrier.

'Don't!' cried Tackleton, with a short, sharp laugh. 'Don't what?'

The Carrier had some faint idea of adding, 'dote upon you.' But, happening to meet the half-closed eye, as it twinkled upon him over the turned-up collar of the cape, which was within an ace of poking it out, he felt it such an unlikely part and parcel of anything to be doted on, that he substituted, 'that she don't believe it?'

'Ah, you dog! You're joking,' said Tackleton.

But the Carrier, though slow to understand the full drift of his meaning, eyed him in such a serious manner, that he was obliged to be a little more explanatory.

'I have the humour,' said Tackleton: holding up the fingers of his left hand, and tapping the forefinger, to imply 'there I am, Tackleton to wit': 'I have the humour, sir, to marry a young wife, and a pretty wife': here he rapped his little finger, to express the Bride; not sparingly, but sharply; with a sense of power. 'I'm able to gratify that humour and I do. It's my whim. But—now look there!'

He pointed to where Dot was sitting, thoughtfully, before the fire; leaning her dimpled chin upon her hand, and watching the bright blaze. The Carrier looked at her, and then at him, and then at her, and then at him again.

'She honours and obeys, no doubt, you know,' said Tackleton; 'and that, as I am not a man of sentiment, is quite enough for *me*. But do you think there's anything more in it?'

'I think', observed the Carrier, 'that I should chuck any man out of window, who said there wasn't.'

'Exactly so,' returned the other with an unusual alacrity of assent. 'To be sure! Doubtless you would. Of course. I'm certain of it. Good night. Pleasant dreams!'

The Carrier was puzzled, and made uncomfortable and uncertain, in spite of himself. He couldn't help showing it, in his manner.

'Good night, my dear friend!' said Tackleton, compassionately. 'I'm off. We're exactly alike, in reality, I see. You won't give us to-morrow evening? Well! Next day you go out visiting, I know. I'll meet you there, and bring my wife that is to be. It'll do her good. You're agreeable? Thank'ee. What's that!'

It was a loud cry from the Carrier's wife: a loud, sharp, sudden cry, that made the room ring, like a glass vessel. She had risen from her seat, and stood like one transfixed by terror and surprise. The Stranger had advanced towards the fire to warm himself, and stood within a short stride of her chair. But quite still.

'Dot!' cried the Carrier. 'Mary! Darling! What's the matter?'

They were all about her in a moment. Caleb, who had been dozing on the cake-box, in the first imperfect recovery of his suspended presence of mind, seized Miss Slowboy by the hair of her head, but immediately apologised.

'Mary!' exclaimed the Carrier, supporting her in his arms. 'Are you ill! What is it? Tell me, dear!'

She only answered by beating her hands together, and falling into a wild fit of laughter. Then, sinking from his grasp upon the ground, she covered her face with her apron, and wept bitterly. And then she laughed again, and then she cried again, and then she said how cold it was, and suffered him to lead her to the fire, where she sat down as before. The old man standing, as before, quite still.

'I'm better, John,' she said. 'I'm quite well now—I—'

'John!' But John was on the other side of her. Why turn her face towards the strange old gentleman, as if addressing him! Was her brain wandering?

'Only a fancy, John dear—a kind of shock—a something coming suddenly before my eyes—I don't know what it was. It's quite gone, quite gone.'

'I'm glad it's gone,' muttered Tackleton, turning the expressive eye all round the room. 'I wonder where it's gone, and what it was. Humph! Caleb, come here! Who's that with the grey hair?'

'I don't know, sir,' returned Caleb in a whisper. 'Never see him before, in all my life. A beautiful figure for a nut-cracker; quite a new model. With a screw-jaw opening down into his waistcoat, he'd be lovely.'

'Not ugly enough,' said Tackleton.

'Or for a firebox, either,' observed Caleb, in deep contemplation, 'what a model! Unscrew his head to put the matches in; turn him heels up'ards for the light; and what a firebox for a gentleman's mantel-shelf, just as he stands!'

'Not half ugly enough,' said Tackleton. 'Nothing in him at all! Come! Bring that box! All right now, I hope?'

'Oh quite gone! Quite gone!' said the little woman, waving him hurriedly away. 'Good night!'

'Good night,' said Tackleton. 'Good night, John Peerybingle! Take care how you carry that box, Caleb. Let it fall, and I'll murder you! Dark as pitch, and weather worse than ever, eh? Good night!'

So, with another sharp look round the room, he went out at the door; followed by Caleb with the wedding-cake on his head.

The Carrier had been so much astounded by his little wife, and so busily engaged in soothing and tending her, that he had scarcely been conscious of the Stranger's presence, until now, when he again stood there, their only guest.

'He don't belong to them, you see,' said John. 'I must give him a hint to go.'

'I beg your pardon, friend,' said the old gentleman, advancing to him; 'the more so, as I fear your wife has not been well; but the Attendant whom my infirmity,' he touched his ears and shook his head, 'renders almost indispensable, not having arrived, I fear there must be some mistake. The bad night which made the shelter of your comfortable cart (may I never have a worse!) so acceptable, is still as bad as ever. Would you, in your kindness, suffer me to rent a bed here?'

'Yes, yes,' cried Dot. 'Yes! Certainly!'

'Oh!' said the Carrier, surprised by the rapidity of this consent. 'Well! I don't object; but, still I'm not quite sure that—'

'Hush!' she interrupted. 'Dear John!'

'Why, he's stone deaf,' urged John.

'I know he is, but—Yes, sir, certainly. Yes! certainly! I'll make him up a bed, directly, John.'

As she hurried off to do it, the flutter of her spirits, and the agitation of her manner, were so strange that the Carrier stood looking after her, quite confounded.

'Did its mothers make it up a Beds then!' cried Miss Slowboy to the Baby; 'and did its hair grow brown and curly, when its caps was lifted off, and frighten it, a precious Pets, a-sitting by the fires!'

With that unaccountable attraction of the mind to trifles, which is often incidental to a state of doubt and confusion, the Carrier, as he walked slowly to and fro, found himself mentally repeating even these absurd words, many times. So many times that he got them by heart, and was still conning them over and over, like a lesson, when Tilly, after administering as much friction to the little bald head with her hand as she thought wholesome (according to the practice of nurses), had once more tied the Baby's cap on.

'And frighten it, a precious Pets, a-sitting by the fires. What frightened Dot, I wonder!' mused the Carrier, pacing to and fro.

He scouted, from his heart, the insinuations of the Toy-merchant, and yet they filled him with a vague, indefinite uneasiness. For, Tackleton was quick and sly; and he had that painful sense, himself, of being a man of slow perception, that a broken hint was always worrying to him. He certainly had no intention in his mind of linking anything that Tackleton had said, with the unusual conduct of his wife, but the two subjects of reflection came into his mind together, and he could not keep them asunder.

The bed was soon made ready; and the visitor, declining all

refreshment but a cup of tea, retired. Then, Dot—quite well again, she said, quite well again—arranged the great chair in the chimney-corner for her husband; filled his pipe and gave it him; and took her usual little stool beside him on the hearth.

She always *would* sit on that little stool. I think she must have had a kind of notion that it was a coaxing, wheedling, little stool.

She was, out and out, the very best filler of a pipe, I should say, in the four quarters of the globe. To see her put that chubby little finger in the bowl, and then blow down the pipe to clear the tube, and, when she had done so, affect to think that there was really something in the tube, and blow a dozen times, and hold it to her eye like a telescope, with a most provoking twist in her capital little face, as she looked down it, was quite a brilliant thing. As to the tobacco, she was perfect mistress of the subject; and her lighting of the pipe, with a wisp of paper, when the Carrier had it in his mouth—going so very near his nose, and yet not scorching it—was Art, high Art.

And the Cricket and the kettle, turning up again, acknowledged it! The bright fire, blazing up again, acknowledged it! The little Mower on the clock, in his unheeded work, acknowledged it! The Carrier, in his smoothing forehead and expanding face, acknowledged it, the readiest of all.

And as he soberly and thoughtfully puffed at his old pipe, and as the Dutch clock ticked, and as the red fire gleamed, and as the Cricket chirped; that Genius of his Hearth and Home (for such the Cricket was) came out, in fairy shape, into the room, and summoned many forms of Home about him. Dots of all ages, and all sizes, filled the chamber. Dots who were merry children, running on before him gathering flowers in the fields; coy Dots, half shrinking from, half yielding to, the pleading of his own rough image; newly-married Dots, alighting at the door, and taking wondering possession of the household keys; motherly little Dots, attended by fictitious Slowboys, bearing babies to be christened; matronly Dots, still young and blooming, watching Dots of daughters, as they danced at rustic balls; fat Dots, encircled and beset by troops of rosy grandchildren; withered Dots, who leaned on sticks, and tottered as they crept along. Old Carriers too, appeared, with blind old Boxers lying at their feet; and newer carts with younger drivers ('Peerybingle Brothers' on the tilt); and sick old Carriers, tended by the gentlest hands; and graves of dead and gone old Carriers, green in the churchyard. And as the Cricket showed him all these things—he saw them plainly, though his eyes were fixed upon the fire—the Carrier's heart grew light and happy, and he thanked his Household Gods with all his might, and cared no more for Gruff and Tackleton than you do.

But, what was that young figure of a man, which the same fairy Cricket set so near Her stool, and which remained there, singly and

alone? Why did it linger still, so near her, with its arm upon the chimney-piece, ever repeating 'Married! and not to me!'

O Dot! O failing Dot! There is no place for it in all your husband's visions; why has its shadow fallen on his hearth!

CHIRP THE SECOND

CALEB PLUMMER and his Blind Daughter lived all alone by themselves, as the Story-books say—and my blessing, with yours to back it I hope, on the Story-books, for saying anything in this workaday world!—Caleb Plummer and his Blind Daughter lived all alone by themselves, in a little cracked nutshell of a wooden house, which was, in truth, no better than a pimple on the prominent red-brick nose of Gruff and Tackleton. The premises of Gruff and Tackleton were the great feature of the street; but you might have knocked down Caleb Plummer's dwelling with a hammer or two, and carried off the pieces in a cart.

If any one had done the dwelling-house of Caleb Plummer the honour to miss it after such an inroad, it would have been, no doubt, to commend its demolition as a vast improvement. It stuck to the premises of Gruff and Tackleton, like a barnacle to a ship's keel, or a snail to a door, or a little bunch of toadstools to the stem of a tree. But it was the germ from which the full-grown trunk of Gruff and Tackleton had sprung; and, under its crazy roof, the Gruff before last, had, in a small way, made toys for a generation of old boys and girls, who had played with them, and found them out, and broken them, and gone to sleep.

I have said that Caleb and his poor Blind Daughter lived here. I should have said that Caleb lived here, and his poor Blind Daughter somewhere else—in an enchanted home of Caleb's furnishing, where scarcity and shabbiness were not, and trouble never entered. Caleb was no sorcerer, but in the only magic art that still remains to us, the magic of devoted, deathless love, Nature had been the mistress of his study; and from her teaching, all the wonder came.

The Blind Girl never knew that ceilings were discoloured, walls blotched and bare of plaster here and there, high crevices unstopped and widening every day, beams mouldering and tending downward. The Blind Girl never knew that iron was rusting, wood rotting,

paper peeling off; the size, and shape, and true proportion of the
dwelling, withering away. The Blind Girl never knew that ugly shapes
of delf and earthenware were on the board; that sorrow and faint-
heartedness were in the house; that Caleb's scanty hairs were turning
greyer and more grey, before her sightless face. The Blind Girl never
knew they had a master, cold, exacting, and uninterested—never
knew that Tackleton was Tackleton in short; but lived in the belief of
an eccentric humourist who loved to have his jest with them, and
who, while he was the Guardian Angel of their lives, disdained to
hear one word of thankfulness.

And all was Caleb's doing; all the doing of her simple father! But
he too had a Cricket on his Hearth; and listening sadly to its music
when the motherless Blind Child was very young, that Spirit had
inspired him with the thought that even her great deprivation might
be almost changed into a blessing, and the girl made happy by these
little means. For all the Cricket tribe are potent Spirits, even though
the people who hold converse with them do not know it (which is
frequently the case); and there are not, in the unseen world, voices
more gentle and more true, that may be so implicitly relied on, or
that are so certain to give none but tenderest counsel, as the Voices in
which the Spirits of the Fireside and the Hearth address themselves
to human kind.

Caleb and his daughter were at work together in their usual
working-room, which served them for their ordinary living-room as
well; and a strange place it was. There were houses in it, finished and
unfinished, for Dolls of all stations in life. Suburban tenements for
Dolls of moderate means; kitchens and single apartments for Dolls
of the lower classes; capital town residences for Dolls of high estate.
Some of these establishments were already furnished according to
estimate, with a view to the convenience of Dolls of limited income;
others could be fitted on the most expensive scale, at a moment's
notice, from whole shelves of chairs and tables, sofas, bedsteads, and
upholstery. The nobility and gentry, and public in general, for whose
accommodation these tenements were designed, lay, here and there,
in baskets, staring straight up at the ceiling; but in denoting their
degrees in society, and confining them to their respective stations
(which experience shows to be lamentably difficult in real life), the
makers of these Dolls had far improved on Nature, who is often
froward and perverse; for they, not resting on such arbitrary marks as

satin, cotton-print, and bits of rag,* had superadded striking personal differences which allowed of no mistake. Thus, the Doll-lady of distinction had wax limbs of perfect symmetry; but only she and her compeers. The next grade in the social scale being made of leather, and the next of coarse linen stuff. As to the common-people, they had just so many matches out of tinder-boxes, for their arms and legs, and there they were—established in their sphere at once, beyond the possibility of getting out of it.

There were various other samples of his handicraft, besides Dolls, in Caleb Plummer's room. There were Noah's Arks, in which the Birds and Beasts were an uncommonly tight fit, I assure you; though they could be crammed in, anyhow, at the roof, and rattled and shaken into the smallest compass. By a bold poetical licence, most of these Noah's Arks had knockers on the doors; inconsistent appendages, perhaps, as suggestive of morning callers and a Postman, yet a pleasant finish to the outside of the building. There were scores of melancholy little carts which, when the wheels went round, performed most doleful music. Many small fiddles, drums, and other instruments of torture; no end of cannon, shields, swords, spears, and guns. There were little tumblers in red breeches, incessantly swarming up high obstacles of red-tape, and coming down, head first, on the other side; and there were innumerable old gentlemen of respectable, not to say venerable, appearance, insanely flying over horizontal pegs, inserted, for the purpose, in their own street doors. There were beasts of all sorts; horses, in particular, of every breed, from the spotted barrel on four pegs, with a small tippet for a mane, to the thoroughbred rocker on his highest mettle. As it would have been hard to count the dozens upon dozens of grotesque figures that were ever ready to commit all sorts of absurdities on the turning of a handle, so it would have been no easy task to mention any human folly, vice, or weakness, that had not its type, immediate or remote, in Caleb Plummer's room. And not in an exaggerated form, for very little handles will move men and women to as strange performances, as any Toy was ever made to undertake.

In the midst of all these objects, Caleb and his daughter sat at work. The Blind Girl busy as a Doll's dressmaker; Caleb painting and glazing the four-pair front of a desirable family mansion.

The care imprinted in the lines of Caleb's face, and his absorbed and dreamy manner, which would have sat well on some alchemist or abstruse student, were at first sight an odd contrast to his occupation, and the trivialities about him. But, trivial things, invented and pursued for bread, become very serious matters of fact; and, apart from this consideration, I am not at all prepared to say, myself, that if Caleb had been a Lord Chamberlain, or a Member of Parliament, or a lawyer, or even a great speculator, he would have dealt in toys one whit less whimsical, while I have a very great doubt whether they would have been as harmless.

'So you were out in the rain last night, father, in your beautiful new great-coat,' said Caleb's daughter.

'In my beautiful new great-coat,' answered Caleb, glancing towards a clothes-line in the room, on which the sackcloth garment previously described was carefully hung up to dry.

'How glad I am you bought it, father!'

'And of such a tailor, too,' said Caleb. 'Quite a fashionable tailor. It's too good for me.'

The Blind Girl rested from her work, and laughed with delight. 'Too good, father! What can be too good for you?'

'I'm half-ashamed to wear it though,' said Caleb, watching the effect of what he said, upon her brightening face; 'upon my word! When I hear the boys and people say behind me, "Hal-loa! Here's a swell!" I don't know which way to look. And when the beggar wouldn't go away last night; and when I said I was a very common man, said, "No, your Honour! Bless your Honour, don't say that!" I was quite ashamed. I really felt as if I hadn't a right to wear it.'

Happy Blind Girl! How merry she was, in her exultation!

'I see you, father,' she said, clasping her hands, 'as plainly, as if I had the eyes I never want when you are with me. A blue coat—'

'Bright blue,' said Caleb.

'Yes, yes! Bright blue!' exclaimed the girl, turning up her radiant face; 'the colour I can just remember in the blessed sky! You told me it was blue before! A bright blue coat—'

'Made loose to the figure,' suggested Caleb.

'Made loose to the figure!' cried the Blind Girl, laughing heartily; 'and in it, you, dear father, with your merry eye, your smiling face, your free step, and your dark hair—looking so young and handsome!'

'Halloa! Halloa!' said Caleb. 'I shall be vain, presently!'

'I think you are, already,' cried the Blind Girl, pointing at him, in her glee. 'I know you, father! Ha, ha, ha! I've found you out, you see!'

How different the picture in her mind, from Caleb, as he sat observing her! She had spoken of his free step. She was right in that. For years and years, he had never once crossed that threshold at his own slow pace, but with a footfall counterfeited for her ear; and never had he, when his heart was heaviest, forgotten the light tread that was to render hers so cheerful and courageous!

Heaven knows! But I think Caleb's vague bewilderment of manner may have half originated in his having confused himself about himself and everything around him, for the love of his Blind Daughter. How could the little man be otherwise than bewildered, after labouring for so many years to destroy his own identity, and that of all the objects that had any bearing on it!

'There we are,' said Caleb, falling back a pace or two to form the better judgment of his work; 'as near the real thing as sixpenn'orth of halfpence is to sixpence. What a pity that the whole front of the house opens at once! If there was only a staircase in it, now, and regular doors to the rooms to go in at! But that's the worst of my calling, I'm always deluding myself, and swindling myself.'

'You are speaking quite softly. You are not tired, father?'

'Tired!' echoed Caleb, with a great burst of animation, 'what should tire me, Bertha? *I* was never tired. What does it mean?'

To give the greater force to his words, he checked himself in an involuntary imitation of two half-length stretching and yawning figures on the mantel-shelf, who were represented as in one eternal state of weariness from the waist upwards; and hummed a fragment of a song. It was a Bacchanalian song,* something about a Sparkling Bowl. He sang it with an assumption of a devil-may-care voice, that made his face a thousand times more meagre and more thoughtful than ever.

'What! You're singing, are you?' said Tackleton, putting his head in at the door. 'Go it! *I* can't sing.'

Nobody would have suspected him of it. He hadn't what is generally termed a singing face, by any means.

'I can't afford to sing,' said Tackleton. 'I'm glad *you* can. I hope you can afford to work too. Hardly time for both, I should think?'

'If you could only see him, Bertha, how he's winking at me!' whispered Caleb. 'Such a man to joke! you'd think, if you didn't know him, he was in earnest—wouldn't you now?'

The Blind Girl smiled and nodded.

'The bird that can sing and won't sing, must be made to sing, they say,' grumbled Tackleton. 'What about the owl that can't sing, and oughtn't to sing, and will sing; is there anything that *he* should be made to do?'

'The extent to which he's winking at this moment!' whispered Caleb to his daughter. 'O, my gracious!'

'Always merry and light-hearted with us!' cried the smiling Bertha.

'O, you're there, are you?' answered Tackleton. 'Poor Idiot!'

He really did believe she was an Idiot; and he founded the belief, I can't say whether consciously or not, upon her being fond of him.

'Well! and being there,—how are you?' said Tackleton, in his grudging way.

'Oh! well; quite well. And as happy as even you can wish me to be. As happy as you would make the whole world, if you could!'

'Poor Idiot!' muttered Tackleton. 'No gleam of reason. Not a gleam!'

The Blind Girl took his hand and kissed it; held it for a moment in her own two hands; and laid her cheek against it tenderly, before releasing it. There was such unspeakable affection and such fervent gratitude in the act, that Tackleton himself was moved to say, in a milder growl than usual:

'What's the matter now?'

'I stood it close beside my pillow when I went to sleep last night, and remembered it in my dreams. And when the day broke, and the glorious red sun—the *red* sun, father?'

'Red in the mornings and the evenings, Bertha,' said poor Caleb, with a woeful glance at his employer.

'When it rose, and the bright light I almost fear to strike myself against in walking, came into the room, I turned the little tree towards it, and blessed Heaven for making things so precious, and blessed you for sending them to cheer me!'

'Bedlam* broke loose!' said Tackleton under his breath. 'We shall arrive at the strait-waistcoat and mufflers soon. We're getting on!'

Caleb, with his hands hooked loosely in each other, stared vacantly before him while his daughter spoke, as if he really were uncertain (I believe he was) whether Tackleton had done anything to deserve her thanks, or not. If he could have been a perfectly free agent, at that moment, required, on pain of death, to kick the Toy-merchant, or fall at his feet, according to his merits, I believe it would have been an even chance which course he would have taken. Yet Caleb knew that with his own hands he had brought the little rose-tree home for her, so carefully, and that with his own lips he had forged the innocent deception which should help to keep her from suspecting how much, how very much, he every day denied himself, that she might be the happier.

'Bertha!' said Tackleton, assuming, for the nonce, a little cordiality. 'Come here.'

'Oh! I can come straight to you! You needn't guide me!' she rejoined.

'Shall I tell you a secret, Bertha?'

'If you will!' she answered, eagerly.

How bright the darkened face! How adorned with light, the listening head!

'This is the day on which little what's-her-name, the spoilt child, Peerybingle's wife, pays her regular visit to you—makes her fantastic Pic-Nic* here; an't it?' said Tackleton, with a strong expression of distaste for the whole concern.

'Yes,' replied Bertha. 'This is the day.'

'I thought so,' said Tackleton. 'I should like to join the party.'

'Do you hear that, father!' cried the Blind Girl in an ecstasy.

'Yes, yes, I hear it,' murmured Caleb, with the fixed look of a sleep-walker; 'but I don't believe it. It's one of my lies, I've no doubt.'

'You see I—I want to bring the Peerybingles a little more into company with May Fielding,' said Tackleton. 'I am going to be married to May.'

'Married!' cried the Blind Girl, starting from him.

'She's such a con-founded Idiot,' muttered Tackleton, 'that I was afraid she'd never comprehend me. Ah, Bertha! Married! Church, parson, clerk, beadle, glass-coach, bells, breakfast, bride-cake, favours, marrow-bones, cleavers,* and all the rest of the tom-foolery. A wedding, you know; a wedding. Don't you know what a wedding is?'

'I know,' replied the Blind Girl, in a gentle tone. 'I understand!'

'Do you?' muttered Tackleton. 'It's more than I expected. Well! On that account I want to join the party, and to bring May and her mother. I'll send in a little something or other, before the afternoon.

A cold leg of mutton, or some comfortable trifle of that sort. You'll expect me?'

'Yes,' she answered.

She had drooped her head, and turned away; and so stood, with her hands crossed, musing.

'I don't think you will,' muttered Tackleton, looking at her; 'for you seem to have forgotten all about it, already. Caleb!'

'I may venture to say I'm here, I suppose,' thought Caleb. 'Sir!'

'Take care she don't forget what I've been saying to her.'

'*She* never forgets,' returned Caleb. 'It's one of the few things she an't clever in.'

'Every man thinks his own geese swans,' observed the Toy-merchant, with a shrug. 'Poor devil!'

Having delivered himself of which remark, with infinite contempt, old Gruff and Tackleton withdrew.

Bertha remained where he had left her, lost in meditation. The gaiety had vanished from her downcast face, and it was very sad. Three or four times, she shook her head, as if bewailing some remembrance or some loss; but, her sorrowful reflections found no vent in words.

It was not until Caleb had been occupied, some time, in yoking a team of horses to a wagon by the summary process of nailing the harness to the vital parts of their bodies, that she drew near to his working-stool, and sitting down beside him, said:

'Father, I am lonely in the dark. I want my eyes, my patient, willing eyes.'

'Here they are,' said Caleb. 'Always ready. They are more yours than mine, Bertha, any hour in the four-and-twenty. What shall your eyes do for you, dear?'

'Look round the room, father.'

'All right,' said Caleb. 'No sooner said than done, Bertha.'

'Tell me about it.'

'It's much the same as usual,' said Caleb. 'Homely, but very snug. The gay colours on the walls; the bright flowers on the plates and dishes; the shining wood, where there are beams or panels; the general cheerfulness and neatness of the building; make it very pretty.'

Cheerful and neat it was wherever Bertha's hands could busy themselves. But nowhere else, were cheerfulness and neatness possible, in the old crazy shed which Caleb's fancy so transformed.

'You have your working dress on, and are not so gallant as when you wear the handsome coat?' said Bertha, touching him.

'Not quite so gallant,' answered Caleb. 'Pretty brisk though.'

'Father,' said the Blind Girl, drawing close to his side, and stealing one arm round his neck, 'tell me something about May. She is very fair?'

'She is indeed,' said Caleb. And she was indeed. It was quite a rare thing to Caleb, not to have to draw on his invention.

'Her hair is dark,' said Bertha, pensively, 'darker than mine. Her voice is sweet and musical, I know. I have often loved to hear it. Her shape—'

'There's not a Doll's in all the room to equal it,' said Caleb. 'And her eyes!—'

He stopped; for Bertha had drawn closer round his neck, and, from the arm that clung about him, came a warning pressure which he understood too well.

He coughed a moment, hammered for a moment, and then fell back upon the song about the sparkling bowl; his infallible resource in all such difficulties.

'Our friend, father, our benefactor. I am never tired you know of hearing about him.—Now, was I ever?' she said, hastily.

'Of course not,' answered Caleb, 'and with reason.'

'Ah! With how much reason!' cried the Blind Girl. With such fervency, that Caleb, though his motives were so pure, could not endure to meet her face; but dropped his eyes, as if she could have read in them his innocent deceit.

'Then, tell me again about him, dear father,' said Bertha. 'Many times again! His face is benevolent, kind, and tender. Honest and true, I am sure it is. The manly heart that tries to cloak all favours with a show of roughness and unwillingness, beats in its every look and glance.'

'And makes it noble,' added Caleb, in his quiet desperation.

'And makes it noble!' cried the Blind Girl. 'He is older than May, father.'

'Ye-es,' said Caleb, reluctantly. 'He's a little older than May. But that don't signify.'

'Oh father, yes! To be his patient companion in infirmity and age; to be his gentle nurse in sickness, and his constant friend in suffering and sorrow; to know no weariness in working for his sake; to watch him, tend him, sit beside his bed and talk to him awake, and pray for him asleep; what privileges these would be! What opportunities for proving all her truth and devotion to him! Would she do all this, dear father?'

'No doubt of it,' said Caleb.

'I love her, father; I can love her from my soul!' exclaimed the Blind Girl. And saying so, she laid her poor blind face on Caleb's shoulder, and so wept and wept, that he was almost sorry to have brought that tearful happiness upon her.

In the mean time, there had been a pretty sharp commotion at John Peerybingle's, for little Mrs. Peerybingle naturally couldn't think of going anywhere without the Baby; and to get the Baby under weigh, took time. Not that there was much of the Baby, speaking of it as a thing of weight and measure, but there was a vast deal to do about and about it, and it all had to be done by easy stages. For instance, when the Baby was got, by hook and by crook, to a certain point of dressing, and you might have rationally supposed that another touch or two would finish him off, and turn him out a tip-top Baby challenging the world, he was unexpectedly extinguished in a flannel cap, and hustled off to bed; where he simmered (so to speak) between two blankets for the best part of an hour. From this state of inaction he was then recalled, shining very much and roaring violently, to partake of— well? I would rather say, if you'll permit me to speak generally—of a slight repast. After which, he went to sleep again. Mrs. Peerybingle took advantage of this interval, to make herself as smart in a small way as ever you saw anybody in all your life; and, during the same short truce, Miss Slowboy insinuated herself into a spencer* of a fashion so surprising and ingenious, that it had no connection with herself, or anything else in the universe, but was a shrunken, dog's-eared, independent fact, pursuing its lonely course without the least regard to anybody. By this time, the Baby, being all alive again, was invested, by the united efforts of Mrs. Peerybingle and Miss Slowboy, with a cream-coloured mantle for its body, and a sort of nankeen raised-pie* for its head; and so in course of time they all three got down to the door, where the old horse had already taken more than the full value of his day's toll out of the Turnpike Trust,* by tearing up the road with his impatient autographs; and whence Boxer might be dimly seen in the remote perspective, standing looking back, and tempting him to come on without orders.

As to a chair, or anything of that kind for helping Mrs. Peerybingle into the cart, you know very little of John, if you think *that* was necessary. Before you could have seen him lift her from the ground, there she was in her place, fresh and rosy, saying, 'John! How *can* you! Think of Tilly!'

If I might be allowed to mention a young lady's legs, on any terms, I would observe of Miss Slowboy's that there was a fatality about them which rendered them singularly liable to be grazed; and that she never effected the smallest ascent or descent, without recording the circumstance upon them with a notch, as Robinson Crusoe marked the days upon his wooden calendar. But as this might be considered ungenteel, I'll think of it.

'John! You've got the Basket with the Veal and Ham-Pie and things, and the bottles of Beer?' said Dot. 'If you haven't, you must turn round again, this very minute.'

'You're a nice little article,' returned the Carrier, 'to be talking about turning round, after keeping me a full quarter of an hour behind my time.'

'I am sorry for it, John,' said Dot in a great bustle, 'but I really could not think of going to Bertha's—I would not do it, John, on any account—without the Veal and Ham-Pie and things, and the bottles of Beer. Way!'

This monosyllable was addressed to the horse, who didn't mind it at all.

'Oh *do* way, John!' said Mrs. Peerybingle. 'Please!'

'It'll be time enough to do that,' returned John, 'when I begin to leave things behind me. The basket's here, safe enough.'

'What a hard-hearted monster you must be, John, not to have said so, at once, and save me such a turn! I declared I wouldn't go to Bertha's without the Veal and Ham-Pie and things, and the bottles of Beer, for any money. Regularly once a fortnight ever since we have been married, John, have we made our little Pic-Nic there. If any-thing was to go wrong with it, I should almost think we were never to be lucky again.'

'It was a kind thought in the first instance,' said the Carrier: 'and I honour you for it, little woman.'

'My dear John,' replied Dot, turning very red, 'don't talk about honouring *me*. Good Gracious!'

'By the bye—' observed the Carrier. 'That old gentleman—'

Again so visibly, and instantly embarrassed!

'He's an odd fish,' said the Carrier, looking straight along the road before them. 'I can't make him out. I don't believe there's any harm in him.'

'None at all. I'm—I'm sure there's none at all.'

'Yes,' said the Carrier, with his eyes attracted to her face by the great earnestness of her manner. 'I am glad you feel so certain of it, because it's a confirmation to me. It's curious that he should have taken it into his head to ask leave to go on lodging with us; an't it? Things come about so strangely.'

'So very strangely,' she rejoined in a low voice, scarcely audible.

'However, he's a good-natured old gentleman,' said John, 'and pays as a gentleman, and I think his word is to be relied upon, like a gentleman's. I had quite a long talk with him this morning: he can hear me better already, he says, as he gets more used to my voice. He told me a great deal about himself, and I told him a great deal about myself, and a rare lot of questions he asked me. I gave him information about my having two beats, you know, in my business; one day to the right from our house and back again; another day to the left from our house and back again (for he's a stranger and don't know the names of places about here); and he seemed quite pleased. "Why, then I shall be returning home to-night your way," he says, "when I thought you'd be coming in an exactly opposite direction. That's capital! I may trouble you for another lift perhaps, but I'll engage not to fall so sound asleep again." He *was* sound asleep, sure-ly!—Dot! what are you thinking of?'

'Thinking of, John? I—I was listening to you.'

'O! That's all right!' said the honest Carrier. 'I was afraid, from the look of your face, that I had gone rambling on so long, as to set you thinking about something else. I was very near it, I'll be bound.'

Dot making no reply, they jogged on, for some little time, in silence. But it was not easy to remain silent very long in John Peerybingle's cart, for everybody on the road had something to say. Though it might only be 'How are you!' and indeed it was very often nothing else, still, to give that back again in the right spirit of cordiality, required, not merely a nod and a smile, but as wholesome an action of the lungs withal, as a long-winded Parliamentary speech. Sometimes, passengers on foot, or horseback, plodded on a little way beside the cart, for the express purpose of having a chat; and then there was a great deal to be said, on both sides.

Then, Boxer gave occasion to more good-natured recognitions of, and by, the Carrier, than half-a-dozen Christians could have done! Everybody knew him, all along the road—especially the fowls and pigs, who when they saw him approaching, with his body all on one side, and his ears pricked up inquisitively, and that knob of a tail making the most of itself in the air, immediately withdrew into remote back settlements, without waiting for the honour of a nearer acquaintance. He had business everywhere; going down all the turnings, looking into all the wells, bolting in and out of all the cottages, dashing into the midst of all the Dame-Schools,* fluttering all the pigeons, magnifying the tails of all the cats, and trotting into the public-houses like a regular customer. Wherever he went, somebody or other might have been heard to cry, 'Halloa! Here's Boxer!' and out came that somebody forthwith, accompanied by at least two or three other somebodies, to give John Peerybingle and his pretty wife, Good Day.

The packages and parcels for the errand cart were numerous; and there were many stoppages to take them in and give them out, which were not by any means the worst parts of the journey. Some people were so full of expectation about their parcels, and other people were so full of wonder about their parcels, and other people were so full of inexhaustible directions about their parcels, and John had such a lively interest in all the parcels, that it was as good as a play. Likewise, there were articles to carry, which required to be considered and discussed, and in reference to the adjustment and disposition of which, councils had to be holden by the Carrier and the senders: at which Boxer usually assisted, in short fits of the closest attention, and long fits of tearing round and round the assembled sages and barking himself hoarse. Of all these little incidents, Dot was the amused and open-eyed spectatress from her chair in the cart; and as she sat there, looking on—a charming little portrait framed to admiration by the tilt—there was no lack of nudgings and glancings and whisperings and envyings among the younger men. And this delighted John the Carrier, beyond measure; for he was proud to have his little wife admired, knowing that she didn't mind it—that, if anything, she rather liked it perhaps.

The trip was a little foggy, to be sure, in the January weather; and was raw and cold. But who cared for such trifles? Not Dot, decidedly. Not Tilly Slowboy, for she deemed sitting in a cart, on any terms, to be the highest point of human joys; the crowning circumstance of earthly hopes. Not the Baby, I'll be sworn; for it's not in Baby nature to be warmer or more sound asleep, though its capacity is great in both respects, than that blessed young Peerybingle was, all the way.

You couldn't see very far in the fog, of course; but you could see a great deal! It's astonishing how much you may see, in a thicker fog than that, if you will only take the trouble to look for it. Why, even to sit watching for the Fairy-rings* in the fields, and for the patches of hoar-frost still lingering in the shade, near hedges and by trees, was a pleasant occupation: to make no mention of the unexpected shapes in which the trees themselves came starting out of the mist, and glided into it again. The hedges were tangled and bare, and waved a multitude of blighted garlands in the wind; but there was no dis-couragement in this. It was agreeable to contemplate; for it made the fireside warmer in possession, and the summer greener in expect-ancy. The river looked chilly; but it was in motion, and moving at a good pace—which was a great point. The canal was rather slow and torpid; that must be admitted. Never mind. It would freeze the sooner when the frost set fairly in, and then there would be skating, and sliding; and the heavy old barges, frozen up somewhere near a wharf, would smoke their rusty iron chimney pipes all day, and have a lazy time of it.

In one place, there was a great mound of weeds or stubble burn-ing; and they watched the fire, so white in the daytime, flaring through the fog, with only here and there a dash of red in it, until, in consequence, as she observed, of the smoke 'getting up her nose,' Miss Slowboy choked—she could do anything of that sort, on the smallest provocation—and woke the Baby, who wouldn't go to sleep again. But Boxer, who was in advance some quarter of a mile or so, had already passed the outposts of the town, and gained the corner of the street where Caleb and his daughter lived; and long before they had reached the door, he and the Blind Girl were on the pavement waiting to receive them.

Boxer, by the way, made certain delicate distinctions of his own, in his communication with Bertha, which persuade me fully that he knew her to be blind. He never sought to attract her attention by looking at her, as he often did with other people, but touched her invariably. What experience he could ever have had of blind people or blind dogs, I don't know. He had never lived with a blind master; nor had Mr. Boxer the elder, nor Mrs. Boxer, nor any of his respectable family on either side, ever been visited with blindness, that I am aware of. He may have found it out for himself, perhaps, but he had got hold of it somehow; and therefore he had hold of Bertha too, by the skirt, and kept hold, until Mrs. Peerybingle and the Baby, and Miss Slowboy, and the basket, were all got safely within doors.

May Fielding was already come; and so was her mother—a little querulous chip* of an old lady with a peevish face, who, in right of having preserved a waist like a bedpost, was supposed to be a most transcendent figure; and who, in consequence of having once been better off, or of labouring under an impression that she might have been, if something had happened which never did happen, and seemed to have never been particularly likely to come to pass—but it's all the same—was very genteel and patronising indeed. Gruff and Tackleton was also there, doing the agreeable, with the evident sensation of being as perfectly at home, and as unquestionably in his own element, as a fresh young salmon on the top of the Great Pyramid.

'May! My dear old friend!' cried Dot, running up to meet her. 'What a happiness to see you.'

Her old friend was, to the full, as hearty and as glad as she; and it really was, if you'll believe me, quite a pleasant sight to see them embrace. Tackleton was a man of taste beyond all question. May was very pretty.

You know sometimes, when you are used to a pretty face, how, when it comes into contact and comparison with another pretty face, it seems for the moment to be homely and faded, and hardly to deserve the high opinion you have had of it. Now, this was not at all the case, either with Dot or May; for May's face set off Dot's, and Dot's face set off May's, so naturally and agreeably, that, as John Perrybingle was very near saying when he came into the room, they ought to have been born sisters—which was the only improvement you could have suggested.

Tackleton had brought his leg of mutton, and, wonderful to relate, a tart besides—but we don't mind a little dissipation when our brides are in the case; we don't get married every day—and in addition to these dainties, there were the Veal and Ham-Pie, and 'things,' as Mrs. Peerybingle called them; which were chiefly nuts and oranges, and cakes, and such small deer.* When the repast was set forth on the board, flanked by Caleb's contribution, which was a great wooden bowl of smoking potatoes (he was prohibited, by solemn compact, from producing any other viands), Tackleton led his intended mother-in-law to the post of honour. For the better gracing of this place at the high festival, the majestic old soul had adorned herself with a cap, calculated to inspire the thoughtless with sentiments of awe. She also wore her gloves. But let us be genteel, or die!*

Caleb sat next his daughter; Dot and her old school-fellow were side by side; the good Carrier took care of the bottom of the table. Miss Slowboy was isolated, for the time being, from every article of furniture but the chair she sat on, that she might have nothing else to knock the Baby's head against.

As Tilly stared about her at the dolls and toys, they stared at her and at the company. The venerable old gentlemen at the street doors (who were all in full action) showed especial interest in the party, pausing occasionally before leaping, as if they were listening to the conversation, and then plunging wildly over and over, a great many times, without halting for breath—as in a frantic state of delight with the whole proceedings.

Certainly, if these old gentlemen were inclined to have a fiendish joy in the contemplation of Tackleton's discomfiture, they had good reason to be satisfied. Tackleton couldn't get on at all; and the more cheerful his intended bride became in Dot's society, the less he liked it, though he had brought them together for that purpose. For he was a regular dog in the manger, was Tackleton; and when they laughed and he couldn't, he took it into his head, immediately, that they must be laughing at him.

'Ah, May!' said Dot. 'Dear, dear, what changes! To talk of those merry school-days makes one young again.'

'Why, you an't particularly old, at any time; are you?' said Tackleton.

'Look at my sober plodding husband there,' returned Dot. 'He adds twenty years to my age at least. Don't you, John?'

'Forty,' John replied.

'How many *you*'ll add to May's, I am sure I don't know,' said Dot, laughing. 'But she can't be much less than a hundred years of age on her next birthday.'

'Ha ha!' laughed Tackleton. Hollow as a drum, that laugh though. And he looked as if he could have twisted Dot's neck, comfortably.

'Dear dear!' said Dot. 'Only to remember how we used to talk, at school, about the husbands we would choose. I don't know how young, and how handsome, and how gay, and how lively, mine was not to be! And as to May's!—Ah dear! I don't know whether to laugh or cry, when I think what silly girls we were.'

May seemed to know which to do; for the colour flushed into her face, and tears stood in her eyes.

'Even the very persons themselves—real live young men—were fixed on sometimes,' said Dot. 'We little thought how things would come about. I never fixed on John I'm sure; I never so much as thought of him. And if I had told you, you were ever to be married to Mr. Tackleton, why you'd have slapped me. Wouldn't you, May?'

Though May didn't say yes, she certainly didn't say no, or express no, by any means.

Tackleton laughed—quite shouted, he laughed so loud. John Peerybingle laughed too, in his ordinary good-natured and contented manner; but his was a mere whisper of a laugh, to Tackleton's.

'You couldn't help yourselves, for all that. You couldn't resist us, you see,' said Tackleton. 'Here we are! Here we are! Where are your gay young bridegrooms now?'

'Some of them are dead,' said Dot; 'and some of them forgotten. Some of them, if they could stand among us at this moment, would not believe we were the same creatures; would not believe that what they saw and heard was real, and we *could* forget them so. No! they would not believe one word of it!'

'Why, Dot!' exclaimed the Carrier. 'Little woman!'

She had spoken with such earnestness and fire, that she stood in need of some recalling to herself, without doubt. Her husband's check was very gentle, for he merely interfered, as he supposed, to shield old Tackleton; but it proved effectual, for she stopped, and said no more. There was an uncommon agitation, even in her silence, which the wary Tackleton, who had brought his half-shut eye to bear upon her, noted closely, and remembered to some purpose too.

May uttered no word, good or bad, but sat quite still, with her eyes cast down, and made no sign of interest in what had passed.

The good lady her mother now interposed, observing, in the first instance, that girls were girls, and byegones byegones, and that so long as young people were young and thoughtless, they would probably conduct themselves like young and thoughtless persons: with two or three other positions of a no less sound and incontrovertible character. She then remarked, in a devout spirit, that she thanked Heaven she had always found in her daughter May, a dutiful and obedient child; for which she took no credit to herself, though she had every reason to believe it was entirely owing to herself. With regard to Mr. Tackleton she said, That he was in a moral point of view an undeniable individual, and That he was in an eligible point of view a son-in-law to be desired, no one in their senses could doubt. (She was very emphatic here.) With regard to the family into which he was so soon about, after some solicitation, to be admitted, she believed Mr. Tackleton knew that, although reduced in purse, it had some pretensions to gentility; and if certain circumstances, not wholly unconnected, she would go so far as to say, with the Indigo Trade,* but to which she would not more particularly refer, had happened differently, it might perhaps have been in possession of wealth. She then remarked that she would not allude to the past, and would not mention that her daughter had for some time rejected the suit of Mr. Tackleton; and that she would not say a great many other things which she did say, at great length. Finally, she delivered it as the general result of her observation and experience, that those marriages in which there was least of what was romantically and sillily called love, were always the happiest; and that she anticipated the greatest possible amount of bliss—not rapturous bliss; but the solid, steady-going article—from the approaching nuptials. She concluded by informing the company that to-morrow was the day she had lived for, expressly; and that when it was over, she would desire nothing better than to be packed up and disposed of, in any genteel place of burial.

As these remarks were quite unanswerable—which is the happy property of all remarks that are sufficiently wide of the purpose—they changed the current of the conversation, and diverted the general attention to the Veal and Ham-Pie, the cold mutton, the potatoes, and the tart. In order that the bottled beer might not be slighted, John Peerybingle proposed To-morrow: the Wedding-Day; and called upon them to drink a bumper to it, before he proceeded on his journey.

For you ought to know that he only rested there, and gave the old horse a bait.* He had to go some four or five miles farther on; and when he returned in the evening, he called for Dot, and took another rest on his way home. This was the order of the day on all the Pic-Nic occasions, and had been, ever since their institution.

There were two persons present, besides the bride and bridegroom elect, who did but indifferent honour to the toast. One of these was Dot, too flushed and discomposed to adapt herself to any small occurrence of the moment; the other, Bertha, who rose up hurriedly, before the rest, and left the table.

'Good bye!' said stout John Peerybingle, pulling on his dread-nought coat.* 'I shall be back at the old time. Good bye all!'

'Good bye John,' returned Caleb.

He seemed to say it by rote, and to wave his hand in the same unconscious manner; for he stood observing Bertha with an anxious wondering face, that never altered its expression.

'Good bye young shaver!' said the jolly Carrier, bending down to kiss the child; which Tilly Slowboy, now intent upon her knife and fork, had deposited asleep (and strange to say, without damage) in a little cot of Bertha's furnishing; 'good bye! Time will come, I suppose, when *you*'ll turn out into the cold, my little friend, and leave your old father to enjoy his pipe and his rheumatics in the chimney corner; eh? Where's Dot?'

'I'm here John!' she said, starting.

'Come, come!' returned the Carrier, clapping his sounding hands. 'Where's the pipe?'

'I quite forgot the pipe, John.'

Forgot the pipe! Was such a wonder ever heard of! She! Forgot the pipe!

'I'll—I'll fill it directly. It's soon done.'

But it was not so soon done, either. It lay in the usual place—the Carrier's dreadnought pocket—with the little pouch, her own work, from which she was used to fill it; but her hand shook so, that she entangled it (and yet her hand was small enough to have come out easily, I am sure), and bungled terribly. The filling of the pipe and lighting it, those little offices in which I have commended her discretion, were vilely done, from first to last. During the whole process, Tackleton stood looking on maliciously with the half-closed eye; which, whenever it met hers—or caught it, for it can hardly be said to have ever met another eye: rather being a kind of trap to snatch it up—augmented her confusion in a most remarkable degree.

'Why, what a clumsy Dot you are, this afternoon!' said John. 'I could have done it better myself, I verily believe!'

With these good-natured words, he strode away, and presently was heard, in company with Boxer, and the old horse, and the cart, making lively music down the road. What time the dreamy Caleb still stood, watching his blind daughter, with the same expression on his face.

'Bertha!' said Caleb, softly. 'What has happened? How changed you are, my darling, in a few hours—since this morning. *You* silent and dull all day! What is it? Tell me!'

'Oh father, father!' cried the Blind Girl, bursting into tears. 'Oh my hard, hard fate!'

Caleb drew his hand across his eyes before he answered her.

'But think how cheerful and how happy you have been, Bertha! How good, and how much loved, by many people.'

'That strikes me to the heart, dear father! Always so mindful of me! Always so kind to me!'

Caleb was very much perplexed to understand her.

'To be—to be blind, Bertha, my poor dear,' he faltered, 'is a great affliction; but—'

'I have never felt it!' cried the Blind Girl. 'I have never felt it, in its fulness. Never! I have sometimes wished that I could see you, or could see him—only once, dear father, only for one little minute— that I might know what it is I treasure up,' she laid her hands upon her breast, 'and hold here! That I might be sure and have it right! And sometimes (but then I was a child) I have wept in my prayers at night, to think that when your images ascended from my heart to Heaven, they might not be the true resemblance of yourselves. But I have never had these feelings long. They have passed away and left me tranquil and contented.'

'And they will again,' said Caleb.

'But, father! Oh my good, gentle father, bear with me, if I am wicked!' said the Blind Girl. 'This is not the sorrow that so weighs me down!'

Her father could not choose but let his moist eyes overflow; she was so earnest and pathetic, but he did not understand her, yet.

'Bring her to me,' said Bertha. 'I cannot hold it closed and shut within myself. Bring her to me, father!'

She knew he hesitated, and said, 'May. Bring May!'

May heard the mention of her name, and coming quietly towards her, touched her on the arm. The Blind Girl turned immediately, and held her by both hands.

'Look into my face, Dear heart, Sweet heart!' said Bertha. 'Read it with your beautiful eyes, and tell me if the truth is written on it.'

'Dear Bertha, Yes!'

The Blind Girl still, upturning the blank sightless face, down which the tears were coursing fast, addressed her in these words:

'There is not, in my soul, a wish or thought that is not for your good, bright May! There is not, in my soul, a grateful recollection stronger than the deep remembrance which is stored there, of the many many times when, in the full pride of sight and beauty, you have had consideration for Blind Bertha, even when we two were children, or when Bertha was as much a child as ever blindness can be! Every blessing on your head! Light upon your happy course! Not the less, my dear May'; and she drew towards her, in a closer grasp; 'not the less, my bird, because, to-day, the knowledge that you are to be His wife has wrung my heart almost to breaking! Father, May, Mary! oh forgive me that it is so, for the sake of all he has done to relieve the weariness of my dark life: and for the sake of the belief you have in me, when I call Heaven to witness that I could not wish him married to a wife more worthy of his goodness!'

While speaking, she had released May Fielding's hands, and clasped her garments in an attitude of mingled supplication and love. Sinking lower and lower down, as she proceeded in her strange confession, she dropped at last at the feet of her friend, and hid her blind face in the folds of her dress.

'Great Power!' exclaimed her father, smitten at one blow with the truth, 'have I deceived her from her cradle, but to break her heart at last!'

It was well for all of them that Dot, that beaming, useful, busy little Dot—for such she was, whatever faults she had, and however you may learn to hate her, in good time—it was well for all of them, I say, that she was there: or where this would have ended, it were hard to tell. But Dot, recovering her self-possession, interposed, before May could reply, or Caleb say another word.

'Come come, dear Bertha! come away with me! Give her your arm, May. So! How composed she is, you see, already; and how good it is of her to mind us,' said the cheery little woman, kissing her upon the forehead. 'Come away, dear Bertha. Come! and here's her good father will come with her; won't you, Caleb? To—be—sure!'

Well, well! she was a noble little Dot in such things, and it must have been an obdurate nature that could have withstood her influence. When she had got poor Caleb and his Bertha away, that they might comfort and console each other, as she knew they only could, she presently came bouncing back,—the saying is, as fresh as any daisy; *I* say fresher—to mount guard over that bridling little piece of consequence in the cap and gloves, and prevent the dear old creature from making discoveries.

'So bring me the precious Baby, Tilly,' said she, drawing a chair to the fire; 'and while I have it in my lap, here's Mrs. Fielding, Tilly, will tell me all about the management of Babies, and put me right in twenty points where I'm as wrong as can be. Won't you, Mrs. Fielding?'

Not even the Welsh Giant,* who, according to the popular expression, was so 'slow' as to perform a fatal surgical operation upon himself, in emulation of a juggling-trick achieved by his arch-enemy at breakfast-time; not even he fell half so readily into the snare prepared for him, as the old lady did into this artful pitfall. The fact of Tackleton having walked out; and furthermore, of two or three people having been talking together at a distance, for two minutes, leaving her to her own resources; was quite enough to have put her on her dignity, and the bewailment of that mysterious convulsion in the Indigo trade, for four-and-twenty hours. But this becoming deference to her experience, on the part of the young mother, was so irresistible, that after a short affectation of humility, she began to enlighten her with the best grace in the world; and sitting bolt upright before the wicked Dot, she did, in half an hour, deliver more infallible domestic recipes and precepts, than would (if acted on) have utterly destroyed and done up that Young Peerybingle, though he had been an Infant Samson.*

To change the theme, Dot did a little needlework—she carried the contents of a whole workbox in her pocket; however she contrived it, I don't know—then did a little nursing; then a little more needlework; then had a little whispering chat with May, while the old lady dozed; and so in little bits of bustle, which was quite her manner always, found it a very short afternoon. Then, as it grew dark, and as it was a solemn part of this Institution of the Pic-Nic that she should perform all Bertha's household tasks, she trimmed the fire, and swept the hearth, and set the tea-board out, and drew the curtain, and lighted a candle. Then she played an air or two on a rude kind of harp, which Caleb had contrived for Bertha, and played them very well; for Nature had made her delicate little ear as choice a one for music as it would have been for jewels, if she had had any to wear. By this time it was the established hour for having tea; and Tackleton came back again, to share the meal, and spend the evening.

Caleb and Bertha had returned some time before, and Caleb had sat down to his afternoon's work. But he couldn't settle to it, poor fellow, being anxious and remorseful for his daughter. It was touching to see him sitting idle on his working-stool, regarding her so wistfully, and always saying in his face, 'Have I deceived her from her cradle, but to break her heart!'

When it was night, and tea was done, and Dot had nothing more to do in washing up the cups and saucers; in a word—for I must come to it, and there is no use in putting it off—when the time drew nigh for expecting the Carrier's return in every sound of distant wheels, her manner changed again, her colour came and went, and she was very restless. Not as good wives are, when listening for their husbands. No, no, no. It was another sort of restlessness from that.

Wheels heard. A horse's feet. The barking of a dog. The gradual approach of all the sounds. The scratching paw of Boxer at the door!

'Whose step is that!' cried Bertha, starting up.

'Whose step?' returned the Carrier, standing in the portal, with his brown face ruddy as a winter berry from the keen night air. 'Why, mine.'

'The other step,' said Bertha. 'The man's tread behind you!'

'She is not to be deceived,' observed the Carrier, laughing. 'Come along, sir. You'll be welcome, never fear!'

He spoke in a loud tone; and as he spoke, the deaf old gentleman entered.

'He's not so much a stranger, that you haven't seen him once, Caleb,' said the Carrier. 'You'll give him house-room till we go?'

'Oh surely John, and take it as an honour.'

'He's the best company on earth, to talk secrets in,' said John. 'I have reasonable good lungs, but he tries 'em, I can tell you. Sit down sir. All friends here, and glad to see you!'

When he had imparted this assurance, in a voice that amply corroborated what he had said about his lungs, he added in his natural tone, 'A chair in the chimney-corner, and leave to sit quite silent and look pleasantly about him, is all he cares for. He's easily pleased.'

Bertha had been listening intently. She called Caleb to her side, when he had set the chair, and asked him, in a low voice, to describe their visitor. When he had done so (truly now; with scrupulous fidelity), she moved, for the first time since he had come in, and sighed, and seemed to have no further interest concerning him.

The Carrier was in high spirits, good fellow that he was, and fonder of his little wife than ever.

'A clumsy Dot she was, this afternoon!' he said, encircling her with his rough arm, as she stood, removed from the rest; 'and yet I like her somehow. See yonder, Dot!'

He pointed to the old man. She looked down. I think she trembled.

'He's—ha, ha, ha!—he's full of admiration for you!' said the Carrier. 'Talked of nothing else, the whole way here. Why, he's a brave old boy. I like him for it!'

'I wish he had had a better subject, John,' she said, with an uneasy glance about the room. At Tackleton especially.

'A better subject!' cried the jovial John. 'There's no such thing. Come, off with the great-coat, off with the thick shawl, off with the heavy wrappers! and a cosy half-hour by the fire! My humble service, Mistress. A game at cribbage, you and I? That's hearty. The cards and board, Dot. And a glass of beer here, if there's any left, small wife!'

His challenge was addressed to the old lady, who accepting it with gracious readiness, they were soon engaged upon the game. At first, the Carrier looked about him sometimes, with a smile, or now and then called Dot to peep over his shoulder at his hand, and advise him on some knotty point. But his adversary being a rigid disciplinarian, and subject to an occasional weakness in respect of pegging more than she was entitled to, required such vigilance on his part, as left him neither eyes nor ears to spare. Thus his whole attention gradually became absorbed upon the cards; and he thought of nothing else, until a hand upon his shoulder restored him to a consciousness of Tackleton.

'I am sorry to disturb you—but a word, directly.'

'I'm going to deal,' returned the Carrier. 'It's a crisis.'

'It is,' said Tackleton. 'Come here, man!'

There was that in his pale face which made the other rise immediately, and ask him, in a hurry, what the matter was.

'Hush! John Peerybingle,' said Tackleton. 'I am sorry for this. I am indeed. I have been afraid of it. I have suspected it from the first.'

'What is it?' asked the Carrier, with a frightened aspect.

'Hush! I'll show you, if you'll come with me.'

The Carrier accompanied him, without another word. They went across a yard, where the stars were shining, and by a little side-door, into Tackleton's own counting-house, where there was a glass window, commanding the ware-room, which was closed for the night. There was no light in the counting-house itself, but there were lamps in the long narrow ware-room; and consequently the window was bright.

'A moment!' said Tackleton. 'Can you bear to look through that window, do you think?'

'Why not?' returned the Carrier.

'A moment more,' said Tackleton. 'Don't commit any violence. It's of no use. It's dangerous too. You're a strong-made man; and you might do murder before you know it.'

The Carrier looked him in the face, and recoiled a step as if he had been struck. In one stride he was at the window, and he saw—

Oh Shadow on the Hearth! Oh truthful Cricket! Oh perfidious Wife!

He saw her, with the old man—old no longer, but erect and gallant—bearing in his hand the false white hair that had won his way into their desolate and miserable home. He saw her listening to him, as he bent his head to whisper in her ear; and suffering him to clasp her round the waist, as they moved slowly down the dim wooden gallery towards the door by which they had entered it. He saw them stop, and saw her turn—to have the face, the face he loved so, so presented to his view!—and saw her, with her own hands, adjust the lie upon his head, laughing, as she did it, at his unsuspicious nature!

He clenched his strong right hand at first, as if it would have beaten down a lion. But opening it immediately again, he spread it out before the eyes of Tackleton (for he was tender of her, even then), and so, as they passed out, fell down upon a desk, and was as weak as any infant.

He was wrapped up to the chin, and busy with his horse and parcels, when she came into the room, prepared for going home.

'Now John, dear! Good night May! Good night Bertha!'

Could she kiss them? Could she be blithe and cheerful in her parting? Could she venture to reveal her face to them without a blush? Yes. Tackleton observed her closely, and she did all this.

Tilly was hushing the Baby, and she crossed and recrossed Tackleton, a dozen times, repeating drowsily:

'Did the knowledge that it was to be its wifes, then, wring its hearts almost to breaking; and did its fathers deceive it from its cradles but to break its hearts at last!'

'Now, Tilly, give me the Baby! Good night, Mr. Tackleton. Where's John, for goodness' sake?'

'He's going to walk, beside the horse's head,' said Tackleton; who helped her to her seat.

'My dear John. Walk? To-night?'

The muffled figure of her husband made a hasty sign in the affirmative; and the false stranger and the little nurse being in their places, the old horse moved off. Boxer, the unconscious Boxer, running on before, running back, running round and round the cart, and barking as triumphantly and merrily as ever.

When Tackleton had gone off likewise, escorting May and her mother home, poor Caleb sat down by the fire beside his daughter; anxious and remorseful at the core; and still saying in his wistful contemplation of her, 'Have I deceived her from her cradle, but to break her heart at last!'

The toys that had been set in motion for the Baby, had all stopped, and run down, long ago. In the faint light and silence, the imperturbably calm dolls, the agitated rocking-horses with distended eyes and nostrils, the old gentlemen at the street-doors, standing half doubled up upon their failing knees and ankles, the wry-faced nutcrackers, the very Beasts upon their way into the Ark, in twos, like a Boarding School out walking, might have been imagined to be stricken motionless with fantastic wonder, at Dot being false, or Tackleton beloved, under any combination of circumstances.

CHIRP THE THIRD

THE Dutch clock in the corner struck Ten, when the Carrier sat down by his fireside. So troubled and griefworn, that he seemed to scare the Cuckoo, who, having cut his ten melodious announcements as short as possible, plunged back into the Moorish Palace again, and clapped his little door behind him, as if the unwonted spectacle were too much for his feelings.

If the little Haymaker had been armed with the sharpest of scythes, and had cut at every stroke into the Carrier's heart, he never could have gashed and wounded it, as Dot had done.

It was a heart so full of love for her; so bound up and held together by innumerable threads of winning remembrance, spun from the daily working of her many qualities of endearment; it was a heart in which she had enshrined herself so gently and so closely; a heart so single and so earnest in its Truth, so strong in right, so weak in wrong; that it could cherish neither passion nor revenge at first, and had only room to hold the broken image of its Idol.

But, slowly, slowly, as the Carrier sat brooding on his hearth, now cold and dark, other and fiercer thoughts began to rise within him, as an angry wind comes rising in the night. The Stranger was beneath his outraged roof. Three steps would take him to his chamber-door. One blow would beat it in. 'You might do murder before you know it,' Tackleton had said. How could it be murder, if he gave the villain time to grapple with him hand to hand! He was the younger man.

It was an ill-timed thought, bad for the dark mood of his mind. It was an angry thought, goading him to some avenging act, that should change the cheerful house into a haunted place which lonely travellers would dread to pass by night; and where the timid would see shadows struggling in the ruined windows when the moon was dim, and hear wild noises in the stormy weather.

He was the younger man! Yes, yes; some lover who had won the heart that *he* had never touched. Some lover of her early choice, of whom she had thought and dreamed, for whom she had pined and pined, when he had fancied her so happy by his side. O agony to think of it!

She had been above-stairs with the Baby, getting it to bed. As he sat brooding on the hearth, she came close beside him, without his knowledge—in the turning of the rack of his great misery, he lost all other sounds—and put her little stool at his feet. He only knew it, when he felt her hand upon his own, and saw her looking up into his face.

With wonder? No. It was his first impression, and he was fain to look at her again, to set it right. No, not with wonder. With an eager and inquiring look; but not with wonder. At first it was alarmed and serious; then, it changed into a strange, wild, dreadful smile of recognition of his thoughts; then, there was nothing but her clasped hands on her brow, and her bent head, and falling hair.

Though the power of Omnipotence had been his to wield at that moment, he had too much of its diviner property of Mercy in his breast, to have turned one feather's weight of it against her. But he could not bear to see her crouching down upon the little seat where he had often looked on her, with love and pride, so innocent and gay; and, when she rose and left him, sobbing as she went, he felt it a relief to have the vacant place beside him rather than her so long cherished presence. This in itself was anguish keener than all, reminding him how desolate he was become, and how the great bond of his life was rent asunder.

The more he felt this, and the more he knew he could have better borne to see her lying prematurely dead before him with their little child upon her breast, the higher and the stronger rose his wrath against his enemy. He looked about him for a weapon.

There was a gun, hanging on the wall. He took it down, and moved a pace or two towards the door of the perfidious Stranger's room. He knew the gun was loaded. Some shadowy idea that it was just to shoot this man like a wild beast, seized him, and dilated in his mind until it grew into a monstrous demon in complete possession of him, casting out all milder thoughts and setting up its undivided empire.

That phrase is wrong. Not casting out his milder thoughts, but artfully transforming them. Changing them into scourges to drive him on. Turning water into blood, love into hate, gentleness into blind ferocity. Her image, sorrowing, humbled, but still pleading to his tenderness and mercy with resistless power, never left his mind; but, staying there, it urged him to the door; raised the weapon to his shoulder; fitted and nerved his finger to the trigger; and cried 'Kill him! In his bed!'

He reversed the gun to beat the stock upon the door; he already held it lifted in the air; some indistinct design was in his thoughts of calling out to him to fly, for God's sake, by the window—

When, suddenly, the struggling fire illumined the whole chimney with a glow of light; and the Cricket on the Hearth began to Chirp!

No sound he could have heard, no human voice, not even hers, could so have moved and softened him. The artless words in which she had told him of her love for this same Cricket, were once more freshly spoken; her trembling, earnest manner at the moment, was again before him; her pleasant voice—O what a voice it was, for making household music at the fireside of an honest man!—thrilled through and through his better nature, and awoke it into life and action.

He recoiled from the door, like a man walking in his sleep, awakened from a frightful dream; and put the gun aside. Clasping his hands before his face, he then sat down again beside the fire, and found relief in tears.

The Cricket on the Hearth came out into the room, and stood in Fairy shape before him.

' "I love it," ' said the Fairy Voice, repeating what he well remembered, ' "for the many times I have heard it, and the many thoughts its harmless music has given me." '

'She said so!' cried the Carrier. 'True!'

' "This has been a happy home, John; and I love the Cricket for its sake!" '

'It has been, Heaven knows,' returned the Carrier. 'She made it happy, always,—until now.'

'So gracefully sweet-tempered; so domestic, joyful, busy, and light-hearted!' said the Voice.

'Otherwise I never could have loved her as I did,' returned the Carrier.

The Voice, correcting him, said 'do'.

The Carrier repeated 'as I did.' But not firmly. His faltering tongue resisted his control, and would speak in its own way, for itself and him.

The Figure, in an attitude of invocation, raised its hand and said:
'Upon your own hearth—'

'The hearth she has blighted,' interposed the Carrier.

'The hearth she has—how often!—blessed and brightened,' said the Cricket; 'the hearth which, but for her, were only a few stones and bricks and rusty bars, but which has been, through her, the Altar of your Home; on which you have nightly sacrificed some petty passion, selfishness, or care, and offered up the homage of a tranquil mind, a trusting nature, and an overflowing heart; so that the smoke from this poor chimney has gone upward with a better fragrance than the richest incense that is burnt before the richest shrines in all the gaudy temples of this world!—Upon your own hearth; in its quiet sanctuary; surrounded by its gentle influences and associations; hear her! Hear me! Hear everything that speaks the language of your hearth and home!'

'And pleads for her?' inquired the Carrier.

'All things that speak the language of your hearth and home, *must* plead for her!' returned the Cricket. 'For they speak the truth.'

And while the Carrier, with his head upon his hands, continued to sit meditating in his chair, the Presence stood beside him, suggesting his reflections by its power, and presenting them before him, as in a glass or picture. It was not a solitary Presence. From the hearthstone, from the chimney, from the clock, the pipe, the kettle, and the cradle; from the floor, the walls, the ceiling, and the stairs; from the cart without, and the cupboard within, and the household implements; from every thing and every place with which she had ever been familiar, and with which she had ever entwined one recollection of herself in her unhappy husband's mind; Fairies came trooping forth. Not to stand beside him as the Cricket did, but to busy and bestir themselves. To do all honour to her image. To pull him by the skirts, and point to it when it appeared. To cluster round it, and embrace it, and strew flowers for it to tread on. To try to crown its fair head with their tiny hands. To show that they were fond of it and loved it; and that there was not one ugly, wicked, or accusatory creature to claim knowledge of it—none but their playful and approving selves.

His thoughts were constant to her image. It was always there.

She sat plying her needle, before the fire, and singing to herself. Such a blithe, thriving, steady little Dot! The fairy figures turned upon him all at once, by one consent, with one prodigious concentrated stare, and seemed to say, 'Is this the light wife you are mourning for!'

There were sounds of gaiety outside, musical instruments, and noisy tongues, and laughter. A crowd of young merry-makers came pouring in, among whom were May Fielding and a score of pretty girls. Dot was the fairest of them all; as young as any of them too. They came to summon her to join their party. It was a dance. If ever little foot were made for dancing, hers was, surely. But she laughed, and shook her head, and pointed to her cookery on the fire, and her table ready spread: with an exulting defiance that rendered her more charming than she was before. And so she merrily dismissed them, nodding to her would-be partners, one by one, as they passed, but with a comical indifference, enough to make them go and drown themselves immediately if they were her admirers—and they must have been so, more or less; they couldn't help it. And yet indifference was not her character. O no! For presently, there came a certain Carrier to the door; and bless her what a welcome she bestowed upon him!

Again the staring figures turned upon him all at once, and seemed to say, 'Is this the wife who has forsaken you!'

A shadow fell upon the mirror or the picture: call it what you will. A great shadow of the Stranger, as he first stood underneath their roof; covering its surface, and blotting out all other objects. But the nimble Fairies worked like bees to clear it off again. And Dot again was there. Still bright and beautiful.

Rocking her little Baby in its cradle, singing to it softly, and resting her head upon a shoulder which had its counterpart in the musing figure by which the Fairy Cricket stood.

The night—I mean the real night: not going by Fairy clocks—was wearing now; and in this stage of the Carrier's thoughts, the moon burst out, and shone brightly in the sky. Perhaps some calm and quiet light had risen also, in his mind; and he could think more soberly of what had happened.

Although the shadow of the Stranger fell at intervals upon the glass—always distinct, and big, and thoroughly defined—it never fell so darkly as at first. Whenever it appeared, the Fairies uttered a general cry of consternation, and piled their little arms and legs, with inconceivable activity, to rub it out. And whenever they got at Dot again, and showed her to him once more, bright and beautiful, they cheered in the most inspiring manner.

They never showed her, otherwise than beautiful and bright, for they were Household Spirits to whom falsehood is annihilation; and being so, what Dot was there for them, but the one active, beaming, pleasant little creature who had been the light and sun of the Carrier's Home!

The Fairies were prodigiously excited when they showed her, with the Baby, gossiping among a knot of sage old matrons, and affecting to be wondrous old and matronly herself, and leaning in a staid, demure old way upon her husband's arm, attempting—she! such a bud of a little woman—to convey the idea of having abjured the vanities of the world in general, and of being the sort of person to whom it was no novelty at all to be a mother; yet in the same breath, they showed her, laughing at the Carrier for being awkward, and pulling up his shirt-collar to make him smart, and mincing merrily about that very room to teach him how to dance!

They turned, and stared immensely at him when they showed her with the Blind Girl; for though she carried cheerfulness and anima-tion with her wheresoever she went, she bore those influences into Caleb Plummer's home, heaped up and running over. The Blind Girl's love for her, and trust in her, and gratitude to her; her own good busy way of setting Bertha's thanks aside; her dexterous little arts for filling up each moment of the visit in doing something useful to the house, and really working hard while feigning to make holiday; her bountiful provision of those standing delicacies, the Veal and Ham-Pie and the bottles of Beer; her radiant little face arriving at the door, and taking leave; the wonderful expression in her whole self, from her neat foot to the crown of her head, of being a part of the establishment—a something necessary to it, which it couldn't be without; all this the Fairies revelled in, and loved her for. And once again they looked upon him all at once, appealingly, and seemed to say, while some among them nestled in her dress and fondled her, 'Is this the wife who has betrayed your confidence!'

More than once, or twice, or thrice, in the long thoughtful night, they showed her to him sitting on her favourite seat, with her bent head, her hands clasped on her brow, her falling hair. As he had seen her last. And when they found her thus, they neither turned nor looked upon him, but gathered close round her, and comforted and kissed her, and pressed on one another to show sympathy and kindness to her, and forgot him altogether.

Thus the night passed. The moon went down; the stars grew pale; the cold day broke; the sun rose. The Carrier still sat, musing, in the chimney corner. He had sat there, with his head upon his hands, all night. All night the faithful Cricket had been Chirp, Chirp, Chirping on the Hearth. All night he had listened to its voice. All night the household Fairies had been busy with him. All night she had been amiable and blameless in the glass, except when that one shadow fell upon it.

He rose up when it was broad day, and washed and dressed himself. He couldn't go about his customary cheerful avocations—he wanted spirit for them—but it mattered the less, that it was Tackleton's wedding-day, and he had arranged to make his rounds by proxy. He thought to have gone merrily to church with Dot. But such plans were at an end. It was their own wedding-day too. Ah! how little he had looked for such a close to such a year!

The Carrier had expected that Tackleton would pay him an early visit; and he was right. He had not walked to and fro before his own door, many minutes, when he saw the Toy-merchant coming in his chaise along the road. As the chaise drew nearer, he perceived that Tackleton was dressed out sprucely for his marriage, and that he had decorated his horse's head with flowers and favours.

The horse looked much more like a bridegroom than Tackleton, whose half-closed eye was more disagreeably expressive than ever. But the Carrier took little heed of this. His thoughts had other occupation.

'John Peerybingle!' said Tackleton, with an air of condolence. 'My good fellow, how do you find yourself this morning?'

'I have had but a poor night, Master Tackleton,' returned the Carrier, shaking his head: 'for I have been a good deal disturbed in my mind. But it's over now! Can you spare me half an hour or so, for some private talk?'

'I came on purpose,' returned Tackleton, alighting. 'Never mind the horse. He'll stand quiet enough, with the reins over this post, if you'll give him a mouthful of hay.'

The Carrier having brought it from his stable, and set it before him, they turned into the house.

'You are not married before noon,' he said, 'I think?'

'No,' answered Tackleton. 'Plenty of time. Plenty of time.'

When they entered the kitchen, Tilly Slowboy was rapping at the Stranger's door; which was only removed from it by a few steps. One of her very red eyes (for Tilly had been crying all night long, because her mistress cried) was at the keyhole; and she was knocking very loud; and seemed frightened.

'If you please I can't make nobody hear,' said Tilly, looking round. 'I hope nobody an't gone and been and died if you please!'

This philanthropic wish, Miss Slowboy emphasised with various new raps and kicks at the door; which led to no result whatever.

'Shall I go?' said Tackleton. 'It's curious.'

The Carrier, who had turned his face from the door, signed to him to go if he would.

So Tackleton went to Tilly Slowboy's relief; and he too kicked and knocked; and he too failed to get the least reply. But he thought of trying the handle of the door; and as it opened easily, he peeped in, looked in, went in, and soon came running out again.

'John Peerybingle,' said Tackleton, in his ear. 'I hope there has been nothing—nothing rash in the night?'

The Carrier turned upon him quickly.

'Because he's gone!' said Tackleton; 'and the window's open. I don't see any marks—to be sure it's almost on a level with the garden: but I was afraid there might have been some—some scuffle. Eh?'

He nearly shut up the expressive eye altogether; he looked at him so hard. And he gave his eye, and his face, and his whole person, a sharp twist. As if he would have screwed the truth out of him.

'Make yourself easy,' said the Carrier. 'He went into that room last night, without harm in word or deed from me, and no one has entered it since. He is away of his own free will. I'd go out gladly at that door, and beg my bread from house to house, for life, if I could so change the past that he had never come. But he has come and gone. And I have done with him!'

'Oh!—Well, I think he has got off pretty easy,' said Tackleton, taking a chair.

The sneer was lost upon the Carrier, who sat down too, and shaded his face with his hand, for some little time, before proceeding.

'You showed me last night,' he said at length, 'my wife; my wife that I love; secretly—'

'And tenderly,' insinuated Tackleton.

'Conniving at that man's disguise, and giving him opportunities of meeting her alone. I think there's no sight I wouldn't have rather seen than that. I think there's no man in the world I wouldn't have rather had to show it me.'

'I confess to having had my suspicions always,' said Tackleton. 'And that has made me objectionable here, I know.'

'But as you did show it me,' pursued the Carrier, not minding him; 'and as you saw her, my wife, my wife that I love'—his voice, and eye, and hand, grew steadier and firmer as he repeated these words: evidently in pursuance of a steadfast purpose—'as you saw her at this disadvantage, it is right and just that you should also see with my eyes, and look into my breast, and know what my mind is, upon the subject. For it's settled,' said the Carrier, regarding him attentively. 'And nothing can shake it now.'

Tackleton muttered a few general words of assent, about its being necessary to vindicate something or other; but he was over-awed by the manner of his companion. Plain and unpolished as it was, it had a something dignified and noble in it, which nothing but the soul of generous honour dwelling in the man could have imparted.

'I am a plain, rough man,' pursued the Carrier, 'with very little to recommend me. I am not a clever man, as you very well know. I am not a young man. I loved my little Dot, because I had seen her grow up, from a child, in her father's house; because I knew how precious she was; because she had been my life, for years and years. There's many men I can't compare with, who never could have loved my little Dot like me, I think!'

He paused, and softly beat the ground a short time with his foot, before resuming.

'I often thought that though I wasn't good enough for her, I should make her a kind husband, and perhaps know her value better than another; and in this way I reconciled it to myself, and came to think it might be possible that we should be married. And in the end it came about, and we *were* married.'

'Hah!' said Tackleton, with a significant shake of the head.

'I had studied myself; I had had experience of myself; I knew how much I loved her, and how happy I should be,' pursued the Carrier. 'But I had not—I feel it now—sufficiently considered her.'

'To be sure,' said Tackleton. 'Giddiness, frivolity, fickleness, love of admiration! Not considered! All left out of sight! Hah!'

'You had best not interrupt me,' said the Carrier, with some sternness, 'till you understand me; and you're wide of doing so. If, yesterday, I'd have struck that man down at a blow, who dared to breathe a word against her, to-day I'd set my foot upon his face, if he was my brother!'

The Toy-merchant gazed at him in astonishment. He went on in a softer tone:

'Did I consider', said the Carrier, 'that I took her—at her age, and with her beauty—from her young companions, and the many scenes of which she was the ornament; in which she was the brightest little star that ever shone, to shut her up from day to day in my dull house, and keep my tedious company? Did I consider how little suited I was to her sprightly humour, and how wearisome a plodding man like me must be, to one of her quick spirit? Did I consider that it was no merit in me, or claim in me, that I loved her, when everybody must, who knew her? Never. I took advantage of her hopeful nature and her cheerful disposition; and I married her. I wish I never had! For her sake; not for mine!'

The Toy-merchant gazed at him, without winking. Even the half-shut eye was open now.

'Heaven bless her!' said the Carrier, 'for the cheerful constancy with which she tried to keep the knowledge of this from me! And Heaven help me, that, in my slow mind, I have not found it out before! Poor child! Poor Dot! *I* not to find it out, who have seen her eyes fill with tears, when such a marriage as our own was spoken of! I, who have seen the secret trembling on her lips a hundred times, and never suspected it till last night! Poor girl! That I could ever hope she would be fond of me! That I could ever believe she was!'

'She made a show of it,' said Tackleton. 'She made such a show of it, that to tell you the truth it was the origin of my misgivings.'

And here he asserted the superiority of May Fielding, who certainly made no sort of show of being fond of *him*.

'She has tried,' said the poor Carrier, with greater emotion than he had exhibited yet; 'I only now begin to know how hard she has tried, to be my dutiful and zealous wife. How good she has been; how much she has done; how brave and strong a heart she has; let the happiness I have known under this roof bear witness! It will be some help and comfort to me, when I am here alone.'

'Here alone?' said Tackleton. 'Oh! Then you do mean to take some notice of this?'

'I mean', returned the Carrier, 'to do her the greatest kindness, and make her the best reparation, in my power. I can release her from the daily pain of an unequal marriage, and the struggle to conceal it. She shall be as free as I can render her.'

'Make *her* reparation!' exclaimed Tackleton, twisting and turning his great ears with his hands. 'There must be something wrong here. You didn't say that, of course.'

The Carrier set his grip upon the collar of the Toy-merchant, and shook him like a reed.

'Listen to me!' he said. 'And take care that you hear me right. Listen to me. Do I speak plainly?'

'Very plainly indeed,' answered Tackleton.

'As if I meant it?'

'Very much as if you meant it.'

'I sat upon that hearth, last night, all night,' exclaimed the Carrier. 'On the spot where she has often sat beside me, with her sweet face looking into mine. I called up her whole life, day by day. I had her dear self, in its every passage, in review before me. And upon my soul she is innocent, if there is One to judge the innocent and guilty!'

Staunch Cricket on the Hearth! Loyal household Fairies!

'Passion and distrust have left me!' said the Carrier; 'and nothing but my grief remains. In an unhappy moment some old lover, better suited to her tastes and years than I; forsaken, perhaps, for me, against her will; returned. In an unhappy moment, taken by surprise, and wanting time to think of what she did, she made herself a party to his treachery, by concealing it. Last night she saw him, in the interview we witnessed. It was wrong. But otherwise than this she is innocent if there is truth on earth!'

'If that is your opinion'—Tackleton began.

'So, let her go!' pursued the Carrier. 'Go, with my blessing for the many happy hours she has given me, and my forgiveness for any pang she has caused me. Let her go, and have the peace of mind I wish her! She'll never hate me. She'll learn to like me better, when I'm not a drag upon her, and she wears the chain I have riveted, more lightly. This is the day on which I took her, with so little thought for her enjoyment, from her home. To-day she shall return to it, and I will trouble her no more. Her father and mother will be here to-day—we had made a little plan for keeping it together—and they shall take her home. I can trust her, there, or anywhere. She leaves me without blame, and she will live so I am sure. If I should die—I may perhaps while she is still young; I have lost some courage in a few hours—she'll find that I remembered her, and loved her to the last! This is the end of what you showed me. Now, it's over!'

'O no, John, not over. Do not say it's over yet! Not quite yet. I have heard your noble words. I could not steal away, pretending to be ignorant of what has affected me with such deep gratitude. Do not say it's over, 'till the clock has struck again!'

She had entered shortly after Tackleton, and had remained there. She never looked at Tackleton, but fixed her eyes upon her husband. But she kept away from him, setting as wide a space as possible between them; and though she spoke with most impassioned earnestness, she went no nearer to him even then. How different in this from her old self!

'No hand can make the clock which will strike again for me the hours that are gone,' replied the Carrier, with a faint smile. 'But let it be so, if you will, my dear. It will strike soon. It's of little matter what we say. I'd try to please you in a harder case than that.'

'Well!' muttered Tackleton. 'I must be off, for when the clock strikes again, it'll be necessary for me to be upon my way to church. Good morning, John Peerybingle. I'm sorry to be deprived of the pleasure of your company. Sorry for the loss, and the occasion of it too!'

'I have spoken plainly?' said the Carrier, accompanying him to the door.

'Oh, quite!'

'And you'll remember what I have said?'

'Why, if you compel me to make the observation,' said Tackleton, previously taking the precaution of getting into his chaise; 'I must say that it was so very unexpected, that I'm far from being likely to forget it.'

'The better for us both,' returned the Carrier. 'Good bye. I give you joy!'

'I wish I could give it to *you*,' said Tackleton. 'As I can't; thank'ee. Between ourselves, (as I told you before, eh?) I don't much think I shall have the less joy in my married life, because May hasn't been too officious about me, and too demonstrative. Good bye! Take care of yourself.'

The Carrier stood looking after him until he was smaller in the distance than his horse's flowers and favours near at hand; and then, with a deep sigh, went strolling like a restless, broken man, among some neighbouring elms; unwilling to return until the clock was on the eve of striking.

His little wife, being left alone, sobbed piteously; but often dried her eyes and checked herself, to say how good he was, how excellent he was! and once or twice she laughed; so heartily, triumphantly, and incoherently (still crying all the time), that Tilly was quite horrified.

'Ow if you please don't!' said Tilly. 'It's enough to dead and bury the Baby, so it is if you please.'

'Will you bring him sometimes, to see his father, Tilly,' inquired her mistress, drying her eyes; 'when I can't live here, and have gone to my old home?'

'Ow if you please don't!' cried Tilly, throwing back her head, and bursting out into a howl—she looked at the moment uncommonly like Boxer. 'Ow if you please don't! Ow, what has everybody gone and been and done with everybody, making everybody else so wretched! Ow-w-w-w!'

The soft-hearted Slowboy trailed off at this juncture, into such a deplorable howl, the more tremendous from its long suppression, that she must infallibly have awakened the Baby, and frightened him into something serious (probably convulsions), if her eyes had not encountered Caleb Plummer, leading in his daughter. This spectacle restoring her to a sense of the proprieties, she stood for some few moments silent, with her mouth wide open; and then, posting off to the bed on which the Baby lay asleep, danced in a weird, Saint Vitus* manner on the floor, and at the same time rummaged with her face and head among the bed-clothes, apparently deriving much relief from those extraordinary operations.

'Mary!' said Bertha. 'Not at the marriage!'

'I told her you would not be there mum,' whispered Caleb. 'I heard as much last night. But bless you,' said the little man, taking her tenderly by both hands, '*I* don't care for what they say. *I* don't believe them. There an't much of me, but that little should be torn to pieces sooner than I'd trust a word against you!'

He put his arms about her and hugged her, as a child might have hugged one of his own dolls.

'Bertha couldn't stay at home this morning,' said Caleb. 'She was afraid, I know, to hear the bells ring, and couldn't trust herself to be so near them on their wedding-day. So we started in good time, and came here. I have been thinking of what I have done,' said Caleb, after a moment's pause; 'I have been blaming myself till I hardly knew what to do or where to turn, for the distress of mind I have caused her; and I've come to the conclusion that I'd better, if you'll stay with me, mum, the while, tell her the truth. You'll stay with me the while?' he inquired, trembling from head to foot. 'I don't know what effect it may have upon her; I don't know what she'll think of me; I don't know that she'll ever care for her poor father afterwards. But it's best for her that she should be undeceived, and I must bear the consequences as I deserve!'

'Mary,' said Bertha, 'where is your hand! Ah! Here it is; here it is!' pressing it to her lips, with a smile, and drawing it through her arm. 'I heard them speaking softly among themselves, last night, of some blame against you. They were wrong.'

The Carrier's Wife was silent. Caleb answered for her.

'They were wrong,' he said.

'I knew it!' cried Bertha, proudly. 'I told them so. I scorned to hear a word! Blame *her* with justice!' she pressed the hand between her own, and the soft cheek against her face. 'No! I am not so blind as that.'

Her father went on one side of her, while Dot remained upon the other: holding her hand.

'I know you all,' said Bertha, 'better than you think. But none so well as her. Not even you, father. There is nothing half so real and so true about me, as she is. If I could be restored to sight this instant, and not a word were spoken, I could choose her from a crowd! My sister!'

'Bertha, my dear!' said Caleb, 'I have something on my mind I want to tell you, while we three are alone. Hear me kindly! I have a confession to make to you, my darling.'

'A confession, father?'

'I have wandered from the truth and lost myself, my child,' said Caleb, with a pitiable expression in his bewildered face. 'I have wandered from the truth, intending to be kind to you; and have been cruel.'

She turned her wonder-stricken face towards him, and repeated 'Cruel!'

'He accuses himself too strongly, Bertha,' said Dot. 'You'll say so, presently. You'll be the first to tell him so.'

'He cruel to me!' cried Bertha, with a smile of incredulity.

'Not meaning it, my child,' said Caleb. 'But I have been; though I never suspected it, till yesterday. My dear blind daughter, hear me and forgive me! The world you live in, heart of mine, doesn't exist as I have represented it. The eyes you have trusted in, have been false to you.'

She turned her wonder-stricken face towards him still; but drew back, and clung closer to her friend.

'Your road in life was rough, my poor one,' said Caleb, 'and I meant to smooth it for you. I have altered objects, changed the characters of people, invented many things that never have been, to make you happier. I have had concealments from you, put deceptions on you, God forgive me! and surrounded you with fancies.'

'But living people are not fancies!' she said hurriedly, and turning very pale, and still retiring from him. 'You can't change them.'

'I have done so, Bertha,' pleaded Caleb. 'There is one person that you know, my dove—'

'Oh father! why do you say, I know?' she answered, in a term of keen reproach. 'What and whom do *I* know! I who have no leader! I so miserably blind.'

In the anguish of her heart, she stretched out her hands, as if she were groping her way; then spread them, in a manner most forlorn and sad, upon her face.

'The marriage that takes place to-day,' said Caleb, 'is with a stern, sordid, grinding man. A hard master to you and me, my dear, for many years. Ugly in his looks, and in his nature. Cold and callous always. Unlike what I have painted him to you in everything, my child. In everything.'

'Oh why,' cried the Blind Girl, tortured, as it seemed, almost beyond endurance, 'why did you ever do this! Why did you ever fill my heart so full, and then come in like Death, and tear away the objects of my love! O Heaven, how blind I am! How helpless and alone!'

Her afflicted father hung his head, and offered no reply but in his penitence and sorrow.

She had been but a short time in this passion of regret, when the Cricket on the Hearth, unheard by all but her, began to chirp. Not merrily, but in a low, faint, sorrowing way. It was so mournful that her tears began to flow; and when the Presence which had been beside the Carrier all night, appeared behind her, pointing to her father, they fell down like rain.

She heard the Cricket-voice more plainly soon, and was conscious, through her blindness, of the Presence hovering about her father.

'Mary,' said the Blind Girl, 'tell me what my home is. What it truly is.'

'It is a poor place, Bertha; very poor and bare indeed. The house will scarcely keep out wind and rain another winter. It is as roughly shielded from the weather, Bertha,' Dot continued in a low, clear voice, 'as your poor father in his sack-cloth coat.'

The Blind Girl, greatly agitated, rose, and led the Carrier's little wife aside.

'Those presents that I took such care of; that came almost at my wish, and were so dearly welcome to me,' she said, trembling; 'where did they come from? Did you send them?'

'No.'

'Who then?'

Dot saw she knew, already, and was silent. The Blind Girl spread her hands before her face again. But in quite another manner now.

'Dear Mary, a moment. One moment? More this way. Speak softly to me. You are true, I know. You'd not deceive me now; would you?'

'No, Bertha, indeed!'

'No, I am sure you would not. You have too much pity for me. Mary, look across the room to where we were just now—to where my father is—my father, so compassionate and loving to me—and tell me what you see.'

'I see', said Dot, who understood her well, 'an old man sitting in a chair, and leaning sorrowfully on the back, with his face resting on his hand. As if his child should comfort him, Bertha.'

'Yes, yes. She will. Go on.'

'He is an old man, worn with care and work. He is a spare, dejected, thoughtful, grey-haired man. I see him now, despondent and bowed down, and striving against nothing. But, Bertha, I have seen him many times before, and striving hard in many ways for one great sacred object. And I honour his grey head, and bless him!'

The Blind Girl broke away from her; and throwing herself upon her knees before him, took the grey head to her breast.

'It is my sight restored. It is my sight!' she cried. 'I have been blind, and now my eyes are open. I never knew him! To think I might have died, and never truly seen the father who has been so loving to me!'

There were no words for Caleb's emotion.

'There is not a gallant figure on this earth,' exclaimed the Blind Girl, holding him in her embrace, 'that I would love so dearly, and would cherish so devotedly, as this! The greyer, and more worn, the dearer, father! Never let them say I am blind again. There's not a furrow in his face, there's not a hair upon his head, that shall be forgotten in my prayers and thanks to Heaven!'

Caleb managed to articulate 'My Bertha!'

'And in my blindness, I believed him', said the girl, caressing him with tears of exquisite affection, 'to be so different! And having him beside me, day by day, so mindful of me always, never dreamed of this!'

'The fresh smart father in the blue coat, Bertha,' said poor Caleb. 'He's gone!'

'Nothing is gone,' she answered. 'Dearest father, no! Everything is here—in you. The father that I loved so well; the father that I never loved enough, and never knew; the benefactor whom I first began to reverence and love, because he had such sympathy for me; All are here in you. Nothing is dead to me. The soul of all that was most dear to me is here—here, with the worn face, and the grey head. And I am NOT blind, father, any longer!'

Dot's whole attention had been concentrated, during this discourse, upon the father and daughter; but looking, now, towards the little Haymaker in the Moorish meadow, she saw that the clock was within a few minutes of striking, and fell, immediately, into a nervous and excited state.

'Father,' said Bertha, hesitating. 'Mary.'

'Yes, my dear,' returned Caleb. 'Here she is.'

'There is no change in *her*. You never told me anything of *her* that was not true?'

'I should have done it, my dear, I am afraid,' returned Caleb, 'if I could have made her better than she was. But I must have changed her for the worse, if I had changed her at all. Nothing could improve her, Bertha.'

Confident as the Blind Girl had been when she asked the question, her delight and pride in the reply and her renewed embrace of Dot, were charming to behold.

'More changes than you think for, may happen though, my dear,' said Dot. 'Changes for the better, I mean; changes for great joy to some of us. You mustn't let them startle you too much, if any such should ever happen, and affect you? Are those wheels upon the road? You've a quick ear, Bertha. Are they wheels?'

'Yes. Coming very fast.'

'I—I—I know you have a quick ear,' said Dot, placing her hand upon her heart, and evidently talking on, as fast as she could, to hide its palpitating state, 'because I have noticed it often, and because you were so quick to find out that strange step last night. Though why you should have said, as I very well recollect you did say, Bertha, "Whose step is that!" and why you should have taken any greater observation of it than of any other step, I don't know. Though as I said just now, there are great changes in the world: great changes: and we can't do better than prepare ourselves to be surprised at hardly anything.'

Caleb wondered what this meant; perceiving that she spoke to him, no less than to his daughter. He saw her, with astonishment, so fluttered and distressed that she could scarcely breathe; and holding to a chair, to save herself from falling.

'They are wheels indeed!' she panted. 'Coming nearer! Nearer! Very close! And now you hear them stopping at the garden-gate! And now you hear a step outside the door—the same step, Bertha, is it not!—and now!'—

She uttered a wild cry of uncontrollable delight; and running up to Caleb put her hands upon his eyes, as a young man rushed into the room, and flinging away his hat into the air, came sweeping down upon them.

'Is it over?' cried Dot.

'Yes!'

'Happily over?'

'Yes!'

'Do you recollect the voice, dear Caleb? Did you ever hear the like of it before?' cried Dot.

'If my boy in the Golden South Americas was alive'—said Caleb, trembling.

'He is alive!' shrieked Dot, removing her hands from his eyes, and clapping them in ecstasy; 'look at him! See where he stands before you, healthy and strong! Your own dear son! Your own dear living, loving brother, Bertha!'

All honour to the little creature for her transports! All honour to her tears and laughter, when the three were locked in one another's arms! All honour to the heartiness with which she met the sunburnt sailor-fellow, with his dark streaming hair, half-way, and never turned her rosy little mouth aside, but suffered him to kiss it, freely, and to press her to his bounding heart!

And honour to the Cuckoo too—why not!—for bursting out of the trap-door in the Moorish Palace like a house-breaker, and hiccoughing twelve times on the assembled company, as if he had got drunk for joy!

The Carrier, entering, started back. And well he might, to find himself in such good company.

'Look, John!' said Caleb, exultingly, 'look here! My own boy from the Golden South Americas! My own son! Him that you fitted out, and sent away yourself! Him that you were always such a friend to!'

The Carrier advanced to seize him by the hand; but, recoiling, as some feature in his face awakened a remembrance of the Deaf Man in the Cart, said:

'Edward! Was it you?'

'Now tell him all!' cried Dot. 'Tell him all, Edward; and don't spare me, for nothing shall make me spare myself in his eyes, ever again.'

'I was the man,' said Edward.

'And could you steal, disguised, into the house of your old friend?' rejoined the Carrier. 'There was a frank boy once—how many years is it, Caleb, since we heard that he was dead, and had it proved, we thought?—who never would have done that.'

'There was a generous friend of mine, once; more a father to me than a friend'; said Edward, 'who never would have judged me, or any other man, unheard. You were he. So I am certain you will hear me now.'

The Carrier, with a troubled glance at Dot, who still kept far away from him, replied, 'Well! that's but fair. I will.'

'You must know that when I left here, a boy,' said Edward, 'I was in love, and my love was returned. She was a very young girl, who perhaps (you may tell me) didn't know her own mind. But I knew mine, and I had a passion for her.'

'You had!' exclaimed the Carrier. 'You!'

'Indeed I had,' returned the other. 'And she returned it. I have ever since believed she did, and now I am sure she did.'

'Heaven help me!' said the Carrier. 'This is worse than all.'

'Constant to her,' said Edward, 'and returning, full of hope, after many hardships and perils, to redeem my part of our old contract, I heard, twenty miles away, that she was false to me; that she had forgotten me; and had bestowed herself upon another and a richer man. I had no mind to reproach her; but I wished to see her, and to prove beyond dispute that this was true. I hoped she might have been forced into it, against her own desire and recollection. It would be small comfort, but it would be some, I thought, and on I came. That I might have the truth, the real truth; observing freely for myself, and judging for myself, without obstruction on the one hand, or presenting my own influence (if I had any) before her, on the other; I dressed myself unlike myself—you know how; and waited on the road—you know where. You had no suspicion of me; neither had—had she,' pointing to Dot, 'until I whispered in her ear at that fireside, and she so nearly betrayed me.'

'But when she knew that Edward was alive, and had come back,' sobbed Dot, now speaking for herself, as she had burned to do, all through this narrative; 'and when she knew his purpose, she advised him by all means to keep his secret close; for his old friend John Peerybingle was much too open in his nature, and too clumsy in all artifice—being a clumsy man in general,' said Dot, half laughing and half crying—'to keep it for him. And when she—that's me, John,' sobbed the little woman—'told him all, and how his sweetheart had believed him to be dead; and how she had at last been over-persuaded by her mother into a marriage which the silly, dear old thing called advantageous; and when she—that's me again, John—told him they were not yet married (though close upon it), and that it would be nothing but a sacrifice if it went on, for there was no love on her side; and when he went nearly mad with joy to hear it; then she—that's me again—said she would go between them, as she had often done before in old times, John, and would sound his sweetheart and be sure that what she—me again, John—said and thought was right. And it WAS right, John! And they were brought together, John! And they were married, John, an hour ago! And here's the Bride! And Gruff and Tackleton may die a bachelor! And I'm a happy little woman, May, God bless you!'

She was an irresistible little woman, if that be anything to the purpose; and never so completely irresistible as in her present transports. There never were congratulations so endearing and delicious, as those she lavished on herself and on the Bride.

Amid the tumult of emotions in his breast, the honest Carrier had stood, confounded. Flying, now, towards her, Dot stretched out her hand to stop him, and retreated as before.

'No, John, no! Hear all! Don't love me any more, John, till you've heard every word I have to say. It was wrong to have a secret from you, John. I'm very sorry. I didn't think it any harm, till I came and sat down by you on the little stool last night. But when I knew by what was written in your face, that you had seen me walking in the gallery with Edward, and when I knew what you thought, I felt how giddy and how wrong it was. But oh, dear John, how could you, could you, think so!'

Little woman, how she sobbed again! John Peerybingle would have caught her in his arms. But no; she wouldn't let him.

'Don't love me yet, please John! Not for a long time yet! When I was sad about this intended marriage, dear, it was because I remembered May and Edward such young lovers; and knew that her heart was far away from Tackleton. You believe that, now. Don't you, John?'

John was going to make another rush at this appeal; but she stopped him again.

'No; keep there, please John! When I laugh at you, as I sometimes do, John, and call you clumsy and a dear old goose, and names of that sort, it's because I love you, John, so well, and take such pleasure in your ways, and wouldn't see you altered in the least respect to have you made a King to-morrow.'

'Hooroar!' said Caleb with unusual vigour. 'My opinion!'

'And when I speak of people being middle-aged, and steady, John, and pretend that we are a humdrum couple, going on in a jog-trot sort of way, it's only because I'm such a silly little thing, John, that I like, sometimes, to act a kind of Play with Baby, and all that: and make believe.'

She saw that he was coming; and stopped him again. But she was very nearly too late.

'No, don't love me for another minute or two, if you please, John! What I want most to tell you, I have kept to the last. My dear, good, generous John, when we were talking the other night about the Cricket, I had it on my lips to say, that at first I did not love you quite so dearly as I do now; that when I first came home here, I was half afraid I mightn't learn to love you every bit as well as I hoped and prayed I might—being so very young, John! But, dear John, every day and hour I loved you more and more. And if I could have loved you better than I do, the noble words I heard you say this morning, would have made me. But I can't. All the affection that I had (it was a great deal John) I gave you, as you well deserve, long, long ago, and I have no more left to give. Now, my dear husband, take me to your heart again! That's my home, John; and never, never think of sending me to any other!'

You never will derive so much delight from seeing a glorious little woman in the arms of a third party, as you would have felt if you had seen Dot run into the Carrier's embrace. It was the most complete, unmitigated, soul-fraught little piece of earnestness that ever you beheld in all your days.

You may be sure the Carrier was in a state of perfect rapture; and you may be sure Dot was likewise; and you may be sure they all were, inclusive of Miss Slowboy, who wept copiously for joy, and wishing to include her young charge in the general interchange of congratulations, handed round the Baby to everybody in succession, as if it were something to drink.

But, now, the sound of wheels was heard again outside the door; and somebody exclaimed that Gruff and Tackleton was coming back. Speedily that worthy gentleman appeared, looking warm and flustered.

'Why, what the Devil's this, John Peerybingle!' said Tackleton. 'There's some mistake. I appointed Mrs. Tackleton to meet me at the church, and I'll swear I passed her on the road, on her way here. Oh! here she is! I beg your pardon, sir; I haven't the pleasure of knowing you; but if you can do me the favour to spare this young lady, she has rather a particular engagement this morning.'

'But I can't spare her,' returned Edward. 'I couldn't think of it.'

'What do you mean, you vagabond?' said Tackleton.

'I mean, that as I can make allowance for your being vexed,' returned the other, with a smile, 'I am as deaf to harsh discourse this morning, as I was to all discourse last night.'

The look that Tackleton bestowed upon him, and the start he gave!

'I am sorry sir,' said Edward, holding out May's left hand, and especially the third finger; 'that the young lady can't accompany you to church; but as she has been there once, this morning, perhaps you'll excuse her.'

Tackleton looked hard at the third finger, and took a little piece of silver-paper, apparently containing a ring, from his waistcoat-pocket.

'Miss Slowboy,' said Tackleton. 'Will you have the kindness to throw that in the fire? Thank'ee.'

'It was a previous engagement, quite an old engagement, that prevented my wife from keeping her appointment with you, I assure you,' said Edward.

'Mr. Tackleton will do me the justice to acknowledge that I revealed it to him faithfully; and that I told him, many times, I never could forget it,' said May, blushing.

'Oh certainly!' said Tackleton. 'Oh to be sure. Oh it's all right. It's quite correct. Mrs. Edward Plummer, I infer?'

'That's the name,' returned the bridegroom.

'Ah, I shouldn't have known you, sir,' said Tackleton, scrutinising his face narrowly, and making a low bow. 'I give you joy sir!'

'Thank'ee.'

'Mrs. Peerybingle,' said Tackleton, turning suddenly to where she stood with her husband; 'I am sorry. You haven't done me a very great kindness, but, upon my life I am sorry. You are better than I thought you. John Peerybingle, I am sorry. You understand me; that's enough. It's quite correct, ladies and gentlemen all, and perfectly satisfactory. Good morning!'

With these words he carried it off, and carried himself off too: merely stopping at the door, to take the flowers and favours from his horse's head, and to kick that animal once, in the ribs, as a means of informing him that there was a screw loose in his arrangements.

Of course it became a serious duty now, to make such a day of it, as should mark these events for a high Feast and Festival in the Peerybingle Calendar for evermore. Accordingly, Dot went to work to produce such an entertainment, as should reflect undying honour on the house and on every one concerned; and in a very short space of time, she was up to her dimpled elbows in flour, and whitening the Carrier's coat, every time he came near her, by stopping him to give him a kiss. That good fellow washed the greens, and peeled the turnips, and broke the plates, and upset iron pots full of cold water on the fire, and made himself useful in all sorts of ways: while a couple of professional assistants, hastily called in from somewhere in the neighbourhood, as on a point of life or death, ran against each other in all the doorways and round all the corners, and everybody tumbled over Tilly Slowboy and the Baby, everywhere. Tilly never came out in such force before. Her ubiquity was the theme of general admiration. She was a stumbling-block in the passage at five-and-twenty minutes past two; a mantrap, in the kitchen at half-past two precisely; and a pitfall in the garret at five-and-twenty minutes to three. The Baby's head was, as it were, a test and touchstone for every description of matter,—animal, vegetable, and mineral. Nothing was in use that day that didn't come, at some time or other, into close acquaintance with it.

Then, there was a great Expedition set on foot to go and find out Mrs. Fielding; and to be dismally penitent to that excellent gentlewoman; and to bring her back, by force, if needful, to be happy and forgiving. And when the Expedition first discovered her, she would listen to no terms at all, but said, an unspeakable number of times, that ever she should have lived to see the day! and couldn't be got to say anything else, except, 'Now carry me to the grave': which seemed absurd, on account of her not being dead, or anything at all like it. After a time, she lapsed into a state of dreadful calmness, and observed, that when that unfortunate train of circumstances had occurred in the Indigo Trade, she had foreseen that she would be exposed, during her whole life, to every species of insult and contumely; and that she was glad to find it was the case; and begged they wouldn't trouble themselves about her,—for what was she? oh, dear! a nobody!—but would forget that such a being lived, and would take their course in life without her. From this bitterly sarcastic mood, she passed into an angry one, in which she gave vent to the remarkable expression that the worm would turn if trodden on; and, after that, she yielded to a soft regret, and said, if they had only given her their confidence, what might she not have had it in her power to suggest! Taking advantage of this crisis in her feelings, the Expedition embraced her; and she very soon had her gloves on, and was on her way to John Peerybingle's in a state of unimpeachable gentility; with a paper parcel at her side containing a cap of state, almost as tall, and quite as stiff, as a mitre.

Then, there were Dot's father and mother to come, in another little chaise; and they were behind their time; and fears were entertained; and there was much looking out for them down the road; and Mrs. Fielding always would look in the wrong and morally impossible direction; and being apprised thereof hoped she might take the liberty of looking where she pleased. At last they came: a chubby little couple, jogging along in a snug and comfortable little way that quite belonged to the Dot family; and Dot and her mother, side by side, were wonderful to see. They were so like each other.

Then, Dot's mother had to renew her acquaintance with May's mother; and May's mother always stood on her gentility; and Dot's mother never stood on anything but her active little feet. And old Dot—so to call Dot's father, I forgot it wasn't his right name, but never mind—took liberties, and shook hands at first sight, and seemed to think a cap but so much starch and muslin, and didn't defer himself at all to the Indigo Trade, but said there was no help for it now; and, in Mrs. Fielding's summing up, was a good-natured kind of man—but coarse, my dear.

I wouldn't have missed Dot, doing the honours in her wedding-gown, my benison on her bright face! for any money. No! nor the good Carrier, so jovial and so ruddy, at the bottom of the table. Nor the brown, fresh sailor-fellow, and his handsome wife. Nor any one among them. To have missed the dinner would have been to miss as jolly and as stout a meal as man need eat; and to have missed the overflowing cups in which they drank The Wedding-Day, would have been the greatest miss of all.

After dinner, Caleb sang the song about the Sparkling Bowl.* As I'm a living man, hoping to keep so, for a year or two, he sang it through.

And, by-the-by, a most unlooked-for incident occurred, just as he finished the last verse.

There was a tap at the door; and a man came staggering in, without saying with your leave, or by your leave, with something heavy on his head. Setting this down in the middle of the table, symmetrically in the centre of the nuts and apples, he said:

'Mr. Tackleton's compliments, and as he hasn't got no use for the cake himself, p'raps you'll eat it.'

And with those words, he walked off.

There was some surprise among the company, as you may imagine. Mrs. Fielding, being a lady of infinite discernment, suggested that the cake was poisoned, and related a narrative of a cake, which, within her knowledge, had turned a seminary for young ladies, blue. But she was overruled by acclamation; and the cake was cut by May, with much ceremony and rejoicing.

I don't think any one had tasted it, when there came another tap at the door, and the same man appeared again, having under his arm a vast brown-paper parcel.

'Mr. Tackleton's compliments, and he's sent a few toys for the Babby. They ain't ugly.'

After the delivery of which expressions, he retired again.

The whole party would have experienced great difficulty in finding words for their astonishment, even if they had had ample time to seek them. But, they had none at all; for, the messenger had scarcely shut the door behind him, when there came another tap, and Tackleton himself walked in.

'Mrs. Peerybingle!' said the Toy-merchant, hat in hand. 'I'm sorry. I'm more sorry than I was this morning. I have had time to think of it. John Peerybingle! I'm sour by disposition; but I can't help being sweetened, more or less, by coming face to face with such a man as you. Caleb! This unconscious little nurse gave me a broken hint last night, of which I have found the thread. I blush to think how easily I might have bound you and your daughter to me, and what a miserable idiot I was, when I took her for one! Friends, one and all, my house is very lonely to-night. I have not so much as a Cricket on my Hearth. I have scared them all away. Be gracious to me; let me join this happy party!'

He was at home in five minutes. You never saw such a fellow. What *had* he been doing with himself all his life, never to have known, before, his great capacity of being jovial! Or what had the Fairies been doing with him, to have effected such a change!

'John! you won't send me home this evening; will you?' whispered Dot.

He had been very near it though!

There wanted but one living creature to make the party complete; and, in the twinkling of an eye, there he was, very thirsty with hard running, and engaged in hopeless endeavours to squeeze his head into a narrow pitcher. He had gone with the cart to its journey's end, very much disgusted with the absence of his master, and stupendously rebellious to the Deputy. After lingering about the stable for some little time, vainly attempting to incite the old horse to the mutinous act of returning on his own account, he had walked into the tap-room and laid himself down before the fire. But suddenly yielding to the conviction that the Deputy was a humbug, and must be abandoned, he had got up again, turned tail, and come home.

There was a dance in the evening. With which general mention of that recreation, I should have left it alone, if I had not some reason to suppose that it was quite an original dance, and one of a most uncommon figure. It was formed in an odd way; in this way. Edward, that sailor-fellow—a good free dashing sort of a fellow he was—had been telling them various marvels concerning parrots, and mines, and Mexicans, and gold dust, when all at once he took it in his head to jump up from his seat and propose a dance; for Bertha's harp was there, and she had such a hand upon it as you seldom hear. Dot (sly little piece of affectation when she chose) said her dancing days were over; *I* think because the Carrier was smoking his pipe, and she liked sitting by him, best. Mrs. Fielding had no choice, of course, but to say *her* dancing days were over, after that; and everybody said the same, except May; May was ready.

So, May and Edward got up, amid great applause, to dance alone; and Bertha plays her liveliest tune.

Well! if you'll believe me, they have not been dancing five minutes, when suddenly the Carrier flings his pipe away, takes Dot round the waist, dashes out into the room, and starts off with her, toe and heel, quite wonderfully. Tackleton no sooner sees this, than he skims across to Mrs. Fielding, takes her round the waist, and follows suit. Old Dot no sooner sees this, than up he is, all alive, whisks off Mrs. Dot in the middle of the dance, and is the foremost there. Caleb no sooner sees this, than he clutches Tilly Slowboy by both hands and goes off at score; Miss Slowboy, firm in the belief that diving hotly in among the other couples, and effecting any number of concussions with them, is your only principle of footing it.

Hark! how the Cricket joins the music with its Chirp, Chirp, Chirp; and how the kettle hums!

*   *   *   *   *   *   *

But what is this! Even as I listen to them, blithely, and turn towards Dot, for one last glimpse of a little figure very pleasant to me, she and the rest have vanished into air, and I am left alone. A Cricket sings upon the Hearth; a broken child's-toy lies upon the ground; and nothing else remains.

D. MACLISE R.A.   JOHN THOMPSON

THE BATTLE OF LIFE

A Love Story

THIS

CHRISTMAS BOOK

IS CORDIALLY INSCRIBED TO MY ENGLISH

FRIENDS IN SWITZERLAND*

PART THE FIRST

ONCE upon a time, it matters little when, and in stalwart England, it matters little where, a fierce battle was fought. It was fought upon a long summer day when the waving grass was green. Many a wild flower formed by the Almighty Hand to be a perfumed goblet for the dew, felt its enamelled cup filled high with blood that day, and shrinking dropped. Many an insect deriving its delicate colour from harmless leaves and herbs, was stained anew that day by dying men, and marked its frightened way with an unnatural track. The painted butterfly took blood into the air upon the edges of its wings. The stream ran red. The trodden ground became a quagmire, whence, from sullen pools collected in the prints of human feet and horses' hoofs, the one prevailing hue still lowered and glimmered at the sun.

Heaven keep us from a knowledge of the sights the moon beheld upon that field, when, coming up above the black line of distant rising-ground, softened and blurred at the edge by trees, she rose into the sky and looked upon the plain, strewn with upturned faces that had once at mothers' breasts sought mothers' eyes, or slumbered happily. Heaven keep us from a knowledge of the secrets whispered afterwards upon the tainted wind that blew across the scene of that day's work and that night's death and suffering! Many a lonely moon was bright upon the battle-ground, and many a star kept mournful watch upon it, and many a wind from every quarter of the earth blew over it, before the traces of the fight were worn away.

They lurked and lingered for a long time, but survived in little things; for, Nature, far above the evil passions of men, soon recovered Her serenity, and smiled upon the guilty battle-ground as she had done before, when it was innocent. The larks sang high above it; the swallows skimmed and dipped and flitted to and fro; the shadows of the flying clouds pursued each other swiftly, over grass and corn and turnip-field and wood, and over roof and church-spire in the nestling town among the trees, away into the bright distance on the borders of the sky and earth, where the red sunsets faded. Crops were sown, and grew up, and were gathered in; the stream that had been crimsoned, turned a water-mill; men whistled at the plough; gleaners and haymakers were seen in quiet groups at work;

sheep and oxen pastured; boys whooped and called, in fields, to scare away the birds; smoke rose from cottage chimneys; sabbath bells rang peacefully; old people lived and died; the timid creatures of the field, and simple flowers of the bush and garden, grew and withered in their destined terms: and all upon the fierce and bloody battle-ground, where thousands upon thousands had been killed in the great fight.

But, there were deep green patches in the growing corn at first, that people looked at awfully. Year after year they re-appeared; and it was known that underneath those fertile spots, heaps of men and horses lay buried, indiscriminately, enriching the ground. The hus-bandmen who ploughed those places, shrunk from the great worms abounding there; and the sheaves they yielded were, for many a long year, called the Battle Sheaves, and set apart; and no one ever knew a Battle Sheaf to be among the last load at a Harvest Home.* For a long time, every furrow that was turned, revealed some fragments of the fight. For a long time, there were wounded trees upon the battle-ground; and scraps of hacked and broken fence and wall, where deadly struggles had been made; and trampled parts where not a leaf or blade would grow. For a long time, no village girl would dress her hair or bosom with the sweetest flower from that field of death: and after many a year had come and gone, the berries growing there, were still believed to leave too deep a stain upon the hand that plucked them.

The Seasons in their course, however, though they passed as lightly as the summer clouds themselves, obliterated, in the lapse of time, even these remains of the old conflict; and wore away such legendary traces of it as the neighbouring people carried in their minds, until they dwindled into old wives' tales, dimly remembered round the winter fire, and waning every year. Where the wild flowers and berries had so long remained upon the stem untouched, gardens arose, and houses were built, and children played at battles on the turf. The wounded trees had long ago made Christmas logs, and blazed and roared away. The deep green patches were no greener now than the memory of those who lay in dust below. The plough-share still turned up from time to time some rusty bits of metal, but it was hard to say what use they had ever served, and those who found them wondered and disputed. An old dinted corslet,* and a helmet, had been hanging in the church so long, that the same weak half-blind old man who tried in vain to make them out above the whitewashed arch, had marvelled at them as a baby. If the host slain upon the field, could have been for a moment reanimated in the forms in which they fell, each upon the spot that was the bed of his untimely death, gashed and ghastly soldiers would have stared in, hundreds deep, at household door and window; and would have risen on the hearths of quiet homes; and would have been the garnered store of barns and granaries; and would have started up between the cradled infant and its nurse; and would have floated with the stream, and whirled round on the mill, and crowded the orchard, and burdened the meadow, and piled the rickyard high with dying men. So altered was the battle-ground, where thousands upon thousands had been killed in the great fight.

Nowhere more altered, perhaps, about a hundred years ago, than in one little orchard attached to an old stone house with a honeysuckle porch; where, on a bright autumn morning, there were sounds of music and laughter, and where two girls danced merrily together on the grass, while some half-dozen peasant women standing on ladders, gathering the apples from the trees, stopped in their work to look down, and share their enjoyment. It was a pleasant, lively, natural scene; a beautiful day, a retired spot; and the two girls, quite unconstrained and careless, danced in the freedom and gaiety of their hearts.

If there were no such thing as display in the world, my private opinion is, and I hope you agree with me, that we might get on a great deal better than we do, and might be infinitely more agreeable company than we are. It was charming to see how these girls danced. They had no spectators but the apple-pickers on the ladders. They were very glad to please them, but they danced to please themselves (or at least you would have supposed so); and you could no more help admiring, than they could help dancing. How they did dance!

Not like opera-dancers.* Not at all. And not like Madame Anybody's finished pupils. Not the least. It was not quadrille dancing, nor minuet dancing, nor even country-dance dancing. It was neither in the old style, nor the new style, nor the French style, nor the English style: though it may have been, by accident, a trifle in the Spanish style, which is a free and joyous one, I am told, deriving a delightful air of off-hand inspiration, from the chirping little castanets. As they danced among the orchard trees, and down the groves of stems and back again, and twirled each other lightly round and round, the influence of their airy motion seemed to spread and spread, in the sun-lighted scene, like an expanding circle in the water. Their streaming hair and fluttering skirts, the elastic grass beneath their feet, the boughs that rustled in the morning air—the flashing leaves, the speckled shadows on the soft green ground—the balmy wind that swept along the landscape, glad to turn the distant windmill, cheerily—everything between the two girls, and the man and team at plough upon the ridge of land, where they showed against the sky as if they were the last things in the world—seemed dancing too.

At last, the younger of the dancing sisters, out of breath, and laughing gaily, threw herself upon a bench to rest. The other leaned against a tree hard by. The music, a wandering harp and fiddle, left off with a flourish, as if it boasted of its freshness; though the truth is, it had gone at such a pace, and worked itself to such a pitch of competition with the dancing, that it never could have held on, half a minute longer. The apple-pickers on the ladders raised a hum and murmur of applause, and then, in keeping with the sound, bestirred themselves to work again like bees.

The more actively, perhaps, because an elderly gentleman, who was no other than Doctor Jeddler himself—it was Doctor Jeddler's house and orchard, you should know, and these were Doctor Jeddler's daughters—came bustling out to see what was the matter, and who the deuce played music on his property, before breakfast. For he was a great philosopher, Doctor Jeddler, and not very musical.

'Music and dancing *to-day!*' said the Doctor, stopping short, and speaking to himself, 'I thought they dreaded to-day. But it's a world of contradictions. Why, Grace, why, Marion!' he added, aloud, 'is the world more mad than usual this morning?'

'Make some allowance for it, father, if it be,' replied his younger daughter, Marion, going close to him, and looking into his face, 'for it's somebody's birth-day.'

'Somebody's birth-day, Puss!' replied the Doctor. 'Don't you know it's always somebody's birth-day? Did you never hear how many new performers enter on this—ha! ha!—it's impossible to speak gravely of it—on this preposterous and ridiculous business called Life, every minute?'

'No, father!'

'No, not you, of course; you're a woman—almost,' said the Doctor. 'By-the-by,' and he looked into the pretty face, still close to his, 'I suppose it's *your* birth-day.'

'No! Do you really, father?' cried his pet daughter, pursing up her red lips to be kissed.

'There! Take my love with it,' said the Doctor, imprinting his upon them; 'and many happy returns of the—the idea!—of the day. The notion of wishing happy returns in such a farce as this,' said the Doctor to himself, 'is good! Ha! ha! ha!'

Doctor Jeddler was, as I have said, a great philosopher, and the heart and mystery of his philosophy was, to look upon the world as a gigantic practical joke; as something too absurd to be considered seriously, by any rational man. His system of belief had been, in the beginning, part and parcel of the battle-ground on which he lived, as you shall presently understand.

'Well! But how did you get the music?' asked the Doctor. 'Poultry-stealers, of course! Where did the minstrels come from?'

'Alfred sent the music,' said his daughter Grace, adjusting a few simple flowers in her sister's hair, with which, in her admiration of that youthful beauty, she had herself adorned it half-an-hour before, and which the dancing had disarranged.

'Oh! Alfred sent the music, did he?' returned the Doctor.

'Yes. He met it coming out of the town as he was entering early. The men are travelling on foot, and rested there last night; and as it was Marion's birthday, and he thought it would please her, he sent them on, with a pencilled note to me, saying that if I thought so too, they had come to serenade her.'

'Ay, ay,' said the Doctor, carelessly, 'he always takes your opinion.'

'And my opinion being favourable,' said Grace, good-humouredly; and pausing for a moment to admire the pretty head she decorated, with her own thrown back; 'and Marion being in high spirits, and beginning to dance, I joined her. And so we danced to Alfred's music till we were out of breath. And we thought the music all the gayer for being sent by Alfred. Didn't we, dear Marion?'

'Oh, I don't know, Grace. How you tease me about Alfred.'

'Tease you by mentioning your lover?' said her sister.

'I am sure I don't much care to have him mentioned,' said the wilful beauty, stripping the petals from some flowers she held, and scattering them on the ground. 'I am almost tired of hearing of him; and as to his being my lover——'

'Hush! Don't speak lightly of a true heart, which is all your own, Marion,' cried her sister, 'even in jest. There is not a truer heart than Alfred's in the world!'

'No—no,' said Marion, raising her eyebrows with a pleasant air of careless consideration, 'perhaps not. But I don't know that there's any great merit in that. I—I don't want him to be so very true. I never asked him. If he expects that I—But, dear Grace, why need we talk of him at all, just now!'

It was agreeable to see the graceful figures of the blooming sisters, twined together, lingering among the trees, conversing thus, with earnestness opposed to lightness, yet, with love responding tenderly to love. And it was very curious indeed to see the younger sister's eyes suffused with tears, and something fervently and deeply felt, breaking through the wilfulness of what she said, and striving with it painfully.

The difference between them, in respect of age, could not exceed four years at most; but Grace, as often happens in such cases, when no mother watches over both (the Doctor's wife was dead), seemed, in her gentle care of her young sister, and in the steadiness of her devotion to her, older than she was; and more removed, in course of nature, from all competition with her, or participation, otherwise than through her sympathy and true affection, in her wayward fancies, than their ages seemed to warrant. Great character of mother, that, even in this shadow and faint reflection of it, purifies the heart, and raises the exalted nature nearer to the angels!*

The Doctor's reflections, as he looked after them, and heard the purport of their discourse, were limited at first to certain merry meditations on the folly of all loves and likings, and the idle imposition practised on themselves by young people, who believed for a moment, that there could be anything serious in such bubbles, and were always undeceived—always!

But the home-adorning, self-denying qualities of Grace, and her sweet temper, so gentle and retiring, yet including so much constancy and bravery of spirit, seemed all expressed to him in the contrast between her quiet household figure and that of his younger and more beautiful child; and he was sorry for her sake—sorry for them both—that life should be such a very ridiculous business as it was.

The Doctor never dreamed of inquiring whether his children, or either of them, helped in any way to make the scheme a serious one. But then he was a Philosopher.

A kind and generous man by nature, he had stumbled, by chance, over that common Philosopher's stone* (much more easily discovered than the object of the alchemist's researches), which sometimes trips up kind and generous men, and has the fatal property of turning gold to dross and every precious thing to poor account.

'Britain!' cried the Doctor. 'Britain! Holloa!'

A small man, with an uncommonly sour and discontented face, emerged from the house, and returned to this call the unceremonious acknowledgement of 'Now then!'

'Where's the breakfast table?' said the Doctor.

'In the house,' returned Britain.

'Are you going to spread it out here, as you were told last night?' said the Doctor. 'Don't you know that there are gentlemen coming? That there's business to be done this morning, before the coach comes by? That this is a very particular occasion?'

'I couldn't do anything, Dr. Jeddler, till the women had done getting in the apples, could I?' said Britain, his voice rising with his reasoning, so that it was very loud at last.

'Well, have they done now?' replied the Doctor, looking at his watch, and clapping his hands. 'Come! make haste! where's Clemency?'

'Here am I, Mister,' said a voice from one of the ladders, which a pair of clumsy feet descended briskly. 'It's all done now. Clear away, gals. Everything shall be ready for you in half a minute, Mister.'

With that she began to bustle about most vigorously; presenting, as she did so, an appearance sufficiently peculiar to justify a word of introduction.

She was about thirty years old, and had a sufficiently plump and cheerful face, though it was twisted up into an odd expression of tightness that made it comical. But the extraordinary homeliness of her gait and manner, would have superseded any face in the world. To say that she had two left legs, and somebody else's arms, and that all four limbs seemed to be out of joint, and to start from perfectly wrong places when they were set in motion, is to offer the mildest outline of the reality. To say that she was perfectly content and satisfied with these arrangements, and regarded them as being no business of hers, and that she took her arms and legs as they came, and allowed them to dispose of themselves just as it happened, is to render faint justice to her equanimity. Her dress was a prodigious pair of self-willed shoes, that never wanted to go where her feet went; blue stockings; a printed gown of many colours, and the most hideous pattern procurable for money; and a white apron. She always wore short sleeves, and always had, by some accident, grazed elbows, in which she took so lively an interest, that she was continually trying to turn them round and get impossible views of them. In general, a little cap placed somewhere on her head; though it was rarely to be met with in the place usually occupied in other subjects, by that article of dress; but from head to foot she was scrupulously clean, and maintained a kind of dislocated tidiness. Indeed, her laudable anxiety to be tidy and compact in her own conscience as well as in the public eye, gave rise to one of her most startling evolutions, which was to grasp herself sometimes by a sort of wooden handle (part of her clothing, and familiarly called a busk), and wrestle as it were with her garments, until they fell into a symmetrical arrangement.

Such, in outward form and garb, was Clemency Newcome; who was supposed to have unconsciously originated a corruption of her own Christian name, from Clementina (but nobody knew, for the deaf old mother, a very phenomenon of age, whom she had supported almost from a child, was dead, and she had no other relation); who now busied herself in preparing the table, and who stood, at intervals, with her bare red arms crossed, rubbing her grazed elbows with opposite hands, and staring at it very composedly, until she suddenly remembered something else she wanted, and jogged off to fetch it.

'Here are them two lawyers a-coming, Mister!' said Clemency, in a tone of no very great good-will.

'Aha!' cried the Doctor, advancing to the gate to meet them. 'Good morning, good morning! Grace, my dear! Marion! Here are Messrs. Snitchey and Craggs. Where's Alfred?'

'He'll be back directly, father, no doubt,' said Grace. 'He had so much to do this morning in his preparations for departure, that he was up and out by daybreak. Good morning, gentlemen.'

'Ladies!' said Mr. Snitchey, 'for Self and Craggs,' who bowed, 'good morning! Miss,' to Marion, 'I kiss your hand.' Which he did.

'And I wish you'—which he might or might not, for he didn't look, at first sight, like a gentleman troubled with many warm outpourings of soul, in behalf of other people, 'a hundred happy returns of this auspicious day.'

'Ha ha ha!' laughed the Doctor thoughtfully, with his hands in his pockets. 'The great farce in a hundred acts!'

'You wouldn't, I am sure,' said Mr. Snitchey, standing a small professional blue bag* against one leg of the table, 'cut the great farce short for this actress, at all events, Doctor Jeddler.'

'No,' returned the Doctor. 'God forbid! May she live to laugh at it, as long as she *can* laugh, and then say, with the French wit,* "The farce is ended; draw the curtain." '

'The French wit', said Mr. Snitchey, peeping sharply into his blue bag, 'was wrong, Doctor Jeddler, and your philosophy is altogether wrong, depend upon it, as I have often told you. Nothing serious in life! What do you call law?'

'A joke,' replied the Doctor.

'Did you ever go to law?' asked Mr. Snitchey, looking out of the blue bag.

'Never,' returned the Doctor.

'If you ever do,' said Mr. Snitchey, 'perhaps you'll alter that opinion.'

Craggs, who seemed to be represented by Snitchey, and to be conscious of little or no separate existence or personal individuality, offered a remark of his own in this place. It involved the only idea of which he did not stand seized and possessed in equal moieties with Snitchey; but he had some partners in it among the wise men of the world.

'It's made a great deal too easy,' said Mr. Craggs.

'Law is?' asked the Doctor.

'Yes,' said Mr. Craggs, 'everything is. Everything appears to me to be made too easy, now-a-days. It's the vice of these times. If the world is a joke (I am not prepared to say it isn't), it ought to be made a very difficult joke to crack. It ought to be as hard a struggle, sir, as possible. That's the intention. But it's being made far too easy. We are oiling the gates of life. They ought to be rusty. We shall have them beginning to turn, soon, with a smooth sound. Whereas they ought to grate upon their hinges, sir.'

Mr. Craggs seemed positively to grate upon his own hinges, as he delivered this opinion; to which he communicated immense effect—being a cold, hard, dry man, dressed in grey and white, like a flint; with small twinkles in his eyes, as if something struck sparks out of them. The three natural kingdoms, indeed, had each a fanciful representative among this brotherhood of disputants; for Snitchey was like a magpie or raven (only not so sleek), and the Doctor had a streaked face like a winter-pippin,* with here and there a dimple to express the peckings of the birds, and a very little bit of pigtail behind that stood for the stalk.

As the active figure of a handsome young man, dressed for a journey, and followed by a porter bearing several packages and baskets, entered the orchard at a brisk pace, and with an air of gaiety and hope that accorded well with the morning, these three drew together, like the brothers of the sister Fates, or like the Graces most effectually disguised, or like the three weird prophets* on the heath, and greeted him.

'Happy returns, Alf!' said the Doctor, lightly.

'A hundred happy returns of this auspicious day, Mr. Heathfield!' said Snitchey, bowing low.

'Returns!' Craggs murmured in a deep voice, all alone.

'Why, what a battery!' exclaimed Alfred, stopping short, 'and one—two—three—all foreboders of no good, in the great sea before me. I am glad you are not the first I have met this morning: I should have taken it for a bad omen. But Grace was the first—sweet, pleasant Grace—so I defy you all!'

'If you please, Mister, *I* was the first you know,' said Clemency Newcome. 'She was walking out here, before sunrise, you remember. I was in the house.'

'That's true! Clemency was the first,' said Alfred. 'So I defy you with Clemency.'

'Ha, ha, ha,—for Self and Craggs,' said Snitchey. 'What a defiance!'

'Not so bad a one as it appears, may be,' said Alfred, shaking hands heartily with the Doctor, and also with Snitchey and Craggs, and then looking round. 'Where are the—Good Heavens!'

With a start, productive for the moment of a closer partnership between Jonathan Snitchey and Thomas Craggs than the subsisting articles of agreement in that wise contemplated, he hastily betook himself to where the sisters stood together, and—however, I needn't more particularly explain his manner of saluting Marion first, and

Grace afterwards, than by hinting that Mr. Craggs may possibly have considered it 'too easy.'

Perhaps to change the subject, Dr. Jeddler made a hasty move towards the breakfast, and they all sat down at table. Grace presided; but so discreetly stationed herself, as to cut off her sister and Alfred from the rest of the company. Snitchey and Craggs sat at opposite corners, with the blue bag between them for safety; the Doctor took his usual position, opposite to Grace. Clemency hovered galvanically about the table, as waitress; and the melancholy Britain, at another and a smaller board, acted as Grand Carver* of a round of beef and a ham.

'Meat?' said Britain, approaching Mr. Snitchey, with the carving knife and fork in his hands, and throwing the question at him like a missile.

'Certainly,' returned the lawyer.

'Do *you* want any?' to Craggs.

'Lean and well done,' replied that gentleman.

Having executed these orders, and moderately supplied the Doctor (he seemed to know that nobody else wanted anything to eat), he lingered as near the Firm as he decently could, watching with an austere eye their disposition of the viands, and but once relaxing the severe expression of his face. This was on the occasion of Mr. Craggs, whose teeth were not of the best, partially choking, when he cried out with great animation, 'I thought he was gone!'

'Now, Alfred,' said the Doctor, 'for a word or two of business, while we are yet at breakfast.'

'While we are yet at breakfast,' said Snitchey and Craggs, who seemed to have no present idea of leaving off.

Although Alfred had not been breakfasting, and seemed to have quite enough business on his hands as it was, he respectfully answered:

'If you please, sir.'

'If anything could be serious,' the Doctor began, 'in such a—'

'Farce as this, sir,' hinted Alfred.

'In such a farce as this,' observed the Doctor, 'it might be this recurrence, on the eve of separation, of a double birth-day, which is connected with many associations pleasant to us four, and with the recollection of a long and amicable intercourse. That's not to the purpose.'

'Ah! yes, yes, Dr. Jeddler,' said the young man. 'It is to the purpose. Much to the purpose, as my heart bears witness this morning; and as yours does too, I know, if you would let it speak. I leave your house to–day; I cease to be your ward to–day; we part with tender relations stretching far behind us, that never can be exactly renewed, and with others dawning yet before us,' he looked down at Marion beside him, 'fraught with such considerations as I must not trust myself to speak of now. Come, come!' he added, rallying his spirits and the Doctor at once, 'there's a serious grain in this large foolish dust-heap, Doctor. Let us allow to–day, that there is One.'

'To–day!' cried the Doctor. 'Hear him! Ha, ha, ha! Of all days in the foolish year. Why, on this day, the great battle was fought on this ground. On this ground where we now sit, where I saw my two girls dance this morning, where the fruit has just been gathered for our eating from these trees, the roots of which are struck in Men, not earth,—so many lives were lost, that within my recollection, generations afterwards, a churchyard full of bones, and dust of bones, and chips of cloven skulls, has been dug up from underneath our feet here. Yet not a hundred people in that battle knew for what they fought, or why; not a hundred of the inconsiderate rejoicers in the victory, why they rejoiced. Not half a hundred people were the better for the gain or loss. Not half-a-dozen men agree to this hour on the cause or merits; and nobody, in short, ever knew anything distinct about it, but the mourners of the slain. Serious, too!' said the Doctor, laughing. 'Such a system!'

'But, all this seems to me', said Alfred, 'to be very serious.'

'Serious!' cried the Doctor. 'If you allowed such things to be serious, you must go mad, or die, or climb up to the top of a mountain, and turn hermit.'

'Besides—so long ago,' said Alfred.

'Long ago!' returned the Doctor. 'Do you know what the world has been doing, ever since? Do you know what else it has been doing? *I* don't!'

'It has gone to law a little,' observed Mr. Snitchey, stirring his tea.

'Although the way out has been always made too easy,' said his partner.

'And you'll excuse my saying, Doctor,' pursued Mr. Snitchey, 'having been already put a thousand times in possession of my opinion, in the course of our discussions, that, in its having gone to law, and in its legal system altogether, I do observe a serious side—now, really, a something tangible, and with a purpose and intention in it—'

Clemency Newcome made an angular tumble against the table, occasioning a sounding clatter among the cups and saucers.

'Heyday! what's the matter there?' exclaimed the Doctor.

'It's this evil-inclined blue bag,' said Clemency, 'always tripping up somebody!'

'With a purpose and intention in it, I was saying,' resumed Snitchey, 'that commands respect. Life a farce, Dr. Jeddler? With law in it?'

The Doctor laughed, and looked at Alfred.

'Granted, if you please, that war is foolish,' said Snitchey. 'There we agree. For example. Here's a smiling country,' pointing it out with his fork, 'once overrun by soldiers—trespassers every man of 'em—and laid waste by fire and sword. He, he, he! The idea of any man exposing himself, voluntarily, to fire and sword! Stupid, wasteful, positively ridiculous; you laugh at your fellow-creatures, you know, when you think of it! But take this smiling country as it stands. Think of the laws appertaining to real property; to the bequest and devise of real property; to the mortgage and redemption of real property; to leasehold, freehold, and copyhold estate; think,' said Mr. Snitchey, with such great emotion that he actually smacked his lips, 'of the complicated laws relating to title and proof of title, with all the contradictory precedents and numerous acts of parliament connected with them; think of the infinite number of ingenious and interminable chancery suits, to which this pleasant prospect may give rise; and acknowledge, Dr. Jeddler, that there is a green spot in the scheme about us! I believe', said Mr. Snitchey, looking at his partner, 'that I speak for Self and Craggs?'

Mr. Craggs having signified assent, Mr. Snitchey, somewhat freshened by his recent eloquence, observed that he would take a little more beef and another cup of tea.

'I don't stand up for life in general,' he added, rubbing his hands and chuckling, 'it's full of folly; full of something worse. Professions of trust, and confidence, and unselfishness, and all that! Bah, bah, bah! We see what they're worth. But you mustn't laugh at life; you've got a game to play; a very serious game indeed! Everybody's playing against you, you know, and you're playing against them. Oh! it's a very interesting thing. There are deep moves upon the board. You must only laugh, Dr. Jeddler, when you win—and then not much. He, he, he! And then not much,' repeated Snitchey, rolling his head and winking his eye, as if he would have added, 'you may do this instead!'

'Well, Alfred!' cried the Doctor, 'what do you say now?'

'I say, sir,' replied Alfred, 'that the greatest favour you could do me, and yourself too I am inclined to think, would be to try sometimes to forget this battle-field and others like it in that broader battle-field of Life, on which the sun looks every day.'

'Really, I'm afraid that wouldn't soften his opinions, Mr. Alfred,' said Snitchey. 'The combatants are very eager and very bitter in that same battle of Life. There's a great deal of cutting and slashing, and firing into people's heads from behind. There is terrible treading down, and trampling on. It is rather a bad business.'

'I believe, Mr. Snitchey,' said Alfred, 'there are quiet victories and struggles, great sacrifices of self, and noble acts of heroism, in it— even in many of its apparent lightnesses and contradictions—not the less difficult to achieve, because they have no earthly chronicle or audience—done every day in nooks and corners, and in little households, and in men's and women's hearts—any one of which might reconcile the sternest man to such a world, and fill him with belief and hope in it, though two-fourths of its people were at war, and another fourth at law; and that's a bold word.'

Both the sisters listened keenly.

'Well, well!' said the Doctor, 'I am too old to be converted, even by my friend Snitchey here, or my good spinster sister, Martha Jeddler; who had what she calls her domestic trials ages ago, and has led a sympathising life with all sorts of people ever since; and who is so much of your opinion (only she's less reasonable and more obstinate, being a woman), that we can't agree, and seldom meet. I was born upon this battle-field. I began, as a boy, to have my thoughts directed to the real history of a battle-field. Sixty years have gone over my head, and I have never seen the Christian world, including Heaven knows how many loving mothers and good enough girls like mine here, anything but mad for a battle-field. The same contradictions prevail in everything. One must either laugh or cry at such stupendous inconsistencies; and I prefer to laugh.'

Britain, who had been paying the profoundest and most melancholy attention to each speaker in his turn, seemed suddenly to decide in favour of the same preference, if a deep sepulchral sound that escaped him might be construed into a demonstration of risibility. His face, however, was so perfectly unaffected by it, both before and afterwards, that although one or two of the breakfast party looked round as being startled by a mysterious noise, nobody connected the offender with it.

Except his partner in attendance, Clemency Newcome; who rousing him with one of those favourite joints, her elbows, inquired, in a reproachful whisper, what he laughed at.

'Not you!' said Britain.

'Who then?'

'Humanity,' said Britain. 'That's the joke!'

'What between master and them lawyers, he's getting more and more addle-headed every day!' cried Clemency, giving him a lunge with the other elbow, as a mental stimulant. 'Do you know where you are? Do you want to get warning?'

'I don't know anything,' said Britain, with a leaden eye and an immovable visage. 'I don't care for anything. I don't make out anything. I don't believe anything. And I don't want anything.'

Although this forlorn summary of his general condition may have been overcharged in an access of despondency, Benjamin Britain—sometimes called Little Britain, to distinguish him from Great; as we might say Young England,* to express Old England with a decided difference—had defined his real state more accurately than might be supposed. For, serving as a sort of man Miles to the Doctor's Friar Bacon,* and listening day after day to innumerable orations addressed by the Doctor to various people, all tending to show that his very existence was at best a mistake and an absurdity, this unfortunate servitor had fallen, by degrees, into such an abyss of confused and contradictory suggestions from within and without, that Truth at the bottom of her well, was on the level surface as compared with Britain in the depths of his mystification. The only point he clearly comprehended, was, that the new element usually brought into these discussions by Snitchey and Craggs, never served to make them clearer, and always seemed to give the Doctor a species of advantage and confirmation. Therefore, he looked upon the Firm as one of the proximate causes of his state of mind, and held them in abhorrence accordingly.

'But this is not our business, Alfred,' said the Doctor. 'Ceasing to be my ward (as you have said) to-day; and leaving us full to the brim of such learning as the Grammar School down here was able to give you, and your studies in London could add to that, and such practical knowledge as a dull old country Doctor like myself could graft upon both; you are away, now, into the world. The first term of probation appointed by your poor father, being over, away you go now, your own master, to fulfil his second desire. And long before your three years' tour among the foreign schools of medicine is finished, you'll have forgotten us. Lord, you'll forget us easily in six months!'

'If I do—But you know better; why should I speak to you!' said Alfred, laughing.

'I don't know anything of the sort,' returned the Doctor. 'What do you say, Marion?'

Marion, trifling with her teacup, seemed to say—but she didn't say it—that he was welcome to forget, if he could. Grace pressed the blooming face against her cheek, and smiled.

'I haven't been, I hope, a very unjust steward in the execution of my trust,' pursued the Doctor; 'but I am to be, at any rate, formally discharged, and released, and what not, this morning; and here are our good friends Snitchey and Craggs, with a bagful of papers, and accounts, and documents, for the transfer of the balance of the trust fund to you (I wish it was a more difficult one to dispose of, Alfred, but you must get to be a great man and make it so), and other drolleries of that sort, which are to be signed, sealed, and delivered.'

'And duly witnessed as by law required,' said Snitchey, pushing away his plate, and taking out the papers, which his partner proceeded to spread upon the table; 'and Self and Craggs having been co-trustees with you, Doctor, in so far as the fund was concerned, we shall want your two servants to attest the signatures—can you read, Mrs. Newcome?'

'I an't married, Mister,' said Clemency.

'Oh! I beg your pardon. I should think not,' chuckled Snitchey, casting his eyes over her extraordinary figure. 'You *can* read?'

'A little,' answered Clemency.

'The marriage service, night and morning, eh?' observed the lawyer, jocosely.

'No,' said Clemency. 'Too hard. I only reads a thimble.'

'Read a thimble!' echoed Snitchey. 'What are you talking about, young woman?'

Clemency nodded. 'And a nutmeg-grater.'

'Why, this is a lunatic! a subject for the Lord High Chancellor!'* said Snitchey, staring at her.

—'If possessed of any property,' stipulated Craggs.

Grace, however, interposing, explained that each of the articles in question bore an engraved motto, and so formed the pocket library* of Clemency Newcome, who was not much given to the study of books.

'Oh, that's it, is it, Miss Grace!' said Snitchey

'Yes, yes. Ha, ha, ha! I thought our friend was an idiot. She looks uncommonly like it,' he muttered, with a supercilious glance. 'And what does the thimble say, Mrs. Newcome?'

'I an't married, Mister,' observed Clemency.

'Well, Newcome. Will that do?' said the lawyer. 'What does the thimble say, Newcome?'

How Clemency, before replying to this question, held one pocket open, and looked down into its yawning depths for the thimble which wasn't there,—and how she then held an opposite pocket open, and seeming to descry it, like a pearl of great price,* at the bottom, cleared away such intervening obstacles as a handkerchief, an end of wax candle, a flushed apple, an orange, a lucky penny, a cramp bone,* a padlock, a pair of scissors in a sheath more expressively describable as promising young shears, a handful or so of loose beads, several balls of cotton, a needle-case, a cabinet collection of curl-papers, and a biscuit, all of which articles she entrusted individually and separately to Britain to hold,—is of no consequence.

Nor how, in her determination to grasp this pocket by the throat and keep it prisoner (for it had a tendency to swing, and twist itself round the nearest corner), she assumed and calmly maintained, an attitude apparently inconsistent with the human anatomy and the laws of gravity. It is enough that at last she triumphantly produced the thimble on her finger, and rattled the nutmeg-grater: the literature of both those trinkets being obviously in course of wearing out and wasting away, through excessive friction.

'That's the thimble, is it, young woman?' said Mr. Snitchey, diverting himself at her expense. 'And what does the thimble say?'

'It says,' replied Clemency, reading slowly round as if it were a tower, 'For-get and For-give.'

Snitchey and Craggs laughed heartily. 'So new!' said Snitchey. 'So easy!' said Craggs. 'Such a knowledge of human nature in it!' said Snitchey. 'So applicable to the affairs of life!' said Craggs.

'And the nutmeg-grater?' inquired the head of the Firm.

'The grater says,' returned Clemency, 'Do as you—wold—be—done by.'

'Do, or you'll be done brown,* you mean,' said Mr. Snitchey.

'I don't understand,' retorted Clemency, shaking her head vaguely. 'I an't no lawyer.'

'I am afraid that if she was, Doctor,' said Mr. Snitchey, turning to him suddenly, as if to anticipate any effect that might otherwise be consequent on this retort, 'she'd find it to be the golden rule* of half her clients. They are serious enough in that—whimsical as your world is—and lay the blame on us afterwards. We, in our profession, are little else than mirrors after all, Mr. Alfred; but we are generally consulted by angry and quarrelsome people who are not in their best looks, and it's rather hard to quarrel with us if we reflect unpleasant aspects. I think', said Mr. Snitchey, 'that I speak for Self and Craggs?'

'Decidedly,' said Craggs.

'And so, if Mr. Britain will oblige us with a mouthful* of ink,' said Mr. Snitchey, returning to the papers, 'we'll sign, seal, and deliver as soon as possible, or the coach will be coming past before we know where we are.'

If one might judge from his appearance, there was every probability of the coach coming past before Mr. Britain knew where *he* was; for he stood in a state of abstraction, mentally balancing the Doctor against the lawyers, and the lawyers against the Doctor, and their clients against both, and engaged in feeble attempts to make the thimble and nutmeg-grater (a new idea to him) square with anybody's system of philosophy; and, in short, bewildering himself as much as ever his great namesake has done with theories and schools. But Clemency, who was his good Genius*—though he had the meanest possible opinion of her understanding, by reason of her seldom troubling herself with abstract speculations, and being always at hand to do the right thing at the right time—having produced the ink in a twinkling, tendered him the further service of recalling him to himself by the application of her elbows; with which gentle flappers* she so jogged his memory, in a more literal construction of that phrase than usual, that he soon became quite fresh and brisk.

How he laboured under an apprehension not uncommon to persons in his degree, to whom the use of pen and ink is an event, that he couldn't append his name to a document, not of his own writing, without committing himself in some shadowy manner, or somehow signing away vague and enormous sums of money; and how he approached the deeds under protest, and by dint of the Doctor's coercion, and insisted on pausing to look at them before writing (the cramped hand, to say nothing of the phraseology, being so much Chinese to him), and also on turning them round to see whether there was anything fraudulent underneath; and how, having signed his name, he became desolate as one who had parted with his property and rights; I want the time to tell. Also, how the blue bag containing his signature, afterwards had a mysterious interest for him, and he couldn't leave it; also, how Clemency Newcome, in an ecstasy of laughter at the idea of her own importance and dignity, brooded over the whole table with her two elbows, like a spread eagle, and reposed her head upon her left arm as a preliminary to the formation of certain cabalistic characters, which required a deal of ink, and imaginary counterparts whereof she executed at the same time with her tongue. Also, how, having once tasted ink, she became thirsty in that regard, as tame tigers are said to be after tasting another sort of fluid, and wanted to sign everything, and put her name in all kinds of places. In brief, the Doctor was discharged of his trust and all its responsibilities; and Alfred, taking it on himself, was fairly started on the journey of life.

'Britain!' said the Doctor. 'Run to the gate, and watch for the coach. Time flies, Alfred.'

'Yes, sir, yes,' returned the young man, hurriedly. 'Dear Grace! a moment! Marion—so young and beautiful, so winning and so much admired, dear to my heart as nothing else in life is—remember! I leave Marion to you!'

'She has always been a sacred charge to me, Alfred. She is doubly so, now. I will be faithful to my trust, believe me.'

'I do believe it, Grace. I know it well. Who could look upon your face, and hear your voice, and not know it! Ah, Grace! If I had your well-governed heart, and tranquil mind, how bravely I would leave this place to-day!'

'Would you?' she answered with a quiet smile.

'And yet, Grace—Sister, seems the natural word.'

'Use it!' she said quickly. 'I am glad to hear it. Call me nothing else.'

'And yet, sister, then,' said Alfred, 'Marion and I had better have your true and steadfast qualities serving us here, and making us both happier and better. I wouldn't carry them away, to sustain myself, if I could!'

'Coach upon the hill-top!' exclaimed Britain.

'Time flies, Alfred,' said the Doctor.

Marion had stood apart, with her eyes fixed upon the ground; but, this warning being given, her young lover brought her tenderly to where her sister stood, and gave her into her embrace.

'I have been telling Grace, dear Marion,' he said, 'that you are her charge; my precious trust at parting. And when I come back and reclaim you, dearest, and the bright prospect of our married life lies stretched before us, it shall be one of our chief pleasures to consult how we can make Grace happy; how we can anticipate her wishes; how we can show our gratitude and love to her; how we can return her something of the debt she will have heaped upon us.'

The younger sister had one hand in his; the other rested on her sister's neck. She looked into that sister's eyes, so calm, serene, and cheerful, with a gaze in which affection, admiration, sorrow, wonder, almost veneration, were blended. She looked into that sister's face, as if it were the face of some bright angel. Calm, serene, and cheerful, the face looked back on her and on her lover.

'And when the time comes, as it must one day,' said Alfred,—'I wonder it has never come yet, but Grace knows best, for Grace is always right—when *she* will want a friend to open her whole heart to, and to be to her something of what she has been to us—then, Marion, how faithful we will prove, and what delight to us to know that she, our dear good sister, loves and is loved again, as we would have her!'

Still the younger sister looked into her eyes, and turned not—even towards him. And still those honest eyes looked back, so calm, serene, and cheerful, on herself and on her lover.

'And when all that is past, and we are old, and living (as we must!) together—close together—talking often of old times,' said Alfred—'these shall be our favourite times among them—this day most of all; and, telling each other what we thought and felt, and hoped and feared at parting; and how we couldn't bear to say good bye——'

'Coach coming through the wood!' cried Britain.

'Yes! I am ready—and how we met again, so happily in spite of all; we'll make this day the happiest in all the year, and keep it as a treble birth-day. Shall we, dear?'

'Yes!' interposed the elder sister, eagerly, and with a radiant smile. 'Yes! Alfred, don't linger. There's no time. Say good bye to Marion. And Heaven be with you!'

He pressed the younger sister to his heart. Released from his embrace, she again clung to her sister; and her eyes, with the same blended look, again sought those so calm, serene, and cheerful.

'Farewell, my boy!' said the Doctor. 'To talk about any serious correspondence or serious affections, and engagements and so forth, in such a—ha, ha, ha!—you know what I mean—why that, of course, would be sheer nonsense. All I can say is, that if you and Marion should continue in the same foolish minds, I shall not object to have you for a son-in-law one of these days.'

'Over the bridge!' cried Britain.

'Let it come!' said Alfred, wringing the Doctor's hand stoutly. 'Think of me sometimes, my old friend and guardian, as seriously as you can! Adieu, Mr. Snitchey! Farewell, Mr. Craggs!'

'Coming down the road!' cried Britain.

'A kiss of Clemency Newcome for long acquaintance' sake! Shake hands, Britain! Marion, dearest heart, good bye! Sister Grace! remember!'

The quiet household figure, and the face so beautiful in its serenity, were turned towards him in reply; but Marion's look and attitude remained unchanged.

The coach was at the gate. There was a bustle with the luggage. The coach drove away. Marion never moved.

'He waves his hat to you, my love,' said Grace. 'Your chosen husband, darling. Look!'

The younger sister raised her head, and, for a moment, turned it. Then, turning back again, and fully meeting, for the first time, those calm eyes, fell sobbing on her neck.

'Oh, Grace. God bless you! But I cannot bear to see it, Grace! It breaks my heart.'

PART THE SECOND

SNITCHEY AND CRAGGS had a snug little office on the old Battle Ground, where they drove a snug little business, and fought a great many small pitched battles for a great many contending parties. Though it could hardly be said of these conflicts that they were running fights—for in truth they generally proceeded at a snail's pace—the part the Firm had in them came so far within the general denomination, that now they took a shot at this Plaintiff, and now aimed a chop at that Defendant, now made a heavy charge at an estate in Chancery, and now had some light skirmishing among an irregular body of small debtors, just as the occasion served, and the enemy happened to present himself. The Gazette* was an important and profitable feature in some of their fields, as in the fields of greater renown; and in most of the Actions wherein they showed their generalship, it was afterwards observed by the combatants that they had had great difficulty in making each other out, or in knowing with any degree of distinctness what they were about, in consequence of the vast amount of smoke by which they were surrounded.

The offices of Messrs. Snitchey and Craggs stood convenient, with an open door down two smooth steps, in the market-place; so that any angry farmer inclining towards hot water, might tumble into it at once. Their special council-chamber and hall of conference was an old back-room up-stairs, with a low dark ceiling, which seemed to be knitting its brows gloomily in the consideration of tangled points of law. It was furnished with some high-backed leathern chairs, garnished with great goggle-eyed brass nails, of which, every here and there, two or three had fallen out—or had been picked out, perhaps, by the wandering thumbs and fore-fingers of bewildered clients. There was a framed print of a great judge in it, every curl in whose dreadful wig had made a man's hair stand on end. Bales of papers filled the dusty closets, shelves, and tables; and round the wainscot there were tiers of boxes, padlocked and fire-proof, with people's names painted outside, which anxious visitors felt themselves, by a cruel enchantment, obliged to spell backwards and forwards, and to make anagrams of, while they sat, seeming to listen to Snitchey and Craggs, without comprehending one word of what they said.

Snitchey and Craggs had each, in private life as in professional existence, a partner of his own. Snitchey and Craggs were the best friends in the world, and had a real confidence in one another; but Mrs. Snitchey, by a dispensation not uncommon in the affairs of life, was on principle suspicious of Mr. Craggs; and Mrs. Craggs was on principle suspicious of Mr. Snitchey. 'Your Snitcheys indeed,' the latter lady would observe, sometimes, to Mr. Craggs; using that imaginative plural as if in disparagement of an objectionable pair of pantaloons, or other articles not possessed of a singular number; 'I don't see what you want with your Snitcheys, for my part. You trust a great deal too much to your Snitcheys, *I* think, and I hope you may never find my words come true.' While Mrs. Snitchey would observe to Mr. Snitchey, of Craggs, 'that if ever he was led away by man he was led away by that man, and that if ever she read a double purpose in a mortal eye, she read that purpose in Craggs's eye.' Notwithstanding this, however, they were all very good friends in general: and Mrs. Snitchey and Mrs. Craggs maintained a close bond of alliance against 'the office,' which they both considered the Blue chamber,* and common enemy, full of dangerous (because unknown) machinations.

In this office, nevertheless, Snitchey and Craggs made honey for their several hives. Here, sometimes, they would linger, of a fine evening, at the window of their council-chamber overlooking the old battle-ground, and wonder (but that was generally at assize time, when much business had made them sentimental) at the folly of mankind, who couldn't always be at peace with one another and go to law comfortably. Here, days, and weeks, and months, and years, passed over them: their calendar, the gradually diminishing number of brass nails in the leathern chairs, and the increasing bulk of papers on the tables. Here, nearly three years' flight had thinned the one and swelled the other, since the breakfast in the orchard; when they sat together in consultation at night.

Not alone; but with a man of thirty, or about that time of life, negligently dressed, and somewhat haggard in the face, but well-made, well-attired, and well-looking, who sat in the arm-chair of state, with one hand in his breast, and the other in his dishevelled hair, pondering moodily. Messrs. Snitchey and Craggs sat opposite each other at a neighbouring desk. One of the fireproof boxes, unpadlocked and opened, was upon it; a part of its contents lay strewn upon the table, and the rest was then in course of passing through the hands of Mr. Snitchey; who brought it to the candle, document by document; looked at every paper singly, as he produced it; shook his head, and handed it to Mr. Craggs; who looked it over also, shook his head, and laid it down. Sometimes they would stop, and shaking their heads in concert, look towards the abstracted client. And the name on the box being Michael Warden, Esquire, we may conclude from these premises that the name and the box were both his, and that the affairs of Michael Warden, Esquire, were in a bad way.

'That's all,' said Mr. Snitchey, turning up the last paper. 'Really there's no other resource. No other resource.'

'All lost, spent, wasted, pawned, borrowed, and sold, eh?' said the client, looking up.

'All,' returned Mr. Snitchey.

'Nothing else to be done, you say?'

'Nothing at all.'

The client bit his nails, and pondered again.

'And I am not even personally safe in England? You hold to that, do you?'

'In no part of the United Kingdom of Great Britain and Ireland,' replied Mr. Snitchey.

'A mere prodigal son* with no father to go back to, no swine to keep, and no husks to share with them? Eh?' pursued the client, rocking one leg over the other, and searching the ground with his eyes.

Mr. Snitchey coughed, as if to deprecate the being supposed to participate in any figurative illustration of a legal position. Mr. Craggs, as if to express that it was a partnership view of the subject, also coughed.

'Ruined at thirty!' said the client. 'Humph!'

'Not ruined, Mr. Warden,' returned Snitchey. 'Not so bad as that. You have done a good deal towards it, I must say, but you are not ruined. A little nursing—'

'A little Devil,' said the client.

'Mr. Craggs,' said Snitchey, 'will you oblige me with a pinch of snuff? Thank you, sir.'

As the imperturbable lawyer applied it to his nose with great apparent relish and a perfect absorption of his attention in the proceeding, the client gradually broke into a smile, and, looking up, said: 'You talk of nursing. How long nursing?'

'How long nursing?' repeated Snitchey, dusting the snuff from his fingers, and making a slow calculation in his mind. 'For your involved estate, sir? In good hands? S. and C.'s, say? Six or seven years.'

'To starve for six or seven years!' said the client with a fretful laugh, and an impatient change of his position.

'To starve for six or seven years, Mr. Warden,' said Snitchey, 'would be very uncommon indeed. You might get another estate by showing yourself, the while. But, we don't think you could do it— speaking for Self and Craggs—and consequently don't advise it.'

'What *do* you advise?'

'Nursing, I say,' repeated Snitchey. 'Some few years of nursing by Self and Craggs would bring it round. But to enable us to make terms, and hold terms, and you to keep terms, you must go away; you must live abroad. As to starvation, we could ensure you some hundreds a-year to starve upon, even in the beginning—I dare say, Mr. Warden.'

'Hundreds,' said the client. 'And I have spent thousands!'

'That,' retorted Mr. Snitchey, putting the papers slowly back into the cast-iron box, 'there is no doubt about. No doubt a—bout,' he repeated to himself, as he thoughtfully pursued his occupation.

The lawyer very likely knew *his* man; at any rate his dry, shrewd, whimsical manner, had a favourable influence on the client's moody state, and disposed him to be more free and unreserved. Or perhaps the client knew *his* man, and had elicited such encouragement as he had received, to render some purpose he was about to disclose the more defensible in appearance. Gradually raising his head, he sat looking at his immovable adviser with a smile, which presently broke into a laugh.

'After all,' he said, 'my iron-headed friend—'

Mr. Snitchey pointed out his partner. 'Self and—excuse me— Craggs.'

'I beg Mr. Craggs's pardon,' said the client. 'After all, my iron-headed friends,' he leaned forward in his chair, and dropped his voice a little, 'you don't know half my ruin yet.'

Mr. Snitchey stopped and stared at him. Mr. Craggs also stared.

'I am not only deep in debt,' said the client, 'but I am deep in—'

'Not in love!' cried Snitchey.

'Yes!' said the client, falling back in his chair, and surveying the Firm with his hands in his pockets. 'Deep in love.'

'And not with an heiress, sir?' said Snitchey.

'Not with an heiress.'

'Nor a rich lady?'

'Nor a rich lady that I know of—except in beauty and merit.'

'A single lady, I trust?' said Mr. Snitchey, with great expression.

'Certainly.'

'It's not one of Dr. Jeddler's daughters?' said Snitchey, suddenly squaring his elbows on his knees, and advancing his face at least a yard.

'Yes!' returned the client.

'Not his younger daughter?' said Snitchey.

'Yes!' returned the client.

'Mr. Craggs,' said Snitchey, much relieved, 'will you oblige me with another pinch of snuff? Thank you! I am happy to say it don't signify, Mr. Warden; she's engaged, sir, she's bespoke. My partner can corroborate me. We know the fact.'

'We know the fact,' repeated Craggs.

'Why, so do I perhaps,' returned the client quietly. 'What of that! Are you men of the world, and did you never hear of a woman changing her mind?'

'There certainly have been actions for breach,' said Mr. Snitchey, 'brought against both spinsters and widows, but, in the majority of cases—'

'Cases!' interposed the client, impatiently. 'Don't talk to me of cases. The general precedent is in a much larger volume than any of your law books. Besides, do you think I have lived six weeks in the Doctor's house for nothing?'

'I think, sir,' observed Mr. Snitchey, gravely addressing himself to his partner, 'that of all the scrapes Mr. Warden's horses have brought him into at one time and another—and they have been pretty numerous, and pretty expensive, as none know better than himself, and you, and I—the worst scrape may turn out to be, if he talks in this way, this having ever been left by one of them at the Doctor's garden wall, with three broken ribs, a snapped collar-bone, and the

Lord knows how many bruises. We didn't think so much of it, at the time when we knew he was going on well under the Doctor's hands and roof; but it looks bad now, sir. Bad? It looks very bad. Doctor Jeddler too—our client, Mr. Craggs.'

'Mr. Alfred Heathfield too—a sort of client, Mr. Snitchey,' said Craggs.

'Mr. Michael Warden too, a kind of client,' said the careless visitor, 'and no bad one either: having played the fool for ten or twelve years. However, Mr. Michael Warden has sown his wild oats now—there's their crop, in that box; and he means to repent and be wise. And in proof of it, Mr. Michael Warden means, if he can, to marry Marion, the Doctor's lovely daughter, and to carry her away with him.'

'Really, Mr. Craggs,' Snitchey began.

'Really, Mr. Snitchey, and Mr. Craggs, partners both,' said the client, interrupting him; 'you know your duty to your clients, and you know well enough, I am sure, that it is no part of it to interfere in a mere love affair, which I am obliged to confide to you. I am not going to carry the young lady off, without her own consent. There's nothing illegal in it. I never was Mr. Heathfield's bosom friend. I violate no confidence of his. I love where he loves, and I mean to win where he would win, if I can.'

'He can't, Mr. Craggs,' said Snitchey, evidently anxious and discomfited. 'He can't do it, sir. She dotes on Mr. Alfred.'

'Does she?' returned the client.

'Mr. Craggs, she dotes on him, sir,' persisted Snitchey.

'I didn't live six weeks, some few months ago, in the Doctor's house for nothing; and I doubted that soon,' observed the client. 'She would have doted on him, if her sister could have brought it about; but I watched them. Marion avoided his name, avoided the subject: shrunk from the least allusion to it, with evident distress.'

'Why should she, Mr. Craggs, you know? Why should she, sir?' inquired Snitchey.

'I don't know why she should, though there are many likely reasons,' said the client, smiling at the attention and perplexity expressed in Mr. Snitchey's shining eye, and at his cautious way of carrying on the conversation, and making himself informed upon the subject; 'but I know she does. She was very young when she made the engagement—if it may be called one, I am not even sure of that—and has repented of it, perhaps. Perhaps—it seems a foppish thing to say, but upon my soul I don't mean it in that light—she may have fallen in love with me, as I have fallen in love with her.'

'He, he! Mr. Alfred, her old playfellow too, you remember, Mr. Craggs,' said Snitchey, with a disconcerted laugh; 'knew her almost from a baby!'

'Which makes it the more probable that she may be tired of his idea,' calmly pursued the client, 'and not indisposed to exchange it for the newer one of another lover, who presents himself (or is presented by his horse) under romantic circumstances; has the not unfavourable reputation—with a country girl—of having lived thoughtlessly and gaily, without doing much harm to anybody; and who, for his youth and figure, and so forth—this may seem foppish again, but upon my soul I don't mean it in that light—might perhaps pass muster in a crowd with Mr. Alfred himself.'

There was no gainsaying the last clause, certainly; and Mr. Snitchey, glancing at him, thought so. There was something naturally graceful and pleasant in the very carelessness of his air. It seemed to suggest, of his comely face and well-knit figure, that they might be greatly better if he chose: and that, once roused and made earnest (but he never had been earnest yet), he could be full of fire and purpose. 'A dangerous sort of libertine,' thought the shrewd lawyer, 'to seem to catch the spark he wants, from a young lady's eyes.'

'Now, observe, Snitchey,' he continued, rising and taking him by the button, 'and Craggs,' taking him by the button also, and placing one partner on either side of him, so that neither might evade him. 'I don't ask you for any advice. You are right to keep quite aloof from all parties in such a matter, which is not one in which grave men like you could interfere, on any side. I am briefly going to review in half-a-dozen words, my position and intention, and then I shall leave it to you to do the best for me, in money matters, that you can: seeing that, if I run away with the Doctor's beautiful daughter (as I hope to do, and to become another man under her bright influence), it will be, for the moment, more chargeable than running away alone. But I shall soon make all that up in an altered life.'

'I think it will be better not to hear this, Mr. Craggs?' said Snitchey, looking at him across the client.

'*I* think not,' said Craggs.—Both listened attentively.

'Well! You needn't hear it,' replied their client. 'I'll mention it, however. I don't mean to ask the Doctor's consent, because he wouldn't give it me. But I mean to do the Doctor no wrong or harm, because (besides there being nothing serious in such trifles, as he says) I hope to rescue his child, my Marion, from what I see—I *know*—she dreads, and contemplates with misery: that is, the return of this old lover. If anything in the world is true, it is true that she dreads his return. Nobody is injured so far. I am so harried and worried here just now, that I lead the life of a flying-fish. I skulk about in the dark, I am shut out of my own house, and warned off my own grounds; but, that house, and those grounds, and many an acre besides, will come back to me one day, as you know and say; and Marion will probably be richer—on your showing, who are never sanguine—ten years hence as my wife, than as the wife of Alfred Heathfield, whose return she dreads (remember that), and in whom or in any man, my passion is not surpassed. Who is injured yet? It is a fair case throughout. My right is as good as his, if she decide in my favour; and I will try my right by her alone. You will like to know no more after this, and I will tell you no more. Now you know my purpose, and wants. When must I leave here?'

'In a week,' said Snitchey. 'Mr. Craggs?'

'In something less, I should say,' responded Craggs.

'In a month,' said the client, after attentively watching the two faces. 'This day month. To-day is Thursday. Succeed or fail, on this day month I go.'

'It's too long a delay,' said Snitchey; 'much too long. But let it be so. I thought he'd have stipulated for three,' he murmured to himself. 'Are you going? Good night, sir!'

'Good night!' returned the client, shaking hands with the Firm. 'You'll live to see me making a good use of riches yet. Henceforth the star of my destiny is Marion!'

'Take care of the stairs, sir,' replied Snitchey; 'for she don't shine there. Good night!'

'Good night!'

So they both stood at the stair-head with a pair of office-candles, watching him down. When he had gone away, they stood looking at each other.

'What do you think of all this, Mr. Craggs?' said Snitchey.

Mr. Craggs shook his head.

'It was our opinion, on the day when that release was executed, that there was something curious in the parting of that pair, I recollect,' said Snitchey.

'It was,' said Mr. Craggs.

'Perhaps he deceives himself altogether,' pursued Mr. Snitchey, locking up the fireproof box, and putting it away; 'or, if he don't, a little bit of fickleness and perfidy is not a miracle, Mr. Craggs. And yet I thought that pretty face was very true. I thought,' said Mr. Snitchey, putting on his great-coat (for the weather was very cold), drawing on his gloves, and snuffing out one candle, 'that I had even seen her character becoming stronger and more resolved of late. More like her sister's.'

'Mrs. Craggs was of the same opinion,' returned Craggs.

'I'd really give a trifle to-night,' observed Mr. Snitchey, who was a good-natured man, 'if I could believe that Mr. Warden was reckoning without his host;* but light-headed, capricious, and unballasted as he is, he knows something of the world and its people (he ought to, for he has bought what he does know, dear enough); and I can't quite think that. We had better not interfere: we can do nothing, Mr. Craggs, but keep quiet.'

'Nothing,' returned Craggs.

'Our friend the Doctor makes light of such things,' said Mr. Snitchey, shaking his head. 'I hope he mayn't stand in need of his philosophy. Our friend Alfred talks of the battle of life,' he shook his head again, 'I hope he mayn't be cut down early in the day. Have you got your hat, Mr. Craggs? I am going to put the other candle out.'

Mr. Craggs replying in the affirmative, Mr. Snitchey suited the action to the word, and they groped their way out of the council-chamber, now dark as the subject, or the law in general.

My story passes to a quiet little study, where, on that same night, the sisters and the hale old Doctor sat by a cheerful fireside. Grace was working at her needle. Marion read aloud from a book before her. The Doctor, in his dressing-gown and slippers, with his feet spread out upon the warm rug, leaned back in his easy-chair, and listened to the book, and looked upon his daughters.

They were very beautiful to look upon. Two better faces for a fireside, never made a fireside bright and sacred. Something of the difference between them had been softened down in three years' time; and enthroned upon the clear brow of the younger sister, looking through her eyes, and thrilling in her voice, was the same earnest nature that her own motherless youth had ripened in the elder sister long ago. But she still appeared at once the lovelier and weaker of the two; still seemed to rest her head upon her sister's breast, and put her trust in her, and look into her eyes for counsel and reliance. Those loving eyes, so calm, serene, and cheerful, as of old.

' "And being in her own home," ' read Marion, from the book; ' "her home made exquisitely dear by these remembrances, she now began to know that the great trial of her heart must soon come on, and could not be delayed. O Home, our comforter and friend when others fall away, to part with whom, at any step between the cradle and the grave" '—

'Marion, my love!' said Grace.

'Why, Puss!' exclaimed her father, 'what's the matter?'

She put her hand upon the hand her sister stretched towards her, and read on; her voice still faltering and trembling, though she made an effort to command it when thus interrupted.

' "To part with whom, at any step between the cradle and the grave, is always sorrowful. O Home, so true to us, so often slighted in return, be lenient to them that turn away from thee, and do not haunt their erring footsteps too reproachfully! Let no kind looks, no well-remembered smiles, be seen upon thy phantom face. Let no ray of affection, welcome, gentleness, forbearance, cordiality, shine from thy white head. Let no old loving word, or tone, rise up in judgment against thy deserter; but if thou canst look harshly and severely, do, in mercy to the Penitent!" '*

'Dear Marion, read no more to-night,' said Grace—for she was weeping.

'I cannot,' she replied, and closed the book. 'The words seem all on fire!'

The Doctor was amused at this; and laughed as he patted her on the head.

'What! overcome by a story-book!' said Doctor Jeddler. 'Print and paper! Well, well, it's all one. It's as rational to make a serious matter of print and paper as of anything else. But dry your eyes, love, dry your eyes. I dare say the heroine has got home again long ago, and made it up all round—and if she hasn't, a real home is only four walls; and a fictitious one, mere rags and ink. What's the matter now?'

'It's only me, Mister,' said Clemency, putting in her head at the door.

'And what's the matter with *you*?' said the Doctor.

'Oh, bless you, nothing an't the matter with me,' returned Clemency—and truly too, to judge from her well-soaped face, in which there gleamed as usual the very soul of good-humour, which, ungainly as she was, made her quite engaging. Abrasions on the elbows are not generally understood, it is true, to range within that class of personal charms called beauty-spots. But it is better, going through the world, to have the arms chafed in that narrow passage, than the temper: and Clemency's was sound and whole as any beauty's in the land.

'Nothing an't the matter with me,' said Clemency, entering, 'but—come a little closer, Mister.'

The Doctor, in some astonishment, complied with this invitation.

'You said I wasn't to give you one before them, you know,' said Clemency.

A novice in the family might have supposed, from her extraordinary ogling as she said it, as well as from a singular rapture or ecstasy which pervaded her elbows, as if she were embracing herself, that 'one,' in its most favourable interpretation, meant a chaste salute. Indeed the Doctor himself seemed alarmed, for the moment; but quickly regained his composure, as Clemency, having had recourse to both her pockets—beginning with the right one, going away to the wrong one, and afterwards coming back to the right one again—produced a letter from the Post-office.

'Britain was riding by on a errand,' she chuckled, handing it to the Doctor, 'and see the mail come in, and waited for it. There's A. H. in the corner. Mr. Alfred's on his journey home, I bet. We shall have a wedding in the house—there was two spoons in my saucer* this morning. Oh Luck, how slow he opens it!'

All this she delivered, by way of soliloquy, gradually rising higher and higher on tiptoe, in her impatience to hear the news, and making a corkscrew of her apron, and a bottle of her mouth. At last, arriving at a climax of suspense, and seeing the Doctor still engaged in the perusal of the letter, she came down flat upon the soles of her feet again, and cast her apron, as a veil, over her head, in a mute despair, and inability to bear it any longer.

'Here! Girls!' cried the Doctor. 'I can't help it: I never could keep a secret in my life. There are not many secrets, indeed, worth being kept in such a—well! never mind that. Alfred's coming home, my dears, directly.'

'Directly!' exclaimed Marion.

'What! The story-book is soon forgotten!' said the Doctor, pinching her cheek. 'I thought the news would dry those tears. Yes. "Let it be a surprise," he says, here. But I can't let it be a surprise. He must have a welcome.'

'Directly!' repeated Marion.

'Why, perhaps not what your impatience calls "directly," ' returned the Doctor; 'but pretty soon too. Let us see. Let us see. To-day is Thursday, is it not? Then he promises to be here, this day month.'

'This day month!' repeated Marion, softly.

'A gay day and a holiday for us,' said the cheerful voice of her sister Grace, kissing her in congratulation. 'Long looked forward to, dearest, and come at last.'

She answered with a smile; a mournful smile, but full of sisterly affection. As she looked in her sister's face, and listened to the quiet music of her voice, picturing the happiness of this return, her own face glowed with hope and joy.

And with a something else; a something shining more and more through all the rest of its expression; for which I have no name It was not exultation, triumph, proud enthusiasm. They are not so calmly shown. It was not love and gratitude alone, though love and gratitude were part of it. It emanated from no sordid thought, for sordid thoughts do not light up the brow, and hover on the lips, and move the spirit like a fluttered light, until the sympathetic figure trembles.

Dr. Jeddler, in spite of his system of philosophy—which he was continually contradicting and denying in practice, but more famous philosophers have done that—could not help having as much interest in the return of his old ward and pupil as if it had been a serious event. So he sat himself down in his easy-chair again, stretched out his slippered feet once more upon the rug, read the letter over and over a great many times, and talked it over more times still.

'Ah! The day was,' said the Doctor, looking at the fire, 'when you and he, Grace, used to trot about arm-in-arm, in his holiday time, like a couple of walking dolls. You remember?'

'I remember,' she answered, with her pleasant laugh, and plying her needle busily.

'This day month, indeed!' mused the Doctor. 'That hardly seems a twelvemonth ago. And where was my little Marion then!'

'Never far from her sister,' said Marion, cheerily, 'however little. Grace was everything to me, even when she was a young child herself.'

'True, Puss, true,' returned the Doctor. 'She was a staid little woman, was Grace, and a wise housekeeper, and a busy, quiet, pleasant body; bearing with our humours and anticipating our wishes, and always ready to forget her own, even in those times. I never knew you positive or obstinate, Grace, my darling, even then, on any subject but one.'

'I am afraid I have changed sadly for the worse, since,' laughed Grace, still busy at her work. 'What was that one, father?'

'Alfred, of course,' said the Doctor. 'Nothing would serve you but you must be called Alfred's wife; so we called you Alfred's wife; and you liked it better, I believe (odd as it seems now), than being called a Duchess, if we could have made you one.'

'Indeed?' said Grace, placidly.

'Why, don't you remember?' inquired the Doctor.

'I think I remember something of it,' she returned, 'but not much. It's so long ago.' And as she sat at work, she hummed the burden of an old song, which the Doctor liked.

'Alfred will find a real wife soon,' she said, breaking off; 'and that will be a happy time indeed for all of us. My three years' trust is nearly at an end, Marion. It has been a very easy one. I shall tell Alfred, when I give you back to him, that you have loved him dearly all the time, and that he has never once needed my good services. May I tell him so, love?'

'Tell him, dear Grace,' replied Marion, 'that there never was a trust so generously, nobly, steadfastly discharged; and that I have loved *you*, all the time, dearer and dearer every day; and O! how dearly now!'

'Nay,' said her cheerful sister, returning her embrace, 'I can scarcely tell him that; we will leave my deserts to Alfred's imagination. It will be liberal enough, dear Marion; like your own.'

With that, she resumed the work she had for a moment laid down, when her sister spoke so fervently: and with it the old song the Doctor liked to hear. And the Doctor, still reposing in his easy-chair, with his slippered feet stretched out before him on the rug, listened to the tune, and beat time on his knee with Alfred's letter, and looked at his two daughters, and thought that among the many trifles of the trifling world, these trifles were agreeable enough.

Clemency Newcome, in the meantime, having accomplished her mission and lingered in the room until she had made herself a party to the news, descended to the kitchen, where her coadjutor, Mr. Britain, was regaling after supper, surrounded by such a plentiful collection of bright pot-lids, well-scoured saucepans, burnished dinner-covers, gleaming kettles, and other tokens of her industrious habits, arranged upon the walls and shelves, that he sat as in the centre of a hall of mirrors. The majority did not give forth very flattering portraits of him, certainly; nor were they by any means unanimous in their reflections; as some made him very long-faced, others very broad-faced, some tolerably well-looking, others vastly ill-looking, according to their several manners of reflecting: which were as various, in respect of one fact, as those of so many kinds of men. But they all agreed that in the midst of them sat, quite at his ease, an individual with a pipe in his mouth, and a jug of beer at his elbow, who nodded condescendingly to Clemency, when she stationed herself at the same table.

'Well, Clemmy,' said Britain, 'how are you by this time, and what's the news?'

Clemency told him the news, which he received very graciously. A gracious change had come over Benjamin from head to foot. He was much broader, much redder, much more cheerful, and much jollier in all respects. It seemed as if his face had been tied up in a knot before, and was now untwisted and smoothed out.

'There'll be another job for Snitchey and Craggs, I suppose,' he observed, puffing slowly at his pipe. 'More witnessing for you and me, perhaps, Clemmy!'

'Lor!' replied his fair companion, with her favourite twist of her favourite joints. 'I wish it was me, Britain!'

'Wish what was you?'

'A-going to be married,' said Clemency.

Benjamin took his pipe out of his mouth and laughed heartily. 'Yes! you're a likely subject for that!' he said. 'Poor Clem!' Clemency for her part laughed as heartily as he, and seemed as much amused by the idea. 'Yes,' she assented, 'I'm a likely subject for that; an't I?'

'*You*'ll never be married, you know,' said Mr. Britain, resuming his pipe.

'Don't you think I ever shall though?' said Clemency, in perfect good faith.

Mr. Britain shook his head. 'Not a chance of it!'

'Only think!' said Clemency. 'Well!—I suppose you mean to, Britain, one of these days; don't you?'

A question so abrupt, upon a subject so momentous, required consideration. After blowing out a great cloud of smoke, and looking at it with his head now on this side and now on that, as if it were actually the question, and he were surveying it in various aspects, Mr. Britain replied that he wasn't altogether clear about it, but— ye-es—he thought he might come to that at last.

'I wish her joy, whoever she may be!' cried Clemency.

'Oh she'll have that,' said Benjamin, 'safe enough.'

'But she wouldn't have led quite such a joyful life as she will lead, and wouldn't have had quite such a sociable sort of husband as she will have,' said Clemency, spreading herself half over the table, and staring retrospectively at the candle, 'if it hadn't been for—not that I went to do it, for it was accidental, I am sure—if it hadn't been for me; now would she, Britain?'

'Certainly not,' returned Mr. Britain, by this time in that high state of appreciation of his pipe, when a man can open his mouth but a very little way for speaking purposes; and sitting luxuriously immovable in his chair, can afford to turn only his eyes towards a companion, and that very passively and gravely. 'Oh! I'm greatly beholden to you, you know, Clem.'

'Lor, how nice that is to think of!' said Clemency.

At the same time, bringing her thoughts as well as her sight to bear upon the candle-grease, and becoming abruptly reminiscent of its healing qualities as a balsam, she anointed her left elbow with a plentiful application of that remedy.

'You see I've made a good many investigations of one sort and another in my time,' pursued Mr. Britain, with the profundity of a sage, 'having been always of an inquiring turn of mind; and I've read a good many books about the general Rights of things and Wrongs of things, for I went into the literary line myself, when I began life.'

'Did you though!' cried the admiring Clemency.

'Yes,' said Mr. Britain: 'I was hid for the best part of two years behind a bookstall, ready to fly out if anybody pocketed a volume; and after that, I was light porter to a stay and mantua-maker,* in which capacity I was employed to carry about, in oilskin baskets, nothing but deceptions—which soured my spirits and disturbed my confidence in human nature; and after that, I heard a world of discussions in this house, which soured my spirits fresh; and my opinion after all is, that, as a safe and comfortable sweetener of the same, and as a pleasant guide through life, there's nothing like a nutmeg-grater.'

Clemency was about to offer a suggestion, but he stopped her by anticipating it.

'Com-bined', he added gravely, 'with a thimble.'

'Do as you wold, you know, and cetrer, eh!' observed Clemency, folding her arms comfortably in her delight at this avowal, and patting her elbows. 'Such a short cut, an't it?'

'I'm not sure,' said Mr. Britain, 'that it's what would be considered good philosophy. I've my doubts about that; but it wears well, and saves a quantity of snarling, which the genuine article don't always.'

'See how you used to go on once, yourself, you know!' said Clemency.

'Ah!' said Mr. Britain. 'But the most extraordinary thing, Clemmy, is that I should live to be brought round, through you. That's the strange part of it. Through you! Why, I suppose you haven't so much as half an idea in your head.'

Clemency, without taking the least offence, shook it, and laughed, and hugged herself, and said, 'No, she didn't suppose she had.'

'I'm pretty sure of it,' said Mr. Britain.

'Oh! I dare say you're right,' said Clemency. 'I don't pretend to none. I don't want any.'

Benjamin took his pipe from his lips, and laughed till the tears ran down his face. 'What a natural you are, Clemmy!' he said, shaking his head, with an infinite relish of the joke, and wiping his eyes. Clemency, without the smallest inclination to dispute it, did the like, and laughed as heartily as he.

'I can't help liking you,' said Mr. Britain; 'you're a regular good creature in your way, so shake hands, Clem. Whatever happens, I'll always take notice of you, and be a friend to you.'

'Will you?' returned Clemency. 'Well! that's very good of you.'

'Yes, yes,' said Mr. Britain, giving her his pipe to knock the ashes out of it; 'I'll stand by you. Hark! That's a curious noise!'

'Noise!' repeated Clemency.

'A footstep outside. Somebody dropping from the wall, it sounded like,' said Britain. 'Are they all a-bed upstairs?'

'Yes, all a-bed by this time,' she replied.

'Didn't you hear anything?'

'No.'

They both listened, but heard nothing.

'I tell you what,' said Benjamin, taking down a lantern. 'I'll have a look round, before I go to bed myself, for satisfaction's sake. Undo the door while I light this, Clemmy.'

Clemency complied briskly; but observed as she did so, that he would only have his walk for his pains, that it was all his fancy, and so forth. Mr. Britain said 'Very likely'; but sallied out, nevertheless, armed with the poker, and casting the light of the lantern far and near in all directions.

'It's as quiet as a churchyard,' said Clemency, looking after him; 'and almost as ghostly too!'

Glancing back into the kitchen, she cried fearfully, as a light figure stole into her view, 'What's that!'

'Hush!' said Marion in an agitated whisper. 'You have always loved me, have you not?'

'Loved you, child! You may be sure I have.'

'I am sure. And I may trust you, may I not? There is no one else just now, in whom I *can* trust.'

'Yes,' said Clemency, with all her heart.

'There is some one out there,' pointing to the door, 'whom I must see, and speak with, to-night. Michael Warden, for God's sake retire! Not now!'

Clemency started with surprise and trouble as, following the direction of the speaker's eyes, she saw a dark figure standing in the doorway.

'In another moment you may be discovered,' said Marion. 'Not now! Wait, if you can, in some concealment. I will come presently.'

He waved his hand to her, and was gone.

'Don't go to bed. Wait here for me!' said Marion, hurriedly. 'I have been seeking to speak to you for an hour past. Oh, be true to me!'

Eagerly seizing her bewildered hand, and pressing it with both her own to her breast—an action more expressive, in its passion of entreaty, than the most eloquent appeal in words,—Marion withdrew; as the light of the returning lantern flashed into the room.

'All still and peaceable. Nobody there. Fancy, I suppose,' said Mr. Britain, as he locked and barred the door. 'One of the effects of having a lively imagination. Halloa! Why, what's the matter?'

Clemency, who could not conceal the effects of her surprise and concern, was sitting in a chair: pale, and trembling from head to foot.

'Matter!' she repeated, chafing her hands and elbows nervously, and looking anywhere but at him. 'That's good in you, Britain, that is! After going and frightening one out of one's life with noises and lanterns, and I don't know what all. Matter! Oh, yes!'

'If you're frightened out of your life by a lantern, Clemmy,' said Mr. Britain, composedly blowing it out and hanging it up again, 'that apparition's very soon got rid of. But you're as bold as brass in general,' he said, stopping to observe her; 'and were, after the noise and the lantern too. What have you taken into your head? Not an idea, eh?'

But, as Clemency bade him good night very much after her usual fashion, and began to bustle about with a show of going to bed herself immediately, Little Britain, after giving utterance to the original remark that it was impossible to account for a woman's whims, bade her good night in return, and taking up his candle strolled drowsily away to bed.

When all was quiet, Marion returned.

'Open the door,' she said; 'and stand there close beside me, while I speak to him, outside.'

Timid as her manner was, it still evinced a resolute and settled purpose, such as Clemency could not resist. She softly unbarred the door: but before turning the key, looked round on the young creature waiting to issue forth when she should open it.

The face was not averted or cast down, but looking full upon her, in its pride of youth and beauty. Some simple sense of the slightness of the barrier that interposed itself between the happy home and honoured love of the fair girl, and what might be the desolation of that home, and shipwreck of its dearest treasure, smote so keenly on the tender heart of Clemency, and so filled it to overflowing with sorrow and compassion, that, bursting into tears, she threw her arms round Marion's neck.

'It's little that I know, my dear,' cried Clemency, 'very little; but I know that this should not be. Think of what you do!'

'I have thought of it many times,' said Marion, gently.

'Once more,' urged Clemency. 'Till to-morrow.' Marion shook her head.

'For Mr. Alfred's sake,' said Clemency, with homely earnestness. 'Him that you used to love so dearly, once!'

She hid her face, upon the instant, in her hands, repeating 'Once!' as if it rent her heart.

'Let me go out,' said Clemency, soothing her. 'I'll tell him what you like. Don't cross the door-step tonight. I'm sure no good will come of it. Oh, it was an unhappy day when Mr. Warden was ever brought here! Think of your good father, darling—of your sister.'

'I have,' said Marion, hastily raising her head. 'You don't know what I do. I *must* speak to him. You are the best and truest friend in all the world for what you have said to me, but I must take this step. Will you go with me, Clemency,' she kissed her on her friendly face, 'or shall I go alone?'

Sorrowing and wondering, Clemency turned the key, and opened the door. Into the dark and doubtful night that lay beyond the threshold, Marion passed quickly, holding by her hand.

In the dark night he joined her, and they spoke together earnestly and long; and the hand that held so fast by Clemency's, now trembled, now turned deadly cold, now clasped and closed on hers, in the strong feeling of the speech it emphasised unconsciously. When they returned, he followed to the door, and pausing there a moment, seized the other hand, and pressed it to his lips. Then, stealthily withdrew.

The door was barred and locked again, and once again she stood beneath her father's roof. Not bowed down by the secret that she brought there, though so young; but with that same expression on her face for which I had no name before, and shining through her tears.

Again she thanked and thanked her humble friend, and trusted to her, as she said, with confidence, implicitly. Her chamber safely reached, she fell upon her knees; and with her secret weighing on her heart, could pray!

Could rise up from her prayers, so tranquil and serene, and bending over her fond sister in her slumber, look upon her face and

smile—though sadly: murmuring as she kissed her forehead, how that Grace had been a mother to her, ever, and she loved her as a child!

Could draw the passive arm about her neck when lying down to rest—it seemed to cling there, of its own will, protectingly and tenderly even in sleep—and breathe upon the parted lips, God bless her!

Could sink into a peaceful sleep, herself; but for one dream, in which she cried out, in her innocent and touching voice, that she was quite alone, and they had all forgotten her.

A month soon passes, even at its tardiest pace. The month appointed to elapse between that night and the return, was quick of foot, and went by like a vapour.

The day arrived. A raging winter day, that shook the old house, sometimes, as if it shivered in the blast. A day to make home doubly home. To give the chimney-corner new delights. To shed a ruddier glow upon the faces gathered round the hearth, and draw each fireside group into a closer and more social league, against the roaring elements without. Such a wild winter day as best prepares the way for shut-out night; for curtained rooms, and cheerful looks; for music, laughter, dancing, light, and jovial entertainment!

All these the Doctor had in store to welcome Alfred back. They knew that he could not arrive till night; and they would make the night air ring, he said, as he approached. All his old friends should congregate about him. He should not miss a face that he had known and liked. No! They should every one be there!

So guests were bidden, and musicians were engaged, and tables spread, and floors prepared for active feet, and bountiful provision made, of every hospitable kind. Because it was the Christmas season, and his eyes were all unused to English holly and its sturdy green, the dancing-room was garlanded and hung with it; and the red berries gleamed an English welcome to him, peeping from among the leaves.

It was a busy day for all of them: a busier day for none of them than Grace, who noiselessly presided everywhere, and was the cheerful mind of all the preparations. Many a time that day (as well as many a time within the fleeting month preceding it), did Clemency glance anxiously, and almost fearfully, at Marion. She saw her paler, perhaps, than usual; but there was a sweet composure on her face that made it lovelier than ever.

At night when she was dressed, and wore upon her head a wreath that Grace had proudly twined about it—its mimic flowers were Alfred's favourites, as Grace remembered when she chose them—that old expression, pensive, almost sorrowful, and yet so spiritual, high, and stirring, sat again upon her brow, enhanced a hundred-fold.

'The next wreath I adjust on this fair head, will be a marriage wreath,' said Grace; 'or I am no true prophet, dear.'

Her sister smiled, and held her in her arms.

'A moment, Grace. Don't leave me yet. Are you sure that I want nothing more?'

Her care was not for that. It was her sister's face she thought of, and her eyes were fixed upon it, tenderly.

'My art,' said Grace, 'can go no farther, dear girl; nor your beauty. I never saw you look so beautiful as now.'

'I never was so happy,' she returned.

'Ay, but there is a greater happiness in store. In such another home, as cheerful and as bright as this looks now,' said Grace, 'Alfred and his young wife will soon be living.'

She smiled again. 'It is a happy home, Grace, in your fancy. I can see it in your eyes. I know it *will* be happy, dear. How glad I am to know it.'

'Well,' cried the Doctor, bustling in. 'Here we are, all ready for Alfred, eh? He can't be here until pretty late—an hour or so before midnight—so there'll be plenty of time for making merry before he comes. He'll not find us with the ice unbroken. Pile up the fire here, Britain! Let it shine upon the holly till it winks again. It's a world of nonsense, Puss; true lovers and all the rest of it—all nonsense; but we'll be nonsensical with the rest of 'em, and give our true lover a mad welcome. Upon my word!' said the old Doctor, looking at his daughters proudly, 'I'm not clear to-night, among other absurdities, but that I'm the father of two handsome girls.'

'All that one of them has ever done, or may do—may do, dearest father—to cause you pain or grief, forgive her,' said Marion, 'forgive her now, when her heart is full. Say that you forgive her. That you will forgive her. That she shall always share your love, and—,' and the rest was not said, for her face was hidden on the old man's shoulder.

'Tut, tut, tut,' said the Doctor gently. 'Forgive! What have I to forgive? Heyday, if our true lovers come back to flurry us like this, we must hold 'em at a distance; we must send expresses out to stop 'em short upon the road, and bring 'em on a mile or two a day, until we're properly prepared to meet 'em. Kiss me, Puss. Forgive! Why, what a silly child you are! If you had vexed and crossed me fifty times a day, instead of not at all, I'd forgive you everything, but such a supplication. Kiss me again, Puss. There! Prospective and retrospective—a clear score between us. Pile up the fire here! Would you freeze the people on this bleak December night! Let us be light, and warm, and merry, or I'll not forgive some of you!'

So gaily the old Doctor carried it! And the fire was piled up, and the lights were bright, and company arrived, and a murmuring of lively tongues began, and already there was a pleasant air of cheerful excitement stirring through all the house.

More and more company came flocking in. Bright eyes sparkled upon Marion; smiling lips gave her joy of his return; sage mothers fanned themselves, and hoped she mightn't be too youthful and inconstant for the quiet round of home; impetuous fathers fell into disgrace for too much exaltation of her beauty; daughters envied her; sons envied him; innumerable pairs of lovers profited by the occasion; all were interested, animated, and expectant.

Mr. and Mrs. Craggs came arm in arm, but Mrs. Snitchey came alone. 'Why, what's become of *him*?' inquired the Doctor.

The feather of a Bird of Paradise in Mrs. Snitchey's turban, trembled as if the Bird of Paradise were alive again, when she said that doubtless Mr. Craggs know. *She* was never told.

'That nasty office,' said Mrs. Craggs.

'I wish it was burnt down,' said Mrs. Snitchey.

'He's—he's—there's a little matter of business that keeps my partner rather late,' said Mr. Craggs, looking uneasily about him.

'Oh—h! Business. Don't tell me!' said Mrs. Snitchey.

'*We* know what business means,' said Mrs. Craggs.

But their not knowing what it meant, was perhaps the reason why Mrs. Snitchey's Bird of Paradise feather quivered so portentously, and why all the pendant bits on Mrs. Cragg's ear-rings shook like little bells.

'I wonder *you* could come away, Mr. Craggs,' said his wife.

'Mr. Craggs is fortunate, I'm sure!' said Mrs. Snitchey.

'That office so engrosses 'em,' said Mrs. Craggs.

'A person with an office has no business to be married at all,' said Mrs. Snitchey.

Then, Mrs. Snitchey said, within herself, that that look of hers had pierced to Craggs's soul, and he knew it; and Mrs. Craggs observed to Craggs, that 'his Snitcheys' were deceiving him behind his back, and he would find it out when it was too late.

Still, Mr. Craggs, without much heeding these remarks, looked uneasily about until his eye rested on Grace, to whom he immediately presented himself.

'Good evening, ma'am,' said Craggs. 'You look charmingly. Your—Miss—your sister, Miss Marion, is she——'

'Oh, she's quite well, Mr. Craggs.'

'Yes—I—is she here?' asked Craggs.

'Here! Don't you see her yonder? Going to dance?' said Grace.

Mr. Craggs put on his spectacles to see the better; looked at her through them, for some time; coughed; and put them, with an air of satisfaction, in their sheath again, and in his pocket.

Now the music struck up, and the dance commenced. The bright fire crackled and sparkled, rose and fell, as though it joined the dance itself, in right good fellowship. Sometimes, it roared as if it would make music too. Sometimes, it flashed and beamed as if it were the eye of the old room: it winked too, sometimes, like a knowing patriarch, upon the youthful whisperers in corners. Sometimes, it sported with the holly-boughs; and, shining on the leaves by fits and starts, made them look as if they were in the cold winter night again, and fluttering in the wind. Sometimes its genial humour grew obstreperous, and passed all bounds; and then it cast into the room, among the twinkling feet, with a loud burst, a shower of harmless little sparks, and in its exultation leaped and bounded, like a mad thing, up the broad old chimney.

Another dance was near its close, when Mr. Snitchey touched his partner, who was looking on, upon the arm.

Mr. Craggs started, as if his familiar had been a spectre.

'Is he gone?' he asked.

'Hush! He has been with me', said Snitchey, 'for three hours and more. He went over everything. He looked into all our arrangements for him, and was very particular indeed. He—Humph!'

The dance was finished. Marion passed close before him, as he spoke. She did not observe him, or his partner; but looked over her shoulder towards her sister in the distance, as she slowly made her way into the crowd, and passed out of their view.

'You see! All safe and well,' said Mr. Craggs. 'He didn't recur to that subject, I suppose?'

'Not a word.'

'And is he really gone? Is he safe away?'

'He keeps to his word. He drops down the river with the tide in that shell of a boat of his, and so goes out to sea on this dark night!—a dare-devil he is—before the wind. There's no such lonely road anywhere else. That's one thing. The tide flows, he says, an hour before midnight—about this time. I'm glad it's over.' Mr. Snitchey wiped his forehead, which looked hot and anxious.

'What do you think,' said Mr. Craggs, 'about—'

'Hush!' replied his cautious partner, looking straight before him. 'I understand you. Don't mention names, and don't let us seem to be talking secrets. I don't know what to think; and to tell you the truth, I don't care now. It's a great relief. His self-love deceived him, I suppose. Perhaps the young lady coquetted a little. The evidence would seem to point that way. Alfred not arrived?'

'Not yet,' said Mr. Craggs. 'Expected every minute.'

'Good.' Mr. Snitchey wiped his forehead again. 'It's a great relief. I haven't been so nervous since we've been in partnership. I intend to spend the evening now, Mr. Craggs.'

Mrs. Craggs and Mrs. Snitchey joined them as he announced this intention. The Bird of Paradise was in a state of extreme vibration, and the little bells were ringing quite audibly.

'It has been the theme of general comment, Mr. Snitchey,' said Mrs. Snitchey. 'I hope the office is satisfied.'

'Satisfied with what, my dear?' asked Mr. Snitchey.

'With the exposure of a defenceless woman to ridicule and remark,' returned his wife. 'That is quite in the way of the office, *that* is.'

'I really, myself,' said Mrs. Craggs, 'have been so long accustomed to connect the office with everything opposed to domesticity, that I am glad to know it as the avowed enemy of my peace. There is something honest in that, at all events.'

'My dear,' urged Mr. Craggs, 'your good opinion is invaluable, but *I* never avowed that the office was the enemy of your peace.'

'No,' said Mrs. Craggs, ringing a perfect peal upon the little bells.

'Not you, indeed. You wouldn't be worthy of the office, if you had the candour to.'

'As to my having been away to-night, my dear,' said Mr. Snitchey, giving her his arm, 'the deprivation has been mine, I'm sure; but, as Mr. Craggs knows—'

Mrs. Snitchey cut this reference very short by hitching her husband to a distance, and asking him to look at that man. To do her the favour to look at him!

'At which man, my dear?' said Mr. Snitchey.

'Your chosen companion; *I'*m no companion to you, Mr. Snitchey.'

'Yes, yes, you are, my dear,' he interposed.

'No, no, I'm not,' said Mrs. Snitchey with a majestic smile. 'I know my station. Will you look at your chosen companion, Mr. Snitchey; at your referee, at the keeper of your secrets, at the man you trust; at your other self, in short.'

The habitual association of Self with Craggs, occasioned Mr. Snitchey to look in that direction.

'If you can look that man in the eye this night,' said Mrs. Snitchey, 'and not know that you are deluded, practised upon, made the victim of his arts, and bent down prostrate to his will by some unaccountable fascination which it is impossible to explain and against which no warning of mine is of the least avail, all I can say is—I pity you!'

At the very same moment Mrs. Craggs was oracular on the cross subject. Was it possible, she said, that Craggs could so blind himself to his Snitcheys, as not to feel his true position? Did he mean to say that he had seen his Snitcheys come into that room, and didn't plainly see that there was reservation, cunning, treachery, in the man? Would he tell her that his very action, when he wiped his forehead and looked so stealthily about him, didn't show that there was something weighing on the conscience of his precious Snitcheys (if he had a conscience), that wouldn't bear the light? Did anybody but his Snitcheys come to festive entertainments like a burglar?— which, by the way, was hardly a clear illustration of the case, as he had walked in very mildly at the door. And would he still assert to her at noon-day (it being nearly midnight), that his Snitcheys were to be justified through thick and thin, against all facts, and reason, and experience?

Neither Snitchey nor Craggs openly attempted to stem the current which had thus set in, but both were content to be carried gently along it, until its force abated. This happened at about the same time as a general movement for a country dance; when Mr. Snitchey proposed himself as a partner to Mrs. Craggs, and Mr. Craggs gallantly offered himself to Mrs. Snitchey; and after some such slight evasions as 'why don't you ask somebody else?' and 'you'll be glad, I know, if I decline,' and 'I wonder you can dance out of the office' (but this jocosely now), each lady graciously accepted, and took her place.

It was an old custom among them, indeed, to do so, and to pair off, in like manner, at dinners and suppers; for they were excellent friends, and on a footing of easy familiarity. Perhaps the false Craggs and the wicked Snitchey were a recognised fiction with the two wives, as Doe and Roe, incessantly running up and down bailiwicks, were with the two husbands: or, perhaps the ladies had instituted, and taken upon themselves, these two shares in the business, rather than be left out of it altogether. But certain it is, that each wife went as gravely and steadily to work in her vocation as her husband did in his, and would have considered it almost impossible for the Firm to maintain a successful and respectable existence, without her laudable exertions.

But now the Bird of Paradise was seen to flutter down the middle; and the little bells began to bounce and jingle in poussette;* and the Doctor's rosy face spun round and round, like an expressive pegtop* highly varnished; and breathless Mr. Craggs began to doubt already, whether country dancing had been made 'too easy,' like the rest of life; and Mr. Snitchey, with his nimble cuts and capers, footed it for Self and Craggs, and half-a-dozen more.

Now, too, the fire took fresh courage, favoured by the lively wind the dance awakened, and burnt clear and high. It was the Genius of the room, and present everywhere. It shone in people's eyes, it sparkled in the jewels on the snowy necks of girls, it twinkled at their ears as if it whispered to them slyly, it flashed about their waists, it flickered on the ground and made it rosy for their feet, it bloomed upon the ceiling that its glow might set off their bright faces, and it kindled up a general illumination in Mrs. Craggs's little belfry.

Now, too, the lively air that fanned it, grew less gentle as the music quickened and the dance proceeded with new spirit; and a breeze arose that made the leaves and berries dance upon the wall, as they had often done upon the trees; and the breeze rustled in the room as if an invisible company of fairies, treading in the footsteps of the good substantial revellers, were whirling after them. Now, too, no feature of the Doctor's face could be distinguished as he spun and spun; and now there seemed a dozen Birds of Paradise in fitful flight; and now there were a thousand little bells at work; and now a fleet of flying skirts was ruffled by a little tempest, when the music gave in, and the dance was over.

Hot and breathless as the Doctor was, it only made him the more impatient for Alfred's coming.

'Anything been seen, Britain? Anything been heard?'

'Too dark to see far, sir. Too much noise inside the house to hear.'

'That's right! The gayer welcome for him. How goes the time?'

'Just twelve, sir. He can't be long, sir.'

'Stir up the fire, and throw another log upon it,' said the Doctor. 'Let him see his welcome blazing out upon the night—good boy!—as he comes along!'

He saw it—Yes! From the chaise he caught the light, as he turned the corner by the old church. He knew the room from which it shone. He saw the wintry branches of the old trees between the light and him. He knew that one of those trees rustled musically in the summer time at the window of Marion's chamber.

The tears were in his eyes. His heart throbbed so violently that he could hardly bear his happiness. How often he had thought of this time—pictured it under all circumstances—feared that it might never come—yearned, and wearied for it—far away!

Again the light! Distinct and ruddy; kindled, he knew, to give him welcome, and to speed him home. He beckoned with his hand, and waved his hat, and cheered out, loud, as if the light were they, and they could see and hear him, as he dashed towards them through the mud and mire, triumphantly.

Stop! He knew the Doctor, and understood what he had done. He would not let it be a surprise to them. But he could make it one, yet, by going forward on foot. If the orchard-gate were open, he could enter there; if not, the wall was easily climbed, as he knew of old; and he would be among them in an instant.

He dismounted from the chaise, and telling the driver—even that was not easy in his agitation—to remain behind for a few minutes, and then to follow slowly, ran on with exceeding swiftness, tried the gate, scaled the wall, jumped down on the other side, and stood panting in the old orchard.

There was a frosty rime upon the trees, which, in the faint light of the clouded moon, hung upon the smaller branches like dead garlands. Withered leaves crackled and snapped beneath his feet, as he crept softly on towards the house. The desolation of a winter night sat brooding on the earth, and in the sky. But, the red light came cheerily towards him from the windows; figures passed and repassed there; and the hum and murmur of voices greeted his ear sweetly.

Listening for hers: attempting, as he crept on, to detach it from the rest, and half-believing that he heard it: he had nearly reached the door, when it was abruptly opened, and a figure coming out encountered his. It instantly recoiled with a half-suppressed cry.

'Clemency,' he said, 'don't you know me?'

'Don't come in!' she answered, pushing him back. 'Go away. Don't ask me why. Don't come in.'

'What is the matter?' he exclaimed.

'I don't know. I—I am afraid to think. Go back. Hark!'

There was a sudden tumult in the house. She put her hands upon her ears. A wild scream, such as no hands could shut out, was heard; and Grace—distraction in her looks and manner—rushed out at the door.

'Grace!' He caught her in his arms. 'What is it! Is she dead!'

She disengaged herself, as if to recognise his face, and fell down at his feet.

A crowd of figures came about them from the house. Among them was her father, with a paper in his hand.

'What is it!' cried Alfred, grasping his hair with his hands, and looking in an agony from face to face, as he bent upon his knee beside the insensible girl. 'Will no one look at me? Will no one speak to me? Does no one know me? Is there no voice among you all, to tell me what it is?'

There was a murmur among them. 'She is gone.'

'Gone!' he echoed.

'Fled, my dear Alfred!' said the Doctor, in a broken voice, and with his hands before his face. 'Gone from her home and us. Tonight! She writes that she has made her innocent and blameless choice—entreats that we will forgive her—prays that we will not forget her—and is gone.'

'With whom? Where?'

He started up, as if to follow in pursuit; but, when they gave way to let him pass, looked wildly round upon them, staggered back, and sunk down in his former attitude, clasping one of Grace's cold hands in his own.

There was a hurried running to and fro, confusion, noise, disorder, and no purpose. Some proceeded to disperse themselves about the roads, and some took horse, and some got lights, and some conversed together, urging that there was no trace or track to follow. Some approached him kindly, with the view of offering consolation; some admonished him that Grace must be removed into the house, and that he prevented it. He never heard them, and he never moved.

The snow fell fast and thick. He looked up for a moment in the air, and thought that those white ashes strewn upon his hopes and misery, were suited to them well. He looked round on the whitening ground, and thought how Marion's foot-prints would be hushed and covered up, as soon as made, and even that remembrance of her blotted out. But he never felt the weather and he never stirred.

PART THE THIRD

THE world had grown six years older since that night of the return. It was a warm autumn afternoon, and there had been heavy rain. The sun burst suddenly from among the clouds; and the old battle-ground, sparkling brilliantly and cheerfully at sight of it in one green place, flashed a responsive welcome there, which spread along the country-side as if a joyful beacon had been lighted up, and answered from a thousand stations.

How beautiful the landscape kindling in the light, and that luxuriant influence passing on like a celestial presence, brightening everything! The wood, a sombre mass before, revealed its varied tints of yellow, green, brown, red: its different forms of trees, with raindrops glittering on their leaves and twinkling as they fell. The verdant meadow-land, bright and glowing, seemed as if it had been blind, a minute since, and now had found a sense of sight wherewith to look up at the shining sky. Corn-fields, hedgerows, fences, homesteads, and clustered roofs, the steeple of the church, the stream, the water-mill, all sprang out of the gloomy darkness smiling. Birds sang sweetly, flowers raised their drooping heads, fresh scents arose from the invigorated ground; the blue expanse above extended and diffused itself; already the sun's slanting rays pierced mortally the sullen bank of cloud that lingered in its flight; and a rainbow, spirit of all the colours that adorned the earth and sky, spanned the whole arch with its triumphant glory.

At such a time, one little roadside Inn, snugly sheltered behind a great elm-tree with a rare seat for idlers encircling its capacious bole, addressed a cheerful front towards the traveller, as a house of entertainment ought, and tempted him with many mute but significant assurances of a comfortable welcome. The ruddy signboard perched up in the tree, with its golden letters winking in the sun, ogled the passer-by, from among the green leaves, like a jolly face, and promised good cheer. The horse-trough, full of clear fresh water, and the ground below it sprinkled with droppings of fragrant hay, made every horse that passed, prick up his ears. The crimson curtains in the lower rooms, and the pure white hangings in the little bedchambers above, beckoned, Come in! with every breath of air. Upon the bright green shutters, there were golden legends about beer and ale, and neat wines, and good beds; and an affecting picture of a brown jug frothing over at the top. Upon the window-sills were flowering plants in bright red pots, which made a lively show against the white front of the house; and in the darkness of the doorway there were streaks of light, which glanced off from the surfaces of bottles and tankards.

On the door-step, appeared a proper figure of a landlord, too; for, though he was a short man, he was round and broad, and stood with his hands in his pockets, and his legs just wide enough apart to express a mind at rest upon the subject of the cellar, and an easy confidence—too calm and virtuous to become a swagger—in the general resources of the Inn. The superabundant moisture, trickling from everything after the late rain, set him off well. Nothing near him was thirsty. Certain top-heavy dahlias, looking over the palings of his neat well-ordered garden, had swilled as much as they could carry—perhaps a trifle more—and may have been the worse for liquor; but the sweetbriar, roses, wall-flowers, the plants at the windows, and the leaves on the old tree, were in the beaming state of moderate company that had taken no more than was wholesome for them, and had served to develop their best qualities. Sprinkling dewy drops about them on the ground, they seemed profuse of innocent and sparkling mirth, that did good where it lighted, softening neglected corners which the steady rain could seldom reach, and hurting nothing.

This village Inn had assumed, on being established, an uncommon sign. It was called The Nutmeg-Grater. And underneath that household word was inscribed, up in the tree, on the same flaming board, and in the like golden characters, By Benjamin Britain.

At a second glance, and on a more minute examination of his face, you might have known that it was no other than Benjamin Britain himself who stood in the doorway—reasonably changed by time, but for the better; a very comfortable host indeed.

'Mrs. B.', said Mr. Britain, looking down the road, 'is rather late. It's tea-time.'

As there was no Mrs. Britain coming, he strolled leisurely out into the road and looked up at the house, very much to his satisfaction. 'It's just the sort of house', said Benjamin, 'I should wish to stop at, if I didn't keep it.'

Then, he strolled towards the garden-paling, and took a look at the dahlias. They looked over at him, with a helpless drowsy hanging of their heads: which bobbed again, as the heavy drops of wet dripped off them.

'You must be looked after,' said Benjamin. 'Memorandum, not to forget to tell her so. She's a long time coming!'

Mr. Britain's better half seemed to be so very much his better half, that his own moiety of himself was utterly cast away and helpless without her.

'She hadn't much to do, I think,' said Ben. 'There were a few matters of business after market, but not many. Oh! here we are at last!'

A chaise-cart, driven by a boy, came clattering along the road: and seated in it, in a chair, with a large well-saturated umbrella spread out to dry behind her, was the plump figure of a matronly woman, with her bare arms folded across a basket which she carried on her knee, several other baskets and parcels lying crowded around her, and a certain bright good nature in her face and contented awkwardness in her manner, as she jogged to and fro with the motion of her carriage, which smacked of old times, even in the distance. Upon her nearer approach, this relish of by-gone days was not diminished; and when the cart stopped at the Nutmeg-Grater door, a pair of shoes, alighting from it, slipped nimbly through Mr. Britain's open arms, and came down with a substantial weight upon the pathway, which shoes could hardly have belonged to any one but Clemency Newcome.

In fact they did belong to her, and she stood in them, and a rosy comfortable-looking soul she was: with as much soap on her glossy face as in times of yore, but with whole elbows now, that had grown quite dimpled in her improved condition.

'You're late, Clemmy!' said Mr. Britain.

'Why, you see, Ben, I've had a deal to do!' she replied, looking busily after the safe removal into the house of all the packages and baskets: 'eight, nine, ten,—where's eleven? Oh! my basket's eleven! It's all right. Put the horse up, Harry, and if he coughs again give him a warm mash to-night. Eight, nine, ten. Why, where's eleven? Oh I forgot, it's all right. How's the children, Ben?'

'Hearty, Clemmy, hearty.'

'Bless their precious faces!' said Mrs. Britain, unbonneting her own round countenance (for she and her husband were by this time in the bar), and smoothing her hair with her open hands. 'Give us a kiss, old man!'

Mr. Britain promptly complied.

'I think,' said Mrs. Britain, applying herself to her pockets and drawing forth an immense bulk of thin books and crumpled papers: a very kennel of dogs'-ears: 'I've done everything. Bills all settled—turnips sold—brewer's account looked into and paid—'bacco pipes ordered—seventeen pound four, paid into the Bank—Doctor Heathfield's charge for little Clem—you'll guess what that is—Doctor Heathfield won't take nothing again, Ben.'

'I thought he wouldn't,' returned Britain.

'No. He says whatever family you was to have, Ben, he'd never put you to the cost of a halfpenny. Not if you was to have twenty.'

Mr. Britain's face assumed a serious expression, and he looked hard at the wall.

'An't it kind of him?' said Clemency.

'Very,' returned Mr. Britain. 'It's the sort of kindness that I wouldn't presume upon, on any account.'

'No,' retorted Clemency. 'Of course not. Then there's the pony—he fetched eight pound two; and that an't bad, is it?'

'It's very good,' said Ben.

'I'm glad you're pleased!' exclaimed his wife. 'I thought you would be; and I think that's all, and so no more at present from yours and cetrer, C. Britain. Ha, ha, ha! There! Take all the papers, and lock 'em up. Oh! Wait a minute. Here's a printed bill to stick on the wall. Wet from the printer's. How nice it smells!'

'What's this?' said Ben, looking over the document.

'I don't know,' replied his wife. 'I haven't read a word of it.'

' "To be sold by Auction," ' read the host of the Nutmeg-Grater, ' "unless previously disposed of by private contract." '

'They always put that,' said Clemency.

'Yes, but they don't always put this,' he returned. 'Look here, "Mansion," &c.—"offices," &c., "shrubberies," &c., "ring fence," &c. "Messrs. Snitchey and Craggs," &c., "ornamental portion of the unencumbered freehold property of Michael Warden, Esquire, intending to continue to reside abroad"!'

'Intending to continue to reside abroad!' repeated Clemency.

'Here it is,' said Britain. 'Look!'

'And it was only this very day that I heard it whispered at the old house, that better and plainer news had been half promised of her, soon!' said Clemency, shaking her head sorrowfully, and patting her elbows as if the recollection of old times unconsciously awakened her old habits. 'Dear, dear, dear! There'll be heavy hearts, Ben, yonder.'

Mr. Britain heaved a sigh, and shook his head, and said he couldn't make it out: he had left off trying long ago. With that remark, he applied himself to putting up the bill just inside the bar window. Clemency, after meditating in silence for a few moments, roused herself, cleared her thoughtful brow, and bustled off to look after the children.

Though the host of the Nutmeg-Grater had a lively regard for his good-wife, it was of the old patronising kind, and she amused him mightily. Nothing would have astonished him so much, as to have known for certain from any third party, that it was she who managed the whole house, and made him, by her plain straightforward thrift, good-humour, honesty, and industry, a thriving man. So easy it is, in any degree of life (as the world very often finds it), to take those cheerful natures that never assert their merit, at their own modest valuation; and to conceive a flippant liking of people for their outward oddities and eccentricities, whose innate worth, if we would look so far, might make us blush in the comparison!

It was comfortable to Mr. Britain, to think of his own condescension in having married Clemency. She was a perpetual testimony to him of the goodness of his heart, and the kindness of his disposition; and he felt that her being an excellent wife was an illustration of the old precept that virtue is its own reward.

He had finished wafering up the bill, and had locked the vouchers for her day's proceedings in the cupboard—chuckling all the time, over her capacity for business—when, returning with the news that the two Master Britains were playing in the coach-house under the superintendence of one Betsey, and that little Clem was sleeping 'like a picture,' she sat down to tea, which had awaited her arrival, on a little table. It was a very neat little bar, with the usual display of bottles and glasses; a sedate clock, right to the minute (it was half-past five); everything in its place, and everything furbished and polished up to the very utmost.

'It's the first time I've sat down quietly to-day, I declare,' said Mrs. Britain, taking a long breath, as if she had sat down for the night; but getting up again immediately to hand her husband his tea, and cut him his bread-and-butter; 'how that bill does set me thinking of old times!'

'Ah!' said Mr. Britain, handling his saucer like an oyster, and disposing of its contents on the same principle.

'That same Mr. Michael Warden,' said Clemency, shaking her head at the notice of sale, 'lost me my old place.'

'And got you your husband,' said Mr. Britain.

'Well! So he did,' retorted Clemency, 'and many thanks to him.'

'Man's the creature of habit,' said Mr. Britain, surveying her, over his saucer. 'I had somehow got used to you, Clem; and I found I shouldn't be able to get on without you. So we went and got made man and wife. Ha! ha! We! Who'd have thought it!'

'Who indeed!' cried Clemency. 'It was very good of you, Ben.'

'No, no, no,' replied Mr. Britain, with an air of self-denial. 'Nothing worth mentioning.'

'Oh yes it was, Ben,' said his wife, with great simplicity; 'I'm sure I think so, and am very much obliged to you. Ah!' looking again at the bill; 'when she was known to be gone, and out of reach, dear girl,

I couldn't help telling—for her sake quite as much as theirs—what I knew, could I?'

'You told it, anyhow,' observed her husband.

'And Dr. Jeddler,' pursued Clemency, putting down her tea-cup, and looking thoughtfully at the bill, 'in his grief and passion turned me out of house and home! I never have been so glad of anything in all my life, as that I didn't say an angry word to him, and hadn't any angry feeling towards him, even then; for he repented that truly, afterwards. How often he has sat in this room, and told me over and over again he was sorry for it!—the last time, only yesterday, when you were out. How often he has sat in this room, and talked to me, hour after hour, about one thing and another, in which he made believe to be interested!—but only for the sake of the days that are gone by, and because he knows she used to like me, Ben!'

'Why, how did you ever come to catch a glimpse of that, Clem?' asked her husband: astonished that she should have a distinct perception of a truth which had only dimly suggested itself to his inquiring mind.

'I don't know, I'm sure,' said Clemency, blowing her tea, to cool it. 'Bless you, I couldn't tell you, if you was to offer me a reward of a hundred pound.'

He might have pursued this metaphysical subject but for her catching a glimpse of a substantial fact behind him, in the shape of a gentleman attired in mourning, and cloaked and booted like a rider on horseback, who stood at the bar-door. He seemed attentive to their conversation, and not at all impatient to interrupt it.

Clemency hastily rose at this sight. Mr. Britain also rose and saluted the guest. 'Will you please to walk up-stairs, sir? There's a very nice room up-stairs, sir.'

'Thank you,' said the stranger, looking earnestly at Mr. Britain's wife. 'May I come in here?'

'Oh, surely, if you like, sir,' returned Clemency, admitting him. 'What would you please to want, sir?'

The bill had caught his eye, and he was reading it.

'Excellent property that, sir,' observed Mr. Britain.

He made no answer; but, turning round, when he had finished reading, looked at Clemency with the same observant curiosity as before. 'You were asking me,' —he said, still looking at her,—

'What you would please to take, sir,' answered Clemency, stealing a glance at him in return.

'If you will let me have a draught of ale,' he said, moving to a table by the window, 'and will let me have it here, without being any interruption to your meal, I shall be much obliged to you.'

He sat down as he spoke, without any further parley, and looked out at the prospect. He was an easy, well-knit figure of a man in the prime of life. His face, much browned by the sun, was shaded by a quantity of dark hair; and he wore a moustache. His beer being set before him, he filled out a glass, and drank, good-humouredly, to the house; adding, as he put the tumbler down again:

'It's a new house, is it not?'

'Not particularly new, sir,' replied Mr. Britain.

'Between five and six years old,' said Clemency; speaking very distinctly.

'I think I heard you mention Dr. Jeddler's name, as I came in,' inquired the stranger. 'That bill reminds me of him; for I happen to know something of that story, by hearsay, and through certain connexions of mine.—Is the old man living?'

'Yes, he's living, sir,' said Clemency.

'Much changed?'

'Since when, sir?' returned Clemency, with remarkable emphasis and expression.

'Since his daughter—went away.'

'Yes! he's greatly changed since then,' said Clemency. 'He's grey and old, and hasn't the same way with him at all; but I think he's happy now. He has taken on with his sister since then, and goes to see her very often. That did him good, directly. At first, he was sadly broken down; and it was enough to make one's heart bleed, to see him wandering about, railing at the world; but a great change for the better came over him after a year or two, and then he began to like to talk about his lost daughter, and to praise her, ay and the world too! and was never tired of saying, with the tears in his poor eyes, how beautiful and good she was. He had forgiven her then. That was about the same time as Miss Grace's marriage. Britain, you remember?'

Mr. Britain remembered very well.

'The sister *is* married then,' returned the stranger. He paused for some time before he asked, 'To whom?'

Clemency narrowly escaped oversetting the tea-board, in her emotion at this question.

'Did *you* never hear?' she said.

'I should like to hear,' he replied, as he filled his glass again, and raised it to his lips.

'Ah! It would be a long story, if it was properly told,' said Clemency, resting her chin on the palm of her left hand, and supporting that elbow on her right hand, as she shook her head, and looked back through the intervening years, as if she were looking at a fire. 'It would be a long story, I am sure.'

'But told as a short one,' suggested the stranger.

'Told as a short one,' repeated Clemency in the same thoughtful tone, and without any apparent reference to him, or consciousness of having auditors, 'what would there be to tell? That they grieved together, and remembered her together, like a person dead; that they were so tender of her, never would reproach her, called her back to one another as she used to be, and found excuses for her! Every one knows that. I'm sure *I* do. No one better,' added Clemency, wiping her eyes with her hand.

'And so,' suggested the stranger.

'And so,' said Clemency, taking him up mechanically, and without any change in her attitude or manner, 'they at last were married. They were married on her birth-day—it comes round again to-morrow—very quiet, very humble like, but very happy. Mr. Alfred said, one night when they were walking in the orchard, "Grace, shall our wedding-day be Marion's birth-day?" And it was.'

'And they have lived happily together?' said the stranger.

'Ay,' said Clemency. 'No two people ever more so. They have had no sorrow but this.'

She raised her head as with a sudden attention to the circumstances under which she was recalling these events, and looked quickly at the stranger. Seeing that his face was turned toward the window, and that he seemed intent upon the prospect, she made some eager signs to her husband, and pointed to the bill, and moved her mouth as if she were repeating with great energy, one word or phrase to him over and over again. As she uttered no sound, and as her dumb motions like most of her gestures were of a very extraordinary kind, this unintelligible conduct reduced Mr. Britain to the confines of despair. He stared at the table, at the stranger, at the spoons, at his wife—followed her pantomime with looks of deep amazement and perplexity—asked in the same language, was it property in danger, was it he in danger, was it she—answered her signals with other signals expressive of the deepest distress and confusion—followed the motions of her lips—guessed half aloud 'milk and water,' 'monthly warning,' 'mice and walnuts'—and couldn't approach her meaning.

Clemency gave it up at last, as a hopeless attempt; and moving her chair by very slow degrees a little nearer to the stranger, sat with her eyes apparently cast down but glancing sharply at him now and then, waiting until he should ask some other question. She had not to wait long; for he said, presently:

'And what is the after history of the young lady who went away? They know it, I suppose?'

Clemency shook her head. 'I've heard,' she said, 'that Doctor Jeddler is thought to know more of it than he tells. Miss Grace has had letters from her sister, saying that she was well and happy, and made much happier by her being married to Mr. Alfred: and has written letters back. But there's a mystery about her life and fortunes, altogether, which nothing has cleared up to this hour, and which—'

She faltered here, and stopped.

'And which'—repeated the stranger.

'Which only one other person, I believe, could explain,' said Clemency, drawing her breath quickly.

'Who may that be?' asked the stranger.

'Mr. Michael Warden!' answered Clemency, almost in a shriek: at once conveying to her husband what she would have had him understand before, and letting Michael Warden know that he was recognised.

'You remember me, sir?' said Clemency, trembling with emotion; 'I saw just now you did! You remember me, that night in the garden. I was with her!'

'Yes. You were,' he said.

'Yes, sir,' returned Clemency. 'Yes, to be sure. This is my husband, if you please. Ben, my dear Ben, run to Miss Grace—run to Mr. Alfred—run somewhere, Ben! Bring somebody here, directly!'

'Stay!' said Michael Warden, quietly interposing himself between the door and Britain. 'What would you do?'

'Let them know that you are here, sir,' answered Clemency, clapping her hands in sheer agitation. 'Let them know that they may hear of her, from your own lips; let them know that she is not quite lost to them, but that she will come home again yet, to bless her father and her loving sister—even her old servant, even me,' she struck herself upon the breast with both hands, 'with a sight of her sweet face. Run, Ben, run!' And still she pressed him on towards the door, and still Mr. Warden stood before it, with his hand stretched out, not angrily, but sorrowfully.

'Or perhaps,' said Clemency, running past her husband, and catching in her emotion at Mr. Warden's cloak, 'perhaps she's here now; perhaps she's close by. I think from your manner she is. Let me see her, sir, if you please. I waited on her when she was a little child. I saw her grow to be the pride of all this place. I knew her when she was Mr. Alfred's promised wife. I tried to warn her when you tempted her away. I know what her old home was when she was like the soul of it, and how it changed when she was gone and lost. Let me speak to her, if you please!'

He gazed at her with compassion, not unmixed with wonder: but he made no gesture of assent.

'I don't think she *can* know,' pursued Clemency, 'how truly they forgive her; how they love her; what joy it would be to them, to see her once more. She may be timorous of going home. Perhaps if she sees me, it may give her new heart. Only tell me truly, Mr. Warden, is she with you?'

'She is not,' he answered, shaking his head.

This answer, and his manner, and his black dress, and his coming back so quietly, and his announced intention of continuing to live abroad, explained it all. Marion was dead.

He didn't contradict her; yes, she was dead! Clemency sat down, hid her face upon the table, and cried.

At that moment, a grey-headed old gentleman came running in: quite out of breath, and panting so much that his voice was scarcely to be recognised as the voice of Mr. Snitchey.

'Good Heaven, Mr. Warden!' said the lawyer, taking him aside, 'what wind has blown——' He was so blown himself, that he couldn't get on any further until after a pause, when he added, feebly, 'you here?'

'An ill wind, I am afraid,' he answered. 'If you could have heard what has just passed—how I have been besought and entreated to perform impossibilities—what confusion and affliction I carry with me!'

'I can guess it all. But why did you ever come here, my good sir?' retorted Snitchey.

'Come! How should I know who kept the house? When I sent my servant on to you, I strolled in here because the place was new to me; and I had a natural curiosity in everything new and old, in these old scenes; and it was outside the town. I wanted to communicate with you, first, before appearing there. I wanted to know what people would say to me. I see by your manner that you can tell me. If it were not for your confounded caution, I should have been possessed of everything long ago.'

'Our caution!' returned the lawyer, 'speaking for Self and Craggs—deceased,' here Mr. Snitchey, glancing at his hat-band, shook his head, 'how can you reasonably blame us, Mr. Warden? It was understood between us that the subject was never to be renewed, and that it wasn't a subject on which grave and sober men like us (I made a note of your observations at the time) could interfere. Our caution too! When Mr. Craggs, sir, went down to his respected grave in the full belief——'

'I had given a solemn promise of silence until I should return, whenever that might be,' interrupted Mr. Warden; 'and I have kept it.'

'Well, sir, and I repeat it,' returned Mr. Snitchey, 'we were bound to silence too. We were bound to silence in our duty towards ourselves, and in our duty towards a variety of clients, you among them, who were as close as wax. It was not our place to make inquiries of you on such a delicate subject. I had my suspicions, sir; but it is not six months since I have known the truth, and been assured that you lost her.'

'By whom?' inquired his client.

'By Doctor Jeddler himself, sir, who at last reposed that confidence in me voluntarily. He, and only he, has known the whole truth, years and years.'

'And you know it?' said his client.

'I do, sir!' replied Snitchey; 'and I have also reason to know that it will be broken to her sister to-morrow evening. They have given her that promise. In the meantime, perhaps you'll give me the honour of your company at my house; being unexpected at your own. But, not to run the chance of any more such difficulties as you have had here, in case you should be recognised—though you're a good deal changed; I think I might have passed you myself, Mr. Warden—we had better dine here, and walk on in the evening. It's a very good place to dine at, Mr. Warden: your own property, by-the-bye. Self and Craggs (deceased) took a chop here sometimes, and had it very comfortably served. Mr. Craggs, sir,' said Snitchey, shutting his eyes tight for an instant, and opening them again, 'was struck off the roll of life too soon.'

'Heaven forgive me for not condoling with you,' returned Michael Warden, passing his hand across his forehead, 'but I'm like a man in a dream at present. I seem to want my wits. Mr. Craggs—yes—I am very sorry we have lost Mr. Craggs.' But he looked at Clemency as he said it, and seemed to sympathise with Ben, consoling her.

'Mr. Craggs, sir,' observed Snitchey, 'didn't find life, I regret to say, as easy to have and to hold as his theory made it out, or he would have been among us now. It's a great loss to me. He was my right arm, my right leg, my right ear, my right eye, was Mr. Craggs. I am paralytic without him. He bequeathed his share of the business to Mrs. Craggs, her executors, administrators, and assigns. His name remains in the Firm to this hour. I try, in a childish sort of a way, to make believe, sometimes, he's alive. You may observe that I speak for Self and Craggs—deceased, sir—deceased,' said the tender-hearted attorney, waving his pocket-handkerchief.

Michael Warden, who had still been observant of Clemency, turned to Mr. Snitchey when he ceased to speak, and whispered in his ear.

'Ah, poor thing!' said Snitchey, shaking his head. 'Yes. She was always very faithful to Marion. She was always very fond of her. Pretty Marion! Poor Marion! Cheer up, Mistress—you *are* married now, you know, Clemency.'

Clemency only sighed, and shook her head.

'Well, well! Wait till to-morrow,' said the lawyer, kindly.

'To-morrow can't bring back the dead to life, Mister,' said Clemency, sobbing.

'No. It can't do that, or it would bring back Mr. Craggs, deceased,' returned the lawyer. 'But it may bring some soothing circumstances; it may bring some comfort. Wait till to-morrow!'

So Clemency, shaking his proffered hand, said she would; and Britain, who had been terribly cast down at sight of his despondent wife (which was like the business hanging its head), said that was right; and Mr. Snitchey and Michael Warden went up-stairs; and there they were soon engaged in a conversation so cautiously conducted, that no murmur of it was audible above the clatter of plates and dishes, the hissing of the frying-pan, the bubbling of saucepans, the low monotonous waltzing of the jack*—with a dreadful click every now and then as if it had met with some mortal accident to its head, in a fit of giddiness—and all the other preparations in the kitchen for their dinner.

To-morrow was a bright and peaceful day; and nowhere were the autumn tints more beautifully seen, than from the quiet orchard of the Doctor's house. The snows of many winter nights had melted from that ground, the withered leaves of many summer times had rustled there, since she had fled. The honeysuckle porch was green again, the trees cast bountiful and changing shadows on the grass, the landscape was as tranquil and serene as it had ever been; but where was she!

Not there. Not there. She would have been a stranger sight in her old home now, even than that home had been at first, without her. But a lady sat in the familiar place, from whose heart she had never passed away; in whose true memory she lived, unchanging, youthful, radiant with all promise and all hope; in whose affection—and it was a mother's now, there was a cherished little daughter playing by her side—she had no rival, no successor; upon whose gentle lips her name was trembling then.

The spirit of the lost girl looked out of those eyes. Those eyes of Grace, her sister, sitting with her husband in the orchard, on their wedding-day, and his and Marion's birth-day.

He had not become a great man; he had not grown rich; he had not forgotten the scenes and friends of his youth; he had not fulfilled any one of the Doctor's old predictions. But in his useful, patient, unknown visiting of poor men's homes; and in his watching of sick beds; and in his daily knowledge of the gentleness and goodness flowering the by-paths of this world, not to be trodden down beneath the heavy foot of poverty, but springing up, elastic, in its track, and making its way beautiful; he had better learned and proved, in each succeeding year, the truth of his old faith. The manner of his life, though quiet and remote, had shown him how often men still entertained angels, unawares,* as in the olden time; and how the most unlikely forms—even some that were mean and ugly to the view, and poorly clad—became irradiated by the couch of sorrow, want, and pain, and changed to ministering spirits with a glory round their heads.

He lived to better purpose on the altered battle-ground perhaps, than if he had contended restlessly in more ambitious lists; and he was happy with his wife, dear Grace.

And Marion. Had *he* forgotten her?

'The time has flown, dear Grace,' he said, 'since then;' they had been talking of that night; 'and yet it seems a long long while ago. We count by changes and events within us. Not by years.'

'Yet we have years to count by, too, since Marion was with us,' returned Grace. 'Six times, dear husband, counting to-night as one, we have sat here on her birth-day, and spoken together of that happy return, so eagerly expected and so long deferred. Ah when will it be! When will it be!'

Her husband attentively observed her, as the tears collected in her eyes; and drawing nearer, said:

'But Marion told you, in that farewell letter which she left for you upon your table, love, and which you read so often, that years must pass away before it *could* be. Did she not?'

She took a letter from her breast, and kissed it, and said 'Yes.'

'That through these intervening years, however happy she might be, she would look forward to the time when you would meet again, and all would be made clear; and that she prayed you, trustfully and hopefully to do the same. The letter runs so, does it not, my dear?'

'Yes, Alfred.'

'And every other letter she has written since?'

'Except the last—some months ago—in which she spoke of you, and what you then knew, and what I was to learn to-night.'

He looked towards the sun, then fast declining, and said that the appointed time was sunset.

'Alfred!' said Grace, laying her hand upon his shoulder earnestly, 'there is something in this letter—this old letter, which you say I read so often—that I have never told you. But to-night, dear husband, with that sunset drawing near, and all our life seeming to soften and become hushed with the departing day, I cannot keep it secret.'

'What is it, love?'

'When Marion went away, she wrote me, here, that you had once left her a sacred trust to me, and that now she left you, Alfred, such a trust in my hands: praying and beseeching me, as I loved her, and as I loved you, not to reject the affection she believed (she knew, she said) you would transfer to me when the new wound was healed, but to encourage and return it.'

'—And make me a proud, and happy man again, Grace. Did she say so?'

'She meant, to make myself so blest and honoured in your love,' was his wife's answer, as he held her in his arms.

'Hear me, my dear!' he said.—'No. Hear me so!'—and as he spoke, he gently laid the head she had raised, again upon his shoulder. 'I know why I have never heard this passage in the letter until now. I know why no trace of it ever showed itself in any word or look of yours at that time. I know why Grace, although so true a friend to me, was hard to win to be my wife. And knowing it, my own! I know the priceless value of the heart I gird within my arms, and thank GOD for the rich possession!'

She wept, but not for sorrow, as he pressed her to his heart. After a brief space, he looked down at the child, who was sitting at their feet playing with a little basket of flowers, and bade her look how golden and how red the sun was.

'Alfred,' said Grace, raising her head quickly at these words. 'The sun is going down. You have not forgotten what I am to know before it sets.'

'You are to know the truth of Marion's history, my love,' he answered.

'All the truth,' she said, imploringly. 'Nothing veiled from me, any more. That was the promise. Was it not?'

'It was,' he answered.

'Before the sun went down on Marion's birth-day. And you see it, Alfred? It is sinking fast.'

He put his arm about her waist, and, looking steadily into her eyes, rejoined:

'That truth is not reserved so long for me to tell, dear Grace. It is to come from other lips.'

'From other lips!' she faintly echoed.

'Yes. I know your constant heart, I know how brave you are, I know that to you a word of preparation is enough. You have said, truly, that the time is come. It is. Tell me that you have present fortitude to bear a trial—a surprise—a shock: and the messenger is waiting at the gate.'

'What messenger?' she said. 'And what intelligence does he bring?'

'I am pledged,' he answered her, preserving his steady look, 'to say no more. Do you think you understand me?'

'I am afraid to think,' she said.

There was that emotion in his face, despite its steady gaze, which frightened her. Again she hid her own face on his shoulder, trembling, and entreated him to pause—a moment.

'Courage, my wife! When you have firmness to receive the messenger, the messenger is waiting at the gate. The sun is setting on Marion's birth-day. Courage, courage, Grace!'

She raised her head, and, looking at him, told him she was ready. As she stood, and looked upon him going away, her face was so like Marion's as it had been in her later days at home, that it was wonderful to see. He took the child with him. She called her back—she bore the lost girl's name—and pressed her to her bosom. The little creature, being released again, sped after him, and Grace was left alone.

She knew not what she dreaded, or what hoped; but remained there, motionless, looking at the porch by which they had disappeared.

Ah! what was that, emerging from its shadow; standing on its threshold! That figure, with its white garments rustling in the evening air; its head laid down upon her father's breast, and pressed against it to his loving heart! O God! was it a vision that came bursting from the old man's arms, and with a cry, and with a waving of its hands, and with a wild precipitation of itself upon her in its boundless love, sank down in her embrace!

'Oh, Marion, Marion! Oh, my sister! Oh, my heart's dear love! Oh, joy and happiness unutterable, so to meet again!'

It was no dream, no phantom conjured up by hope and fear, but Marion, sweet Marion! So beautiful, so happy, so unalloyed by care and trial, so elevated and exalted in her loveliness, that as the setting sun shone brightly on her upturned face, she might have been a spirit visiting the earth upon some healing mission.

Clinging to her sister, who had dropped upon a seat and bent down over her—and smiling through her tears—and kneeling, close before her, with both arms twining round her, and never turning for an instant from her face—and with the glory of the setting sun upon her brow, and with the soft tranquillity of evening gathering around them—Marion at length broke silence; her voice, so calm, low, clear, and pleasant, well-tuned to the time.

'When this was my dear home, Grace, as it will be now again—'

'Stay, my sweet love! A moment! O Marion, to hear you speak again!'

She could not bear the voice she loved so well, at first.

'When this was my dear home, Grace, as it will be now again, I loved him from my soul. I loved him most devotedly. I would have died for him, though I was so young. I never slighted his affection in my secret breast for one brief instant. It was far beyond all price to me. Although it is so long ago, and past, and gone, and everything is wholly changed, I could not bear to think that you, who love so well, should think I did not truly love him once. I never loved him better, Grace, than when he left this very scene upon this very day. I never loved him better, dear one, than I did that night when *I* left here.'

Her sister, bending over her, could look into her face, and hold her fast.

'But he had gained, unconsciously,' said Marion, with a gentle smile, 'another heart, before I knew that I had one to give him. That heart—yours, my sister!—was so yielded up, in all its other tenderness, to me; was so devoted, and so noble; that it plucked its love away, and kept its secret from all eyes but mine—Ah! what other eyes were quickened by such tenderness and gratitude!—and was content to sacrifice itself to me. But, I knew something of its depths. I knew the struggle it had made. I knew its high, inestimable worth to him, and his appreciation of it, let him love me as he would. I knew the debt I owed it. I had its great example every day before me. What you had done for me, I knew that I could do, Grace, if I would, for you. I never laid my head down on my pillow, but I prayed with tears to do it. I never laid my head down on my pillow, but I thought of Alfred's own words on the day of his departure, and how truly he had said (for I knew that, knowing you) that there were victories gained every day, in struggling hearts, to which these fields of battle were as nothing. Thinking more and more upon the great endurance cheerfully sustained, and never known or cared for, that there must be, every day and hour, in that great strife of which he spoke, my trial seemed to grow light and easy. And He who knows our hearts, my dearest, at this moment, and who knows there is no drop of bitterness or grief—of anything but unmixed happiness—in mine, enabled me to make the resolution that I never would be Alfred's wife. That he should be my brother, and your husband, if the course I took could bring that happy end to pass; but that I never would (Grace, I then loved him dearly, dearly!) be his wife!'

'O Marion! O Marion!'

'I had tried to seem indifferent to him;' and she pressed her sister's face against her own; 'but that was hard, and you were always his true advocate. I had tried to tell you of my resolution, but you would never hear me; you would never understand me. The time was drawing near for his return. I felt that I must act, before the daily intercourse between us was renewed. I knew that one great pang, undergone at that time, would save a lengthened agony to all of us. I knew that if I went away then, that end must follow which *has* followed, and which has made us both so happy, Grace! I wrote to good Aunt Martha, for a refuge in her house: I did not then tell her all, but something of my story, and she freely promised it. While I was contesting that step with myself, and with my love of you, and home, Mr. Warden, brought here by an accident, became, for some time, our companion.'

'I have sometimes feared of late years, that this might have been,' exclaimed her sister; and her countenance was ashy-pale. 'You never loved him—and you married him in your self-sacrifice to me!'

'He was then,' said Marion, drawing her sister closer to her, 'on the eve of going secretly away for a long time. He wrote to me, after leaving here; told me what his condition and prospects really were; and offered me his hand. He told me he had seen I was not happy in the prospect of Alfred's return. I believe he thought my heart had no part in that contract; perhaps thought I might have loved him once, and did not then; perhaps thought that when I tried to seem indifferent, I tried to hide indifference—I cannot tell. But I wished that you should feel me wholly lost to Alfred—hopeless to him—dead. Do you understand me, love?'

Her sister looked into her face, attentively. She seemed in doubt.

'I saw Mr. Warden, and confided in his honour; charged him with my secret, on the eve of his and my departure. He kept it. Do you understand me, dear?'

Grace looked confusedly upon her. She scarcely seemed to hear.

'My love, my sister!' said Marion, 'recall your thoughts a moment; listen to me. Do not look so strangely on me. There are countries, dearest, where those who would abjure a misplaced passion, or would strive against some cherished feeling of their hearts and conquer it, retire into a hopeless solitude, and close the world against themselves and worldly loves and hopes for ever. When women do so, they assume that name which is so dear to you and me, and call each other Sisters. But, there may be sisters, Grace, who, in the broad world out of doors, and underneath its free sky, and in its crowded places, and among its busy life, and trying to assist and cheer it and to do some good,—learn the same lesson; and who, with hearts still fresh and young, and open to all happiness and means of happiness, can say the battle is long past, the victory long won. And such a one am I! You understand me now?'

Still she looked fixedly upon her, and made no reply.

'Oh Grace, dear Grace,' said Marion, clinging yet more tenderly and fondly to that breast from which she had been so long exiled, 'if you were not a happy wife and mother—if I had no little namesake here—if Alfred, my kind brother, were not your own fond husband—from whence could I derive the ecstasy I feel to-night! But, as I left here, so I have returned. My heart has known no other love, my hand has never been bestowed apart from it. I am still your maiden sister, unmarried, unbetrothed: your own loving old Marion, in whose affection you exist alone and have no partner, Grace!'

She understood her now. Her face relaxed; sobs came to her relief; and falling on her neck, she wept and wept, and fondled her as if she were a child again.

When they were more composed, they found that the Doctor, and his sister good Aunt Martha, were standing near at hand, with Alfred.

'This is a weary day for me,' said good Aunt Martha, smiling through her tears, as she embraced her nieces; 'for I lose my dear companion in making you all happy; and what can you give me, in return for my Marion?'

'A converted brother,' said the Doctor.

'That's something, to be sure,' retorted Aunt Martha, 'in such a farce as—'

'No, pray don't,' said the Doctor penitently.

'Well, I won't,' replied Aunt Martha. 'But, I consider myself ill used. I don't know what's to become of me without my Marion, after we have lived together half-a-dozen years.'

'You must come and live here, I suppose,' replied the Doctor. 'We shan't quarrel now, Martha.'

'Or you must get married, Aunt,' said Alfred.

'Indeed,' returned the old lady, 'I think it might be a good specula-tion if I were to set my cap at Michael Warden, who, I hear, is come home much the better for his absence in all respects. But as I knew him when he was a boy, and I was not a very young woman then, perhaps he mightn't respond. So I'll make up my mind to go and live with Marion, when she marries, and until then (it will not be very long, I dare say) to live alone. What do *you* say, Brother?'

'I've a great mind to say it's a ridiculous world altogether, and there's nothing serious in it,' observed the poor old Doctor.

'You might take twenty affidavits of it if you chose, Anthony,' said his sister; 'but nobody would believe you with such eyes as those.'

'It's a world full of hearts,' said the Doctor, hugging his younger daughter, and bending across her to hug Grace—for he couldn't separate the sisters; 'and a serious world, with all its folly—even with mine, which was enough to have swamped the whole globe; and it is a world on which the sun never rises, but it looks upon a thousand bloodless battles that are some set-off against the miseries and wick-edness of Battle-Fields; and it is a world we need be careful how we libel, Heaven forgive us, for it is a world of sacred mysteries, and its Creator only knows what lies beneath the surface of His lightest image!'

You would not be the better pleased with my rude pen, if it dis-sected and laid open to your view the transports of this family, long severed and now reunited. Therefore, I will not follow the poor Doctor through his humbled recollection of the sorrow he had had, when Marion was lost to him; nor will I tell how serious he had found that world to be, in which some love, deep-anchored, is the portion of all human creatures; nor how such a trifle as the absence of one little unit in the great absurd account, had stricken him to the ground. Nor how, in compassion for his distress, his sister had, long ago, revealed the truth to him by slow degrees, and brought him to the knowledge of the heart of his self-banished daughter, and to that daughter's side.

Nor how Alfred Heathfield had been told the truth, too, in the course of that then current year; and Marion had seen him, and had promised him, as her brother, that on her birth-day, in the evening, Grace should know it from her lips at last.

'I beg your pardon, Doctor,' said Mr. Snitchey, looking into the orchard, 'but have I liberty to come in?'

Without waiting for permission, he came straight to Marion, and kissed her hand, quite joyfully.

'If Mr. Craggs had been alive, my dear Miss Marion,' said Mr. Snitchey, 'he would have had great interest in this occasion. It might have suggested to him, Mr. Alfred, that our life is not too easy perhaps; that, taken altogether, it will bear any little smoothing we can give it; but Mr. Craggs was a man who could endure to be convinced, sir. He was always open to conviction. If he were open to conviction, now, I—this is weakness. Mrs. Snitchey, my dear,'—at his summons that lady appeared from behind the door, 'you are among old friends.'

Mrs. Snitchey having delivered her congratulations, took her husband aside.

'One moment, Mr. Snitchey,' said that lady. 'It is not in my nature to take up the ashes of the departed.'

'No, my dear,' returned her husband.

'Mr. Craggs is—'

'Yes, my dear, he is deceased,' said Snitchey.

'But I ask you if you recollect,' pursued his wife, 'that evening of the ball? I only ask you that. If you do; and if your memory has not entirely failed you, Mr. Snitchey; and if you are not absolutely in your dotage; I ask you to connect this time with that—to remember how I begged and prayed you, on my knees—'

'Upon your knees, my dear?' said Mr. Snitchey.

'Yes,' said Mrs. Snitchey, confidently, 'and you know it—to beware of that man—to observe his eye—and now to tell me whether I was right, and whether at that moment he knew secrets which he didn't choose to tell.'

'Mrs. Snitchey,' returned her husband, in her ear, 'Madam. Did you ever observe anything in *my* eye?'

'No,' said Mrs. Snitchey, sharply. 'Don't flatter yourself.'

'Because, Madam, that night,' he continued, twitching her by the sleeve, 'it happens that we both knew secrets which we didn't choose to tell, and both knew just the same professionally. And so the less you say about such things the better, Mrs. Snitchey; and take this as a warning to have wiser and more charitable eyes another time. Miss Marion, I brought a friend of yours along with me. Here! Mistress!'

Poor Clemency, with her apron to her eyes, came slowly in, escorted by her husband; the latter doleful with the presentiment, that if she abandoned herself to grief, the Nutmeg-Grater was done for.

'Now, Mistress,' said the lawyer, checking Marion as she ran towards her, and interposing himself between them, 'what's the matter with *you*?'

'The matter!' cried poor Clemency.—When, looking up in wonder, and in indignant remonstrance, and in the added emotion of a great roar from Mr. Britain, and seeing that sweet face so well remembered close before her, she stared, sobbed, laughed, cried, screamed, embraced her, held her fast, released her, fell on Mr. Snitchey and embraced him (much to Mrs. Snitchey's indignation), fell on the Doctor and embraced him, fell on Mr. Britain and embraced him, and concluded by embracing herself, throwing her apron over her head, and going into hysterics behind it.

A stranger had come into the orchard, after Mr. Snitchey, and had remained apart, near the gate, without being observed by any of the group; for they had little spare attention to bestow, and that had been monopolised by the ecstasies of Clemency. He did not appear to wish to be observed, but stood alone, with downcast eyes; and there was an air of dejection about him (though he was a gentleman of a gallant appearance) which the general happiness rendered more remarkable.

None but the quick eyes of Aunt Martha, however, remarked him at all; but, almost as soon as she espied him, she was in conversation with him. Presently, going to where Marion stood with Grace and her little namesake, she whispered something in Marion's ear, at which she started, and appeared surprised; but soon recovering from her confusion, she timidly approached the stranger, in Aunt Martha's company, and engaged in conversation with him too.

'Mr. Britain,' said the lawyer, putting his hand in his pocket, and bringing out a legal-looking document, while this was going on, 'I congratulate you. You are now the whole and sole proprietor of that

freehold tenement, at present occupied and held by yourself as a licensed tavern, or house of public entertainment, and commonly called or known by the sign of the Nutmeg-Grater. Your wife lost one house, through my client Mr. Michael Warden; and now gains another. I shall have the pleasure of canvassing you for the county,* one of these fine mornings.'

'Would it make any difference in the vote if the sign was altered, sir?' asked Britain.

'Not in the least,' replied the lawyer.

'Then,' said Mr. Britain, handing him back the conveyance, 'just clap in the words, "and Thimble," will you be so good; and I'll have the two mottoes painted up in the parlour instead of my wife's portrait.'

'And let me,' said a voice behind them; it was the stranger's— Michael Warden's; 'let me claim the benefit of those inscriptions. Mr. Heathfield and Dr. Jeddler, I might have deeply wronged you both. That I did not, is no virtue of my own. I will not say that I am six years wiser than I was, or better. But I have known, at any rate, that term of self-reproach. I can urge no reason why you should deal gently with me. I abused the hospitality of this house; and learnt by my own demerits, with a shame I never have forgotten, yet with some profit too I would fain hope, from one', he glanced at Marion, 'to whom I made my humble supplication for forgiveness, when I knew her merit and my deep unworthiness. In a few days I shall quit this place for ever. I entreat your pardon. Do as you would be done by! Forget and Forgive!'

TIME—from whom I had the latter portion of this story, and with whom I have the pleasure of a personal acquaintance of some five-and-thirty years' duration—informed me, leaning easily upon his scythe, that Michael Warden never went away again, and never sold his house, but opened it afresh, maintained a golden mean of hospitality, and had a wife, the pride and honour of that country-side, whose name was Marion. But, as I have observed that Time confuses facts occasionally, I hardly know what weight to give to its authority.

THE HAUNTED MAN
AND
THE GHOST'S BARGAIN

A Fancy for Christmas Time

CONTENTS

CHAPTER I

THE GIFT BESTOWED

EVERYBODY said so.

Far be it from me to assert that what everybody says must be true. Everybody is, often, as likely to be wrong as right. In the general experience, everybody has been wrong so often, and it has taken in most instances such a weary while to find out how wrong, that the authority is proved to be fallible. Everybody may sometimes be right; 'but *that's* no rule,' as the ghost of Giles Scroggins says in the ballad.*

The dread word, GHOST, recalls me.

Everybody said he looked like a haunted man. The extent of my present claim for everybody is, that they were so far right. He did.

Who could have seen his hollow cheek, his sunken brilliant eye; his black attired figure, indefinably grim, although well-knit and well-proportioned; his grizzled hair hanging, like tangled sea-weed, about his face,—as if he had been, through his whole life, a lonely mark for the chafing and beating of the great deep of humanity,—but might have said he looked like a haunted man?

Who could have observed his manner, taciturn, thoughtful, gloomy, shadowed by habitual reserve, retiring always and jocund never, with a distraught air of reverting to a bygone place and time, or of listening to some old echoes in his mind, but might have said it was the manner of a haunted man?

Who could have heard his voice, slow-speaking, deep, and grave, with a natural fulness and melody in it which he seemed to set himself against and stop, but might have said it was the voice of a haunted man?

Who that had seen him in his inner chamber, part library and part laboratory,—for he was, as the world knew, far and wide, a learned man in chemistry, and a teacher on whose lips and hands a crowd of aspiring ears and eyes hung daily,—who that had seen him there, upon a winter night, alone, surrounded by his drugs and instruments and books; the shadow of his shaded lamp a monstrous beetle on the wall, motionless among a crowd of spectral shapes raised there by the flickering of the fire upon the quaint objects around him; some of these phantoms (the reflection of glass vessels that held liquids), trembling at heart like things that knew his power to uncombine them, and to give back their component parts to fire and vapour;— who that had seen him then, his work done, and he pondering in his chair before the rusted grate and red flame, moving his thin mouth as if in speech, but silent as the dead, would not have said that the man seemed haunted and the chamber too?

Who might not, by a very easy flight of fancy, have believed that everything about him took this haunted tone, and that he lived on haunted ground?

His dwelling was so solitary and vault-like,—an old, retired part of an ancient endowment for students, once a brave edifice planted in an open place, but now the obsolete whim of forgotten architects; smoke-age-and-weather-darkened, squeezed on every side by the over-growing of the great city, and choked, like an old well, with stones and bricks; its small quadrangles, lying down in very pits formed by the streets and buildings, which, in course of time, had been constructed above its heavy chimney stacks; its old trees, insulted by the neighbouring smoke, which deigned to droop so low when it was very feeble and the weather very moody; its grass-plots, struggling with the mildewed earth to be grass, or to win any show of compromise; its silent pavements, unaccustomed to the tread of feet, and even to the observation of eyes, except when a stray face looked down from the upper world, wondering what nook it was; its sun-dial in a little bricked-up corner, where no sun had straggled for a hundred years, but where, in compensation for the sun's neglect, the snow would lie for weeks when it lay nowhere else, and the black east wind would spin like a huge humming-top, when in all other places it was silent and still.

His dwelling, at its heart and core—within doors—at his fireside— was so lowering and old, so crazy, yet so strong, with its worm-eaten beams of wood in the ceiling, and its sturdy floor shelving downward to the great oak chimney-piece; so environed and hemmed in by the pressure of the town, yet so remote in fashion, age and custom; so quiet, yet so thundering with echoes when a distant voice was raised or a door was shut,—echoes, not confined to the many low passages and empty rooms, but rumbling and grumbling till they were stifled in the heavy air of the forgotten Crypt where the Norman arches were half-buried in the earth.

You should have seen him in his dwelling about twilight, in the dead winter time.

When the wind was blowing, shrill and shrewd, with the going down of the blurred sun. When it was just so dark, as that the forms of things were indistinct and big—but not wholly lost. When sitters by the fire began to see wild faces and figures, mountains and abysses, ambuscades and armies, in the coals. When people in the streets bent down their heads and ran before the weather. When those who were obliged to meet it, were stopped at angry corners, stung by wandering snow-flakes alighting on the lashes of their eyes,—which fell too sparingly, and were blown away too quickly, to leave a trace upon the frozen ground. When windows of private houses closed up tight and warm. When lighted gas began to burst forth in the busy and the quiet streets fast blackening otherwise. When stray pedestrians, shivering along the latter, looked down at the glowing fires in kitchens, and sharpened their sharp appetites by sniffing up the fragrance of whole miles of dinners.

When travellers by land were bitter cold, and looked wearily on gloomy landscapes, rustling and shuddering in the blast. When mariners at sea, outlying upon icy yards, were tossed and swung above the howling ocean dreadfully. When lighthouses, on rocks and headlands, showed solitary and watchful; and benighted sea-birds breasted on against their ponderous lanterns, and fell dead. When little readers of story-books, by the firelight, trembled to think of Cassim Baba* cut into quarters, hanging in the Robbers' Cave, or had some small misgivings that the fierce little old woman with the crutch, who used to start out of the box in the merchant Abudah's bedroom,* might, one of these nights, be found upon the stairs, in the long, cold, dusky journey up to bed.

When, in rustic places, the last glimmering of daylight died away from the ends of avenues; and the trees, arching overhead, were sullen and black. When, in parks and woods, the high wet fern and sodden moss and beds of fallen leaves, and trunks of trees, were lost to view, in masses of impenetrable shade. When mists arose from dyke, and fen, and river. When lights in old halls and in cottage windows, were a cheerful sight. When the mill stopped, the wheel-wright and the blacksmith shut their workshops, the turnpike-gate closed, the plough and harrow were left lonely in the fields, the labourer and team went home, and the striking of the church clock had a deeper sound than at noon, and the churchyard wicket would be swung no more that night.

When twilight everywhere released the shadows, prisoned up all day, that now closed in and gathered like mustering swarms of ghosts. When they stood lowering, in corners of rooms, and frowned out from behind half-opened doors. When they had full possession of unoccupied apartments. When they danced upon the floors, and walls, and ceilings of inhabited chambers, while the fire was low, and withdrew like ebbing waters when it sprung into a blaze. When they fantastically mocked the shapes of household objects, making the nurse an ogress, the rocking-horse a monster, the wondering child half-scared and half-amused, a stranger to itself,—the very tongs upon the hearth, a straddling giant* with his arms a-kimbo, evidently smelling the blood of Englishmen, and wanting to grind people's bones to make his bread.

When these shadows brought into the minds of older people, other thoughts, and showed them different images. When they stole from their retreats, in the likenesses of forms and faces from the past, from the grave, from the deep, deep gulf, where the things that might have been, and never were, are always wandering.

When he sat, as already mentioned, gazing at the fire. When, as it rose and fell, the shadows went and came. When he took no heed of them, with his bodily eyes; but, let them come or let them go, looked fixedly at the fire. You should have seen him, then.

When the sounds that had arisen with the shadows, and come out of their lurking places at the twilight summons, seemed to make a deeper stillness all about him. When the wind was rumbling in the chimney, and sometimes crooning, sometimes howling, in the house. When the old trees outside were so shaken and beaten, that one querulous old rook, unable to sleep, protested now and then, in a feeble, dozy, high-up 'Caw!' When, at intervals, the window trembled, the rusty vane upon the turret-top complained, the clock beneath it recorded that another quarter of an hour was gone, or the fire collapsed and fell in with a rattle.

—When a knock came at his door, in short, as he was sitting so, and roused him.

'Who's that?' said he. 'Come in!'

Surely there had been no figure leaning on the back of his chair, no face looking over it. It is certain that no gliding footstep touched the floor, as he lifted up his head with a start, and spoke. And yet there was no mirror in the room on whose surface his own form could have cast its shadow for a moment; and Something had passed darkly and gone!

'I'm humbly fearful, sir,' said a fresh-coloured busy man, holding the door open with his foot for the admission of himself and a wooden tray he carried, and letting it go again by very gentle and careful degrees, when he and the tray had got in, lest it should close noisily, 'that it's a good bit past the time to-night. But Mrs. William has been taken off her legs so often——'

'By the wind? Ay! I have heard it rising.'

'—By the wind, sir—that it's a mercy she got home at all. Oh dear, yes. Yes. It was by the wind, Mr. Redlaw. By the wind.'

He had, by this time, put down the tray for dinner, and was employed in lighting the lamp, and spreading a cloth on the table. From this employment he desisted in a hurry, to stir and feed the fire, and then resumed it; the lamp he had lighted, and the blaze that rose under his hand, so quickly changing the appearance of the room, that it seemed as if the mere coming in of his fresh red face and active manner had made the pleasant alteration.

'Mrs. William is of course subject at any time, sir, to be taken off her balance by the elements. She is not formed superior to *that*.'

'No,' returned Mr. Redlaw good-naturedly, though abruptly.

'No, sir. Mrs. William may be taken off her balance by Earth; as, for example, last Sunday week, when sloppy and greasy, and she going out to tea with her newest sister-in-law, and having a pride in herself, and wishing to appear perfectly spotless though pedestrian. Mrs. William may be taken off her balance by Air; as being once over-persuaded by a friend to try a swing at Peckham Fair,* which acted on her constitution instantly like a steam-boat. Mrs. William may be taken off her balance by Fire; as on a false alarm of engines at her mother's, when she went two miles in her night-cap. Mrs. William may be taken off her balance by Water; as at Battersea,* when rowed into the piers by her young nephew, Charley Swidger junior, aged twelve, which had no idea of boats whatever. But these are elements. Mrs. William must be taken out of elements for the strength of *her* character to come into play.'

As he stopped for a reply, the reply was 'Yes,' in the same tone as before.

'Yes, sir. Oh dear, yes!' said Mr. Swidger, still proceeding with his preparations, and checking them off as he made them. 'That's where it is, sir. That's what I always say myself, sir. Such a many of us Swidgers!—Pepper. Why there's my father, sir, superannuated keeper and custodian of this Institution, eigh-ty-seven year old. He's a Swidger!—Spoon.'

'True, William,' was the patient and abstracted answer, when he stopped again.

'Yes, sir,' said Mr. Swidger. 'That's what I always say, sir. You may call him the trunk of the tree!—Bread. Then you come to his successor, my unworthy self—Salt—and Mrs. William, Swidgers both.—Knife and fork. Then you come to all my brothers and their families, Swidgers, man and woman, boy and girl. Why, what with cousins, uncles, aunts, and relationships of this, that, and t'other degree, and what-not degree, and marriages, and lyings-in, the Swidgers—Tumbler—might take hold of hands, and make a ring round England!'

Receiving no reply at all here, from the thoughtful man whom he addressed, Mr. William approached him nearer, and made a feint of accidentally knocking the table with a decanter, to rouse him. The moment he succeeded, he went on, as if in great alacrity of acquiescence.

'Yes, sir! That's just what I say myself, sir. Mrs. William and me have often said so. "There's Swidgers enough," we say, "without *our* voluntary contributions,"—Butter. In fact, sir, my father is a family in himself—Castors*—to take care of; and it happens all for the best that we have no child of our own, though it's made Mrs. William rather quiet-like, too. Quite ready for the fowl and mashed potatoes, sir? Mrs. William said she'd dish in ten minutes when I left the Lodge?'

'I am quite ready,' said the other, waking as from a dream, and walking slowly to and fro.

'Mrs. William has been at it again, sir!' said the keeper, as he stood warming a plate at the fire, and pleasantly shading his face with it. Mr. Redlaw stopped in his walking, and an expression of interest appeared in him.

'What I always say myself, sir. She *will* do it! There's a motherly feeling in Mrs. William's breast that must and will have went.'

'What has she done?'

'Why, sir, not satisfied with being a sort of mother to all the young gentlemen that come up from a wariety of parts, to attend your courses of lectures at this ancient foundation—it's surprising how stone-chaney* catches the heat this frosty weather, to be sure!' Here he turned the plate, and cooled his fingers.

'Well?' said Mr. Redlaw.

'That's just what I say myself, sir,' returned Mr. William, speaking over his shoulder, as if in ready and delighted assent. 'That is exactly where it is, sir! There ain't one of our students but appears to regard Mrs. William in that light. Every day, right through the course, they puts their heads into the Lodge, one after another, and have all got something to tell her, or something to ask her. "Swidge" is the appellation by which they speak of Mrs. William in general, among themselves, I'm told; but that's what I say, sir. Better be called ever so far out of your name, if it's done in real liking, than have it made ever so much of, and not cared about! What's a name for? To know a person by. If Mrs. William is known by something better than her name—I allude to Mrs. William's qualities and disposition— never mind her name, though it *is* Swidger, by rights. Let 'em call her Swidge, Widge, Bridge—Lord! London Bridge, Blackfriars, Chelsea, Putney, Waterloo, or Hammersmith Suspension—if they like!'

The close of this triumphant oration brought him and the plate to the table, upon which he half laid and half dropped it, with a lively sense of its being thoroughly heated, just as the subject of his praises entered the room, bearing another tray and a lantern, and followed by a venerable old man with long grey hair.

Mrs. William, like Mr. William, was a simple, innocent-looking person, in whose smooth cheeks the cheerful red of her husband's official waistcoat was very pleasantly repeated. But whereas Mr. William's light hair stood on end all over his head, and seemed to draw his eyes up with it in an excess of bustling readiness for anything, the dark brown hair of Mrs. William was carefully smoothed down, and waved away under a trim tidy cap, in the most exact and quiet manner imaginable. Whereas Mr. William's very trousers hitched themselves up at the ankles, as if it were not in their iron-grey nature to rest without looking about them, Mrs. William's neatly-flowered skirts—red and white, like her own pretty face— were as composed and orderly, as if the very wind that blew so hard out of doors could not disturb one of their folds. Whereas his coat had something of a fly-away and half-off appearance about the collar and breast, her little bodice was so placid and neat, that there should have been protection for her, in it, had she needed any, with the roughest people. Who could have had the heart to make so calm a bosom swell with grief, or throb with fear, or flutter with a thought of shame! To whom would its repose and peace have not appealed against disturbance, like the innocent slumber of a child!

'Punctual, of course, Milly,' said her husband, relieving her of the tray, 'or it wouldn't be you. Here's Mrs. William, sir!—He looks lonelier than ever tonight,' whispering to his wife, as he was taking the tray, 'and ghostlier altogether.'

Without any show of hurry or noise, or any show of herself even, she was so calm and quiet, Milly set the dishes she had brought upon the table,—Mr. William, after much clattering and running about, having only gained possession of a butter-boat of gravy, which he stood ready to serve.

'What is that the old man has in his arms?' asked Mr. Redlaw, as he sat down to his solitary meal.

'Holly, sir,' replied the quiet voice of Milly.

'That's what I say myself, sir,' interposed Mr. William, striking in with the butter-boat. 'Berries is so seasonable to the time of year!—Brown gravy!'

'Another Christmas come, another year gone!' murmured the Chemist, with a gloomy sigh. 'More figures in the lengthening sum of recollection that we work and work at to our torment, till Death idly jumbles all together, and rubs all out. So, Philip!' breaking off, and raising his voice, as he addressed the old man standing apart, with his glistening burden in his arms, from which the quiet Mrs. William took small branches, which she noiselessly trimmed with her scissors, and decorated the room with, while her aged father-in-law looked on much interested in the ceremony.

'My duty to you, sir,' returned the old man. 'Should have spoke before, sir, but know your ways, Mr. Redlaw—proud to say—and wait till spoke to! Merry Christmas, sir, and happy New Year, and many of 'em. Have had a pretty many of 'em myself—ha, ha!—and may take the liberty of wishing 'em. I'm eighty-seven!'

'Have you had so many that were merry and happy?' asked the other.

'Ay, sir, ever so many,' returned the old man.

'Is his memory impaired with age? It is to be expected now,' said Mr. Redlaw, turning to the son, and speaking lower.

'Not a morsel of it, sir,' replied Mr. William. 'That's exactly what I say myself, sir. There never was such a memory as my father's. He's the most wonderful man in the world. He don't know what forgetting means. It's the very observation I'm always making to Mrs. William, sir, if you'll believe me!'

Mr. Swidger, in his polite desire to seem to acquiesce at all events, delivered this as if there were no iota of contradiction in it, and it were all said in unbounded and unqualified assent.

The Chemist pushed his plate away, and, rising from the table, walked across the room to where the old man stood looking at a little sprig of holly in his hand.

'It recalls the time when many of those years were old and new, then?' he said, observing him attentively, and touching him on the shoulder. 'Does it?'

'Oh many, many!' said Philip, half awaking from his reverie. 'I'm eighty-seven!'

'Merry and happy, was it?' asked the Chemist, in a low voice. 'Merry and happy, old man?'

'May-be as high as that, no higher,' said the old man, holding out his hand a little way above the level of his knee, and looking retrospectively at his questioner, 'when I first remember 'em! Cold, sunshiny day it was, out a-walking, when some one—it was my mother as sure as you stand there, though I don't know what her blessed face was like, for she took ill and died that Christmas time— told me they were food for birds. The pretty little fellow thought— that's me, you understand—that birds' eyes were so bright, perhaps, because the berries that they lived on in the winter were so bright. I recollect that. And I'm eighty-seven!'

'Merry and happy!' mused the other, bending his dark eyes upon the stooping figure, with a smile of compassion. 'Merry and happy— and remember well!'

'Ay, ay, ay!' resumed the old man, catching the last words. 'I remember 'em well in my school time, year after year, and all the merry-making that used to come along with them. I was a strong chap then, Mr. Redlaw; and, if you'll believe me, hadn't my match at foot-ball within ten mile. Where's my son William? Hadn't my match at foot-ball, William, within ten mile!'

'That's what I always say, father!' returned the son promptly, and with great respect. 'You ARE a Swidger, if ever there was one of the family!'

'Dear!' said the old man, shaking his head as he again looked at the holly. 'His mother—my son William's my youngest son—and I, have sat among 'em all, boys and girls, little children and babies, many a year, when the berries like these were not shining half so bright all round us, as their bright faces. Many of 'em are gone; she's gone; and my son George (our eldest, who was her pride more than all the rest!) is fallen very low: but I can see them, when I look here, alive and healthy, as they used to be in those days; and I can see him, thank God, in his innocence. It's a blessed thing to me, at eighty-seven.'

The keen look that had been fixed upon him with so much earnestness, had gradually sought the ground.

'When my circumstances got to be not so good as formerly, through not being honestly dealt by, and I first come here to be custodian,' said the old man, '—which was upwards of fifty years ago—where's my son William? More than half a century ago, William!'

'That's what I say, father,' replied the son, as promptly and duti-fully as before, 'that's exactly where it is. Two times ought's an ought, and twice five ten, and there's a hundred of 'em.'

'It was quite a pleasure to know that one of our founders—or more correctly speaking,' said the old man, with a great glory in his subject and his knowledge of it, 'one of the learned gentlemen that helped endow us in Queen Elizabeth's time, for we were founded afore her day—left in his will, among the other bequests he made us, so much to buy holly, for garnishing the walls and windows, come Christmas. There was something homely and friendly in it. Being but strange here, then, and coming at Christmas-time, we took a liking for his very picter that hangs in what used to be, anciently, afore our ten poor gentlemen commuted for an annual stipend in money, our great Dinner Hall.—A sedate gentleman in a peaked beard, with a ruff round his neck, and a scroll below him, in old English letters, "Lord! keep my memory green!" You know all about him, Mr. Redlaw?'

'I know the portrait hangs there, Philip.'

'Yes, sure, it's the second on the right, above the panelling. I was going to say—he has helped to keep *my* memory green, I thank him; for, going round the building every year, as I'm a-doing now, and freshening up the bare rooms with these branches and berries, freshens up my bare old brain. One year brings back another, and that year another, and those others numbers! At last, it seems to me as if the birth-time of our Lord was the birth-time of all I have ever had affection for, or mourned for, or delighted in,—and they're a pretty many, for I'm eighty-seven!'

'Merry and happy,' murmured Redlaw to himself.

The room began to darken strangely.

'So you see, sir,' pursued old Philip, whose hale wintry cheek had warmed into a ruddier glow, and whose blue eyes had brightened while he spoke, 'I have plenty to keep, when I keep this present season. Now, where's my quiet Mouse? Chattering's the sin of my time of life, and there's half the building to do yet, if the cold don't freeze us first, or the wind don't blow us away, or the darkness don't swallow us up.'

The quiet Mouse had brought her calm face to his side, and silently taken his arm, before he finished speaking.

'Come away, my dear,' said the old man. 'Mr. Redlaw won't settle to his dinner, otherwise, till it's cold as the winter. I hope you'll excuse me rambling on, sir, and I wish you good night, and, once again, a merry—'

'Stay!' said Mr. Redlaw, resuming his place at the table, more, it would have seemed from his manner, to reassure the old keeper, than in any remembrance of his own appetite. 'Spare me another moment, Philip. William, you were going to tell me something to your excellent wife's honour. It will not be disagreeable to her to hear you praise her. What was it?'

'Why, that's where it is, you see, sir,' returned Mr. William Swidger, looking towards his wife in considerable embarrassment. 'Mrs. William's got her eye upon me.'

'But you're not afraid of Mrs. William's eye?'

'Why, no, sir,' returned Mr. Swidger, 'that's what I say myself. It wasn't made to be afraid of. It wouldn't have been made so mild, if that was the intention. But I wouldn't like to—Milly!—him, you know. Down in the Buildings.'

Mr. William, standing behind the table, and rummaging disconcertedly among the objects upon it, directed persuasive glances at Mrs. William, and secret jerks of his head and thumb at Mr. Redlaw, as alluring her towards him.

'Him, you know, my love,' said Mr. William. 'Down in the Buildings. Tell, my dear. You're the works of Shakspeare in comparison with myself. Down in the Buildings, you know, my love.—Student.'

'Student?' repeated Mr. Redlaw, raising his head.

'That's what I say, sir!' cried Mr. William, in the utmost animation of assent. 'If it wasn't the poor student down in the Buildings, why should you wish to hear it from Mrs. William's lips? Mrs. William, my dear—Buildings.'

'I didn't know,' said Milly, with a quiet frankness, free from any haste or confusion, 'that William had said anything about it, or I wouldn't have come. I asked him not to. It's a sick young gentleman, sir —and very poor, I am afraid—who is too ill to go home this holiday-time, and lives, unknown to any one, in but a common kind of lodging for a gentleman, down in Jerusalem Buildings. That's all, sir.'

'Why have I never heard of him?' said the Chemist, rising hurriedly. 'Why has he not made his situation known to me? Sick!—give me my hat and cloak. Poor!—what house?—what number?'

'Oh, you mustn't go there, sir,' said Milly, leaving her father-in-law, and calmly confronting him with her collected little face and folded hands.

'Not go there?'

'Oh dear, no!' said Milly, shaking her head as at a most manifest and self-evident impossibility. 'It couldn't be thought of!'

'What do you mean? Why not?'

'Why, you see, sir,' said Mr. William Swidger, persuasively and confidentially, 'that's what I say. Depend upon it, the young gentleman would never have made his situation known to one of his own sex. Mrs. William has got into his confidence, but that's quite different. They all confide in Mrs. William; they all trust *her*. A man, sir, couldn't have got a whisper out of him; but woman, sir, and Mrs. William combined—!'

'There is good sense and delicacy in what you say, William,' returned Mr. Redlaw, observant of the gentle and composed face at his shoulder. And laying his finger on his lip, he secretly put his purse into her hand.

'Oh dear no, sir!' cried Milly, giving it back again. 'Worse and worse! Couldn't be dreamed of!'

Such a staid matter-of-fact housewife she was, and so unruffled by the momentary haste of this rejection, that, an instant afterwards, she was tidily picking up a few leaves which had strayed from between her scissors and her apron, when she had arranged the holly.

Finding, when she rose from her stooping posture, that Mr. Redlaw was still regarding her with doubt and astonishment, she quietly repeated—looking about the while, for any other fragments that might have escaped her observation:

'Oh dear no, sir! He said that of all the world he would not be known to you, or receive help from you —though he is a student in your class. I have made no terms of secrecy with you, but I trust to your honour completely.'

'Why did he say so?'

'Indeed I can't tell, sir,' said Milly, after thinking a little, 'because I am not at all clever, you know; and I wanted to be useful to him in making things neat and comfortable about him, and employed myself that way. But I know he is poor, and lonely, and I think he is somehow neglected too.—How dark it is!'

The room had darkened more and more. There was a very heavy gloom and shadow gathering behind the Chemist's chair.

'What more about him?' he asked.

'He is engaged to be married when he can afford it,' said Milly, 'and is studying, I think, to qualify himself to earn a living. I have seen, a long time, that he has studied hard and denied himself much—How very dark it is!'

'It's turned colder, too,' said the old man, rubbing his hands. 'There's a chill and dismal feeling in the room. Where's my son William? William, my boy, turn the lamp, and rouse the fire!'

Milly's voice resumed, like quiet music very softly played:

'He muttered in his broken sleep yesterday afternoon, after talking to me' (this was to herself) 'about some one dead, and some great wrong done that could never be forgotten; but whether to him or to another person, I don't know. Not *by* him, I am sure.'

'And, in short, Mrs. William, you see—which she wouldn't say herself, Mr. Redlaw, if she was to stop here till the new year after this next one—' said Mr. William, coming up to him to speak in his ear, 'has done him worlds of good! Bless you, worlds of good! All at home just the same as ever—my father made as snug and comfortable— not a crumb of litter to be found in the house, if you were to offer fifty pound ready money for it—Mrs. William apparently never out of the way—yet Mrs. William backwards and forwards, backwards and forwards, up and down, up and down, a mother to him!'

The room turned darker and colder, and the gloom and shadow gathering behind the chair was heavier.

'Not content with this, sir, Mrs. William goes and finds, this very night, when she was coming home (why it's not above a couple of hours ago), a creature more like a young wild beast than a young child, shivering upon a door-step. What does Mrs. William do, but brings it home to dry it, and feed it, and keep it till our old Bounty of food and flannel is given away, on Christmas morning! If it ever felt a fire before, it's as much as ever it did; for it's sitting in the old Lodge chimney, staring at ours as if its ravenous eyes would never shut again. It's sitting there, at least,' said Mr. William, correcting himself, on reflection, 'unless it's bolted!'

'Heaven keep her happy!' said the Chemist aloud, 'and you too, Philip! and you, William! I must consider what to do in this. I may desire to see this student, I'll not detain you longer now. Good night!'

'I thank'ee, sir, I thank'ee!' said the old man, 'for Mouse, and for my son William, and for myself. Where's my son William? William, you take the lantern and go on first, through them long dark passages, as you did last year and the year afore. Ha, ha! *I* remember—though I'm eighty-seven! "Lord, keep my memory green!" It's a very good prayer, Mr. Redlaw, that of the learned gentleman in the peaked beard, with a ruff round his neck—hangs up, second on the right above the panelling, in what used to be, afore our ten poor gentlemen commuted, our great Dinner Hall. "Lord keep my memory green!" It's very good and pious, sir. Amen! Amen!'

As they passed out and shut the heavy door, which, however carefully withheld, fired a long train of thundering reverberations when it shut at last, the room turned darker.

As he fell a-musing in his chair alone, the healthy holly withered on the wall, and dropped—dead branches.

As the gloom and shadow thickened behind him, in that place where it had been gathering so darkly, it took, by slow degrees,—or out of it there came, by some unreal, unsubstantial process—not to be traced by any human sense,—an awful likeness of himself.

Ghastly and cold, colourless in its leaden face and hands, but with his features, and his bright eyes, and his grizzled hair, and dressed in the gloomy shadow of his dress, it came into his terrible appearance of existence, motionless, without a sound. As *he* leaned his arm upon the elbow of his chair, ruminating before the fire, *it* leaned upon the chair-back, close above him, with its appalling copy of his face looking where his face looked, and bearing the expression his face bore.

This, then, was the Something that had passed and gone already. This was the dread companion of the haunted man!

It took, for some moments, no more apparent heed of him, than he of it. The Christmas Waits* were playing somewhere in the distance, and, through his thoughtfulness, he seemed to listen to the music. It seemed to listen too.

At length he spoke; without moving or lifting up his face.

'Here again!' he said.

'Here again!' replied the Phantom.

'I see you in the fire,' said the haunted man; 'I hear you in music, in the wind, in the dead stillness of the night.'

The Phantom moved its head, assenting.

'Why do you come, to haunt me thus?'

'I come as I am called,' replied the Ghost.

'No. Unbidden,' exclaimed the Chemist.

'Unbidden be it,' said the Spectre. 'It is enough. I am here.'

Hitherto the light of the fire had shone on the two faces—if the dread lineaments behind the chair might be called a face—both addressed towards it, as at first, and neither looking at the other. But, now, the haunted man turned, suddenly, and stared upon the Ghost. The Ghost, as sudden in its motion, passed to before the chair, and stared on him.

The living man, and the animated image of himself dead, might so have looked, the one upon the other. An awful survey, in a lonely and remote part of an empty old pile of building, on a winter night, with the loud wind going by upon its journey of mystery—whence, or whither, no man knowing since the world began—and the stars, in unimaginable millions, glittering through it, from eternal space, where the world's bulk is as a grain, and its hoary age is infancy.

'Look upon me!' said the Spectre. 'I am he, neglected in my youth, and miserably poor, who strove and suffered, and still strove and suffered, until I hewed out knowledge from the mine where it was buried, and made rugged steps thereof, for my worn feet to rest and rise on.'

'I *am* that man,' returned the Chemist.

'No mother's self-denying love,' pursued the Phantom, 'no father's counsel, aided *me*. A stranger came into my father's place when I was but a child, and I was easily an alien from my mother's heart. My parents, at the best, were of that sort whose care soon ends, and whose duty is soon done; who cast their offspring loose, early, as birds do theirs; and, if they do well, claim the merit; and, if ill, the pity.'

It paused, and seemed to tempt and goad him with its look, and with the manner of its speech, and with its smile.

'I am he,' pursued the Phantom, 'who, in this struggle upward, found a friend. I made him—won him—bound him to me! We worked together, side by side. All the love and confidence that in my earlier youth had had no outlet, and found no expression, I bestowed on him.'

'Not all,' said Redlaw, hoarsely.

'No, not all,' returned the Phantom. 'I had a sister.'

The haunted man, with his head resting on his hands, replied 'I had!' The Phantom, with an evil smile, drew closer to the chair, and resting its chin upon its folded hands, its folded hands upon the back, and looking down into his face with searching eyes, that seemed instinct with fire, went on:

'Such glimpses of the light of home as I had ever known, had streamed from her. How young she was, how fair, how loving! I took her to the first poor roof that I was master of, and made it rich. She came into the darkness of my life, and made it bright.—She is before me!'

'I saw her, in the fire, but now. I hear her in music, in the wind, in the dead stillness of the night,' returned the haunted man.

'*Did* he love her?' said the Phantom, echoing his contemplative tone. 'I think he did once. I am sure he did. Better had she loved him less—less secretly, less dearly, from the shallower depths of a more divided heart!'

'Let me forget it,' said the Chemist, with an angry motion of his hand. 'Let me blot it from my memory!'

The Spectre, without stirring, and with its unwinking, cruel eyes still fixed upon his face, went on:

'A dream, like hers, stole upon my own life.'

'It did,' said Redlaw.

'A love, as like hers', pursued the Phantom, 'as my inferior nature might cherish, arose in my own heart. I was too poor to bind its object to my fortune then, by any thread of promise or entreaty. I loved her far too well, to seek to do it. But, more than ever I had striven in my life, I strove to climb! Only an inch gained, brought me something nearer to the height. I toiled up! In the late pauses of my labour at that time—my sister (sweet companion!) still sharing with me the expiring embers and the cooling hearth,—when day was breaking, what pictures of the future did I see!'

'I saw them, in the fire, but now,' he murmured. 'They come back to me in music, in the wind, in the dead stillness of the night, in the revolving years.'

'—Pictures of my own domestic life, in after-time, with her who was the inspiration of my toil. Pictures of my sister, made the wife of my dear friend, on equal terms—for he had some inheritance, we none—pictures of our sobered age and mellowed happiness, and of the golden links, extending back so far, that should bind us, and our children, in a radiant garland,' said the Phantom.

'Pictures', said the haunted man, 'that were delusions. Why is it my doom to remember them too well!'

'Delusions,' echoed the Phantom in its changeless voice, and glaring on him with its changeless eyes. 'For my friend (in whose breast my confidence was locked as in my own), passing between me and the centre of the system of my hopes and struggles, won her to himself, and shattered my frail universe. My sister, doubly dear, doubly devoted, doubly cheerful in my home, lived on to see me famous, and my old ambition so rewarded when its spring was broken, and then—'

'Then died,' he interposed. 'Died, gentle as ever, happy, and with no concern but for her brother. Peace!'

The Phantom watched him silently.

'Remembered!' said the haunted man, after a pause. 'Yes. So well remembered, that even now, when years have passed, and nothing is more idle or more visionary to me than the boyish love so long outlived, I think of it with sympathy, as if it were a younger brother's or a son's. Sometimes I even wonder when her heart first inclined to him, and how it had been affected towards me.—Not lightly, once, I think.—But that is nothing. Early unhappiness, a wound from a hand I loved and trusted, and a loss that nothing can replace, outlive such fancies.'

'Thus,' said the Phantom, 'I bear within me a Sorrow and a Wrong. Thus I prey upon myself. Thus, memory is my curse; and, if I could forget my sorrow and my wrong, I would!'

'Mocker!' said the Chemist, leaping up, and making, with a wrathful hand, at the throat of his other self. 'Why have I always that taunt in my ears?'

'Forbear!' exclaimed the Spectre in an awful voice. 'Lay a hand on me, and die!'

He stopped midway, as if its words had paralysed him, and stood looking on it. It had glided from him; it had its arm raised high in warning; and a smile passed over its unearthly features as it reared its dark figure in triumph.

'If I could forget my sorrow and wrong, I would,' the Ghost repeated. 'If I could forget my sorrow and wrong, I would!'

'Evil spirit of myself,' returned the haunted man, in a low, trembling tone, 'my life is darkened by that incessant whisper.'

'It is an echo,' said the Phantom.

'If it be an echo of my thoughts—as now, indeed, I know it is,' rejoined the haunted man, 'why should I, therefore, be tormented? It is not a selfish thought. I suffer it to range beyond myself. All men and women have their sorrows,—most of them their wrongs; ingratitude, and sordid jealousy, and interest, besetting all degrees of life. Who would not forget their sorrows and their wrongs?'

'Who would not, truly, and be the happier and better for it?' said the Phantom.

'These revolutions of years, which we commemorate,' proceeded Redlaw, 'what do *they* recall! Are there any minds in which they do not re-awaken some sorrow, or some trouble? What is the remembrance of the old man who was here to-night? A tissue of sorrow and trouble.'

'But common natures,' said the Phantom, with its evil smile upon its glassy face, 'unenlightened minds and ordinary spirits, do not feel or reason on these things like men of higher cultivation and profounder thought.'

'Tempter,' answered Redlaw, 'whose hollow look and voice I dread more than words can express, and from whom some dim foreshadowing of greater fear is stealing over me while I speak, I hear again an echo of my own mind.'

'Receive it as a proof that I am powerful,' returned the Ghost.

'Hear what I offer! Forget the sorrow, wrong, and trouble you have known!'

'Forget them!' he repeated.

'I have the power to cancel their remembrance—to leave but very faint, confused traces of them, that will die out soon,' returned the Spectre. 'Say! It is done?'

'Stay!' cried the haunted man, arresting by a terrified gesture the uplifted hand. 'I tremble with distrust and doubt of you; and the dim fear you cast upon me deepens into a nameless horror I can hardly bear.—I would not deprive myself of any kindly recollection, or any sympathy that is good for me, or others. What shall I lose, if I assent to this? What else will pass from my remembrance?'

'No knowledge; no result of study; nothing but the intertwisted chain of feelings and associations, each in its turn dependent on, and nourished by, the banished recollections. Those will go.'

'Are they so many?' said the haunted man, reflecting in alarm.

'They have been wont to show themselves in the fire, in music, in the wind, in the dead stillness of the night, in the revolving years,' returned the Phantom scornfully.

'In nothing else?'

The Phantom held its peace.

But, having stood before him, silent, for a little while, it moved towards the fire; then stopped.

'Decide!' it said, 'before the opportunity is lost!'

'A moment! I call Heaven to witness,' said the agitated man, 'that I have never been a hater of my kind,—never morose, indifferent, or hard, to anything around me. If, living here alone, I have made too much of all that was and might have been, and too little of what is, the evil, I believe, has fallen on me, and not on others. But, if there were poison in my body, should I not, possessed of antidotes and knowledge how to use them, use them? If there be poison in my mind, and through this fearful shadow I can cast it out, shall I not cast it out?'

'Say,' said the Spectre, 'is it done?'

'A moment longer!' he answered hurriedly. '*I would forget it if I could!* Have *I* thought that, alone, or has it been the thought of thousands upon thousands, generation after generation? All human memory is fraught with sorrow and trouble. My memory is as the memory of other men, but other men have not this choice. Yes,

I close the bargain. Yes! I WILL forget my sorrow, wrong, and trouble!'

'Say,' said the Spectre, 'is it done?'

'It is!'

'IT IS. And take this with you, man whom I here renounce! The gift that I have given, you shall give again, go where you will. Without recovering yourself the power that you have yielded up, you shall henceforth destroy its like in all whom you approach. Your wisdom has discovered that the memory of sorrow, wrong, and trouble is the lot of all mankind, and that mankind would be the happier, in its other memories, without it. Go! Be its benefactor! Freed from such remembrance, from this hour, carry involuntarily the blessing of such freedom with you. Its diffusion is inseparable and inalienable from you. Go! Be happy in the good you have won, and in the good you do!'

The Phantom, which had held its bloodless hand above him while it spoke, as if in some unholy invocation, or some ban; and which had gradually advanced its eyes so close to his, that he could see how they did not participate in the terrible smile upon its face, but were a fixed, unalterable, steady horror; melted before him and was gone.

As he stood rooted to the spot, possessed by fear and wonder, and imagining he heard repeated in melancholy echoes, dying away fainter and fainter, the words, 'Destroy its like in all whom you approach!' a shrill cry reached his ears. It came, not from the passage beyond the door, but from another part of the old building, and sounded like the cry of some one in the dark who had lost the way.

He looked confusedly upon his hands and limbs, as if to be assured of his identity, and then shouted in reply, loudly and wildly; for there was a strangeness and terror upon him, as if he too were lost.

The cry responding, and being nearer, he caught up the lamp, and raised a heavy curtain in the wall, by which he was accustomed to pass into and out of the theatre where he lectured,—which adjoined his room. Associated with youth and animation, and a high amphitheatre of faces which his entrance charmed to interest in a moment, it was a ghostly place when all this life was faded out of it, and stared upon him like an emblem of Death.

'Halloa!' he cried. 'Halloa! This way! Come to the light!' When, as he held the curtain with one hand, and with the other raised the lamp and tried to pierce the gloom that filled the place, something rushed past him into the room like a wild-cat, and crouched down in a corner.

'What is it?' he said, hastily.

He might have asked 'What is it?' even had he seen it well, as presently he did when he stood looking at it gathered up in its corner.

A bundle of tatters, held together by a hand, in size and form almost an infant's, but, in its greedy, desperate little clutch, a bad old man's. A face rounded and smoothed by some half-dozen years, but pinched and twisted by the experiences of a life. Bright eyes, but not youthful. Naked feet, beautiful in their childish delicacy,—ugly in the blood and dirt that cracked upon them. A baby savage, a young monster, a child who had never been a child, a creature who might live to take the outward form of man, but who, within, would live and perish a mere beast.

Used, already, to be worried and hunted like a beast, the boy crouched down as he was looked at, and looked back again, and interposed his arm to ward off the expected blow.

'I'll bite,' he said, 'if you hit me!'

The time had been, and not many minutes since, when such a sight as this would have wrung the Chemist's heart. He looked upon it now, coldly; but, with a heavy effort to remember something—he did not know what—he asked the boy what he did there, and whence he came.

'Where's the woman?' he replied. 'I want to find the woman.'

'Who?'

'The woman. Her that brought me here, and set me by the large fire. She was so long gone, that I went to look for her, and lost myself. I don't want you. I want the woman.'

He made a spring, so suddenly, to get away, that the dull sound of his naked feet upon the floor was near the curtain, when Redlaw caught him by his rags.

'Come! you let me go!' muttered the boy, struggling, and clenching his teeth. 'I've done nothing to you. Let me go, will you, to the woman!'

'That is not the way. There is a nearer one,' said Redlaw, detaining

him, in the same blank effort to remember some association that ought, of right, to bear upon this monstrous object. 'What is your name?'

'Got none.'

'Where do you live?'

'Live! What's that?'

The boy shook his hair from his eyes to look at him for a moment, and then, twisting round his legs and wrestling with him, broke again into his repetition of 'You let me go, will you? I want to find the woman.'

The Chemist led him to the door. This way,' he said, looking at him still confusedly, but with repugnance and avoidance, growing out of his coldness. 'I'll take you to her.'

The sharp eyes in the child's head, wandering round the room, lighted on the table where the remnants of the dinner were.

'Give me some of that!' he said, covetously.

'Has she not fed you?'

'I shall be hungry again to-morrow, sha'n't I? Ain't I hungry every day?'

Finding himself released, he bounded at the table like some small animal of prey, and hugging to his breast bread and meat, and his own rags, all together, said:

'There! Now take me to the woman!'

As the Chemist, with a new-born dislike to touch him, sternly motioned him to follow, and was going out of the door, he trembled and stopped.

'The gift that I have given, you shall give again, go where you will!'

The Phantom's words were blowing in the wind, and the wind blew chill upon him.

'I'll not go there, to-night,' he murmured faintly.

'I'll go nowhere to-night. Boy! straight down this long-arched passage, and past the great dark door into the yard,—you see the fire shining on the window there.'

'The woman's fire?' inquired the boy.

He nodded, and the naked feet had sprung away. He came back with his lamp, locked his door hastily, and sat down in his chair, covering his face like one who was frightened at himself.

For now he was, indeed, alone. Alone, alone.

CHAPTER II

THE GIFT DIFFUSED

A SMALL man sat in a small parlour, partitioned off from a small shop by a small screen, pasted all over with small scraps of newspapers. In company with the small man, was almost any amount of small children you may please to name—at least, it seemed so; they made, in that very limited sphere of action, such an imposing effect, in point of numbers.

Of these small fry, two had, by some strong machinery, been got into bed in a corner, where they might have reposed snugly enough in the sleep of innocence, but for a constitutional propensity to keep awake, and also to scuffle in and out of bed. The immediate occasion of these predatory dashes at the waking world, was the construction of an oyster-shell wall in a corner, by two other youths of tender age; on which fortification the two in bed made harassing descents (like those accursed Picts and Scots who beleaguer the early historical studies of most young Britons), and then withdrew to their own territory.

In addition to the stir attendant on these inroads, and the retorts of the invaded, who pursued hotly, and made lunges at the bedclothes, under which the marauders took refuge, another little boy, in another little bed, contributed his mite of confusion to the family stock, by casting his boots upon the waters,* in other words, by launching these and several small objects inoffensive in themselves, though of a hard substance considered as missiles, at the disturbers of his repose,—who were not slow to return these compliments.

Besides which, another little boy—the biggest there, but still little—was tottering to and fro, bent on one side, and considerably affected in his knees by the weight of a large baby, which he was supposed, by a fiction that obtains sometimes in sanguine families, to be hushing to sleep. But oh! the inexhaustible regions of contemplation and watchfulness into which this baby's eyes were then only beginning to compose themselves to stare, over his unconscious shoulder!

It was a very Moloch* of a baby, on whose insatiate altar the whole existence of this particular young brother was offered up a daily sacrifice. Its personality may be said to have consisted in its never being quiet, in any one place, for five consecutive minutes, and never going to sleep when required. 'Tetterby's baby' was as well known in the neighbourhood as the postman or the pot-boy. It roved from door-step to door-step, in the arms of little Johnny Tetterby, and lagged heavily at the rear of troops of juveniles who followed the Tumblers or the Monkey, and came up, all on one side, a little too late for everything that was attractive, from Monday morning until Saturday night. Wherever childhood congregated to play, there was little Moloch making Johnny fag and toil. Wherever Johnny desired to stay, little Moloch became fractious, and would not remain. Whenever Johnny wanted to go out, Moloch was asleep, and must be watched. Whenever Johnny wanted to stay at home, Moloch was awake, and must be taken out. Yet Johnny was verily persuaded that it was a faultless baby, without its peer in the realm of England; and was quite content to catch meek glimpses of things in general from behind its skirts, or over its limp flapping bonnet, and to go stagger-ing about with it like a very little porter with a very large parcel, which was not directed to anybody, and could never be delivered anywhere.

The small man who sat in the small parlour, making fruitless attempts to read his newspaper peaceably in the midst of this dis-turbance, was the father of the family, and the chief of the firm described in the inscription over the little shop front, by the name and title of A. TETTERBY AND CO., NEWSMEN. Indeed, strictly speaking, he was the only personage answering to that designation; as Co. was a mere poetical abstraction, altogether baseless and impersonal.

Tetterby's was the corner shop in Jerusalem Buildings. There was a good show of literature in the window, chiefly consisting of picture-newspapers out of date, and serial pirates,* and footpads. Walking-sticks, likewise, and marbles, were included in the stock in trade. It had once extended into the light confectionery line; but it would seem that those elegancies of life were not in demand about Jerusalem Buildings, for nothing connected with that branch of commerce remained in the window, except a sort of small glass lan-tern containing a languishing mass of bull's-eyes, which had melted in the summer and congealed in the winter until all hope of ever getting them out, or of eating them without eating the lantern too, was gone for ever. Tetterby's had tried its hand at several things. It had once made a feeble little dart at the toy business; for, in another lantern, there was a heap of minute wax dolls, all sticking together upside down, in the direst confusion, with their feet on one another's heads, and a precipitate of broken arms and legs at the bottom. It had made a move in the millinery direction, which a few dry, wiry bonnet-shapes remained in a corner of the window to attest. It had fancied that a living might lie hidden in the tobacco trade, and had stuck up a representation of a native of each of the three integral portions of the British empire, in the act of consuming that fragrant weed; with a poetic legend attached, importing that in one cause they sat and joked, one chewed tobacco, one took snuff, one smoked; but nothing seemed to have come of it—except flies. Time had been when it had put a forlorn trust in imitative jewellery, for in one pane of glass there was a card of cheap seals, and another of pencil-cases, and a mysterious black amulet of inscrutable intention, labelled ninepence. But, to that hour, Jerusalem Buildings had bought none of them. In short, Tetterby's had tried so hard to get a livelihood out of Jerusalem Buildings in one way or other, and appeared to have done so indifferently in all, that the best position in the firm was too evidently Co.'s; Co., as a bodiless creation,* being untroubled with the vulgar inconveniences of hunger and thirst, being chargeable neither to the poor's-rates* nor the assessed taxes, and having no young family to provide for.

Tetterby himself, however, in his little parlour, as already mentioned, having the presence of a young family impressed upon his mind in a manner too clamorous to be disregarded, or to comport with the quiet perusal of a newspaper, laid down his paper, wheeled, in his distraction, a few times round the parlour, like an undecided carrier-pigeon, made an ineffectual rush at one or two flying little figures in bed-gowns that skimmed past him, and then, bearing suddenly down upon the only unoffending member of the family, boxed the ears of little Moloch's nurse.

'You bad boy!' said Mr. Tetterby, 'haven't you any feeling for your poor father after the fatigues and anxieties of a hard winter's day, since five o'clock in the morning, but must you wither his rest, and corrode his latest intelligence, with *your* wicious tricks? Isn't it enough, sir, that your brother 'Dolphus is toiling and moiling in the fog and cold, and you rolling in the lap of luxury with a—with a baby, and everything you can wish for,' said Mr. Tetterby, heaping this up as a great climax of blessings, 'but must you make a wilderness of home, and maniacs of your parents? Must you, Johnny? Hey?' At each interrogation, Mr. Tetterby made a feint of boxing his ears again, but thought better of it, and held his hand.

'Oh, father!' whimpered Johnny, 'when I wasn't doing anything, I'm sure, but taking such care of Sally, and getting her to sleep. Oh, father!'

'I wish my little woman would come home!' said Mr. Tetterby, relenting and repenting, 'I only wish my little woman would come home! I ain't fit to deal with 'em. They make my head go round, and get the better of me. Oh, Johnny! Isn't it enough that your dear mother has provided you with that sweet sister?' indicating Moloch; 'isn't it enough that you were seven boys before, without a ray of gal, and that your dear mother went through what she *did* go through, on purpose that you might all of you have a little sister, but must you so behave yourself as to make my head swim?'

Softening more and more, as his own tender feelings and those of his injured son were worked on, Mr. Tetterby concluded by embracing him, and immediately breaking away to catch one of the real delinquents. A reasonably good start occurring, he succeeded, after a short but smart run, and some rather severe cross-country work under and over the bedsteads, and in and out among the intricacies of the chairs, in capturing his infant, whom he condignly punished, and bore to bed. This example had a powerful, and apparently, mesmeric influence* on him of the boots, who instantly fell into a deep sleep, though he had been, but a moment before, broad awake, and in the highest possible feather. Nor was it lost upon the two young architects, who retired to bed, in an adjoining closet, with great privacy and speed. The comrade of the Intercepted One also shrinking into his nest with similar discretion, Mr. Tetterby, when he paused for breath, found himself unexpectedly in a scene of peace.

'My little woman herself,' said Mr. Tetterby, wiping his flushed face, 'could hardly have done it better! I only wish my little woman had had it to do, I do indeed!'

Mr. Tetterby sought upon his screen for a passage appropriate to be impressed upon his children's minds on the occasion, and read the following.

' "It is an undoubted fact that all remarkable men have had remarkable mothers, and have respected them in after life as their best friends." Think of your own remarkable mother, my boys,' said Mr. Tetterby, 'and know her value while she is still among you!'

He sat down in his chair by the fire, and composed himself, cross-legged, over his newspaper.

'Let anybody, I don't care who it is, get out of bed again,' said Tetterby, as a general proclamation, delivered in a very soft-hearted manner, 'and astonishment will be the portion of that respected contemporary!'—which expression Mr. Tetterby selected from his screen. 'Johnny, my child, take care of your only sister, Sally; for she's the brightest gem that ever sparkled on your early brow.'

Johnny sat down on a little stool, and devotedly crushed himself beneath the weight of Moloch.

'Ah, what a gift that baby is to you, Johnny!' said his father, 'and how thankful you ought to be! "It is not generally known," Johnny,' he was now referring to the screen again, ' "but it is a fact ascertained, by accurate calculations, that the following immense percentage of babies never attain to two years old;* that is to say—" '

'Oh, don't, father, please!' cried Johnny. 'I can't bear it, when I think of Sally.'

Mr. Tetterby desisting, Johnny, with a profounder sense of his trust, wiped his eyes, and hushed his sister.

'Your brother 'Dolphus,' said his father, poking the fire, 'is late to-night, Johnny, and will come home like a lump of ice. What's got your precious mother?'

'Here's mother, and 'Dolphus too, father!' exclaimed Johnny, 'I think.'

'You're right!' returned his father, listening. 'Yes, that's the footstep of my little woman.'

The process of induction, by which Mr. Tetterby had come to the conclusion that his wife was a little woman, was his own secret. She would have made two editions of himself, very easily. Considered as an individual, she was rather remarkable for being robust and portly; but considered with reference to her husband, her dimensions became magnificent. Nor did they assume a less imposing proportion, when studied with reference to the size of her seven sons, who were but diminutive. In the case of Sally, however, Mrs. Tetterby had asserted herself, at last; as nobody knew better than the victim

Johnny, who weighed and measured that exacting idol every hour in the day.

Mrs. Tetterby, who had been marketing, and carried a basket, threw back her bonnet and shawl, and sitting down, fatigued, commanded Johnny to bring his sweet charge to her straightway, for a kiss. Johnny having complied, and gone back to his stool, and again crushed himself, Master Adolphus Tetterby, who had by this time unwound his Torso out of a prismatic comforter,* apparently interminable, requested the same favour. Johnny having again complied, and again gone back to his stool, and again crushed himself, Mr. Tetterby, struck by a sudden thought, preferred the same claim on his own parental part. The satisfaction of this third desire completely exhausted the sacrifice, who had hardly breath enough left to get back to his stool, crush himself again, and pant at his relations.

'Whatever you do, Johnny,' said Mrs. Tetterby, shaking her head, 'take care of her, or never look your mother in the face again.'

'Nor your brother,' said Adolphus.

'Nor your father, Johnny,' added Mr. Tetterby.

Johnny, much affected by this conditional renunciation of him, looked down at Moloch's eyes to see that they were all right, so far, and skilfully patted her back (which was uppermost), and rocked her with his foot.

'Are you wet, 'Dolphus, my boy?' said his father. 'Come and take my chair, and dry yourself.'

'No, father, thank'ee,' said Adolphus, smoothing himself down with his hands. 'I an't very wet, I don't think. Does my face shine much, father?'

'Well, it *does* look waxy, my boy,' returned Mr. Tetterby.

'It's the weather, father,' said Adolphus, polishing his cheeks on the worn sleeve of his jacket. 'What with rain, and sleet, and wind, and snow, and fog, my face gets quite brought out into a rash sometimes. And shines, it does—oh, don't it, though!'

Master Adolphus was also in the newspaper line of life, being employed by a more thriving firm than his father and Co., to vend newspapers at a railway station, where his chubby little person, like a shabbily disguised Cupid, and his shrill little voice (he was not much more than ten years old), were as well known as the hoarse panting of the locomotives, running in and out. His juvenility might have been at some loss for a harmless outlet, in this early application to traffic, but for a fortunate discovery he made of a means of entertaining himself, and of dividing the long day into stages of interest, without neglecting business. This ingenious invention, remarkable, like many great discoveries, for its simplicity, consisted in varying the first vowel in the word 'paper,' and substituting, in its stead, at different periods of the day, all the other vowels in grammatical succession. Thus, before daylight in the winter time, he went to and fro, in his little oilskin cap and cape, and his big comforter, piercing the heavy air with his cry of 'Morn–ing Pa–per!' which, about an hour before noon, changed to 'Morn–ing Pep–per!' which, at about two, changed to 'Morn–ing Pip–per!' which, in a couple of hours, changed to 'Morn–ing Pop–per!' and so declined with the sun into 'Eve–ning Pup–per!' to the great relief and comfort of this young gentleman's spirits.

Mrs. Tetterby, his lady–mother, who had been sitting with her bonnet and shawl thrown back, as aforesaid, thoughtfully turning her wedding–ring round and round upon her finger, now rose, and divesting herself of her out–of–door attire, began to lay the cloth for supper.

'Ah, dear me, dear me, dear me!' said Mrs. Tetterby. 'That's the way the world goes!'

'Which is the way the world goes, my dear?' asked Mr. Tetterby, looking round.

'Oh, nothing!' said Mrs. Tetterby.

Mr. Tetterby elevated his eyebrows, folded his newspaper afresh, and carried his eyes up it, and down it, and across it, but was wandering in his attention, and not reading it.

Mrs. Tetterby, at the same time, laid the cloth, but rather as if she were punishing the table than preparing the family supper; hitting it unnecessarily hard with the knives and forks, slapping it with the plates, dinting it with the salt–cellar, and coming heavily down upon it with the loaf.

'Ah, dear me, dear me, dear me!' said Mrs. Tetterby. 'That's the way the world goes!'

'My duck,' returned her husband, looking round again, 'you said that before. Which is the way the world goes?'

'Oh, nothing!' said Mrs. Tetterby.

'Sophia!' remonstrated her husband, 'you said *that* before, too.'

'Well, I'll say it again if you like,' returned Mrs. Tetterby. 'Oh nothing—there! And again if you like, oh nothing—there! And again if you like, oh nothing —now then!'

Mr. Tetterby brought his eye to bear upon the partner of his bosom, and said, in mild astonishment:

'My little woman, what has put you out?'

'I'm sure *I* don't know,' she retorted. 'Don't ask me. Who said I was put out at all? *I* never did.'

Mr. Tetterby gave up the perusal of his newspaper as a bad job, and, taking a slow walk across the room, with his hands behind him, and his shoulders raised—his gait according perfectly with the resignation of his manner—addressed himself to his two eldest offspring.

'Your supper will be ready in a minute, 'Dolphus,' said Mr. Tetterby. 'Your mother has been out in the wet, to the cook's shop, to buy it. It was very good of your mother so to do. *You* shall get some supper too, very soon, Johnny. Your mother's pleased with you, my man, for being so attentive to your precious sister.'

Mrs. Tetterby, without any remark, but with a decided subsidence of her animosity towards the table, finished her preparations, and took, from her ample basket, a substantial slab of hot pease pudding wrapped in paper, and a basin covered with a saucer, which, on being uncovered, sent forth an odour so agreeable, that the three pair of eyes in the two beds opened wide and fixed themselves upon the banquet. Mr. Tetterby, without regarding this tacit invitation to be seated, stood repeating slowly, 'Yes, yes, your supper will be ready in a minute, 'Dolphus—your mother went out in the wet, to the cook's shop, to buy it. It was very good of your mother so to do'—until Mrs. Tetterby, who had been exhibiting sundry tokens of contrition behind him, caught him round the neck, and wept.

'Oh, 'Dolphus!' said Mrs. Tetterby, 'how could I go and behave so?'

This reconciliation affected Adolphus the younger and Johnny to that degree, that they both, as with one accord, raised a dismal cry, which had the effect of immediately shutting up the round eyes in the beds, and utterly routing the two remaining little Tetterbys, just then stealing in from the adjoining closet to see what was going on in the eating way.

'I am sure, 'Dolphus,' sobbed Mrs. Tetterby, 'coming home, I had no more idea than a child unborn——'

Mr. Tetterby seemed to dislike this figure of speech, and observed, 'Say than the baby, my dear.'

'—Had no more idea than the baby,' said Mrs. Tetterby.— 'Johnny, don't look at me, but look at her, or she'll fall out of your lap and be killed, and then you'll die in agonies of a broken heart, and serve you right.—No more idea I hadn't than that darling, of being cross when I came home; but somehow, 'Dolphus——' Mrs. Tetterby paused, and again turned her wedding-ring round and round upon her finger.

'I see!' said Mr. Tetterby. 'I understand! My little woman was put out. Hard times, and hard weather, and hard work, make it trying now and then. I see, bless your soul! No wonder! 'Dolf, my man,' continued Mr. Tetterby, exploring the basin with a fork, 'here's your mother been and bought, at the cook's shop, besides pease pudding, a whole knuckle of a lovely roast leg of pork, with lots of crackling left upon it, and with seasoning gravy and mustard quite unlimited. Hand in your plate, my boy, and begin while it's simmering.'

Master Adolphus, needing no second summons, received his portion with eyes rendered moist by appetite, and withdrawing to his particular stool, fell upon his supper tooth and nail. Johnny was not forgotten, but received his rations on bread, lest he should, in a flush of gravy, trickle any on the baby. He was required, for similar reasons, to keep his pudding, when not on active service, in his pocket.

There might have been more pork on the knucklebone,—which knucklebone the carver at the cook's shop had assuredly not forgotten in carving for previous customers—but there was no stint of seasoning, and that is an accessory dreamily suggesting pork, and pleasantly cheating the sense of taste. The pease pudding, too, the gravy and mustard, like the Eastern rose in respect of the nightingale,* if they were not absolutely pork, had lived near it; so, upon the whole, there was the flavour of a middle-sized pig. It was irresistible to the Tetterbys in bed, who, though professing to slumber peacefully, crawled out when unseen by their parents, and silently appealed to their brothers for any gastronomic token of fraternal affection. They, not hard of heart, presenting scraps in return, it resulted that a party of light skirmishers in night-gowns were careering about the parlour all through supper, which harassed Mr. Tetterby exceedingly, and once or twice imposed upon him the necessity of a charge, before which these guerilla troops retired in all directions and in great confusion.

Mrs. Tetterby did not enjoy her supper. There seemed to be something on Mrs. Tetterby's mind. At one time she laughed without reason, and at another time she cried without reason, and at last she laughed and cried together in a manner so very unreasonable that her husband was confounded.

'My little woman,' said Mr. Tetterby, 'if the world goes that way, it appears to go the wrong way, and to choke you.'

'Give me a drop of water,' said Mrs. Tetterby, struggling with herself, 'and don't speak to me for the present, or take any notice of me. Don't do it!'

Mr. Tetterby having administered the water, turned suddenly on the unlucky Johnny (who was full of sympathy), and demanded why he was wallowing there, in gluttony and idleness, instead of coming forward with the baby, that the sight of her might revive his mother. Johnny immediately approached, borne down by its weight; but Mrs. Tetterby holding out her hand to signify that she was not in a condition to bear that trying appeal to her feelings, he was interdicted from advancing another inch, on pain of perpetual hatred from all his dearest connections; and accordingly retired to his stool again, and crushed himself as before.

After a pause, Mrs. Tetterby said she was better now, and began to laugh.

'My little woman,' said her husband, dubiously, 'are you quite sure you're better? Or are you, Sophia, about to break out in a fresh direction?'

'No, 'Dolphus, no,' replied his wife. 'I'm quite myself.' With that, settling her hair, and pressing the palms of her hands upon her eyes, she laughed again.

'What a wicked fool I was, to think so for a moment!' said Mrs. Tetterby. 'Come nearer, 'Dolphus, and let me ease my mind, and tell you what I mean. Let me tell you all about it.'

Mr. Tetterby bringing his chair closer, Mrs. Tetterby laughed again, gave him a hug, and wiped her eyes.

'You know, 'Dolphus, my dear,' said Mrs. Tetterby, 'that when I was single, I might have given myself away in several directions. At one time, four after me at once; two of them were sons of Mars.'

'We're all sons of Ma's, my dear,' said Mr. Tetterby, 'jointly with Pa's.'

'I don't mean that,' replied his wife, 'I mean soldiers—serjeants.'

'Oh!' said Mr. Tetterby.

'Well, 'Dolphus, I'm sure I never think of such things now, to regret them; and I'm sure I've got as good a husband, and would do as much to prove that I was fond of him, as——'

'As any little woman in the world,' said Mr. Tetterby. 'Very good. *Very* good.'

If Mr. Tetterby had been ten feet high, he could not have expressed a gentler consideration for Mrs. Tetterby's fairy-like stature; and if Mrs. Tetterby had been two feet high, she could not have felt it more appropriately her due.

'But you see, 'Dolphus,' said Mrs. Tetterby, 'this being Christmas-time, when all people who can, make holiday, and when all people who have got money, like to spend some, I did, somehow, get a little out of sorts when I was in the streets just now. There were so many things to be sold—such delicious things to eat, such fine things to look at, such delightful things to have—and there was so much calculating and calculating necessary, before I durst lay out a six-pence for the commonest thing; and the basket was so large, and wanted so much in it; and my stock of money was so small, and would go such a little way;—you hate me, don't you, 'Dolphus?'

'Not quite,' said Mr. Tetterby, 'as yet.'

'Well! I'll tell you the whole truth,' pursued his wife, penitently, 'and then perhaps you will. I felt all this, so much, when I was trudging about in the cold, and when I saw a lot of other calculating faces and large baskets trudging about, too, that I began to think whether I mightn't have done better, and been happier, if—I hadn't—' the wedding-ring went round again, and Mrs. Tetterby shook her downcast head as she turned it.

'I see,' said her husband quietly; 'if you hadn't married at all, or if you had married somebody else?'

'Yes,' sobbed Mrs. Tetterby. 'That's really what I thought. Do you hate me now, 'Dolphus?'

'Why no,' said Mr. Tetterby, 'I don't find that I do, as yet.'

Mrs. Tetterby gave him a thankful kiss, and went on.

'I begin to hope you won't, now, 'Dolphus, though I am afraid I haven't told you the worst. I can't think what came over me. I don't know whether I was ill, or mad, or what I was, but I couldn't call up anything that seemed to bind us to each other, or to reconcile me to my fortune. All the pleasures and enjoyments we had ever had—*they* seemed so poor and insignificant, I hated them. I could have trodden on them. And I could think of nothing else, except our being poor, and the number of mouths there were at home.'

'Well, well, my dear,' said Mr. Tetterby, shaking her hand encouragingly, 'that's truth after all. We *are* poor, and there *are* a number of mouths at home here.'

'Ah! but, Dolf, Dolf!' cried his wife, laying her hands upon his neck, 'my good, kind, patient fellow, when I had been at home a very little while—how different! Oh, Dolf, dear, how different it was! I felt as if there was a rush of recollection on me, all at once, that softened my hard heart, and filled it up till it was bursting. All our struggles for a livelihood, all our cares and wants since we have been married, all the times of sickness, all the hours of watching, we have ever had, by one another, or by the children, seemed to speak to me, and say that they had made us one, and that I never might have been, or could have been, or would have been, any other than the wife and mother I am. Then, the cheap enjoyments that I could have trodden on so cruelly, got to be so precious to me—oh so priceless, and dear!—that I couldn't bear to think how much I had wronged them; and I said, and say again a hundred times, how could I ever behave so, 'Dolphus, how could I ever have the heart to do it!'

The good woman, quite carried away by her honest tenderness and remorse, was weeping with all her heart, when she started up with a scream, and ran behind her husband. Her cry was so terrified, that the children started from their sleep and from their beds, and clung about her. Nor did her gaze belie her voice, as she pointed to a pale man in a black cloak who had come into the room.

'Look at that man! Look there! What does he want?'

'My dear,' returned her husband, 'I'll ask him if you'll let me go. What's the matter? How you shake!'

'I saw him in the street, when I was out just now. He looked at me, and stood near me. I am afraid of him.'

'Afraid of him! Why?'

'I don't know why—I—stop! husband!' for he was going towards the stranger.

She had one hand pressed upon her forehead, and one upon her breast; and there was a peculiar fluttering all over her, and a hurried unsteady motion of her eyes, as if she had lost something.

'Are you ill, my dear?'

'What is it that is going from me again?' she muttered, in a low voice. 'What *is* this that is going away?'

Then she abruptly answered: 'Ill? No, I am quite well,' and stood looking vacantly at the floor.

Her husband, who had not been altogether free from the infection of her fear at first, and whom the present strangeness of her manner did not tend to reassure, addressed himself to the pale visitor in the black cloak, who stood still, and whose eyes were bent upon the ground.

'What may be your pleasure, sir,' he asked, 'with us?'

'I fear that my coming in unperceived,' returned the visitor, 'has alarmed you; but you were talking and did not hear me.'

'My little woman says—perhaps you heard her say it,' returned Mr. Tetterby, 'that it's not the first time you have alarmed her to-night.'

'I am sorry for it. I remember to have observed her, for a few moments only, in the street. I had no intention of frightening her.'

As he raised his eyes in speaking, she raised hers. It was extraordinary to see what dread she had of him, and with what dread he observed it—and yet how narrowly and closely.

'My name,' he said, 'is Redlaw. I come from the old college hard by. A young gentleman who is a student there, lodges in your house, does he not?'

'Mr. Denham?' said Tetterby.

'Yes.'

It was a natural action, and so slight as to be hardly noticeable; but the little man, before speaking again, passed his hand across his forehead, and looked quickly round the room, as though he were sensible of some change in its atmosphere. The Chemist, instantly transferring to him the look of dread he had directed towards the wife, stepped back, and his face turned paler.

'The gentleman's room,' said Tetterby, 'is up-stairs, sir. There's a more convenient private entrance; but as you have come in here, it will save your going out into the cold, if you'll take this little staircase,' showing one communicating directly with the parlour, 'and go up to him that way, if you wish to see him.'

'Yes, I wish to see him,' said the Chemist. 'Can you spare a light?'

The watchfulness of his haggard look, and the inexplicable distrust that darkened it, seemed to trouble Mr. Tetterby. He paused; and looking fixedly at him in return, stood for a minute or so, like a man stupefied, or fascinated.

At length he said, 'I'll light you, sir, if you'll follow me.'

'No,' replied the Chemist, 'I don't wish to be attended, or announced to him. He does not expect me. I would rather go alone. Please to give me the light, if you can spare it, and I'll find the way.'

In the quickness of his expression of this desire, and in taking the candle from the newsman, he touched him on the breast. Withdrawing his hand hastily, almost as though he had wounded him by accident (for he did not know in what part of himself his new power resided, or how it was communicated, or how the manner of its reception varied in different persons), he turned and ascended the stair.

But when he reached the top, he stopped and looked down. The wife was standing in the same place, twisting her ring round and round upon her finger. The husband, with his head bent forward on his breast, was musing heavily and sullenly. The children, still clustering about the mother, gazed timidly after the visitor, and nestled together when they saw him looking down.

'Come!' said the father, roughly. 'There's enough of this. Get to bed here!'

'The place is inconvenient and small enough,' the mother added, 'without you. Get to bed!'

The whole brood, scared and sad, crept away; little Johnny and the baby lagging last. The mother, glancing contemptuously round the sordid room, and tossing from her the fragments of their meal, stopped on the threshold of her task of clearing the table, and sat down, pondering idly and dejectedly. The father betook himself to the chimney-corner, and impatiently raking the small fire together, bent over it as if he would monopolise it all. They did not interchange a word.

The Chemist, paler than before, stole upward like a thief; looking back upon the change below, and dreading equally to go on or return.

'What have I done!' he said, confusedly. 'What am I going to do!'

'To be the benefactor of mankind,' he thought he heard a voice reply.

He looked round, but there was nothing there; and a passage now shutting out the little parlour from his view, he went on, directing his eyes before him at the way he went.

'It is only since last night,' he muttered gloomily, 'that I have remained shut up, and yet all things are strange to me. I am strange to myself. I am here, as in a dream. What interest have I in this place, or in any place that I can bring to my remembrance? My mind is going blind!'

There was a door before him, and he knocked at it. Being invited, by a voice within, to enter, he complied.

'Is that my kind nurse?' said the voice. 'But I need not ask her. There is no one else to come here.'

It spoke cheerfully, though in a languid tone, and attracted his attention to a young man lying on a couch, drawn before the chimney-piece, with the back towards the door. A meagre scanty stove, pinched and hollowed like a sick man's cheeks, and bricked into the centre of a hearth that it could scarcely warm, contained the fire, to which his face was turned. Being so near the windy house-top, it wasted quickly, and with a busy sound, and the burning ashes dropped down fast.

'They chink when they shoot out here,' said the student, smiling, 'so, according to the gossips, they are not coffins, but purses.* I shall be well and rich yet, some day, if it please God, and shall live perhaps to love a daughter Milly, in remembrance of the kindest nature and the gentlest heart in the world.'

He put up his hand as if expecting her to take it, but, being weakened, he lay still, with his face resting on his other hand, and did not turn round.

The Chemist glanced about the room;—at the student's books and papers, piled upon a table in a corner, where they, and his extinguished reading-lamp, now prohibited and put away, told of the attentive hours that had gone before this illness, and perhaps caused it;—at such signs of his old health and freedom, as the out-of-door attire that hung idle on the wall;—at those remembrances of other and less solitary scenes, the little miniatures upon the chimney-piece, and the drawing of home;—at that token of his emulation, perhaps, in some sort, of his personal attachment too, the framed engraving of himself, the looker-on. The time had been, only yesterday, when not one of these objects, in its remotest association of interest with the living figure before him, would have been lost on Redlaw. Now, they were but objects; or, if any gleam of such connexion shot upon him, it perplexed, and not enlightened him, as he stood looking round with a dull wonder.

The student, recalling the thin hand which had remained so long untouched, raised himself on the couch, and turned his head.

'Mr. Redlaw!' he exclaimed, and started up.

Redlaw put out his arm.

'Don't come nearer to me. I will sit here. Remain you, where you are!'

He sat down on a chair near the door, and having glanced at the young man standing leaning with his hand upon the couch, spoke with his eyes averted towards the ground.

'I heard, by an accident, by what accident is no matter, that one of my class was ill and solitary. I received no other description of him, than that he lived in this street. Beginning my inquiries at the first house in it, I have found him.'

'I have been ill, sir,' returned the student, not merely with a modest hesitation, but with a kind of awe of him, 'but am greatly better. An attack of fever—of the brain, I believe—has weakened me, but I am much better. I cannot say I have been solitary, in my illness, or I should forget the ministering hand that has been near me.'

'You are speaking of the keeper's wife,' said Redlaw.

'Yes.' The student bent his head, as if he rendered her some silent homage.

The Chemist, in whom there was a cold, monotonous apathy, which rendered him more like a marble image on the tomb of the man who had started from his dinner yesterday at the first mention of this student's case, than the breathing man himself, glanced again at the student leaning with his hand upon the couch, and looked upon the ground, and in the air, as if for light for his blinded mind.

'I remembered your name,' he said, 'when it was mentioned to me down-stairs, just now; and I recollect your face. We have held but very little personal communication together?'

'Very little.'

'You have retired and withdrawn from me, more than any of the rest, I think?'

The student signified assent.

'And why?' said the Chemist; not with the least expression of interest, but with a moody, wayward kind of curiosity. 'Why? How comes it that you have sought to keep especially from me, the knowledge of your remaining here, at this season, when all the rest have dispersed, and of your being ill? I want to know why this is?'

The young man, who had heard him with increasing agitation, raised his downcast eyes to his face, and clasping his hands together, cried with sudden earnestness and with trembling lips:

'Mr. Redlaw! You have discovered me. You know my secret!'

'Secret?' said the Chemist, harshly. '*I* know?'

'Yes! Your manner, so different from the interest and sympathy which endear you to so many hearts, your altered voice, the constraint there is in everything you say, and in your looks,' replied the student, 'warn me that you know me. That you would conceal it, even now, is but a proof to me (God knows I need none!) of your natural kindness, and of the bar there is between us.'

A vacant and contemptuous laugh was all his answer.

'But, Mr. Redlaw,' said the student, 'as a just man, and a good man, think how innocent I am, except in name and descent, of participation in any wrong inflicted on you, or in any sorrow you have borne.'

'Sorrow!' said Redlaw, laughing. 'Wrong! What are those to me?'

'For Heaven's sake,' entreated the shrinking student, 'do not let the mere interchange of a few words with me change you like this, sir! Let me pass again from your knowledge and notice. Let me occupy my old reserved and distant place among those whom you instruct. Know me only by the name I have assumed, and not by that of Longford—'

'Longford!' exclaimed the other.

He clasped his head with both his hands, and for a moment turned upon the young man his own intelligent and thoughtful face. But the light passed from it, like the sunbeam of an instant, and it clouded as before.

'The name my mother bears, sir,' faltered the young man, 'the name she took, when she might, perhaps, have taken one more honoured. Mr. Redlaw,' hesitating, 'I believe I know that history. Where my information halts, my guesses at what is wanting may supply something not remote from the truth. I am the child of a marriage that has not proved itself a well-assorted or a happy one. From infancy, I have heard you spoken of with honour and respect—with something that was almost reverence. I have heard of such devotion, of such fortitude and tenderness, of such rising up against the obstacles which press men down, that my fancy, since I learnt my little lesson from my mother, has shed a lustre on your name. At last, a poor student myself, from whom could I learn but you?'

Redlaw, unmoved, unchanged, and looking at him with a staring frown, answered by no word or sign.

'I cannot say,' pursued the other, 'I should try in vain to say, how much it has impressed me, and affected me, to find the gracious traces of the past, in that certain power of winning gratitude and confidence which is associated among us students (among the humblest of us, most) with Mr. Redlaw's generous name. Our ages and positions are so different, sir, and I am so accustomed to regard you from a distance, that I wonder at my own presumption when I touch, however lightly, on that theme. But to one who—I may say, who felt no common interest in my mother once—it may be something to hear, now that is all past, with what indescribable feelings of affection I have, in my obscurity, regarded him; with what pain and reluctance I have kept aloof from his encouragement, when a word of it would have made me rich; yet how I have felt it fit that I should hold my course, content to know him, and to be unknown. Mr. Redlaw,' said the student, faintly, 'what I would have said, I have said ill, for my strength is strange to me as yet; but for anything unworthy in this fraud of mine, forgive me, and for all the rest forget me!'

The staring frown remained on Redlaw's face, and yielded to no other expression until the student, with these words, advanced towards him, as if to touch his hand, when he drew back and cried to him:

'Don't come nearer to me!'

The young man stopped, shocked by the eagerness of his recoil, and by the sternness of his repulsion; and he passed his hand, thoughtfully, across his forehead.

'The past is past,' said the Chemist. 'It dies like the brutes. Who talks to me of its traces in my life? He raves or lies! What have I to do with your distempered dreams? If you want money, here it is. I came to offer it; and that is all I came for. There can be nothing else that brings me here,' he muttered, holding his head again, with both his hands. 'There *can* be nothing else, and yet——'

He had tossed his purse upon the table. As he fell into this dim cogitation with himself, the student took it up, and held it out to him.

'Take it back, sir,' he said proudly, though not angrily. 'I wish you could take from me, with it, the remembrance of your words and offer.'

'You do?' he retorted, with a wild light in his eyes. 'You do?'

'I do!'

The Chemist went close to him, for the first time, and took the purse, and turned him by the arm, and looked him in the face.

'There is sorrow and trouble in sickness, is there not?' he demanded, with a laugh.

The wondering student answered, 'Yes.'

'In its unrest, in its anxiety, in its suspense, in all its train of physical and mental miseries?' said the Chemist, with a wild unearthly exultation. 'All best forgotten, are they not?'

The student did not answer, but again passed his hand, confusedly, across his forehead. Redlaw still held him by the sleeve, when Milly's voice was heard outside.

'I can see very well now,' she said, 'thank you, Dolf. Don't cry, dear. Father and mother will be comfortable again, to-morrow, and home will be comfortable too. A gentleman with him, is there!'

Redlaw released his hold, as he listened.

'I have feared, from the first moment,' he murmured to himself, 'to meet her. There is a steady quality of goodness in her, that I dread to influence. I may be the murderer of what is tenderest and best within her bosom.'

She was knocking at the door.

'Shall I dismiss it as an idle foreboding, or still avoid her?' he muttered, looking uneasily around.

She was knocking at the door again.

'Of all the visitors who could come here,' he said, in a hoarse alarmed voice, turning to his companion, 'this is the one I should desire most to avoid. Hide me!'

The student opened a frail door in the wall, communicating where the garret-roof began to slope towards the floor, with a small inner room. Redlaw passed in hastily, and shut it after him.

The student then resumed his place upon the couch, and called to her to enter.

'Dear Mr. Edmund,' said Milly, looking round, 'they told me there was a gentleman here.'

'There is no one here but I.'

'There has been some one?'

'Yes, yes, there has been some one.'

She put her little basket on the table, and went up to the back of the couch, as if to take the extended hand—but it was not there. A little surprised, in her quiet way, she leaned over to look at his face, and gently touched him on the brow.

'Are you quite as well to-night? Your head is not so cool as in the afternoon.'

'Tut!' said the student, petulantly, 'very little ails me.'

A little more surprise, but no reproach, was expressed in her face, as she withdrew to the other side of the table, and took a small packet of needlework from her basket. But she laid it down again, on second thoughts, and going noiselessly about the room, set everything exactly in its place, and in the neatest order; even to the cushions on the couch, which she touched with so light a hand, that he hardly seemed to know it, as he lay looking at the fire. When all this was done, and she had swept the hearth, she sat down, in her modest little bonnet, to her work, and was quietly busy on it directly.

'It's the new muslin curtain for the window, Mr. Edmund,' said Milly, stitching away as she talked. 'It will look very clean and nice, though it costs very little, and will save your eyes, too, from the light. My William says the room should not be too light just now, when you are recovering so well, or the glare might make you giddy.'

He said nothing; but there was something so fretful and impatient in his change of position, that her quick fingers stopped, and she looked at him anxiously.

'The pillows are not comfortable,' she said, laying down her work and rising. 'I will soon put them right.'

'They are very well,' he answered. 'Leave them alone, pray. You make so much of everything.'

He raised his head to say this, and looked at her so thanklessly, that, after he had thrown himself down again, she stood timidly pausing. However, she resumed her seat, and her needle, without having directed even a murmuring look towards him, and was soon as busy as before.

'I have been thinking, Mr. Edmund, that *you* have been often thinking of late, when I have been sitting by, how true the saying is, that adversity is a good teacher. Health will be more precious to you, after this illness, than it has ever been. And years hence, when this time of year comes round, and you remember the days when you lay here sick, alone, that the knowledge of your illness might not afflict those who are dearest to you, your home will be doubly dear and doubly blest. Now, isn't that a good, true thing?'

She was too intent upon her work, and too earnest in what she said, and too composed and quiet altogether, to be on the watch for any look he might direct towards her in reply; so the shaft of his ungrateful glance fell harmless, and did not wound her.

'Ah!' said Milly, with her pretty head inclining thoughtfully on one side, as she looked down, following her busy fingers with her eyes. 'Even on me—and I am very different from you, Mr. Edmund, for I have no learning, and don't know how to think properly—this view of such things has made a great impression, since you have been lying ill. When I have seen you so touched by the kindness and attention of the poor people down-stairs, I have felt that you thought even that experience some repayment for the loss of health, and I have read in your face, as plain as if it was a book, that but for some trouble and sorrow we should never know half the good there is about us.'

His getting up from the couch, interrupted her, or she was going on to say more.

'We needn't magnify the merit, Mrs. William,' he rejoined slightingly. 'The people down-stairs will be paid in good time, I dare say, for any little extra service they may have rendered me; and perhaps they anticipate no less. I am much obliged to you, too.'

Her fingers stopped, and she looked at him.

'I can't be made to feel the more obliged by your exaggerating the case,' he said. 'I am sensible that you have been interested in me, and I say I am much obliged to you. What more would you have?'

Her work fell on her lap, as she still looked at him walking to and fro with an intolerant air, and stopping now and then.

'I say again, I am much obliged to you. Why weaken my sense of what is your due in obligation, by preferring enormous claims upon me? Trouble, sorrow, affliction, adversity! One might suppose I had been dying a score of deaths here!'

'Do you believe, Mr. Edmund,' she asked, rising and going nearer to him, 'that I spoke of the poor people of the house, with any reference to myself? To me?' laying her hand upon her bosom with a simple and innocent smile of astonishment.

'Oh! I think nothing about it, my good creature,' he returned. 'I have had an indisposition, which your solicitude—observe! I say solicitude—makes a great deal more of, than it merits; and it's over, and we can't perpetuate it.'

He coldly took a book, and sat down at the table.

She watched him for a little while, until her smile was quite gone, and then returning to where her basket was, said gently:

'Mr. Edmund, would you rather be alone?'

'There is no reason why I should detain you here,' he replied.

'Except—' said Milly, hesitating, and showing her work.

'Oh! the curtain,' he answered, with a supercilious laugh. 'That's not worth staying for.'

She made up the little packet again, and put it in her basket. Then, standing before him with such an air of patient entreaty that he could not choose but look at her, she said:

'If you should want me, I will come back willingly. When you did want me, I was quite happy to come; there was no merit in it. I think you must be afraid, that, now you are getting well, I may be troublesome to you; but I should not have been, indeed. I should have come no longer than your weakness and confinement lasted. You owe me nothing; but it is right that you should deal as justly by me as if I was a lady—even the very lady that you love; and if you suspect me of meanly making much of the little I have tried to do to comfort your sick room, you do yourself more wrong than ever you can do me. That is why I am sorry. That is why I am very sorry.'

If she had been as passionate as she was quiet, as indignant as she was calm, as angry in her look as she was gentle, as loud of tone as she was low and clear, she might have left no sense of her departure in the room, compared with that which fell upon the lonely student when she went away.

He was gazing drearily upon the place where she had been, when Redlaw came out of his concealment, and came to the door.

'When sickness lays its hand on you again,' he said, looking fiercely back at him, '—may it be soon!—Die here! Rot here!'

'What have you done?' returned the other, catching at his cloak.

'What change have you wrought in me? What curse have you brought upon me? Give me back myself!'

'Give me back *my*self!' exclaimed Redlaw like a madman. 'I am infected! I am infectious! I am charged with poison for my own mind, and the minds of all mankind. Where I felt interest, compassion, sympathy, I am turning into stone. Selfishness and ingratitude spring up in my blighted footsteps. I am only so much less base than the wretches whom I make so, that in the moment of their transformation I can hate them.'

As he spoke—the young man still holding to his cloak—he cast him off, and struck him: then, wildly hurried out into the night air where the wind was blowing, the snow falling, the cloud-drift sweeping on, the moon dimly shining, and where, blowing in the wind, falling with the snow, drifting with the clouds, shining in the moonlight, and heavily looming in the darkness, were the Phantom's words, 'The gift that I have given, you shall give again, go where you will!'

Whither he went, he neither knew nor cared, so that he avoided company. The change he felt within him made the busy streets a desert, and himself a desert, and the multitude around him, in their manifold endurances and ways of life, a mighty waste of sand, which the winds tossed into unintelligible heaps and made a ruinous confusion of. Those traces in his breast which the Phantom had told him would 'die out soon,' were not, as yet, so far upon their way to death, but that he understood enough of what he was, and what he made of others, to desire to be alone.

This put it in his mind—he suddenly bethought himself, as he was going along, of the boy who had rushed into his room. And then he recollected, that of those with whom he had communicated since the Phantom's disappearance, that boy alone had shown no sign of being changed.

Monstrous and odious as the wild thing was to him, he determined to seek it out, and prove if this were really so; and also to seek it with another intention, which came into his thoughts at the same time.

So, resolving with some difficulty where he was, he directed his steps back to the old college, and to that part of it where the general porch was, and where, alone, the pavement was worn by the tread of the students' feet.

The keeper's house stood just within the iron gates, forming a part of the chief quadrangle. There was a little cloister outside, and from that sheltered place he knew he could look in at the window of their ordinary room, and see who was within. The iron gates were shut, but his hand was familiar with the fastening, and drawing it back by thrusting in his wrist between the bars, he passed through softly, shut it again, and crept up to the window, crumbling the thin crust of snow with his feet.

The fire, to which he had directed the boy last night, shining brightly through the glass, made an illuminated place upon the ground. Instinctively avoiding this, and going round it, he looked in at the window. At first, he thought that there was no one there, and that the blaze was reddening only the old beams in the ceiling and the dark walls; but peering in more narrowly, he saw the object of his search coiled asleep before it on the floor. He passed quickly to the door, opened it, and went in.

The creature lay in such a fiery heat, that, as the Chemist stooped to rouse him, it scorched his head. So soon as he was touched, the boy, not half awake, clutched his rags together with the instinct of flight upon him, half rolled and half ran into a distant corner of the room, where, heaped upon the ground, he struck his foot out to defend himself.

'Get up!' said the Chemist. 'You have not forgotten me?'

'You let me alone!' returned the boy. 'This is the woman's house—not yours.'

The Chemist's steady eye controlled him somewhat, or inspired him with enough submission to be raised upon his feet, and looked at.

'Who washed them, and put those bandages where they were bruised and cracked?' asked the Chemist, pointing to their altered state.

'The woman did.'

'And is it she who has made you cleaner in the face, too?'

'Yes, the woman.'

Redlaw asked these questions to attract his eyes towards himself, and with the same intent now held him by the chin, and threw his wild hair back, though he loathed to touch him. The boy watched his eyes keenly, as if he thought it needful to his own defence, not knowing what he might do next; and Redlaw could see well that no change came over him.

'Where are they?' he inquired.

'The woman's out.'

'I know she is. Where is the old man with the white hair, and his son?'

'The woman's husband, d'ye mean?' inquired the boy.

'Aye. Where are those two?'

'Out. Something's the matter, somewhere. They were fetched out in a hurry, and told me to stop here.'

'Come with me,' said the Chemist, 'and I'll give you money.'

'Come where? and how much will you give?'

'I'll give you more shillings than you ever saw, and bring you back soon. Do you know your way to where you came from?'

'You let me go,' returned the boy, suddenly twisting out of his grasp. 'I'm not a–going to take you there. Let me be, or I'll heave some fire at you!'

He was down before it, and ready, with his savage little hand, to pluck the burning coals out.

What the Chemist had felt, in observing the effect of his charmed influence stealing over those with whom he came in contact, was not nearly equal to the cold vague terror with which he saw this baby-monster put it at defiance. It chilled his blood to look on the immovable impenetrable thing, in the likeness of a child, with its sharp malignant face turned up to his, and its almost infant hand, ready at the bars.

'Listen, boy!' he said. 'You shall take me where you please, so that you take me where the people are very miserable or very wicked. I want to do them good, and not to harm them. You shall have money, as I have told you, and I will bring you back. Get up! Come quickly!' He made a hasty step towards the door, afraid of her returning.

'Will you let me walk by myself, and never hold me, nor yet touch me?' said the boy, slowly withdrawing the hand with which he threatened, and beginning to get up.

'I will!'

'And let me go before, behind, or anyways I like?'

'I will!'

'Give me some money first then, and I'll go.'

The Chemist laid a few shillings, one by one, in his extended hand. To count them was beyond the boy's knowledge, but he said 'one,' every time, and avariciously looked at each as it was given, and at the donor. He had nowhere to put them, out of his hand, but in his mouth; and he put them there.

Redlaw then wrote with his pencil on a leaf of his pocket-book, that the boy was with him; and laying it on the table, signed to him to follow. Keeping his rags together, as usual, the boy complied, and went out with his bare head and his naked feet into the winter night.

Preferring not to depart by the iron gate by which he had entered, where they were in danger of meeting her whom he so anxiously avoided, the Chemist led the way, through some of those passages among which the boy had lost himself, and by that portion of the building where he lived, to a small door of which he had the key. When they got into the street, he stopped to ask his guide—who instantly retreated from him—if he knew where they were.

The savage thing looked here and there, and at length, nodding his head, pointed in the direction he designed to take. Redlaw going on at once, he followed, somewhat less suspiciously; shifting his money from his mouth into his hand, and back again into his mouth, and stealthily rubbing it bright upon his shreds of clothes, as he went along.

Three times, in their progress, they were side by side. Three times they stopped, being side by side. Three times the Chemist glanced down at his face, and shuddered as it forced upon him one reflection.

The first occasion was when they were crossing an old church-yard, and Redlaw stopped among the graves, utterly at a loss how to connect them with any tender, softening, or consolatory thought.

The second was, when the breaking forth of the moon induced him to look up at the Heavens, where he saw her in her glory, sur-rounded by a host of stars he still knew by the names and histories which human science has appended to them; but where he saw noth-ing else he had been wont to see, felt nothing he had been wont to feel, in looking up there, on a bright night.

The third was when he stopped to listen to a plaintive strain of music, but could only hear a tune, made manifest to him by the dry mechanism of the instruments and his own ears, with no address to any mystery within him, without a whisper in it of the past, or of the future, powerless upon him as the sound of last year's running water, or the rushing of last year's wind.

At each of these three times, he saw with horror that, in spite of the vast intellectual distance between them, and their being unlike each other in all physical respects, the expression on the boy's face was the expression on his own.

They journeyed on for some time—now through such crowded places, that he often looked over his shoulder thinking he had lost his guide, but generally finding him within his shadow on his other side; now by ways so quiet, that he could have counted his short, quick, naked footsteps coming on behind—until they arrived at a ruinous collection of houses, and the boy touched him and stopped.

'In there!' he said, pointing out one house where there were scattered lights in the windows, and a dim lantern in the doorway, with 'Lodgings for Travellers' painted on it.

Redlaw looked about him; from the houses, to the waste piece of ground on which the houses stood, or rather did not altogether tumble down, unfenced, undrained, unlighted, and bordered by a sluggish ditch; from that, to the sloping line of arches, part of some neighbouring viaduct or bridge with which it was surrounded, and which lessened gradually, towards them, until the last but one was a mere kennel for a dog, the last a plundered little heap of bricks; from that, to the child, close to him, cowering and trembling with the cold, and limping on one little foot, while he coiled the other round his leg to warm it, yet staring at all these things with that frightful likeness of expression so apparent in his face, that Redlaw started from him.

'In there!' said the boy, pointing out the house again. 'I'll wait.'

'Will they let me in?' asked Redlaw.

'Say you're a doctor,' he answered with a nod. 'There's plenty ill here.'

Looking back on his way to the house-door, Redlaw saw him trail himself upon the dust and crawl within the shelter of the smallest arch, as if he were a rat. He had no pity for the thing, but he was afraid of it; and when it looked out of its den at him, he hurried to the house as a retreat.

'Sorrow, wrong, and trouble,' said the Chemist, with a painful effort at some more distinct remembrance, 'at least haunt this place, darkly. He can do no harm, who brings forgetfulness of such things here!'

With these words, he pushed the yielding door, and went in.

There was a woman sitting on the stairs, either asleep or forlorn, whose head was bent down on her hands and knees. As it was not easy to pass without treading on her, and as she was perfectly regardless of his near approach, he stopped, and touched her on the shoulder. Looking up, she showed him quite a young face, but one whose bloom and promise were all swept away, as if the haggard winter should unnaturally kill the spring.

With little or no show of concern on his account, she moved nearer to the wall to leave him a wider passage.

'What are you?' said Redlaw, pausing, with his hand upon the broken stair-rail.

'What do you think I am?' she answered, showing him her face again.

He looked upon the ruined Temple of God, so lately made, so soon disfigured; and something, which was not compassion—for the springs in which a true compassion for such miseries has its rise, were dried up in his breast—but which was nearer to it, for the moment, than any feeling that had lately struggled into the darkening, but not yet wholly darkened, night of his mind—mingled a touch of softness with his next words.

'I am come here to give relief, if I can,' he said. 'Are you thinking of any wrong?'

She frowned at him, and then laughed; and then her laugh prolonged itself into a shivering sigh, as she dropped her head again, and hid her fingers in her hair.

'Are you thinking of a wrong?' he asked, once more.

'I am thinking of my life,' she said, with a momentary look at him.

He had a perception that she was one of many, and that he saw the type of thousands, when he saw her, drooping at his feet.

'What are your parents?' he demanded.

'I had a good home once. My father was a gardener, far away, in the country.'

'Is he dead?'

'He's dead to me. All such things are dead to me. You a gentleman, and not know that!' She raised her eyes again, and laughed at him.

'Girl!' said Redlaw, sternly, 'before this death, of all such things, was brought about, was there no wrong done to you? In spite of all that you can do, does no remembrance of wrong cleave to you? Are there not times upon times when it is misery to you?'

So little of what was womanly was left in her appearance, that now, when she burst into tears, he stood amazed. But he was more amazed, and much disquieted, to note that in her awakened recollection of this wrong, the first trace of her old humanity and frozen tenderness appeared to show itself.

He drew a little off, and in doing so, observed that her arms were black, her face cut, and her bosom bruised.

'What brutal hand has hurt you so?' he asked.

'My own. I did it myself!' she answered quickly.

'It is impossible.'

'I'll swear I did! He didn't touch me. I did it to myself in a passion, and threw myself down here. He wasn't near me. He never laid a hand upon me!'

In the white determination of her face, confronting him with this untruth, he saw enough of the last perversion and distortion of good surviving in that miserable breast, to be stricken with remorse that he had ever come near her.

'Sorrow, wrong, and trouble!' he muttered, turning his fearful gaze away. 'All that connects her with the state from which she has fallen, has those roots! In the name of God, let me go by!'

Afraid to look at her again, afraid to touch her, afraid to think of having sundered the last thread by which she held upon the mercy of Heaven, he gathered his cloak about him, and glided swiftly up the stairs.

Opposite to him, on the landing, was a door, which stood partly open, and which, as he ascended, a man with a candle in his hand, came forward from within to shut. But this man, on seeing him, drew back, with much emotion in his manner, and, as if by a sudden impulse, mentioned his name aloud.

In the surprise of such a recognition there, he stopped, endeavouring to recollect the wan and startled face. He had no time to consider it, for, to his yet greater amazement, old Philip came out of the room, and took him by the hand.

'Mr. Redlaw,' said the old man, 'this is like you, this is like you, sir! you have heard of it, and have come after us to render any help you can. Ah, too late, too late!'

Redlaw, with a bewildered look, submitted to be led into the room. A man lay there, on a truckle-bed, and William Swidger stood at the bedside.

'Too late!' murmured the old man, looking wistfully into the Chemist's face; and the tears stole down his cheeks.

'That's what I say, father,' interposed his son in a low voice. 'That's where it is, exactly. To keep as quiet as ever we can while he's a-dozing, is the only thing to do. You're right, father!'

Redlaw paused at the bedside, and looked down on the figure that was stretched upon the mattress. It was that of a man, who should have been in the vigour of his life, but on whom it was not likely the sun would ever shine again. The vices of his forty or fifty years' career had so branded him, that, in comparison with their effects upon his face, the heavy hand of time upon the old man's face who watched him had been merciful and beautifying.

'Who is this?' asked the Chemist, looking round.

'My son George, Mr. Redlaw,' said the old man, wringing his hands. 'My eldest son, George, who was more his mother's pride than all the rest!'

Redlaw's eyes wandered from the old man's grey head, as he laid it down upon the bed, to the person who had recognised him, and who had kept aloof, in the remotest corner of the room. He seemed to be about his own age; and although he knew no such hopeless decay and broken man as he appeared to be, there was something in the turn of his figure, as he stood with his back towards him, and now went out at the door, that made him pass his hand uneasily across his brow.

'William,' he said in a gloomy whisper, 'who is that man?'

'Why you see, sir,' returned Mr. William, 'that's what I say, myself. Why should a man ever go and gamble, and the like of that, and let himself down inch by inch till he can't let himself down any lower!'

'Has *he* done so?' asked Redlaw, glancing after him with the same uneasy action as before.

'Just exactly that, sir,' returned William Swidger, 'as I'm told. He knows a little about medicine, sir, it seems; and having been wayfaring towards London with my unhappy brother that you see here,' Mr. William passed his coat-sleeve across his eyes, 'and being lodging up-stairs for the night—what I say, you see, is that strange companions come together here sometimes—he looked in to attend upon him, and came for us at his request. What a mournful spectacle, sir! But that's where it is. It's enough to kill my father!'

Redlaw looked up, at these words, and, recalling where he was and with whom, and the spell he carried with him—which his surprise had obscured—retired a little, hurriedly, debating with himself whether to shun the house that moment, or remain.

Yielding to a certain sullen doggedness, which it seemed to be a part of his condition to struggle with, he argued for remaining.

'Was it only yesterday,' he said, 'when I observed the memory of this old man to be a tissue of sorrow and trouble, and shall I be afraid, to-night, to shake it? Are such remembrances as I can drive away, so precious to this dying man, that I need fear for *him*? No! I'll stay here.'

But he stayed, in fear and trembling none the less for these words; and, shrouded in his black cloak with his face turned from them, stood away from the bedside, listening to what they said, as if he felt himself a demon in the place.

'Father!' murmured the sick man, rallying a little from his stupor.

'My boy! My son George!' said old Philip.

'You spoke, just now, of my being mother's favourite, long ago. It's a dreadful thing to think now, of long ago!'

'No, no, no:' returned the old man. 'Think of it. Don't say it's dreadful. It's not dreadful to me, my son.'

'It cuts you to the heart, father.' For the old man's tears were falling on him.

'Yes, yes,' said Philip, 'so it does; but it does me good. It's a heavy sorrow to think of that time, but it does me good, George. Oh, think of it too, think of it too, and your heart will be softened more and more! Where's my son William? William, my boy, your mother loved him dearly to the last, and with her latest breath said, "Tell him I forgave him, blessed him, and prayed for him." Those were her words to me. I have never forgotten them, and I'm eighty-seven!'

'Father!' said the man upon the bed, 'I am dying, I know. I am so far gone, that I can hardly speak, even of what my mind most runs on. Is there any hope for me beyond this bed?'

'There is hope,' returned the old man, 'for all who are softened and penitent. There is hope for all such. Oh!' he exclaimed, clasping his hands and looking up, 'I was thankful, only yesterday, that I could remember this unhappy son when he was an innocent child. But what a comfort it is, now, to think that even God himself has that remembrance of him!'

Redlaw spread his hands upon his face, and shrunk like a murderer.

'Ah!' feebly moaned the man upon the bed. 'The waste since then, the waste of life since then!'

'But he was a child once,' said the old man. 'He played with children. Before he lay down on his bed at night, and fell into his guiltless rest, he said his prayers at his poor mother's knee. I have seen him do it, many a time; and seen her lay his head upon her breast, and kiss him. Sorrowful as it was to her, and to me, to think of this, when he went so wrong, and when our hopes and plans for him were all broken, this gave him still a hold upon us, that nothing else could have given. Oh, Father, so much better than the fathers upon earth! Oh, Father, so much more afflicted by the errors of thy children! take this wanderer back! Not as he is, but as he was then, let him cry to thee, as he has so often seemed to cry to us!'

As the old man lifted up his trembling hands, the son, for whom he made the supplication, laid his sinking head against him for support and comfort, as if he were indeed the child of whom he spoke.

When did man ever tremble, as Redlaw trembled, in the silence that ensued! He knew it must come upon them, knew that it was coming fast.

'My time is very short, my breath is shorter,' said the sick man, supporting himself on one arm, and with the other groping in the air, 'and I remember there is something on my mind concerning the man who was here just now. Father and William—wait!—is there really anything in black, out there?'

'Yes, yes, it is real,' said his aged father.

'Is it a man?'

'What I say myself, George,' interposed his brother, bending kindly over him. 'It's Mr. Redlaw.'

'I thought I had dreamed of him. Ask him to come here.'

The Chemist, whiter than the dying man, appeared before him. Obedient to the motion of his hand, he sat upon the bed.

'It has been so ripped up, to-night, sir,' said the sick man, laying his hand upon his heart, with a look in which the mute, imploring agony of his condition was concentrated, 'by the sight of my poor old father, and the thought of all the trouble I have been the cause of, and all the wrong and sorrow lying at my door, that—'

Was it the extremity to which he had come, or was it the dawning of another change, that made him stop?

'—that what I *can* do right, with my mind running on so much, so fast, I'll try to do. There was another man here. Did you see him?'

Redlaw could not reply by any word; for when he saw that fatal sign he knew so well now, of the wandering hand upon the fore-head, his voice died at his lips. But he made some indication of assent.

'He is penniless, hungry, and destitute. He is completely beaten down, and has no resource at all. Look after him! Lose no time! I know he has it in his mind to kill himself.'

It was working. It was on his face. His face was changing, hardening, deepening in all its shades, and losing all its sorrow.

'Don't you remember? Don't you know him?' he pursued.

He shut his face out for a moment, with the hand that again wandered over his forehead, and then it lowered on Redlaw, reckless, ruffianly, and callous.

'Why, d—n you!' he said, scowling round, 'what have you been doing to me here! I have lived bold, and I mean to die bold. To the Devil with you!'

And so lay down upon his bed, and put his arms up, over his head and ears, as resolute from that time to keep out all access, and to die in his indifference.

If Redlaw had been struck by lightning, it could not have struck him from the bedside with a more tremendous shock. But the old man, who had left the bed while his son was speaking to him, now returning, avoided it quickly likewise, and with abhorrence.

'Where's my boy William?' said the old man hurriedly. 'William, come away from here. We'll go home.'

'Home, father!' returned William. 'Are you going to leave your own son?'

'Where's my own son?' replied the old man.

'Where? why, there!'

'That's no son of mine,' said Philip, trembling with resentment. 'No such wretch as that, has any claim on me. My children are pleasant to look at, and they wait upon me, and get my meat and drink ready, and are useful to me. I've a right to it! I'm eighty-seven!'

'You're old enough to be no older,' muttered William, looking at him grudgingly, with his hands in his pockets. 'I don't know what good you are, myself. We could have a deal more pleasure without you.'

'*My* son, Mr. Redlaw!' said the old man. '*My* son, too! The boy talking to me of *my* son! Why, what has he ever done to give me any pleasure, I should like to know?'

'I don't know what you have ever done to give *me* any pleasure,' said William, sulkily.

'Let me think,' said the old man. 'For how many Christmas times running, have I sat in my warm place, and never had to come out in the cold night air; and have made good cheer, without being disturbed by any such uncomfortable, wretched sight as him there? Is it twenty, William?'

'Nigher forty, it seems,' he muttered. 'Why, when I look at my father, sir, and come to think of it,' addressing Redlaw, with an impatience and irritation that were quite new, 'I'm whipped if I can see anything in him but a calendar of ever so many years of eating and drinking, and making himself comfortable, over and over again.'

'I—I'm eighty-seven,' said the old man, rambling on, childishly and weakly, 'and I don't know as I ever was much put out by anything. I'm not going to begin now, because of what he calls my son. He's not my son. I've had a power of pleasant times. I recollect once—no, I don't—no, it's broken off. It was something about a game of cricket and a friend of mine, but it's somehow broken off. I wonder who he was—I suppose I liked him? And I wonder what became of him—I suppose he died? But I don't know. And I don't care, neither; I don't care a bit.'

In his drowsy chuckling, and the shaking of his head, he put his hands into his waistcoat-pockets. In one of them he found a bit of holly (left there, probably last night), which he now took out, and looked at.

'Berries, eh?' said the old man. 'Ah! It's a pity they're not good to eat. I recollect, when I was a little chap about as high as that, and out a-walking with—let me see—who was I out a-walking with?—no, I don't remember how that was. I don't remember as I ever walked with any one particular, or cared for any one, or any one for me. Berries, eh? There's good cheer when there's berries. Well; I ought to have my share of it, and to be waited on, and kept warm and comfortable; for I'm eighty-seven, and a poor old man. I'm eigh-ty-seven. Eigh-ty-seven!'

The drivelling, pitiable manner in which, as he repeated this, he nibbled at the leaves, and spat the morsels out; the cold, uninterested eye with which his youngest son (so changed) regarded him; the determined apathy with which his eldest son lay hardened in his sin;—impressed themselves no more on Redlaw's observation; for he broke his way from the spot to which his feet seemed to have been fixed, and ran out of the house.

His guide came crawling forth from his place of refuge, and was ready for him before he reached the arches.

'Back to the woman's?' he inquired.

'Back, quickly!' answered Redlaw. 'Stop nowhere on the way.'

For a short distance the boy went on before; but their return was more like a flight than a walk, and it was as much as his bare feet could do, to keep pace with the Chemist's rapid strides. Shrinking from all who passed, shrouded in his cloak, and keeping it drawn closely about him, as though there were mortal contagion in any fluttering touch of his garments, he made no pause until they reached the door by which they had come out. He unlocked it with his key, went in, accompanied by the boy, and hastened through the dark passages to his own chamber.

The boy watched him as he made the door fast, and withdrew behind the table, when he looked round.

'Come!' he said. 'Don't you touch me! You've not brought me here to take my money away.'

Redlaw threw some more upon the ground. He flung his body on it immediately, as if to hide it from him, lest the sight of it should tempt him to reclaim it; and not until he saw him seated by his lamp, with his face hidden in his hands, began furtively to pick it up. When he had done so, he crept near the fire, and, sitting down in a great chair before it, took from his breast some broken scraps of food, and fell to munching, and to staring at the blaze, and now and then to glancing at his shillings, which he kept clenched up in a bunch, in one hand.

'And this,' said Redlaw, gazing on him with increased repugnance and fear, 'is the only one companion I have left on earth.'

How long it was before he was aroused from his contemplation of this creature, whom he dreaded so—whether half an hour, or half the night—he knew not. But the stillness of the room was broken by the boy (whom he had seen listening) starting up, and running towards the door.

'Here's the woman coming!' he exclaimed.

The Chemist stopped him on his way, at the moment when she knocked.

'Let me go to her, will you?' said the boy.

'Not now,' returned the Chemist. 'Stay here. Nobody must pass in or out of the room now. Who's that?'

'It's I, sir,' cried Milly. 'Pray, sir, let me in!'

'No! not for the world!' he said.

'Mr. Redlaw, Mr. Redlaw, pray, sir, let me in.'

'What is the matter?' he said, holding the boy.

'The miserable man you saw, is worse, and nothing I can say will wake him from his terrible infatuation. William's father has turned childish in a moment. William himself is changed. The shock has been too sudden for him; I cannot understand him; he is not like himself. Oh, Mr. Redlaw, pray advise me, help me!'

'No! No! No!' he answered.

'Mr. Redlaw! Dear sir! George has been muttering, in his doze, about the man you saw there, who, he fears, will kill himself.'

'Better he should do it, than come near me!'

'He says, in his wanderings, that you know him; that he was your friend once, long ago; that he is the ruined father of a student here—my mind misgives me, of the young gentleman who has been ill. What is to be done? How is he to be followed? How is he to be saved? Mr. Redlaw, pray, oh, pray, advise me! Help me!'

All this time he held the boy, who was half-mad to pass him, and let her in.

'Phantoms! Punishers of impious thoughts!' cried Redlaw, gazing round in anguish. 'Look upon me! From the darkness of my mind, let the glimmering of contrition that I know is there, shine up, and show my misery! In the material world, as I have long taught, nothing can be spared; no step or atom in the wondrous structure could be lost, without a blank being made in the great universe.* I know, now, that it is the same with good and evil, happiness and sorrow, in the memories of men. Pity me! Relieve me!'

There was no response, but her 'Help me, help me, let me in!' and the boy's struggling to get to her.

'Shadow of myself! Spirit of my darker hours!' cried Redlaw, in distraction. 'Come back, and haunt me day and night, but take this gift away! Or, if it must still rest with me, deprive me of the dreadful power of giving it to others. Undo what I have done. Leave me benighted, but restore the day to those whom I have cursed. As I have spared this woman from the first, and as I never will go forth

again, but will die here, with no hand to tend me, save this creature's
who is proof against me,—hear me!'

The only reply still was, the boy struggling to get to her, while he
held him back; and the cry, increasing in its energy, 'Help! let me in.
He was your friend once, how shall he be followed, how shall he be
saved? They are all changed, there is no one else to help me, pray,
pray, let me in!'

CHAPTER III

THE GIFT REVERSED

NIGHT was still heavy in the sky. On open plains, from hill-tops, and
from the decks of solitary ships at sea, a distant low-lying line, that
promised by-and-by to change to light, was visible in the dim horizon; but its promise was remote and doubtful, and the moon was
striving with the night-clouds busily.

The shadows upon Redlaw's mind succeeded thick and fast to one
another, and obscured its light as the night-clouds hovered between
the moon and earth, and kept the latter veiled in darkness. Fitful and
uncertain as the shadows which the night-clouds cast, were their
concealments from him, and imperfect revelations to him; and, like
the night-clouds still, if the clear light broke forth for a moment, it
was only that they might sweep over it, and make the darkness
deeper than before.

Without, there was a profound and solemn hush upon the ancient
pile of buildings, and its buttresses and angles made dark shapes
of mystery upon the ground, which now seemed to retire into the
smooth white snow and now seemed to come out of it, as the moon's
path was more or less beset. Within, the Chemist's room was
indistinct and murky, by the light of the expiring lamp; a ghostly
silence had succeeded to the knocking and the voice outside; nothing
was audible but, now and then, a low sound among the whitened
ashes of the fire, as of its yielding up its breath. Before it on the
ground the boy lay fast asleep. In his chair, the Chemist sat, as he had
sat there since the calling at his door had ceased—like a man turned
to stone.

At such a time, the Christmas music he had heard before, began to play. He listened to it at first, as he had listened in the churchyard; but presently—it playing still, and being borne towards him on the night-air, in a low, sweet, melancholy strain—he rose, and stood stretching his hands about him, as if there were some friend approaching within his reach, on whom his desolate touch might rest, yet do no harm. As he did this, his face became less fixed and wondering; a gentle trembling came upon him; and at last his eyes filled with tears, and he put his hands before them, and bowed down his head.

His memory of sorrow, wrong, and trouble, had not come back to him; he knew that it was not restored; he had no passing belief or hope that it was. But some dumb stir within him made him capable, again, of being moved by what was hidden, afar off, in the music. If it were only that it told him sorrowfully the value of what he had lost, he thanked Heaven for it with a fervent gratitude.

As the last chord died upon his ears, he raised his head to listen to its lingering vibration. Beyond the boy, so that his sleeping figure lay at its feet, the Phantom stood, immovable and silent, with its eyes upon him.

Ghastly it was, as it had ever been, but not so cruel and relentless in its aspect—or he thought or hoped so, as he looked upon it, trembling. It was not alone, but in its shadowy hand it held another hand.

And whose was that? Was the form that stood beside it indeed Milly's, or but her shade and picture? The quiet head was bent a little, as her manner was, and her eyes were looking down, as if in pity, on the sleeping child. A radiant light fell on her face, but did not touch the Phantom; for, though close beside her, it was dark and colourless as ever.

'Spectre!' said the Chemist, newly troubled as he looked, 'I have not been stubborn or presumptuous in respect to her. Oh, do not bring her here. Spare me that!'

'This is but a shadow,' said the Phantom; 'when the morning shines seek out the reality whose image I present before you.'

'Is it my inexorable doom to do so?' cried the Chemist.

'It is,' replied the Phantom.

'To destroy her peace, her goodness; to make her what I am myself, and what I have made of others!'

'I have said, "seek her out," ' returned the Phantom. 'I have said no more.'

'Oh, tell me,' exclaimed Redlaw, catching at the hope which he fancied might lie hidden in the words. 'Can I undo what I have done?'

'No,' returned the Phantom.

'I do not ask for restoration to myself,' said Redlaw. 'What I abandoned, I abandoned of my own will, and have justly lost. But for those to whom I have transferred the fatal gift; who never sought it; who unknowingly received a curse of which they had no warning, and which they had no power to shun; can I do nothing?'

'Nothing,' said the Phantom.

'If I cannot, can any one?'

The Phantom, standing like a statue, kept his gaze upon him for a while; then turned its head suddenly, and looked upon the shadow at its side.

'Ah! Can she?' cried Redlaw, still looking upon the shade.

The Phantom released the hand it had retained till now, and softly raised its own with a gesture of dismissal. Upon that, her shadow, still preserving the same attitude, began to move or melt away.

'Stay,' cried Redlaw with an earnestness to which he could not give enough expression. 'For a moment! As an act of mercy! I know that some change fell upon me, when those sounds were in the air just now. Tell me, have I lost the power of harming her? May I go near her without dread? Oh, let her give me any sign of hope!'

The Phantom looked upon the shade as he did—not at him—and gave no answer.

'At least, say this—has she, henceforth, the consciousness of any power to set right what I have done?'

'She has not,' the Phantom answered.

'Has she the power bestowed on her without the consciousness?'

The Phantom answered: 'Seek her out.' And her shadow slowly vanished.

They were face to face again, and looking on each other, as intently and awfully as at the time of the bestowal of the gift, across the boy who still lay on the ground between them, at the Phantom's feet.

'Terrible instructor,' said the Chemist, sinking on his knee before it, in an attitude of supplication, 'by whom I was renounced, but by whom I am revisited (in which, and in whose milder aspect, I would fain believe I have a gleam of hope), I will obey without inquiry, praying that the cry I have sent up in the anguish of my soul has been, or will be, heard, in behalf of those whom I have injured beyond human reparation. But there is one thing—'

'You speak to me of what is lying here,' the Phantom interposed, and pointed with its finger to the boy.

'I do,' returned the Chemist. 'You know what I would ask. Why has this child alone been proof against my influence, and why, why have I detected in its thoughts a terrible companionship with mine?'

'This,' said the Phantom, pointing to the boy, 'is the last, completest illustration of a human creature, utterly bereft of such remembrances as you have yielded up. No softening memory of sorrow, wrong, or trouble enters here, because this wretched mortal from his birth has been abandoned to a worse condition than the beasts, and has, within his knowledge, no one contrast, no humanising touch, to make a grain of such a memory spring up in his hardened breast. All within this desolate creature is barren wilderness. All within the man bereft of what you have resigned, is the same barren wilderness. Woe to such a man! Woe, tenfold, to the nation that shall count its monsters such as this, lying here, by hundreds, and by thousands!'

Redlaw shrunk, appalled, from what he heard.

'There is not,' said the Phantom, 'one of these—not one—but shows a harvest that mankind MUST REAP. From every seed of evil in this boy, a field of ruin is grown that shall be gathered in, and garnered up, and sown again in many places in the world, until regions are overspread with wickedness enough to raise the waters of another Deluge. Open and unpunished murder in a city's streets would be less guilty in its daily toleration, than one such spectacle as this.'

It seemed to look down upon the boy in his sleep. Redlaw, too, looked down upon him with a new emotion.

'There is not a father,' said the Phantom, 'by whose side in his daily or his nightly walk, these creatures pass; there is not a mother among all the ranks of loving mothers in this land; there is no one risen from the state of childhood, but shall be responsible in his or her degree for this enormity. There is not a country throughout the earth on which it would not bring a curse. There is no religion upon

earth that it would not deny; there is no people upon earth it would
not put to shame.'

The Chemist clasped his hands, and looked, with trembling fear
and pity, from the sleeping boy to the Phantom, standing above him
with its finger pointing down.

'Behold, I say,' pursued the Spectre, 'the perfect type of what it
was your choice to be. Your influence is powerless here, because from
this child's bosom you can banish nothing. His thoughts have been in
"terrible companionship" with yours, because you have gone down
to his unnatural level. He is the growth of man's indifference; you
are the growth of man's presumption. The beneficent design of
Heaven is, in each case, overthrown, and from the two poles of the
immaterial world you come together.'

The Chemist stooped upon the ground beside the boy, and, with
the same kind of compassion for him that he now felt for himself,
covered him as he slept, and no longer shrunk from him with
abhorrence or indifference.

Soon, now, the distant line on the horizon brightened, the darkness faded, the sun rose red and glorious, and the chimney stacks
and gables of the ancient building gleamed in the clear air, which
turned the smoke and vapour of the city into a cloud of gold. The
very sun-dial in his shady corner, where the wind was used to spin
with such un-windy constancy, shook off the finer particles of snow
that had accumulated on his dull old face in the night, and looked
out at the little white wreaths eddying round and round him.
Doubtless some blind groping of the morning made its way down
into the forgotten crypt so cold and earthy, where the Norman
arches were half buried in the ground, and stirred the dull deep sap
in the lazy vegetation hanging to the walls, and quickened the slow
principle of life within the little world of wonderful and delicate
creation which existed there, with some faint knowledge that the
sun was up.

The Tetterbys were up, and doing. Mr. Tetterby took down the
shutters of the shop, and, strip by strip, revealed the treasures of the
window to the eyes, so proof against their seductions, of Jerusalem
Buildings. Adolphus had been out so long already, that he was
halfway on to Morning Pepper. Five small Tetterbys, whose ten
round eyes were much inflamed by soap and friction, were in the
tortures of a cool wash in the back kitchen; Mrs. Tetterby

presiding. Johnny, who was pushed and hustled through his toilet with great rapidity when Moloch chanced to be in an exacting frame of mind (which was always the case), staggered up and down with his charge before the shop door, under greater difficulties than usual; the weight of Moloch being much increased by a complication of

defences against the cold, composed of knitted worsted-work, and forming a complete suit of chain-armour, with a head-piece and blue gaiters.

It was a peculiarity of this baby to be always cutting teeth. Whether they never came, or whether they came and went away again, is not in evidence; but it had certainly cut enough, on the showing of Mrs. Tetterby, to make a handsome dental provision for the sign of the Bull and Mouth. All sorts of objects were impressed for the rubbing of its gums, notwithstanding that it always carried, dangling at its waist (which was immediately under its chin), a bone ring, large enough to have represented the rosary of a young nun. Knife-handles, umbrella-tops, the heads of walking-sticks selected from the stock, the fingers of the family in general, but especially of Johnny, nutmeg-graters, crusts, the handles of doors, and the cool knobs on the tops of pokers, were among the commonest instruments indiscriminately applied for this baby's relief. The amount of electricity that must have been rubbed out of it in a week, is not to be calculated. Still Mrs. Tetterby always said 'it was coming through, and then the child would be herself'; and still it never did come through, and the child continued to be somebody else.

The tempers of the little Tetterbys had sadly changed with a few hours. Mr. and Mrs. Tetterby themselves were not more altered than their offspring. Usually they were an unselfish, good-natured, yielding little race, sharing short-commons* when it happened (which was pretty often) contentedly and even generously, and taking a great deal of enjoyment out of a very little meat. But they were fighting now, not only for the soap and water, but even for the breakfast which was yet in perspective. The hand of every little Tetterby was against the other little Tetterbys; and even Johnny's hand—the patient, much-enduring, and devoted Johnny—rose against the baby! Yes, Mrs. Tetterby, going to the door by a mere accident, saw him viciously pick out a weak place in the suit of armour where a slap would tell, and slap that blessed child.

Mrs. Tetterby had him into the parlour by the collar, in that same flash of time, and repaid him the assault with usury thereto.

'You brute, you murdering little boy,' said Mrs. Tetterby. 'Had you the heart to do it?'

'Why don't her teeth come through, then,' retorted Johnny, in a loud rebellious voice, 'instead of bothering me? How would you like it yourself?'

'Like it, sir!' said Mrs. Tetterby, relieving him of his dishonoured load.

'Yes, like it,' said Johnny. 'How would you? Not at all. If you was me, you'd go for a soldier. I will, too. There an't no babies in the army.'

Mr. Tetterby, who had arrived upon the scene of action, rubbed his chin thoughtfully, instead of correcting the rebel, and seemed rather struck by this view of a military life.

'I wish I was in the army myself, if the child's in the right,' said Mrs. Tetterby, looking at her husband, 'for I have no peace of my life here. I'm a slave—a Virginia slave'; some indistinct association with their weak descent on the tobacco trade perhaps suggested this aggravated expression to Mrs. Tetterby. 'I never have a holiday, or any pleasure at all, from year's end to year's end! Why, Lord bless and save the child,' said Mrs. Tetterby, shaking the baby with an irritability hardly suited to so pious an aspiration, 'what's the matter with her now?'

Not being able to discover, and not rendering the subject much clearer by shaking it, Mrs. Tetterby put the baby away in a cradle, and, folding her arms, sat rocking it angrily with her foot.

'How you stand there, 'Dolphus,' said Mrs. Tetterby to her husband. 'Why don't you do something?'

'Because I don't care about doing anything,' Mr. Tetterby replied.

'I am sure *I* don't,' said Mrs. Tetterby.

'I'll take my oath *I* don't,' said Mr. Tetterby.

A diversion arose here among Johnny and his five younger brothers, who, in preparing the family breakfast table, had fallen to skirmishing for the temporary possession of the loaf, and were buffeting one another with great heartiness; the smallest boy of all, with precocious discretion, hovering outside the knot of combatants, and harassing their legs. Into the midst of this fray, Mr. and Mrs. Tetterby both precipitated themselves with great ardour, as if such ground were the only ground on which they could now agree; and having, with no visible remains of their late soft-heartedness, laid about them without any lenity, and done much execution, resumed their former relative positions.

'You had better read your paper than do nothing at all,' said Mrs. Tetterby.

'What's there to read in a paper?' returned Mr. Tetterby, with excessive discontent.

'What?' said Mrs. Tetterby. 'Police.'

'It's nothing to me,' said Tetterby. 'What do I care what people do, or are done to.'

'Suicides,' suggested Mrs. Tetterby.

'No business of mine,' replied her husband.

'Births, deaths, and marriages, are those nothing to you?' said Mrs. Tetterby.

'If the births were all over for good and all to-day; and the deaths were all to begin to come off to-morrow; I don't see why it should interest me, till I thought it was a-coming to my turn,' grumbled Tetterby. 'As to marriages, I've done it myself. I know quite enough about *them*.'

To judge from the dissatisfied expression of her face and manner, Mrs. Tetterby appeared to entertain the same opinions as her husband; but she opposed him, nevertheless, for the gratification of quarrelling with him.

'Oh, you're a consistent man,' said Mrs. Tetterby, 'an't you? You, with the screen of your own making there, made of nothing else but bits of newspapers, which you sit and read to the children by the half-hour together!'

'Say used to, if you please,' returned her husband. 'You won't find me doing so any more. I'm wiser, now.'

'Bah! wiser, indeed!' said Mrs. Tetterby. 'Are you better?'

The question sounded some discordant note in Mr. Tetterby's breast. He ruminated dejectedly, and passed his hand across and across his forehead.

'Better!' murmured Mr. Tetterby. 'I don't know as any of us are better, or happier either. Better, is it?'

He turned to the screen, and traced about it with his finger, until he found a certain paragraph of which he was in quest.

'This used to be one of the family favourites, I recollect,' said Tetterby, in a forlorn and stupid way, 'and used to draw tears from the children, and make 'em good, if there was any little bickering or discontent among 'em, next to the story of the robin redbreasts in the wood. "Melancholy case of destitution. Yesterday a small man, with a baby in his arms, and surrounded by half-a-dozen ragged little ones, of various ages between ten and two, the whole of whom were evidently in a famishing condition, appeared before the worthy magistrate, and made the following recital:"—Ha! I don't understand it, I'm sure,' said Tetterby; 'I don't see what it has got to do with us.'

'How old and shabby he looks,' said Mrs. Tetterby, watching him. 'I never saw such a change in a man. Ah! dear me, dear me, dear me, it was a sacrifice!'

'What was a sacrifice?' her husband sourly inquired.

Mrs. Tetterby shook her head; and without replying in words, raised a complete sea-storm about the baby, by her violent agitation of the cradle.

'If you mean your marriage was a sacrifice, my good woman—' said her husband.

'I *do* mean it,' said his wife.

'Why, then I mean to say,' pursued Mr. Tetterby, as sulkily and surlily as she, 'that there are two sides to that affair; and that *I* was the sacrifice; and that I wish the sacrifice hadn't been accepted.'

'I wish it hadn't, Tetterby, with all my heart and soul I do assure you,' said his wife. 'You can't wish it more than I do, Tetterby.'

'I don't know what I saw in her,' muttered the newsman, 'I'm sure:—certainly, if I saw anything, it's not there now. I was thinking so, last night, after supper, by the fire. She's fat, she's ageing, she won't bear comparison with most other women.'

'He's common-looking, he has no air with him, he's small, he's beginning to stoop, and he's getting bald,' muttered Mrs. Tetterby.

'I must have been half out of my mind when I did it,' muttered Mr. Tetterby.

'My senses must have forsook me. That's the only way in which I can explain it to myself,' said Mrs. Tetterby, with elaboration.

In this mood they sat down to breakfast. The little Tetterbys were not habituated to regard that meal in the light of a sedentary occupation, but discussed it as a dance or trot; rather resembling a savage ceremony, in the occasional shrill whoops, and brandishings of bread and butter, with which it was accompanied, as well as in the intricate filings off into the street and back again, and the hoppings up and down the doorsteps, which were incidental to the performance. In the present instance, the contentions between these Tetterby children for the milk-and-water jug, common to all, which stood upon the table, presented so lamentable an instance of angry passions risen very high indeed, that it was an outrage on the memory of Doctor Watts.* It was not until Mr. Tetterby had driven the whole herd out at the front door, that a moment's peace was secured; and even that was broken by the discovery that Johnny had surreptitiously come back, and was at that instant choking in the jug like a ventriloquist,* in his indecent and rapacious haste.

'These children will be the death of me at last!' said Mrs. Tetterby, after banishing the culprit. 'And the sooner the better, I think.'

'Poor people,' said Mr. Tetterby, 'ought not to have children* at all. They give *us* no pleasure.'

He was at that moment taking up the cup which Mrs. Tetterby had rudely pushed towards him, and Mrs. Tetterby was lifting her own cup to her lips, when they were both stopped, as if they were transfixed.

'Here! Mother! Father!' cried Johnny, running into the room. 'Here's Mrs. William coming down the street!'

And if ever, since the world began, a young boy took a baby from a cradle with the care of an old nurse, and hushed and soothed it tenderly, and tottered away with it cheerfully, Johnny was that boy, and Moloch was that baby, as they went out together!

Mr. Tetterby put down his cup; Mrs. Tetterby put down her cup. Mr. Tetterby rubbed his forehead; Mrs. Tetterby rubbed hers. Mr. Tetterby's face began to smooth and brighten; Mrs. Tetterby's face began to smooth and brighten.

'Why, Lord forgive me,' said Mr. Tetterby to himself, 'what evil tempers have I been giving way to? What has been the matter here!'

'How could I ever treat him ill again, after all I said and felt last night!' sobbed Mrs. Tetterby, with her apron to her eyes.

'Am I a brute,' said Mr. Tetterby, 'or is there any good in me at all? Sophia! My little woman!'

' 'Dolphus dear,' returned his wife.

'I—I've been in a state of mind,' said Mr. Tetterby, 'that I can't abear to think of, Sophy.'

'Oh! It's nothing to what I've been in, Dolf,' cried his wife in a great burst of grief.

'My Sophia,' said Mr. Tetterby, 'don't take on. I never shall forgive myself. I must have nearly broke your heart, I know.'

'No, Dolf, no. It was me! Me!' cried Mrs. Tetterby.

'My little woman,' said her husband, 'don't. You make me

reproach myself dreadful, when you show such a noble spirit. Sophia, my dear, you don't know what I thought. I showed it bad enough, no doubt; but what I thought, my little woman!'—

'Oh, dear Dolf, don't! Don't!' cried his wife.

'Sophia,' said Mr. Tetterby, 'I must reveal it. I couldn't rest in my conscience unless I mentioned it. My little woman—'

'Mrs. William's very nearly here!' screamed Johnny at the door.

'My little woman, I wondered how,' gasped Mr. Tetterby, supporting himself by his chair, 'I wondered how I had ever admired you—I forgot the precious children you have brought about me, and thought you didn't look as slim as I could wish. I—I never gave a recollection,' said Mr. Tetterby, with severe self-accusation, 'to the cares you've had as my wife, and along of me and mine, when you might have had hardly any with another man, who got on better and was luckier than me (anybody might have found such a man easily I am sure); and I quarrelled with you for having aged a little in the rough years you have lightened for me. Can you believe it, my little woman? I hardly can myself.'

Mrs. Tetterby, in a whirlwind of laughing and crying, caught his face within her hands, and held it there.

'Oh, Dolf!' she cried. 'I am so happy that you thought so; I am so grateful that you thought so! For I thought that you were common-looking, Dolf; and so you are, my dear, and may you be the commonest of all sights in my eyes, till you close them with your own good hands. I thought that you were small; and so you are, and I'll make much of you because you are, and more of you because I love my husband. I thought that you began to stoop; and so you do, and you shall lean on me, and I'll do all I can to keep you up. I thought there was no air about you; but there is and it's the air of home, and that's the purest and the best there is, and GOD bless home once more, and all belonging to it, Dolf!'

'Hurrah! Here's Mrs. William!' cried Johnny.

So she was, and all the children with her; and as she came in, they kissed her, and kissed one another, and kissed the baby, and kissed their father and mother, and then ran back and flocked and danced about her, trooping on with her in triumph.

Mr. and Mrs. Tetterby were not a bit behind-hand in the warmth of their reception. They were as much attracted to her as the children were; they ran towards her, kissed her hands, pressed round her, could not receive her ardently or enthusiastically enough. She came among them like the spirit of all goodness, affection, gentle consideration, love, and domesticity.

'What! are *you* all so glad to see me, too, this bright Christmas morning?' said Milly, clapping her hands in a pleasant wonder. 'Oh dear, how delightful this is!'

More shouting from the children, more kissing, more trooping round her, more happiness, more love, more joy, more honour, on all sides, than she could bear.

'Oh dear!' said Milly, 'what delicious tears you make me shed. How can I ever have deserved this! What have I done to be so loved?'

'Who can help it!' cried Mr. Tetterby.

'Who can help it!' cried Mrs. Tetterby.

'Who can help it!' echoed the children, in a joyful chorus. And they danced and trooped about her again, and clung to her, and laid their rosy faces against her dress, and kissed and fondled it, and could not fondle it, or her, enough.

'I never was so moved', said Milly, drying her eyes, 'as I have been this morning. I must tell you, as soon as I can speak.—Mr. Redlaw came to me at sunrise, and with a tenderness in his manner, more as if I had been his darling daughter than myself, implored me to go with him to where William's brother George is lying ill. We went together, and all the way along he was so kind, and so subdued, and seemed to put such trust and hope in me, that I could not help crying with pleasure. When we got to the house, we met a woman at the door (somebody had bruised and hurt her, I am afraid) who caught me by the hand, and blessed me as I passed.'

'She was right,' said Mr. Tetterby. Mrs. Tetterby said she was right. All the children cried out she was right.

'Ah, but there's more than that,' said Milly. 'When we got up-stairs, into the room, the sick man who had lain for hours in a state from which no effort could rouse him, rose up in his bed, and, bursting into tears, stretched out his arms to me, and said that he had led a mis-spent life, but that he was truly repentant now, in his sorrow for the past, which was all as plain to him as a great prospect, from which a dense black cloud had cleared away, and that he entreated me to ask his poor old father for his pardon and his blessing, and to say a prayer beside his bed. And when I did so, Mr. Redlaw joined in it so fervently, and then so thanked and thanked me, and thanked Heaven, that my heart quite overflowed, and I could have done nothing but sob and cry, if the sick man had not begged me to sit down by him,—which made me quiet of course. As I sat there, he held my hand in his until he sunk in a doze; and even then, when I withdrew my hand to leave him to come here (which Mr. Redlaw was very earnest indeed in wishing me to do), his hand felt for mine, so that some one else was obliged to take my place and make believe to give him my hand back. Oh dear, oh dear,' said Milly, sobbing. 'How thankful and how happy I should feel, and do feel, for all this!'

While she was speaking, Redlaw had come in, and, after pausing for a moment to observe the group of which she was the centre, had silently ascended the stairs. Upon those stairs he now appeared again; remaining there, while the young student passed him, and came running down.

'Kind nurse, gentlest, best of creatures,' he said, falling on his knee to her, and catching at her hand, 'forgive my cruel ingratitude!'

'Oh dear, oh dear!' cried Milly innocently, 'here's another of them! Oh dear, here's somebody else who likes me. What shall I ever do!'

The guileless, simple way in which she said it, and in which she put her hands before her eyes and wept for very happiness, was as touching as it was delightful.

'I was not myself,' he said. 'I don't know what it was—it was some consequence of my disorder perhaps—I was mad. But I am so no longer. Almost as I speak, I am restored. I heard the children crying out your name, and the shade passed from me at the very sound of it. Oh don't weep! Dear Milly, if you could read my heart, and only know with what affection and what grateful homage it is glowing, you would not let me see you weep. It is such deep reproach.'

'No, no,' said Milly, 'it's not that. It's not indeed. It's joy. It's wonder that you should think it necessary to ask me to forgive so little, and yet it's pleasure that you do.'

'And will you come again? and will you finish the little curtain?'

'No,' said Milly, drying her eyes, and shaking her head. 'You won't care for *my* needlework now.'

'Is it forgiving me, to say that?'

She beckoned him aside, and whispered in his ear.

'There is news from your home, Mr. Edmund.'

'News? How?'

'Either your not writing when you were very ill, or the change in your handwriting when you began to be better, created some suspicion of the truth; however that is—but you're sure you'll not be the worse for any news, if it's not bad news?'

'Sure.'

'Then there's some one come!' said Milly.

'My mother?' asked the student, glancing round involuntarily towards Redlaw, who had come down from the stairs.

'Hush! No,' said Milly.

'It can be no one else.'

Indeed,' said Milly, 'are you sure?'

'It is not——' Before he could say more, she put her hand close upon his mouth.

'Yes it is!' said Milly. 'The young lady (she is very like the miniature, Mr. Edmund, but she is prettier) was too unhappy to rest without satisfying her doubts, and came up, last night, with a little servant-maid. As you always dated your letters from the college, she came there; and before I saw Mr. Redlaw this morning, I saw her. *She* likes me too!' said Milly. 'Oh dear, that's another!'

'This morning! Where is she now?'

'Why, she is now,' said Milly, advancing her lips to his ear, 'in my little parlour in the Lodge, and waiting to see you.'

He pressed her hand, and was darting off, but she detained him.

'Mr. Redlaw is much altered, and has told me this morning that his memory is impaired. Be very considerate to him, Mr. Edmund; he needs that from us all.'

The young man assured her, by a look, that her caution was not ill-bestowed; and as he passed the Chemist on his way out, bent respectfully and with an obvious interest before him.

Redlaw returned the salutation courteously and even humbly, and looked after him as he passed on. He drooped his head upon his hand too, as trying to re-awaken something he had lost. But it was gone.

The abiding change that had come upon him since the influence of the music, and the Phantom's reappearance, was, that now he truly felt how much he had lost, and could compassionate his own condition, and contrast it, clearly, with the natural state of those who were around him. In this, an interest in those who were around him was revived, and a meek, submissive sense of his calamity was bred, resembling that which sometimes obtains in age, when its mental powers are weakened, without insensibility or sullenness being added to the list of its infirmities.

He was conscious that, as he redeemed, through Milly, more and more of the evil he had done, and as he was more and more with her, this change ripened itself within him. Therefore, and because of the attachment she inspired him with (but without other hope), he felt that he was quite dependent on her, and that she was his staff in his affliction.

So, when she asked him whether they should go home now, to where the old man and her husband were, and he readily replied 'yes'—being anxious in that regard—he put his arm through hers, and walked beside her; not as if he were the wise and learned man to whom the wonders of nature were an open book, and hers were the uninstructed mind, but as if their two positions were reversed, and he knew nothing, and she all.

He saw the children throng about her, and caress her, as he and she went away together thus, out of the house; he heard the ringing of their laughter, and their merry voices; he saw their bright faces, clustering around him like flowers; he witnessed the renewed contentment and affection of their parents; he breathed the simple air of their poor home, restored to its tranquillity; he thought of the unwholesome blight he had shed upon it, and might, but for her, have been diffusing then; and perhaps it is no wonder that he walked submissively beside her, and drew her gentle bosom nearer to his own.

When they arrived at the Lodge, the old man was sitting in his chair in the chimney-corner, with his eyes fixed on the ground, and his son was leaning against the opposite side of the fireplace, looking at him. As she came in at the door, both started, and turned round towards her, and a radiant change came upon their faces.

'Oh dear, dear, dear, they are pleased to see me like the rest!' cried Milly, clapping her hands in an ecstasy, and stopping short. 'Here are two more!'

Pleased to see her! Pleasure was no word for it. She ran into her husband's arms, thrown wide open to receive her, and he would have been glad to have her there, with her head lying on his shoulder, through the short winter's day. But the old man couldn't spare her. He had arms for her too, and he locked her in them.

'Why, where has my quiet Mouse been all this time?' said the old man. 'She has been a long while away. I find that it's impossible for me to get on without Mouse. I—where's my son William?—I fancy I have been dreaming, William.'

'That's what I say myself, father,' returned his son. '*I* have been in an ugly sort of dream, I think. How are you, father? Are you pretty well?'

'Strong and brave, my boy,' returned the old man.

It was quite a sight to see Mr. William shaking hands with his father, and patting him on the back, and rubbing him gently down with his hand, as if he could not possibly do enough to show an interest in him.

'What a wonderful man you are, father!—How are you, father? Are you really pretty hearty, though?' said William, shaking hands with him again, and patting him again, and rubbing him gently down again.

'I never was fresher or stouter in my life, my boy.'

'What a wonderful man you are, father! But that's exactly where it is,' said Mr. William, with enthusiasm. 'When I think of all that my father's gone through, and all the chances and changes, and sorrows and troubles, that have happened to him in the course of his long life, and under which his head has grown grey, and years upon years have gathered on it, I feel as if we couldn't do enough to honour the old gentleman, and make his old age easy.—How are you, father? Are you really pretty well, though?'

Mr. William might never have left off repeating this inquiry, and shaking hands with him again, and patting him again, and rubbing him down again, if the old man had not espied the Chemist, whom until now he had not seen.

'I ask your pardon, Mr. Redlaw,' said Philip, 'but didn't know you were here, sir, or should have made less free. It reminds me, Mr. Redlaw, seeing you here on a Christmas morning, of the time when you was a student yourself, and worked so hard that you was backwards and forwards in our Library even at Christmas-time. Ha! ha! I'm old enough to remember that; and I remember it right well, I do, though I am eighty-seven. It was after you left here that my poor wife died. You remember my poor wife, Mr. Redlaw?'

The Chemist answered yes.

'Yes,' said the old man. 'She was a dear creetur.—I recollect you come here one Christmas morning with a young lady—I ask your pardon, Mr. Redlaw, but I think it was a sister you was very much attached to?'

The Chemist looked at him, and shook his head. 'I had a sister,' he said vacantly. He knew no more.

'One Christmas morning,' pursued the old man, 'that you come here with her—and it began to snow, and my wife invited the young lady to walk in, and sit by the fire that is always a-burning on Christmas Day in what used to be, before our ten poor gentlemen commuted, our great Dinner Hall. I was there; and I recollect, as I was stirring up the blaze for the young lady to warm her pretty feet by, she read the scroll out loud, that is underneath that picter. "Lord, keep my memory green!" She and my poor wife fell a-talking about it; and it's a strange thing to think of, now, that they both said (both being so unlike to die) that it was a good prayer, and that it was one they would put up very earnestly, if they were called away young, with reference to those who were dearest to them. "My brother," says the young lady—"My husband," says my poor wife.—"Lord, keep his memory of me green, and do not let me be forgotten!" '

Tears more painful, and more bitter than he had ever shed in all his life, coursed down Redlaw's face. Philip, fully occupied in recalling his story, had not observed him until now, nor Milly's anxiety that he should not proceed.

'Philip!' said Redlaw, laying his hand upon his arm, 'I am a stricken man, on whom the hand of Providence has fallen heavily, although deservedly. You speak to me, my friend, of what I cannot follow; my memory is gone.'

'Merciful Power!' cried the old man.

'I have lost my memory of sorrow, wrong, and trouble,' said the Chemist, 'and with that I have lost all man would remember!'

To see old Philip's pity for him, to see him wheel his own great chair for him to rest in, and look down upon him with a solemn sense of his bereavement, was to know, in some degree, how precious to old age such recollections are.

The boy came running in, and ran to Milly.

'Here's the man,' he said, 'in the other room. I don't want *him*.'

'What man does he mean?' asked Mr. William.

'Hush!' said Milly.

Obedient to a sign from her, he and his old father softly withdrew. As they went out, unnoticed, Redlaw beckoned to the boy to come to him.

'I like the woman best,' he answered, holding to her skirts.

'You are right,' said Redlaw, with a faint smile. 'But you needn't fear to come to me. I am gentler than I was. Of all the world, to you, poor child!'

The boy still held back at first, but yielding little by little to her urging, he consented to approach, and even to sit down at his feet. As Redlaw laid his hand upon the shoulder of the child, looking on him with compassion and a fellow-feeling, he put out his other hand to Milly. She stooped down on that side of him, so that she could look into his face; and after silence, said:

'Mr. Redlaw, may I speak to you?'

'Yes,' he answered, fixing his eyes upon her. 'Your voice and music are the same to me.'

'May I ask you something?'

'What you will.'

'Do you remember what I said, when I knocked at your door last night? About one who was your friend once, and who stood on the verge of destruction?'

'Yes. I remember,' he said, with some hesitation.

'Do you understand it?'

He smoothed the boy's hair—looking at her fixedly the while, and shook his head.

'This person,' said Milly, in her clear, soft voice, which her mild eyes, looking at him, made clearer and softer, 'I found soon afterwards. I went back to the house, and, with Heaven's help, traced him. I was not too soon. A very little and I should have been too late.'

He took his hand from the boy, and laying it on the back of that hand of hers, whose timid and yet earnest touch addressed him no less appealingly than her voice and eyes, looked more intently on her.

'He *is* the father of Mr. Edmund, the young gentleman we saw just now. His real name is Longford.—You recollect the name?'

'I recollect the name.'

'And the man?'

'No, not the man. Did he ever wrong me?'

'Yes.'

'Ah! Then it's hopeless—hopeless.'

He shook his head, and softly beat upon the hand he held, as though mutely asking her commiseration.

'I did not go to Mr. Edmund last night,' said Milly.—'You will listen to me just the same as if you did remember all?'

'To every syllable you say.'

'Both, because I did not know, then, that this really was his father, and because I was fearful of the effect of such intelligence upon him, after his illness, if it should be. Since I have known who this person is, I have not gone either; but that is for another reason. He has long been separated from his wife and son—has been a stranger to his home almost from this son's infancy, I learn from him—and has abandoned and deserted what he should have held most dear. In all that time he has been falling from the state of a gentleman, more and more, until—' she rose up, hastily, and going out for a moment, returned, accompanied by the wreck that Redlaw had beheld last night.

'Do you know me?' asked the Chemist.

'I should be glad,' returned the other, 'and that is an unwonted word for me to use, if I could answer no.'

The Chemist looked at the man, standing in self-abasement and degradation before him, and would have looked longer, in an ineffectual struggle for enlightenment, but that Milly resumed her late position by his side, and attracted his attentive gaze to her own face.

'See how low he is sunk, how lost he is!' she whispered, stretching out her arm towards him, without looking from the Chemist's face. 'If you could remember all that is connected with him, do you not think it would move your pity to reflect that one you ever loved (do not let us mind how long ago, or in what belief that he has forfeited), should come to this?'

'I hope it would,' he answered. 'I believe it would.'

His eyes wandered to the figure standing near the door, but came back speedily to her, on whom he gazed intently, as if he strove to learn some lesson from every tone of her voice, and every beam of her eyes.

'I have no learning, and you have much,' said Milly; 'I am not used to think, and you are always thinking. May I tell you why it seems to me a good thing for us to remember wrong that has been done us?'

'Yes.'

'That we may forgive it.'

'Pardon me, great Heaven!' said Redlaw, lifting up his eyes, 'for having thrown away thine own high attribute!'

'And if,' said Milly, 'if your memory should one day be restored, as we will hope and pray it may be, would it not be a blessing to you to recall at once a wrong and its forgiveness?'

He looked at the figure by the door, and fastened his attentive eyes on her again; a ray of clearer light appeared to him to shine into his mind, from her bright face.

'He cannot go to his abandoned home. He does not seek to go there. He knows that he could only carry shame and trouble to those he has so cruelly neglected; and that the best reparation he can make them now, is to avoid them. A very little money carefully bestowed, would remove him to some distant place, where he might live and do no wrong, and make such atonement as is left within his power for the wrong he has done. To the unfortunate lady who is his wife, and to his son, this would be the best and kindest boon that their best friend could give them—one too that they need never know of; and to him, shattered in reputation, mind, and body, it might be salvation.'

He took her head between his hands, and kissed it, and said: 'It shall be done. I trust to you to do it for me, now and secretly; and to tell him that I would forgive him, if I were so happy as to know for what.'

As she rose, and turned her beaming face towards the fallen man, implying that her mediation had been successful, he advanced a step, and without raising his eyes, addressed himself to Redlaw.

'You are so generous,' he said, '—you ever were—that you will try to banish your rising sense of retribution in the spectacle that is before you. I do not try to banish it from myself, Redlaw. If you can, believe me.'

The Chemist entreated Milly, by a gesture, to come nearer to him; and, as he listened, looked in her face, as if to find in it the clue to what he heard.

'I am too decayed a wretch to make professions; I recollect my own career too well, to array any such before you. But from the day on which I made my first step downward, in dealing falsely by you, I have gone down with a certain, steady, doomed progression. That, I say.'

Redlaw, keeping her close at his side, turned his face towards the speaker, and there was sorrow in it. Something like mournful recognition too.

'I might have been another man, my life might have been another life, if I had avoided that first fatal step. I don't know that it would have been. I claim nothing for the possibility. Your sister is at rest, and better than she could have been with me, if I had continued even what you thought me: even what I once supposed myself to be.'

Redlaw made a hasty motion with his hand, as if he would have put that subject on one side.

'I speak,' the other went on, 'like a man taken from the grave. I should have made my own grave, last night, had it not been for this blessed hand.'

'Oh dear, he likes me too!' sobbed Milly, under her breath. 'That's another!'

'I could not have put myself in your way, last night, even for bread. But to-day, my recollection of what has been is so strongly stirred, and is presented to me, I don't know how, so vividly, that I have dared to come at her suggestion, and to take your bounty, and to thank you for it, and to beg you, Redlaw, in your dying hour, to be as merciful to me in your thoughts, as you are in your deeds.'

He turned towards the door, and stopped a moment on his way forth.

'I hope my son may interest you for his mother's sake. I hope he may deserve to do so. Unless my life should be preserved a long time, and I should know that I have not misused your aid, I shall never look upon him more.'

Going out, he raised his eyes to Redlaw for the first time. Redlaw, whose steadfast gaze was fixed upon him, dreamily held out his hand. He returned and touched it—little more—with both his own—and bending down his head, went slowly out.

In the few moments that elapsed, while Milly silently took him to the gate, the Chemist dropped into his chair, and covered his face with his hands. Seeing him thus, when she came back, accompanied by her husband and his father (who were both greatly concerned for him), she avoided disturbing him, or permitting him to be disturbed; and kneeled down near the chair to put some warm clothing on the boy.

'That's exactly where it is. That's what I always say, father!' exclaimed her admiring husband. There's a motherly feeling in Mrs. William's breast that must and will have went!'

'Ay, ay,' said the old man; 'you're right. My son William's right!'

'It happens all for the best, Milly dear, no doubt,' said Mr. William, tenderly, 'that we have no children of our own; and yet I sometimes wish you had one to love and cherish. Our little dead child that you built such hopes upon, and that never breathed the breath of life—it has made you quiet-like, Milly.'

'I am very happy in the recollection of it, William dear,' she answered. 'I think of it every day.'

'I was afraid you thought of it a good deal.'

'Don't say afraid; it is a comfort to me; it speaks to me in so many ways. The innocent thing that never lived on earth, is like an angel to me, William.'

'You are like an angel to father and me,' said Mr. William, softly. 'I know that.'

'When I think of all those hopes I built upon it, and the many times I sat and pictured to myself the little smiling face upon my bosom that never lay there, and the sweet eyes turned up to mine that never opened to the light,' said Milly, 'I can feel a greater tenderness, I think, for all the disappointed hopes in which there is no harm. When I see a beautiful child in its fond mother's arms, I love it all the better, thinking that my child might have been like that, and might have made my heart as proud and happy.'

Redlaw raised his head, and looked towards her.

'All through life, it seems by me,' she continued, 'to tell me something. For poor neglected children, my little child pleads as if it were alive, and had a voice I knew, with which to speak to me. When I hear of youth in suffering or shame, I think that my child might have come to that, perhaps, and that God took it from me in his mercy. Even in age and grey hair, such as father's is at present: saying that it too might have lived to be old, long and long after you and I were gone, and to have needed the respect and love of younger people.'

Her quiet voice was quieter than ever, as she took her husband's arm, and laid her head against it.

'Children love me so, that sometimes I half fancy—it's a silly fancy, William—they have some way I don't know of, of feeling for my little child, and me, and understanding why their love is precious to me. If I have been quiet since, I have been more happy, William, in a hundred ways. Not least happy, dear, in this—that even when my little child was born and dead but a few days and I was weak and sorrowful, and could not help grieving a little, the thought arose, that if I tried to lead a good life, I should meet in Heaven a bright creature, who would call me, Mother!'

Redlaw fell upon his knees, with a loud cry.

'O Thou,' he said, 'who through the teaching of pure love, has graciously restored me to the memory which was the memory of Christ upon the cross, and of all the good who perished in His cause, receive my thanks, and bless her!'

Then, he folded her to his heart; and Milly, sobbing more than ever, cried, as she laughed, 'He is come back to himself! He likes me very much indeed, too! Oh dear, dear, dear me, here's another!'

Then, the student entered, leading by the hand a lovely girl, who was afraid to come. And Redlaw so changed towards him, seeing in him and his youthful choice, the softened shadow of that chastening passage in his own life, to which, as to a shady tree, the dove so long imprisoned in his solitary ark might fly for rest and company, fell upon his neck, entreating them to be his children.

Then, as Christmas is a time in which, of all times in the year, the memory of every remediable sorrow, wrong, and trouble in the world around us, should be active with us, not less than our own experiences, for all good, he laid his hand upon the boy, and, silently calling Him to witness who laid His hand on children in old time, rebuking, in the majesty of His prophetic knowledge, those who kept them from Him,* vowed to protect him, teach him, and reclaim him.

Then, he gave his right hand cheerily to Philip, and said that they would that day hold a Christmas dinner in what used to be, before the ten poor gentlemen commuted, their great Dinner Hall; and that they would bid to it as many of that Swidger family, who, his son had told him, were so numerous that they might join hands and make a ring round England, as could be brought together on so short a notice.

And it was that day done. There were so many Swidgers there, grown up and children, that an attempt to state them in round numbers might engender doubts, in the distrustful, of the veracity of this history. Therefore the attempt shall not be made. But there they were, by dozens and scores—and there was good news and good hope there, ready for them, of George, who had been visited again by his father and brother, and by Milly, and again left in a quiet sleep. There, present at the dinner, too, were the Tetterbys, including young Adolphus, who arrived in his prismatic comforter, in good time for the beef. Johnny and the baby were too late, of course, and came in all on one side, the one exhausted, the other in a supposed state of double-tooth; but that was customary, and not alarming.

It was sad to see the child who had no name or lineage, watching the other children as they played, not knowing how to talk with them, or sport with them, and more strange to the ways of childhood than a rough dog. It was sad, though in a different way, to see what an instinctive knowledge the youngest children there, had of his being different from all the rest, and how they made timid approaches to him with soft words, and touches, and with little presents, that he might not be unhappy. But he kept by Milly, and began to love her— that was another, as she said!—and, as they all liked her dearly, they were glad of that, and when they saw him peeping at them from behind her chair, they were pleased that he was so close to it.

All this, the Chemist, sitting with the student and his bride that was to be, and Philip, and the rest, saw.

Some people have said since, that he only thought what has been herein set down; others, that he read it in the fire, one winter night about the twilight time; others, that the Ghost was but the representation of his own gloomy thoughts, and Milly the embodiment of his better wisdom. *I* say nothing.

—Except this. That as they were assembled in the old Hall, by no other light than that of a great fire (having dined early), the shadows once more stole out of their hiding-places, and danced about the room, showing the children marvellous shapes and faces on the walls, and gradually changing what was real and familiar there, to what was wild and magical. But that there was one thing in the Hall, to which the eyes of Redlaw, and of Milly and her husband, and of the old man, and of the student, and his bride that was to be, were often turned, which the shadows did not obscure or change. Deepened in its gravity by the firelight, and gazing from the darkness of the panelled wall like life, the sedate face in the portrait, with the beard and ruff, looked down at them from under its verdant wreath of holly, as they looked up at it; and, clear and plain below, as if a voice had uttered them, were the words

Lord, Keep my Memory Green.

APPENDIX 1

'What Christmas Is, As We Grow Older'

TIME was, with most of us, when Christmas Day encircling all our limited world like a magic ring, left nothing out for us to miss or seek; bound together all our home enjoyments, affections, and hopes; grouped everything and every one around the Christmas fire; and made the little picture shining in our bright young eyes, complete.

Time came, perhaps, all too soon, when our thoughts overleaped that narrow boundary; when there was some one (very dear, we thought then, very beautiful, and absolutely perfect) wanting to the fulness of our happiness; when we were wanting too (or we thought so, which did just as well) at the Christmas hearth by which that some one sat; and when we intertwined with every wreath and garland of our life that some one's name.

That was the time for the bright visionary Christmases which have long arisen from us to show faintly, after summer rain, in the palest edges of the rainbow! That was the time for the beatified enjoyment of the things that were to be, and never were, and yet the things that were so real in our resolute hope that it would be hard to say, now, what realities achieved since, have been stronger!

What! Did that Christmas never really come when we and the priceless pearl* who was our young choice were received, after the happiest of totally impossible marriages, by the two united families previously at daggers-drawn on our account? When brothers and sisters in law who had always been rather cool to us before our relationship was effected, perfectly doted on us, and when fathers and mothers overwhelmed us with unlimited incomes? Was that Christmas dinner never really eaten, after which we arose, and generously and eloquently rendered honour to our late rival, present in the company, then and there exchanging friendship and forgiveness, and founding an attachment, not to be surpassed in Greek or Roman story,* which subsisted until death? Has that same rival long ceased to care for that same priceless pearl, and married for money, and become usurious? Above all, do we really know, now, that we should probably have been miserable if we had won and worn the pearl, and that we are better without her?

That Christmas when we had recently achieved so much fame;
when we had been carried in triumph somewhere, for doing something great and good; when we had won an honoured and ennobled
name, and arrived and were received at home in a shower of tears of
joy; is it possible that *that* Christmas has not come yet?

And is our life here, at the best, so constituted that, pausing as we
advance at such a noticeable milestone in the track as this great
birthday, we look back on the things that never were, as naturally and
full as gravely as on the things that have been and are gone, or have
been and still are? If it be so, and so it seems to be, must we come to
the conclusion that life is little better than a dream, and little worth
the loves and strivings that we crowd into it?

No! Far be such miscalled philosophy from us, dear Reader, on
Christmas Day! Nearer and closer to our hearts be the Christmas
spirit, which is the spirit of active usefulness, perseverance, cheerful
discharge of duty, kindness and forbearance! It is in the last
virtues especially, that we are, or should be, strengthened by the
unaccomplished visions of our youth; for, who shall say that they
are not our teachers to deal gently even with the impalpable nothings
of the earth!

Therefore, as we grow older, let us be more thankful that the circle
of our Christmas associations and of the lessons that they bring,
expands! Let us welcome every one of them, and summon them to
take their places by the Christmas hearth.

Welcome, old aspirations, glittering creatures of an ardent fancy,
to your shelter underneath the holly! We know you, and have not
outlived you yet. Welcome, old projects and old loves, however fleeting, to your nooks among the steadier lights that burn around us.
Welcome, all that was ever real to our hearts; and for the earnestness
that made you real, thanks to Heaven! Do we build no Christmas
castles in the clouds now? Let our thoughts, fluttering like butterflies
among these flowers of children, bear witness! Before this boy, there
stretches out a Future, brighter than we ever looked on in our old
romantic time, but bright with honour and with truth. Around this
little head on which the sunny curls lie heaped, the graces sport, as
prettily, as airily, as when there was no scythe within the reach of
Time to shear away the curls of our first-love. Upon another girl's
face near it—placider but smiling bright—a quiet and contented
little face, we see Home fairly written. Shining from the word, as

rays shine from a star, we see how, when our graves are old, other hopes than ours are young, other hearts than ours are moved; how other ways are smoothed; how other happiness blooms, ripens, and decays—no, not decays, for other homes and other bands of children, not yet in being nor for ages yet to be, arise, and bloom and ripen to the end of all!

Welcome, everything! Welcome, alike what has been, and what never was, and what we hope may be, to your shelter underneath the holly, to your places round the Christmas fire, where what is sits open-hearted! In yonder shadow, do we see obtruding furtively upon the blaze, an enemy's face? By Christmas Day we do forgive him! If the injury he has done us may admit of such companionship, let him come here and take his place. If otherwise, unhappily, let him go hence, assured that we will never injure nor accuse him.

On this day we shut out Nothing!

'Pause,' says a low voice. 'Nothing? Think!'

'On Christmas Day, we will shut out from our fireside, Nothing.'

'Not the shadow of a vast City where the withered leaves* are lying deep?' the voice replies. 'Not the shadow that darkens the whole globe? Not the shadow of the City of the Dead?'

Not even that. Of all days in the year, we will turn our faces towards that City upon Christmas Day, and from its silent hosts bring those we loved, among us. City of the Dead, in the blessed name wherein we are gathered together at this time, and in the Presence that is here among us according to the promise, we will receive, and not dismiss, the people who are dear to us!

Yes. We can look upon these children angels* that alight, so solemnly, so beautifully among the living children by the fire, and can bear to think how they departed from us. Entertaining angels unawares,* as the Patriarchs did, the playful children are unconscious of their guests; but we can see them—can see a radiant arm around one favourite neck, as if there were a tempting of that child away. Among the celestial figures there is one, a poor mis-shapen boy on earth,* of a glorious beauty now, of whom his dying mother said it grieved her much to leave him here, alone, for so many years as it was likely would elapse before he came to her—being such a little child. But he went quickly, and was laid upon her breast, and in her hand she leads him.

There was a gallant boy, who fell, far away upon a burning sand beneath a burning sun, and said, 'Tell them at home, with my last love, how much I could have wished to kiss them once, but that I died contented and had done my duty!' Or there was another, over whom they read the words, 'Therefore we commit his body to the deep,' and so consigned him to the lonely ocean and sailed on. Or there was another, who lay down to his rest in the dark shadow of great forests, and, on earth, awoke no more. O shall they not, from sand and sea and forest, be brought home at such a time?

There was a dear girl—almost a woman*—never to be one—who made a mourning Christmas in a house of joy, and went her trackless way to the silent City. Do we recollect her, worn out, faintly whispering what could not be heard, and falling into that last sleep for weariness? O look upon her now! O look upon her beauty, her serenity, her changeless youth, her happiness! The daughter of Jairus* was recalled to life, to die; but she, more blest, has heard the same voice, saying unto her, 'Arise for ever!'

We had a friend who was our friend from early days, with whom we often pictured the changes that were to come upon our lives, and merrily imagined how we would speak, and walk, and think, and talk, when we came to be old. His destined habitation in the City of the Dead received him in his prime. Shall he be shut out from our Christmas remembrance? Would his love have so excluded us? Lost friend, lost child, lost parent, sister, brother, husband, wife, we will not so discard you! You shall hold your cherished places in our Christmas hearts, and by our Christmas fires; and in the season of immortal hope, and on the birthday of immortal mercy, we will shut out Nothing!

The winter sun goes down over town and village; on the sea it makes a rosy path, as if the Sacred tread were fresh upon the water.* A few more moments, and it sinks, and night comes on, and lights begin to sparkle in the prospect. On the hill-side beyond the shapelessly-diffused town, and in the quiet keeping of the trees that gird the village-steeple, remembrances are cut in stone, planted in common flowers, growing in grass, entwined with lowly brambles around many a mound of earth. In town and village, there are doors and windows closed against the weather, there are flaming logs heaped high, there are joyful faces, there is healthy music of voices. Be all ungentleness and harm excluded from the temples of the Household Gods, but be those remembrances admitted with tender encouragement! They are of the time and all its comforting and peaceful reassurances; and of the history that reunited even upon earth the living and the dead;* and of the broad beneficence and goodness that too many men have tried to tear to narrow shreds.

APPENDIX 2

Dickens's Reading Version of *A Christmas Carol*

[DICKENS's first public reading of *A Christmas Carol* took place on 27 December 1853, and he seems to have used the same marked-up copy for the next seventeen years, making additional cuts and underlinings, or adding notes to himself ('Low', 'Cheerful Narrative', 'Mystery', 'Action', and so on) as his performance of the story developed. This 'prompt-copy' was an ordinary printed edition, the pages of which were stuck on to larger sheets of paper, in order to leave more space for revisions and short bridging sections of narrative where a large cut had been made, and were then bound into a handsome octavo volume. Given how many performances he undertook, this volume seems to have ended up being treated by Dickens more as a prop than an aide-mémoire. Even when he forgot his lines, Dickens did not necessarily look to his prompt-copy in the way that an actor who dries on stage might look to a stage manager in the wings: 'I have got to know the Carol so well', he wrote from America in 1868, 'that I can't remember it, and occasionally go dodging about in the wildest manner to pick up lost pieces.' The prompt-copy from which the following pages have been reproduced is now in the Berg Collection of the New York Public Library.]

The clerk promised that he would; and Scrooge walked out with a growl. The office was closed in a twinkling, and the clerk, with the long ends of his white comforter dangling below his waist (for he boasted no great-coat), went down a slide ~~on Corn-hill~~, at the end of a lane of boys, twenty times, in honour of its being Christmas-eve, and then ran home ~~to Camden Town~~ as hard as he could pelt, to play at blindman's-buff.

Tone to mystery

Scrooge took his melancholy dinner in his usual melancholy tavern; and having read all the news-papers, and beguiled the rest of the evening with his banker's-book, went home to bed. He lived in chambers which had once belonged to his deceased partner. They were a gloomy suite of rooms, in a lowering pile of building up a yard, where it had so little business to be, that one could scarcely help fancying it must have run there when it was a young house, playing at hide-and-seek with other houses, and have forgotten the way out again. It was old enough now, and dreary enough, for nobody lived in it but Scrooge, the other rooms being

The building

all let out as offices. The yard was so dark that
even Scrooge, who knew its every stone, was fain to
grope with his hands. The fog and frost so hung
about the black old gateway of the house, that it
seemed as if the Genius of the Weather sat in
mournful meditation on the threshold.

Now, it is a fact, that there was nothing at all
particular about the knocker on the door except that
it was very large. It is also a fact, that Scrooge
had seen it night and morning during his whole
residence in that place; also that Scrooge had as little
of what is called fancy about him as any man in
the City of London, even including—which is a bold
word—the corporation, aldermen, and livery. Let
it also be borne in mind that Scrooge had not bestowed
one thought on Marley, since his last mention of his
seven years' dead partner that afternoon. And then
let any man explain to me, if he can, how it happened
that Scrooge, having his key in the lock of the door,
saw in the knocker, without its undergoing any
intermediate process of change: not a knocker, but
Marley's face.

of this house

c 2

EXPLANATORY NOTES

In these notes I have occasionally drawn upon previous editions of the Christmas Books, in particular Michael Hearn's *Annotated Christmas Carol* (New York and London, 1976), Michael Slater's Penguin edition of the *Christmas Books* (Harmondsworth, 1971) and the earlier Oxford World's Classics *Christmas Books, including 'A Christmas Carol'* edited by Ruth Glancy (Oxford, 1988). I have also benefited from the unpublished notes compiled by T. W. Hill, Honorary Secretary of the Dickens Fellowship, 1914–19, and Honorary Treasurer, 1932–47, now in the archives of the *Dickensian*. Specific debts are indicated by the author's name in parentheses following the note. All biblical references are to the King James Bible (1611).

A CHRISTMAS CAROL

9 *'Change*: the Royal Exchange, the financial centre of London, situated between Threadneedle Street and Cornhill. The original building had burned down in 1838, and a replacement was under construction at the time *A Christmas Carol* was being written.

the wisdom of our ancestors: a phrase popular with Tory politicians and often mocked by Dickens. When he had some dummy books made for his study in Tavistock House, one series carried the title *The Wisdom of Our Ancestors*, with individual volumes labelled *Ignorance, Superstition, The Block, The Stake, The Rack, Dirt* and *Disease*. (Slater)

assign . . . legatee: legal expressions; an assign is one to whom the property and affairs of the deceased are transferred; a legatee is one who is bequeathed what remains of an estate after all debts have been paid. (Hearn)

Hamlet's Father . . . taking a stroll at night: Hamlet, I. i, in which the disappearance of the Ghost of Old Hamlet is associated with a Christmas legend: 'Some say that ever 'gainst that season comes | Wherein our Saviour's birth is celebrated, | The bird of dawning singeth all night long.' In Dickens's original manuscript, this paragraph continued with some further, equally sturdy comments on Hamlet's state of mind: 'Perhaps you think Hamlet's intellects were strong. I doubt it. If you could have such a son tomorrow, depend upon it, you would find him a poser. He would be thought a most impractical fellow to deal with, and however creditable he might be to his family, he would prove a special incumbrance in his lifetime, trust me.'

10 *dog-days*: the period 3 July to 11 August, when the dog-star Sirius rises and sets with the sun; popular belief has it that dogs can be driven mad by the summer heat.

10 *didn't know where to have him*: (slang) didn't know how to affect him.

'*came down*': (slang) gave money.

'*nuts*': (slang) a great pleasure.

11 '*Humbug!*': nonsense; originally a fraud or sham.

13 *Bedlam*: popular nickname of the Hospital of St Mary of Bethlehem, founded in the fourteenth century as an institution for the insane. In 1812 it was moved to a new building in Lambeth, which currently houses the Imperial War Museum.

14 *Union workhouses*: the Poor Law Amendment Act of 1834, heavily criticized by Dickens in *Oliver Twist* (1837–8), grouped parishes together into 'poor law unions' which established workhouses (popularly known as 'Unions') to house the destitute.

decrease the surplus population: a reference to the theories of the Revd Thomas Malthus (1766–1834), who argued in the second edition of his *Essay on the Principles of Population* (1803) that anyone who could not be supported by his parents, and whose labour was not wanted by society, 'has no claim of *right* to the smallest portion of food, and, in fact, has no business to be where he is. At nature's mighty feast there is no cover for him. She tells him to be gone . . .'

flaring links: torches made of cloth dipped in pitch or tar; nineteenth-century travellers could hire a 'link-boy' or 'link' to light their way along the streets.

15 *Saint Dunstan . . . lusty purpose*: St Dunstan (924–88), patron saint of armourers, blacksmiths, goldsmiths, locksmiths, and musicians. In his *Child's History of England* (1851–3), Dickens recounts the legend that Dunstan was once at work in his forge when the devil looked in through the window and tried to tempt him to a life of pleasure, 'whereupon, having his pincers in the fire, red hot, he seized the devil by the nose and put him to such pain, that his bellowings were heard for miles and miles . . .'

'*God bless you . . . dismay!*': a revision of the traditional Christmas carol, printed in William Sandys's *Christmas Carols, Ancient and Modern* (1833), which begins 'God rest you merry, gentlemen, | Let nothing you dismay.'

16 *next morning*: 26 December, known in the UK as Boxing Day from the tradition of giving presents of money ('Christmas boxes') to servants and tradesmen, was an ordinary working day until an Act of Parliament turned it into a Bank Holiday in 1871. (Slater)

Cornhill: a street in London's banking district, between two and three miles from Camden Town, where many City clerks and their families lived.

blindman's-buff: a traditional game in which one player is blindfolded and is playfully pushed about while he tries to catch and identify one or more of the others; it is played by Mr Pickwick at Dingly Dell in chapter 28 of *The Pickwick Papers* (1837).

corporation, aldermen, and livery: the Corporation is the governing body of the City of London, the senior members of which are called Alderman; Liverymen, who had the power to elect the City of London's Mayor and local government officials, were members of one of the ancient trade guilds, deriving their name from the distinctive dress (livery) worn by their members.

17 *Marley's face*: an echo of the transformation scene in E. T. A. Hoffmann's story 'The Golden Pot' (1814), translated by Carlyle in 1827. Dickens had earlier written about 'the physiognomy of street-door knockers' in *Sketches by Boz* (1839).

   a bad young Act of Parliament: a reference to Daniel O'Connell, the Irish lawyer and MP nicknamed 'the Liberator', who is said to have boasted that he could drive a coach drawn by six horses through a loosely worded Act.

   splinter-bar: a cross-bar in a carriage or coach to which the traces are attached.

18 *dip*: a candle, made by dipping a wick several times in melted tallow.

   the ancient Prophet's rod: a reference to the story of Aaron's rod (Exodus 7: 12) which was turned into a serpent and swallowed the serpents conjured up by Pharaoh's magicians.

19 *Marley had no bowels*: a pun on the literal sense of bowels, meaning 'entrails' or 'innards', and its metaphorical sense of 'pity' or 'compassion', drawing on 1 John 3: 17: 'But whoso hath this world's good, and seeth his brother have need, and shutteth up his bowels of compassion from him, how dwelleth the love of God in him?' (Hearn)

21 *'to a shade'*: to a degree, punning on 'shade' as a ghost.

22 *the bandage round its head*: during the nineteenth century bandages were often wrapped around the chin and head of the dead, in order to keep the mouth closed and prevent it from producing an unseemly post-mortem leer. (Hearn)

23 *Ward*: a night watchman; the 'wards' were the 26 parishes of London.

24 *when the bell tolls One*: another echo of *Hamlet*, I. i.

26 *Invisible World*: the realm of departed spirits, and a phrase often used in the nineteenth century to describe anything thought to lurk beyond the human senses or powers of reason. Dickens's lifelong ambivalence is discussed in Harry Stone, *Dickens and the Invisible World: Fairy Tales, Fantasy and Novel-Making* (Bloomington, Ind.: Indiana University Press, 1979).

27 *repeater*: a watch or clock able to strike the hour and quarter hour when a button is pressed.

   a mere United States' security: during the 1830s, individual States borrowed heavily from foreign investors to finance large public projects such as the building of railways and canals, and the financial crisis of

1837 left many of them unable to repay their debts; the schemes quickly became a byword for something worthless or fraudulent.

28 *now a thing with one arm . . . melted away*: an echo of Ariel in *The Tempest* (I. ii. 196–201).

29 *The voice was soft and gentle. Singularly low*: an echo of Lear's description of his dead daughter Cordelia: 'Her voice was ever soft, | Gentle and low' (*King Lear*, V. iii. 271–2).

'bonneted': to 'bonnet' someone is to pull their hat down over their eyes. In *Sketches by Boz* (1836–7), Dickens describes how two young wags in a coffee-house 'varied their amusement by "bonneting" the proprietor', while in chapter 44 of *The Pickwick Papers* (1837) Sam Weller mistakenly 'bonnets' his own father.

30 *his heart leap up*: an allusion to one of Dickens's favourite poems, Wordsworth's 'My heart leaps up', which ends 'The Child is father of the Man; | And I could wish my days to be | Bound each to each by natural piety.'

31 *plain deal forms*: long benches made from unvarnished deal wood or pine.

Not a latent echo . . . to his tears: the situation and phrasing echo Tennyson's poem 'Mariana' (1830).

Ali Baba: the hero of 'Ali Baba and the Forty Thieves' from *The Arabian Nights*, a collection of popular tales that first reached England via the French translation of Antoine Galland (1704–8) and was often reprinted during the eighteenth and nineteenth centuries. Dickens first read it as a child, possibly in Jonathan Scott's six-volume edition of 1811, and it remained one of his favourite books; in the essay 'A Christmas Tree' (1850) he recalls the magical effect of his childhood reading: 'Oh, now all common things become uncommon and enchanted to me! All lamps are wonderful; all rings are talismans. Common flower-pots are full of treasure, with a little earth scattered on the top; trees are for Ali Baba to hide in . . .'

Valentine . . . and his wild brother, Orson: the heroes of a fifteenth-century French romance, first translated into English in the early sixteenth century as *The History of two Valyannte Brethren, Valentyne and Orson*, which became a popular children's story. After the twin brothers are separated at birth, Valentine is raised as a knight in the king's court, while Orson is carried off by a bear and becomes a wild man of the woods. (Glancy)

32 *the Princess*: in the *Arabian Nights* story 'Nur-ed-Din and his Son and Shems-ed-Din and his Daughter', the daughter is forced to marry the Sultan's groom, who is an ugly hunchback. Thanks to the help of a genie and a fairy, at the wedding Nur-ed-Din's son replaces the Groom, who is held upside-down all night. At dawn the son is carried away by the fairy and left at the gates of Damascus 'in his shirt and drawers'.

There goes Friday . . . the little creek: a reference to Daniel Defoe's *Robinson*

Crusoe (1719), another favourite story of Dickens's childhood, in which Crusoe first sees Man Friday swimming across the creek to escape from cannibals. Dickens later recalled the same scene in his essay 'Nurse's Stories' (1860): 'No face is ever reflected in the waters of the little creek which Friday swam across when pursued by his two brother cannibals with sharpened stomachs.'

34 *Welsh wig*: a woollen cap.

organ of benevolence: according to the Victorian pseudo-science of phrenology, personal qualities were determined by the shape of the skull, which phrenologists divided up into forty sections or 'organs', each of which was supposed to govern one particular mental or moral faculty. The 'organ of benevolence' was located near the top of the forehead. Dickens's references to phrenology are usually sceptical: in *Great Expectations* (1860–1), Magwitch describes how, as a homeless child thrown into prison, interfering adults 'measured my head, some on 'em,—they had better a measured my stomach'. Dickens himself had been given a phrenological examination on 5 February 1842, in Worcester, Massachusetts, by the leading American practitioner Lorenzo N. Fowler, who reported that Dickens possessed a small organ of veneration, indicating that he 'is not serious nor respectful', but that his largest organ was benevolence, suggesting that he 'feels lively sympathy for distress; does good to all.' (Hearn)

35 *porter*: a dark brown beer, especially popular with porters and other manual workers.

negus: wine (usually port or sherry) mixed with hot water, sweetened with sugar, and sometimes flavoured with lemon and spices.

36 *'Sir Roger de Coverley'*: an English country-dance named after a character in Addison's *Spectator* (1711–14). In 'Where We Stopped Growing' (1853), Dickens explained that adults who remain young in spirit 'have not outgrown Sir Roger de Coverley'; according to R. H. Horne in *A New Spirit of the Age* (1844), Dickens himself was 'very much given to dancing Sir Roger de Coverley'.

'cut': in dancing, to jump into the air while rapidly criss-crossing the feet.

37 *A golden one*: according to Exodus 32: 1–35, Aaron constructed a golden idol in the shape of a calf, in defiance of holy law, while Moses was on Mount Sinai.

39 *the celebrated herd in the poem*: an allusion to Wordsworth's poem 'Written in March': 'The cattle are grazing, | Their heads never raising; | There are forty feeding like one!'

42 *free-and-easy sort*: sporting types; a 'free-and-easy' was a place that catered for young men about town who enjoyed smoking, drinking, singing, and gambling.

acquainted with a move or two . . . equal to the time-of-day: (slang) on the ball, streetwise.

42 *pitch-and-toss*: a street gambling game in which coins are tossed at a target, and the player whose coin lands nearest is allowed to throw all the remaining coins up in the air and claim those that land face up.

43 *spontaneous combustion*: a much disputed Victorian medical theory that corrupt human bodies could become so unstable that they exploded. Dickens was attacked by a number of critics, particularly George Henry Lewes, for being ghoulishly unscientific after making Krook die of spontaneous combustion in *Bleak House*.

twelfth-cakes: large decorated cakes, traditionally eaten on Twelfth Night (6 January) to mark the end of Christmas festivities.

46 *Norfolk Biffins*: red cooking apples.

gold and silver fish: live carp in glass bowls were commonly available from grocers and street-sellers in the nineteenth century; according to Henry Mayhew's *London Labour and the London Poor* (1851) there were over seventy sellers in London alone. (Hearn)

47 *for Christmas daws to peck at*: 'for people to find fault with', an echo of Iago's speech in *Othello*, I. i ('I will wear my heart upon my sleeve | For daws to peck at').

carrying their dinners to the bakers' shops: bakers were forbidden by law to bake bread on Sundays or Christmas Day, but were allowed to cook food (mostly joints of meat and pies) brought to them, often by those who were too poor to afford proper cooking facilities of their own.

48 *close these places on the Seventh Day*: between 1832 and 1837 Sir Andrew Agnew (1793–1849) repeatedly attempted to introduce a Sunday Observance Bill in the House of Commons, which would have closed the bakeries and severely limited opportunities for the poor to enjoy themselves on their day off. Dickens had signalled his opposition to Agnew in an 1836 pamphlet *Sunday Under Three Heads. As It is; As Sabbath Bills would make it; As it might be made*.

'Bob': a shilling.

49 *twice-turned gown*: a dress that has been altered twice, either to bring it in line with fashion or to achieve extra wear from the material.

50 *blood horse*: a thoroughbred racehorse.

copper: a large metal container, originally made of copper but now more often iron, mainly used for washing laundry.

who made lame beggars walk, and blind men see: a reference to the miracles of healing performed by Christ, as related in John 5: 1–10 and Mark 8: 22–6.

51 *half-a-quartern*: 1¼ fluid ounces, or about 35 ml.

53 *good long rest*: milliners' apprentices were notoriously overworked and underpaid; in *Sketches by Boz* (1839), Dickens reported that they were among 'the hardest worked, the worst paid, and too often, the worst used class of the community'. (Hearn)

54 *burial-place of giants*: Cornwall is home to many legends involving giants, including 'Jack the Giant Killer', and was visited by Dickens in 1842 in order to investigate the appalling conditions of child workers in the tin mines.

55 *grog*: rum and water, traditionally drunk by sailors, and named after the grogram coat of Admiral Vernon, who in 1740 ordered that the sailors' ration of rum should be watered down. (Glancy)

57 *tucker*: a detachable frilly collar worn over the breast.

58 *Glee or Catch*: a glee is an unaccompanied song for three or more voices; a catch is a round for several voices who 'catch' one another's words as they overlap in performance.

59 *loved her love to admiration with all the letters of the alphabet*: a parlour game in which each player has to compose a series of sentences based on letters of the alphabet. In *Our Mutual Friend* (1864–5) the dolls' dressmaker Jenny Wren plays an idiosyncratic version of the game when giving some clues about her profession: 'I love my love with a B because she's Beautiful; I hate my love with a B because she is Brazen; I took her to the sign of the Blue Boar, and I treated her with Bonnets; her name's Bouncer, and she lives in Bedlam.'

How, When, and Where: a parlour game in which players take it in turn to ask 'How do you like it?', 'When do you like it?', 'Where do you like it?'

best Whitechapel: the working-class east London suburb of Whitechapel was known for the quality of its metalwork, including the manufacture of needles; 'Not a wery nice neighbourhood', according to Sam Weller in chapter 22 of *The Pickwick Papers* (1837).

61 *little brief authority*: alluding to *Measure for Measure*, II. ii. 119–24: '. . . man, proud man! | Dress'd in a little brief authority | . . . Plays such fantastic tricks before high heaven | As makes the angels weep.'

65 *black gloves*: these were routinely provided for mourners at middle-class funerals.

Old Scratch: a nickname for the Devil, from the Old Norse *skratta*, a goblin.

66 *beetling*: overhanging.

67 *pick holes in each other's coats*: (slang) quarrel with each other.

68 *screw*: (slang) a miser or skinflint.

70 *withdraw the veil*: from Plato onwards the veil has been used to suggest what is hidden or inaccessible to human understanding, in particular what lies beyond the barrier of death. It was especially common in the nineteenth century, as religious and scientific speculation continued to press against the limits of human knowledge: Tennyson's *In Memoriam* (1850) asks 'What hope of answer, or redress?— | Behind the veil, behind the veil', while George Eliot's *The Lifted Veil* (1859) features a character who confesses a secret that seemed to have died with her, after she is brought back to life with a blood transfusion.

70 *this is thy dominion!*: an echo of biblical phrasing, e.g. Romans 6: 9: 'Knowing that Christ being raised from the dead dieth no more; death hath no more dominion over him.'

72 *'And he took a child . . . in the midst of them'*: Matthew 18: 2, one of Dickens's favourite passages of the Bible, which he frequently set in opposition to the sort of 'gloomy theology' characterized by the Murdstones in chapter 48 of *David Copperfield*, which 'made all children out to be a nest of vipers (though there *was* a child once set in the midst of the Disciples)'.

75 *choked up with too much burying*: a common nineteenth-century complaint, dramatized by Dickens in *Bleak House* (1852–3), in which the crossing-sweeper Jo recalls that Nemo's corpse was buried in the graveyard 'wery nigh the top. They was obliged to stamp upon it to git it in.'

78 *Laocoön*: the Trojan priest who tried to persuade his fellow citizens not to bring the fatal wooden horse into their city. In punishment the goddess Athena sent two huge sea serpents to crush Laocoön and his sons to death. The scene is vividly depicted in a piece of Roman sculpture displayed in the Vatican, which became central to discussions of how successfully art could represent human emotions following the publication of G. E. Lessing's influential treatise *Laokoon* (1766).

79 *'Walk-ER!'*: 'Walker' is nineteenth-century Cockney slang roughly equivalent to 'Come off it!' or 'Get away!'; it is a favourite exclamation of Sam Weller's father in *The Pickwick Papers* (1837).

   Joe Miller: an eighteenth-century actor famous for his comic quips; the collection *Joe Miller's Jests* was first published in 1739, and was frequently revised and reprinted during Dickens's lifetime.

83 *smoking bishop*: a hot drink made with red wine, oranges, sugar, and spices, so called because it is said to be the same colour as a bishop's cassock.

   Total Abstinence Principle: a joking reference to temperance campaigners, many of them associated with the Methodist movement, who encouraged the public to 'take the pledge' by swearing to avoid all alcoholic drinks.

THE CHIMES

88 *an old church*: Dickens's model seems to have been St Dunstan-in-the-West, Fleet Street, which is the church depicted in Doyle and Stanfield's illustration for the first edition. In fact St Dunstan's in 1844 was not an old church: the medieval building (mentioned in *Barnaby Rudge*) had been pulled down in 1830, to be replaced by a new church designed by John Shaw. (Hill)

   Henry the Eighth had melted down their mugs: as part of his break with the Catholic Church, Henry VIII dissolved the English monasteries and redistributed much of their property to his own nobles.

89 *ticket-porter*: a London street-porter who usually wore a white apron and

displayed his licence like a badge. By 1861 Henry Mayhew's *London Labour and the London Poor* was describing them as a dying breed.

90 *teetotums*: a teetotum is a small top spun around with the fingers, applied figuratively to things that are unsteady or in a whirl: Thackeray's *Roundabout Papers* (1860) asks 'Who knows how long that dear teetotum happiness can be made to spin without toppling over?'

tap: a room in a tavern in which liquors are kept on tap.

95 *laughing gas*: nitrous oxide, whose nickname was coined to describe the exhilarating effects caused when it is inhaled. Discovered in 1793 by the English scientist Joseph Priestley, in the 1840s it was experimented with as an alternative anaesthetic to ether. Some of Dickens's readers may have witnessed its effects in scientific demonstrations, but many more would have experienced them at first hand through the travelling medicine shows and carnivals which encouraged the public to pay a small price to inhale a minute's worth of the gas.

Polonies: pork sausages.

Pettitoes: pigs' trotters.

chitterlings: pigs' intestines, sometimes filled with minced meat to make a kind of sausage.

100 *pepper-and-salt*: cloth made of interwoven dark and light threads, giving a flecked or speckled appearance.

Alderman Cute: a caricature of Sir Peter Laurie (1778–1861), a Middlesex magistrate noted for his bluff humour and common sense, and for his ability to talk to offenders in language they could understand.

bills of mortality: the 109 parishes in and around London, named after the regular recording of deaths in this area carried out by the London Company of Parish Clerks from the late sixteenth century onwards. (Slater)

101 *he's a robber*: a riposte to the review of *A Christmas Carol* in the *Westminster Review* (June 1844), the journal most closely associated with the political economists Dickens despised, which had concluded that 'Who went without turkey and punch in order that Bob Cratchit might get them—for, unless there were turkeys and punch in surplus, some one must go without—is a disagreeable reflection kept wholly out of sight.'

the good old times!: Dickens frequently attacked those who were content to ruminate nostalgically on the past while ignoring its cruelty and misery; in *American Notes* (1842), for example, he scoffed at 'those good old customs of the good old times which made England, even so recently as in the reign of the Third King George, in respect of her criminal code and prison regulations, one of the most bloody-minded and barbarous countries on the earth.' This reference to 'the good old times' is all that remains of an earlier draft of *The Chimes*, cut on the advice of John Forster, in which Dickens set out to satirize the 'Young England' movement: a group of aristocratic Tory MPs led by Benjamin Disraeli who favoured a return to a feudal system of government, in which 'Each knew his place: king, peasant, peer, or priest, | The greatest owned connexion with the least; | From rank to rank the generous feeling ran, | And linked society as man to man' (Lord John Manners, *England's Trust*, 1841).

101 *Strutt's Costumes*: *Strutt's Costumes. A Complete View of the Dress and Habits of the People of England* (1796–9) by the antiquarian Joseph Strutt; a new edition had come out in 1842. Maclise's 1842 painting of Dickens's children shows one of them studying this work. (Slater)

102 *'chaff'*: (slang) to banter or tease.

103 *Methuselah*: according to Genesis 5: 27 Methuselah lived to the age of 969.

104 *We reduced it to a mathematical certainty long ago!*: a reference to nineteenth-century political economists, many of them influenced by Thomas Malthus (see note on *A Christmas Carol*, p. 14), who seemed to reduce all of human life to a matter of statistics by arguing that the poor should not marry until they could afford to support a family.

105 *the church-service*: the Litany in the Book of Common Prayer refers to 'all sick persons and young children', described by Dickens as 'that beautiful passage' in chapter 6 of *American Notes* (1842).

Put all suicide Down: in 1841 Laurie had begun a campaign to put a stop to the crime of attempted suicide, which was especially prevalent among the poor, by sentencing offenders to prison and hard labour. In 1844 he committed a woman to trial for attempting to poison herself, observing that 'He had put an end to persons attempting to drown themselves; he would now try the same cure for attempted poisoning.' (Slater)

108 *His place was the ticket*: a reference to the phrase 'That's the ticket', meaning what is wanted or expected; this was a new piece of slang in 1844: the *OED*'s first recorded use is from 1838.

110 *the Poor Man's Friend*: on 6 April 1844 *Punch* published an article by Douglas Jerrold which described Lord Brougham, the Whig ex-Chancellor, as 'the poor man's friend'. It was intended ironically: Brougham had come under attack for presenting himself as a champion of working people, while revealing in his speeches to the Lords on the 1844 Factory Bill that his real attitude towards the poor was at best insensitive and at worst indifferent. (Slater)

112 *put down*: punning on two senses of the phrase: to suppress and to put to death.

pinking and eyelet-holing: decorating cloth by cutting scalloped edges or small holes.

music on the new system: the system of notation originally devised by Sarah Glover (1785–1867) and developed by John Curwen in 1843, which used sol-fa syllables and their initial letters for the notes of the scale, and divided the bar by colons, dots, and inverted commas. (Glancy)

113 *Vagabond*: an allusion to the Vagrancy Act of 1824, which gave Justices of the Peace the power to arrest and imprison 'Vagabonds and Incorrigible Rogues'.

118 *the Union*: the workhouse. See note on *A Christmas Carol*, p. 14.

121 *Solomon*: the famously wise and just King of Israel. 1 Kings 3: 16–28 tells the story of how he adjudicated between the rival claims of two women to be the mother of the same child.

 My wits are wool-gathering: indulging in wandering thoughts or idle fancies, so called from the practice of gathering up tufts of wool left by sheep on bushes and fences.

122 *a woman who had laid her desperate hands . . . her young child*: alluding to the notorious case of Mary Furley, who was sentenced to death for infanticide on 16 April 1844 after she had tried to drown herself and her young child rather than return to the workhouse where the child had been ill-treated. Following a public outcry in which Dickens played a leading role (his 'Threatening Letter to Thomas Hood from an Ancient Gentleman' was published in *Hood's Magazine*, May 1844), the sentence was commuted to seven years' transportation. (Slater)

125 *Black are the brooding clouds . . . can tell*: Edward Bulwer-Lytton noted that this passage unconsciously borrowed the 'style and manner of expression' from his novel *Zanoni* (1842).

133 *skittles—with his tenants!*: one idea put forward by the 'Young England' movement (see note on p. 101) was that landowners could reinforce paternalistic ties by playing games with their tenants.

 bluff King Hal: Henry VIII, the 'horrors' of whose reign are described by Dickens in *A Child's History of England*, chapter 28: 'We now come to King Henry the Eighth, whom it has been too much the fashion to call "Bluff King Hal" and "Burly King Harry" and other fine names; but whom I shall take the liberty of calling, plainly, one of the most detestable villains that ever drew breath.'

135 *Daniel*: one of the apocryphal additions to the Bible tells the story of how the clever young lawyer Daniel saved Susannah from a false charge of adultery.

136 *You've drunk the Labourer*: 'the health of the labourer' was a traditional toast that landowners and farmers made to their workers at agricultural dinners; a number of Victorian commentators noted the irony of a custom that involved raising a glass to men who were paid only starvation wages.

138 *'Whither thou goest . . . Nor thy God my God!'*: a reversal of the promise made in Ruth 1: 16: 'And Ruth said . . . whither thou goest, I will go; and whence thou lodgest, I will lodge: thy people shall be my people, and thy God my God.'

143 *He suffered her to sit beside His feet, and dry them with her hair*: a reference to Mary Magdalene, the penitent prostitute forgiven by Christ (Luke 7: 38).

146 *Sally Lunns*: a kind of teacake, eaten hot with butter, supposedly named after the woman who invented the recipe in Bath at the end of the eighteenth century.

146 *the cream and marrow*: an alternative to 'pith and marrow', meaning the central or essential part of something.

150 *Like Fighting Cocks*: 'to live like fighting cocks' is a slang phrase meaning to live in luxury; fighting cocks were well fed in order to increase their size and strength.

151 *runaway carriage-doubles*: a popular pastime amongst London children was to knock twice upon the door of a grand house and then run away; the double-knock may have been intended to mimic a signal used to indicate the arrival of visitors in a carriage. (Slater)

153 *There'll be a Fire to-night*: the lighting of hayricks by farm labourers, driven to arson by low wages and poor living conditions, was a particular concern at the time of writing; the *Annual Register* (1844) noted that 102 cases had been reported in 1843, a considerable rise on the average figure of 49 in 1838–42. (Slater)

154 *preached upon a Mount*: the Sermon on the Mount, described in Matthew 5–7.

wearied and lay down to die: probably alluding to a passage in Carlyle's recently published *Past and Present* (1843), which describes how an Irish widow in Edinburgh was refused help by one charity after another 'till she had exhausted them all; till her strength and heart failed her: she sank down in typhus-fever; died . . .' (Slater)

159 *marrow-bones and cleavers*: refers to the custom at popular festivities of using a butcher's chopper to beat out a clinking rhythm on large bones, a cheap alternative to more sophisticated forms of music.

flip: a hot drink made with spirits, beer, and sugar, sometimes with the addition of an egg.

161 *Dorsetshire*: changed from Hertfordshire in the proofs to reflect the worsening reputation of Dorset as a county where the rural poor lived and worked in especially abject conditions. On 28 April 1844, *Lloyd's Weekly London Newspaper* printed a letter signed 'A Dorsetshire Land-lord' which claimed that unless these conditions were improved, they would 'produce a revolution not less frightful than that which France has been subjected to'. (Slater)

THE CRICKET ON THE HEARTH

164 *Lord Jeffrey*: Francis Jeffrey (1773–1850), a founder and editor of the *Edinburgh Review*, godfather to Dickens's third son (Francis Jeffrey Dickens), and the novelist's self-designated 'Critic Laureate'. He had been warmly appreciative of Dickens's sympathetic treatment of the poor in *The Chimes*, and later praised *The Battle of Life* for its 'generous sentiments'.

165 *convulsive little Haymaker*: probably a figure of Father Time carrying his scythe, a popular ornament on the top of Dutch clocks. (Hill)

pattens: wooden shoes. The reference to Euclid (below) indicates that Mrs Peerybingle's are made with iron patten rings, designed to raise the soles off the ground.

the first proposition in Euclid: a geometrical exercise designed to show the construction of an equilateral triangle on a finite straight line; the points of the triangle are situated on two intersecting circles, which is the pattern made by the iron rings on Dot's pattens.

166 *the Royal George*: an English warship that sank at Spithead in 1782; efforts to raise her had repeatedly failed.

169 *dot and carry*: usually 'dot and carry one', an expression used in elementary arithmetic, meaning to set down the units and carry over the tens to the next column of figures. (Glancy)

171 *'How doth the little'*: from 'Against Idleness and Mischief', the twentieth of Isaac Watts's *Divine and Moral Songs for Children* (1715): 'How doth the little busy bee | Improve each shining hour | And gather honey all the day | From every opening flower.' Lewis Carroll parodies the verse as 'How doth the little crocodile' in *Alice's Adventures in Wonderland* (1865).

172 *the luckiest thing in all the world!*: a singing cricket in the house is considered good luck in a number of cultures; traditionally, crickets have even been kept in small cages to prevent luck from escaping the house.

175 *The Old Gentleman*: (slang) the Devil.

176 *the other six*: an allusion to the legend of the Seven Sleepers of Ephesus. As recounted in chapter 33 of Gibbon's *The History of the Decline and Fall of the Roman Empire* (1776–88), seven Christian youths, who had been imprisoned in a cave by the Roman emperor Decius, fell into a miraculous sleep until they were accidentally discovered 187 years later. (Slater)

house lamb: a lamb raised by hand, either as a pet or to provide especially succulent flesh. Dickens enjoyed blurring the distinction: chapter 15 of *The Uncommercial Traveller* recalls his nurse's stories of Captain Murderer, whose cannibal appetites meant that 'On his marriage morning, he always caused both sides of the way to church to be planted with curious flowers; and when his bride said, "Dear Captain Murderer, I never saw flowers like these before: what are they called?" he answered, "They are called Garnish for house-lamb," and laughed at his ferocious practical joke in a horrid manner, disquieting the minds of the noble bridal company, with a very sharp show of teeth.'

178 *Philosopher's stone*: a mythical substance which medieval and Renaissance alchemists searched for in the hope that it would transmute ordinary substances into gold.

179 *What's the damage?*: how much do I owe you?

180 *Pony-nightmare*: an oddly tautologous way of describing a nightmare, which originally referred to a feeling of being 'hag-ridden' while asleep by a female spirit or monster. The expression does not appear in *OED*.

190 *such arbitrary marks as satin, cotton-print, and bits of rag*: Dickens often draws attention to the absurdity of distinguishing different classes by their clothing, probably influenced by Carlyle's satirical 'Clothes Philosophy' in *Sartor Resartus* (1838). (Slater)

192 *Bacchanalian song*: a drinking song, after Bacchus, the Roman god of wine.

193 *Bedlam*: see note to *A Christmas Carol*, p. 13.

194 *Pic-Nic*: used here in its original sense to mean 'A fashionable social entertainment in which each person present contributed a share of the provisions' (*OED* 1a).

marrow-bones, cleavers: see note to *The Chimes*, p. 159.

197 *spencer*: a kind of close-fitting jacket or bodice.

nankeen raised-pie: a kind of hat made from buff-coloured cloth (a raised pie is one that does not require the support of a dish).

Turnpike Trust: turnpikes were public highways on which tolls were collected, and were managed by trustees or commissioners.

200 *Dame-Schools*: elementary schools for children, mostly run by women, and often satirized for the poor quality of their teaching. Dickens offers a comic portrait of one such school in chapter 7 of *Great Expectations* (1860–1).

201 *Fairy-rings*: 'A circular band of grass differing in colour from the grass around it, a phenomenon supposed in popular belief to be produced by fairies when dancing; really caused by the growth of certain fungi' (*OED*).

202 *chip*: the main sense is that she is small and thin, with the added implication perhaps that she is also dry and dull (*OED*, 'chip' 5).

203 *such small deer*: *King Lear*, III. iv. 123–4: 'But mice and rats and such small deer | Have been Tom's food for seven long year.'

let us be genteel, or die!: Dickens frequently pokes fun at people who dress to impress, with no fewer than nineteen allusions to the wearing of gloves as a mark of gentility. (Hill)

205 *Indigo Trade*: until the development of a synthetic substitute, all blue textiles (including the serge uniforms worn by the British police force) were dyed with natural indigo, which was the subject of a fiercely competitive trade in India and other countries.

206 *bait*: a snack or light refreshment taken on a journey.

dreadnought coat: a thick coat designed to withstand severe weather, also known as a 'fearnought'.

209 *Welsh Giant*: in the fairy-tale 'Jack the Giant Killer', Jack tricks the giant by stuffing his breakfast into a leather bag hidden in his shirt, and then slitting it open. The giant, wanting to copy this trick, slits open his own stomach and falls down dead. The story makes several reappearances in Dickens's fiction, including once as a circus routine in *Hard Times* (1854), admiringly described by the lisping Mr Sleary: 'That'h Jack the Giant Killer—piethe of comic infant bithnith.'

Samson: the legendary strongman and last of the Judges of Israel; his exploits are described in Judges 13–16.

226 *Saint Vitus*: Saint Vitus's Dance, originally a name given to the dancing madness (*choreomania*) which spread through Europe in the fifteenth century, was later extended to refer to a medical disorder, usually occurring in early life, characterized by convulsions and involuntary muscular contractions. It derives from the old German tradition of dancing in front of a statue of St Vitus to ensure good health.

238 *the song about the Sparkling Bowl*: there are several popular songs in this vein, such as 'The Flowing Bowl' ('Fill the bowl with sparkling nectar'); a more literary example Dickens may have had in his mind's ear is Thomas Gray's 'The Bard': 'Fill high the sparkling bowl, | The rich repast prepare'. Chapter 7 of *The Pickwick Papers* (1836–7) records 'a song (supposed to have been sung by Mr. Jingle), in which the words "bowl" "sparkling" "ruby" "bright" and "wine" are frequently repeated at short intervals'.

THE BATTLE OF LIFE

246 *MY ENGLISH FRIENDS IN SWITZERLAND*: Dickens lived in Lausanne between June and November 1846, and although he was depressed by the 'mighty dull little town' and the spectacle of its native inhabitants (many of whom were deformed due to iodine deficiencies), he forged a strong friendship there with the Hon. Richard Watson (1800–52) and his wife Lavinia (1816–88) which lasted for the rest of his life.

248 *Harvest Home*: the occasion or time of bringing home the last of the harvest.

corslet: a piece of defensive armour covering the body.

249 *opera-dancers*: ballet had been an integral part of opera performance since its introduction by Jean-Baptiste Lully during the reign of Louis XIV (1638–1715).

252 *Great character of mother ... to the angels*: a Victorian commonplace, given memorable expression in Samuel Smiles's account of one mother, as reported by her daughter, in his best-selling *Self-Help* (1859): 'When she entered the room it had the effect of immediately raising the tone of the conversation, and as if purifying the moral atmosphere—all seeming to breathe more freely, and stand more erectly.'

253 *Philosopher's stone*: see note to *The Cricket on the Hearth*, p. 178.

255 *blue bag*: the bag used by junior barristers to carry legal papers is traditionally blue.

the French wit: Rabelais, whose dying words were reported to have been 'Tirez le rideau: la farce est jouée.'

256 *winter-pippin*: an apple.

the sister Fates ... the Graces ... the three weird prophets: in Greek mythology, the Fates are three old women who spin the threads of life and decide when each person's thread should be cut. The Graces are Zeus' daughters, usually depicted as three intertwined bodies, symbolizing beauty, nobility, and purity. The weird prophets are the three witches in Shakespeare's *Macbeth*.

257 *Grand Carver*: an especially skilful carver of meat, also known as a 'First Carver'.

261 *Young England*: see note to *The Chimes*, p. 101.

man Miles to the Doctor's Friar Bacon: in Robert Greene's comic play *Friar Bacon, and Friar Bungay* (1594), the two friars make a brass head and enlist the Devil's help to make it talk. They are told that they will only have one chance to hear it speak, but their servant Miles fails to wake them when the moment arrives and the head smashes on the floor.

263 *Lord High Chancellor*: as the highest legal authority in the land, he had official jurisdiction over lunatics.

pocket library: small editions of popular books, designed to be slipped into a pocket, were often published in the nineteenth century; in 1889 Routledge's Pocket Library included a 14 cm-high edition of *The Battle of Life*.

pearl of great price: Matthew 13: 46 compares the kingdom of heaven to a merchant 'Who, when he found one pearl of great price, went and sold all that he had, and bought it.'

a lucky penny, a cramp bone: a penny with a hole in it was thought to bring good luck; the kneecap of a sheep was thought to be a charm against cramp. In *Martin Chuzzlewit* (1842–4), Mrs Gamp explains how Mrs Harris carries a tin containing 'two cramp-bones, a bit o' ginger, and a grater like a blessed infant's shoe'.

264 *done brown*: (slang) 'cheated' or 'got the better of'.

the golden rule: traditionally, 'Do as you would be done by' (from Matthew 7: 12).

a mouthful: a small quantity.

good Genius: one of two mutually opposed spirits (the other being an evil Genius) supposed to attend each person throughout his or her life, here meaning that Clemency is a powerful influence for good on Mr Britain's character and fortune.

flappers: a flapper is someone who arouses the attention or jogs the memory of another, so named after Swift's satire on absent-minded scientists in *Gulliver's Travels* (1726) each of whom employs a Flapper 'gently to strike with his Bladder the Mouth of him who is to speak, and the Right Ear of him . . . to whom the Speaker addresseth himself'.

268 *The Gazette*: one of three government publications (*The London Gazette, The Edinburgh Gazette*, and *The Dublin Gazette*) which listed bankruptcies, official appointments, military promotions, and other public notices.

269 *Blue chamber*: an allusion to the fairy-tale of Bluebeard, whose wife enters a forbidden room in his castle and there discovers the bodies of his former wives.

270 *prodigal son*: in Luke 15: 11–32 Christ tells the parable of the wastrel son whose return is celebrated by his father with a feast: 'For this my son was dead, and is alive again; he was lost, and is found.'

276 *reckoning without his host*: refusing to consider anyone else's opinions, literally adding up his bill without consulting the tavern-keeper.

277 ' *"And being in her own home . . . the Penitent"* ': written by Dickens himself, but paraphrasing a series of Victorian commonplaces about the place of the home in social and moral life.

278 *two spoons in my saucer*: according to popular superstition, two spoons accidentally placed on the same saucer indicates that a wedding will take place soon; it can also mean that the person on whose saucer they appear will marry twice, or that she will have twins.

283 *stay and mantua-maker*: a dressmaker who specializes in corsets (stays) and gowns (mantuas).

294 *poussette*: a move in country dancing in which couples join hands and spin around.

pegtop: a pear-shaped spinning top, set in action by the rapid uncoiling of a string wound around it.

310 *jack*: a machine for turning the spit when roasting meat.

311 *how often men still entertained angels, unawares*: see Hebrews 13: 2, alluding to the visit of three angels to Abraham (Genesis 18: 3). Dickens's essay 'What Christmas Is, As We Grow Older' (1851), reprinted as Appendix 1, describes how the spirits of dead children cluster around the family hearth at Christmas time: 'Entertaining angels unawares, as the Patriarchs did, the playful children are unconscious of their guests; but we can see them.'

321 *canvassing you for the county*: as a freehold landowner, Britain is now eligible to vote in the election of members to the House of Commons. (Glancy)

THE HAUNTED MAN

325 *the ballad*: according to the old ballad, Giles Scroggins dies before he can marry his sweetheart Molly Brown. His ghost then appears to her, crying 'O Molly you must go with I'; when she refuses, pointing out 'I am not dead, you fool', he replies, 'Vy, that's no rule.'

327 *Cassim Baba*: Ali Baba's brother in the *Arabian Nights*, who learns how to get into the cave of the forty thieves, but then forgets the password and is unable to escape before the thieves return.

the merchant Abudah's bedroom: a reference to 'The Talisman of Oromanes' in the popular collection of Persian stories *Tales of the Genii*, translated by 'Sir Charles Morell' [James Ridley] in 1764, in which the merchant is nightly accused of delaying his search for the talisman of Oromanes by 'a diminutive old hag' who appears shaking her crutches from a small box in his bedroom. The story was one that Dickens recalled from his childhood (see 'Nurse's Stories' in _The Uncommercial Traveller_); he refers to the same scene in chapter 5 of _Martin Chuzzlewit_ (1842–4).

328 _a straddling giant_: from the traditional English fairy-tale _Jack the Giant Killer_, where the giant Blunderbore hunts Jack with the cry 'Fee fi fo fum | I smell the blood of an Englishman. | Be he alive or be he dead, | I'll grind his bones to make my bread.'

329 _Peckham Fair_: a rowdy annual event, lasting up to three weeks, that was held in the Peckham Road until 1827, when it was abolished as a nuisance. (Hill)

Battersea: the original Battersea Bridge was a wooden structure built in 1770–1, and boats were often wrecked by colliding with one of the piers while attempting to shoot the arches. The present bridge dates from 1886–90. (Slater)

330 _Castors_: sugar, salt, or pepper shakers.

331 _stone-chaney_: hard pottery made by mixing together clay and flint ('chaney' is a dialect variant of 'china').

339 _The Christmas Waits_: a band of musicians and carol singers who go from door to door at Christmas offering seasonal music in return for small sums of money.

348 _casting his boots upon the waters_: revising Ecclesiastes 11: 1: 'Cast thy bread upon the waters: for thou shalt find it after many days.'

Moloch: in 2 Kings 23: 10, Moloch is the god of the Ammonites, who sacrificed children to him; in _Paradise Lost_, Milton depicts him as one of Satan's chief henchmen.

349 _serial pirates_: hack writers often published cheap plagiarisms of Dickens's novels ('serial' puns on his preference for serial publication and the fact that many plagiarists were repeat offenders), which he was unable to prevent due to the inadequate copyright laws; he unsuccessfully took one publisher to court for a piracy of _A Christmas Carol_ in 1844.

350 _bodiless creation_: an imaginary person, alluding to _Hamlet_, III. iv. 133–4: 'This bodiless creation ecstasy | Is very cunning in.'

poor's-rates: a local tax intended to support the workhouses and other forms of poor relief.

351 _mesmeric influence_: hypnotic powers, named after Franz Anton Mesmer (1734–1815), who launched a Europe-wide craze in the late eighteenth century, and led to mesmerism being a popular and much debated Victorian medical fad. Dickens was an enthusiastic practitioner: see Fred Kaplan, _Dickens and Mesmerism: The Hidden Springs of Fiction_ (Princeton: Princeton University Press, 1975).

352 _immense percentage of babies never attain to two years old_: Dickens gives

more details of Victorian infant mortality rates in *The Uncommercial Traveller* (1861), writing in the voice of an anxious father: 'I learn from the statistical tables that one child in five dies within the first year of its life; and one child in three, within the fifth' ('Births. Mrs Meek, of a Son').

353 *comforter*: a long woollen scarf.

356 *like the Eastern rose in respect of the nightingale*: probably an allusion to 'The Veiled Prophet of Khorassan', the first tale in Thomas Moore's *Lalla Rookh* (1817): 'There's a bower of roses by Bendemeer's stream | And the nightingales sing round it all the day long; | In the time of my childhood 'twas like a sweet dream | To sit in the roses and hear the bird's song.' (Hill)

362 *they are not coffins, but purses*: 'Coffins out of the fire are hollow oblong cinders spurted from it, and are a sign of coming death . . . If the cinder . . . is round, it is a purse and means prosperity' (recorded in I. Opie and M. Tatum (eds.), *A Dictionary of Superstitions*, Oxford: Oxford University Press, 1989). (Slater)

383 *no step or atom . . . the great universe*: drawing on the Law of Conservation of Matter, first formulated by Antoine-Laurent de Lavoisier (1743–94), which states that over time matter and energy are neither created nor destroyed, but merely change their form.

390 *short-commons*: insufficient food.

394 *Doctor Watts*: No. 17 of Isaac Watts's *Divine Songs for Children* (1715), on 'Love between Brothers and Sisters', contains the lines 'But, children, you should never let | Such angry passions rise; | Your little hands were never made | To tear each other's eyes.' (Slater)

choking in the jug like a ventriloquist: Victorian ventriloquists were celebrated for their ability to throw voices into a range of hollow objects, from milk jugs to snuff-boxes. Dickens was more suspicious, and satirized their patter in *The Uncommercial Traveller* (1861): '[The bee] will be with difficulty caught in the hand of Monsieur the Ventriloquist—he will escape—he will again hover—at length he will be recaptured by Monsieur the Ventriloquist, and will be with difficulty put into the bottle' ('In the French-Flemish Country').

Poor people . . . ought not to have children: a commonplace of Victorian economic and moral thought, drawing on Thomas Malthus's *Essay on the Principle of Population* (1798). See note to *A Christmas Carol*, p. 14.

407 *rebuking . . . those who kept them from Him*: see Matthew 19: 13–14.

APPENDIX 1: 'What Christmas Is, As
We Grow Older'

409 *priceless pearl*: Matthew 13: 46.

Greek or Roman story: a number of classical legends, such as the story of Damon and Pythias, celebrate powerful friendships between men. Given the looming presence of death in his description, Dickens may also have had in mind the heroic exploits of the Spartan army, founded and organized on ties of comradeship that led to friends dying for or with one another.

411 *withered leaves*: the traditional comparison of ghosts to dead leaves can be traced back through Virgil, *Aeneid* vi, to Homer, *Iliad* vi; later sources that may have been in Dickens's mind include Dante, *Inferno*, iii. 112–14, and P. B. Shelley, 'Ode to the West Wind'.

these children angels: a common Victorian idea, and one that Dickens returned to throughout his career; closer to home, he may have had in mind his infant daughter Dora, who died on 14 April 1851.

Entertaining angels unawares: see note to *The Battle of Life*, p. 311.

poor mis-shapen boy on earth: many of Dickens's fictional children are handicapped or deformed (Smike in *Nicholas Nickleby*, Tiny Tim in *A Christmas Carol*, Jenny Wren in *Our Mutual Friend*). Here the reference is probably to his crippled nephew Harry, who died in January 1849; his mother, Dickens's much-loved sister Fanny Burnett, had died in September 1848.

412 *a dear girl—almost a woman*: Mary Hogarth, the younger sister of Dickens's wife Catherine, whose sudden death aged 17 on 7 May 1837 left Dickens prostrated with grief. Dickens idolized her in life and idealized her in death; she appears lightly disguised in a number of his stories, as discussed by Michael Slater in *Dickens and Women* (London: J. M. Dent, 1983).

daughter of Jairus: Mark 5: 35–43.

the Sacred tread were fresh upon the water: Mark 6: 46–62.

413 *the living and the dead*: a secular echo of the Apostles' Creed from the Book of Common Prayer, which describes how all people will be brought together when Christ returns 'to judge the quick and the dead'.